THE MERMAID'S PENDANT

LeAnn Neal Reilly

ZEPHON
BOOKS

Boston

Zephon Books USA
3 Billings Way
Framingham, MA 01701

First published in the United States by Zephon Books in 2010.
First paperback edition: April 2010
First Kindle edition: April 2010

The characters and events portrayed in this book are fictitious. Any
similarity to real persons, living or dead, is coincidental and not intended
by the author.

ISBN: 9780982687505 (paperback)
ISBN: 9780982687512 (Kindle)

Book design by LeAnn Neal Reilly
Front cover image by Sean F. Boggs, SFB Photographics, Inc. / iStockphoto
Goddess pendant by Emmett A. Hamilton III

Text set in Cambria.

Printed in the United States of America.

To Scott

Without you, nothing happens.

To Ashlyn, Gwyneth, and Liam

When I grow up, I will write a book titled: *Everything I Needed to Learn About Reading I Learned From My Children.*

Volume I

An

Ordinary Drowning

The whole world has now been so ransacked that there is little room in these times for the imagination to play; but in mediaeval days travelers brought back such wonderful stories, some of them true, and others, perhaps, a little wanting in that respect, of the things that they had seen, that almost anything seemed a possibility.

F. Edward Hulme, Natural History: Lore and Legend

One

❧

IT TOOK TWO HOURS AND TEN MINUTES for John Wilkerson's fantasy about escaping to paradise to evaporate in the dry Caribbean air. Two hours on a ferry and a short walk around Culebra, a small island off the east coast of Puerto Rico, and John had to face up to the truth. But then, it was his own fault. He should have known that any island that resembled Disney's Neverland from an aerial photo must, at ground level, have more than a few flaws. He should have known not to invent something too fantastic to believe.

Unfortunately, he'd spent months conjuring up images of Culebra, known as the Last Spanish Virgin. Months invested in visions of dark-haired, buxom wenches with castanets on their slender hands and tiers of flounces swirling around their ankles. For weeks before he left Pittsburgh, he heard Spanish guitars thrumming and waves rushing when he drifted off to sleep at night, his girlfriend Zoë coiled around his body. Once or twice he even saw the sheen on the forehead of an *hacienda* owner in his mind's eye. When he and Zoë went to the Squirrel Cage after their day's research at Carnegie Mellon, he now drank rum instead of Yuengling's. And every now and then he caught the delicate scent of frangipani entwined with the mineral intensity of saltwater. He always darted a glance at Zoë whenever he remembered the scent of frangipani. His first love in high school, a bubbly artist named Tilda, had worn frangipani.

These visions stayed with him until he got to Puerto Rico. Instead of chartering a flight to Culebra from San Juan, John spent two bucks on the sleek double-decker ferry from Fajardo. When he arrived at the ferry dock, he found dozens of beachgoers lounging on hard-plastic coolers, holding beach towels and floats, and chatting with more energy than he had at eight a.m. Many drank Medalla or Bud Light, already getting a start on their beach weekend. He heard a toddler's cries and witnessed a mother in tube top and shorts, her thighs pockmarked with cellulite and a bandana around the curlers in her hair, shush the child. John's images of an island paradise wavered a bit but still held.

For the first hour on the ferry, he saw nothing but a steely smudge along the eastern horizon where Culebra should be. There wasn't much to do except listen to a CD of Van Morrison and watch the Caribbean, but then his batteries ran dry and he discovered that he hadn't packed replacements. Dropping the CD player in disgust, he ignored the smells of fried food and the rapid flow of Spanish around him. As he leaned over the ferry's railing on the upper deck, John studied the pixelated surface of the ocean, surprised at how much it resembled a poorly compressed movie. Choppy shades of blue, gray, and white jerked and resolved into water and foam and then fractured again into blocks of color. He blinked, rubbed his eyes and lifted his gaze to the horizon.

The steely smudge lingered and without landmarks to confirm the ferry's passage, John's mind played tricks on him. The constant sounds of wind and rushing water convinced him that the ferry labored on a watery treadmill—one which he feared would break down any moment like the taxi he took to the dock—but gradually he discerned the smudge growing and clarifying into a mountainous outcropping of sere green and dusty brown. Except for a smattering of white structures along the northern shoreline, Culebra appeared unsettled. A frontier outpost.

4

As they approached Dewey, Culebra's one and only town, the last rosy tinge faded from John's vision and reality settled in. No winsome *señoritas*, no Spanish guitars, no *haciendas*. Old men in tank tops sat on two benches in front of a short block of shops painted in dusty pastels. The small plaza with its tree benches, picnic tables, and old-fashioned streetlights across from the squat terminal with its wall of glass-block windows only made John long for the more stately colonial plazas in Old San Juan. Just beyond the main block, red-and-white columns for a drawbridge reared up behind the tired shops.

As he waited behind a father laden with sand pails, a mountain of beach towels, and an open Medalla, John shifted from foot to foot. At last the father lurched away and John shouldered his backpack, grabbed his bag, and disembarked into paradise, two hours and ten minutes after getting on the ferry.

After a quick tour of downtown Dewey, he returned to the *público* stop near the dock. Four people waited in the sparse shade across the street, talking and drinking beer. Half a block away, a liquor store did a brisk business from foot traffic, including some graying *gringos* who looked more than a bit pickled from sun and drink. When the *público* finally came, John walked all the way to the back, slid into a seat, and stared out the window. His dreams of colonial villas teeming with bougainvillea and surrounded by lush green landscaping had died, and they'd died hard. He glared at the arid and hilly terrain during the whole ten-minute ride to Playa Flamenco, supposedly one of the world's ten best beaches. The architecture relied on the ubiquitous cinderblock and no amount of bright-red blooms softened their angles. At least Wean Hall, in whose bowels his networking lab resided, daunted. These homes just depressed.

When he saw the rusty chain-link fence around the camping area and the sandy field that stood for a parking lot, John almost went back to Dewey. The backpack and bag weighed his arms down and he propped himself against the fence with his eyes closed until he could bring himself to rouse the dozing Culebrense in the shack

5

identified as the camp office. The man shrugged when John asked about renting a locker. John rolled his eyes and turned on his heel, dragging the bags with him. He halfway hid them among some guinea grass near a tree trunk.

Through the palms and over a small rise, laughter and loud music from the mob of weekend beachgoers repelled John from Playa Flamenco and back to the *público*. He'd eaten *huevos rancheros* hours before and his stomach demanded more *cocina criolla*, more Puerto Rican food, before he headed off for snorkeling. The Pepto pink of Señorita's, a two-story guesthouse, drew him in the glare of early afternoon. He enjoyed lunch there so much that his disappointment in not finding paradise began fading and when he rented snorkeling gear, the primitive machine for swiping credit cards only added to Culebra's growing rustic charm. It was time to find out if the snorkeling and diving around Culebra redeemed it altogether.

Half an hour later, he strode toward the trail to Carlos Rosario, a reef that the dive-shop owner had raved about. At the trailhead, he stopped long enough to read the sign posted on the chain-link fence that warned against straying off the trail and into an area littered with U.S. Navy ordnance. John's chest tightened, threatening a familiar panic attack, and he took a step back. Three carefully controlled exhalations seemed to relax his breathing, but he took three more for good measure and stepped onto the lonely, risky path.

A strip of white sand and ocean met him at trail's end. Nothing but the delicious sound of waves sighing against the shore and an occasional wild cry overhead from a seabird. The crystalline color of the water seduced his screen-weary eyes and something let go of him, some grip of asphalt and glass-walled office buildings, and he breathed in deeply. Even if he saw nothing but rocks and hermit crabs, the surreal blue saltwater against a clear Caribbean sky redeemed his trip, made Culebra a paradise, cellulite thighs and cinderblock eyesores be damned.

A hundred feet out he saw the shadow of coral reef. To the south, a narrow canal separated Culebra from a large cay. The dive-shop owner had recommended the canal for a first snorkel dive. Of course, the guy had warned against snorkeling alone, but alone with nature was *exactly* what he wanted to be. He'd return to the Carlos Rosario reef after he'd gotten his feet wet in the canal. Grinning at his weak joke, he whistled a short tune. Even weak jokes were funny when Zoë wasn't around.

To get a better idea of what he was getting himself into, John dropped his gear on some bare ground among the clusters of cactus and guinea grass near the trail and climbed a twisted mangrove to look out over the canal. From this height, he saw clumps of turtle grass in the shallow waters where fish of all sizes darted in and out of the swaying blades. Besides the fish and dozens of birds surfing along air currents, not another soul intruded upon his peace. Satisfied with his reconnaissance, he climbed down, stripped off his t-shirt and snatched up the snorkel, goggles, and flippers.

John hadn't snorkeled since senior year at Berkeley, but once he plunged his face underwater he wondered why he'd waited so long to do it again. He'd descended into another world, vast and silent except for the regular gurgle of his breathing in the tube. All around him, organic shapes defied right angles and straight lines, flat planes and intersecting sides. Colors ranging from subdued to garish—but never dull as concrete or bland as limestone—enticed his city-weary eyes. There was a mystery here, a truth so sublime that it defied easy expression into variable and quantity.

He swayed on the current, gazing at parrotfish with their hooked beaks darting among the blue tangs. A squadron of sergeant majors soared over the reef south of him, their black stripes flashing as they banked and turned. Copper-colored squirrelfish with their big brown eyes, ocean surgeonfish, and slender needlefish swarmed ahead of him. Here was primeval life, unaware and unconcerned about the self-important ambition of computer scientists in their office cubicles overgrown with cable and whirring disk drives.

An image of Zoë, tall and sinewy, wavered to life in front of him. His chest tightened and memory overlay his view of trumpet fish hovering among tan sea whips as thick as fingers. Darkness overwhelmed him. He tugged at remembered covers that clung to his torso and legs, but they only entangled him more tightly. Yanking at edges, clumps under his back—anything he could grab onto—he kicked out and then his vision cleared until he saw that a flipper had snagged on some turtle grass.

He panted into the snorkel and waited, his heart racing. Behind him, Zoë's weight shifted and she coiled her arms around his torso, binding him. John blinked and the underwater tableau reappeared. Large yellowtail snapper, a bright yellow stripe racing down their sides to their yellow tails, drifted past. As John turned to follow, an octopus lunged from nowhere at a yellowtail. Writhing arms pinned the hapless fish to the ocean floor. In seconds, it was all over. The octopus injected the yellowtail with poison and stuffed it into its beak.

John flinched. His heart stuttered and thudded. He kicked away from the violent death, but a flipper again caught on turtle grass. His arms thrashed. Spears of sunlight, bubbles, sea grass upended his vision. Then a terrible thing happened. His lips lost their seal on the breathing tube. Saltwater choked him. He flung his face above the surface and spit out the tube. Gasped a breath. Choked and sputtered. Flailed under again, losing the goggles. Struggled out into sunlight, coughing and sucking at the air. He slipped under; pushed up again. Missed a breath, slid down. Inhaled more water. Ears ringing, he popped up a final time. Then he swatted once at the water before slipping under the surface. The heaviness of saltwater filled his lungs just as two arms grabbed him from behind and pulled him free of the water. The pressure in his lungs eased and the pounding in his brain faded to black.

Dizzy awareness returned to him. He couldn't focus his eyes. Everything was a blur. His shoulder and side hurt. His chest spasmed. He coughed weakly, but something soft and firm wrapped his mouth. He wanted to lift a hand to brush it away, but his arm refused to move and he coughed again. The pressure on his mouth lifted and then he retched warm saltwater until nothing came up. He continued to heave and shake. Someone laid a hand on his back; a gentle vibration spread through his torso, soothing his retching.

The hand remained while he breathed. The dizziness subsided gradually. He had no idea how much time had passed and cared only for the implacable ground beneath him, the concerned fingers on his back. When he felt that he could move without causing the world to spin, he rolled to see his rescuer. The hand dropped away and he felt bereft. His eyes, still clouded by saltwater, refused to focus on her face. He had an impression of luminous skin, and two bare breasts peeking through a curtain of dark hair.

"Thank you." The words croaked from his ravaged throat. Then he passed out again.

༄༅།།

John's savior sat some minutes, watching him. Then she leaned forward and pressed several fingertips to his neck, feeling for his pulse. It was there, strong and steady. She let her hand slide along the skin of his jaw, brushing the hair away from his cheek. She put a light fingertip on his mouth, now a warm red. Her lips tingled and she leaned her face closer—perhaps she could press her lips there again? He moaned and rolled his head against the stones. The mermaid snatched her hand back and waited, her breath held, but he didn't move again. She didn't touch him a second time; instead, she caressed the hard muscles of his calves with her gaze. She looked away from his feet though. One still wore one of those pseudo-flippers that always made her shiver.

She had, of course, seen countless humans before—snorkeling and diving, on shore and on deck. But she'd never *touched* one before, never felt the dry skin that prickled with fine hairs. This man overwhelmed her. Already the sun had evaporated most of the water on his chest, which was covered with dark hair. Not like a merman, smooth and sleek and slender. His chest, shoulders, and hips were wider and his frame bulkier. His flesh was a different color, too. He was pale but not shark-belly pale like the *mer* people.

His skin held warmth, the warmth of sun-bleached wood. Only his long dark hair resembled a merman's. Her nostrils flared at his scent. She had no words to describe it other than hot and dry, but she used those words for the shore and he didn't smell like the shore. He smelled like the wind from distant lands.

A voice, sandy and familiar, abraded her thoughts. "What have you done, young one?"

The mermaid looked up to see an ancient woman as gnarled and twisted as the roots of the trees that grew at the shore's edge. The woman picked her way across the stones toward the place where the mermaid sat. She stopped a few feet away. Freeing her bag, which the mermaid had always seen at her waist, the old woman rummaged around for a few moments before withdrawing something. Then she came forward and nudged John with her foot. He didn't stir.

"Pulled him out of the water, did you? Cough up all the water he breathed in?" The mermaid nodded. "And his heart's beat is still strong?" The mermaid nodded again. "He'll live then."

She bent and tugged the flipper from the man's foot. When it came off, the mermaid let a sharp sound escape her.

The ancient one laughed, a sound like dry stones shifting. "You think he's strange? No wonder you find him so interesting, girl." She smiled. It spread like seal oil on water. "I can help him, if you'd like." She paused and waited. The mermaid stole a glance at the man and nodded. "This herb tincture will rouse him. I'll see to it that he's recovered his senses and can walk. You'd best get going. I'll tell him I found him here."

The mermaid nodded again. After one more look at the unconscious man, she propelled herself backward with her hands, her tail lifted slightly above the stones. Once she was in the water, she paused, her gaze taking in the wide stance of the ancient woman, who stood over the stranger as though he were *her* bounty from the waters. Was this all there was to saving a man's life?

Before she could lower herself underwater and speed away, the old woman called to her.

"Oh, yes, young one, I need some turtle grass, and a sea cucumber. And one of those pink sea urchins, you know the ones."

There was nothing of the usual promise of a human artifact or any stories about the human world on this island. The mermaid nodded. It was the old woman's price for keeping her secret.

❧❧❧

When John regained consciousness, he found a wizened old woman hunched over him holding what looked like a mini-bar liquor bottle. But its rank liquid was no whiskey that he'd ever smelled. Upon seeing her wild, white hair and a burning right eye in a face like a walnut, he sat up quickly. She chortled and hunkered down, her ragged skirt splayed across her bony knees.

"So, you don't like the smell? Strong it is. Just be glad you aren't dead, then, and can smell it." Her voice crackled. Her accent was odd, not like the locals.

John shook his head, trying to clear the confusion that still hung over his thoughts. "Who ...?"

The old woman just sat there and looked at him. He cleared his throat and began again.

"Who pulled me from the water?"

"You were pulled from the water?"

"Yes." A cough interrupted him. "Almost drowned."

"What'd he look like?"

He shifted his position on the rocky shore, bracing himself and pushing his hair out of his eyes. "Not he, she."

"She? Then you did see her?" The woman's voice was sharp.

"No." He shook his head. "Not really."

The old woman at first said nothing; instead, she wrapped the top of the bottle with a bit of cloth and then tied that with a bit of string. She dropped this bottle into a bag that lay on the rocks behind her before turning to face him again.

Finally, she spoke. "You were lying on the beach. You were breathing; you weren't dead. That's when I put my tincture under your nose."

John recalled the foul odor of the tincture, grateful that she hadn't poured it down his throat. "Thanks."

"It's little enough I did." She shrugged. "If you want a doctor, there's one in the *pueblo*, across the plaza from the dock. But you're all right."

Without waiting for him to agree, she picked up her bag and slung it over her shoulder. She headed toward the east and the low-growing shrubs there. Not sure what he should do or say next, John sat watching her go. As she reached the edge of the rocks, the old woman turned for a parting shot.

"You should thank God for your life." She raised her chin toward the water of the canal and continued, "The ocean is as lethal as it's lovely. You'd do well to remember."

She disappeared into the shrubs and darkening shadows, going who knew where. John, feeling chastised, sat for a long moment before studying the rocks near where he'd been laying. There was nothing to show how he'd gotten ashore, no footprints, no drag marks. No way of knowing where his rescuer had come from or gone to. Why hadn't she stayed around?

Two
૯૩

JOHN LEVERAGED HIMSELF to his feet before shaking gripped him. He sat down again, hard, on the stony shore. His heart seized up and he flushed hot and cold before it resumed beating. Turning to look at the canal, he thought that he saw his snorkel floating north but the fractured sunlight dazzled him and he couldn't be sure. His second flipper and mask had disappeared into the deceptive water. The shaking intensified. He'd almost lost his life in an out-of-the-way corner of the Caribbean. The silence of the empty shore confirmed how fantastic his rescue had been.

Maybe his rescuer was still close. The thought impelled him to his feet and a mad, yet fruitless, search of the scrub around the shore. Whatever girl? woman? superwoman? had pulled him to safety must have hightailed it along the path back to Carlos Rosario. Or maybe there was access from the nearby Tamarindo Estates. Zoë would have stood over him, hands on hips and smirk on lips, until he'd stumbled upright with his head hanging. Frustration filled him, drowning his shock. He couldn't remember what she looked like. A bleary memory of long, wet hair that could have been any color swam across his mind's eye, panning out into a clearer image of breasts, small and strangely vulnerable. If ever he saw those breasts again, he'd recognize his rescuer—and cover her up. Given

13

that he wasn't likely to see any other breasts than Zoë's for the foreseeable future, his frustration magnified ten-fold.

A nagging bladder drew him from his predicament and the mundane act of pissing behind a tree brought him back to himself. He felt as empty as the stony shoreline, as blank as the impervious waves, drained and hollow from his struggle. He couldn't stand here all day, longing for an ephemeral sprite to reappear and finish saving him. Maybe he wanted some magical creature to enter his life so badly that he half-believed that she had, but nothing had changed from the time he'd gone under to the time he'd awakened on shore: the sun would still set tonight on dreamless sleep and tomorrow it would rise on unfulfilled fantasies.

He looked around, trying to get his bearings. Directly opposite him rose the jagged outlines of a cay. He'd have to take the path back north toward Carlos Rosario where he'd left his gear. There was no way he was getting back into the water. He'd gone only a couple of feet along the path when a prickling sensation along his spine caused him to stop. Yet when he looked behind him, he saw nothing but the regular lapping of water on stone. No one watched him.

By the time he returned to the Playa Flamenco campground, his frustration and emptiness had bottomed out into resignation. He was accustomed to the hilly terrain of Pittsburgh but had no stamina for Culebra's dry heat or the uneven trail. His head hurt and his throat had constricted around a layer of dust. He'd earned a sunburn from going so long without a t-shirt. All he wanted now was air conditioning, low lights, and a cold drink. A shower was out of the question. He wouldn't get one of those until Zoë arrived in two weeks and they stayed at Tamarindo Estates.

Against all expectation, there weren't any places to retreat to near here, not even a stand to buy a bottle of water or a soda. He'd known that Culebra was undeveloped, a "hidden jewel in the Caribbean," but why hadn't someone set up at least one thatched-roof shack with an ice tub filled with drinks and a hot-dog steamer? No wonder all those people on the ferry had lugged those huge coolers with them. One of the world's ten best beaches and you were on your own. He'd hiked into wildernesses with more civilization.

He consulted the island map that he'd gotten at the dive shop. The closest restaurant outside Dewey was at Tamarindo Estates, but it only opened on the weekend for lunch and dinner. He suspected that it was what passed for nice on Culebra. He didn't want to wait two hours while covered in trail dust to order a beer there. Tamarindo Estates *was* the only place near where he'd almost drowned, but he couldn't be sure that his rescuer had any connection to it. And really, what would he say? Any of your guests like to swim topless in the canal?

There weren't many other options. On the way back into town, there was only The Happy Landing Café near the airport. Beyond that, there appeared to be only two or three standalone eateries in Dewey. Either way, he was on foot. The prospect didn't appeal to him, but he decided that he could kill a few birds with one weary trip: he'd rent a bike, report the lost gear, and get a beer and dinner. So he settled on Isla Encantada, which was back near the dive shop. It sounded more appealing anyway, even if Culebra had turned out to be far from enchanted.

He regretted his decision to walk into Dewey after taking an hour to get there. If he hadn't stopped at The Happy Landing Café for a bottle of water, he might have passed out along the way. A lone black stallion standing along the highway oddly tempted him, but when he took a step in its direction, it bolted.

The bike shop owner had just stuck his key into the shop's lock when John came limping up. He smiled and opened up anyway, chatting the whole time it took John to fill out a form and for him to swipe John's credit card. John didn't have the same luck with the dive shop, however. It was already closed even though it was only four-thirty in the afternoon. He didn't mind. If he didn't get a cold Medalla in the next ten minutes, he might combust and his ashes float away on the wind over the harbor, Ensenada Honda. He was that dry.

15

Isla Encantada had none of Señorita's refinements. That is to say, it wasn't pastel. It didn't have strings of white Christmas lights and tropical flowers. There was no Hemingway doppelganger at the bar. The tables were wooden, their surfaces pockmarked and oiled by countless palms and fingers. It didn't serve Nuevo Caribbean cuisine with thin-sliced plantain chips and entrees drizzled with garlic-scented sauce. No, Isla Encantada served traditional *tostones*, monstrous *pastelillos de carne, paella* teeming with shrimp and spiny lobster, and heavy *arroz con dulce*. This was a place Culebrense sons came to eat when they couldn't eat their mother's cooking. John, who wasn't a Culebrense son but the boyfriend of a virulent vegetarian, restricted himself to *estofado de garbanzos*, a thick chickpea stew with pumpkin and cabbage. He washed it down with Medalla and ice water. He tried to pace himself, but he drank more beer and water than he'd ever consumed at one sitting.

He sank against his chair back and looked around the dim restaurant. A barrel-chested Culebrense with a hairy caterpillar of a mustache stood talking to a younger Culebrense behind the bar. Four young men sat at one of the ten tables in the dining area. A small dance floor with worn, sooty parquet took up the rest of the space. John grimaced at his reflection in the floor-to-ceiling mirror on the far wall. He wondered what kind of musicians used the stands waiting in the corner.

Too bad no lovely *señoritas* sat sipping *sangria* at the bar. Not that it mattered, anyway. He wasn't as smooth as his friend Stefan. Or maybe not as carefree and immoral. He could never seek out a one-night stand, Zoë or no Zoë. At the thought of his girlfriend, John looked around the bar even though she wasn't there. That's when he saw the old woman at a table by the door. She nodded at him and raised her beer bottle. John nodded back and shifted his gaze away. Something about her gave him the willies.

The barrel-chested man approached with a Medalla.

"*Hola, mi amigo.* Medalla?" He didn't wait for John's answer, just set the bottle next to John's empty. "May I?" He gestured to the chair across from John.

John shrugged and nodded.

"So, you like our island, *señor*?" The man had brought an extra Medalla for himself. He sipped it and waited.

John shifted in his seat. His backside ached and he found himself thinking about the hard campground where he planned to sleep tonight. "I dunno. Haven't seen much of it yet."

The big man nodded. "Not much to see, unless you like seabirds and turtles."

"Playa Flamenco as amazing as they say?"

"*Sí, señor.* Not so much when the beachgoers from the mainland infest it like sand fleas. They will be gone tomorrow. Then you will see for yourself."

"Weekend only?"

The man nodded. "My name is Tomás. I own Isla Encantada. You like my wife's cooking, no?"

"*Sí.*" John smiled, his first since he'd gotten to Culebra. "My name's John." They shook hands. "So, what's there to do around here at night? Any good music?" He indicated the music stands with a sideways tilt of his head.

"We have a four-piece group. A guitar and kettle drum. A trumpet. And *maracas*, of course. It's the best on *la isla*. You stay and listen, no?"

"Is there a lot of music on Culebra?"

"Sometimes at Señorita's. No one is there now." Tomás sipped his beer. "We are *muy rústico* here, *señor*. There are more roosters and wild horses than *turistas*. I am the only one open past eleven on the weekend. An hour."

"Wow. Zoë's gonna love that."

"*Cómo?*"

"Oh, nothing." He shrugged. "It's not what I expected is all."

"You came to snorkel perhaps? The reefs, they bring many *norteamericanos*."

"Actually, I came to scuba dive. I'm going out over the Trench in a couple of weeks."

"Treasure hunting? The Trench is graveyard to many Spanish galleons."

"No, no. Too deep, *amigo*. It's a research trip. Underwater geology." John laughed. "Of course, I almost drowned in the canal today so maybe I shouldn't go."

Tomás appeared shocked. "The canal? Luís Peña?"

John nodded, sheepish. "Long story, Tomás. Never would have made it back to shore without somebody pulling me in."

Tomás frowned. "You snorkeled alone then? You are *suerte*, lucky, *señor*, that someone came along at the right time. As I have already said, not many *turistas* come here and the *puertoriqueños* stay on Playa Flamenco. The Culebrenses, they don't often snorkel."

"Well, whoever she was, she saved my life."

Tomás started. "She? A woman pulled you from the canal?"

"Yeah," John laughed. "Must be some kind of superhero to pluck me out of the water and drag me to shore so fast."

Tomás looked thoughtful. "What did she look like, this woman?"

"Don't really know. My eyes were full of saltwater. I was throwing it up, too." John paused. "Actually, now that you ask, I'm getting this distinct image of her." He frowned heavily, concentrating on the startling and clear vision that popped into his mind.

"She's got outrageously curly hair"—here he demonstrated with two hands hovering around his head—"the color of an old penny and eyes the color of the shallows around Culebra. And ..." here John hesitated, "and she didn't have anything on. No shirt. No swimsuit. *Nada*."

"You saw her?" Tomás sounded excited. "You really saw this woman, *señor*?"

John's confusion mushroomed. "No. No." Anger sharpened the edge of his voice and he shook his head. "*Lo siento*, Tomás. I'm not angry with you. It's just that I know I didn't see her clearly, but I have this distinct image of her. Like I already know her."

18

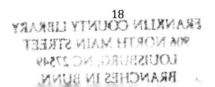

Tomás pursed his lips and nodded. He sipped his beer and then, his gaze directed at his beer label as though seeing for the first time, he asked, "What happened to her, *Señor* Juan? Did she tell you her name?"

"That's the odd thing. I passed out. When I woke up, she was gone. But that old woman—" John inclined his head toward the old woman, who sat smoking and reading a book—"was there. Stuck a foul-smelling liquid under my nose. Claims she found me on the shore, no one else there."

Tomás's gaze slid toward Ana and back. "Ana?"

"You know her?"

"Yes, everyone knows Ana, *señor*. Some more than most. Some wish they knew her less."

"What's that mean?"

Tomás kept his gaze on his hands, which were wrapped around his empty Medalla bottle. "Some say she is a *bruja*, a witch, *señor*."

John looked at the other man for a moment, trying to gauge his meaning. "You're kidding? A witch?"

Tomás shrugged. "One man's superstition is another man's explanation."

"She's just some sort of herbalist. Crossed with a bag lady. Scary looking, but a witch?" John heard incredulity twist his voice.

"Some say she is also *del mar*."

"'*Del mar*'? 'Of the sea'?"

"This woman, the one who pulled you from the sea. Perhaps she was not altogether a woman."

"What's that mean?" John studied the other man's face but saw only seriousness in his eyes. "What else is there? A mermaid?" He laughed and looked away.

Tomás looked at Ana. He picked at the label on his bottle and shook his head. "Sí, *loco*, *loco*. Just a crazy explanation for your mystery, *Señor* Juan. A story to tell your friends when you go home."

John frowned. "I'd rather know who she is, Tomás. I just don't have any idea how to track her down."

"You could post a flyer here. Nearly everyone comes here at one time or another."

"A flyer?" John pursed his lips. "Sure. Why not?" He tilted the last of the beer into his mouth. "Time for me to head back to the campground. I'll catch the music another time. Nearly drowning has worn me out. What I owe you?"

After he settled the bill—trying without success to pay the friendly Tomás for the last Medalla—John biked back to Playa Flamenco. The heat had fled with the sunset and a languor slowed his peddling. He passed a few Culebrenses enjoying the evening from their porches. They waved and called hello and he answered in kind. There were only a handful of cars on the road to the north, and none past the airport. The acrid smell of dry thorn acacia and asphalt subsided beneath the cool mineral scent of ocean water. The sky was the color of honeydew, oozing thousands of white seed-stars. Bougainvillea, its rich red muted, added mystery to the dusk. John thought the world looked unutterably lovely, tranquil and complete. He was alive and he had no one to thank. His gratitude wouldn't stay inside though.

"I'm alive!" he yelled into the gloaming. Startled horses whinnied and broke across the highway in front of him. He bellowed, a pure animal sound of pleasure, and coasted down an incline, his hands fluttering above his head.

Later, as he lay listening to laughter from the weekenders still partying on the beach, he wondered again how he was going to find her, the vulnerable woman with the crazy hair and haunting eyes who'd saved him from drowning. He tossed on the sandy ground for more than an hour, replaying the rescue. Where was she, this woman *del mar*? Something tickled his thoughts and ran down his spine. He popped up in his sleeping bag. Again, he had the feeling that someone was watching him, but he could see nothing, just dark shapes of trees and snoring bodies. He strained his hearing, but only voices and waves reached him. He might have sat up half the night, waiting, but a breeze caressed his face. Its touch urged him to slide back down, to close his eyes, to dream.

Ana climbed the hidden path beyond her house toward Playa Tamarindo. Overhead, sooty terns fluttered like kites without string. Before she reached the summit, her rooster crowed, but her sleepy hens would ignore him. They wouldn't leave their straw-lined beds until she jostled them looking for eggs. She paused at a small stand of tamarind trees and studied the full-length pods hanging from the branches. Their pliant shells needed another six weeks to fill out with a sweet-sour pulp and become brittle enough to pluck. Given the number of pods, she'd have pulp for a dozen vials of diarrhea medicine, a jar of burn salve, and a vial of abortifacient—and still have enough to make three or four kegs of tamarind ale. If she didn't harvest them quickly, the birds might feast on them first. Her cadre of laughing gulls forgot their training as messengers and spies every spring to gorge on ripe tamarind pods.

While she stood there, one fluttered to a branch at her head. Seaweed affixed a lace murex shell to its leg.

"What's this, Ai?"

Ana slipped a small pair of scissors from the bag at her waist and snipped the seaweed. The lace murex dropped into her palm. She fingered it, turning it over and studying its lacy spines and ridges. Then she rubbed it around her palm several times, humming and chanting under her breath. When she'd released the message, she put the shell into the bag. The gull cocked its head and opened its beak, laughing at her.

"Of course you did well. The midwife in Guadaloupe still watches. She'll signal when the winds turn ferocious. All right, all right." She reached into a pocket of her skirt, pulled out a rectangle of dried tamarind pulp, and broke off a corner. "Don't be so greedy or you'll shit yourself silly, Ai."

She tossed the bit into the air where the gull snatched it. As she walked on, a sea of thorny acacia and guinea grass, unremarkable yet as familiar to her as the thicket of lines on the back of her hands, rolled away. She didn't have to look over her shoulder to know the acacia and guinea grass swallowed up her steps. No one could follow her unless she wanted him to.

At the shore, she sensed the mermaid, maybe close, maybe far—but not too far. So she squatted at the water's edge and rummaged through the wet stones. She'd gathered five when a shift in the air tingled her ears. The mermaid had released her glamour, the magic spell of disguise used by the *mer*.

"It's good you returned." Ana spoke without looking up from her work. "You must be warned." She swiveled to face the mermaid. "That *idiota americano* is looking for you."

He'll see what I mean him to.

"Then careful what you mean, young one."

But ....

"No buts. Stay away until he's gone."

The mermaid tossed her head, reminding Ana of the proud stallion who nipped the wild mares and shied away from everyone, even her. She launched herself from the water, arcing over backward in defiant grace, her sinewy tail slapping the water's surface. The air wavered around her and she swelled into a portly manatee as saltwater and foam showered Ana. A sheet of droplets glittered in the early sunlight, but Ana saw the mermaid torpedoing through the canal anyway.

Ana sat back on her heels and studied the mermaid's wake with narrowed eyes. She must continue to follow the stranger, but more importantly she must find some way to distract him. She'd heard him at Isla Encantada, she'd heard his desire to find his rescuer. He would never find the mermaid on his own, of course, but his thoughts would be open to her. The besotted fool would linger around the edges of Culebra, hoping to catch his thoughts. He would draw her, like a homing pigeon, to him.

A smile lifted her face. Perhaps she, Ana, could call him to *her*. She'd caught him thinking of dark-haired, dark-eyed Spanish beauties and long limbs entwined, glistening as they moved against each other. He would soon forget the mystery woman who'd saved his life when he'd become intoxicated with a flesh-and-blood siren. It would be done.

She plucked up her skirt and waded into the shallows to gather more stones, shells, and seaweed. Muttering, she placed these around the edge of the small beach. She returned to the water and searched until she found a small sea star. At her touch, it flexed its arms but could not move fast enough to escape. She carried the dripping animal to the largest stone on the beach and laid it there. From the bag at her waist, she pinched a bit of dried cactus powder and, muttering again, outlined the sea star.

It poured its life into her hands and into her plans.

Three
⁕

WHEN JOHN WOKE AT SIX A.M. the next morning, cool sand and crisp light buoyed him. Sometime in the night, he'd freed himself from his sleeping bag, which lay in a heap at his feet. He stretched and grunted, reaching overhead and breathing deeply. He sighed and released the stretch. Overhead, terns and gulls fluttered, their sharp cries counterpointing the rhythmic *shoosh-shoosh* of the waves. Palm and acacia leaves tangoed with a flirty breeze tangy with salt. John closed his eyes and sighed again. All his senses had heightened. Sounds were clearer, smells sharper. Even his sunburn had cooled.

Sitting up, he scooped some sand and let its powder slip through his fingers. It was as fine as confectioner's sugar and almost as white. An urge overcame him and he scooped up more and rubbed it into his stubble. The sand felt less gritty than he did. He grinned. He was alive and he'd never felt better.

His stomach rumbled. He was hungry. He rummaged in his backpack and found a Snickers bar. Breakfast of champions it was not, but it would do for now.

It wasn't until he bent over his sleeping bag, smoothing it before rolling, that he remembered the dream. It was less a vision than a memory of movement, a flowing along dark, swift currents

24

studded with lights and teeming with music. Infinity swirled at his feet and forever arched over his head. He'd been without form, yet he'd been everything. He'd traveled alone, silent—yet not alone. A multitude of others swam beside him. Together, they swam always, yet they needed no destination. Once recalled, the dream disappeared like smoke on the breeze. Even though he'd lost its details, it left a sense of fulfillment in its wake.

He hummed and stepped over snoring campers toward the Portajohns. That's when Zoë's absence hit him. He hadn't slept away from her in nine months. A shadow crossed the sun and he glanced up reflexively. The morning brightened even before his eyes adjusted, but his peace faded. He shook himself. He needed to find the mystery woman.

Not knowing what else to do, John decided to return to the scene of his rescue. Perhaps, in the clear light of early morning, he'd be able to spot some clue that he'd missed from the day before. The hike over the Carlos Rosario trail only added to his perplexity. There was no good reason to think that a stranger happened to be hiking along this trail, heard his floundering in the canal, dove in and pulled him out, and then returned to her hike post-haste. It just didn't make any sense at all. The Luís Peña Canal was a destination, not someplace anyone would just pass by. And what had brought Ana, the local witch woman, to the shore with her pungent herbal medicine?

The trail ended near the quiet little beach where his rescuer had brought him. John searched the perimeter of the shore again, but the only thing that he found out of the ordinary was a shriveled sea star lying exposed on a large rock. He was the last one to know anything about sea animals, but it seemed a strange place to find a sea star. There was something forlorn about it. He touched it with the tip of his finger. Out here, it was nothing but some tern's morning meal. He cradled it on his palm and turned to face the canal.

The last thing that he wanted to do was go back into the ocean. He stood for a minute or two, studying the impervious water—

water that had nearly swallowed him. He looked again at the sea star, desiccated when it should have been moist, living. He was too late to save it, but he couldn't leave the sea star lying on the stones. Returning the helpless creature to the ocean was the best he could do to set things right. He owed it to the woman who'd risked her life to save his. Holding his breath, he took a step into the canal. The water was blood warm and silky. It caressed his thighs and urged him deeper. He sighed and sank to his knees. Beneath him, the sand shifted to accommodate him. He lowered the sea star below the surface and watched as the water lifted its husk off his palm and carried it away. The current swirled around him, alive and tender. Like being naked and draped in satin sheets. He knew that he was alone. He saw nothing through the crystalline water, not even a darting fish, yet fingers stroked his calves and thighs, toyed with his hair, caressed his shoulders. A hallucinatory torso pressed against him, arms encircled his neck and he bent forward....

The water turned playful, rolling and ducking him. John, water sheeting over his face, laughed and began splashing. Somewhere in the back of his mind, he realized that he'd look totally bonkers to anyone who stumbled upon him, but he didn't care. Nothing held him back, entangled him, under this infinite sky.

"Where's my lady *del mar* when I need her?" He didn't realize that he'd spoken aloud until he heard an answer.

"Will I do?" Ana stood at the mouth of the trail; her wild white hair spun wisps around her face. "Or are you looking for something else? You seem recovered."

John hung suspended in the water, which had lost its charm. He felt vulnerable to the old woman's sharp gaze. "I am."

As dainty and graceful as a mountain goat, the old woman picked her way across the stony shore. She squatted down and toyed with some broken bits of shells. "Saw your flyer at Isla Encantada. Think to catch your mermaid, eh?" Her rough voice stayed even, but John heard the scorn in it.

"I never said that."

"Tomás thinks you did."

26

John sighed. "No."

"Don't believe in mermaids, do you? Why not? Maybe one is swimming right beside you." The old woman's right eye glittered. "Close to us vile humans, eh?" She chortled.

John squirmed. "Look, you see who pulled me out of the canal or not?"

"I saw no woman. Either there's a lady *del mar* or you made the whole thing up."

"Why would I do that?"

"Hm." She picked at some seaweed on the sand, swirling its limp strands on the stones. "Ask yourself."

He had to get out of the water, fast. He lurched upright and strode to the shore, water spraying from his quick arms. He stopped next to her, but she didn't look at him. "I'm not making this up. I didn't imagine nearly drowning. I didn't imagine the woman who saved me." He paused and then braved a question. "Do you know more than you're telling?"

She swiveled and looked up at him. A sly smile oiled her wrinkled cheeks. "Maybe I pulled you out."

John ignored her. "How'd you happen to find me?"

Ana shrugged, stood up, and brushed her hands on her threadbare skirt. "Came here to gather this and that for my remedies."

"Maybe you're not the only one who gathers 'this and that' for her remedies."

"Perhaps." She shrugged again. "Whatever makes you happy."

John watched her bend over the stones, dismissing him. He didn't need to stay and watch her pick over rocks, to have her pick over his story. What did it matter what she thought? He'd already passed her and reached the trail before something in her manner made him turn around. She seemed to scour the rock where he'd found the sea star. After a minute, she turned to stare at him.

"Maybe Tomás has found her for you."

"I'll ask. Good hunting." He nodded and turned back to the trail.

If he'd felt perplexed before, now he felt angry. He stopped walking after ten minutes and closed his eyes. The memory of saltwater filling his lungs choked him. Fresh panic shocked his heart into erratic beating. His eyes flew open. Brilliant light haloed his vision in the rising heat. He *had* almost drowned. But. He tried to recall the feel of her arms around him or the sound of her voice. All he summoned was a feeling of warm security, of relief from suffocation. Had his oxygen-starved brain hallucinated her? The inexplicable image of curly hair and brilliant blue eyes returned as if to confirm this.

John returned to his campsite. He couldn't go to Isla Encantada for hours. He didn't want to read. He couldn't snorkel. He wanted to know who had pulled him out of the water. He wanted to know why she'd left him. He stuck the island map into the waistband of his shorts and hopped onto the bike. He would distract himself with a tour of the island. He peddled so furiously that he lost himself under the hard blue sky until a headache pounded its way into his blank mind and made him acknowledge his need for water.

When he got back to Dewey, John headed for Isla Encantada where water and a cold Medalla waited. Tomás nodded and smiled when John caught his eye and brought a bottle over before John could order.

"*Gracias.*"

"*De nada, Señor Juan.*"

"Some water too, please."

"*Sí.*"

John noticed a woman at the bar. He couldn't see her face, but her dark hair cascaded over her shoulders; her flamingo-pink skirt and white blouse popped against the brown of her skin. He stole looks at her through lunch. No one came to meet her. She flirted with the bartender and made Tomás blush. Her husky, Bette Davis voice drifted across the dining area and insinuated itself into John's ears. He began to wonder why he'd never picked women up in bars. He'd just worked up the courage to motion Tomás over when a man slid onto the stool next to her.

John watched as the newcomer leaned into the woman's shoulder and said something. The woman answered, shaking her head and shifting away. She lit a cigarette and propped her elbow on the bar between them. From John's vantage point, it was a clear rejection. He waited for the other man to take the hint, but he didn't. Instead, he snapped his fingers at the bartender and ordered something without taking his eyes off of the woman. The bartender set two beers down, his eyes sliding from the woman—who'd grown into John's Caribbean fantasy—to the man, who ignored the bartender to lean again toward the woman. The bartender hustled away but not before John saw the nervous flash on his face.

When the newcomer put his hand on the small of the woman's back, she shrugged it away. The man put it back. That's when John acted. His chair scraped against the floor and he stood before he knew what he was doing. The newcomer turned and stared at him.

"*Una problema, señor?*" The man's flat dark eyes telegraphed a challenge.

It wicked all the moisture from John's throat. He stood there, suspended between his seat and a certain confrontation.

The woman swiveled and looked at him, smoke painting a ghostly filigree around her. She smiled. White teeth brightened her face. "*No problema*, Jesus. This is *mi amigo*, the one I was to meet. Right?" Her dusky voice never rose yet John heard her across the room.

His own voice returned. "Yes."

The lithe Caribbean beauty slid from her stool and slinked toward him. John saw bare feet with peeping pink toenails. She met him, slipped her arm through his, and winked. "Buy me a beer, my friend?" She smelled of cloves and something hot and fecund. John nearly swooned.

"Of course." He started to guide her to a chair when Jesus blocked the way.

"*Gringo.*" Jesus' breath stank of hops and something sour. "I never forget. Never. " His flat eyes regarded John. He looked at the woman. "You and I will meet later, *mi alma dulce.*"

She laughed, a throaty, wild sound. "I will be all the sweeter, *mi guapetón.*"

Jesus stroked a fingertip along her forearm. "*Igual que la fruta.* Until then." He shot a final glance at John and left Isla Encantada.

John let a shaky breath out and helped the woman into a seat. She reached for the dregs of his Medalla and tilted the bottle to her mouth. John watched as she swallowed. She kept her eyes on his.

"So." She passed a hand across her lips. John noticed that they were the color of pomegranate seeds, slightly swollen and glistening. "You are visiting Culebra?"

He nodded.

She smiled at Tomás who brought over two frosted bottles of Medalla. "*Gracias.*" He stuttered a nearly inaudible reply and left. "The beer is in my hand, my friend. Now, perhaps, we share names?"

John grinned. "I'm John."

"*Hola*, John. I am Raimunda." She tucked a strand of dark hair behind her ear, which was oddly shriveled against her smooth cheek. "You have come for the beach and the fish, my friend?"

"That's the plan. What gave me away?"

She shrugged and tipped up her bottle to drink. "That is why most *norteamericanos* come. Others? They run away from their demons and hide here on the Island of the Snake."

"'Island of the Snake?'"

"*Culebra.*" It sounded slightly dangerous when Raimunda said it. "Did you not know that you are on the Island of the Snake?" She watched him closely. Her right eye drooped a little. John found it enticing.

"And? *Are* there snakes here?"

Raimunda looked at him from between lowered eyelashes. "Not enough, some would say."

John's eyes widened. "And what do *you* say?"

"I say, my friend, there are always snakes if you know how to find them."

"I bet you're a regular snake charmer."

She tipped a modest face and the hair behind her ear slipped free. John wanted to reach over and push it back but he couldn't bring himself to touch her.

"You see my flyer?" He tilted his head toward the wall next to the door. She followed his motion with her gaze.

"That was you?" It was her turn to widen her eyes.

"'Fraid so. Do you like to swim?"

"Sometimes. *Por qué?*"

John looked at his hands, which were wrapped around the half-empty Medalla. She didn't match his mental image of his rescuer, but he wanted her to. "Someone pulled me out yesterday. I would've drowned."

"Oh, no! That is terrible, my friend. No, no I could never save you." She shifted so that she leaned closer. Her husky voice lowered. It caressed his jaw on its way into his ears. "I am *muy débil*. How you say? Weak. I am only *una mujer*. How pull I such a big man from the water?" Here she touched his arm.

John lifted his Medalla and drained it. At the moment, finding his mystery woman seemed less compelling.

She slid the bottles to the side of their table and took one of his hands in her own. "It matters not, my friend. I can make you even more glad to be alive."

⅌⅌⅌

The mermaid circled the canal over and over and over, long after a glaring Ana left the shore. She worried the water over the hapless sea star. A hot, foul stench rose off of it, poisoning the water for a tail's length around it. Its death stank of cruel purpose, not natural release. She hovered over it for long seconds and then darted away toward the spot where the man last treaded water. Here, a different kind of echo altogether colored the water's essence. It was soft, luminous, and warm still. When she'd had more than she could stand from the sea star's final resting spot, she returned to the man's echo and renewed herself.

She'd hardly touched him last night. She'd found him after hours of searching along the coasts until she'd detected him on the northern shore. She'd drawn upon the dark energy of the earth and walked on temporary legs to his sleeping place. His sleep was hollow and yet heavy, devoid of nurturing dreams. He'd come from a far place where something had bound his soul, delicate as a sooty tern chick, in a filament as light and unbreakable as whale sinew. She tested this binding, finding that it had loosened a bit. There was hope then. She could send him dreams and free him entirely.

She lay next to him and sent visions into him as he slept. His dark hair covered her cheek and tickled her nose. She nuzzled the musky hollow beneath his arm. He smelled rich, his salty body excretions becoming his own human cologne, the breath of plants, and cool night air. He smelled like the promise of life. Next to his sharp odor, the *mer* males she knew smelled faint and diffuse, pale and unreal.

In the time between night and day, before the sky lightens with the sun's approach, the mermaid drew away from his warm, dry body. He sighed and she watched his sleeping face as long as she dared. When the shifting light sharpened his features, she stole away to the ocean. A gossamer thread connected them now. It was enough. She could trace him, could follow where he went.

She'd followed him to the place where she'd left him the day before. That's when she realized that he was looking for her. The gossamer thread binding them grew a little sturdier, a little more permanent. His thoughts were open to her and she urged him into the water. He came, bringing the lifeless sea star. She felt his pity and sorrow for the small animal and it moved her. When he lowered its husk, she sent it away on the current. She couldn't restrain herself any longer and she swam around him, running hidden hands along his thighs and up his flank. He radiated heat. She wanted it to weld them.

As soon as he sensed this, she backed away and they began to splash and roll. His deep laugh surprised her. She'd never heard laughter quite like it before and that too captured her. If she could elicit that again and again it would never be enough.

When he said, "Where's my lady *del mar* when I need her?" she knew that it was time to reveal herself.

At that moment, the old woman spoke. The mermaid's glamour wavered, but it held steady under the old woman's jagged gaze. The gossamer thread linking her and the man attenuated and flattened but didn't break. Heart skipping, she swam between him and the old woman, who came closer to the water, squatted, fingered bits of shell. The old woman radiated menace. Then she asked the man the unthinkable.

"Don't believe in mermaids, do you? Why not? Maybe one is swimming right beside you. Close to us vile humans, eh?" The old woman laughed, a sound of broken shells tossed on stone. The mermaid knew that she laughed at both of them. When the man wriggled behind her, she looked back at him. She recognized embarrassment. And denial.

Disconcerted, the mermaid swam to a safe distance where she observed as the man spoke to the old woman, saw him stop and scrutinize her search. She felt his perplexity when the old woman reached the rock where the sea star had lain. Unlike the stranger to whom she'd given her heart, this search troubled the mermaid. It troubled her a great deal.

Four

❦

ON MONDAY MORNING John awakened with an implacable urge to go to the cay across Luís Peña Canal, an urge that went far beyond any desire to be alone on his own private rock, beyond the fear of the ocean crouching in his brain stem. It had all the force of ravenous hunger, of raging thirst, of insatiable lust. After nearly drowning, he would have put off coming back to the dive shop to schedule diving lessons—his stated reason for coming to Culebra— except that he needed to rent a kayak *today* to quell this urge.

So he returned to Chris's Sunken Reef Dive Shop, a dusty storefront carpeted in beige and lined on one side with racks of snorkels, masks, and flippers, as soon as the shop opened, which happened to be ten a.m. Chris, a slouching tanned man with a phone cradled between jaw and shoulder, waved him in before disappearing into the back room. While he waited, John studied the shop more carefully than he had on Saturday. An assortment of artifacts—links of rusty chain, several spikes embedded in worm-eaten planking, and disintegrating portholes—studded the opposite wall along with other less certain items. What appeared to be a palm-size, dark-orange cannonball served as star to a solar system that included ancient handles and a dozen verdigris lengths of metal that may have been fasteners (of what, John had no clue)

34

before the sea laid claim to them. The real treasure, presumably from Chris's underwater adventures, resided in a glass case that divided the shop. Inside, three dark gray plates—pewter, John guessed—lay in state along with flat oval gold rings and several heavy coins stamped with a cross surrounded by lions and what looked like castle towers. An emerald, the size of a teardrop, and flakes of gold held the place of honor in the center of the case.

John tapped his fingers against the smudged glass, his lips compressed and his chest tight. Chris had been friendly and chatty on Saturday, saying it was good to see someone from the States in the off-season, and told John that his diving schedule was wide open for the next two weeks. John knew that getting certified to dive was more important than satisfying an insane need to spend the day on a deserted cay, but he just couldn't think beyond renting a kayak. Would this genial guy deny him one after he confessed that he'd lost the snorkeling gear in Luís Peña Canal?

He found out two minutes later when Chris, his mutt Murphy at his heels, strolled through the doorway from the back office. He carried a flat wooden box that looked like it had been rescued from the wreck of a Spanish galleon. John would love to see what was inside.

"Hey," Chris said. He set the box on the counter between them. "I thought I'd see you today."

That made John nervous. "Why?"

Chris pursed his lips, opened the box. It contained receipts for the shop. John's disappointment couldn't overshadow his anxiety at Chris's next words, however. "I saw the flyer at Isla Encantada. I figured you lost the gear."

John closed his eyes, took a breath, squared his shoulders, and looked at Chris. "Yes, I did."

Chris shook his head slightly. Sighed. Then he pulled out the top receipt and noted something on it. "Shoulda made you wear a vest. I'm gonna have to charge you for the gear."

For the first time since the near-drowning, John felt like an idiot. "I still have these." He held out the mesh bag that stored the gear and the lone flipper.

Chris accepted them, his face thoughtful. "Well, I can use the mesh bag, but no one's lost a leg to shark bite in years." He grinned at John's dumbfounded look and laid the items aside. "A new set will cost me seventy dollars."

"No problem." John handed Chris a credit card, simultaneously relieved that his stupidity was out in the open and angry with himself for the cost. And then he remembered that the cost had nearly been his life and he let the anger go. Instead, while Chris swiped the card, he screwed up his courage. Time to ask. "I don't suppose I can talk you into renting me a kayak?"

Chris dropped the card machine into the box and shut it with a satisfying snick. He studied John while scratching his stubbly chin. "Kayaking alone? Depends. Where you plan to go?"

That was the best John could hope for. At least Chris hadn't said no outright.

"To the cay across the canal." He paused, took a breath. "Listen, I've been white-water kayaking with friends since high school. The trip to the cay will be a piece of cake after all the rapids I've gone over."

Chris nodded. "I believe you, but I'm gonna need to know what happened the other day, before I take you out in open water. That is, if you still wanna dive."

John looked out the window. He'd gotten the kayak, but he still needed the lessons. All the coursework and confined diving in Pittsburgh meant nothing without the open-water dives. What else could he say about his accident? He returned his gaze to the lanky instructor and then looked down at the glass case. The emerald winked at him.

"I have these attacks sometimes. They've always been at night before so I didn't expect this one."

Chris's large eyes grew larger. "Attacks? Like your heart? Man, that's not something I think we should mess with."

John's mouth went dry. How would he make what happened sound mundane? "No, nothing like that. I just wake up sometimes feeling like the room is going to swallow me." He sounded weak. He spread his fingers on the counter, forced an easy grin and some apology into his voice. "What can I say? Thought of my girlfriend and suddenly I couldn't breathe. Got some water down my gullet and suddenly I was drowning."

Chris frowned. "Tell the truth, that makes me a little nervous." He turned, pulled a thick navy binder down from a shelf behind him, and plopped it onto the counter between them. "But it's probably covered under the standard release form."

John nodded. He waited while Chris considered the situation out loud.

"You won't be diving alone, of course."

"Right." John nodded again.

"And you gotta do well on my quiz before we go out."

"No problem." John knew he could ace any written test—he always did well on paper.

Chris scratched his chin again. It sounded like sandpaper. After what seemed like forever but was probably only ten seconds, he made up his mind.

"If you start to feel that way again, give me a sign—hands at your throat works for me—and I'll drag you up. Also, you gotta wear a full-face mask." He waited for John's nod before grinning. The lantern of his large white teeth lit up his long face. "Now that's settled, I gotta ask: is it true that some woman pulled you out?"

"Afraid so." John shifted his feet, shrugged, and smiled. "Any idea who she was?"

"Maybe. What'd she look like?" Chris's eyes had taken on a funny light, especially given how serious he'd been only seconds before. Later, John would wonder uneasily if he'd misread Chris the whole time or if he'd turned into a whack job only after hearing John's story.

"Not sure. I was a little out of it."

"Did you see breasts?" Chris sounded eager; breasts might do that, but the fact that he'd even asked the question stunned John.

"Y-yes," he said. "Is that relevant?"

Chris's grin had grown excited. "Maybe. I've seen one or two of them but never so close to the island."

"Of who?" The change that had come over Chris surprised John. Worse yet, he couldn't follow Chris's narrative. "How many women swim alone and naked around here?"

Chris blinked as though the question caught him by surprise. "Women? No women swim alone and naked around here."

John began to feel exasperated, but he pushed it down. It would do no good to let it out; who knows how Chris's mood would shift. "I'm sorry. What are we talking about then?"

Chris's expression lightened. "The *gente del mar*. I've seen them several times."

"*Gente del mar*'? People of the sea?" Even when he translated it into English, John didn't understand as quickly as he should. When he did, incredulity flickered through his thoughts, and then died down. He smiled. "I see you talked to Tomás. He teased me too."

Chris, who'd been staring out the window and muttering to himself, a little smile curling his mouth, stopped and focused on John. "No one's teasing you. I *have* seen mermaids. And so have other Culebrenses. Pablo and Jorge, the guys who work on my boat, talk about seeing mermaids. ..."

"The oceans are such a huge mystery," John said, choosing his words carefully.

Chris's smile faded. "You think I'm one of those people who believe in UFOs and the Bermuda Triangle, don't you?"

John couldn't meet Chris's eyes. "I didn't say that."

Awkward silence padded the space between them. John looked down at the consent form that Chris had left on the counter. One man's fish might be another's mermaid. Who was he to decide? He looked at Chris, who watched him, shrugged again, and smiled.

"A mermaid's certainly better than a giant squid."

Chris smiled back. "I bet you see her again. I'd take you out, panic attacks and all, just for the chance to be with you when you do."

ىهىهى

After leaving the dive shop, John spent the rest of the morning in Dewey. Chris, although he'd agreed to rent a kayak, had stipulated that he needed to check on John for his own peace of mind. What that meant was that John had to wait until tomorrow. So he shopped for supplies at the *mercado*, picking up a Caribbean soda made with tamarind syrup, peanut butter, a loaf of bread, and a half a dozen oranges. He'd brought a camp stove and enamelware for some of his meals but only halfheartedly tossed four cans of beans into his basket. He'd suspected that camping would test his devotion to Zoë's diet, but he hadn't expected the dearth of good vegetarian convenience foods. He'd have to make do with fruit, imported chips and candy bars, and purified water from the main island. One good thing about Zoë's visit in twelve days: breakfast came with their room at Tamarindo Estates.

When he came out of the *mercado*, he stopped on the sidewalk, clutching his bag of supplies and blinking in the brilliance of the late morning. For perhaps the first time in recent memory, he had no agenda, no goal to accomplish or activity to pursue. Even the intense desire to go to Luís Peña had lost its edge. As he stood there, an unexpected tide of nostalgia surged in him. At 26, he couldn't be justified in missing his youth, in missing the free hours frittered away during summer. Or weekends. Or holidays. The lazy, hazy time spent daydreaming on soft spring mornings instead of tapping away at his keyboard or reading a textbook. But he did miss his youth. More often than not, he turned away from the beckoning green world outside his graduate office. More often than not, he spent hours below ground in a bunker euphemistically called a research lab.

He'd brought a book, of course, Lewis Thomas's *Late Night Thoughts on Listening to Mahler's Ninth Symphony*, but at the moment it seemed like pulling it out qualified as an assignment. A

39

must-do, focused and probing. He wanted—no, he hungered for—diffuse, unplanned, open-ended wandering. After some time, a man pushed past him, lifting his reverie for an instant. Rubbing his forehead in a vain attempt to control his thoughts, he saw his bike and understood that he needed to get on and ride. Unlike his almost-frantic tour of the island yesterday, he peddled only strongly enough to keep the bike going and gradually his thoughts unspooled into emptiness.

His surroundings melted and merged into a living Impressionist artwork, a stained-glass filter that blocked out details of baked asphalt and dusty scrub. He'd lost two hours this way when a nagging ache in the pit of his stomach brought him back to the needs of his body. In his moving meditation, he'd managed to bike back to town—a very good thing because the back of his neck and his forearms had started to burn even though he'd slathered them with sun block.

He walked slowly into a deli, blinking his dazzled eyes in the sudden dimness. A plump, middle-aged American woman in an apron stood muttering with a clipboard before a cooler. She glanced up and smiled; her large eyes and upswept wrinkles promised old-fashioned hospitality and good cheer. She piled shredded carrots on top of a mound of hummus and feta, jabbed an olive-adorned toothpick into the sprouted-grain bun, and grabbed a large handful of plantain chips to wedge into the basket next to his sandwich. Seeing him settled at a table, she returned to her inventory and left him to his book.

John read through the heat of the afternoon, sucking in Thomas's essays with all the fervor of a man dying of thirst. Here was a kindred mind, a scientist and music lover driven beyond the myopic world of hypothesis, controlled setting, calibrated instruments, and precise measurements. To life beyond lab specimens. Even though Thomas's palpable fear of a nuclear holocaust no longer held the urgency it must have once excited, his genuine sense of wonder at the beautiful complexity of the natural world more than made up for its appearance in the lead essay. His willingness to tackle the dark side of modern technology, to pull back and consider the intricate connections among humans, life, and science both gratified and disturbed John.

He left the deli, stuffed in body and in thought. This time when he peddled toward Punta Soldado at the tip of the southern peninsula, coasting on the downhill stretches, he returned again to Thomas's observations about the Earth. At the end of the paved road, he left his bike at the top of a steep hill and picked his way down a rutted dirt path to the rocky beach. He snapped a few photos and then sat down on a boulder near the water. The sun hung low in the sky, its reflection a golden fractal.

After a minute or two, he dug the essays from his backpack and flipped again to a sentiment that had grabbed him:

> Of all celestial bodies within reach or view, as far as we can see, out to the edge, the most wonderful and marvelous and mysterious is turning out to be our own planet earth. There is nothing to match it anywhere, not yet anyway.

Lewis Thomas was right, of course: the Earth was one of the seven wonders of the modern world, one hidden beneath the feet of all those urban souls who tramped unconsciously upon its skin, forever busy with their self-important tasks. His own vision had long been clouded, his own soul long troubled. On impulse, he rose and climbed back up the hill where he could look out at the blue horizon and marvel at its vastness. No one noticed it, this vastness, sitting inside a cubicle or walking along a sidewalk surrounded by houses or office buildings. But here, where there was nothing to obscure his vision, to bring the world down to his size, it was clear just how wide the sky was and just how small *he* was.

He glanced at his watch for the first time in hours. There was still time before the sun set to write a few postcards. He thumbed through glossy photos of old San Juan with its Spanish colonial fort and images of Caribbean parrots, orange and green and yellow like sweet-and-sour lollipops with beaks and claws. What should he send to Zoë? Historic buildings or living creatures? What would he write in the two-inch by two-inch square that would strike the right balance between "having a good time" and "it's no big deal that I'm here without you"?

After shuffling through the postcards, he sighed and decided to put off writing. Instead, he pulled out one of Punta Soldado that he'd bought this morning and scrawled a note to Stefan, who'd joked about John never returning to Pittsburgh:

> *They named this point of land after a soldier who*
> *went AWOL when he came to Culebra. I feel like*
> *going AWOL, too. The beauty of the ocean calls to*
> *me, like a siren.*

What would Zoë think if he admitted that Culebra answered some primeval need in him? She'd take it personally, of course. An image of her large black eyes radiating angry hurt flickered to life in front of his eyes. Perhaps he'd better keep his note chatty and impersonal. After staring toward the setting sun for ten minutes, he finally wrote this on the back of a postcard of Ensenada Honda, Dewey's harbor:

> *Jackpot! I've found the last unspoiled spot in the*
> *Caribbean. No casinos, no swanky resorts. I'm up*
> *with the rooster, literally. Lots to see, do. The food's*
> *great and the locals are friendly. I'll call this*
> *weekend to talk about our plans.*

He'd filled the four square inches; his writer's block had unfrozen once he'd discovered the appropriately casual tone supplied by the exclamation "jackpot." There was hardly room to sign his note, but he hesitated anyway. He never wrote a closing in an email to her, but a handwritten note demanded one. If he signed just his name, would that be intimate enough? Did she expect a "love" or would "cheers," just squeezed in, do? He waited for the answer and when it came, he knew that he couldn't write "love" no matter what she expected. If he was going to fall in love with her, it hadn't happened yet. He was still falling. So he signed only "John."

He stayed at Punta Soldado until the sun sank into the water, its brilliance extinguished in the rhythmic blue. Afterwards, he biked in the deepening dusk through town until he reached Isla Encantada. Standing just inside the entrance, he searched the dim interior, but only a handful of customers sat at the bar drinking. Tomás looked out from behind them and when he caught John's eye, nodded and returned to drying a rack of glasses.

The scent of hot corn oil and fried dough made John's stomach grumble. He ordered *arepas* stuffed with *queso* and a Medalla. The dumplings' flaky crust tasted so wonderful that he found himself ordering more. Tomás grinned at him when the waitress brought over a second plate heaped with extra *arepas*. John ate these so quickly that the bubbling cheese burned his palate, but still his stomach felt hollow. Perhaps he'd better order something more sustaining, something more basic like rice and beans. When the waitress set the bowl of *arroz con habichuelas* in front of him, he started to sigh until he caught sight of the chunk of ham, a dark pink iceberg floating in a sea of rich brown. Even then, he almost tasted it. His mouth watered while he struggled against the complex scent of cilantro, garlic, and smoked meat. The waitress, who'd come to check on his food, saved him from himself. He sent the bowl back untouched.

Tomás came over looking concerned. "The *arroz con habichuelas*, they are bad, *señor*? They are *una especialidad de mi esposa*."

John squirmed and made an embarrassed face. "I'm sure they're *deliciosa*, Tomás. But I don't eat ham."

Tomás's face cleared. "Oh, I see, *señor*. *No problema*. I will tell her to make you some without."

"You don't have to do that."

"Oh, it's *no problema*. Many people, they don't like ham. We often eat it without ourselves."

Thankfully Tomás hurried away before John could protest again. He longed for the ham, but everything tasted so good here that he shouldn't give in to his baser cravings, even though the hollowness in the pit of his stomach had spread down his thighs. To distract himself while he waited for the vegetarian beans and rice, he pulled Zoë's postcard out and laid it on the table to consider.

Fifteen minutes later, the waitress deposited another bowl in front of him with a *thunk*. John looked at her, but she'd already turned, disapproval in her meaty shoulders. John shrugged and scooped up a mouthful of the savory beans and rice. Before he could stop himself, he'd shoveled the contents of the bowl into his maw. Afterwards, he still felt empty. He'd hardly begun to study the menu when Raimunda, pink and brown and luscious, sauntered into his line of vision. She stopped at his table, a hand-rolled cigarette dangling from her fingers. She smiled, her dark eyes bold.

"Find your mystery woman yet?" He couldn't believe how attractive he found her husky voice. The hollow feeling spread to his chest.

"Nope." John hoped that he sounded casual. He nodded toward a seat. "You'll have to do."

Raimunda sat down and pulled her chair closer to his. "Buy me a beer?"

John waved the waitress over and ordered two Medallas. Raimunda put soft fingers on his wrist. He felt rather than heard his stomach growl.

"A plate of *alcapurrias*, too. You do not mind?" She smiled. "I am ravenous."

When the basket of deep-fried yucca fritters arrived, John's stomach did rumble aloud. He smiled and shrugged and focused on his order of *sorullos*, a cornmeal "log" stuffed with cheese.

Raimunda picked up one of the *alcapurrias*, broke it in half, and offered it to him. John shook his head, but his gaze stayed on the tantalizing deep-orange pocket filled with what looked like ground beef. Raimunda took a dainty bite from her half, and John could almost taste the savory meat-and-yucca.

"Have some, my friend," Raimunda said and brought the *alcapurria* nearer to his nose.

They sat that way for an eternity while John's heartbeat filled his head and hunger filled his whole body. He leaned over and took a deliberate, large bite from the fritter. It was his first taste of beef in almost a year and it tasted out of this world. He took another bite, his lips brushing Raimunda's fingers as she popped the last of the *alcapurria* into his mouth. She said nothing, just pushed the basket closer to him.

He ate three more orders of *alcapurrias* before the hollowness inside him had been satiated. He'd had no idea how hungry he'd been until the relief at not being hungry left him drowsy and unfocused. He slouched in his chair and played with the label that he'd stripped from his Medalla bottle. Through its brown glass, he saw Zoë's postcard lying under an empty basket. Grease spots speckled his handwriting. He found that he didn't care.

They sat drinking and talking for another half an hour. A few more customers wandered in and the conversation at the bar grew lively, but no one looked their way. John let words slip from his mouth, too overwhelmed by Raimunda's scent, her throaty laugh, the hollow at the base of her neck, to have more than a passing interest in the sound of his own voice. He floated just outside his head, detached from himself and yet aware of how hot he was, how slick his palms were on his thighs. When Raimunda edged her seat closer, he knew only the reality of the pulse fluttering in her throat.

"Let's leave." She spoke low, sending a thrill through him.

"You got someplace in mind?" He heard the tremor in his voice.

She stood up. Held out her hand. "Come, *gringo*."

They left his bike outside Isla Encantada. She held his hand in her warm, dry one and led him through Dewey, past the disapproving Catholic Church and the darkly officious post office. A few Culebrenses congregated on lit porches drinking beer and listening to tinny radios, their warm laughter muffling John's steps.

Raimunda padded along on cat's feet. On the far side of the plaza a couple of sailors sauntered into the liquor store, but the *pueblo* was otherwise deserted at this hour. No one called out to them or even looked their way—they were wraiths. Near the clinic, Raimunda turned west and headed away from town. John tried to picture where they were going, but a fuzzy Culebra map only flickered and died in his memory.

They walked close to each other, Raimunda's arm grazing his every so often. As she moved, she exuded the spicy scent of cloves and musk that he already associated with her. It made him lightheaded. Perhaps Raimunda clicked no castanets nor seductively twirled any long skirts, but in her company he had no desire to meet a *señorita*. He'd just begun to wonder where she was leading him when he saw the sign for Playa Melones, a small stony beach near the southern tip of the canal. Except for a red navigation light glowing at the tip of a thin tower on the point, only the sound of lapping waves and the pungent odor of seaweed and salt greeted them.

Before John could speak, Raimunda sank down onto her knees and tugged at a sandal strap. She braced her shoulder against his thigh and lifted his foot to remove the loosened shoe, running her warm fingers lightly up his calf afterwards. John let his hand drift to her shoulder where it rested among soft dark hair. He leaned into her as she stripped the other sandal off. Again she caressed his calf. Gooseflesh sprung up in the wake of her fingers, which traveled as far as his shorts. Just as they tickled the skin under the hem, she jumped up and pulled John toward the water. As soon as their feet touched the wet stones, she ran ahead of him on the thin strip of beach.

John stood, gasping faintly.

"Catch me, *gringo*," Raimunda called over her shoulder.

His legs carried him forward before his mind had chosen to act. As John ran after her, she swerved into the ocean. Water swirled around his ankles before he realized what he'd done and stopped.

She appeared not to notice and continued until the water reached her thighs. She turned around to face him.

"You must follow me to catch me, my friend," she said. The warm huskiness of her voice made the night intimate. "Rescue *me*."

The soft sibilance of her *rescue* twined around him, tugged him toward her even though the rush of the water urged him to stay safe on shore. Heart pounding, he waded deeper, his eyes locked onto Raimunda, her head dark against the night sky and her face hidden in shadow. And then she turned and headed toward the path of flickering moonlight caressing the waves. Without warning, she slid under the surface and disappeared. John's heart lanced his throat and he lunged toward the spot that she'd last been standing. Water cascaded over his head as he plunged into the suffocating ocean and grabbed for her. His hand closed on her hair. He snatched her head up and stumbled back until his feet touched the bottom.

They stood there, panting, faces dark and streaming.

"What did you say last night about making me glad to be alive?" The words tumbled out of him. Beyond recall.

For an answer, Raimunda pressed her chest against his and leaned in to kiss him. Her hot, salty mouth clung to his. The water tugged at their shoulders, pulled at their legs. But it could not separate them.

৵৵৵

John woke up late the next morning, headachy and stiff—and bemused. He'd only had three or four beers last night, but the fuzzy feeling between his ears and along his tongue testified to former intoxication, as though the forbidden beef, or Raimunda, had made him drunk. He sat up and rubbed his temples, squinting against the light. He'd slept heavily, dreamlessly. A sense of regret filled him as he realized this. He'd missed something. Or someone. Regret and peevishness sharpened the ache between his eyes, but he managed to shoulder them aside as he ate a cold breakfast of bread and cheese. He had the campground to himself now that the weekend beachgoers had returned to the mainland so he left his sleeping bag unrolled when he left to go kayaking. He biked into town, passing parents kissing children good-bye at the school. It was a familiar, if unexpected sight. That sealed it. No paradise contained a school.

He arrived at Luís Peña around nine-thirty and rowed around to the north side of the cay to the small beach there. Like much of the larger Culebra, the uninhabited Luís Peña Cay was covered with low-growing vegetation, stunted trees and dense shrubs; at its highest point, south of the beach, it reached nearly five hundred feet. Even though it was a nature preserve, day trips for hikes, snorkeling and swimming were allowed. Still, he was almost guaranteed to have the entire cay to himself on a Tuesday morning in March. He'd maneuvered his kayak without any difficulty, gliding smoothly and silently over the innocuous seawater, its clear depths hiding no dangers. After securing the kayak, he set out to explore the cay, taking forty-five minutes to walk its perimeter. By the time he returned to the beach, the fuzzy fatigue had burned off in the morning sun, taking his black feelings with it.

While he drank some water, he imagined that he was Robinson Crusoe. Castaway and forced to survive by his wits. No hard drives. No fluorescent lights. No windowless lab space. Just him, his hands, and what God and nature provided. An image of himself, woolly bearded and tanned sinew, filled his mind. He laughed. He wouldn't last three days let alone twenty-eight years. Still chuckling, he stripped off his sweaty t-shirt and shorts, leaving them to dry on a rock. After a few minutes, he added his sweaty underwear, too.

He considered the ocean before him. Unlike the fear that had gripped him last night when Raimunda beckoned him into the water, this gently lapping expanse promised peace. As long as he went no deeper than waist high, he should be fine. He wandered fifteen feet into the water, which was too warm to cool off in, and swam across the length of the small bay twice. The desire to separate from his body as it moved, to recapture the sweet blankness that had freed him as he'd cycled yesterday afternoon flitted in his thoughts, but a shadow on his spirit stoppered them inside his head. He flipped over onto his back and floated, his hearing muffled by seawater and his eyes dazzled by the sun.

Seabirds streamed overhead like bits of windblown confetti. He tried to distinguish different species, but outside of the laughing gulls he was familiar with and a variety of pelican, the rest remained unknown—just as his rescuer remained unknown. She was one more element of nature, inextricably linked to Culebra's beauty and serenity.

As if conjured up by this thought, an upside-down face blocked his view of the sky.

"Ahhh!" He pulled his feet to the sandy bottom to right himself. His heart zigzagged and his breathing sped up.

Saltwater streamed into his eyes and blinded him. He swiped at the water running down his forehead. When he could see again, he realized that a young woman swam nearby.

"You scared the shit out of me." Even as he said this, his heart righted itself and his breathing calmed.

She flinched and backed away from him.

He regretted his words, the sharpness of his voice. He extended a hand toward her. "No, don't go. I didn't mean to yell at you. You just surprised me, that's all." Could this be his mystery woman? Only her face, her hair plastered to her head, appeared above the water's surface. Hard to know if she had the hair or the breasts to be the one.

She stopped backing away and came closer. She certainly had the eyes, though. Her eyes mirrored the color of the sea. "I'm sorry," she said. "I wanted to make sure you're all right." Innocent concern turned her musical voice grave.

"All right? Why wouldn't I be all right?" Confusion and discomfort tangled his voice. His thoughts were as opaque as the water around him, full of the sand that he'd stirred up, shielding his nakedness only temporarily. He refused to look down, to call her attention to it.

"The last time I saw someone floating alone, she—well, she didn't need any help." Something in her voice, some slight hitch, alerted him. He saw unhappiness cloud her wonderful eyes.

"I take it she'd drowned?" He asked this gently, as if the word might startle her into darting away. She couldn't go until he knew for certain if she were the one that he'd been looking for, if she were the one who'd saved *him* from drowning.

The unhappiness surged into tears; she nodded but said nothing. He wanted to wipe them away, but he didn't dare touch her. He tried to console her with words instead. "It wasn't your fault, you know."

Again she nodded and the tears shone on her cheeks. He looked beyond her and then over his shoulder to the beach. He saw no other kayak and he was sure that he would have heard a water taxi or other boat.

Seeing him searching, she looked away and said in slow words as though uncertain that she should admit to such a fabulous tale, "I swam from the other side of the cay." She'd stopped crying. Her brief tears struck him as natural as a summer shower.

"Really? I was told no one swam alone around here."

"I don't do it often. My father doesn't like me to go far from my family." Her remarkable blue eyes, like stained glass, held his. An electric shock leapt between them.

"Ah." It was his turn to look away. He knew that the water around him had cleared and he was entirely at her mercy. He knew what she would see if he didn't get a handle on himself. He had to keep her talking, had to work up the courage to ask her if she'd pulled him from the canal. "So you live around here?"

"Yes." Her eyes slid away again, fortunately not down. "My father's a fisherman."

So far so good. Time for introductions.

"I'm John." When she said nothing, he continued, "Do you have a name?"

She bit her lower lip, reminding him of his sister Cassie when she was in high school. He wasn't any good at guessing a woman's age, except for some vague sense that she was too young or too old, some rough guideline for the tenor of their interactions. The lip biting signaled extreme youth. Surely too young to have the breasts

50

he'd seen. Too young to pull a grown man, thrashing and gasping, to shore.

"Never mind. I'm sure your parents wouldn't want you to tell me your name."

Her next words confirmed his suspicions about her youth. "I don't care what my father wants and my mother's dead." Still she didn't tell him her name. Instead, she asked, "Where're your pants?"

Heat rose in John's cheeks. He looked down, not to verify her statement but to hide his embarrassment. Nothing like exposing himself to a pubescent girl. At least he'd controlled himself in time—he didn't have *that* on his conscience. "I thought I was alone. I was sweaty after walking around."

"Oh, so it's not your custom to swim naked?"

"Now that you mention it, I'd like to get dressed."

With as much dignity as he could muster, he swam to the beach and stood up, walking toward the rock where his clothes lay without turning to see if she'd followed. He pulled his briefs and shorts on before looking over his shoulder. She remained behind.

"Aren't you coming out?" Perhaps she feared him. They were alone, after all.

After a moment, she swam closer and stood up. When she did, John understood why she'd hesitated. Except for a pair of tan cargo shorts that looked a lot like his, she wore nothing else. Heat flooded John's face again.

"Here." He tossed her his t-shirt. She caught it and looked at it before looking back at him. She didn't seem nearly as disconcerted as he felt. "Please put it on."

Shrugging, she pulled the t-shirt over her head. Her hair left large dark patches on the shoulders and the shirt clung to her wet breasts, negating the concealment of the cloth and testing his theory about her age. *She's too young*, he repeated to himself. *Dangerously young.* Every aspect of her behavior pointed to innocence and vulnerability. She walked over to the rock and sat down and began to comb out the tangles in her hair with her fingers.

"And you asked why I was naked? No wonder your father doesn't want you to go too far from your family." John stopped, thinking. "Maybe you should get back to him. I'd hate for him to show up and see you're wearing my shirt."

She looked down. "He wouldn't be happy, no." She made no move to leave, however.

John frowned at her. She seemed too slight to pull a flailing man out of the canal, but he couldn't help himself. Too young or too slight, everything else fit. He had to ask.

"Did you save me from drowning a couple of days ago?"

He watched her toy with a strand of damp hair; her eyes followed the pelicans walking stiff legged through the shallows not far from them.

"Yes, I did," she said at last without looking at him.

At her words, a thrill sparked the tender of his curiosity and ignited some strong emotion in him. He damped it down, as much to calm himself as to keep from scaring her. *Go slowly*, he told himself.

"Please, I'd really like to know your name."

She looked at him and he fell into the immense blue of her eyes. In that instant, he recognized the face that he'd described to Tomás. Why had he ever doubted it? "Tamarind. I'm Tamarind."

"Like the trees?" When she nodded, he thought, *How fitting. A water sprite with a wood nymph's name.* She really was the embodiment of a natural element. He went on, "I'm sorry if I sounded rude a moment ago, Tamarind."

She cocked her head, looking for the world like an inquisitive bird. "Are you going now, John?"

"No." He couldn't say *I can't go now that I know who saved my life. I need to know more about you.* Instead, he said, "I brought lunch. Would you like some?"

"Lunch?" She sounded perplexed.

"It's not much. Just some oranges and peanut butter sandwiches." He retrieved his backpack from the kayak and pulled out the food. She hadn't moved from her perch. He held up an orange in one hand and two peanut butter sandwiches in the other.

When Tamarind said nothing, he came over and sat on the sand at her feet. She watched him slide a sandwich out of its clear baggie and bite into it.

"Would you like to try some?" he offered, holding out the other sandwich.

"Yes!" A smile transformed her small face, which was tucked into a bed of drying hair that already showed signs of wildness. John thought he saw bits of seaweed in it as befitting a water sprite. Just like a sprite, she was small, perhaps only as tall as his shoulder, and delicately built. She was definitely too young. Maybe not even in high school.

Ignoring the proffered sandwich, she leaned over and bit into John's. After a few chews, she started coughing and gagging.

"What?" Fear clutched John's chest. He leaned in and put his hand on her shoulder. "Are you choking?"

In response Tamarind began digging into her mouth. John watched her with mixed astonishment and fascination. Bits of peanut butter and bread clung to its corners and flecked her cheeks. She spit without turning her head away, her tongue pushing the tenacious paste that had been her sandwich out of her mouth. At last, she wiped the mush away with the back of her hand. She appeared totally unaware that her actions could be perceived as curious at best, disgusting at worst. John surprised himself by finding her lack of social awareness appealing. Clearly she hadn't been molded yet in the rough world of adolescence.

"Mmmnuhh!" She screwed her face up. "What *is* that?"

John's own sandwich lay forgotten in his lap. "All that because you've never tasted a peanut butter sandwich before?"

Tamarind tossed her head a little and the tangles of her hair fluttered around her face. He wanted to brush it away, like a big brother taking care of his kid sister. He'd fixed Cassie's hair when she was little. "It clung to the inside of my mouth, like a tongue crab."

"Tongue crab? What's that?"

Tamarind's brow creased as she thought. "A tiny crab that crawls into a fish's mouth. It latches onto the fish's tongue and drinks its blood. The tongue shrivels up and falls off." She caught his expression and laughed. It was a delightful gurgle. "Don't worry. The crab becomes the fish's tongue."

"I can see you're going to be a bundle of fascinating facts." John smiled and put his sandwich away.

Tamarind didn't seem to hear him. She dropped off the rock and waded out into the water.

"Hey, I'm sorry. I don't mind your stories," he said, standing up.

She waved a hand toward him. "I'll be right back."

He sat and watched as she entered the water and began swimming what looked like the butterfly but so fluidly and gracefully that she appeared to glide through the water. She swam out about fifty yards and disappeared. He waited, his chest tightening and his throat closing, but she popped to the surface before his head began to pound. This time, when she swam back, she didn't use her arms, which she held in front of her as though she were a human torpedo. She managed to get her feet beneath her and rose in one smooth movement, her hands cupped together. For no reason, John thought of primordial life emerging from the oceans. He kept his eyes on her face and avoided looking at her transparent t-shirt.

Tamarind approached him, her liquid blue eyes bringing some of the sea with them. She held out her hands. John peered at them. At first, he thought that she'd brought back a jellyfish, but then he realized that it was a mess of translucent, worm-like creatures with little round white eyes with black centers—like those wiggly eyes children used in crafts.

"Your turn," she said and held up one of the creatures pinched between forefinger and thumb.

"Uh, what is it?" John asked, stalling. The creatures were squirming.

"Baby reef fish," she said and popped a whole handful, like peanuts or popcorn, into her mouth.

Could he tell her that he didn't eat fish? But he'd eaten beef last night. In for a penny, in for a pound. Besides, she'd clearly never had peanut butter before and *she* hadn't hesitated. Maybe he could just spit his out, too? John swallowed and reached for one of the larvae, grasping its slippery body. It squirted from his grip and dropped in the sand.

Tamarind laughed, leaned over, and dropped several into his mouth, as though he were a seal. Or baby bird. He didn't chew. He swallowed. It was like swallowing salty noodles. Not so bad after all, but he'd pass on doing it again.

"Thanks." His voice came out as a croak.

She finished eating the tiny fish from her palm, sucking the last three between her lips. John shrugged; he'd watched enough cable television to know that people of different cultures ate all kinds of things. Fish seemed rather benign in comparison to insects. Or snakes.

She lifted her face to the sky and smiled, an unself-consciously happy upturn that rendered her eyes half moons of pleasure. Particles of food still outlined the corners of her mouth and there was a smear of peanut butter in her hair, but she was oblivious to them. Instead, she started humming a tune. John had never heard anything like it before. The vibrations thrummed through her torso as if her ribcage were a tuning fork. He heard variations in pitch emanating from her throat, serving as a nice counterpoint to the bass of her body. She clicked her tongue against her teeth at the same time. John sank his feet into the warm sand of the beach and closed his eyes to listen. His spirit soared into the cerulean above them. When she stopped, he dropped back into himself.

"Why'd you stop?" He looked at her. Whatever she'd done, she'd gifted him with the sweet blankness that he'd experienced on his bike ride.

"Do you ever fly up with the birds?" she asked. In the space of a heartbeat, she went on, "Do you ever go underwater, I mean, way underwater or do you only use one of those tubes and stay near the surface?"

"I'm trying to learn to dive, but—"

"Where'd you come from? Is it far from here?"

"I'm from Pittsburgh, which takes two short flights to get here. I—"

She didn't wait for more but leaped up. "It was very pleasant meeting you, John. Thank you for the shirt. I hope to see you again."

She laid a cool, moist hand onto his cheek and looked at him unsmilingly. After a moment, the spectacular smile split her face again and lit her eyes, and then she backed away from him without looking at the ocean.

"Wait!"

But she only waved and turned to run into the shallow water. When the water reached her thighs, she flung herself into the next wave. John saw a tangle of arms and hair as she surged away from him.

"Wait," he repeated to himself. He didn't know what else to say.

When she looked back at him, her laughter danced like sunlight on waves. And then she disappeared around the point toward the canal.

⋟⋟⋟

That evening, John ventured south over the drawbridge to the Dockside, as much to avoid running into Raimunda as for a change of culinary pace. Isla Encantada was small and intimate, and he'd be a sitting duck if she showed up. He'd had all day to consider what he'd done last night and he still didn't know how it had happened. He wasn't a saint by any means, but he knew where his boundaries were. At least, he thought that he'd known. Raimunda had waltzed right over them as if they didn't exist. As if she had a secret code that bypassed his system programming. The question was: would Zoë believe him? Would she forgive him? They lived together; it mattered a great deal what he did with another woman, to himself as much as to Zoë. Stefan, if he knew, would grin and offer to buy him a beer.

John asked the waitress to seat him as far from the entrance as possible and she led him to a small table next to the canal. While he waited for his order, he drank iced tea and composed a speech to Zoë, but no matter how many times he tried, nothing he said sounded plausible or defensible. He stayed there all evening trying to find the words, sitting in an ever-increasing cloud of mosquitoes who dined on his penitent flesh until the waitress gently shooed him out.

Five

☙

WHEN IT FINALLY CAME TIME for John to strap on an oxygen tank and drop sixty feet to the ocean floor, he found that nearly drowning no longer dominated his thoughts. He couldn't look at the Caribbean without seeing Tamarind's luminous eyes—everything else about the sea receded into meaninglessness. He hadn't entirely lost his fear. It had just moved inside a plexi-glass box inside his mind: he could see his irrational self pounding and mouthing words, but it had been reduced to wild gestures that he ignored.

He met Chris at his shop. Chris had lost the feral gleam in his eyes and never mentioned the *gente del mar* while they loaded gear with Pablo and Jorge onto his boat. His no-nonsense demeanor and thorough checklist turned the lights out in John's anxiety box. As they worked, he told John what to expect at Amberjack—the reef southwest of Culebra named for the silver fish that clustered in schools there. The currents were variable, for good and for bad, but nothing that a neophyte couldn't handle. John started to look forward to it, to see himself surrounded by water and breathing fine.

They'd boarded the boat and were casting away when he caught sight of Raimunda slouching against a corrugated building on shore, one knee bent under her tiered skirt. Even from a distance, warm, spicy smoke from her cigarette drifted over the cool smell of saltwater, mesmerizing and insistent. A familiar hollowness filled John. He nearly cried out to Chris to reverse course and tie up again, but he clinched his jaw instead and wrenched his gaze forward to the brilliant horizon. The scent of clove lingered like regret until Culebra had shrunk into a dark speck.

While they sailed, an ominous patch of clouds obscured the sun. Pablo and Jorge shielded their eyes and muttered to each other, but as quickly as it had appeared, the patch blew away. Chris pulled out photo albums with hundreds of pictures of fish, crustaceans, coral, and seaweed from dives he'd taken throughout the Caribbean. John nodded and murmured over as many pictures as he deemed polite. Perhaps it was the protective sheet overlaying the images, but the sea life looked plastic and posed.

Chris closed the creaky cover on the last album. "I've been everywhere. Always come back to Culebra though. It isn't the best diving in the world, but there's something about the waters around this little rock in the ocean. It's not just that they're so clear. There's something, I don't know, something *eternal*. Something bigger than us here."

John, who'd let the sound of the engine lull him into a trance, stirred and stretched. He'd been thinking of Tamarind's crazy hair and infectious laugh. The outrageous way she'd spit out her food, the graceful speed of her swimming. He'd tried to recall her humming, but he could only identify its absence. He tugged himself back to the present and Chris, who sat rubbing the album cover.

"I guess Culebra really is the 'Enchanted Isle,'" he said. It was the first thing that came to mind.

Chris looked at John out of the corner of his eye. His introspective mood visibly changed. "Think you'll see your mermaid?"

The question didn't surprise John. It didn't bother him as much as it would have two days ago. "Maybe."

"Ah-ha! You've already seen her again." Chris studied him. "She's pulling you under her spell."

A dolphin broke the surface of the water. John watched as it leapt beside the boat, racing them. An image of himself riding on its back filled his mind, echoing his dream from the morning after his rescue. "I met the girl who pulled me out, yes."

Chris beamed. "What'd I tell you?"

John smiled at him. "She's a scrawny young thing." He almost said, *Too young for me*. He didn't. Instead, he pointed out the obvious. "With legs."

Chris grinned. "Oh, yeah. They can put on legs, walk on shore. I'll bet you cold cash you won't find it easy to go back to Pittsburgh next week."

It was clear that Chris couldn't be talked from his irrational belief. But how irrational was it? How had Tamarind pulled him, a 165-pound male, from eight feet of ocean? She'd grabbed him as he slipped under that last time. Perhaps that explained it....

John shoved the doubt aside and ended their debate with a joke. "Don't tell my girlfriend that. She'll come down here and kick my ass all the way back if I don't."

Chris shook his head and stowed the albums away in watertight bags. As he headed below decks to put them into a locker, he called over his shoulder, "I came to Culebra to escape my girlfriend. Best thing I ever did."

৵৵৵

At Amberjack, they descended through warm, clear water to a bottom where tan-colored soft corals sprouted, sheltering tiny black-and-yellow-striped wrasses. A sharp, brief twinge of fear erupted through John's mental restraint, but it was too late. He succumbed to the press of water overhead, gave into it—and found himself free to mingle with a teeming world of alien life. Even as John watched, the wrasses set up cleaning stations there to rid barracudas and orange hogfish of parasites. Not far from the coral lay a long line of rocks where delicate sponges and red and black deep-water gorgonians blossomed in a rich brocade, large French angels gliding among them. At the end of the row of rocks a cabin-sized boulder jutted off the flat sand. A school of amberjack swirled around John, many of them larger than his torso. Here Chris urged him to shoot some photos.

As John floated over the boulder with his waterproof disposable at his eye, he heard—or rather felt—humming like the song Tamarind had hummed the day before. The weight of the water around him disappeared and colors brightened. Yet when he looked around he saw nobody but Chris, who hovered nearby. Chris turned his palm up, questioning. He grabbed at his own throat with two hands before repeating the upturned palm. John shook his head vigorously and brought the camera again to his eye. No panic assailed him now. He'd shed his fear as easily as a sea snake shed its skin.

୬୬୬

In the warm air afterwards, his body weighed more and the nerves in his skin tingled, exposed. The fiberglass deck burned his bare soles, but John scarcely noticed. As he moved around the deck, he swayed to the rhythm of his afternoon dive even though the boat rocked little. When they returned to Chris's dock in the harbor, they tied the boat up and began stowing gear in the lockers. Voices further down the dock, the thin cries of seabirds, and the sawing of outboard motors out in the harbor all washed over him after the deep silence of Amberjack.

"John." Tamarind's odd voice startled him.

Looking up, he saw her standing on the dock in his t-shirt and the same pair of cargo shorts that she'd worn the day before and still barefoot. Copper-colored hair corkscrewed around her face, obscuring her eyes in the breeze. A smile radiated through the mess.

"Hey, Tamarind! And here I was afraid I'd never see that t-shirt again."

Chris paused behind him at that moment and said in a low voice, "I'd be afraid I'd never see what's in that t-shirt again."

Raising his voice, he said, "Go on. I can take care of the rest of this. See you tomorrow then."

John nodded, grabbed his backpack and slipped on his sandals before stepping up onto the dock.

"Your father anchor somewhere close by?"

"Yes." She matched his pace as he walked. "What were you doing? Fishing?"

"Nope. That guy—Chris," here he gestured behind him, "is keeping an eye on me while I dive. We went out to Amberjack today."

"Keeping an eye on you? What does that mean?"

John looked at her, but it was a serious question. "Watch. Dive with me in case I try to drown myself again."

"Oh. Well, then, that makes sense. You obviously have a lot to learn."

"Gee, thanks."

She stopped. "Did I say something wrong?"

John sighed and turned toward her. "No, no. I guess I'm not used to hearing such brutal honesty, except from my—my friend Zoë. But she enjoys it."

"Enjoys it?" She appeared to think for a moment. "It's not that I enjoy or don't enjoy it. I just tell the truth. We were all babies once."

John looked at her for a long moment. "I believe you." He heard the surprise in his voice and hurried on. "Do you dive?"

She looked away and started walking again. "Yes."

"Do you want to dive with me tomorrow then? Chris won't mind." He didn't say that Chris would salivate at the chance to dive with a mermaid. He didn't think that he could say that with a straight face.

"I haven't ... with the things you use."

"Really?" They walked along in silence while he pondered what she meant. He imagined Chris grinning. He went on slowly, thinking aloud, "You dive like pearl divers? That's amazing! How long can you stay down?"

She looked at him, her eyes wide but said nothing.

"Well, I don't know much about them, but I think there are some people who can dive pretty deep and stay there for a minute or two to look for oysters. Where'd you learn to dive without equipment?"

"I don't know." She looked away from him.

"You don't know?"

"We've always dived without things, all of us."

"All of you?"

"All of my family."

"Why? Why does your family dive? Is it for your livelihood?"

"'Livelihood'? What's that?" Again, the eyes that haunted his dreams jolted him as she turned to look at him.

"To bring up stuff to sell. Like the pearl divers."

She shrugged. "We just do. We dive because we can."

"Oh, well, that's a good enough reason." He looked at her, but her crazy hair hid her features. He rushed on. "I think it'd be pretty cool to see you in action. That's if you'd show me."

She didn't say anything, her head bent to look at the street onto which they'd just stepped. John changed the subject.

"Can you do that humming thing again? It was unbelievable! I felt like I'd just had a full night's sleep *and* a massage. I can't remember being so relaxed and alert."

Without answering, Tamarind began humming. This time, the throat-level hum skipped along in a decidedly upbeat melody. They walked for several minutes with the heat of the afternoon rising from the pavement around them. John, looking at Tamarind's feet, wondered if they'd developed protective calluses or if her humming blocked out all burning sensation in them. He was about to ask her if she wanted to join him for lunch when she abruptly stopped humming. He glanced aside. Her gaze had frozen forward.

"I've got to go. Perhaps I'll see you tomorrow." A note of panic sounded in her voice.

"Wait! Tell me where I can find you."

She didn't answer; instead she turned down a side street and hurried away. John started to call after her when a small movement caused him to look ahead. Ana sat cross-legged under a palm tree forty feet away, a large mat in front of her. Sunlight glinted on numerous small objects around her. When John's gaze met hers, she folded her hands into her scrawny lap and nodded. The lightness following Tamarind's humming drained away into the scorching pavement. A gull laughed overhead. John looked up reflexively and bird crap dropped onto his bare shoulder.

That night, Raimunda found him at his camping spot at Flamenco Beach. When she finally slept, John lay on his back staring at the stars for a long time. He found that, if he focused on the distant wash of wave on shore, he could remember Tamarind's song. He imagined that it sounded like the music of the ancient seas, of the primordial ooze that birthed every living thing.

෴෴෴

When John went out on his second dive with Chris, he looked for Tamarind at the dock, but she never appeared. This time, no humming reached him underwater, but he played the memory of her last tune over and over in his head like that refrain by Sheryl Crow—*All I wanna do is have some fun.* Whether it actually kept his panic at bay or only acted as a placebo, he had no way of knowing. On his third and final dive on Friday, he hummed to himself behind his mask. Chris flashed him a thumbs-up at the end of the dive and John knew that he'd earned his certification. He looked for Tamarind again after they docked, but she didn't show up. Much to his relief neither did Raimunda that night.

Now that he'd completed his training, John had several days to explore other areas of Culebra, especially its National Wildlife Refuge—and to lose himself in its dusty isolation. He planned to check out Playa Brava and Playa Resaca on the north coast where leatherback turtles swam ashore every spring to lay their eggs in sandy nests. But his trek wouldn't soothe him: his inexplicable unfaithfulness simmered in his unquiet spirit. He prayed instead that hard hiking might exorcise Raimunda. A part of him, the altar boy part, the part that cared that he hadn't been to Mass since his grandmother died, sought absolution on the hilly terrain east of Flamenco.

But first, he had to call Zoë. To hear her voice for the first time in a week, to tell her. He woke too early, anxiety curdling his stomach. Forgoing breakfast, he tried to read to pass the time. He'd already finished *Late Night Listening to Mahler's Ninth Symphony* so he read through the proposal for his research mission again, trying to focus on the marine geology, which wasn't his area. When it was late enough, he biked into Dewey to use Chris's phone. Chris, his large eyes drooping, yawned and led him to the room in the back where an old black phone sat on a metal desk. He waved at John, yawned again, and left.

Zoë sounded groggy when she answered. "God, John! Do you have to call so early?"

"Sorry. I forgot you're in the middle of your paper." Had she been too busy to notice that he hadn't written to her?

"You don't know the half of it." Already she sounded alert. True to her nature, she warmed to her subject in zero to thirty. "Dan's decided we need to run some new simulations before we submit the final paper and I've been working eighteen-hour days all week."

Sympathy, played well, could distract her. "He's out of his freakin' mind. Who does that any way?"

"A man who knows everyone in the security world and can get all the extensions he wants. I'm sleeping in today as an act of rebellion." She paused. Her voice turned silky. "When I get down there next Saturday, there's no way I'm sleeping at the beach. This island of yours might be paradise, but I don't need to do penance to be let in, do I?"

"No, of course not. I've already booked a cottage." Let her think that Culebra was a 'paradise,' something from a travel brochure. *He'd* be doing penance when she arrived. "It overlooks the ocean."

"Beautiful." She paused. "Had any luck diving?"

"Yeah, it went much better than I'd hoped. I won't have any trouble." The truth hadn't found its way to his tongue so he chattered on. "I saw some amazing sea life last week. It was like I'd descended into a Disney theme park, the colors were that bright."

"I told you there's nothing like snorkeling along a reef." Zoë's familiar smugness nettled him; he seized onto it to keep from drowning. "I'm looking forward to getting in some snorkeling. How's Playa Flamenco? Every bit as beautiful as you read?"

He counted to three, let out a steady breath. When he spoke, he sounded casual. "Oh, absolutely. A mile of pristine white sand, which unfortunately is crowded with drunk campers on the weekend. I took the ferry over with a few hundred last Saturday. They start drinking at eight a.m. and sleep at the beach."

So much for letting her think Culebra was a paradise. At least he'd told the truth. Maybe it would be easier to admit that he'd slept with another woman now.

"Okay, I'll cross Playa Flamenco off the list, then. Too bad, I was looking forward to sunbathing topless." The silkiness returned, inviting him to banter, but he couldn't respond in kind. He changed the topic to get his legs under him, to give him control.

"I've been going over the proposal again. The geology, what I understand of it, is incredibly fascinating. These guys don't really know what they're going to see down there, and it's rife with speculation. I'm beginning to appreciate just how important this is. It's like we're going to the moon for the first time."

"Not thinking about changing careers, are you?" It was a throwaway question.

More truth leaked out, surprising John as he said it. "I wonder sometimes."

If she'd understood him, she would have mined this vein for all of its worth, but Zoë didn't follow up. She appeared to have another, more serious issue to confront.

"So, have you met anybody on Culebra? Any sassy *señoritas*?" Her voice was light, playful, but John knew better.

Now was the time to tell her. He squirmed, grateful that she couldn't see his face. He couldn't see hers, either, and in that moment he knew that he couldn't tell her over the phone. He'd have to take his punches in person.

"Except for the weekends, this place is pretty quiet. There's a guy here who is Hemingway's double. He was talking to a couple of American college students the other day. I guess I could've sat at the bar with them, but I just satisfied myself with speculating about what brought them here. Other than that, I've spent most of my time with a guy from the dive shop."

Zoë must not have heard the tremor in his voice, only the escapism.

"You've got a week ahead of you with nothing to do except visit some sea-turtle nesting grounds and drink beer? I really wish I could've gotten away sooner to be with you. But *I'm* not blessed with an advisor who thinks it's okay to start spring break a couple of weeks early."

"What?" John feigned exaggerated ignorance. He could hide in humor now that the crisis had passed. "I'm here preparing for my mission."

"Yeah, yeah. Save it for the envious geeks you call friends. What are you *really* going to do with yourself? Daydream about what you're going to do to me when I finally get there?"

John ignored the question. "When *are* you getting here?"

"I'm flying into Dewey at 10 Friday morning where I'm sure you'll be waiting impatiently to see me."

"Impatient isn't the word," he said—honesty hidden in humor. Another relief to his sore conscience, even if it was indirect. "I'll see you on Friday then."

"Okay, I'll see you on Friday. And John—I love you." She'd slipped it in, just when he'd thought that he was home free.

John mumbled good-bye and hung up. He took the ponytail holder out of his hair and raked his fingers through the thick strands a couple of times, looking out toward the horizon. He shrugged and twisted the holder around his hair again. He'd delayed the catharsis of confession; now all he could do was to throw himself into his hike.

67

He picked up his backpack and set out for Playa Resaca, the nearest of the two nesting beaches. As he hiked the tortuous mile and a half, his mind emptied and he soaked in the mid-morning sun like a solar cell. He wasn't serene and detached as he'd been on the bike ride; on the contrary, he experienced an exquisite awareness of his body in its surroundings. The sun burned the back of his neck and forearms and that knowledge consumed him until he focused on his straining hamstrings and calves. He felt the heaviness of his footfalls on the steep boulder-lined trail that led him 650 feet upwards through a forest of cupey and jaguey, whose stilt-like roots shaded orchids, succulent bromeliads, and agave with their stiff, sword-shaped leaves. The still air clung to him like a wetsuit and he stopped frequently to drink water and shoot photographs. Once he arrived at the eastern side of the mountain, the trail plunged to the shore; and by the end of his hike, he panted and his skin was slick with sweat.

Playa Resaca—"bottom of the sack" in Spanish—was nearly as beautiful as Playa Flamenco; Mount Resaca and the rugged terrain that he'd hiked sheltered the beach and it remained deserted, even this late in the morning. John surveyed Playa Resaca for several minutes, resting from his trek and sipping water. He could well understand why the leatherbacks would avoid the noisier Playa Flamenco for this beach; he himself preferred its solitude. When his breathing had evened out, he continued through the thorny scrub toward the other main nesting beach, Playa Brava, where he would take a quick dip.

Playa Brava was much like Playa Resaca: sheltered and deserted. Here, however, the surf was much stronger; hence its name: "the rough one." John walked along the length of beach, imagining awkward turtles swimming onto the shore. Once they had cleared the water, their powerful flippers would be nearly useless in the clinging sand; they would manage to propel themselves across the beach with the drive to bury their eggs on land.

John paused in mid-stride.

Why do female sea turtles split their lives between sea and land? Why do they leave their eggs alone and vulnerable? Surely beaches are no safer than the sandy ocean bottom?

He looked up at the bright, flat sky.

There must be hawks or something who like turtle eggs. Come to think of it so do people and other animals. Why do leatherback turtles risk the survival of their species by leaving the ocean?

No answer came to him. As he stood, caught by these sudden questions, a lone seagull glided overhead, arcing over his spot. John watched, turning to follow it. The gull laughed and sped away toward the west.

Hot, hungry and unable to sustain a coherent mental struggle, he strode back to his backpack, which he'd left under a tree. He sat with his back against the trunk and pulled a sandwich and chips out. As he ate, he glanced idly up at the tree, which had numerous small green fruits resembling crabapples growing on it. He'd seen fruit trees all over the island: orange, lime, banana, guava, and mango. Perhaps the fruit of this tree was also edible, even if he wasn't familiar with it. He'd take some back with him to Dewey and ask a local what it was and if he could eat it.

He'd finished his lunch, including an orange and a banana, and stood up to pluck one of the fruits when a woman's voice behind him said, "No, don't touch it."

His fingers slipped from the fruit, which fell to the ground at his feet. He turned to face Tamarind, who stood fifteen feet away.

"Tamarind! You surprised me." He heard the happiness in his voice but didn't have time to wonder at it.

She stepped toward him. "The fruit of the *manchineel* tree is very poisonous."

John shook his head, smiling. "I wasn't going to eat it, if that's what you thought. I'm not *that* stupid."

She frowned, her eyes a vivid blue-green. "It's dangerous even to touch. It bleeds white. It burns."

John stood and gazed at her. She held his gaze for a moment but then tilted her head and stared off into the tree line. Strands of damp hair lifted off her neck and danced along a finger of breeze.

He teased her, hoping that she'd look at him. "Saved again in the nick of time. How'd you find me? You following me?"

She turned and looked back toward the water. "Yes."

"I don't know whether to be flattered or worried." Still teasing, he took a step toward her.

"Worried? Why?" When she looked at him, her amazing eyes had widened.

"I'm just not used to being stalked." He grinned at the thought of this girl stalking anybody.

She kept her gaze on him. He'd aroused her curiosity. "'Stalked'? What does 'stalked' mean?"

"Follow someone around a lot without him knowing it."

She tossed her head and the breeze caught her tangled hair and pulled it away from her face. "Now you know I'm following you. Maybe I'll stop." Here she stuck her hands in the pockets of her cargo shorts and turned away from him.

John darted forward and caught her arm before she could walk more than a step. Her skin and hair smelled salty. "No you don't. Your abrupt exits are unnerving. Besides, I know you're not stalking me. Stalkers don't usually act the part of guardian angel."

She didn't try to escape; if anything she shifted closer. "Guardian angel?"

"My protector. Please, stay for a while." He gestured to the tree where he'd been sitting and sat down. "No more peanut butter sandwiches, I promise."

She squatted on the sand, imitating his posture. "How's your diving?"

John realized that he hadn't stopped grinning. "Well, I passed my test so now I'm certified! You'll have to come up with another reason to follow me around."

She wrapped her arms around her knees and stared at the sand near her feet. She said nothing. His grin faded. Maybe he'd gone too far.

John took a long pull on his water bottle and changed the subject. "You know when the sea turtles start coming in to lay their eggs?"

Tamarind pushed a clump of hair behind her ear where it sprang immediately to freedom. "They come to land after the rain starts, perhaps in a week or two."

"You ever helped out with counting eggs or monitoring beach conditions?"

"No. But my family helps out whenever we see any on their way here."

"How d'you do that? You can't put out a beacon or anything, right? I thought lights distracted the turtles from finding their nesting spots."

She shrugged. "We do whatever we can. Turtles aren't very smart. They eat anything that looks like a jellyfish. You people dump a lot of garbage."

"You sound like a marine biologist." As he spoke, he idly traced her name in front of his toes with his fingertip.

Tamarind shifted so that she could bend her face nearer to the sand. Her elbows jutted out on either side of her torso and her hair fell over her face in riotous deluge as she studied the letters, the layer nearest her slender neck damp and smelling of the sea. For an instant, John thought he saw the iridescence of mother of pearl at the top of her spine, but when he squinted for a better look, her smooth skin was bare. She wore no jewelry at all.

"What's that?" She pointed at his tracing. "I've seen that before."

"I should hope so. It's your name." He touched each letter as he called it out. "T-a-m-a-r-i-n-d. Tamarind."

"It is?" She didn't look at him. Instead, she reached her forefinger out and drew over the letters. Under her breath she repeated their names. Then she traced the letters again under his, repeating them as she did so.

"You can't read?" He said this gently but surprise still colored his voice.

"No."

Something in the way that she hunched her shoulders told him not to ask anything else about the topic. She shifted back onto her buttocks and draped her arms around her bent knee. She hummed a bit, as though trying out a tune and then began in earnest. As abruptly as she began, she stopped.

"Did you come just to learn to dive?"

"Pretty much. I came to spend a couple of weeks getting used to the water for a research mission I'm going on next week. I got seasick once and needed to get my sea legs before I sail."

"Sea legs?" Then she laughed the same delightful burble that he'd heard when they first met. He hadn't realized that he'd wanted to hear it again until now. "*I* have sea legs and I want land legs!"

Turning to squint at the sky, he shaded his eyes with his hand. "I also came to spend some time away from a computer screen and cinderblock walls." It felt safe to let that out.

"So you aren't going to be here much longer?"

"Just another week. Then it's back to the salt mines."

"There's a lot of salt in the sea." She looked serious.

John whooped, a head-thrown-back, hand-slapping-thigh reaction. "That's priceless! I'll have to use that next time I want to take off when I should be working."

A sound in the bushes behind them caused John to turn around. A dark-haired, brown-skinned man wearing a khaki shirt and pants emerged from the path and stopped short when he saw them. He smiled, white teeth splitting his brown face. John guessed that he was a park ranger.

"*Hola.*"

"*Hola.*"

"*Hablás Español?*" When John shook his head, he went on. "This isn't the best beach for swimming, you know. The current here is very strong."

"No problem. We're just enjoying the view."

The man looked at Tamarind, who sat humming and tracing in the sand. He grinned again. "I see what you mean. It's especially lovely today."

John ignored the comment and he leaned closer to her. He almost put his arm around her but stopped himself. "I was wondering. You got all the volunteers you need this year to help count leatherback eggs?"

The ranger, who'd been rummaging through a large olive-green duffel, paused to think.

"Another pair of hands, they would make the work grow lighter." Another grin sent a sparkle to his eyes.

"Thanks." After the ranger walked away from them, John turned to Tamarind and smiled. "Maybe you should volunteer. I get the feeling you're going to need something to do after I'm gone."

"I can always find some other tourist to 'stalk.' You're not much different from sea turtles, you know."

Six

∽

Zoë arrived on Culebra the following Friday morning, an Amazon warrior barely civilized for life among unevolved men. John met her at the airport in a rented Suzuki Samurai and they drove to Tamarindo Estates to check in and drop off her gear. As Zoë dropped her duffel bag onto the queen-sized bed, she turned, lifted her arms and snaked them around John's neck.

"God, am I glad to be here. This trip has been one nightmare after another. First, some guy copped a feel outside the airport while I waited at the taxi stand. He wasn't even very subtle about it, just grabbed my ass as he walked by me on the sidewalk. The employees at the Marriott weren't much better. The man behind the counter slid the room key into my palm, rubbing his fingertips suggestively over my wrist. Then the bellhop just happened to caress my hand as he reached for my bag. What pigs."

"I doubt they would've pressed their attentions any more than that. If they did, you could've just kicked the shit out of them. Isn't that what you study for?" John said this as casually as he could, aware that he spoke for himself as much as some yokel in San Juan.

"That's hardly the point, John! I shouldn't have to depend on Tae Kwon Do when I'm traveling in the U.S. Puerto Rico isn't exactly the third world." She nuzzled the side of his neck. "Mmm. You smell good enough to eat, even if I *am* a vegetarian."

Her lips burned along the flesh of his neck, washing stillness down him as effectively as a fast-acting poison. He just managed to speak before the process was complete. It was a lame attempt to beg for forgiveness. "Where would the fun be if you didn't have some real jerks to deal with now and again? It's got to get pretty boring policing the misogynists at CMU."

"You're just thrilled that these guys make you look so good." She kissed him, pressing her whole torso against his. "It's been too long since we made love."

She pulled away long enough to close the curtains on the window overlooking the canal. Then she twined herself around him again as if she feared his escape, but she had nothing to fear. He was already paralyzed.

"Time to change that."

❧❧❧

Later, John drove her around the island, or as much of it as was accessible by road.

"Not much to see, really." They turned north toward Playa Flamenco. "The beach is world-class, of course, but nothing else is here."

"It's just because it's not built up, John. Some people would think that was a good thing, you know." She paused. "So whadya have planned for me this weekend, besides showing me how much you missed me?" At these words, she slid her left hand up his right thigh and into his crotch, squeezing gently.

John kept his eyes on the road.

"Actually, I wondered what you'd think about going out for some deep-sea fishing. There's a crusty old barnacle around here with a forty-three-foot yacht, the Sakitumi. That is, if battling big fish in the name of *sport* appeals to you." He held his breath. Given her rabid form of vegetarianism, he expected her to spit fire. He had no idea what had prompted him to antagonize her this way.

75

She stunned him with her answer. "How Hemingway. I'd love to go. Absolutely."

She leaned against the passenger door and looked out the open window. The breeze as they drove dared to lift her heavy hair and caress her neck. In her dark sunglasses and black camisole, she reminded John of a Hollywood starlet, exuding sex appeal as cloying as night-blooming jasmine.

"Maybe a little development wouldn't hurt," she said after a few moments as they drove south on 251 toward town. "Something that would help pay to clean this place up."

"What? You don't like having such an unobstructed view to the terraced dump?" John had forgotten the dump until it came into view and the sarcasm in his voice surprised him.

"Not in paradise I don't. They should plant some of those bright red flowers—what are they called?—in front of the trash."

"Bougainvillea. I think you're thinking of that. Or maybe hibiscus."

It took John only an hour to drive the circuit of the island's main roads. Perhaps it was Zoë's presence or the view from the driver's seat of the Samurai, but John surveyed all of Culebra's eyesores for the first time in two weeks. As they neared Dewey, they saw cramped cinderblock houses huddling along narrow streets. Boats rested on concrete blocks in the patches of land that constituted yards and everywhere they saw more trash: pipes, tires, and beer cans. Zoë wrinkled her nose and shifted away from the window. Even after they drove south past Dewey and left the houses behind, lines creased her forehead. Little existed on the southern and eastern arms of Culebra beyond a few side roads leading to homes that, from their vantage point, seemed to promise privacy to transplanted *gringos*. But for John, the trip away from Dewey reminded him of the serenity that he'd discovered while visiting the Enchanted Isle: every rise in the road brought views of the ocean, vivid against the sere brown and dusty green of the landscape.

Culebra exists only to draw the spirit to the sea around it. On the heels of this thought, Tamarind's ethereal blue eyes tantalized John's memory, but he shoved the image aside. Funny that he should think about a slip of a girl with crazy hair and incessant questions while Zoë's head rested on his shoulder—Zoë deserved better. He turned the Samurai onto the road to Tamarindo Estates.

"Wow, that was short and sweet. After a winter in Pittsburgh, this sun is a godsend, but I wouldn't want to live here." She hadn't moved even though he'd parked; instead, she ran her fingers along his forearm and the back of his hand.

John switched off the engine and looked down at her black hair, glossy and thick. She was too close; there wasn't enough room in the cabin of the Samurai to tell her the explosive news that he must tell her. So he settled for what he hoped was conciliatory humor. "Between the macho males and the roaming roosters, it's probably not the best place for you."

Lunch was larger and more gourmet than John had eaten for most of the past week; he'd hoarded his money and eaten only one meal out—a cheeseburger at Señorita's where he'd avoided seeing Raimunda, who managed to find him at the camp anyway. He had no idea why she kept seeking him out; more to the point, he couldn't understand the queer state that came over him whenever she appeared. He felt at the mercy of his lust, his rational thought subsumed to the white heat radiating from his groin. At these times, a shadow fell over his spirit that left him in a funk until he went to sleep; and then the dream returned and washed away the darkness as oil is washed from skin. He felt cleaner, but a vile residue still remained. And then Tamarind would arrive somewhere on his journeys about the shore or cays and her smile was the sun burning away the clinging mist of night.

He shook his head as Zoë addressed him while they waited for their Nuevo Caribbean chickpea stew. *Now* was not the time to think of either of these island women.

"I need to call the vet's before we go snorkeling. Stella had to have surgery on Wednesday and she's staying there while I'm away."

"I bet that's expensive." It was perfunctory; he and Zoë's cat had never gotten along and it was even harder to fake concern after two weeks away from the mercurial tortoiseshell.

"Yeah. It's got me thinking I should consider veterinary school after I finish my Ph.D." She paused. "So Heath Garrett's just been named as faculty researcher of the year. He won a two million grant from ARPA. But that's not all. The rumor's going around that he's sleeping with his administrative assistant and she's married with two kids."

"You sound shocked." His tone was casual; he kept his eyes on his flatware, the water glass, anything but Zoë's face. He felt as though he'd been slung up on a meat hook, however, and his chest tightened.

"I am. The man's got no scruples. Can't he at least bang someone from another department?"

He had to defend Dr. Garrett although he couldn't stand the arrogant prick. Struggling around the feeling that his left lung had collapsed, he spoke in reasoned words. "C'mon, he's a geek, Zoë. He doesn't have any social skills and he's not meeting many women holed up in that lab of his. He's probably grateful to have the attentions of anything remotely female."

"Are you speaking from experience? If so, I'm not sure that's a compliment." Had he misheard? Was there menace in her voice?

He picked up his ice water, choked on a sip, and wiped his mouth with his napkin. Time to take the self-deprecating route, seasoned with truth. He forced himself to look at her. "Oh, please. You know damn well you're out've my league. That makes me an extra-grateful geek."

Zoë preened. "True, too true. I expect you'll show me how grateful later."

Beneath the table, John felt her bare foot on his calf. He thought of the crescent kicks she often whizzed past his cheeks as they walked around campus. Once, she'd misjudged the distance to his head and connected with a kick. His ears rang for the rest of the afternoon. She'd apologized and given him a thorough body massage later, but he still couldn't think of her feet without vestigial tinnitus.

"So you got your paper out, I take it?" John sipped at his Medalla.

"Thanks to yours truly, we not only got it out but the data from the last-minute experiments actually got verified, graphed, and explained coherently. Not a single person on my project can write his way out of a wet paper sack without me."

"Good you know your own worth." Not that he'd ever doubted that she did, but he meant it: women computer scientists often had to be their own champions even in so-modern an era as the mid-1990s. It felt good to be genuine and straightforward.

Zoë picked up one of his hands with both of hers and rubbed his fingers with the pad of her thumbs. John wanted to take his hand away, to build on his slight honesty, but he couldn't.

"Okay, so that wasn't so modest," she said. "But I'm really speaking out of frustration. I hate to work so hard on research and have it documented by illiterate buffoons. Just because they can write an elegant piece of code or practically visualize where all the locks and keys go in a system doesn't mean they get a pass when it comes to explaining what they did."

"Not everyone's as well rounded as you. And take it from me, most people can't write their way out of a wet paper sack. You should see the Trench proposal. I had to annotate it heavily during the kick-off meeting. Luckily for me Dave Pendergrass speaks better than he writes or I'd be completely lost."

"Now you're really asking for something special." She wagged a finger at him. "I never said I expected these guys to explain their work to people outside the field. God, that's too much to ask for."

"That's why the most brilliant scientists—Hawking, Sagan, Wilson, Gould, Glieck, Feynman—" John freed his hand to tick them off on his fingers, "stand out. They bring science to the masses.

Maybe it's your destiny to illuminate computer security issues for the average person. There certainly need to be more women science writers."

"Ugh. Forget it. I just want to win the Turing Award." She smiled a coquette's smile and John remembered their first meeting last September at an IC event for new grad students. She'd ignored Stefan's full frontal assault and bestowed all her dazzling, dark radiance on *him*. No matter what happened between them, he'd never forget the thrill of being her choice and the heady first days of their dating.

"Now *that* would be a glass ceiling worth breaking." He raised his Medalla and smiled, his empty hand dropped to his lap and freedom.

Zoë picked up her beer in toast. "Here's to the future. May it bring us many worthy research problems, outstanding recognition, and plenty of time to bask in the glory together."

John raised his beer and dipped his head, wondering if he'd promised something with his acquiescence that he couldn't honor.

જ્જ્જ્

John woke the next day stiffer and more tired than he'd been after two weeks of sleeping on the ground, even after hiking. He'd dreamt odd fragments filled with wraiths and foreboding. In one, Tamarind floated in shallow water, her arms uplifted to the sky; instead of skinny legs, a scaly, muscular mermaid's tail undulated beneath her perky breasts. In another, Zoë crouched at the edge of a cliff overlooking the water, unblinking eyes staring at something, her black hair loose and tangled. When he tried to call out to her, she looked at him with zombie eyes, dark and devoid of life. At the same time, he saw Raimunda standing behind her, swaying and smirking. Then, as dreams tend to do, everything discernible dissolved, only to be replaced by fleeting snatches of color and emotion that left him feeling uneasy.

He found himself alone in bed. He lay along one edge, his right arm dangling and his pillow covering his head. Lifting his face, he studied Zoë's pillow. An irregular hollow wafted back a faint trace

80

of spicy perfume. Her presence lingered there in some memory of density and form. He could not have relaxed into the expanse of the bed now any more than when she'd actually lain next to him. After a moment, he rolled onto his back and looked at the ceiling fan in the clear early light, restless until he realized that he couldn't hear the sound of surf or the sharp cries of seabirds. Releasing his breath at the thought, he pivoted on the bed and stood up. In the bathroom he took a piss, relishing the luxury of standing in a clean, lit bathroom first thing in the morning. He wanted to shave again— he'd already showered and shaved the night before—but he settled for brushing his teeth and washing his face. In the mirror, the dark stubble gave his face a haggard appearance.

Outside their cottage, Zoë practiced Tae Kwon Do on a bare patch near the main building. She'd pulled her hair back with a plain silver clip and wore a tank top—sans bra—and black Lycra bicycle shorts. Although her face was free of makeup, her bare feet revealed deep-red polish on the toenails. There was no mistaking her physical strength. As John leaned against the rough stucco wall watching, she put her well-trained body through its paces, gracefully and forcefully lifting her legs in a variety of kicks that he'd seen knock expert martial artists on their butts. She breathed heavily and her skin glistened. Several minutes passed before she noticed him. When she did, she bowed toward him before bending over to grab her sandals off the rocky ground.

John stayed against the safety of the wall. "Morning."

"Hey." She squinted at him, smiled. "Ready for breakfast?"

"Sure."

Together, they walked to the main building's lobby where a continental breakfast had been laid out on a long table. They chose several items and sat out on the patio where they could look out over the canal while they ate.

"It's nice to get yogurt and coffee for a change," John said as he sat down. "I don't mind sleeping at the beach, but I'm getting tired of eating peanut butter sandwiches or dry granola for breakfast."

"No wonder you're looking so skinny." Zoë put a hand under his t-shirt and rubbed his chest. "Do we have enough time before we need to be at the dock?" Her voice sounded husky.

"'fraid not. It's the first time all week that a rooster didn't wake me and I slept in a bit. We need to get going, actually." He hoped that she couldn't hear the relief that threaded his voice.

"Too bad." She leaned over and nibbled his neck.

"Zoë, please." John pulled away from the fiery touch of her mouth, but he regretted the reflex at once. He put a conciliatory hand on her forearm. "Let's just eat and go, okay?"

She sat back and looked at him, frowning. His cover was blown, no doubt about it. "No problem, chief. I guess snagging a flailing fish is much more enticing than boning your girlfriend, who you haven't seen in two weeks." John winced at her crudity.

They ate in silence and Zoë, who finished first, stood up without waiting for John and cleared off her dishes. John finished his coffee without hurrying. He found Zoë a few minutes later waiting in the Samurai, her profile stormy. As if answering her mood, it rained as they drove into Dewey—enough to wet the pavement on the highway and lighten the air. During the brief shower, a single cloud paused as it glided overhead and then the sky was bright, without a trace of cumulous. Afterwards, there came renewed birdsong along the coast, vigorous and joyful after the storm's interruption. What had seemed dry and tired in their surroundings only moments before was simultaneously sharper and softer, more vivid.

By the time they'd reached the dock and boarded their fishing boat, Zoë appeared more relaxed than she had at the outset of their drive. John hoped that she'd let his insult go. Several damp strands of hair, not used to being confined for long, had escaped the silver clip and now softened the angles of her face. She asked John to rub some sun block on her shoulders and upper back, sitting patiently and relaxed while his hands worked it into her skin. He was required to wait upon her to redeem himself. If fortune smiled on him, no more would be asked of him on this outing.

It wasn't likely she'd handle his infidelity with such equanimity, however.

John watched half a dozen seabirds—dark filaments against a bright sky—fly high overhead. If he could escape into the heavens with them, would he? No. The gravity of his conscience anchored him here, with Zoë. Once he'd managed to tell her about Raimunda, adding the insult of an extended leave from grad school would probably suit her just fine.

They were met at the gangway by their captain, Captain Joe, who had the mien of a New England lobsterman: taciturn, angular, and tanned. He didn't look as though he belonged on a Caribbean island skippering a boat for green-gilled landlubbers out on a sporting cruise. John couldn't help wondering what had brought Captain Joe to Culebra—a cheating wife? a drinking habit? a lobster boat lost in a storm?—but he also didn't have any doubts that the silent skipper would take them straightaway to the best fishing available in the waters off the coast. Captain Joe, true to appearances, said little beyond the necessary once all the would-be anglers had boarded: life jackets were to be worn at all times, no one was going to risk his life trying to reel in a big one, and he, Captain Joe, was the sole arbiter of what was and wasn't safe on his vessel.

Two other couples joined them. After several minutes, it became clear to John and Zoë that these two couples had planned their vacations together—and that something was going on between two of them that the other two didn't know about. John wasn't tuned into such things, but shortly after they'd gotten underway Zoë poked him with her elbow and whispered in his ear to watch the furtive manner in which the man in the baseball cap touched the dark-haired woman's elbow, shoulder or hip. The first time it happened, John wondered why Zoë would think that such a small, light touch meant anything. Then he realized that the man wearing the baseball cap seemed to be obsessed: he touched the dark-haired woman so regularly that his actions resembled a reflex or a tic. Even still, that wouldn't have struck him as odd if the man hadn't been sitting most of the time with his arm draped around his wife's shoulders. Watching them, John wondered if unfaithfulness is always so obvious to outsiders.

To John's surprise, Captain Joe headed straight for Amberjack; he hadn't realized that amberjacks were a sport fish during his diving session there last week, and he said as much to Captain Joe.

The skipper squinted at him, his left eye nearly shut. "They ain't too flashy, not like a marlin or a shark, but they ain't too easy to catch, either. Any number of hotshot fishermen from the States come here and guffaw over what looks like an easy catch. But the jacks, they tax your tackle and your stamina like few other fish do. If you hook one, you'll have the fight of your life."

John's question had elicited more than Captain Joe's usual elliptical phrases and nonverbal grunts. He took this as a sign of the crusty old man's respect for the fish and not him, a "hotshot fishermen" by virtue of his origins. He didn't have a problem with this until Zoë, not he, won the fight with one of these *pez fuerte*, earning a high spot in Captain Joe's hierarchy of regard.

While they were still underway, but not more than five hundred yards from Amberjack, the captain baited a forty-pound test line off the stern of the Sakitumi with some squid. When one of the other passengers asked what he was doing, he said that the squid was leaving a downside scent, much like an erratic, wounded baitfish on the retrieve would. With any luck, he'd snag one of the jacks and then some of its comrades would follow it to the surface where they'd all have a better chance of catching them with their lighter tackle.

After he'd set anchor at the site, Captain Joe came around and helped them bait their rods with frozen chum, then demonstrated the appropriate way to hold a deep-sea rod and reel: the end of the rod placed under the left armpit while the right hand reeled in the line. Zoë, who was left-handed and used to reversing all instructions, slid her rod under her right armpit and waited for something to bite. It didn't take long. John immediately felt a tug on his line, but just as quickly he lost the jack without setting a hook.

In the process, he himself was hooked. For a while, he wasn't aware of Zoë's efforts to handle her own tackle; it wasn't until he heard Captain Joe's sharp intake of breath and a muttered "take it easy" next to him that he realized that Zoë had managed to snag something big. When he turned to watch, his own rod loose in his hands, he discovered that Zoë had found a rather unorthodox method for setting a hook: she now held her rod between her thighs.

It turned out to be an extremely effective means for catching a twenty-pound amberjack. Zoë was able to choke up on the rod past the reel, gaining better leverage, and use her entire body weight to fight her fish. John was so entranced by her performance that he nearly lost his own rod overboard when another jack hooked onto his line. Together, they fought their individual catches, John simply trying to keep his line from crossing Zoë's, Zoë bent on bringing her fish to the surface to see it. His jack eventually got away, but not until after Zoë had hauled in her amazing catch.

Dripping and red-faced with exhaustion, she turned to John while Captain Joe, his foot on the line next to the jack, cut the still-quivering fish free.

"He put up a fight but in the end I was tougher."

Seven

☙

TAMARIND HOVERED JUST UNDER THE SURFACE of the water, watching John standing on the boat above her. She recognized the old man who stood behind and to the side of John—she'd tailed his boat countless times through the waters to the south and west of Culebra. When she'd first happened upon his boat, she grew excited at the prospect of observing a human outside of the forbidden shores of Culebra, but her excitement quickly evaporated. Many times he dropped anchor miles out from the harbor and sat on his deck alone, drinking something. Under his white hat, his face resembled the warped and weathered texture of an old tree branch that had drifted far from land, preserved from natural decay by the salt air. Even from a safe distance in the water, Tamarind could see that his eyes captured no light from the water's surface. She no longer studied him for clues about humans. She satisfied herself with racing his boat instead.

Today he walked between John and five other humans, each holding a long stick with a glittering lure hanging from it and into a cloud of large silver amberjacks. Dead Branch, as she thought of the old man, stopped behind the woman nearest John and touched her forearm. The woman didn't acknowledged Dead Branch's presence,

86

engrossed instead in flinging the lure away from the boat. Once, her lure caught around John's and she scowled at him.

As if it's his fault!

For a while, Tamarind refrained from swimming closer to the fish as she usually did if she found humans trying to catch them. Stupid as they were, fish of all kinds reacted to diverse stimuli, from sight and pheromones to vibration and water pressure. They probably swarmed the water around the boat because one of their comrades had already been caught and they scented a meal. Yet if she swam at their periphery, they would scatter, ignoring the lure. She didn't do this. Instead, she wrapped the seal glamour around her and waited to see how this sport would progress.

One of the fish abruptly swerved and swallowed John's lure. He gave a shout and pulled up on the stick he held. Dead Branch and the woman near John, whom Tamarind had dubbed Black Urchin, both moved closer. The amberjack zipped away from the boat and Tamarind saw John struggle to maintain a hold on his stick. Black Urchin leaned closer and gestured to John, perhaps giving him advice. The frown on his face deepened, whether from the advice or the battle, Tamarind couldn't be sure. She flipped her tail and headed for the fish, trying to corral it so that she could lull it into submission with her humming, but after zigzagging against John's line in the time that it took her to change direction, the amberjack broke free. As she expected, it wandered a bit before sensing one of its cohort and rejoining the school.

Dead Branch and Black Urchin stood side by side now. The old man spoke into her ear and she nodded, but John seemed absorbed in fiddling with the base of his stick. He hooked another glittering lure onto a line and concentrated on launching this new lure over the side of the boat. Tamarind no longer waited.

Switching her glamour to mirror the water around her, she headed toward the school. The amberjacks dispersed, but they didn't swim far. The smell of squid and their dead comrade permeated the water in which the innocuous lures undulated. Tamarind hummed a bit and rolled, gathering up scent particles in the palm of her hands and rippling these diaphanous globes through the swells and away from the fishers. The amberjacks darted a hundred different directions as the globes burst their scents in new underwater pockets. Tamarind laughed and tugged on the nearest piece of squid. Someone at the top tugged back.

Humming and swaying on the currents, Tamarind yanked at every flashing lure within fifty feet of the boat. Several times she broke the lures off with enough line to tie them onto a necklace for herself. Then she had an idea. Swimming toward a small group of amberjacks, she hummed to keep them from leaving their safe haven. She grabbed one, which rested in her grasp without twitching, and raced back to the boat. It took her a moment, but she finally identified Black Urchin's lure. She hummed some more and brought the amberjack closer to the wicked barb. It opened its mouth docilely and swallowed. Tamarind clutched onto the fish and sped toward the open ocean. The line followed her for several long moments before Black Urchin managed to stop her run. That's when Tamarind swerved, diving deep and rolling right.

Laughing again, she zipped and dodged with the amberjack, which continued to lie calmly in her hands. Black Urchin struggled to slow her down, but Tamarind, who often played games with dolphins, could have swum all day if she'd wanted to do so. After a few dozen passes, she swam back to the boat, letting Black Urchin reel in her line bit by bit. When she'd gotten close enough to see John wrestling with his own amberjack, she gave one last tug on the fish in her hands and then let go. She could have broken the line at the last maneuver, but just knowing this satisfied her. Let Black Urchin think that she'd won.

Rolling toward John's line, Tamarind saw that it floated free without amberjack or lure. She looked around, but the school had moved on. Tucking her arms to her side, she glided to the surface where she watched Black Urchin and Dead Branch grappling with the still-quivering amberjack. The woman's wet face shone, but she exuded triumph. When Tamarind looked towards John's face, she

88

saw admiration and something else. Something she couldn't name, but it made her uneasy nevertheless.

ক্ষক্ষক্ষ

On the trip back to shore, an animated Zoë talked with Captain Joe, asking numerous questions about bait, tackle, the difference between amberjacks and the showier sport fish—marlin, shark, mahi mahi. If John hadn't known better, he would believe that Zoë had softened her stance on eating any flesh, whether from a fowl, a fish, or a four-legged mammal. Scowling, he noticed how patiently Captain Joe answered her questions, how the old man offered her a soda without saying a word to the others. He saw Captain Joe's admiring glances at Zoë's full breasts, her damp tank top clinging to them.

The old goat. Like he has any hope of catching his own quivering trophy. His jealousy surprised and confused him. His anger, unfocused as it was, flared. He closed his eyes and breathed. Until this moment, he hadn't understood how volatile his emotions had grown on the Island of the Snake. He wasn't sure he liked feeling so out of control.

John swiveled around in his chair and watched the bow of the boat as they neared Culebra. His eye caught a glimpse of something in the water near their boat, something dark, which disappeared just as he turned his head for a better look. Perhaps it was a harbor porpoise, or a seal—maybe even a small whale. Whatever it had been, it was larger than the amberjack that Zoë had hauled on board and had disappeared under the boat with incredible speed. He thought about asking Captain Joe what it might have been but then changed his mind when he saw that the other man was still engrossed in conversation with Zoë.

They got back into port about twelve-thirty. John waited while Zoë posed on-board for the requisite photo documenting her catch, and then he had to wait further while she got advice from Captain Joe about where to take the twenty-pounder to have it cleaned, filleted, flash frozen, and shipped. It wasn't right, she said, to waste something that other people would eat, startling John again. After eating a late lunch at the Dockside, they split up so that Zoë could shop in some of the little artisan boutiques that exist in the smallest tourist area, those tenacious barnacles hanging onto an uncertain livelihood derived from the whims of sporadic shoppers. John had already bought souvenirs—some earrings for Cassie, a hair clip for his mom, a fountain pen carved from driftwood for his dad, and a t-shirt for Stefan who was chauffeuring him to and from the airport. So he headed to Señorita's and drank several Medallas in a dark corner instead.

"*Hola, gringo.*" Raimunda had found him. She sat down at the table across from him. "Buy me a beer?" After the bright morning out to sea, the shadows of the restaurant turned her white blouse and brilliant-orange skirt lurid.

John nodded and raised his hand to flag down his waitress. After she left, he looked at Raimunda. "I'm afraid that this is the last beer I can buy you."

"Why?" She leaned forward to grab his hands where they lay on the table. The neck of her blouse hung open to reveal bare breasts like an offering. "Is today your last day on this fair island?"

"Almost. But that's not why. Remember my girlfriend? She's here now and she's not good with sharing." For the first time since falling under Raimunda's spell, John's lust churned with disgust. He felt sick. His head throbbed. Images of Zoë practicing crescent kicks merged with her triumphant smile after catching her trophy and the randy leer on Captain Joe's face.

Raimunda accepted the Medalla from the waitress and lifted it high, sucking half of it down in a single drink. She wiped the corners of her mouth with a delicate thumb and forefinger.

"Too bad," she said at last. "But all good things must end."

She leaned back and slung her right arm over the back of the chair before raising her feet to the chair next to John. Her skirt fell away to reveal her legs, brown and slender.

"I am a tolerant woman." She smiled. "If your girlfriend should bore you, I would be happy to meet you at Playa Melones for a private goodbye."

John smiled but refrained from caressing the calf that skimmed his left thigh. A wave of nausea swept through him at the thought.

"I must decline out of concern for your safety. And mine, I'm afraid." He tried to smile and grimaced instead. "My girlfriend has spent years learning how to kick the shit out of any bastard who tries to hurt her. I've already earned a serious ass-kicking as it is."

"Ah." Raimunda toyed with the label on her beer bottle. "Perhaps she's not the best woman for you, my friend."

John scowled and gulped too big a mouthful of beer. Choking a little on the effervescence, he felt tears prick the corners of his eyes. For the first time since he'd nearly drowned in the canal, he felt his environment shrink around him. Señorita's pastel-pink, green, and yellow walls loomed over him. Sweat slicked his palms, his shirt stuck to his armpits, and his face grew hot.

Raimunda squinted at him but said nothing. She swilled the remnants of her beer without taking her eyes off of him. After what seemed like half an hour but must have only been a minute, the walls receded and the breeze from the overhead fan dried John. A chill streaked up and down his spine and faded away. John leaned his forehead into his left hand, which was propped up by his elbow on the tabletop.

"You must be careful when you drink your beer."

"Yes. No. I mean, that was more than a careless swig. I felt like the walls had shrunk around me so much that I was suffocating. I couldn't breathe for a moment."

"Your girlfriend must have quite some hold on you, my friend." How had he never noticed how feral her grin seemed? Her teeth, small and sharp, gleamed in the dull restaurant.

John closed his eyes, willing her to go away. She didn't.

"Look, you don't know me. I'd rather not discuss my girlfriend with you."

Raimunda pulled her feet down from the chair and leaned forward until her face came within inches of his, still propped in his hand.

"I know what your mouth tastes like. I know what your hands feel like on my body. I know what you feel like inside me." She paused and held his gaze with her own. "I know what desperation feels like, *gringo*. Desperation and escape."

She stood up. "Don't worry. I'll leave you to your misery, my friend."

John watched as she turned, her hair thick on her shoulders. In the dim light of the restaurant, her skirt glowed. He couldn't take his eyes off her hips as they swayed up the stairs and out into the Culebra sunlight.

✍✍✍

Zoë's head ached after so much sun and wind on the Sakitumi and she suspected that her sun block had either worn off or that John had applied it haphazardly. After leaving him outside the Dockside, she headed straight for Mayte's supermarket—shaking her head at the generous use of the term "super"—to look for water, Tylenol, and Aloe Vera lotion. She bought a bottle of water, but after drinking some of it, she wished that she'd purchased a Diet Coke instead. Studying the label, she saw that it wasn't spring water at all but distilled water. It tasted awful, like salty dishwater.

She left Mayte's and headed southwest toward the ferry dock and the lowering sun. Along the way, she passed Dewey's two churches, one Methodist, the other Catholic. A red rooster bobbed ahead and across the street from her, proudly leading several smaller hens to some unfathomable destination downtown. As she got closer to the intersection with the road in front of the ferry dock, she noticed a brightly painted figure leaning against a tree. Not having seen any other local art, she paused and studied it. The figure's staring eyes unnerved her and she wondered if Culebra had any practitioners of Santeria or voodoo. On a nearby abandoned building someone had spray painted the words *Culebra para los Culebrenses*. Together, the figure and words presaged some eruption of cruelty or of violence against interlopers. She shivered and hurried away toward the bright plaza.

Zoë passed the island's tiny post office and a Chinese restaurant on her left. Both appeared deserted, exacerbating her foreboding. Ahead, the pink and gray concrete blazed. A solitary figure sat under a tree on the small plaza. As Zoë got closer, she saw that it was a wizened old woman who sat on a mat or blanket. Dozens of small bottles and bags lay in neat rows before her. The old woman's head nodded and her hands lay loose in her lap. Napping. Which made a lot of sense in this stultifying heat.

Ignoring the cool lure of the seawater near the dock, Zoë turned away from the withered form. A heat vise clamped around her forehead and temples. If she didn't find an open, air-conditioned shop along this stretch of downtown waterfront, she'd have to head to the liquor store at the far end of the street and hope that the owner wouldn't throw her out for loitering. A door opened ahead of her with a jingle and she drew close enough to see a line drawing of a mermaid and the words "The Mermaid's Purse" on a sign protruding from the storefront. Sighing, she picked up her pace and reached the door panting.

Inside, air conditioning took the edge off the swelter but disappointed Zoë's hopes. Scowling, she barely returned the owner's greeting and drifted over to the far corner of the shop to pretend to study the cotton batik dresses until her headache abated.

"You'd look good in the red or the blue," the owner, a deeply tanned, champagne blonde, called. "Although I think the red is more dramatic."

Zoë lifted the colorful fabric away from the hanger and studied it. "I don't know. I wear a lot of black."

The woman came out from behind her desk and walked over to the rack where she folded her arms and appraised Zoë.

"Black is good, but red is bold, especially this color of red. It's *flamboyan* red. You're too early to see the blossoms of the *flamboyan* tree, but they're unmistakable. Try it on and see how it makes you feel."

Zoë accepted the dress and headed to the single, closet-like dressing room in the back. She thanked her lucky stars that her skin had dried and didn't stick to the cotton. The material draped nicely along her hips and the camisole fit well, not too loose along the seams and not too tight across the bust. The dressing room lacked a mirror so she stepped out into the store. The woman waited for her.

"Sweet Mother! You look fantastic!"

Zoë smoothed the skirt. "You think so? Or are you just trying to sell me a dress?"

"Well, sure, I'm trying to sell you a dress. But I don't need to lie to you. I'd kill to look like that in one of those dresses. You buy that, and you'll be the best advertising I could get. Just to show you how happy I am to see someone look so good in one of my dresses, I'll take twenty-five percent off."

Zoë laughed. "Okay, okay! You sold me. I just hope you're not feeding me a line...."

She kept the dress on and paid for it along with three turquoise and lime t-shirts emblazoned with a mermaid. When she stepped out into the plaza again, she scarcely noticed the heat that accosted her. The solitary figure no longer napped on the plaza but stared at Zoë, who felt a tingle. Was it curiosity? Whatever it was, it compelled her toward the figure. As she approached, the woman's face clarified within her crazy white hair and crumpled skin. She peered at Zoë, who saw that a milky cloud swirled over her left iris. She was half-blind then, and harmless.

"What's all this?"

The woman shrugged. "Just some tinctures for stomachache or headache or diarrhea."

"Are you some kind of folk healer?"

The woman grinned, showing small, even teeth. "You might say so. Sometimes I heal other things, like broken hearts."

"Really?" Zoë stepped forward a single step and then stopped. "Good grief! What am I doing? The Caribbean sun must have fried my brains good." She turned to go.

"Ah, a skeptic. I just thought a woman who wore such a vivid color might take a chance for the right man."

Zoë turned back. She stood looking down at the herbal remedies, trying to discern whether any of the bottles or bags held any merit. Nothing appeared especially enticing to her inexpert eyes.

"Is he here on Culebra with you?"

"Who? Oh, yes. '*The right man.*' Yes, he's here."

"That dress is sure to get his attention."

"I sure hope so. Being away from me for two weeks sure hasn't whet his appetite any."

The old woman sat up and stared at Zoë, her blue eye intent. "Perhaps it's another woman."

Zoë, who had been idly rubbing a small glass bottle in front of her, blinked. "Another woman?"

"Here." The old woman picked up a green glass bottle in the shape of a tiny flask, slid it into Zoë's limp palm and pressed her fingers closed with both hands. "Just a drop of this will spike his lust for you and drive away all thoughts of other women."

Zoë murmured something without being sure whether she said thanks or if she muttered nonsense. A fierce headache swelled and the next few minutes grew confused. She didn't know whether a heat haze blurred her vision or whether sun block got into her eyes, creating a film over her sight. She clutched the bottle to her chest and whirled away from the old cretin. Scurrying across the street, she wasn't aware of her steps or her surroundings. A cloud passed overhead, dimming her vision. Her heartbeat fluttered against her ribs. Almost as quickly as the cloud appeared, it scuttled away again and Zoë plunged down the street away from the plaza. She no longer felt the old woman's piercing gaze on her back and her heart settled into its usual rhythm. She held her hand open in front of her.

"Fucking garbage."

She looked around for a trashcan but saw none nearby. For a moment she considered smashing the bottle against the side of the nearest building, but then she caught sight of the painted figure and realized that she hadn't paid for the promised aphrodisiac. Just thinking about returning to pay the creepy old witch made her shudder. She looked again at the innocuous little bottle and then hid it in the pocket of her skirt.

When she descended into Señorita's colorful cave, she stopped at the bottom of the stairs to let her eyes adjust. At first, she didn't see John because she thought he'd be waiting at the bar, but only Hemingway's double sat there drowsing over an empty pint glass. She finally saw John sitting at a table in a dark corner. He stared out toward the small canal on the far side of the restaurant and his forearms rested on the table. A full glass of beer stood untouched in front of him. When she walked over to stand at his side, he didn't stir.

"Is this seat taken?"

"What?" He looked at her. Catching her eye, he looked away quickly but not before she'd seen something there. Fear? Guilt? "Uh, no."

She slid into the seat. "You're on your fourth beer already? Drinking alone is a bad sign."

John refused to look at her. "I haven't even touched this one."

"I see that." Zoë picked it up and sipped it. "What is it?"

"A Heineken. They don't have any microbrews around here."

"Ugh. How can you drink so much of it?"

He shrugged. "It beats the water."

She sighed and stretched her legs under the table. "That's true. I bought a bottle of something euphemistically called water earlier and gagged on it."

Silence fell between them while the waitress came at last to collect the empty glasses and take Zoë's drink order.

"Did you get enough souvenirs?" John watched his hands playing with his Heineken bottle. As if nothing else mattered.

"Just a few t-shirts." She held up the bag. "And this fabulous dress." She winced at the bitterness in her voice. He still hadn't looked her in the eye. "John."

Now he looked up at her. His green eyes were opaque in the dim light.

"John, I–" She paused. "Is something wrong? You don't seem as relaxed as I expected for two weeks away from the gray skies of Pittsburgh and the dungeon we lovingly call our office building."

He seemed to struggle with focusing on her words. His lips worked a bit before he got an answer out. "There's nothing wrong. I'm just really wiped out from the boat ride. I can't believe you've got enough stamina to traipse around to gift shops after that struggle with the amberjack."

"I do feel like I'm hung over. Another reason to avoid this." She tipped the beer glass slightly, studying the amber liquid, which glowed in the dimness. She couldn't bring herself to push harder, not here. Not now. Maybe later, when they were alone.

"Well, tank up on some bottled spring water here and then let's head back to the room. Maybe a nap is in order. I've got just the island hangout for tonight."

Eight
ভ

TAMARIND WAITED UNTIL BLACK URCHIN walked away from the old woman before she shifted her cloaking glamour to the aspect that she'd worn for John. When she felt certain that no one else ventured out during the heat of the afternoon, she sidled over to the woman, who busied herself with wrapping her sundry bottles and tins into the woven mat. Tamarind watched the efficient brown arms, little more than bone and sinew, as they scuttled around. She knew that the old woman kept her waiting.

"You're an idiot, young one." The old woman didn't raise her eyes from her task.

Tamarind flinched but said nothing.

"I told you to stay away from that man, that he's dangerous. His woman is on the island."

Tamarind's glamour wavered, but she clamped down on her control.

"His woman?"

Now the ancient woman did look at her. She put a hand-rolled clove cigarette into her mouth and then lit it. After a moment, fragrant smoke clouded the air between them. "The term is 'girlfriend.' That was her in the red dress."

Tamarind bit her lip. "That was his girlfriend?"

"Yup."

"She's as prickly as a long-spined urchin."

The old woman barked a laugh. "For one so foolish, your description's apt. Nevertheless, he's leaving the island with her."

Tamarind tossed her head. "No, he's not."

The old woman looked at her for a long moment. "Ah, you know something."

"Perhaps."

"He's coming back to Culebra, isn't he?"

The wind off the sound surged through the spirals of Tamarind's hair, blocking her vision in a tangle of fine copper.

"Yes. He says he wants to volunteer to count sea-turtle eggs."

"And you want to try winning his heart, don't you? It's not enough for you to sneak around on the island after I warned you. Now you want me to help you. Help you put off those lovely legs of yours?" The old woman blew scented smoke out of the corner of her mouth.

"Yes."

"There is a way to put off your tail. But it's dangerous and painful, not to be done on a whim. Your father won't let you do it if he finds out."

"He's not going to find out."

The old woman sucked on her clove cigarette again. Its scented smoke obscured her withered face, but Tamarind felt the sting of her barbed gaze.

"You'll put your tail off, but you don't really understand what it'll cost you." She paused but went on again before Tamarind could say anything. "It's a terrible transformation, young one. You may die or worse—you may live but be horribly disfigured, neither mermaid nor human. Are you ready for that?"

A chill tickled Tamarind's chest, but she nodded.

"It won't be enough, you know. It takes more than legs. You've got to learn how to walk among humans. Are you really willing to give up all that being a mermaid means? For some man?"

"Yes."

The old woman threw the cigarette stub on the ground and pressed it into the earth with a calloused sole. "I don't think you've got it in you to make it as a human."

There was a long silence. Laughing gulls mocked them from the fringe of mangrove trees along the nearby coastline. Tamarind studied the birds.

"You won't help me then?"

The old woman sighed and then turned back to her bundle. "I've warned you, but you're the one who has to choose, not me. I'll help you, but my help doesn't come without a price."

"What do you want? Cone snails? Jellyfish? Sea anemone? "

"Ha! Those are hardly enough for my help. No. You've got to be my servant and work off the debt until the rainy season ends."

Before Tamarind could accept these terms, the old woman spoke one last time.

"And your legs disappear, too, unless you mate with this human. That's why I want you to search your heart to make sure he's worth all you're risking. If so, return to me after the first rain."

ৡৡৡ

Tamarind wandered as far inland as the power she drew from the sea allowed her. With each step, the air around her threatened to suck moisture from her core and out through her pores. Each breath she drew seared her throat and lungs. After only a few dozen steps her head ached and her thoughts swam inside her head. She collapsed on the sidewalk under a *flamboyan* tree, wondering how she ever thought that she could sustain herself long enough to find John. Culebra might be a small island for a mermaid to swim around, but it might as well be a trip to the other side of the world for her to cross by land.

She looked up into staring eyes in the *flamboyan* tree behind her. In the space between two breaths, she switched to her cloaking glamour. When her heart calmed down a bit, she realized that the eyes and face belonged to a painted figure. The resemblance to *mer* art left at particular underwater meeting places reassured her. While she rested, she examined the distinctive dot pattern and wide mouth, the sightless eyes. Just as she began to hum to herself—a low, even hum devoid of clicking—she realized that someone had passed her on the sidewalk on the way to the plaza.

100

She turned her head in time to see John pause and look around him, his eyebrows drawn together under a cap. When his gaze swept past her and moved around to the other side of the street, she switched aspects again.

"John."

He jumped. "Good grief, Tamarind! How in the world do you keep sneaking up on me like that?" He sounded annoyed. And something else that she wasn't sure about.

"Lucky, I guess." She held her breath until he changed subjects.

"Well, it's a good thing you found me. I had no idea how to find you and I'm getting set to meet my research boat in an hour. I wanted to say good bye before I left."

"Is your girlfriend gone?" For some reason, her voice burned her on the way out.

John squinted and hefted his backpack up onto his shoulder. "My girlfriend?" He sounded startled.

Tamarind plucked some pebbles from the sidewalk and tossed them across the street. "I saw her walking with you a couple of days ago."

"Ah. Well." He cleared his throat and looked away. "She's not my girlfriend. Not anymore."

"Hmm." Tamarind kept her eyes down on the perfect legs that she projected, but she wanted to hum in ecstasy. She'd read him right after all; he *was* happy to see her. Almost as good, she'd been right about Black Urchin, and Ana had been wrong.

"Hey, I volunteered both of us to help with the sea turtles. The ranger seemed really happy to have extra volunteers." He paused for a moment. "Why are you sitting on the sidewalk anyway? Do you want to wait at the pier with me until my mates show up?"

"Maybe." Her heartbeat picked up again. "Maybe not. I think it's too hot here and I need a swim."

"C'mon, we'll go into the liquor store and get some cold drinks."

"Okay."

He waited for her to get up and together they walked around the corner to the plaza and on to the liquor store in the corner. He smelled strange, not dusty with the natural scent of his body in the sun. Out of the corner of her eye, she studied his profile. No coarse hairs darkened the smooth skin of his cheeks and his hair lay coiled neatly in a dark ponytail on his upper back. His skin had darkened so that he looked like a native of Culebra. Her glance drifted down to his feet, visible within the straps of his sandals, and up his legs again. Fine dark hair softened their angles. A strong urge to stroke those curves, to press her fingertips into the hollow around his knee and down the ridge of shin, filled her.

She realized that John had said something. "What?"

"Let's stop in this shop here before we get drinks."

She looked up at the sign over the entranceway. A woman with a tail instead of legs floated on an unnatural blue sea. Tamarind recognized the markings next to her as letters—some of them appeared in the written version of the name that she'd adopted.

"What's in here?"

John, in the act of opening the door, looked at her. "You've never been inside this shop?"

Several strands of hair blew into her face as a breeze off the harbor rushed past her and into the open door. She pulled at them to clear her vision. "No. Should I have?"

"I guess not. It's a gift shop for tourists after all."

He held the door and waved her in. She held her head up and stepped inside, blinking in the dimmer light. Her diving membrane slid over her eyes where it stayed, momentarily beyond her ability to control it.

"Do you like this?" John held up a vivid blue item.

Tamarind turned away from him and headed toward a display of shells, blinking to raise the membrane. It stayed in place.

"Is something wrong?" John stood behind her so close she could feel heat rising from his torso, and his breath tickled the hair on her neck. "I didn't mean to offend you. I just wanted to get you a gift."

Tamarind began humming and clicking and turned away from him to head to the t-shirt rack. Despite her unsteady heartbeat, she knew that she had to calm down in order to raise the membrane. She had no ready excuse for John if he glimpsed the thin blue layer over her eyes. Near the t-shirt rack she saw the dark eye coverings that many people on Culebra wore and grabbed a pair to try on just as John halted behind her again.

"Tamarind."

She twirled around and looked at him through the dark layer.

"We don't have to look around. We can go on over and get something to drink."

"It's okay. I just had a little trouble seeing when we first came in, that's all."

John nodded, but a shadow remained around his eyes. He followed her as she walked through the racks but didn't say anything more about what they saw hanging there.

"How about this one?" A woman with hair the color of the sand on Playa Flamenco and skin nearly as brown as a tamarind pod stood next to the rack holding the same vivid blue piece that John had spotted. "It would look lovely next to that mass of wavy hair of yours."

Tamarind continued humming, low inside herself to keep her mental grasp on her glamour, and turned to face the woman. The color of the material captured the brilliance of the afternoon sky around Culebra. She reached out and traced a fingertip against it. It was smooth, soft.

"The dressing room's over there," The woman pointed to a door in the corner. When Tamarind didn't move, she lifted the hanger off of the rack and held out the item to her.

Tamarind noticed that the woman wore clothing that resembled the blue material in texture if not color. So she accepted the item and walked to the dressing room. Once inside she looked more closely at the shape of the clothing. It appeared to be identical to what the woman wore. She took the eyewear off, grateful that John wouldn't see the diving membrane, which still covered her eyes. She concentrated for a moment until the image of the t-shirt and shorts that she'd borrowed from John disappeared. Then she pulled the blue material over her head and stepped out of the dressing room.

"Wow! Don't you look fabulous! That dress looks like it was cut to your figure! I must be doing something right because you're the second woman in two days to put one of my pieces on who looks absolutely amazing."

"We'll take it." John pulled his wallet out of his backpack.

Tamarind turned to go back to the dressing room to change.

"No, leave it on."

"Yeah, you must wear that around for me," the woman said. "I'll give you a bag for your other things. And I'll give you the same discount I gave the other woman."

"Oh, and add in the sunglasses, too. Just don't put them on yet. The blue in the dress really draws out the blue of your eyes."

Tamarind gasped and felt her temples. She'd left the sunglasses in the dressing room.

John looked at her while the woman ran his credit card. "You look amazing." His eyes never left her face.

A bouncy hum filled her upper chest before she could stop it and she found herself trilling a string of clicks with her tongue. She looked away from John. The diving membrane slid behind her eyelids, but she let her hair cover her face anyway.

"Here's a bag."

Tamarind snatched it from the woman's hand and rushed into the dressing room. For a moment the small space suffocated her and then she reminded herself how to breathe air. She picked the sunglasses up from the bench where she'd left them and returned to the shop. John waited for her by the door, chatting with the woman.

"Thanks for the tip," he said as Tamarind joined them. "Ready to go get something to drink?"

"Sure."

They left the shop and continued down the sidewalk toward the liquor store. The heat radiated from the concrete and reflected back at them from the glass storefronts. Tamarind felt her pulse throb in her left temple and a sharp pain pierced her left eye. She had never felt so dry in her life, not even when she sunned herself on a nearby cay. When they stood in front of the coolers in the liquor store at last, she opened the door and let the cold air wash over her. The pain in her eye disappeared, but her body cried out for water.

"What'll you have?" John held a bottle of something dark in his hand.

"Water." She plucked a bottle out and opened it.

John laughed and went to pay for their drinks. While he stood in front of the register, she tipped the water up and let half the bottle flow down her throat without taking a breath.

"What are you drinking?"

"Coke."

"Can I try some?"

"You've never had Coke before? I thought it was the drink of millions. Here." He handed her the bottle and she tipped it up as she'd done with the water. The Coke burned its way down her throat and left a sharp pain in her upper chest. She coughed and choked.

"Hey, take it easy, okay?" John snatched the Coke from her hand and patted her bare upper back. Even in her distress, his fingertips raised starfish bumps.

Air pressure rolled its way from her chest to her throat, much as it had done when she was young and she'd surfaced too quickly from a great depth. She opened her mouth to cry out and a tremendous ripping sound emitted. For the first time since she'd come on land to look for John, she felt all right.

John looked at her, his eyes wide. Then he threw his head back and laughed the deep laugh that she loved, until he panted. His cap fell off his head, but he didn't seem to notice; he just put his thumb and his forefinger in the inside corners of his eyes and stretched the lower half of his face. Gradually, his breathing slowed to normal and his eyes cleared. He grinned at her, then bent down and retrieved his cap off the floor.

"Holy crap, girl! That was mighty impressive. If fishing doesn't pan out for you, you might want to challenge some frat boys to belching contests."

"It doesn't do that to you?" Her heartbeat tapped against her ribcage.

"Well, sure, if I tip it back like you just did. But I've had a little more experience with carbonation, I guess. Just sip it slowly."

He handed her the bottle again and this time she only took a mouthful. It fizzed inside her mouth as bubbles popped against her palate, but after she swallowed the pressure remained normal. On impulse, she tipped the bottle up again. The pressure rose a bit in her chest. Grinning, she parted her lips and urged the trapped air up with her diaphragm. A smaller belch sounded.

John grinned but reached out for the Coke bottle. "All right, enough of that. C'mon, walk me to the marina."

The walk from the liquor store tried her stamina, but the water she'd drunk kept the pains and parched sensation from returning. Once they arrived at the dock, she was close enough to draw on the power of the water to sustain her. John dropped his backpack and sat down on the dock's edge. Tamarind sat next to him. Her lower half, dangling above the water in the harbor, sucked energy into itself.

"You look a lot better than you did a little while ago. I guess Coke revived you."

Tamarind pulled the sunglasses out of her bag and put them on. "It's like looking through Coke."

"That's one way to put it, I guess." He said nothing for a moment. "I'm looking forward to coming back here in a couple of weeks and counting turtle eggs with you. I don't know what I'm going to tell my thesis advisor, but I'm not ready to go back to Pittsburgh yet."

"Is that why she's not your girlfriend anymore?" She didn't look at him. Instead, she bit her lip and swung her lower half back and forth.

106

"Partly." He rushed on, his voice hurrying away from the subject. "Hey, listen, I've got something for you." He bent toward his backpack and rummaged inside it. "Remember I took the ferry to Fajardo last week? Well, I drove to San Juan and while I was there I got these books for you."

He held them out to her. She took them and looked at the drawings on the covers. They clearly depicted creatures of some sort, but while they had recognizable faces, arms, and legs, they looked like nothing that she'd seen, either underwater or on Culebra. The creatures reminded her a little of the outline of the woman with the fish's tail on the sign over the shop.

"They're all written by Dr. Seuss. *Green Eggs and Ham*, *The Cat in the Hat*, *Horton Hears a Who*, *Red Fish Blue Fish*. All the classics."

She squirmed and frowned at him. "I told you I don't know how to read."

"I know. I'm going to teach you."

Tamarind looked at the books with their brightly colored covers again. Her eyes stung behind the sunglasses.

"Did I say something wrong?" John sounded worried.

"No." She tossed her head and squeezed her eyelids until the stinging stopped. "No. I can't wait for you to teach me."

There was a shout from fifty feet out in the harbor and John stood up. Suddenly, it was time for him to go. Tamarind shoved the books into her bag, ready to cloak herself as soon as John boarded and no longer noticed her. After the crew of the ship tied off and lowered the gangplank, John turned and ruffled her hair.

"Don't stalk any other tourists while I'm gone." He ascended the narrow bridge from the dock to the ship.

She didn't change her aspect even though he never turned around to look at her again. Instead, she caressed his calves with her gaze and hugged the bag of books to her chest.

"I won't," she said to his retreating form.

❧❧❧

Ana squatted on the shore at La Playa Tamarindo, peering at the stones, seaweed, and shells arranged there. Overhead, a darkening cloudbank obscured the morning sun and the ever-present chatter of birds had hushed to stillness; in moments, the season's first rain pelted her and disturbed the outlines of her question before Mother Sea. This by itself was an omen, one that foretold that Father Sky would mediate the outcome. Even before she'd come to the beach this morning, Ana's intuition had spoken to her about the violence of the upcoming season and the oracle had just confirmed her suspicions. The hurricanes that blew through the Caribbean every summer and fall would be especially numerous, and one would batter her little island late in the season after pummeling the islands further south.

While this prediction disturbed her, Ana wanted to know something entirely unrelated to the future weather. She wanted to know whether the mermaid would return and accept her conditions for help, and if so, how she would fare during the transformation. This latter was a question that she wouldn't have dared to ask in her youth, but she was growing more tired—and lonelier than she would have thought possible—and she was willing to risk Mother Sea's ire by asking it. When she'd first returned to Culebra and taken up her role as healer and diviner, she'd been reluctant to aid the occasional mermaid who called upon her; as the years passed, she began to realize that a time would come when she'd no longer be able to carry out her duties. Now, she feared that each opportunity to help a mermaid become human might also be her last to find a protégée.

Ana rearranged the artifacts on the shore before her, adding a few shells here, removing a few stones there. She asked Mother Sea what the mermaid's immediate fate would be and waited, scarcely breathing. After several moments, seawater fingered her code.

Rubbing between her brows, she sighed and sat back on her haunches. The unequivocal oracle had shown that the mermaid would return and accept the conditions of her metamorphosis; and, blessed be the Creator, she would not only survive but would indeed have put off her tail. This was as much as she could hope to learn today and she would not be allowed to ask any more questions regarding the mermaid for at least one cycle of the moon. But it wasn't enough to satisfy her, to assure her that all would turn out as she wished. It occurred to her that she could get at some of what she wanted to know by asking a question about the man who had captured the mermaid's heart.

She leaned forward onto her knees, eagerly rearranging her artifacts while the rain fell.

Mother, will this human take the mermaid away with him after the rains end?

The waves, which lapped at her arrangement even as she placed the items, surged and obliterated all but a few of them. Satisfied, Ana picked up the remaining shells and stones and placed them within a small canvas sack. The oracle had suggested that John would leave the island alone, but she had seen her own hand in it and knew that this wasn't a certainty, only a probability. She must take every opportunity to ensure that what the oracle said came to pass.

Nine

❦

TAMARIND WATCHED FROM THE SECURITY of mangrove roots along the northern edge of the Luís Peña Canal as the old woman stooped over a section of beach, frowning at some detritus there. This was not the first time that the old woman had spent long moments contemplating seaweed and shells, yet Tamarind still had no insight into what she was doing. After a few moments, the old woman leaned forward and rearranged some of the items around her and then Mother Sea flowed forward, the foamy edge of Her waves caressing them. All at once, Tamarind understood that the old woman was communicating with Mother Sea. *Mer* people, living in symbiosis with Mother Sea, did not speak with Her. She embraced them, gave them refuge, provided power for them to draw upon to protect themselves, both underwater and on shore. She never spoke to them.

The old woman leaned forward a second time, moving bits of shell, seaweed, and stone. This time, Mother Sea rushed forward before she'd finished, sucking most of her items into the canal. Instead of appearing angry or upset, she appeared relieved. She gathered the remaining stones and shells and tucked them into a small bag, then rose and turned away from the shore.

Tamarind waited a moment. She had only to walk on borrowed power to the old woman's house. *What if reality is less wonderful*

110

than my vague fantasies? Will I wish I hadn't risked so much for so little?

Closing her eyes and lifting her chin, she sent her thoughts out to the water around her to transform her tail into a pair of human legs; she would store some energy within her mind, doling it out along the short walk to the old woman's house. She swam until her new feet reached the bottom of the canal, then stood up and walked from the clinging grip of Mother Sea. As she walked, the rain tapered off and stopped altogether; by the time she reached the edge of La Playa Tamarindo, the sun shone overhead.

When Tamarind arrived at the old woman's squat cinderblock house, she was sitting in the doorway smoking a clove cigarette. Her good eye sparkled, alive in her shriveled features. She didn't smile. Tamarind's stomach churned and her glamour wavered. She came closer to the old woman, transfixed. Even though the sun was bright, she felt cold. For the first time that she could remember, the hum that always waited inside her core had fled, leaving her empty.

"I've been waiting for you, young one. You agree to my condition?"

"Ye—" Her dry throat trapped her voice. She cleared her throat forcefully. "Yes."

The old woman's eye flashed; she bent and smashed the stub of her clove cigarette into the ground. Smoke continued to drift up around her head, twining like ghostly seaweed. She unfurled herself and disappeared into her dark house. Tamarind hesitated, unsure whether she should follow, but the old woman reappeared holding a clear container filled with a dark brown liquid, its surface faintly hissing.

"Here, drink this."

Tamarind took the container from the old woman's outstretched hand. As she did, she caught sight of a silvery sheen between the fingers and nearly dropped the smooth container. She steadied her hand and raised it to her lips. Its contents hissed, reminding her of John's Coke. She sucked in some of the liquid, tiny bubbles rising from its surface and popping on her cheeks. The liquid's heat slid furiously down her throat and consumed her. Her heart responded as wildly as a netted fish, flopping against her ribs. Just as she started to back away from the old woman, the heat subsided, leaving a strangely sweet taste.

"Drink all of it."

The old woman watched as Tamarind lifted the container again, choking on the first drops of liquid. She wanted to spit it out, to throw the container down and run away, but its heat rooted her and the old woman's eye compelled her to finish it. This time, the liquid lost some of its heat. Tamarind flushed, just as she did after an afternoon lying on a sheltered beach. Her thoughts loosened and swam away from her.

The old woman took the container before it could slip from her grasp. She was about to take a step on her borrowed legs when, to her surprise and horror, she found that her glamour had vanished and she lay on her side. She called for her father, but her mind's voice refused to escape her head.

"Don't bother. He can't hear you this far inland and the beer has dulled your mental energies." She paused. "I didn't poison you. The beer will fortify you for your coming ordeal—it's all I have to help you, but it'll wear off soon enough."

Tamarind tried to latch onto the old woman's words, but they darted about like tiny fish among coral.

"Gather yourself and follow me." The old woman turned away from Tamarind and walked toward some low bushes.

Tamarind blinked. She hadn't moved when the old woman stopped by some guinea grass, coarse and thick, and turned her glittering eye onto her. Tamarind leaned over and put her forearms onto the ground and felt the familiar surge of energy into her upper body. Mustering her focus, she pulled her limp tail into the air where it hung suspended over her head and lurched across the ground on her hands. Panting, she dropped down near the guinea grass. The old woman stooped and parted two clumps with her hands until Tamarind saw a long cleft in the ground. Smaller ridges and fissures surrounded this narrow opening, which was almost entirely obscured once the grasses sprang back to their normal places. Tamarind scooted closer on her belly.

"You must enter this cave, young one. Not head first but with your tail."

Tamarind wasn't sure how she could fit inside the cleft, but she nodded and pushed herself sideways until her tail neared it. It was just wide enough to accommodate the muscles of her tail once she'd tilted her flippers and eased them into the opening. She grunted as she backed herself into the earth, which widened out after the lower half of her tail had disappeared inside it. The soil was warm, clinging to her skin, yielding and conforming to her. And then her flippers pushed against unyielding earth and her torso hung over the lip of the fissure, half in and half out.

"I can't go any further."

"You will, you will."

Before Tamarind could puzzle over her words, the old woman let go of the overhanging branches, concealing her with their leaves. She considered pushing her way out of this cave and through the branches, but her willpower drained away into the earth instead. The old woman returned and told her to drink something sweetish, slightly salty and viscous. She nearly retched, but the old woman held the cup to her lips and gripped her jaw until she'd swallowed it all. In moments, she felt dizzy and incoherent, alternately hot and cold.

The old woman left her alone for some time—Tamarind had no idea how long—only to return with a pot filled with a pungent salve. The old woman dipped a finger into the pot and traced it along Tamarind's forehead and cheekbones, all the while muttering. She set the pot onto the ground, grasped Tamarind's shoulders and, simultaneously lifting and pushing, slid her further back into the cave. Tamarind cried out as her tail bent against the rear wall and doubled underneath her. Her whole torso now fit inside, but her shoulders wedged at the entrance until the old woman twisted them into alignment; then the old woman leaned her whole weight into Tamarind until her head disappeared inside the lip of the cave.

Tamarind heard a sound and she realized that she was sobbing. The cave, which had initially conformed to her in a comforting way, now painfully immobilized her. She couldn't have escaped if she'd wanted to and, now sober, she knew that even the old woman could not pry her out. Blood pounded in her ears and she nearly lost consciousness, but she fought it and her tears. After a few moments, she mastered her breath and as it slowed she grew calm.

The cave was darker than the deepest cave she'd ever swum within, moist and almost airless. The pain in her tail was terrible, but now that she'd regained control of her thoughts, she believed that she could survive this ordeal. She had to stay focused. Neither it, nor the old woman, would get the best of her. A paroxysm of pain gripped her. It was in her midsection and it was everywhere, all at once. Her head arched away from her flippers, bringing her mouth toward the cave's opening. A scream ripped the air and she scarcely knew that it came from her. She had no idea how long the pain seized her, but at last it subsided and she panted in her airless space. From outside the cave came faint noises. In the suffocating stillness, the smell of the old woman's clove cigarette reached her.

Tamarind clung to the scent while the next pain squeezed her. She had no idea when it would quit wracking her body, but every time it ceased, she prayed that it was over. Still pain rose to overtake her and soon there were hardly two breaths between waves, hardly enough time for her to gasp out a plea.

"Please." And the next time the pain hit her, "I can't!" And then, "Oh, Mother," and she vomited into what little space she had.

After that, she said no more because she no longer had any thoughts. Each new round of pain rode upon the heels of the last so that she could no longer distinguish them as separate assaults even if she'd been capable of doing so. Time had no meaning for her and she couldn't have said if moments or days passed. Groans rolled over her lips with the immutability of waves. Yet long before her voice failed, the pain began to lessen.

She grew aware of her hands digging into the soft soil around her torso: they'd gouged deep holes in her agony. Pain still shuddered through her lower body, but she knew herself again. Before she could do more than note this return of awareness, she felt an indomitable urge to unfold herself.

"Wait, wait, young one!"

Tamarind had no idea what was happening to her, but she fought the urge to push against the constricting earth. She felt the old woman's fingers dig into the cleft and clamp onto her shoulders.

"Now."

A new insistence filled Tamarind and she gave into it; deep inside her she knew that this was the struggle that would free her. As she pushed, the old woman pulled her head clear of the cave wall and the pain in her lower body eased. The old woman let go of one shoulder and then quickly brushed loose soil and vomit from her eyes and out of her clogged nostrils. Tamarind sucked in air and laughed.

Another need to push gripped her. The old woman barely grasped her shoulders in time to twist them through the narrow cleft. With an odd *shlucking* sound Tamarind slid out onto the cool ground and lay not far from the cave's entrance. She closed her eyes, but not before she saw that it was night. She heard the old woman bustling around her, but she wanted only to sprawl on the ground. She lay there without moving until the old woman rolled her over onto her back, startling her with the light in her hand. Pushing up onto her elbows, she held one hand out; the other shielded her eyes.

"Leave me alone."

"Look at yourself."

Tamarind peered down her torso toward her tail. She was covered in mud and something else: in the light's glow, she caught sight of blood. Her blood. She was so shocked that at first she didn't register the oddness of her tail under all the obscuring muck. When she did, she saw that it was no longer gray but fish-belly white. It was no longer strong and muscular but atrophied and knobby. Where her strong flippers had been, she saw two stubs.

"Don't understand, do you?"

"Understand?"

"Perhaps this will help."

The old woman turned back toward the bushes, dark and indistinct against the lighter sky. Overhead, tiny pricks of white, scattered where Father Sky had thrown them, glittered. She knelt, setting her lamp on the ground and then leaned into what must be the cave's entrance. For a long moment all was silent and Tamarind began to shiver. The old woman sat back, something sagging and dark in her hands.

When she turned around, Tamarind's breath caught at the base of her throat. *My tail.*

Where it had been hard and convex, filled with muscle, bone and sinew, her tail was now hardly more than a shell. As she watched, the old woman spread it out for her so that she could see the inside lining. It was veined and knotted, quilted with blood-purple fat and long strips of shredded muscle and torn ligaments. At its center, strung like beads on a necklace, she could see oblong vertebrae spanning the length of the tail, disappearing at last among the cartilage of her flippers.

Tamarind tore her gaze from the remnants of her tail and looked again at herself. Now what she saw were unmistakably legs, thin and wobbly looking but legs nevertheless. She pushed herself up into a sitting position.

"I did it! I put off my tail!"

"That you did." The old woman had lit another clove cigarette and now took a long drag on it. "Help me bury it."

Tamarind blinked. She rolled onto her side, pausing to look at the night sky. After several moments, the old woman cleared her throat. It was a harsh, rattling noise like the sound of pebbles inside a desiccated crab shell. Gripping her lower lip with her teeth, Tamarind pulled herself along the ground to the spot where the old woman waited. Once she was there, the old woman knelt down and together they dug a shallow trench with their hands and lay her tail in it.

When Tamarind awoke later, the sun sailed overhead and hunger hollowed her to her new toes. She lay on a thick, rough cloth on the floor inside the old woman's house, which was filled with the scent of fish, among other odors that she didn't recognize. Blood and soil caked her skin and her lower body burned near where her new legs extended from her torso. She was about to call out for help when the old woman appeared in the doorway to her house.

"Awake are you? Lots of new sensations? Bet most of them aren't pleasant."

Tamarind nodded and licked her lips. She couldn't speak.

"First things first. Let's get you outside so you can empty your bladder. After, food, drink and a bath."

She came over and helped Tamarind sit upright; Tamarind's head spun and she clutched the old woman's arm.

"That's it, take it slowly."

Tamarind gathered her concentration from where it had scattered and pushed herself up onto her feet. If the old woman hadn't pulled at the same time and steadied her, she might not have made it. Twice she stumbled and once she actually fell, pulling the old woman down beside her. It took five minutes before they were both standing outside the house in the sunshine.

"Don't go far. Squat down here. I'll clean it up later."

The old woman never let go of her arm as she slunk down onto her new haunches. She sat there until the old woman told her to urinate.

"I don't know how."

"Yes you do. Focus on your functions. Remember what it felt like to empty your bladder in the sea."

Tamarind nodded and withdrew her thoughts into herself. At last, she could remember the feeling that came whenever she released her bladder. She triggered that release now. Hot urine shot out between her shins, splattering her. As it hit the ground, she saw a trickle of blood from between her legs. After the ache and burning from her over-full bladder had drained away, she felt her soreness as well.

"You'll bleed for awhile, maybe a whole moon. Then you'll bleed again, once each moon. All human women do."

As she stood up, Tamarind clutched the old woman's arm. "Will I always feel so tender in the place between my legs?"

The old woman removed the stub of her cigarette and tossed it onto the damp ground where it hissed and stopped burning.

"No, you'll heal. The only time you'll feel sore is if you copulate with a man."

The old woman steadied Tamarind against her side and led her back to the shade inside her dwelling.

"Do humans also have difficulty mating their minds?"

The old woman ignored the question and shuffled Tamarind to a far corner where she made her sit on something hard and round that was raised from the ground by several long sticks of wood.

"Don't mind how hard it is. I didn't want to get your blanket wet."

She turned to a flat surface that was raised higher than the one Tamarind sat on and pulled a shallow container of water towards her. In it was a small cloth, which she rung out before carefully wiping Tamarind's face. She hadn't forgotten Tamarind's question, however.

"Humans don't mate their minds. Sometimes two humans grow close. They appear to share a mind, but they can't mate the way *mer* do." The old woman bathed the rest of her with gentle hands. "For humans, mating is temporary and absurd. They try to make up for it by committing their will to each other. They call this 'marriage.' It's as flawed as humans are."

"Marriage." Tamarind tried the word out.

"I was married once. Didn't last more than ten rainy seasons. *Couldn't* have lasted much longer."

"What happened to your husband?"

"Don't know and don't care." The old woman's pincer-like fingers gripped Tamarind's thighs as she scrubbed the dirt away. "When it's dark, go to the resort not far from here and use the beach showers."

"Why do I have to go when it's dark?"

"They don't want you to use the showers, young one. Don't worry about why. Just don't let anyone see you." She dropped the filthy cloth behind her and stood up. "Time to get you some food."

The old woman walked over to the shiny vessel, which emitted a fish-scented cloud. Picking up a flat stick with an appendage that looked like a curled hand, she scooped up some of the liquid and poured it into a shallow container near her. This she set on the flat surface, simultaneously handing Tamarind a shiny object.

"What is it?" Tamarind held the object in her hand before waving it in front of her.

The old woman laughed. "Got a lot to learn, don't you? This," she said, touching the object in Tamarind's hand, "is a spoon. This is a bowl filled with fish broth." She mimed using the spoon to dip up the broth and bring it to her lips.

Tamarind wasted no time in tasting the broth. As she ate, the old woman pulled something out of an opening in the front of her clothes and tossed it next to the bowl.

"Crackers to eat with the broth. Dip them in." She paused. "Since we're naming things, I'm Ana."

Tamarind hardly paused in spooning in the broth; she grabbed crackers and dipped them into the bowl. Ana chortled so loudly that Tamarind looked up at her, the crackers halfway to her mouth.

"No, no, young one! Tear the plastic bag open to get the crackers!"

As Tamarind watched, Ana took the bag from her and pulled at one end of it until it split open like a skate's membrane. Out tumbled several white crackers. Ana laid the bag next to Tamarind's bowl and pursed her lips, her hands on her hips.

"What are we going to call you?"

"Tamarind," Tamarind told her between gulps of broth.

Ana looked surprised. Then she smiled, the first smile to curl the corner of her single eye and lift her whole face upward.

"Yes, Tamarind. That's what we'll call you."

Ten
ও

JOHN WAITED FOR TAMARIND in the gathering dark at the bottom of the hill next to the service road that led to Tamarindo Estates. Since returning to Culebra two weeks ago, he'd driven nightly to the same spot and waited for her silhouette to descend toward him, the last of the day's sunlight her aura. Tonight, he'd waited for twenty minutes and still she hadn't appeared. To the northwest, sooty terns streamed toward their nesting grounds on the tip of the Flamenco Peninsula, their black oblongs parting and merging in a fast flow against the lemon-orange layer of sky above the treetops.

He drummed his fingers along the steering wheel and then picked up his flashlight and checked it again to make sure the batteries still had enough juice. He popped the glove compartment and verified again that there were spare batteries. On the floorboard of the Samurai rested his backpack with water and soda bottles, chips, sandwiches, mosquito repellent and a copy of *The Lion, The Witch, and The Wardrobe.* He switched on the radio, leaned against the driver's side door, and closed his eyes. A new guest had arrived mid-morning at Posada La Diosa where he'd rented a room since his return from the Trench mission and he'd been unable to sleep until nearly noon. If Tamarind didn't arrive soon, he might fall asleep.

Humming reached his ears before the sound of her feet on the pavement. Stirring, he sat and looked up the hill. As usual, she skipped barefoot toward him, her corkscrew hair jouncing with each little leap. She wore the mermaid t-shirt that he'd bought her from The Mermaid's Purse and a pair of shorts that were too big for her. Every fifth skip she stopped and hitched them up. When she reached him, he saw that she sucked on a Popsicle. Orange stained her upper lip and tongue.

"It's about time you got here. We're going to be late."

She shrugged. "So? The turtles won't get there until it's dark. We've got time."

She came around to the passenger side and got in. Hearing the music, she leaned forward and began pushing buttons on the radio.

"Please buckle up so I can go."

"Oh, yeah, right." She stuck what was left of the Popsicle into her mouth and reached around her right shoulder for the belt. After she'd clicked the belt into its slot, she reached for the radio again. When she found a station playing Lito Peña's *Yo Vivo Enamorado*, she stopped jabbing, turned the volume up and began singing along. John smiled to himself as she rocked in time with the music, the Popsicle dripping everywhere as her arm swung wide.

"I bet you'd be fun at Isla Encantada." He started the Samurai and u-turned south onto 251. An image of Tamarind dancing around the restaurant's worn floor teased his inner eye. All at once, he knew that he wanted to hold her. Would it feel as though he held a will o' the wisp? Or danced to the music of the spheres?

"Isla Encantada? What's that?"

"You don't get out much do you? Your father must keep you on a tight leash. It's a bar that has live music on the weekends."

"'Tight leash'? What's that mean?"

Mentioning her father made him squirm. He couldn't take Tamarind into his arms as he wanted if she was as young as he feared she was. "Never mind. It's just a figure of speech. But that reminds me. Are you twenty-one?"

"Twenty-one?"

121

"Twenty-one years old." An image of Zoë slithered into his thoughts, but he shoved it into oblivion. She'd tried to insist that they were taking a break, not breaking up. What would she think about him hitting on a girl who looked and acted younger than his sister?

"Oh, I'm way older than that. Why?"

"You have to be twenty-one to dance at Isla Encantada. Do you have some sort of ID?"

She stopped rocking. "ID? No, I don't have any ID." She sounded as if she didn't know what he was talking about, though.

"Don't worry." John patted her head, letting his fingers linger just long enough to feel the surprising softness of the tangles. "I've never seen them check. I just wanted to be sure for my own peace of mind."

"Piece of mind? Which piece of your mind needs to know how old I am?"

John laughed. "The biggest piece."

They drove along without speaking for a while, listening to more *boricua* jazz. John turned north after they reached Laguna del Flamenco. The road ended short of Playa Resaca; they'd have to leave the car and hike over the same hilly terrain that John had first hiked over in late March. He turned the radio down before they reached the place where they'd park the Samurai.

"I brought a book that I want to read to you while we wait."

Tamarind looked at him. Even in the growing darkness, the blue of her eyes astounded him. Hair fell into her eyes, but she didn't seem to notice. "You brought a book? Where is it? Can I see it? What's it about?"

"Whoa, whoa! All in good time. Let's just say it's a classic of children's literature and I'm looking forward to reading it to you."

Tamarind hummed a bit and looked out the window. Without warning, she leaned over and kissed his right hand. "Thank you." Her voice sounded thick.

Fifteen minutes later they'd caught up with the four other volunteers and the National Wildlife Refuge park ranger who all sat as far inland as they could on blankets, talking quietly. All but Jesus smiled and waved John and Tamarind over to join them. When he'd found himself skewered by Jesus' hot glare the first night that they'd watched for leatherbacks, John braced himself for the inevitable angry confrontation. Jesus said nothing, however, about their first meeting and John stopped worrying about a destructive scuffle among the sea-turtle nests. Even so, he often caught the other man's eyes watching him.

In the deepening twilight, everyone brought out sandwiches and chips and listened to Pablo describe the time a nesting leatherback dug several holes before finally laying her eggs. When he finished, no one spoke for a while. The last of the sun's light faded from the horizon and the sky gradually deepened from a honeydew melon to pale blue and finally, deep blue. Stars extruded through the velvety backdrop of sky like diamond studs in a jeweler's display.

John snapped on his flashlight and pulled out *The Lion, The Witch, and The Wardrobe*. Although he read quietly to Tamarind, the other volunteers clearly listened in and refrained from speaking. He'd read only two sentences when she interrupted him.

"'War raids'? What are those?"

"This book is set during World War Two when the Germans bombed London, kind've like when the U.S. Navy used to bomb Culebra."

Next to him, she shivered. "I remember that."

John looked toward her, but the darkness obscured her features. Her wild hair appeared black against the royal sky, the stars crowning her with a glittering diadem. He laid his hand on top of hers where it rested on the blanket. "So I guess you can relate to the children in this book, huh?"

Tamarind shifted. "I guess." She spoke so quietly that John strained to hear her.

He waited, but she said nothing more and no one else spoke about the bombing or one of the former targets, an abandoned tank now rusting on Carlos Rosario—along with unexploded bombs amidst the island's largest nesting grounds. So he picked up the book and continued reading. After a while, he lost himself to the reading, to the story of the children playing hide and seek in the strange old country house to which they'd been sent. Underneath it rode the rhythmic wash of water on white sand and the taste of salt on the air. He'd read a third of the book when one of the other volunteers spoke in a low voice.

"Our first mother has arrived."

Everyone turned toward the beach, now illuminated only by moonlight. A leatherback—a large one, perhaps fifteen hundred pounds—emerged from the water and heaved herself across the sand toward them. They melted back into the tree line and waited until she found the spot she wanted and dug furiously at the sand. When she finished digging the tear-shaped egg cavity, Pablo came forward and lifted her rear flipper so that the rest of them had a clear view of the eggs as they dropped into the sand. Serena counted the large, fertile eggs and Inez counted the small, infertile ones. John and Tamarind measured the turtle after she'd finished laying her eggs. As she held the tape measure next to the leatherback's beak, Tamarind wiped the salty tears from the sea-turtle's eyes with reverent fingers. Jesus documented everything and took a picture of the leatherback—at six and a half feet from beak to tail, she was the largest seen on Culebra in several years.

The leatherback buried her eggs and turned toward the sea, throwing sand behind her to cover her tracks. They all watched her go. Tamarind stood away from John as she did every time a leatherback struggled back across the beach, her lips pursed and her eyes unfocused. She hummed faintly and the air around her seemed to vibrate slightly. When the sea turtle gained the wet edge of beach and seawater reached to embrace it, Tamarind sighed and relaxed her stance.

"She's safe again," she always said to anyone listening.

≈≈≈

Nightly turtle watch lasted through June. John picked Tamarind up every evening on 251 near Tamarindo Estates and dropped her

124

off before dawn in the same place. Even though he urged her to let him walk her home, she always said no. The one time that he'd ignored her and followed her up the access road, she'd disappeared almost in front of his eyes. When he finally turned to head back down to the Samurai after calling for her for fifteen minutes, she jumped out of the scrub along the roadside, shouted, and laughed when he yelled out in surprise. Then she dashed up the road and out of sight still laughing. Tonight he just waited until she'd bounced up the hill like a schoolgirl and then followed a ways behind until he saw her approach a squat cinderblock building a hundred yards off the road to the southeast. It was an odd place for a house, so far from town where most of the Culebrenses lived. As far as John could tell, Tamarind's only neighbors besides the resort were wild horses and lizards. He never saw anyone greet her.

During their weeks watching for turtles, he finished reading *The Lion, The Witch, and The Wardrobe* and then the five successive books in the Narnia series. Pablo, Serena, and Inez huddled close, listening, but Jesus prowled along the edge of the beach as a panther paces near a water hole, waiting for quarry. While he read, John watched the flashlight beam that bounced among the acacia, wary at the other man's restless energy. As long it wasn't directed at him, he wouldn't worry.

Besides straining his eyes on dim text, John spent a small fortune on batteries for his flashlight over the course of their turtle watch. One night, when only a single turtle braved the trip from shallows to sandy beach, he drained two sets of spare batteries.

"I'll be glad when I can read to you during the day," he said after the flashlight dimmed so low that he had to shut it off or they'd be forced to wait for sunrise to walk back to the Samurai. "This is becoming expensive."

Tamarind sat so close to him that long spirals of her hair rested on his bare upper arm. The toes of her left foot, powdered with sand, brushed his whenever she dug them into the beach. She smelled salty and earthy at the same time.

"Don't you have to leave soon? I think maybe this is the last leatherback we'll see this season."

"I'm thinking about staying longer. I wrote a research paper based on my experience from the Trench mission. My advisor's okay with me staying as long as I keep getting work done." But Zoë was *not* okay with it. She'd found out where he was staying from Stefan and started leaving him phone messages with Valerie, the owner of the guesthouse where he'd rented a room. She'd written, too. He just couldn't bring himself to be as blunt with her as he should be.

"Oh."

"Still working on reading *Green Eggs and Ham*?"

She didn't answer right away. In the dark, John felt her swaying and guessed that she still traced her finger through the sand at her side.

"Yes," she said finally. "All the letters looked like bird scratching in sand for a while, but two days ago when I looked, the scratches rearranged themselves in front of my eyes. Some of the words look just like themselves now."

"You'll have to read to me then." He looked out toward the horizon, which lightened toward dawn. Fifteen feet away from them on the beach, the other volunteers sat talking quietly. "I haven't taken you dancing yet. The first Friday after the watch ends, I'll pick you up at the same time and we'll go grab some dinner first. How's that sound?"

Tamarind had grown still. "I've never gone dancing."

"Don't worry." He put his hand on her back. The heat from her skin warmed his palm through the cotton of her t-shirt. "I've seen you dance every day for the past six weeks and you'll put everyone else to shame."

"As long as I don't have to read to them."

A few days later, Teresa Jimenez, the refuge manager, called an end to the season's turtle watch. All the volunteers met at Señorita's at sunset that day to drink beer and poke fun at each other in the brighter lights of the restaurant. John had forgotten the burnish of

126

Tamarind's hair, the peculiar blue of her eyes. For all that she drank only Coke—albeit several of them—her face flushed as the evening wore on. She even imitated birdcalls for their group with astounding accuracy.

He couldn't remember the last time that he'd been out with a group of people, chatting and drinking, and having such a good time. Probably last fall, around the time he and Zoë met. Even Jesus seemed relaxed, his sleepy eyelids minimizing his flat gaze and lending him a seductive air. John suspected that Jesus remained as alert as ever, however.

Half an hour later, Jesus proved John's suspicions right.

"Do you know what 'Culebra' means, Juanito?" He'd taken to calling John by the diminutive, but John knew that it had nothing to do with affection.

Everyone stopped talking to listen.

"Yes. 'Snake.'"

"Ah, *bueno*, good." Jesus toyed with the neck of his Medalla bottle. "There are no snakes on this island. Why is it 'snake island' then?"

"I dunno."

Inez spoke. Where she'd been red-faced and laughing only seconds before, she was very serious. "To remind us about the snake, the evil, that lives at the heart of paradise."

Serena picked up where Inez left off. "There cannot be an *isla encantada* without a *culebra*. Some say a great snake sleeps at the heart of the island, waiting for the end of the world when it will hunt again."

Jesus sneered. "These two, they are *virginal*. They do not understand, Juanito. *Pero tú comprendes, sí?* You want to show our little bird of paradise here the true meaning of *culebra*. You don't have it in you, though."

"What does that mean?" Tamarind's voice broke their locked gazes.

Pablo, who'd had too much to drink, slurred his words. "Means Jesus is jealous."

"Jealous? Why?" Tamarind looked at Jesus, puzzled.

"Not jealous. Just waiting. Waiting for you to fly from this spineless worm. When you do, *mi reina*, I will be ready."

The evening's mood soured after that. Inez and Serena, darting looks at Jesus, made excuses for leaving. Pablo, lurching to his feet, declared that he needed to get up early to go out on a dive and asked Jesus to walk him the five blocks to his apartment. Jesus finished his beer and dropped some cash on the table as he stood to go. He looked down on John and Tamarind but said nothing more. They watched him trail Pablo out Señorita's door, his posture sober and cocky. They didn't move or say a word until the waitress came five minutes later, and then John roused and said that it was time to head out.

As he drove Tamarind home, he reminded her of his promise.

"Looks like we're going dancing tomorrow."

"It's Friday?"

"Yup."

"Okay then." She looked out the window at the moon-washed road for several moments, but then a song on the radio caught her attention and she hummed along with it and tapped her fingers on the doorframe.

"Tamarind?" His voice had grown deep in seriousness.

She turned to look at him. "Yes?"

"Forget about Jesus. We've got bad blood between us, that's all. It isn't about you."

"'Bad blood'?" Has he hurt you, John?" She'd sat up straight, her face in darkness against the moonlight.

"No, of course not. 'Bad blood' is just a saying. It means we've disagreed before."

"Oh."

Something in her voice, in its small uncertainty, caused him to reach out and push the hair from her face. Tendrils curled around his fingers almost as if they were alive. "See you around sunset, then?" He spoke gently.

She nodded. "I'll be here."

When John let her out at the bottom of the hill, he watched her silhouette shrink against the pricks of starlight until it winked out at the top. With her disappearance, the night diminished and became ordinary. Even the music on the radio sounded tinny and weak. He quickly turned and drove back south into town and bed.

Tamarind leaned against a palm tree waiting for him the following evening. She wore the blue dress that he'd bought her before he left the island in early April. For the first time since he'd known her, her hair looked combed and smooth curls lay sedately on her shoulders. Shell hair ornaments clipped long strands together in small bunches away from her face, and around her neck hung lures on transparent fishing line. But her feet were still bare.

She slid into her seat.

"You look great. You even make bare feet look dressed up."

Tamarind looked down at her feet as she pulled her door shut. "Should I have worn shoes then?"

"No, no. Wouldn't look natural on you, I think."

"Feet do?"

He glanced over as he pulled away and saw her looking down at her feet. Another glance told him that she wiggled her toes.

"I've never seen anyone whose feet look more natural on her than yours do on you." Out of the corner of his eye he sensed her looking at him. He grinned.

"We're going to the Dockside for dinner. Is that okay?"

"Sure."

They chatted about books during the ten minutes it took to get to the Dockside. John wanted her to take the ferry with him to San Juan and visit a bookstore.

"Really? You'd really take me with you?"

"Sure. You should get to help pick out the next books I read you. I also need to pick up some supplies, if you don't mind tagging along that is."

"Oh, no, I don't mind." She vibrated a low hum; a few soft clicks escaped her mouth.

"You know you hum and click all the time? I'm starting to be able to tell what all the different pitches, tempos, and volumes mean. I'm guessing you're being polite. Am I right?"

"No. I'm excited. And scared."

"Really?" He looked at her. "Well, I'll try not to disappoint you then."

The Dockside had few customers this hour in the off-season. The waitress led them to a two-person table looking out over the canal where they ordered *buñuelos de queso*, *mojo isleño*, and *tembleque*. John ordered a Medalla and watched with a smile as Tamarind ordered a Coke.

"How do you like your fish?"

Tamarind wrinkled her nose and sliced off a tiny wedge from the *mojo isleño*. "Not much. I can hardly taste the fish with all the other flavors. I like my fish fresher, too."

"How do you normally eat it? I thought this garlic sauce was popular in Puerto Rico."

"Oh. Well, we usually eat our fish raw."

"Like sushi?" At her puzzled look, he said, "That's what the Japanese call raw fish, seaweed, and rice. You'd probably like it."

"It sounds good. How do you like to eat fish?"

John sipped his beer. "I don't normally eat fish or animal flesh. I'm a vegetarian, but it's hard to stick with it here on the island so I've been eating fish." He figured that there was no need to mention his brief deviation into beef.

"No fish?" Tamarind sounded shocked. "Why not? I thought everybody ate fish."

"I guess there's a lot of reasons." John ticked off some of the issues that Zoë had given him when she insisted he become a vegetarian. They still seemed reasonable. "Mostly, it's not sustainable. I mean, huge fishing boats come along and trawl with their nets, scooping up whatever gets trapped in them. The fish can't possibly keep reproducing fast enough and sometimes other creatures die simply because they're caught in the net. Plus, I think it's healthier to cut out fish and meat."

"It's not because you don't like to eat fish?"

"No, actually, I love fish, especially sushi."

"But you don't want to kill them to eat them? Didn't you go fishing here?"

John squirmed a bit. "Yeah, but that's not what I find objectionable. It's kind've hard to explain, but it doesn't bother me if somebody catches a few fish using a rod and bait. That's just not how most people get fish in the U.S."

"Oh. Okay."

They fell silent. Tamarind continued to pick at her *mojo isleño*.

John decided to rescue her. "You don't have to finish that."

She sighed and pushed the fish aside. She dipped a tentative spoon into the coconut custard. "The *tembleque*'s good, though."

"Anyone who loves Coke as much as you do obviously has a sweet tooth."

Tamarind began rubbing the tip of her tongue over her teeth. "How do I know which one? None of them taste sweet."

John laughed. "Sorry! That just means you like to eat sweet things."

Tamarind frowned. "I always get it wrong."

He put his hand briefly on hers. "I love the way you get it. I feel like I'm looking at the world through fresh eyes when I'm with you. It's wonderful."

Tamarind blushed and dipped the spoon back into the *tembleque*.

They drove to Isla Encantada twenty minutes later and found the live music just getting going. Even in the dim lighting, John recognized Jesus in the far corner. To his surprise—and relief—he recognized Jesus' date as well. Raimunda's voluptuous curves and luxuriant hair were unmistakable. He didn't know what relieved him more: Jesus having a date or Raimunda's near-feral sexuality being contained. A small sound at his side made him look down to see Tamarind gazing at Jesus. John squeezed her hand and smiled.

Tamarind said nothing but sidled closer to John, who forgot all about Jesus at her nearness and led her onto the dance floor. She watched John and imitated his movements, but after John ordered a beer she drank half of it without taking a breath. She closed her eyes when she returned to the dance floor and appeared to listen to something in the music audible only to her. John couldn't take his eyes from her, barely dancing. She looked like a poem set to music.

They might have danced minutes or hours. The heat of bodies, the dim interior and flashes of mirror and lights, the beat of drums and the sound of Spanish—all these cocooned John in a timeless world. At last Tamarind opened eyes in a flushed face and grabbed John's hand.

"Let's get out of here!" She pulled him to the door and outside into the cooler, though still warm, Caribbean night. "I need water."

"We can get something to drink inside."

"No, no. I need to swim."

The cocoon had split open and the night air touched a fingertip to John's damp forehead. The need for full immersion in water of any kind seized him after she spoke.

"Me too. Let's get out of here."

John headed north toward Playa Tamarindo, but Tamarind tugged on his arm when they approached the right onto 250. He turned as she directed and they headed east. He'd driven this route only one other time since coming to Culebra—the time that Zoë visited and they'd driven around the whole island. Even so, he'd kayaked and cruised the eastern shore and visited Culebrita and its hundred-year-old lighthouse so he knew the eastern shoreline. Since 250 ended at Playa Zoni, he thought he knew where Tamarind intended for them to go. However, not long after the road bore sharply to the north, she asked him to pull over.

"Here. I want to show you Puerto del Manglar."

After he'd parked the Samurai along the deserted two-lane road, they descended a rocky path toward the lagoon, which was bordered by a narrow muddy rim. A westerly breeze passed over the water and cooled their skin. Around them and along the shoreline of the lagoon, darker mangrove trees framed the night sky where stars lay scattered in brilliant disarray.

John tilted his face up to the dome of the night sky over them.

"I'm an explorer at the end of the world," he said. In the still night, his quiet voice seemed loud to him. "Thanks for showing me this place."

"Wait. There's something else you need to see." Tamarind bent down and picked something up from the ground. When she tossed whatever it was into the still waters, the incandescent filament of its plunge lit up the lagoon before his eyes. "There are tiny creatures that live in this water that react to movement by lighting up."

"Like underwater fireflies?"

John turned to Tamarind, but she'd already lifted her dress over her head and dropped it on the ground at her feet, sighing. She wore nothing under the dress. As he watched her stride into the phosphorescent water, thousands of the tiny creatures shimmered like blue-green fire along the surface of her skin and in the patch of hair between her legs. Around them, the *coquí* frog sang its distinctive refrain and mosquitoes hummed.

He took a step forward and then stopped. Tamarind swam in the obsidian water, her strokes luminous and eerie.

"I thought you were hot from dancing." Tamarind lay on her back fifty feet away looking at him, her torso elevated from the surface of the lagoon. Neon streaked the surrounding water as she stroked to stay afloat.

"I was."

"You're not now? Is something wrong?"

"No—yes. Sometimes I feel a little like I'm suffocating."

She swam closer, her eyes never leaving his face. "Is that how you felt the day I pulled you from the canal?"

"Yes."

"I know how you feel. Sometimes I find it hard to breathe when I'm out of water."

John remembered her swimming. "Coming from you, that makes perfect sense."

She stood up and walked to him, her small breasts high and their nipples taut. Seawater fell from her in a glowing sheet. When she reached him, she took his right hand in her left. He felt her vibrating hum through the skin of his palm.

"I'll take care of you." She lifted his t-shirt over his head while he stood there, shivering. "You're cold?" Her hands, normally cool and moist, felt warm against his shoulders.

She stepped closer and wrapped her arms around his torso, pressing against him. Her heat seeped into his skin and he shivered more. She laid her head against his chest and hummed louder. John closed his eyes and breathed. After a moment he realized that Tamarind breathed in unison with him and he felt warmer. Something inside his chest unlocked and his lungs expanded to let in air. Slowly he lifted his left hand and cupped the back of her head. She didn't move or halt her humming.

John shifted so that Tamarind looked up at him. In the dark he saw only starlight reflected in her eyes; her hair, so carefully clipped up earlier in the evening, curved around her face in damp clumps. He lowered his mouth to hers and tasted salt.

"Counting turtle eggs? You're so full of shit, John." Zoë's voice sliced through the night around them. "Care to introduce me to your naked friend?"

Eleven

JOHN STOOD ON THE BERM between the road and the lagoon with the dripping woman shrinking beside him. He dipped his head and stepped sideways, blocking Zoë's view.

"Wha-what are you doing here?" He didn't look at her.

"Fuck if I know!" Her voice cracked on the last word and she clinched her hands at her side. "I believed you when you said you were sorry about fucking another woman, that you cared about me. I believed you when you said you just needed to get away from grad school for a while, spend some time in the surf and sand. I came down here to give you a second chance."

Her words flew at him. She almost wished that they were stilettos, and she didn't mean those ridiculous neck-breakers that Barbie dolls wore.

He turned and said something Zoë couldn't hear to his date. She scurried in the direction of the Samurai parked thirty feet from them.

"I didn't lie to you." John turned back to face her.

"So I'm supposed to believe that this-this—" She flung her arm in the direction of the Samurai. "That you haven't been fucking this island bitch all summer?"

The moon had risen over them, bringing John's features into sharp relief. Shadows underneath his eyes obscured their expression.

"You're supposed to believe that I never intended to hurt you." He raised his hand toward her—to ward off her next words or to console her, she didn't know which.

"My God! Even now you're dancing around the truth! You think you love her, don't you?"

John dropped his hand and said nothing.

"What is she to you? Someone not too educated to forget her place? You're an asshole, John, and I can't believe I've been tearing myself up over you. Let me show you what a real woman does when a man tries to make a fool out of her."

Before he could anticipate her or even protest, she lifted her right knee to her chest, rising onto the ball of her left foot. A fraction of a second later her right heel connected with his solar plexus, sending him flying away from her. He landed on the soft mud at the edge of Puerto del Manglar. She followed the kick up with a dash and a swing of her left leg that stopped short of his head; as she stood over him, panting, she knew he got the message: she could knock his block off if she chose. Then, after a long moment, she lowered her foot and turned away.

ᴥᴥᴥ

Ana hunkered within the scant shade of her doorway, her good eye squinted against the mid-afternoon light. Smoke from her clove cigarette curled and wafted until it was snared within the strands of her coarse hair. On a grass mat before her was a mound of tamarind pods, nearly ten pounds, that she'd collected this morning after scouring the ground near the tamarind trees along the coast; it was the first of the season's fruit. She'd already washed each pod and now broke them into smaller pieces, leaving the outer shell and seeds with the pulp and tossing them into a large cast-iron pot at her right side. Reach, grasp, snap, snap, snap. Her body swayed and rocked as she worked, her movements efficient and easy; only the sounds of birds competed with her radio, now playing Latin salsa behind her.

After she'd finished breaking the tamarind pods, Ana built a fire under a cast-iron frame ten feet from her house. She hauled the pot to the frame and lifted it onto a hook over the flames. Next, she poured in twice as much spring water as fruit from her cache of bottled water and stirred the tamarind around in it, her left hand drifting to the stub of cigarette in her mouth before removing it; as she stirred, a spicy scent of tamarind fruit insinuated itself through the cloying smoke. She stirred until the water began to darken and the pulp separated from the shells and seeds. These she strained from the pot with a long-handled sieve and saved in a wooden bowl for later use in lotions and syrups for a wide-range of ailments.

She let the water simmer for ten minutes or so before she tossed in a handful of cloves, allspice and black peppercorns, then slices of lime and ginger. She breathed the vapors rising from her brew and sighed before sinking down again on her heels under the shade of a nearby tree and waiting for the fruit and spices to flavor the water fully. A slight breeze stirred the air around her, drying the sweat from between her flaccid breasts and lifting the ends of her hair from her cheeks.

When she'd judged that the decoction was sufficiently spiced, she strained out the spices and fruit. Near the wooden bowl into which she deposited these spent flavorings sat two five-pound bags of palm sugar; she added these slowly to the pot, stirring until she had a thin syrup. She let this syrup boil for several minutes and then doused the fire under the pot. As the syrup cooled, she ladled it into a large glass bottle (which one of the Culebrenses had given her as payment for curing his diarrhea) filled with several gallons of purified water. Now the brew was cool enough for the yeast, which she'd already dissolved in warm water. Her task was nearly over: she would watch the fermentation over the next two weeks, adding sugar whenever it seemed to slow down. By the end of that time, it would be drinkable; in a month, it would be a spicy beer.

Ana had brewed a variety of other wines and beers from Culebra's fruits, but none tasted nearly as good as tamarind beer and she'd long since abandoned any other recipes that she'd tested. Even though she had no one but herself to please, she'd found that more than a few of the locals preferred her tamarind beer to commercial beers and she was able to sell a cup here and there for far more than that which a bottle of Medalla garnered.

She lifted the full bottle of fermenting brew into her decrepit refrigerator, its once-white exterior now chipped and pockmarked from a lifetime of use. It was one of the few modern conveniences that she'd grudgingly adopted from her previous life as a sailor's wife, but one which earned her respect for its ability to make her life more pleasant and pay for itself. It, a warming plate, and a radio were the only appliances that she owned.

Now that she'd finished brewing, she pulled out a smaller, two-and-a-half gallon bottle of finished beer from one of the higher shelves in the refrigerator and poured herself a cup. She took the cup and a fresh clove cigarette and returned to the doorway of her single room to wait for the rain that she smelled in the air.

A hush descended over the afternoon as the sun reached its zenith and all of the Creator's wildlife dozed in its heat. Even Ana grew sleepy in the still warmth, her head drooping over her cup and her hand holding the cigarette growing limp. Gentle fingers saved her from being burned and woke her with their cool touch. Struggling awake, Ana lifted her face. Seeing the mermaid, she shifted on her heels and brought her cup up to her mouth. It wouldn't do for the young one to guess that she'd been waiting for her. She drained the last of the tamarind beer, its fiery descent into her stomach bracing her, and set the cup down. She rose to face Tamarind, who still held her burning cigarette.

"I'll take that."

Tamarind handed it to her, her forehead puckered. The young one looked so much like Ana herself had before she'd married her sailor that a deep soreness settled in her chest, but this time there was no tamarind beer to fortify her nerves. Even if she had a mirror, Ana knew that Tamarind would not recognize her own innocence and vulnerability within it.

"You've been gone all night." She said, her voice gruff from the heartache, and took a drag. "Did you manage to win your legs by mating with that man?"

The muscles in Tamarind's face tightened. Ana noticed that her dress, originally brilliant blue, was dusty and torn in several places.

"Did he hurt you? Tell me and I'll brew him a special potion. Or I'll call on Mother Sea and curse him to the seventh generation!"

Tamarind sank into a squat and folded her arms across her chest. Her corkscrew hair concealed her face.

"He didn't hurt me the way you think. We went dancing last night and I took him to Puerto Manglar to show him the glowing ones. Then he kissed me."

She stopped, but Ana said nothing. Instead, she went inside and returned with a cup of the tamarind beer. She handed it to Tamarind, who gulped some of it and winced.

"His girlfriend appeared at just that moment. Her anger pulsed from her—it nearly overwhelmed my senses. John asked me to wait in his Samurai, but I could still hear them talking." She paused long enough to sip the tamarind beer. "Then she kicked him in the chest. He fell hard and she nearly kicked him in the head, but she didn't. I could tell she wanted to though."

Ana dropped her cigarette butt onto the hard ground and twisted her heel on it. "Ah. Did he plead with her?"

"No, he lay on the ground, clutching at his chest. I waited until she left to go to him, but he said nothing to me, just waved me back into the Samurai. When he finally got in, he said it was time for me to go home. He dropped me off at the bottom of the hill."

"Where've you been then?"

Tamarind looked into her cup as though she looked at it for the first time and didn't like what she saw. "Just wandering—and swimming. I couldn't sleep anyway."

Ana gripped Tamarind's chin and made her look up. "I warned you to stay away from him. He's not worth the pain you've already been through. Don't let him hurt you anymore."

"His girlfriend said he thinks he loves me."

"Bah! She said that in the heat of the moment. Even if she's right, he's not to be trusted. Look how he's hurt her. I doubt he knows what he wants. And as hurt and angry as she is, I bet you a colossal squid for dinner she'd take him back if he asked her to."

Tamarind stood up. "I need another swim."

"Go and have one. But keep in mind, young one: you win this man, you're not likely to live close to the ocean. You won't be able to swim whenever your heart troubles you."

Tamarind frowned. Without speaking, she turned toward the hidden path to Playa Tamarindo and trudged away.

Ana lit another clove cigarette and took a deep drag, her eyes all the while on Tamarind's hunched shoulders. After Tamarind disappeared over the rise, she smiled and exhaled smoke, which lingered around her face pleasantly.

ഛഛഛ

John's head ached. His head and torso felt as if they'd been hollowed out and then stuffed with a mix of sandpaper and wool. He groaned and rolled over onto his side, misjudging how close he was to the edge of the bed. He crashed against the floor hard, but the pain receded quickly as he realized that the air washing over his face was cool. Looking up to the clock on his bedside table, he read 4:08 p.m.

He lay there for a long time. The headache only grew sharper and his tongue, now swollen and hairy inside his mouth, commandeered his thoughts once he noticed its state. With willpower alone, he pushed himself into a seated position, wincing as an invisible pick plunged through his skull and out his left eye. He remembered enough to focus his energy on standing up and getting into the bathroom where water and ibuprofen awaited him. His legs had fallen asleep while he lay on the floor and prickles danced up and down his calves and out his toes as he hobbled across the room.

Every act of getting ready took much longer than it should have, but by dinnertime John had managed to shower, shave, and dress in clean clothes. He still felt tired, but his headache no longer plagued him and the gallon of water that he'd ingested one cup at a

140

time had returned his tissues to their normal fullness. A residue clung to his tongue even though he'd brushed it with toothpaste.

He walked to Señorita's and asked for a table in the corner away from James, the ever-present double of Ernest Hemingway that he'd seen during his first stay on Culebra. James would happily buy him a hair of the dog, but John didn't feel like listening to his exploits or his complaints this evening. When Janelle came to take his order, she clucked and grasped his chin in her free hand to tilt his face toward the light.

"Sweetie! You look like someone mugged you! Are you all right?"

John shrugged and pulled away. "Just too much to drink, Janelle. I'll be fine tomorrow."

"I'll bring you a club soda with lemon. Order something healthy, too. No fries, hear?"

John sank back into his chair after Janelle brought him his drink and fussed over him. He kept his eyes on the tiled tabletop, but there was no one around to meet his gaze. Although the weekend beachgoers arrived on the ferry this morning, Playa Flamenco absorbed their numbers and town remained quiet. Very few tourists came to Culebra during the summer—that hot, dry hurricane season—and no one followed John into Señorita's for the next half an hour. After she delivered his food, Janelle retreated to a barstool next to James and across from Tim, the bartender, and the three of them gossiped in the otherwise empty restaurant. John cut up his fish and lifted food into his mouth, but every bite tasted like sawdust.

He heard laughter near the entranceway just as he finished eating as much of his dinner as he could swallow. Looking, he caught sight of Raimunda. Wearing a tight t-shirt and blue jeans, she stood gazing up at Pablo, whose right arm curled around her waist. So. She was a free agent, but he knew that, didn't he? Maybe he should renew their relationship. Same terms as before, even if he didn't have a girlfriend anymore. He didn't know how he felt about Zoë. Or Tamarind. He did know how he felt about Raimunda. It was

141

lust, plain and simple. And he deserved the funk that swallowed him every time it came over him. John pushed his plate away from him without taking his eyes from her and put his feet up on the seat of the chair opposite him. When Janelle came to collect the plate, he put his hand on her wrist and ordered a Medalla.

"If you say so, honey," she said, but he only half heard.

John watched Raimunda as he sipped his beer. She never turned to look at him but kept her attention on Pablo and the bottle of beer Janelle brought her. When Pablo left Raimunda to head to the bathroom, John tipped his beer up and drained it before pushing his chair back with a loud squeak. At the sound, Raimunda turned to watch him, a smile twitching at the corners of her mouth.

"*Hola, gringo.*"

"*Buenas noches.*" He sat down in an empty chair. "I came to steal you away from Pablo."

She smirked and lifted her beer to her mouth. John watched her throat pulse as she swallowed. Above the collar of the t-shirt, a small shell pendant rested in the hollow at the base of her throat. She touched the tip of her tongue to her upper lip as she set the bottle down in front of her.

"Perhaps I don't wish to be stolen away, *mi amigo.*"

John leaned forward and traced the inside of her upper arm with his index finger. "Perhaps I don't care what you want," he said into her ear.

Raimunda laughed and tossed her hair out of her face. "Oh, I think you care what I want all right."

John picked up her hand from where it rested on the table and pulled it into his lap. "I know what you want."

"John? *Qué pasa?*" Pablo materialized not far from them.

Raimunda slid her hand up and around her beer bottle before Pablo reached the table. John wondered if Pablo had seen.

"Not much, *amigo.* Just saying hello to Raimunda."

"John and I are old friends," she said as Pablo sat down. John saw her hand disappear under the table and he imagined it on Pablo's thigh. From the look on Pablo's face, he'd guessed right.

"Well, it was good to see you two, but I'll leave you alone to enjoy your dinner." John stood.

Pablo, whose eyes had fastened on Raimunda's ripe mouth, barely nodded. "*Hasta la vista*, John."

John walked around Dewey for the next hour, passing by Señorita's entrance a dozen times before Pablo and Raimunda finally left together. He watched Pablo weave down the sidewalk north toward his apartment. Raimunda propped him up as he chattered incomprehensibly next to her; she intermittently uttered soothing sounds in response to his commentary. After they'd gone fifty yards, John followed them. When they reached Pablo's apartment, Raimunda folded her arms and leaned against the wall of the building while Pablo tried to insert his key into the deadbolt. John waited until he'd caught her eye and pointed to Pablo, then shook his head and pointed to himself. Raimunda grinned and took Pablo's arm. Waving to John over her shoulder, she took the key from Pablo and unlocked the door. Pablo nearly fell into the building as she swung the door open and away from him.

John waited, his lips compressed. After only a few minutes, Raimunda reappeared in the doorway—alone. She scanned the far sidewalk and when her eyes met John's, she smiled and leaned again, this time onto the doorframe. John strode toward her; when he reached her, he gripped her elbows.

"Pablo can't hold his beer, can he?"

She shrugged. "He's sitting on his sofa muttering in front of his TV. Good thing he's got a satellite dish."

"Let's go find out if I know what you want."

Raimunda rose up on her toes and kissed him, hard. "I want exactly what you want, *gringo*."

She threaded her fingers through his and together they walked toward Posada La Diosa and his room there.

143

Twelve
ভ

WET SAND CLUNG TO JOHN'S BARE FEET as he strolled along the strip of Isla Verde beach owned by the Ritz-Carlton's San Juan Hotel. He heard dozens of voices from other conference attendees as they spilled through the hotel's doors to the beachfront, chattering without seeing the beauty in front of them. He'd already presented the paper that he'd written about the difficulties in storing and accessing large amounts of digital video while onboard a marine research ship. He'd escaped the ongoing presentations and milling graduate students as soon as the last questioner scurried out of his particular conference room on the way to another talk. Somewhere inside, his advisor deftly worked his industry contacts, always looking for a way to turn a spark of interest into funding.

"Hey, man, you look like you should be combing the beach for loose change, the way you've got your pants rolled up like that," said a voice several feet behind him.

John whirled. His friend Stefan stood at the edge of the manicured lawn holding a wineglass and a notepad.

"And you look like Eddie Murphy in *Beverly Hills Cop* when he lied his way into the Beverly Hills Hotel. You ever think maybe a t-shirt and blue jeans weren't the best things to wear to the Ritz?"

John walked over to where Stefan stood. "Have they put out lunch yet?"

Stefan nodded and raised the wineglass to his mouth. "The wine's actually pretty crappy. But I doubt too many of the others will notice. They're too wrapped up in debating optimal bit rates and lossless compression. They don't have our refined sensitivities."

"We'll just have to make do with the hotel buffet for lunch, but tonight I'll take you across the street to this Cuban place I know, *Metropole*. They have the best *moros y cristianos* in Puerto Rico. Their *pastelitos* are also very tasty. I eat there about once a week now."

They turned and made their way toward the Vista Mar Terrace where the largest number of graduate students, faculty members, and industry researchers now congregated around open bars and tables laden with crudités, cheese and crackers, and fresh fruit. When they'd managed to fill their small plates and gotten full glasses of wine, they positioned themselves in a corner furthest from the building and chatted between bites.

"So I met Elí Arroyo López from Polytech last night at the reception. He's very excited to have an 'exchange' student as he puts it for the summer. He told me that he's been working for some time to create a real department instead of offering a single EE degree."

John popped a water cracker laden with Brie into his mouth, chewed and swallowed. "Elí's a good guy with a lot of ambitions for his beloved PUPR. Who knows? Maybe he's prescient about the need for high-tech degrees in Puerto Rico. A lot of people are talking about India these days, but Elí thinks there's a large pool of talent closer to home."

"You getting a lot of work done here? I read your paper in the proceedings and it looks like you might have yourself a thesis topic percolating in there."

"Actually, I've been working on another research paper for the Video IR Symposium in October. It's amazing how much work you can get done when you don't really know anyone."

145

"No? I thought maybe there were one or two women in this tropical paradise."

John shrugged and looked down at his plate. "I've been spending weekends on Culebra where I have some friends. Some of them happen to be women."

"That explains why Zoë's been a regular storm cloud around the CS department. You two still together?"

"No." John didn't elaborate.

"Ah. Well, no wonder you're in no hurry to get back to Pittsburgh." Stefan grinned, his Cheshire-cat grin. It irritated John. "Let me know if you need a place to stay when you get back."

"I'm in no hurry to get back to Pittsburgh because I needed a break, Stefan." John set his empty wineglass down on the terrace wall a little harder than he intended. A passing waiter glared at him as he rescued it. "My time away from CMU hasn't been wasted. I've seen endangered leatherback turtles struggle onto dark beaches where they exhaust themselves digging pits for their eggs, which they leave, trusting that the next generation will survive the greediness and stupidity of people. I've also spent a lot of time teaching an illiterate woman how to read. Compared to those two activities, worrying about which RAID scheme works best for video storage seems a tad inconsequential."

"So what's the answer then? Chuck it all and live on a Caribbean island?"

John looked out over the horizon. "If I figure out a way to do it, I just might."

Later that night, John left the window looking out on La Isla Verde open. The moon illuminated his suite so well that he found himself unable to sleep until long after he lay down on the Egyptian cotton sheets. He slept without knowing he slept, or so he came to believe. In the vivid light, he saw Tamarind standing framed in the window. She wore the blue batik dress that she'd worn the night that they went dancing and even in the shadows around her head he could see the hue of her eyes. Pearls studded her hair, which flowed as smooth as water around her head; abalone and obsidian ornaments dangled from her ears and neck. She studied his face without smiling, but her eyes hinted at mirth. After a moment, she hummed and clicked until John lost the dream and sank into sleep.

ومومو

Ana trod barefoot over the dusty path toward Playa Tamarindo, her calloused feet insensitive to the hard stones and uneven ground. The dry heat burned her lungs as it had done for more years than she cared to remember, but she knew that she had long passed the point where she could choose a different home, a better life. Above her, her favorite laughing gull hovered protectively and occasionally dropped down to her shoulder and chuckled reprovingly in her ear.

She stopped just as the path began to descend again toward the shore and peered down through the opening in the thorny scrub ahead of her to Tamarind's scraggly-haired silhouette embossed against the night sky. Around the motionless form emanated an aura like a grease slick on wet pavement. Seeing it, Ana's breath quickened and she bit her lower lip. Half the rainy season had already passed and still the mermaid pined for the weak, lustful man that she'd saved from a watery death. Ana could no longer wait for Tamarind to abandon her mad hope for something more to happen with John. She must entice her with a powerful alternative.

ومومو

Shifting her buttocks a little, Tamarind shoved her feet against the stones in front of her and lifted her face into the breeze, her eyes closed. The fan-leafed palms and tamarind trees lining the beach's edge whispered as the breeze tickled their leaves and the ocean *shush-shushed* them; otherwise, the reverent night was silent beneath the moon overhead. She felt the strength of the trees rooting down into the ground and she leaned into their strength, wanting to draw it into herself and keep it there.

"So. I find you here." A raspy voice and the scent of cloves came from behind her.

Tamarind didn't answer; she only closed her eyes.

"T'won't do you any good to sit here and moon over that idiot."

147

"What business is it of yours what I'm doing?" She didn't look at the old woman.

For a moment she heard nothing; then she felt Ana's presence next to her on the stones.

"None of my business, that's what. I'm neither kin nor friend to you. But I speak from experience, young one." She paused. "I was once a mermaid like you and also fell in love with a human man."

Tamarind stared at Ana. "What happened?"

Ana shrugged and sucked hard on her clove cigarette without looking from the distant horizon. The sound of burning paper and her harsh exhale mingled with the rich scent of clove. "Not important what happened. All you need to know is I put off my tail for love. Long after I left this island behind, I found myself alone. Came back here and begged the island midwife to undo what she'd done, to send me back to the waves. She said it was impossible for me. I was no longer the same person; I might die trying to put a tail on again. I insisted anyway, saying I was as likely to die from grief."

She turned to look at Tamarind. Both opaque eyes appeared blind in the starlight.

"Obviously didn't work. But it wasn't a complete failure. Instead of dying, I lost only the sight in my eye. If you'd been paying attention, you'd've seen the *mer* in me. I still hear *mer* speech, though not like I once did. Along my flanks are pores for sensing movement underwater." She smoothed the side of her shirt. "Mine no longer work. Only give the Culebrenses something to gossip about."

Tamarind studied Ana in the brilliant moonlight. She thought that she must always have known. Signs of the *mer* showed clearly on the old woman: she had a bit of webbing between her fingers, almost indiscernible now from the loose skin of old age, and her eye, piercing as it was, was the changeable blue of Mother Sea.

"Why are you telling me all this?"

"Because, unlike you, I didn't really have a choice. I tried to force my way back, but it wasn't my fate. You gotta choice."

"What choice? When the rainy season ends, I'll revert back to being *mer*. You said I couldn't remain human unless I consummated my love with John."

"Yeah, I did say that. But you can keep your legs if you copulate with any human male while you're transformed."

Tamarind started to speak, but Ana cut her off. "I'm getting old and need an apprentice, Tamarind. There's always been a midwife. She tells the *dragos* what she can about the humans on her island. She casts and keeps glamours. Sometimes she helps a *mer* put off a tail. Took me a while to see I'd been chosen, but I came to accept my fate."

Her last words hung, heavy as ripe tamarind pods on slender branches, over them.

"You're offering me the choice of becoming a midwife, like you? To remain human?" Tamarind paused, shaking her head. "I don't want to be human if I can't be with John."

Ana squinted her eye before pushing the stub of her clove cigarette into the stones at her side. She exhaled smoke in twin streams from her nostrils. It writhed and expanded in front of her face. "Don't have to decide now. You still have time before the rains end. Think over my offer. That's all I ask, young one."

Tamarind noticed the book that lay on the ground near Ana like a dark smudge in the moonlight. Thick, with a dirty cloth cover that was torn and water-stained, its yellowed pages exuded age—and *power*. She'd seen Ana consulting this book numerous times, but Ana had always guarded it and said that it was for no one's eyes but her own.

"You can't read," Ana said the first time that Tamarind asked about it. "What's the point in looking at a book when you don't have any idea what it says?"

At the time, Tamarind shrugged and said nothing. Now it lay between them like a promise. Ana saw where her gaze fell and she put withered fingers on it.

"Intrigued by my book?"

Tamarind looked at the old woman's face. Ana gazed back at her with a mild expression. So she picked the book up with reverent fingers and pulled it into her lap. Her eyes, used to the dimmer underwater world, had no difficulty distinguishing details, faint as they were. Turning pages as fragile as dried seaweed, she glimpsed lists of herbs, spices, sea creatures and underwater plants—many items were words that she didn't recognize from her short reading experience. Underneath the lists, she saw directions for preparing the items and instructions for keeping and administering the final preparations. In the margins, there were handwritten notes and occasional drawings.

"I'll teach you to read it."

Tamarind nearly responded that she already knew how to read before something stopped her short; she blinked instead and recalled that Ana had tempted her a long time with the key to human learning.

"Why should I believe that you'd teach me how to read?"

"Because it's the midwife's book. If you're gonna take my place one day, you have to be able to read it."

Tamarind bit her lower lip. "I haven't said I'll take your place."

"True." Ana nodded, the clove cigarette clamped between her first two fingers where it dangled in front of her. "When you do, you'll find many, many useful recipes and spells. The method for helping a *mer* put off her tail—and the method for putting it on again—to name a few. Become my apprentice and I'll show you how to do lots of amazing things."

Tamarind continued to turn the pages and to run her fingertips over the contents. On a page two-thirds of the way through the book she squinted at instructions for transforming someone into a temporary copy of another, living or dead. As long as the caster had some item that belonged to the person being copied, something taken from the body, then an elaborate potion could be brewed and distilled that transformed the caster for one turn of the day. She frowned.

"Tell me, young one. Where is it your father thinks you've been all this time?"

Tamarind's frown deepened. "I let him think that I went to the Hidden Caves of Camuy for training with the *mer* elders."

"Ah." Ana rummaged in the small pouch she wore on a long strap around her neck. After a moment, she pulled out another clove cigarette and a small object that glistened in the moonlight. Muttering something that might have been a spell, she raised the disc to one end of the cigarette and sucked on the other until a thin plume of smoke appeared near the disc. "So your father intends for you to be a *dragos*. He sees the same qualities in you I do. We just don't have the same ideas about how best to help the *mer*."

She smoked the cigarette in silence while Tamarind continued turning pages in the book. A laughing gull flew over their heads, a dark speck that spiraled around them until it had descended low enough to land on Ana's shoulder. Tamarind had never seen a bird flying at this time of night before. She watched the bird nuzzle Ana's cheek and appear to whisper in her ear. When the laughing gull cocked its head and turned a bright eye on Tamarind, she thought it studied her coldly. It again whispered in Ana's ear and the old woman laughed. Tamarind ignored them and struggled to read more spells in the waning moonlight.

"What's he gonna think when he finds out you spent the rainy season with me?"

"I don't know."

"Yes you do. You just don't know why he hates humans so much. I do. It's because of your mother."

Tamarind sat up straighter. "What do you know about my mother?"

"Enough. She was the first mermaid I tried to help put off her tail."

"What? What lie are you telling me, old woman?" She'd never spoken to Ana so rudely before; she'd caught a residue of thought from the former *mer* and responded to its flash of visceral ugliness.

"No lie." The gull laughed at them and launched itself into the air above their heads. "Just like you, she mooned about wherever she could see humans: beaches, boats, cays. And, just like you, she fixated on one, a boat captain. And one day, she came to me and asked me to help her put off her tail."

"But how did she know you could help her? I didn't know about you before we met. I certainly didn't know *mer* could put off their tails."

"Ah, that's because your father drowned the knowledge among your community. If any remember, he's forbidden them from sharing it among the others."

"But—but Mother was a mermaid! I was very young, it's true, but I still remember her. If she'd been human, how could she and my father have mated, let alone had six daughters?"

"Yeah, she was a mermaid when she died." Ana picked up a clove cigarette. Her lined face seemed to shrivel even more and her eye no longer blazed. "Her tail never came off. I remember the sound she made when I eased her out of the ground. Like a baby seal mewing. Her tail bruised and bloodied, one tip broken and limp—it still haunts me.

"Something in her mind died that day. Her thoughts frothed and foamed. Your father loved her before she came to me, though she never returned his love. He took her, poor wounded thing, and mated with her. His strength kept her safe for a while and you and your sisters were born. But she couldn't stay away from humans and kept wandering toward them."

Here Ana stopped and sucked on her cigarette so long that Tamarind thought that the story must be done. She was about to ask Ana why she had told her all this about her mother, when Ana began to speak again.

"I've thought about that spell of transforming over and over. I just can't be sure it wasn't my fault it failed."

Tamarind hesitated a moment. "Is that why Father kept us from knowing about your powers?"

"No." Ana looked away. "Putting off the tail has always been dangerous for *mer*. He didn't blame me for that. No, he didn't want any of you to know how to become human because he despises humans."

"Because Mother was so fascinated by them?"

"That's partly why, young one." Ana brought her eye to Tamarind's face with visible effort. "But it has more to do with the fact a human killed her and very nearly killed him, too."

Thirteen

ᚙ

ANA STUDIED THE SMOKING STUB between her fingers without meeting Tamarind's eyes. After it had burned almost to her fingertips, she leaned forward and sunk it into the seawater caressing the stones around their feet. It hissed briefly. She flicked the remains into the tree line behind them. Time to wield the truth like a shark's tooth.

"It's more than ten rainy seasons since I found your father on Luís Peña. Back then I could still swim. Swam over there to look for birds' eggs. That day, I finished gathering all the eggs I could carry and went up to the beach to look for seaweed. That's when I came across your father, bleeding his life into the sand.

"Took all my strength to wrestle him onto his back so I could clean his wound and get a better look. Can't tell you, young one, how scary that terrible hole in his shoulder was—never seen anything like it! Worse, I never cared for anyone so badly hurt. Whatever had done it was still in him and I had to get it out, and get it out quick. But everything was on Culebra, all my healing salves, all my infusions and tinctures, all my tools—not to mention my book.

"Fear turned me into rigid coral. I couldn't act. My thoughts swam. I cried out to Mother Sea but blood pounded in my head.

154

Breath stuck in my throat. Couldn't hear Her answer. Then I remembered what my teacher had told me: listen to the sound of the waves and breathe with them. I closed my eyes until I had their rhythm, until I *became* their rhythm.

"I knew what to do when I opened my eyes. Couldn't swim over here and back in time, let alone bring everything. Had to bring him around, no matter how dazed he'd be, and then reach into his mind and direct it. Your father has a very strong mind—*very strong*. I knew it would take everything I had to save him. I reached into my pouch for the eggs, cracked them with my thumb and forefinger like so"—Ana demonstrated with a quick motion of her hand—"and sucked them all down.

"I entered his mind like a thief and pried my fingers into his wound. He groaned, a horrible sound like the rending of wood in fierce water, and his eyes fluttered. I kept poking until I found it.

"Couldn't tell what it was, just that it was very hard and warm—and sharp. It moved a little as I prodded but didn't come loose. It reached deep into his shoulder. I was so absorbed I forgot your father and kept jiggling it back and forth to dislodge it. While I was busy, he groaned again and then his pain stung me.

"'Do you seek to kill me, you who are chosen as healer?' he asked.

"'If I did, oh *dragos*, first and foremost among *mer*, I would have left you to die where I found you,' I answered.

"I ignored his rigid body and harsh breathing because I sensed he was going to slip away from me. I tightened my grip on his mind instead.

"*Come here*, I ordered using *mer* speech.

"He fought me. I kept my wits and drew upon the power of the water. He didn't fight long before I found myself looking through his eyes as well as my own. Pain rolled over me. I vomited and almost let go, but I expected this. Focused on breathing to shut off awareness of that part of his mind. In, out, in, out, in, out—until I felt nothing else.

"I threw a glamour around us and pushed against the power of the cay. Mother Sea pulled us down quicker than I expected, and saltwater slapped us hard. It stung your father's wound. I struggled to master both of us. Then, slowly, we moved around Luís Peña and on to Playa Tamarindo. It was excruciating, but I kept breathing and continued to draw strength from Mother Sea.

"We reached Playa Tamarindo finally. I was nearly beyond my limit. Got your father behind some scrub before I had to let his mind go. Got enough energy back to throw a glamour on him while I was gone. I reached home, clumsy and slow, dizzy and sick to my stomach, but I managed to find my book. Then I filled my pouch with a small knife, a candle and matches, some seaweed and a needle, and tamarind paste.

"I stumbled back. He was still unconscious and so pale he might have been bleached coral. The blood on his shoulder had congealed into a sticky black mass. I sank down on my knees and dumped my pouch out onto the rocks next to him. My fingers trembled as I lit the candle. Then I held the knife blade in the flame until it glowed. I let it cool a little before I started probing the wound with its tip. Your father didn't stir or make a sound. Scared me more than anything else. I decided to slice the wound a little deeper and probe some more. This time the object moved! Got the blade's point under it and managed to pry it up. It was the broken tip of a harpoon.

"Know what a harpoon looks like?" She didn't give the stunned mermaid a chance to respond. "I didn't spend too much time looking at it. I dropped it and heated the end of my needle. Then I threaded some seaweed into it and sewed the wound closed. It bled again, making my fingers sticky and the work hard, but I pressed the heel of my hand against your father's shoulder until he stopped bleeding. I washed the wound, spread some of the tamarind paste over the stitches, and wrapped some clean rags over it.

"After that, I collapsed. We must've laid there for most of a day and no human found us, thank the Creator. When I woke, I saw your father was also awake. He was in great pain, but he didn't have a fever. That's when he told me what happened to your mother."

Here Ana reached out and took Tamarind's hand. Its clammy skin was firm and smooth against her veined and wrinkled one. She ignored the spark of sympathy it engendered and her voice grew gruffer. Time for the climax of her story.

"Your mother was swimming alone near the cay the humans call Cayo Lobo, away from Culebra and towards the Hidden Caves. She saw a boat there, and not having any shred of sense, swam up to it. Your father had asked your eldest sister to keep watch over her, so as soon as your sister saw what your mother was doing, she called for him. He wasn't close by because he thought the outer cays safe enough. Didn't know anything about drug runners."

"Drug runners?"

"Men who sneak around with pills and powders and herbs outlawed by some humans because they're so powerful and dangerous, for the mind and the body. Drug runners are nothing more than bottom feeders—violent and mad. They saw your mother and dragged her out of the water, probably thinking she was spying on them. When they saw her tail, they dropped her back into the water and started throwing things off the boat at her but she didn't leave. Your father got there just as one of the drug runners picked up a harpoon. He grabbed your mother and dove underwater, swimming as fast as he could with her to Luís Peña. When he came up, he realized two things: the harpoon had caught him as he dove and your mother was dead. She had a large black hole in her cheek, but he didn't know how or when it got there."

Tamarind pulled her hand from Ana's grasp, leaned over her legs and dropped her face into the tent of her hands. She didn't move or say anything as Ana finished her story.

"Your father hid on Playa Tamarindo until he got strong enough to swim back to a hidden cove on the far side of Luís Peña where your mother's body lay. He took her to an underwater cave far east of Culebra and entombed her on a ledge under piles of sea rocks and bits of coral. I hadn't wanted him to swim so far so soon, but I didn't bother saying anything to him. He came to see me only once afterwards so I could check the scar on his shoulder. I gave him an infusion to help him heal faster and get his strength back.

"I haven't seen or spoken to him since."

అఅఅ

At the bottom of the service road to Tamarindo Estates, John slowed the Samurai and stopped, his foot resting on the brake while he looked up the hill through the dusty windshield. Finding Tamarind in the tangle of thorn acacia, stunted tamarind trees, and cactuses posed no real difficulty, but still he hesitated. For the first time since he'd found an apartment in San Juan and traveled back to Culebra for long weekends, Tamarind had not waited for him at the ferry dock when he arrived. He drove on to Posada La Diosa where Valerie sat in her kitchen sipping lemonade and crafting wire jewelry for sale at The Mermaid's Purse. Since he'd left for San Juan, Tamarind sometimes hung out talking with Valerie and learned how to shape and twist wire into jewelry from her. She'd created some unique pieces after only a few lessons that Valerie sold for her in San Juan and as far away as New York, and Valerie helped her spend the money on clothes and hair accessories. Valerie had only the neighborhood stray cat with her today, however.

"Seen Tamarind?"

"Nope. Come to think of it, I haven't seen her all week."

"Huh." John set his backpack and travel bag down on the floor next to the table. "It's not like her to miss the ferry."

"Maybe she's tired of waiting for you, John." Valerie clipped the end off of a piece of wire and looked up at him.

John refused to meet her eyes. Instead, he walked to the cabinet where Valerie kept drinking glasses and took one out. He poured some lemonade and sat down.

"That's pretty cool." He pointed to the piece she worked on. "What is it? A pregnant woman?"

Valerie slipped a long strand of her graying-blond hair behind a delicate ear and picked up her lemonade, which she sipped. "Well, yes, she is. But not just any pregnant woman, John. She's the Goddess, the Divine Mother, that many cultures worshipped before

158

the Judeo-Christian patriarchy tried to eradicate Her. She's always shown with a large belly and breasts because She symbolizes fertility, of the mind and spirit as well as the body."

"Does something like that sell well?"

"Oh, I can't make Her fast enough for the two shops I supply in New York. Chuck's always telling me I have to return and open my own shop, but I told him he doesn't get it. I need to be here on Culebra to channel the Goddess. In New York, I only channel lots of cappuccinos while running from meeting to stressful meeting."

"You don't ever look like you get stressed."

"Oh, don't let my serene appearance fool you. I spent a dozen years as an aggressive media buyer in New York. I *lived* on stress until I realized it was making me sick."

"Is Chuck still moving here in September?"

Valerie sighed and shrugged. "Apparently, he hasn't quite topped off his retirement funds as he'd like. I keep telling him that he won't want much once he gets here, but he's not ready to give up the game yet. Whatever. I'm not going anywhere."

She set her lemonade down and returned to the Goddess figure. "I did see Ana, the old woman who sells herbal remedies in town, a couple of days ago. I showed her one of the pieces of jewelry that Tamarind made and she knew somehow that I hadn't made it. She got very excited and practically gave me some of her most expensive remedies to buy it. When I asked her if she knew Tamarind, she told me that Tamarind is her apprentice and has been staying with her all summer."

"Funny, Tamarind never mentioned her. I thought all this time she lived at home with her father and sisters. Does this Ana live out near Tamarindo Estates?"

"Yeah, not far west of 251. You can't really miss it. It's a one-room cinderblock house with a dirt front porch and a chicken coop out back. The wild horses and laughing gulls really love her and she brews this wicked ale from a mash made from tamarind pods."

"Wait a second. Do you mean that scary-looking old woman who sits on the plaza selling herbal remedies?" John frowned. He'd gotten the distinct impression that Tamarind avoided Ana. He knew that *he* did. "Tamarind's staying with her and learning her arts?"

Valerie nodded. "That's what Ana said anyway. Why don't you go out there and talk to Tamarind yourself? You look about as forlorn as a puppy sitting in the rain while his owner doesn't see him from the kitchen window."

"Whatever that means." John stood up and rubbed the stray cat's head where it lay on the table among Valerie's jewelry-making supplies. "Don't worry about me for dinner. I'll grab something to eat at Isla Encantada."

Ten minutes later, he waited at the bottom of the hill leading to Ana's house in the growing heat of afternoon. Tamarind didn't magically appear to save him the trip so he slipped the gearshift into drive and eased the gas pedal down. At the top of the hill, he parked the Samurai and walked the rest of the way on foot toward the cinderblock house to which he'd followed Tamarind nightly in June. A few brown hens meandered through the dirt patch beaten in front of the low-gray building, but no one sat in the rusty aluminum chairs outside the front door.

He knocked on the door, but when no one answered, he walked around to the back where the chicken coop and what looked like an apartment building for birds stood. To his surprise, several laughing gulls poked their heads out of the holes in the stacked wooded compartments and eyed him curiously. A rooster strutted around the side of the low cinderblock wall and crowed when he saw John. John jumped a bit and relaxed. The spicy warmth of clove insinuated itself in his nostrils as he stood there facing the vigilant rooster.

"She's not here," rasped a woman behind him.

John turned to face Ana. He hadn't been this close to her since March. Her white hair wove a fine mesh around her miniature features. The drooping lid of one eye lent her a sinister air. She stood with her arms crossed loosely over her chest, a hand-rolled cigarette smoking in one upraised hand.

"How do you know who I'm looking for?"

"Don't sound so belligerent, *gringo*. Would you believe I can tell the future?" She laughed at his response. "Okay. Scratch that. I saw you and Tamarind in town more than once. And she told me you might come looking for her."

"She did? Where is she?"

Ana narrowed her eye and took a drag on the clove cigarette. "I'm not sure she wants to see you." The words issued forth in an effluence of hot smoke.

"Why not? Why can't she tell me herself?"

Ana dropped her cigarette arm and walked a few feet away from him. Several laughing gulls fluttered out of their nests and hovered around her head. Reaching into her apron, she tossed bits of something into the air around her. The birds lunged and snapped for them. One bird, bigger and faster than the others, managed to shoulder aside another gull and snatch its catch away from it. This bird landed on Ana's shoulder, looked directly at John and laughed, and then began to preen itself.

"This is a small island, *mi amigo*. Some have seen you here and there. Sometimes you are with Tamarind, sometimes you are with another woman. Perhaps you understand how people in such a small place as this love to gossip."

"Where is she?" He gritted his teeth as he spoke.

"Carlos Rosario, not far from the nesting grounds on the peninsula, gathering seaweed and bird dung." Just as John started to turn and go she called out to him. "From what Tamarind told me about your fight with your girlfriend, it sounds like you have quite a way with women, *gringo*." Her laugh rang in his ears.

He said nothing but returned to his Samurai and drove to the parking lot next to Playa Flamenco. He hadn't visited this beach since his first weeks in Culebra, but it took him only moments to find the head of the trail leading to the beach locals called Impact Beach. He walked the narrow dirt trail among dusty, drooping plants while overhead terns and brown boobies patrolled the skies where Navy bombers once descended upon decoy targets. The effulgent sun scorched his vision and parched him until his forehead ached and his crown burned. At last the trail ended at Carlos Rosario.

The beach appeared deserted. Then John recognized Tamarind's shape on the far side where she kneeled among the tall grasses. He halted on the beach and watched her as she searched, tendrils of her unmistakable hair floating on invisible air currents around her head. When she looked up and saw him, he smiled and waved. She didn't wave back.

John trotted over to where she waited, her face never leaving his and her arms still.

"Hey." He stood close enough to see the blue of her eyes.

"Hello."

"You weren't at the dock today."

"No." She turned back to combing through the grasses near her.

"I brought you a book. *Grimm's Fairy Tales*. I enjoyed it when I learned to read to myself." He held the book out, but she didn't turn back to him. After a moment, he slid it back into his backpack.

"Is something wrong, Tamarind?" His voice caught on her name. "That old woman you're living with—Ana—she said you didn't want to see me. Can I ask why?"

Tamarind sighed and sat up. She pulled out a small bottle of something and poured it into her left palm before rubbing her hands together. After a moment she lifted a bottle of what looked like water from the ground near her left knee and poured it over her hands. When she finished, she wiped them dry on her shorts and then she pushed her hair out of her eyes, only to have the wind send it fluttering into them again.

"It's been a long week, John. I have a lot of things to do and you shouldn't expect to see me at the dock any more when you come to Culebra." She stood up and pulled the burlap tote next to her feet up onto her shoulder.

John fell into step beside her as she walked across the beach toward the path. "No problem, I understand. So, dinner at Isla Encantada and then I'll read some of these fairy tales to you?"

Tamarind stopped and looked at him. "Actually, I have a date to go dancing with Jesus tonight." She started walking again. "Maybe we'll see you there later with Raimunda."

John said nothing until she reached the head of the trail. "Yeah, sure."

Tamarind waved over her shoulder without slowing down. "You can keep the book. I've got plenty to read right now. Thanks anyway." Her last words drifted back to him as she disappeared around a turn in the path.

Overhead, a seagull laughed as it bobbed and glided away toward the south.

Fourteen
ᏆᏚ

TAMARIND WAITED UNTIL ANA LEFT for Dewey with her bag full
of remedies, love potions, charms, and the secret cache of poisons
that she didn't know Tamarind had discovered. Although Ana had
already spent the morning in town waiting for weekend vacationers
from the ferry, she'd returned because a wealthy patron from San
Juan had arrived unexpectedly with a special request. Tamarind
had grown used to Ana's frequent absences to treat wealthy locals
and so she bided her time until Ana had gone from sight. When the
old woman disappeared over the hill on the path toward the road,
Tamarind shut the door and headed toward the shore.

Not far from the water she stopped on the path and crouched
down. Moving several rocks and chanting under her breath,
Tamarind released the cloaking spell that she'd used to hide her
clothes and hair ornaments. She hummed for the first time all
week, clicking through several octaves in a complex melody familiar
to every *mer*. She checked over her growing collection of items and
then stood up, removed her shorts and dirty t-shirt, and walked
into the water until it was over her head. She lay back on the
buoyant saltwater and stared above her where terns and brown-
footed boobies played games in the cerulean sky. Around her, the
water mirrored their antics. If she closed her vestigial earflaps

against the water and wove a glamour between herself and the edges of her vision, she could imagine that she drifted on air currents with the sea birds. When one landed on the surface of the water not far from her, she shifted her head and studied it.

After a long time, Tamarind released the glamour. The horizon and the uneven outline of Culebra's plant life disturbed her soak so she rolled onto her stomach and kicked toward the shore. Walking from the water on her own legs almost made up for the struggle to move against the inherent power of the lagoon.

She noticed that the lapping waves had deposited several shells and strands of seaweed near where she emerged. She stopped to look at them. Their resting places suggested that they'd been placed there by design, but she had no idea what they meant. In a moment a wave fingered the closest shell, lifting it a bit and sliding it into the design further. All at once, Tamarind understood that Mother Sea sought to tell her something. Sinking down, she cracked her knees on the slippery stones, plunged her hands into the water, and closed her eyes.

Mother, I don't understand. What are you trying to tell me?

Her thoughts flowed from her fingertips into the current and for a moment she felt tension fill her and something powerful surged around her mind, but the meaning was lost. A residue of fear and warning remained as the power drained out of her.

Tamarind slapped the stones with both palms and stood up, water dripping from her hair and shoulders. She closed her eyes again and let out an audible breath. After a moment she hummed softly and gestured. Her fingers pulled continuous warm air strands over her body and hair. When her hair and skin had dried she uttered a single word and sliced the air in front of her with her right hand. The air calmed.

She returned to the hoard of clothes and searched around until she found the patterned halter dress that Valerie had helped her find on her first shopping expedition to San Juan two weeks ago. Even as she picked it up from the bundle and slipped it over her head, the memory of that trip played itself before her mind's eye.

Gray asphalt ribbons hosted multitudes of cars like speeding schools of amberjack while concrete and glass buildings hemmed them all around. Her chest tightened at the images and she remembered John's words about having difficulty breathing sometimes.

After she tied the halter around her neck, she stepped into a pair of panties. She'd lingered in the lingerie store where the feel of silk on her fingertips engrossed her so long that Valerie laughed at her and strode around the store to pluck pairs from tables without a second glance. If she hadn't spent so long gazing at the tern earlier, she might have scattered the panties around her on the warm stones and tried them on one by one. Should she live to be half the age of a *mer* elder, she would never grow accustomed to the feel of silk rubbing against her crotch as she walked, the way the elastic encircled her upper thighs and the material hugged her buttocks. As she repacked her clothes, she shoved the red wisp of material that Valerie called a thong deep into the bottom of the bag. The power suggested in that triangle made her heart beat faster.

She extracted the smaller bag that Valerie had given her along with a variety of barrettes, hair bands, and hair clips. None of the manmade items worked half as well as her shell ornaments, but the sticky, thick liquids and foams that Valerie showed her how to use tamed her hair so well that the fragile things sufficed. Even so, the colors and patterns of the plastic pieces rivaled the beauty of her former underwater home and the crystals had no equal in her experience, except for the reflection of stars on the night sea.

At last she found the large flat barrette crusted with sparkling cabochons. She laid it alongside her thigh while she squirted a mound of fragrant foam into her palm. She distributed the foam between her hands and then worked it through her hair. She plucked through her curls with the long tines of a comb and then gathered a handful from either side and clasped the barrette around it. The mirror in her small bag reflected the tiny stones in her hair when she glanced at the stranger that she'd become within in its hard edges.

Done transforming herself, Tamarind stowed all of her human possessions back beneath the stones and reset the protective glamour. No prying eyes could discern where she'd hidden them. She glanced at the late afternoon sky and stuck her tongue out to taste the relative humidity of the air because her skin always felt dry since she'd put off her tail. Slowly she headed back to Ana's where she waited to walk the twenty minutes to Isla Encantada. Once the sun kissed the horizon, she set off barefoot toward the access road.

Jesus sat outside the restaurant on the curb talking to some of his friends. When he happened to look up and see her fifty feet away, a grin split his dark face and he leaped up. His deep brown eyes gleamed.

"Look at you, *mi chica linda*! We're going to make everyone else look like clumsy beasts tonight." He took her hands in his and held her arms up so that he could look at her. "Ah, I have dreamed of this all summer."

Still holding her left hand, he turned to face his friends. "I told you. I am the luckiest man on Culebra. Come, *cariño*, let's go get something to drink."

They went in and found a table not far from the bar. As she sat down, Tamarind felt a prickling along her flanks and the sides of her neck where *mer* sensory pores still pocked her skin. She looked around and saw John sitting in a far corner, staring at her. Their gazes met, and for the few seconds that they held, Tamarind felt shock rise up her spine and electricity pulse in her brain. Then, as in her brief contact with Mother Sea, the charge flowed away. This time, her arms and legs trembled.

She turned back to Jesus and slapped the table with an open palm. "Where's my drink?"

He startled, then grinned. "Only tell me what you'd like to drink and it's yours, *mi corazón*."

"Beer. I'd like to have a beer."

ৡৡৡ

John ordered another Tom Collins even before finishing his first. In the dark of Isla Encantada he could see only indistinct shapes where Tamarind and Jesus sat, but he'd recognize her profile under a burqa. Tamarind sat sideways to him so that he glimpsed little flashes from the barrette she wore as it caught what ambient light existed. When she leaned over to speak to Jesus, he saw in the candlelight that her tame curls cascaded across her shoulders and framed her face. As she laughed, candlelight caressed a reflective pendant at her collarbone. She laughed a lot—especially after drinking from the dark bottle Jesus brought her from the bar. After their earlier eye contact, she never came over to say hi or even turned in his direction. The snub hurt more than he could have imagined.

John scowled and sipped from his Tom Collins. He glanced at the door, but Raimunda didn't saunter through it wearing a clinging white shirt and ruffled skirt. Several Culebrenses came in and settled down at neighboring tables while the band fiddled with keyboard and drums before their set. The smell of fried food reached his nose as a waitress emerged from the kitchen with a plate of yellowtail snapper and plantains. He'd skipped dinner and should have been hungry, but his stomach only tumbled.

He switched to drinking *coquitos* on his third drink and the coconut and rum congealed in his knotted gut. Then the band began playing and the din tunneled into his brain unopposed. He leaned his face into his raised hands and massaged his temples with his thumbs. When he looked up, he saw Tamarind and Jesus dancing. She had eyes only for Jesus, who led her in the peculiar rolling gait of the salsa; his arm wrapped around her waist and his stomach pressed against hers. The small triangle of chest above her dress shone and the dim light glittered off the pendant and the stones in her barrette as they danced. Her delicate feet, as bare as always, lifted and settled on the tiled floor.

"*Hola, gringo,*" said Raimunda at his side. "She's a tasty bit, that one is, isn't she?" She leaned over and kissed him, long and hard. "But I'm a full meal, *mi amigo.*"

John said nothing as she sat down on his left side and held up her hand to signal the waitress. While she waited for her beer, Raimunda leaned closer to him, her hand on his inner thigh. She nuzzled his neck and nibbled his ear. John lifted his *coquito* and drained it.

"Let's dance," he said and stood up, his chair scraping loudly.

He pulled Raimunda to her feet. She grabbed her Medalla, tilted it at her mouth, and gulped half of it down as he strode to the dance floor ahead of her. When John pulled her into his arms, she laughed and clutched the half-full bottle between them. As they danced, John closed his eyes and focused on the music. Raimunda sinuated about him, her full breasts brushing now against his upper arm, now against his chest.

John abruptly lurched from the dance floor and out through the entrance. Bending over, he braced his hands against his thighs and breathed in.

"Too much to drink?" Raimunda leaned against the doorway, her arms crossed.

John breathed in and out several times before standing up. "No, I'm fine. Let's go back in."

They walked back into the stuffy restaurant, Raimunda's arm entwined in his and her hip rubbing his thigh. John's gaze traveled to the dance floor where Tamarind and Jesus still rocked and swayed to the loud Latin music.

"I'm going to the toilet."

"No problem, *mi amigo*. I'll just wait at the table and order another Medalla, on you." She smiled and dipped her eyelashes.

John went to the men's room and gripped the white porcelain rim of the pedestal sink. In the harsh fluorescence, he stared at his reflection in the mirror. He looked like a madman: strands of hair had escaped his ponytail holder, darkly misting the outlines of his pale face; his wide eyes suggested that he'd just witnessed his mother being raped and his father shot. Closing his eyes for a moment, he leaned his head back and expelled his breath. Then he turned on the cold water and splashed handfuls over his face. When his eyes had relaxed and his breathing had evened out, he turned off the water, dried his hands, and made his way to the bar. Raimunda sat looking toward the dance floor, a bottle cradled in her hands.

"You know that guy over there?" John gestured with his chin toward the dance floor.

Tomás, who'd been talking to the bartender, looked up and out at Jesus. "*Sí*, Señor Juan." He shrugged. "He's well known around Culebra, especially by the women."

"What's that supposed to mean?"

"He's, how you say it? A ladies' man? Most of the ladies like him."

"Most? What's that mean?"

"Some say he isn't always sensitive about whether a *mujer* wants to be with him or not."

"Are you talking about date rape?"

Tomás shrugged again. "Who am I to say? Me, I think women always find something to complain about. If it's not the way they look, it's how much money we spend on them."

"I believe in the old adage 'where there's smoke there's fire.'" John stared at the couple. "Some women just don't know they're going to get burnt."

He looked at Tomás until the older Culebrense looked away. Then Tomás nodded and turned back to the bartender. John left the bar and headed toward Tamarind and Jesus. When he reached them, Jesus saw him first and swung Tamarind out and away before embracing her. Jesus smiled at John over Tamarind's head.

"Look, *mi dulcinea*, it's John. Hey, *amigo*, what's up?" His grin didn't reach his eyes, as flat and malevolent as ever. "This time, I get the bird of paradise, no?"

"No." John turned toward Tamarind. "Tamarind, dance with me."

Jesus spoke for her. "She's with me. *Comprende*?"

Tamarind, her smooth curls already frizzing from heat and sweat, lifted her chin and looked at Jesus. "Don't worry, Jesus. It's just a dance. I'll be right back."

Jesus slipped his arm around her waist, tight. "Just one dance, *cariño*. I am—how you say *un amante celoso*? A jealous lover." He turned to John. "Take good care of her, *amigo*, or you'll answer to me."

Jesus nuzzled Tamarind's neck before kissing it, his eyes on John. She tolerated the kiss but looked embarrassed. Jesus sauntered back to their table and grabbed his beer. When he turned to watch John and Tamarind dancing, he crossed one arm over his stomach while the other kept the bottle within easy reach of his mouth. John didn't look at Raimunda.

He placed one hand around Tamarind's waist and took her hand with the other. He glanced over at Jesus and smiled as if he meant it. As they danced, he spoke through his teeth; he found it difficult to take his eyes off of the small Culebrense waiting for Tamarind at the edge of the dance floor. "Tamarind, you need to be careful with Jesus."

"Why?" Heat from her seeped through his t-shirt and the front of his pants. She smelled salty and like something else—like a mix of seaweed, sand, and sunshine. She smelled like freedom.

"Because he's got a reputation for liking women. A lot of women."

"So? You seem to like a lot of women yourself."

A different heat scalded his neck and seeped out his palms. "That may be true, but I never force myself on anyone."

"Force yourself on anyone?" Tamarind screwed up her brows. "I don't know what you're talking about, John. I really must get back to Jesus. I think Raimunda—that's her, isn't it?—is waiting for you."

The song still played but Tamarind halted where she was and disengaged herself from John's grip. Slipping out of his arms, she skipped over to where Jesus sat and held her hands out to him.

John didn't remain on the dance floor to see Tamarind and Jesus dancing again. Instead, he returned to his table and leaned over Raimunda. Her dark hair smelled faintly of cloves and musk. He'd tried, and it hurt like hell.

"What was that about a meal? I'm hungry."

She smiled and slid the neck of the bottle suggestively into her hollowed mouth before sipping. Then she licked the rim without taking her eyes from his face. "Let's go where we can discuss this in private."

John helped her to her feet and they walked out of Isla Encantada holding hands. He'd left the Samurai at Posada La Diosa so they walked south along 251 toward town. Here and there a few people sat on their patios in the dark, talking and listening to music. Sometimes the glow of cigarettes and the clink of glass joined the sounds of voices and Latin jazz energized the low-key gatherings, but the parties remained contained.

Valerie's light still glowed in her room, but darkness shrouded the rest of the guesthouse. A black shape darted in front of John's feet as he reached the front stoop and he nearly tripped over the stray cat that had adopted Valerie. It growled when he stepped on its tail and hissed as he stumbled away. Raimunda laughed, but the cat refused to come near her when she bent down and reached out a hand for it. John pulled out his key and turned to the side so that the moon illuminated the lock. While he fumbled to insert the key, Raimunda—still bent over—ran her hand along his calf.

They moved without speaking down the hall toward John's room. John left the light off and pulled Raimunda in after him, groaning before kissing her and shutting the door. They tore at shirts, John pushing aside the low neckline of Raimunda's peasant blouse and grasping her full breast. He pulled his face from hers, rolling her nipple between his thumb and forefinger and then descended upon the hardened flesh with a hot mouth.

Raimunda raked fingers through his hair and then tugged at her skirt. Together, they worked at the button at his waistband and struggled to lower his shorts to a safe enough distance for him to climb out of them. Then they stumbled nearer to his bed before launching themselves at it. Now John clawed, kneaded, pinched, and sucked at every inch of flesh beneath him while Raimunda's long hair cloaked him in clove and something spicy sweet. Grasping a handful, he wound it around his hand and pulled her face closer to his.

"Tamarind."

"I'll be whoever you want me to be, *amigo*. Just fuck me."

John's chest seized and his breath stopped. The airless room encapsulated him and he couldn't move, couldn't think—couldn't see in the suffocating black. Collapsing, he trapped Raimunda under him. She responded by squirming and kicking until she'd managed to roll him off of her and onto the bed.

"What the hell is wrong with you, *gringo*? You're as hard as obsidian one moment and limp as seaweed the next—and you nearly crush me!" She sat up and pushed him away from her.

John opened his mouth, but nothing came in or out. Pricks of light danced in front of his vision. His blood roared in his ears. He felt Raimunda get off the bed and sensed rather than heard her search on the floor for her blouse and skirt. He tried to remember the sound of Tamarind's humming, to feel her arms around him again as she promised to take care of him, but he couldn't snag the memory and he felt the darkness winning. As he lost consciousness, he heard the door to his room click shut.

৵৵৵

Ana scurried into the plaza near the ferry dock, her bag slung over her shoulder. She didn't have much time. She laid the bag on a concrete table and pulled out the wire-wrapped Goddess that she'd bartered from Valerie, the hair that she'd taken from Tamarind's sleeping mat, and the potion that she'd brewed using both items. Next came a copy of the destroyed blue batik dress, the one that John had bought for Tamarind weeks ago and that she'd worn the night they'd gone dancing. Muttering and turning, she waved her right hand in the air until the cloaking glamour reflected the night plaza seamlessly around her. Should anyone wander into the plaza, he'd see only empty tables next to the dock.

173

Stepping out of her skirt and blouse, Ana lifted the batik dress over her head and let it drop down over her shoulders. She squinted down at her discarded clothes and frowned. Muttering again, she wove both of her hands in the air above them. Now a small pile of paper cups and wrappers littered the pavement.

She lifted the bottle from the table and hefted it in her palm. So small, yet so crucial. She slid her thumbnail into and around the wax seal and then pushed the stopper out. A minute pop issued and she felt infinitesimal droplets as pockets of gas burst against the skin on the back of her hand. She waited until the bottle grew warm in her palm and then she tipped it up and let it slide down her throat in one breathless gulp. She coughed and wiped her lips with the back of her hand. Her book said that the potion needed time to spread throughout her body, trailing change with it, but she had been a midwife a long time and had developed her own techniques, ones that improved upon the original.

She grasped the wire Goddess and rubbed the beads that Tamarind had so carefully bound there. Tamarind had also bound some of her own essence as well and Ana sought it now. Closing her eyes and whispering a chant, she drew upon the charm to speed her transformation. After only a few breaths, she opened her eyes again. It was done.

Fifteen
♋

JOHN CAME TO WITH A SENSE OF URGENCY. The room around him vibrated with the aftereffects of sound and he waited, certain an alarm or clap of thunder would rend the air. He heard nothing but the harsh rasp of his own breathing in the stifling dark. Sitting up, heart pounding, he tried to think. He glanced at the clock and saw that Isla Encantada had closed an hour ago. He groaned and twisted on the bed until his feet touched the floor and the clothes he'd left there. Without searching for the light first, he found his t-shirt and shorts and put them on. His sandals still lay just inside the door where he'd kicked them earlier and he slid them on, fumbling with the straps.

The stray cat passed him in the hallway, this time rubbing against his calves and purring. John ignored her and walked quietly past Valerie's door. Once outside, he glanced toward her window and saw that it was dark. He hurried down the sidewalk. Everyone had long since gone to sleep in town; no streetlights lit his way. Only the sound of water lapping at the canal and the squeak of his sandals on pavement broke the utter silence.

He didn't know where he planned to go, but he walked north on 250. At this hour in Isla Verde in San Juan, people wandered streets laughing and chatting while cars cruised along the *avenida*. Casinos

175

and restaurants catered to restless tourists and young lovers, but here on Culebra, only wind and water spirits kept him company. After a few minutes, he heard voices and he picked up his pace. A young couple—he sat on the stoop and she stood between his bent knees with his hands on her hips—talked in the shadows of a doorway. John recognized the young man's tennis shoes and his date's ponytail. They were college students from the U.S. who'd bought a *Let's Go! Puerto Rico* and had arrived on Culebra a week ago. Hearing his footsteps, they stopped talking and glanced in his direction. John waved. They waved back and he kept on walking.

As he'd already known it would, Isla Encantada stood dark and empty when he came up to its entrance. He sat down on the curb outside the restaurant and propped his head in his hands. Darkness enveloped him like an old friend, its soothing arm laid across his shoulders. He smelled the dust from the sun-baked pavement around him, stale beer and cigarettes, old cooking oil, salt air and something else—a thin tang of green life holding out against the strength of the ocean on one side and the indifferent crush of humanity on the other.

Looking up, he studied the sky. It loomed impassively above, innumerable tiny twinkles mocking him. Culebra was a tiny island and he was just a speck on it. He sat still, staring at this yawning chasm, waiting for it to swallow him and blot out everything. Eventually the mosquitoes hummed so loudly in his ears that they compelled him to his feet in search of a better place to loiter. He shuffled onto 250 where not even the shadows had voices any more, his gaze polishing the rough pavement just a couple of feet in front of his sandals. He'd reached the fork in the road where 250 split into one-way streets, but just as he thought to stay on the left and continue toward Posada La Diosa, he spied something gleaming on the sidewalk at the fork. Bending down, he saw that it was one of Valerie's wire-wrapped Goddesses. He picked it up, tossing it lightly in his palm and then absentmindedly rubbing the largest stone in its globular belly with his thumb.

An urge struck him to take the other fork before heading west and then north again toward Playa Melones. He hadn't been to Playa Melones since April when Raimunda had led him there for the first time. The soft squeak of his sandals' rubber soles sounded eerily loud in the still street where obsidian storefronts glimmered darkly at his passage. He needed to reach Playa Melones and the waves that whispered along its slight expanse.

Ten minutes later, John left the low buildings of Dewey behind and his sandals crunched on the thin gravel lining the path to the beach. He'd walked so quickly from town after finding the Goddess that a flush warmed him. He scowled at his pace but didn't slow down until he'd reached the water's edge. He gripped the wire figure in his hand so hard that it bit into his flesh. He scarcely noticed this, however, until it began to burn as if it contained a heating element. Yelping, John dropped the Goddess.

"What the fuck!" He sucked on his palm.

That's when he heard a low sound, a moan of pain, from a mound of vegetation not far north from where he stood. Forgetting his own pain for the moment, he went to investigate. There was a break in the shrubbery and he crept up near it, not willing to barge in without seeing who and what lay before him. As he knelt down, he shot a glance around the deserted beach, suddenly aware of his isolation. He saw no one else.

Shivering, John held his burnt palm off of the stony ground and leaned closer to the opening in the thick vegetation. When he caught sight of the forms writhing on the ground in front of him, John stifled a laugh. He started to rise cautiously from his knees until the sound of his rising caught the attention of the woman lying sprawled beneath the frantic man. In the sharp-edged moonlight, there was no mistaking Tamarind. Their eyes met and she smiled, a wide smile that reflected the light.

For a moment, John's throat constricted so painfully that he thought that he might be suffering an anaphylactic reaction. Swallowing hard, he nodded slightly at her and stood up without any more effort to quiet his movements. He took a step or two backwards and then swiveled on his left heel. Even though he could no longer see her face, John felt the strength of Tamarind's gaze on his back as he lurched back across the sand and the path leading to town. As he passed by the spot where the wire Goddess lay after searing him, the stone in its belly glowed as if mocking him.

John squeezed his lips together and pushed his shoulders back. He walked faster and faster until he was running and panting and he didn't stop until he'd reached Posada La Diosa. Even then, even as he struggled with the finicky lock on the front door and tiptoed down the main hall towards his room, his body quivered with the need for running. As he lay back onto his empty bed, his chest heaved. He gave himself over to the feeling of running, running as if he flew, running as if his legs would never tire. He fell asleep running on an infinite route through the clouds.

❧❧❧

The next morning, the sun woke John early. His upper back ached, his forehead ached, and fine sandpaper lined his throat. Blinking and squinting against the glare that accosted him through the wide-planked shades, he groaned and eased himself onto his side. After several more moments pinned to the mattress by an implacable bar of sunlight, he groaned again and swung his legs over the side. Dead weights that they were, his legs dropped to the floor, but his upper body refused to comply with their pull and remained leaning against the mattress. His whole body felt like a punching bag the day after the heavyweight champion pummeled it, and for a long time the strain on his waist from the awkward twisting of his upper and lower halves failed to compare.

At last his bladder chimed in with its burning fullness and he had to ignore the stabbing pain through his left eye and the wave of nausea that rose up as he leveraged his upper body away from the bed with his hands. He managed to piss into the toilet before the nausea overwhelmed him and then he collapsed onto his knees, clutching at the cool porcelain bowl as he threw up hot fermented *coquitos* into it. The sour tang of bile and partially digested coconut

178

milk clashed with the acid of his urine, causing him to heave until the spasms echoed in his abdomen reflexively.

He gripped the edge of the bowl for a moment before pushing the handle down and standing up on trembling legs. His reflection grimaced at him as he gulped a mouthful of water and swished it around his nasty mouth. Although it helped, he couldn't rid himself of the taste until he'd brushed his teeth and tongue.

Still weak, he managed to return to his room and find a pair of shorts and t-shirt on the floor of the closet that didn't look too rumpled and smelled faintly of salt water. He pulled these on, buckled his sandals onto his feet and slid his sunglasses over his fragile eyes. Then he set out for the only *mercado* open at this hour, Mayte's. He needed Tylenol and whatever liquid that his queasy stomach would tolerate. Later, when he returned to Posada La Diosa, he would try drinking coffee, but he doubted that he'd eat much.

"Stefan would laugh at me, getting hung over on only three drinks."

Only the stray cat laying on the sun-warmed stoop heard him and she simply purred in response. Small yellow-and-black bananaquits squeaked nearby as they fluttered between several messy, globe-shaped nests and the bowls of sugar that Valerie left along the canal for them. John watched the bits of wild brightness dart for several moments, and then he sighed and headed into the morning sun toward Mayte's. When he got there a handful of Culebrenses shopped for necessities—eggs, bread, rice, beans— and a couple of them leaned against the counter, chatting with the dour owner, Luisa. They ignored John as he toured the aisles looking for Seven-Up and Tylenol. He'd just found the over-the-counter drugs when Sister Maria Margarita from La Virgin Del Mar entered the aisle from the other end.

"*Buenos días*, John." She stopped, holding a basket over her right forearm, and looked him up and down. "You don't look so good. Too much sun and sand or too much Medalla?"

"Neither." John grimaced. "Look, Sister, I won't be coming to Mass any more. I've decided it's time to return to Pittsburgh and get back to work on my research."

She nodded, pursing her lips. "There is a time for everything, as the wise man says. It is for you to judge when is your time to leave us, though I am sorry to see you go."

"Being here has done me a lot of good, Sister. I used to sit on one of the *playas* sometimes and just stare out at the endless blue without thinking anything at all, just listening to my own breathing. I can really breathe here."

"You can always breathe, John. You just need to remember how. God will remind you, you must trust in that."

She placed her free hand briefly on his forearm and squeezed. She smiled a little and walked on down the aisle. John watched her for a moment and then he returned to his immediate search for pain medication.

❧❧❧

Tamarind waited outside Ana's house on the plot of bare earth that served as a porch, her feet curled under her on the aluminum chair. She watched the sooty terns take to the sky as the sun diluted it to pale saffron tinged with a deeper salmon along the horizon. In a stunted tamarind tree not far from where she sat, a laughing gull perched on a lower branch, its head half-tucked under a wing and a single bright eye watching her. She wondered if it was Ana's favorite and whether Ana had set it to spy on her.

Ana still slept inside. She hadn't come home until nearly dawn. Tamarind had returned last night from Isla Encantada to find the cinderblock house dark and empty. At first, she'd been relieved that Ana wasn't there to catch her in her clothes and makeup, but she'd managed to hide them away and scrub her face with saltwater and still Ana hadn't returned. She sat for a while in the moonlit doorway studying the constellations that John had taught her. *Mer* folk also had names for the stars, but they'd grouped them differently and identified these groups with way stations undersea. There was the Great Coral Passage, the Deep Blue Hole, and the Cave of the

180

Ancestors. Viewing them last night had brought saltwater to her eyes.

Humming, she studied her bare feet. Over the past few weeks, calluses had grown on the balls of her toes and her heels. Even though she continued to find the ground rough and the pavement painfully hot, she still couldn't tolerate wearing shoes. John had often teased her about looking like an urchin and when she'd finally asked him how bare feet made her look like the prickly sea creature, he'd only laughed.

"No, not that kind of urchin, silly. I mean a child who lives on the street without anyone to care for her."

So that's how John saw her: an unloved orphan.

After another couple of hours, Tamarind decided to go inside to get something to eat. She brought out some plantain chips and a jar of peanut butter with a spoon. John had also laughed at her craving for salty snacks and asked her if she smoked pot. When she got upset after learning that pot was a name for an illegal plant that some people smoked, he quit teasing her.

She'd finished the bag of plantain chips when she heard a throat being cleared behind her and smelled a familiar scent of clove.

"You were out late last night." Tamarind didn't look around at Ana.

"Uh-huh." Ana sat down next to her. "It happens. How'd your date with Jesus go?"

Tamarind shrugged. "Fine. It was fine."

"That doesn't sound so positive."

"I don't know if I can do this, Ana. The best part of the evening was when John watched us dance together. After he left, I spent all my time keeping Jesus' hands away from me. He's like an octopus. It was exhausting."

Ana bit her thumb, her clove cigarette balanced between her first two fingers. Smoke caressed her forehead. "You only have to put up with him once, young one. Then you're free of all men."

Tamarind opened the jar of peanut butter but eschewed the spoon that she'd brought. Sticking her forefinger into the jar, she scooped out a large dollop and licked neatly at it.

"Raimunda reminded me of someone."

Ana dragged on her cigarette. "Oh, yeah?" Smoke streamed along with the words.

"Yeah, but I don't know who." Tamarind twisted the lid back on the jar and looked at Ana for a moment. "John looked like thunder when they left together. I don't think he's with her anymore."

"And you think maybe he'll come to his senses and be with you now?" Ana laughed. It was a choppy, rough sound. "I wouldn't bet my legs on it, young one. The sooner you forget him, the better off you'll be. Mark my words."

Tamarind shrugged again and stood up. "I'm going for a swim. My throat's as dry as a piece of driftwood this morning."

Ana watched Tamarind trudge up the path toward the beach. She wore only a white t-shirt and shorts. After being briefly tamed the night before, the long kinks of her copper hair reveled at the sun's familiar touch. Her legs, where they showed below the fabric of her shorts, had grown as gracefully muscular as a dancer's. She watched until Tamarind had disappeared from sight and then she smiled.

Tamarind continued on down toward the playa, but she had no intention of swimming beyond a quick sustaining dunk. After wetting herself completely, she shook out her hair and then dried most of the saltwater from her skin and hair. Already, she felt less parched and stiff. She pulled John's t-shirt back over her head and stepped into the shorts. She glanced toward the secret path to see if Ana had followed her, but the old woman had not. After a moment, she knelt down and arranged several rocks on the shore at the outlet of the path, humming a bit while scooping handfuls of seawater over them. If Ana should happen to walk this way, she would forget why she'd come to the playa and have a strong urge to return to her house. It was the best Tamarind could do on Ana's own turf.

She got up then and hurried toward Tamarindo Estates and the road toward 251. By the time she reached Posada La Diosa, she felt dry and worn out even though it was only mid-morning. Her feet and calves ached from her haste.

Valerie sat outside on her patio next to the canal, drinking coffee and twisting wire jewelry. Behind her, a yellow and black bananaquit fluttered around the feeder that Valerie kept filled with sugar water. On the pavers at her feet, a black cat lay on its side licking its front paws in the sunshine. Tamarind watched the tiny bird for a moment and the ache in her legs disappeared. Then, drawing on the water in the canal to restore her further, she hummed a purr to the cat, which stopped licking and looked at her. It blinked once and purred back.

"That's a pretty amazing trick you have. You're a pretty amazing girl, aren't you?" When she looked at Tamarind that way, Tamarind thought Valerie knew her secret. "Want to help make some pieces today?"

"Yeah, sure."

Tamarind sat down and began gathering necessary bits and tools. Valerie had plenty of wire, but her store of polished stones had grown low and nothing appealed to Tamarind. She picked up some wire and began twisting a figure anyway. She could add a stone later.

"Do you know someone named Raimunda?"

Valerie snipped a bit of wire before answering. "No, can't say that I do. Why, should I?"

Tamarind bit her lower lip and twisted a tight spiral. "Well, I thought you might if John's been bringing her around here."

"Ah, that's what this is about." Valerie put her piece down and took a sip from her coffee. "Last night, he brought someone home but I heard her screaming at him not long after they got here. I don't think she stayed long."

She watched Tamarind deftly twist two arms and a head for her Goddess.

"There aren't any good stones here." She fingered the pile in front of her. "Of course, some might tell you to go ahead and put in any old stone you find and what you've got will be good enough. I say you have to wait for the right stone for your Goddess to be polished and set carefully into Her form. The love and care you take will be nothing short of pure magic. But I think you know that, don't you, Tamarind?"

She held up the Goddess that she'd been working on. In its belly was an inferior stone, dull and pockmarked.

"See? This one doesn't have any power with the wrong stone. Now take this stone here." She picked up a dull blue one. "This stone looks rather unimpressive in its current state. But I can tell by its shape and color that it's actually rather rare. It's a blue moonstone. Blue moonstone symbolizes the water signs in the zodiac. It's supposed to make wearers more receptive so they recognize the truth and to bring them dreams. It's also said to calm emotions so two lovers can see their future together without fear or pain."

She paused and looked steadily at Tamarind.

"You know, I think you should have this one, Tamarind. If you're patient and wait for it to be polished, you may find that this moonstone is exactly the right stone for your Goddess."

Valerie slipped the milky-blue stone into Tamarind's palm and closed her fingers around it. "Just take care of it, Tamarind. Something this rare won't come across your path again. I know it."

Tamarind looked into Valerie's eyes. Swallowing hard against a dry throat, she nodded and squeezed the blue moonstone even tighter. She would keep the promise of this stone against her heart as long as necessary.

Sixteen
ೞ

JOHN FELT THE SOLID PRESENCE of the hills between the Pittsburgh airport and the Fort Pitt Tunnel as his friend Stefan's car climbed and plunged. Once through the tunnel, his gaze embraced downtown—"dahntahn" in the vernacular—and the point where the Allegheny and the Monongahela Rivers met to form the Ohio. As they passed over the Monongahela, he could see the dark bulk of Three Rivers Stadium across from the Point State Park. He'd missed so many of the Pirates' summer home games.

The drive from the airport to Stefan's place in Squirrel Hill took only half an hour; Stefan asked no questions and John volunteered nothing. They chatted about inconsequential things, the latest gossip in the CS department, the incoming first years, the big grant won for a robotics project. They headed to the Squirrel Cage where Stefan's favorite waitress, the one John used to tease him was his soul mate, brought them hand-formed hamburgers and black-and-tans. Pittsburgh residents and grad students filled the booths of the dark bar, their cigarettes and chatter comforting to John. He'd had no idea how fond that he'd grown of this former steel town or how much he'd missed its coffee houses and bagel shops. When they'd finished dinner, he urged Stefan to cross over Murray Avenue to the Eat'n Park for dessert.

Stefan's last roommate had graduated in May and he hadn't yet found a new one. John viewed the available bedroom, which was still furnished in low-budget melamine from the popular Swedish furniture store, and thanked Stefan for letting Zoë dump his clothes and books there. He'd get the rest of his stuff from storage later, after he'd had time to get back into the groove at school. Dropping his bags near the door, he went over to the window facing the street and opened it wide to the muggy August evening. He stood inhaling the mingled smells of exhaust and baked motor oil and listening to the sounds from Murray Avenue where people laughed and talked at outdoor tables or walked between restaurants and shops. Underneath it all the sound of cars washed like the waves on Culebra's beaches. He'd returned to the place he belonged, but he'd left his soul behind.

When he lay down on the bed's bare mattress, no dreams graced his sleep.

⋯⋯

As soon as John walked onto the Carnegie Mellon campus, he saw his advisor. Steve appeared surprised to see his errant graduate student—and exceptionally happy. His surprise at seeing John lasted about two minutes, long enough for John to cross the quad to the main entrance to Wean Hall.

"Hey, John! You have impeccable timing," he said when John got within five feet of him. "I've been working on a funding application for ARPA and it would really help our cause if you update your Web site with the digital stills and video from the mission."

As nearly all his colleagues did, Steve constantly sought sources of funding and the Defense Department's Advance Research Projects Agency proved to be one of the best.

"Yeah, no problem. What's the timeframe like?"

"Paul Stoddard is visiting next Monday so you don't have much time, John, but I think you could get something decent together by then. We don't have to show Paul much—he's got the capacity to make a leap or two, if we can just show him the outlines of what you've been working on. I had this idea just yesterday after I poked around your Pitt-Woods Hole site and I wanted to talk with you about it."

"Go ahead." John trailed Steve through the lobby of Wean. "Oh, hey, wait. I've got to get a cup of coffee here. It's been months since I've had a good cup of Joe."

Steve kept talking while John ordered. "You've got a lot of great images from the Puerto Rican Trench, John, but they don't give a big picture of the place. I mean, this trench is five miles below sea level and what you've got is a view from a few hundred feet above it."

"So what're you proposing? I'm not sure how my expertise in networked RAID and streaming video is very useful for presenting the image data."

Steve ordered a decaf latte from the cart. "Well, no, you don't have the expertise—yet. But I think you should go talk with Ken Abel in the computer-vision group. What I'm thinking is that your image data might be the source for a modeling program that puts it all together into bigger segments."

John sipped his coffee carefully; it burned his tongue nonetheless. "This sounds like a helluva lot of work. What happened to the work I was planning to do on my proposal?"

Steve gripped his own coffee and looked squarely at John. "Look, John, I'm not one to give anyone advice on how to live his life—what's done is done. But let's face it: you've been gone for nearly five months and now you've got to do a little extra to redeem yourself. Six months ago, I could've let you stick with your original plan. But now, I think you'd do well to labor on something a little more glamorous, if you know what I mean."

John adjusted his backpack higher onto his shoulder. He could feel his chest tightening, his esophagus narrowing. What Steve was suggesting—no, ordering—was that he write a less evolutionary research plan and jump into a riskier technical challenge, one that might not result in a feasible working solution in the end. He said nothing for a few moments, instead focusing on breathing. A faint humming echoed in his memory and his chest released. When he and Steve made it to the Networking and Storage Lab, he spoke.

"Okay, you're the boss. There's a faint chance that I could actually write a proposal before Black Friday."

"That's the ticket." Steve opened the lab door. "Nothing like a high-stakes deadline to get the old adrenaline pumping and the mental juices flowing. I'll ping you in a few days to see how it's going."

A week later, John, ensconced in his office in the bowels of Wean Hall, had begun tackling the new thesis proposal when his friend Puneet poked his head into the lab.

"So it's true—you *have* returned from paradise! They say all good things must come to an end and here you are slaving in the dungeon already."

John grinned. "You know Steve, Puneet. He can drive a slave with the best of 'em. Besides, there's a corollary to your saying: eventually, you have to pay the piper. And that's what I'm doing."

Puneet walked into the lab and stood next to John's chair where he could see John's monitor. "Yikes! Don't tell me you're working on a proposal."

"Okay, I won't tell you. But don't act surprised when Catherine posts the date for my proposal talk before the end of the semester."

"So soon? Man, you're setting a bad standard for the rest of us. How long have you been here, anyway?"

"This will be my fourth year."

"What's your rush? Don't you have another semester or two before you're really under pressure to propose?"

"Not after taking a five-month vacation—at least, that's how it's perceived around here."

"Oh." Puneet drew out the sound as if it were a three-syllable word. "Look, I know you're busy, but maybe you could come up out of your underground dwelling and go to lunch with me. It's a glorious day outside and you don't see too many of those in Pittsburgh."

"No, you don't. Where should we go?"

"Mad Mex."

They walked into Oakland and spent most of lunch talking at length about what it was like to run away from research for a while.

"I don't know what happened to me, Puneet. There was something about Culebra—I don't know what exactly. I just found myself sitting for long hours staring at the surreal blue ocean. I even wondered if I could open up a microbrewery there and turn the local soda, el Tamarindo, into a wicked Snake Island Ale. Still sounds like a good idea, actually."

Puneet grinned. "No doubt, John, no doubt. That idea is definitely enticing." He toyed with his fork, tilting it this way and that so that it threw light shards onto the ceiling. "Especially when code won't flow. Or you despair that you've chosen a topic that's just another math problem, one only pointy-eared geeks care about."

"You're not afraid of that, are you?" John let his voice register his incredulity. For all his surface levity, Puneet was one of the most focused, most disciplined, graduate students he knew. "Don't be. What you're working on will protect our country's most important secrets."

"Me? I'm just building a more elegant lock for network security. That's enough to make me want to take up auto mechanics sometimes." Puneet laid the fork next to his plate and looked at John. His dark eyes, usually dancing with humor, were direct and sober. "John, you don't have to run away to an island in shame and frustration. You're going to help advance what science understands about the oceans. That's monumental, if you ask me." He paused. "So, tell me, what are you planning to propose?"

Puneet listened as John described the raw data he'd collected in the Puerto Rico Trench and his original plans to write special algorithms for storing and retrieving it over a high-speed network. When he heard Steve's revised standard for what constituted proposal-level work his eyes widened, but he said nothing until John had outlined the problem and described how he'd solve it.

"That's good, John. You sound like you're jumping in with both feet. But I think you've got a bigger technical problem than how to

189

build a system that enables both quick-and-dirty analysis on-board ship and more detailed analysis after the survey is over. Those are really two sides of the same issue. No, the problem is more fundamental than that. I'm not a geologist and I don't know what the current state of knowledge is on the seabed, but I wouldn't bet that a generic algorithm is going to allow you to filter out all the noise from your video so that you can cleanly model the Trench landscape."

John frowned and pushed his plate away from him. "I guess that is a naive approach to take. But I should think the geologists have a pretty good idea what most of the noises are so all I have to do is pick Dave Gibbons' brain and write a few more algorithms. I'm not saying it'll be a piece of cake, but I'm not worried it's impossible."

Puneet nodded. "You're probably right. Still, I'd be prepared, if I were you, for a few surprises along the way. The oceans are the last great, uncharted territory on Earth. I don't think we know a tenth there is to know about them. That's why what you're doing is so valuable."

John said nothing, but he kept thinking about Puneet's remarks all the way back to campus. He was so engrossed that he didn't see Zoë until he'd almost bumped into her as she stood chatting with a group of friends outside Wean. As soon as they made eye contact, the chatter died down among her friends and one by one they all drifted away, though most stayed just out of earshot. Puneet murmured something polite and continued into Wean, leaving John alone with his ex-girlfriend.

"So." Zoë eyed him. "Back at last? Bring any mermaids back with you? Or have you grown up after dallying so long in the tropical sun?"

John winced and broke eye contact first.

"Ah." He could have shaved with her tone. "You came to your senses then? Playing Pygmalion isn't your strong suit?"

John expelled his breath, but little air returned to fill the void. "Listen, Zoë, I'm sorry you're still upset with me. But I think it's in both our interests if we agree to a truce right here and now—CMU just isn't a big enough campus for us to be at each other's throats."

Zoë squared her shoulders and stood straighter, her book bag falling down her right arm unnoticed. She appeared to consider his words. For the first time, he noticed that her dark hair had been cut level with her chin, swinging at an angle to the back of her head. Her makeup, always minimal—foundation and powder to cover less-than-perfect skin—was now a bit more obvious, though applied with a light touch. Her nails were still short and unpolished so he suspected that she hadn't abandoned her Tae Kwon Do or sports. The style of her clothes remained clearly in the black-is-artsy-and-cool realm—her Doc Marten boots added a good two inches to her five-nine height—but they were less secondhand-store chic and more mall-hip. Zoë had always drawn attention wherever she went, but now she demanded it.

"I don't see why not." She shrugged. "It's not as though I've gone to pieces over our breakup—I've moved on. You just gave me a shock, that's all."

John nodded and felt his chest ease. He was about to offer to buy her a coffee sometime when a rather tall man dressed in black jeans, red t-shirt, and black leather jacket came up behind Zoë from the direction of the fine arts building and put his hand familiarly on Zoë's forearm.

"Hey, Zoë." When she turned to face him, he gave her a kiss. "I've finished fixing the problems with the design of the gallery for the new student union and I thought I'd come and take you to Buns'n Udders for coffee."

Zoë caught John's eye, smirking. "Sure, Greg. I was just saying goodbye to my friend John here. John, this is Greg Moreland; he's a prof in the architecture department."

Greg barely glanced toward John. "Hey, nice to meet you."

"Nice to meet you, too."

John watched them head into Wean Hall, presumably to take the elevator to the first floor where they could take the shortcut through the parking lot behind Wean to Forbes Avenue. Zoë threaded her arm through Greg's as they walked, never glancing back at him.

ہے ہے ہے

A month later, John biked into CMU in an early-morning shower that left him drenched; in a few weeks, he'd be forced to drive again to campus to avoid the cold, but today it was still warm enough for biking while wet. A few leaves had fallen already and wet clumps of them clung to the edges of Schenley Drive and Frew Street and to the sidewalks. Students and staff alike, indistinguishable from each other in their yellow rain slickers and backpacks, hurried to shelter wherever he looked. When he came up to the fourth floor of Wean later in the afternoon for a cup of coffee, he saw that the day remained gray and overcast, bathing the lobby in its steely light.

After he'd grabbed his coffee, he planned to go up to Steve's office on the sixth floor and drop off his latest chapter, the first one not rehashing old material. He had a surprise for Steve: instead of proposing to pursue a limited number of algorithms for recognizing underwater objects in order to model the environment captured in his Trench video, he planned to design a genetic algorithm that learned as it filtered out common noises. He'd already toyed with some basic genetic algorithms for fun when he'd gotten tired of working on networking problems for Steve and had set up a Web page of genetic haikus that "evolved" as visitors voted on lines that they liked best. It hadn't been anything fancy, but he'd gotten some notice and inspired a few other grad students to write more advanced algorithms.

If Steve didn't keep him too long glancing over his proposal's new direction, John planned to take a break for a couple of hours and drop in on a talk by some guys from Pixar over in Porter Hall, one of whom was James Wilson, a former member of the graphics group. Half an hour later, he and Steve were headed over to Porter, laughing about the current crop of first years, who were both a tad too uptight and a little too business-oriented, when Zoë fell into step at his side. He managed to say hi in an even voice and to keep talking as the three of them walked together. Zoë said little, her long legs easily keeping stride with them, her arms swinging slightly and her hair pushed behind her ear. A spicy scent warmed the autumn air between them and enveloped her in a soft, invisible cocoon.

"So you think they're gonna show some outtakes from *Toy Story*?" Zoë asked as if her presence wasn't explosive.

"Absolutely." Steve eyed them but said nothing.

"You planning to see it when it comes out?" John thought that he knew Zoë's answer.

"Sure—are you asking me to go?" She swiveled her head and leveled her gaze on him.

John blinked. "Yeah, why not?"

The conversation halted as they reached the door to Porter and another group of CS grad students came up behind them. Members of the combined group conjectured about how much Disney had influenced the work of the Pixar animators and storytellers, but Zoë said nothing more. She remained at John's side, however, and when he sat down next to Steve, she took the seat at his left. He became preternaturally aware of her forearm brushing against his, the swell of her breasts beneath her red camisole, the smell of her perfume.

When did she start wearing perfume?

Without bidding, images of Zoë, naked and sweaty above him, haunted his thoughts, overriding texture algorithms and rendering pipelines.

He didn't remember much of the talk afterwards and later told Steve that he'd been too consumed with his proposal to focus on what was being said. Zoë chose to take her leave outside Porter, murmuring something about an appointment on the other side of campus and then she was gone with the crowd spilling from the auditorium. John watched her go, her hair swinging confidently about her face and her lovely legs encased in black tights under a black-and-white checked mini-skirt. He remembered them wrapped around his torso.

"That's one cool customer." Steve's voice broke his reverie.

"What?"

"Nothing, John, nothing at all." Steve grinned.

Slowly, John walked back to his office. When he got there, Stefan half sat on the long table next to his desk, one leg on the floor and the other bent in front of him, chatting with John's office mate, Patrick. Stefan gestured for some time with his long fingers as he talked, his long face animated and his dark eyes gleaming underneath the overhang of his choppy brown hair. John sat down and began to type.

"Oy, it looks like John hasn't got the time o'day for you."

Stefan's hands stilled in mid-air as he turned his face toward John.

"Hey, man! What's up with you? You look like you just ate some unmarked leftovers in the lounge refrigerator. Steve ridin' you hard these days?"

John stopped typing and leaned back in his chair. He stomach roiled.

"No more than I deserve." He pinched the bridge of his nose between his thumb and forefinger. "What's up? Going to tonight's IC at Gilgenoff's house?"

Stefan grinned. "Absolutely. You have to ask? Have you seen that new first year? Astrid? She's smokin'."

"No, I got better things to do these days."

"Once burned? Anyway, that's not why I'm here, actually. I just saw CNN in the student center and there's another tropical storm developing in the Caribbean. They're already talking about naming it Marilyn. With all the hurricanes coming through these days, I guess you got outta there in the nick of time, man."

John blinked rapidly and frowned. "No shit?"

"Would I lie to you?"

John rubbed his palms along the sides of his head and rocked around in his chair. "Dewey's got one of the safest harbors in the Caribbean," he said, more to himself than to Stefan and Patrick. "It's been a really busy season, but nothing's come close to Culebra, not even Luis. I'm sure they're in no danger."

"You look more than a little worried, my man. Don't tell me you forgot to love 'em and leave 'em."

John, who sat staring at a pile of tech reports next to Stefan on the table, missed this last remark. "What?"

"Nothing, nothing. Hey, wanna come with me tonight to Gilgenoff's?"

John heard Stefan, but he still had difficulty processing his words. "Uh, what? Oh, yeah, sure. I'll be here until you come and get me. Loads to do."

"Okay, I'll swing by at 6:30. But, hey, John, do me a favor and find another ride if I happen to hit it off with Astrid, okay?"

"Sure, sure." John waved Stefan away.

He sat immobile long after Stefan had gone whistling down the hall. He didn't move, in fact, until Patrick rolled his own chair over and very gently pushed John around to face his workstation and put his fingers on the keys.

≪≪≪

Tamarind stood outside Ana's house frowning at the sky, her hands on her hips and her hair teased by the wind. Yesterday, she'd heard the news on Ana's radio that a ferocious storm terrified the humans living on the islands south and west of Culebra and she knew, even without Ana's oyster-tight lips, that this storm would scour Culebra long before it blew itself out. Among the *mer*, it was said that these devastating winds and waves were the result of angry quarrels between Mother Sea and Father Sky and, until these two elements made peace, the *mer* sought refuge in the Hidden Caves. Without a doubt they swam there now, her father's mind urging her family and community to swim faster while his strength bolstered the flagging energies of the older *mer* and his will compelled the youngest to stay on task. When they arrived, he would discover her deceit.

She studied the sky, gauged the feel of the air on her skin, and tested the humidity with her tongue. Each hour the air pressure dropped further. Her experience and her instinct told her that they must find shelter before the storm hit in two days. While she stood

195

there, Ana squatted at the shore, arranging shells, pebbles, and seaweed into an elaborate and inexplicable design. Tamarind had no idea what more Ana hoped to learn from Mother Sea. She dug hard fingertips into her hipbones and waited.

A laughing gull glided silently over the spot where Ana stood. Tamarind frowned at it before turning on her heel. She flopped down into an aluminum chair outside Ana's front door and nudged a big toe around the basket that Ana had packed that morning. It reminded her of the first-aid kit that the park rangers brought along for their turtle watches. She didn't recognize all of the vials and baggies, but Ana had included tamarind-and-lemon syrup for an antiseptic, a diluted cone-snail extract for numbing a small area, and a plankton tincture spiked with turtle grass and algae as a sedative.

She reached into her pocket and pulled out the moonstone that Valerie had given her. Just this week they'd traveled to San Juan and a jeweler that Valerie knew there. The jeweler had studied the gem for some time before lifting her eyepiece and smiling at them.

"Valerie, this is a beautiful specimen. Where'd you get it?"

Valerie shrugged. "I have a friend in New York who keeps a lookout for me. Cabochon cut, do you think?"

The jeweler rolled the moonstone between her fingers before answering. "No, I wouldn't. This one needs to become a bead. Then I can polish it on my wheel for you, but it will take some time."

"No, that won't be necessary. We'll polish it by hand."

The jeweler nodded and pulled her eyepiece down again. "So what are you going to use it for? It's so fine. You could make it the centerpiece of a pendant. Make a lot of money on it, too."

"It's not for sale. It's a gift for a friend." At her words, Valerie smiled at Tamarind.

When they picked the moonstone up later, all its knobby edges had been sheared away and it shimmered expectantly. Tamarind held the bead in her palm and raised it to the light. For the first time, she understood that transforming power existed outside of the sea. Even after she'd slid the moonstone into her pocket, its light called to her fingers and she rubbed it without being aware that she did.

Today while she waited for Ana to return from communing with Mother Sea, she polished the moonstone as she'd done every free moment since their return from San Juan. Valerie had given her a strip of clean felt and a small jar of tin oxide paste.

"A wheel would polish it faster but not better. Besides, I rather believe in the lore around this gem. By polishing it yourself, you make it your own. Just remember to keep the tin oxide moist."

"How will I know when it's done?"

A smile lifted the corners of Valerie's mouth. "I imagine you'll know."

Smooth and cool, the bead disappeared beneath the white paste. Wrapping a corner of the felt around it, she rubbed it against her palm and hummed. She thought of John, who had left Culebra weeks before without saying good-bye and she wondered if he still worked in San Juan. For the season that she'd known him, Mother Sea and Father Sky had quarreled frequently. Valerie told her that the summer storms this year had destroyed homes and businesses on islands all around them. Now, as the time that she had human legs drew to a close, it seemed that Culebra too would suffer.

Tamarind stopped humming and rubbing the moonstone. She brought her eyes back from buffing the sky and looked at her hands. The tin oxide paste rimed the felt dangling between her fingers but a thin layer still lay upon the moonstone like dust, or heartbreak. She lifted the bead up on a flat palm to her mouth and exhaled warm breath over it. Then, with a delicate fingertip, she wiped away the last of the paste. The moonstone gleamed, aloof and invincible, against her grimy palm. It was time to set it into the womb of the Goddess.

Seventeen

CB

ANA FELT THE AIR LESSENING AROUND HER by incremental degrees even as she knelt on the wet stones quizzing Mother Sea. The storm she sensed had started far off to the east a week before and it gained power as it headed their way. The Culebrenses might not even sense the danger yet—it had been a long time since a hurricane had blown through their harbor. She would do what she could to warn and protect them, but strength no longer surged through her when she called on Mother Sea. Instead, she hoped for a generous upwelling to sustain her through the trial ahead of her.

"What's this?" She fingered the seaweed and coral laid out before her that Mother Sea had licked. She sat back on her haunches.

Mother Sea swept them into a pile beside her.

Ana moved several palm-sized stones aside and buried a horseshoe-crab shell into the resulting depression. Around this, she rimmed seaweed topped with oyster shells and the carcass of a sea star. Ocean lapped at the structure until it had filled in all crevices and nothing remained but a salty pool. Ana closed her good eye and stuck the fingers of her right hand into this water. An image of Tamarind's father filled her mind's eye.

"Ah, of course."

She made to draw her hand out of the water when another image replaced the first. This time, she saw Tamarind. The mermaid's lower half wavered as if distorted by water and a tail, dark gray like a manatee's, appeared under her transparent legs. Even though the rainy season had weeks to go, she understood at once from this image that Tamarind's transformation would be decided one way or another by the coming storm.

Pulling her hand out at last, Ana sat back and sighed. She plucked the dead sea star and several shells from the ground around her and slid them into the small sack propped against a rock behind her. She unfolded her legs and stood upright. Her knees ached from being bent so long.

A laughing gull surfed the air in front of her face, its wings tipping to control its descent until it landed on the rock next to her sack. On its foot, twine secured a roll of paper.

"Thank you, Ai my love." She snipped the twine with her scissors and absentmindedly pulled some tamarind pulp from her apron for the gull. It had been a long time since she'd received a written message.

The midwife who lived on Guadaloupe had sent this one. She had read the signs of the brewing storm and tracked it as it came closer to the islands. Now a hurricane that the humans called Marilyn, it had passed southwest of her island on a course for the U.S. Virgin Islands. Its current trajectory put it on a path to cross over the eastern coast of Puerto Rico and Culebra. She estimated its arrival in less than two days.

Ana looked up as the gull wobbled into the sky.

"Hey, Ai!" She threw it another, larger, bit of tamarind pulp. The bird snatched it from the air, flapped once around Ana's head laughing softly, and then headed back to its home. It would have to hurry to miss the rising winds.

ৼৼৼ

John woke in the early dawn on September 15th, its pale glow filtering through the blinds in the northern wall of his guestroom in Culebra. Something was wrong, but it took him several minutes to realize that the morning was eerily silent. Every weekend for nearly five months, he'd awakened daily to the cries of thousands of brown boobies, laughing gulls, and a variety of terns at their nesting grounds on Flamenco Peninsula and, in the nearby lagoons, competing calls from brown pelicans, Bahamas pintails, masked ducks, and ruddy ducks. Then he remembered that Hurricane Marilyn appeared to be headed straight for Culebra, and he knew why the birds were silent.

Late last night when he arrived back on the island after taking a charter flight with a pilot, who made no secret that he thought John had lost his marbles, he went straight to Posada La Diosa. Valerie sat listening to her radio in her kitchen. When she caught sight of him, she jumped up from her chair, threw her arms around his neck and squeezed him hard.

"You're a welcome sight! I've been pretty nonchalant this season, even though Luís gave everyone else a scare. But after what Hugo did to us, I'm not sure I can weather Marilyn by myself."

"I don't know what help I'll be." He looked down at Valerie's jewelry-making supplies and the wire-wrapped pieces laying there. "Is Tamarind still making jewelry with you?"

Valerie went to the refrigerator and pulled out a pitcher of lemonade, which she poured into two glasses.

"Here." She handed him one. "While we still have electricity, we should enjoy cold drinks. Yeah, I see Tamarind a few times a week. We've been going to San Juan every now and then. She's never been off this island so I've made it my duty to educate her a bit, take her to museums, shopping, whatever."

John nodded once and sipped his lemonade.

Valerie sat down at her table and studied him. "But that's not what you wanted to know is it? She's not seeing anyone. I think she's still stuck on you."

"Is she still staying with that old hag, Ana?"

"John! That's a horrible thing to say! Ana's rough around the edges, I'll give you that, but she does a lot of good for the folks around here."

"I'm not a big fan of herbal lore and witchcraft."

"Don't knock what you don't understand, John. To paraphrase Shakespeare, there are more things in heaven and earth than you dream of, my boy. And, yes, Tamarind still lives with Ana."

"Do you think she'll be safe there?"

"I think Ana's one tough cookie who's weathered a lot. I think she'll know when to run for cover. But if you're so worried about Tamarind, why don't you go find her?"

John hadn't left town to look for her this morning, even though the hurricane watch had been upgraded around midnight to a warning. Instead, he'd gone to the ferry dock with Valerie to help unload a shipment of plywood, nails, and water. Everyone's mouths remained in tight lines, even the people that John knew and greeted. Today, everyone would be consumed with boarding up windows and buying supplies. And then they'd wait.

Somewhere in the small guesthouse, he heard a door slam and then low voices. Luís had already spooked most of the guests away from Culebra, and only one other of Posada La Diosa's guests planned to stay through the coming storm. He got out of bed, dressed hastily and went into the bathroom to piss and brush his teeth. He'd borrowed Stefan's cell phone so that he could call his parents before the storm hit—thank God he'd be able to reach them if the power went out. After he'd grabbed a bagel or something like it, he'd head over to the Sunken Reef Dive Shop and help Chris secure his boat in the marina and finish boarding up the windows in the shop. After that, he'd make sure that Valerie had gotten enough bottled water and groceries to last for a few days.

He arrived at the dive shop to find Chris already hammering at the piece of three-quarter-inch plywood he held over his front door; the larger sheet for the front window lay propped against the side of the shop. Chris said only "hey" when he saw John and handed him the bucket of nails to hold. Together, they finished boarding up all the glass surfaces for the shop before heading to the marina to add a few more lines from the dive boat to its mooring at the dock. As they worked, John paused frequently to stare at the southern horizon, which seemed a little darker to his searching eyes; even though the weather was still mostly sunny, the wind had picked up considerably. By the time they'd finished at the marina, it was mid-morning.

John wished Chris good luck, then almost ran all the way back to Posada La Diosa where he came across Valerie trying to herd the stray cat from the neighborhood into her door with her foot, her hands filled with grocery bags. The stupid animal refused to enter the half-opened screen door, instead insisting on winding itself around Valerie's ankles until she nearly tripped. Bending down, John swooped the cat through the door and left it in the entranceway where it stood mewling in outrage. Valerie, clucking, urged John to grab the bag of cat food just outside the door and feed the cat to make up for its rough handling. John held the cat back with one hand while he reached through the half-open door for the food, and then squatted down to feed the stray, which purred vociferously. John laughed at how greedily, yet delicately, it ate its meal.

"Hey, Johnny. I have a couple cases of bottled water in the back of my Jeep. Can you bring them in for me?"

"Sure, no problem."

She came out with him to unload still more bags. John hiked the box of bottled water onto his shoulder and followed Valerie into Posada La Diosa. Valerie had already set the other remaining guest to boarding up the windows to his room, and his hammering blended with the hammering echoing up and down the street. She took the bottled water from John and directed him to the back porch where there were sheets of plywood propped against the guesthouse wall, an open paper bag of nails, and a couple of hammers. Grabbing a handful of nails, he tucked them into a front pocket of his shorts, slid the hammer's claws into his waistband, and then lifted a piece of plywood before heading toward the northwest end of the guesthouse and the window to his room. On this side of the guesthouse, which was less sheltered by the surrounding buildings, the gusts of wind were strong enough to whip his ponytail into his face and eyes. Still, he managed to nail the plywood securely in place without too much struggle and he prayed silently that all their efforts would be unnecessary.

When he returned to the back porch, Valerie was waiting for him.

"Why don't you come in and grab a sandwich? It might be a long couple of days and you don't need to start skipping meals now."

Valerie made hummus sandwiches and poured lemonade for both of them. They sat at the kitchen island eating and listening to Latin pop on the radio. Before they'd finished, reports from Miami aired. Although Marilyn currently moved toward St. Croix at more than 70 miles per hour, forecasters didn't expect her to strengthen beyond category one once she passed St. Croix. Still, she would reach Culebra before midnight.

"Dear God, why do they have to use the term 'strengthen'? It sounds so positive, like what you do for someone who has a bad back or weak immune system." Valerie licked the tip of her index finger and pressed it against the crumbs on the counter. She was about to stand up when John spoke again.

"Do you remember what you said about Shakespeare last night? You know, about more things in heaven and earth than I dream of?"

"Yes." She pushed her empty plate and glass away from her and bent her head in an attitude of listening with all her attention.

"Well, I've had some pretty vivid dreams in the last six months, nearly all of them on Culebra. For most of the time I was back in Pittsburgh, I didn't have any dreams—it was like I slept in a coma while I was there. And then two nights ago, I dreamt again about Tamarind."

"Again?"

"Yeah. One time, when I was in San Juan, I dreamt she'd come into my room and, you know, did that humming thing she does. But she looked and sounded so real I nearly reached out and touched her. A couple of nights ago, I dreamt that she was in my apartment with me and she looked frightened. She asked me to come back to Culebra before the storm hit."

Valerie squinted her eyes before standing up to get a cup of coffee. "Dreams are powerful messengers."

"This was more than my subconscious trying to tell me something, Val. Look, I know this sounds crazy, but I think Tamarind really came to me somehow, that she needs me."

"You must not believe too seriously or you'd have gone to find her before now."

John stuck his fingertips into his hair, pulling out long strands from his once-neat ponytail. "I believe it, but I also don't believe it. I believed it enough to get on a plane and come here, but now that I'm here all these doubts crowd in my head and I can't bring myself to face her."

Valerie sipped her coffee and Latin pop filled the silence around them. After a moment, she spoke as if measuring out each syllable.

"John, did you happen to hear the phrase *del mar* while you were here this summer?"

John scowled and stared at his empty plate. "Yeah, I did. From Tomás and Chris. They suggested the woman who saved me from drowning back when I first got here was *del mar*. I thought Tomás was mocking me. And Chris? I just thought Chris had a lunatic edge."

Valerie looked at him, her lips pursed. She tapped the counter with her fingertips and then sighed noisily. "Look, this will probably sound nuttier to you than your theory about Tamarind achieving astral projection, but I think Tamarind is a mermaid."

John choked on the swallow of lemonade he'd just attempted. "Wha-at?"

"Okay, I know you're a rational, science-type of guy, Johnny, but hear me out. Mermaids have been a part of the mythology of any number of peoples around the world—from India, China and Japan to Native America. Maybe there's some basis for these myths."

"Mermaids are about as real as leviathans."

Valerie played with her napkin. "Actually, some scientists have proposed that leviathans might be a prehistoric ancestor to modern snakes."

"But that just means that mermaids are really dolphins or–or manatees. Not some half-person, half-fish."

"Once I read this book. I think it was called *The Aquatic Ape*. Anyway, the author hypothesized that if marine life crawled out of the primordial oceans and adapted to land, what's to say that some of the primates that evolved didn't go back into the ocean?"

John said nothing. He remembered thinking about what motivated sea turtles to split their time between land and sea. On the face of it, the idea of a primate heading for the ocean and adapting to it wasn't so outrageous.

"I guess." He laid his hands on the counter and studied them. "But why hasn't anyone confirmed this theory? Why are mermaids still just myths? Beyond a cheesy Tom Hanks movie and kitsch in resort towns, no one has ever seen a mermaid."

"That's not true. Why do you think the Culebrenses talk about the *gente del mar*? In fact, many natives of the Caribbean whisper about them. They say they walk in human form among us, that they protect the sea turtles and reefs, and that they bring vital sea life to help heal humans. They even say some of the *mer* folk fall in love with humans and leave the sea to be with their chosen loves.

"Besides, if you were a merman, would you willingly swim up to a human and announce what you were? If it were me, I'd probably stay as far from shore as I could. But Tamarind isn't me, is she?"

"No, she's not. So, what do you propose I do? Ask her outright?"

"Sure? Why not? Can't be any worse than asking her if her spirit leaves her body behind and travels to visit you, can it?"

"No, I guess not."

"Astral projection couldn't work for her anyway. Mermaids don't have spirits."

Eighteen
ଔ

RAIMUNDA SAT AT THE BAR OF ISLA ENCANTADA watching
Tomás and the bartender, Enrique, nailing plywood over the bar's
windows. She sipped her Medalla and nibbled on the stale *surullitos*
resting on a small platter near her right hand. Every few moments
her eyes slid to the door, which remained closed despite her
vigilance. After a while, she pulled a packet of cigarette papers from
the bag that hung at her waist and a handful of her special tobacco
mix. Sprinkling a pinch onto a paper, she rolled a tapered tube,
licked the edge of the paper, and lit it. As she sucked the sweet,
spicy smoke into her mouth, she heard the door creak behind her.

She kept her face forward, the hand holding the cigarette
propped up on an elbow next to her on the bar. Her lips curved at
the corners. She set the cigarette into the ashtray next to her and
picked up the Medalla.

"*Mi sirenita.*" Jesus kissed the back of her neck. "Somehow I
knew I'd find you here, when everyone else is working so hard to
save themselves."

She shrugged. "Why work when I don't have to?"

He sat on the barstool next to her. "Ah, yes, *mi alma dulce.* You
live in a cave, don't you?"

"Always trying to find out where I live, *mi guapetón*? Let's just say that my home *es inexpugnable. Comprende*?"

"Well, not every woman is as *agradable* as you, *mi reina*. Sometimes I need some loving arms to welcome me."

"*Necesitas no más que llamarme buscarme.*" She sipped her beer. "Was it not a few weeks ago I saw you here, *mi amigo*, with that *chica deliciosa? Cómo se llama?* Tamarind?"

Enrique interrupted them to ask Jesus what he wanted to drink. After the bartender left to get another Medalla, Jesus picked up a *surullito* and broke it between his thumb and forefinger. Cornmeal crumbs powdered the counter in front of him.

"*Sí*, we were together that night. She was very coy and left here alone, only to show up later and drag me away, begging me to fuck her. *Pero no la he visto en mucho tiempo.* It's as though she doesn't want me to see her."

"I've seen her." Raimunda pulled on her cigarette, her lips making a slight smacking noise as they clasped and released it. "She was at the *norteamericano* bar, the Dockside, a few days later. She complained she hadn't had a good lay *todo el verano*."

"*Es la verdad?*"

"*Sí. Te mentiría?* I was very surprised, *mi amigo*, very surprised. I listened while she told *todas las mujeres* about how small the cock was on her last fuck, smaller than that of the *norteamericano*."

Enrique clanked Jesus' Medalla onto the bar. Raimunda saw his eyes flicker at her last words, but he said nothing, only took Jesus' money and returned to his inventory in the back.

"*Esa bruja! Le voy a demostrar mi miembre*! How do I find this bitch?"

"She's known to stay with *la mujer vieja* Ana."

Jesus swigged his entire beer in one breath and slammed the empty bottle down. "*Perdóname, mi preciosa.* I must go find *este puta joven* and teach her a lesson *no olvidará nunca*."

"What's your hurry, *mi amor*? Stay with me and have another *cerveza. Ahora no es el tiempo*."

"Wrong, *cariño*. Now *es el tiempo perfecto*. Once the hurricane hits Culebra, only those with a death wish will venture from the safety of their houses. We will have *mucho tiempo estar solos juntos*. Tamarind will think again before complaining to *los gringos*."

"*Ah, ya veo. Buena suerte, mi amigo. Buena suerte.*"

Raimunda watched as Jesus dropped out of his barstool and loped away to the entrance. In the dim light from the boarded-up windows on either side of the door, she recognized the appetite of the man scorned, the single-minded focus of the predator.

৵৵৵

Even above the noise of the wind, Tamarind heard the sound of a car motor on the hill road from town and her heart leapt. But when she saw the battered old Pontiac through a gap in the scrub, she knew that it wasn't John and turned to look toward the canal so that the stranger wouldn't see the disappointment in her gaze. The car rattled to a stop not far from her and a man in a red shirt blooming with hibiscus and gray polyester slacks jumped out, the car's engine idling loudly.

"*Señorita, dónde está Señora Ana? Mi esposa necesita ayuda ahora, por favor.*"

By now, Tamarind was used to people driving, walking, and riding horses or bikes to Ana's door at all hours of the day, although they had rarely shown such urgency. None of the Culebrenses had seemed very surprised to see Tamarind and she sometimes wondered if they attributed her presence to the power of Ana's magic—for all they knew, Ana had conjured her up from lifeless dust. Shrugging, she accepted their conclusions—they weren't entirely wrong anyway—and did nothing that would cause them to think differently. The Creator had allowed her to remain unknown among these humans and she must be careful not to invite suspicion to herself.

Without a word, she gestured for this latest supplicant to wait before sprinting away toward the beach, reveling in the feel of her toes pounding on the stony ground and the wind in her hair. At the edge of the beach, Ana waited for Tamarind, her knees under her

208

chin as she squatted, her single eye glinting even though the sun no longer shone. She unfurled herself and stood up. Together, they hurried back up the hidden path toward the man, whose anxiety manifested itself in rapid, unceasing Spanish.

"*Señora Ana! Señora Ana*!" The man shouted even before he saw them. "*Es el tiémpo. El bebé va nacer pronto. Vengate con migo, por favor.*"

Ana smiled widely when she came out onto the hill. "I've been expecting you, Jaime. Only Carme would have the bad luck to have a baby in a hurricane."

Jaime crossed himself. "*Madre de Diós! Digáme si ellos estén bien.*"

"You think you're having a son? '*Ellas' estén bien, muy bien*, if we leave now. Tamarind, you must come with me and help."

Tamarind, who stared beyond the Pontiac where the road disappeared over a hill, started at Ana's command and looked at them with narrowed eyes. "Me? What do you mean?"

Ana swiveled on her haunches to look up at Tamarind; her hands flitted in the air around her. "Look, young one, there's a mother about to give birth. She's in a lot of pain and needs my help. And I need yours. So stop thinking about yourself and go back to my place. We're going to need a few things."

Tamarind's mouth opened, but she shut it again. Nodding, she listened as Ana told her exactly what to get before returning to the house on heavy feet. Inside, Ana's chickens chuckled nervously from a temporary roost in one corner. She finished gathering the midwife's book, some scissors, and the medicine basket when she remembered the moonstone Goddess that she'd hidden down on Playa Tamarindo along with all of her other belongings. Wrapping a cloaking glamour around herself, she slipped out of the door while Ana and Jaime secured a tarp over the chicken coop and the wooden seagull house. Ana had sent all of the seagulls away days ago to nesting areas on the Puerto Rico mainland. After the storm hit, they would fly over the islands and return to her with news from other midwives.

Tamarind reached Playa Tamarindo and quickly released the cloaking spell guarding her horde of human artifacts. She ignored the pile of clothes and hair ornaments carefully tucked inside and snatched the moonstone Goddess up. There wasn't much time and she had no idea if she'd mastered the necessary spell from the midwife's book. Clutching it to her chest, she closed her eyes and murmured. She squatted, still murmuring and touched the seawater that surged restlessly toward her. A thrill ran through her fingers. On impulse, she popped up and hurried over to the scrub along the edge of the shore. Squatting again, she dug away at the roots of the closest low-growing bush and stuck her fingertips into the earth. Again she murmured. A new power tasted her skin and tickled her hand, unfamiliar and rich. When it flowed through her veins, it had none of the wild impatience of Mother Sea. Rather, it filled her with the dark, steady scent of the cavern where she'd gained her legs.

This new power stayed with her while she climbed away from the beach, her calf muscles straining against the incline and the soles of her feet aching from the stones and uneven ground. In the cavern of her fist, the moonstone glowed as if lit from within and the wires embossed themselves on her palm. She hummed a bit, deep and low, and several clicks skittered across her palate. Overhead, the flat gray sky waited, impervious and implacable. As she crested the top of the hill behind Ana's house, rising winds waylaid her, nearly knocking her off her feet and back down the hidden path.

Her hair fluttered into her face and then two arms wrapped around her, one around her mouth and the other around her torso. She dropped the Goddess. Fingers from the hand over her mouth pressed hard into her nostrils, asphyxiating her. From somewhere off to her right, she heard a hoarse shout and then the pulsating of her blood drowned out all other sounds. She squirmed and kicked a heel into flesh and bone. A kaleidoscope of vivid colors whirled across her vision before disappearing into soft, soundless charcoal.

When her senses returned, she found her arms wrenched behind her and her wrists tied tightly together. Her ankles too were tied together and she lay on her side in the back of a moving vehicle. A gag bit the corners of her mouth and choked her dry tongue; some rough cloth covered her eyes. Beneath her, unidentifiable objects dug into her side and the reek of old fried foods, the bitter tang of stale beer, and the slightly sweetish scent of something else mingled together and assailed her. A sharp ache threatened to split her forehead and nausea burbled in her gut. In her current condition, so far from sea and unable even to manipulate the fine drops of water in the air around her with her fingers, she had no hope of calling on any magic, let alone producing a cloaking spell for herself.

Gusts of wind rocked the vehicle and a male voice swore in Spanish. The voice sounded familiar, but her headache interfered with her ability to concentrate. She waited, trying to hum around the gag, but her chest refused to expand against the restraint of her arms. Just when she thought that she might vomit into the gag and choke, the vehicle veered and abruptly halted. The driver opened his door and got out; whatever they'd ridden in rocked in reflex. He swung open the door near her feet and cool, humid air caressed her soles.

Her captor leaned in and caressed her upper thigh, murmuring unintelligibly. Tamarind desperately soaked up as much of the moisture in the air around her feet as she could. Still, she felt parched.

Father, help me. The thought formed before she recognized it.

When the unknown abductor tugged her toward him, her feet touched the earth and again she felt the strange power flow through her soles. She urged it to fill her and something responded to her silent plea, swirling through her chest and into the far reaches of her mind. Almost she felt as if she could understand it. Seconds later, he launched her up and over his shoulder and her stomach heaved dangerously.

John. Why didn't you come for me?

The wind wrestled with her abductor as he walked and he cursed again. It snatched his words away and Tamarind sensed a thread of anger in its swift fingers—anger separate from the passion brewing the hurricane. The new power in her blood sang in response. Tamarind slumped against the shoulder he carried her over and waited.

He stopped and fiddled with something in front of him. She tentatively stretched a toe behind her. Her bare feet didn't recognize the smooth, hard surface. Abruptly he opened a door and the wind howled past them as he stepped forward. Tamarind sensed the room around them before he turned and pushed the door shut, leaning against it for a long moment. In the sudden quiet, his breathing sounded harsh and uneven. After a moment, he pulled her from his shoulder and she tumbled onto the floor, hitting her head and bruising her back. When he spoke this time, she recognized the voice. Its caress chilled her.

"Ah, *mi cariño*. That was *muy dificil*. But now we're alone, I can assure you that it was worth it."

Jesus knelt over her and rolled her onto her side. Then she felt the cold blade he wielded as he cut the bindings on her ankles. Pain prickled through her feet along with the rush of blood. He cut the blindfold away from her eyes, dragging the flat of the blade across her cheek as she looked at him for the first time in more than a month.

He clicked his tongue and shook his head slightly. "So wide, your eyes, *mi dulcinea*. Perhaps you are surprised to see me after all this time spent ignoring me. Perhaps you guess I have heard the stories you have been telling about me and you are afraid."

The gag wedged Tamarind's tongue back into her throat, which was so dry that she could only shake her head.

"Ah, *mi reina*, you pretended innocence all those weeks of turtle watching. Innocence when that *gringo* looked at you lustfully every night on the beach, innocence when I took you dancing and tried to touch you. But you weren't innocent when you returned and led me

212

to Playa Melones to fuck, and you aren't innocent now. You know exactly what I'm talking about."

As he spoke, he used the tip of the knife to toy with several strands of hair near her left ear.

"Even when you came back that night, you wouldn't let me touch your hair." His voice sounded husky, strange. "Your hair. It's almost alive. You must be so proud of it. Too proud, perhaps."

The blade caught and tugged at the strands for a moment.

"There are some that say you are *del mar*, but I, I say you are nothing but a foolish woman."

He held up the severed strands for her to see, watching her eyes as he lifted them to his nose and inhaled. He dropped the strands onto her face and laughed as she blinked to clear hair from her vision. She was still blinking against the scratchy filaments rubbing against her eyeballs when he leaned over. Even so, she caught the bright flash of steel through the tangle of hair against her cheek.

Nineteen
 confirms

MARILYN BATTERED ST. CROIX, only 65 miles away, throughout the afternoon on its way north to the other U. S. Virgin Islands, St. John and St. Thomas, and Culebra. John, driving Valerie's Jeep north on Route 251, refused to turn the radio on and listen to the reports from Miami. He met almost no one on the way to Ana's small house; only a single black car turned east at the intersection of 251 and 250, away from Dewey. Many Culebrenses had fled their homes for the safety of the shelter built with relief money after Hugo had ripped through the island in 1989. Some huddled in the largest public buildings: the school and its library, the clinic and ferry terminal, and the two churches. Most of the owners of the guesthouses, including Valerie, had opened their doors to anyone looking for a place to hide.

John, his elbow propped on the window frame, looked out at the landscape as he drove. The treetops danced against the buttermilk sky and tired shrubs rustled, imitating the constant shushing of the ocean enclosing Culebra. Under a stand of palm trees on the east side of 251, a herd of wild horses huddled. The whites of their eyes showed even from a distance. Nothing else moved, on land or in sky. Valerie told John that morning that the seabirds had risen in dark sheets from their nesting grounds over the past few days and streamed away to the northeast and safety. The air, heavy and hot, smelled like kindling and dust—overriding the faint metallic scent of the ocean.

In the silence, he heard Tamarind's voice, clear and musical. Anguish rippled its edges.

John slowed down and looked around, half expecting to see Tamarind sitting next to him, her bare feet hanging out the window and her corkscrew hair filling the cabin. But no mischievous eyes peeked back at him, no fingers tapped in time with the radio on the seat beside him. Instead, an image of Tamarind hunched under the low-hanging night sky when he'd read *The Lion, The Witch, and The Wardrobe* to her filled his mind. Her rounded shoulders burned themselves on his soul's retina.

He'd just reached the access road to Tamarindo Estates when a dented blue Pontiac crested the hill and roared toward him. He almost ignored it, but then he caught sight of Ana's wild white hair as the driver turned south onto 251. Quickly he turned the Jeep around and followed after the speeding car, alternately banging on the horn and flashing the high beams. The driver didn't notice him until he'd turned onto 250 and even then he refused to stop, only slowing down enough for John to come along his left side. John leaned over while driving and jerked down the passenger window.

"Hey, you, Ana! Where's Tamarind!"

She looked at him. The contrast between her brilliant blue eye and the cloudy left one silenced the howl of the wind and the rumble of the two engines. In her look, she subsumed life and death. When she smiled, a chill split his cranium and discharged along his spine. Something gleamed on her breast.

John swerved the Jeep toward the Pontiac.

The driver swore in Spanish as the Jeep rammed his car and pulled hard on the wheel to veer away from John.

"Pull over, *amigo*!"

The driver darted glances at John and pulled ahead of him, but John punched the accelerator and swerved in front of the Pontiac. The old car went right and skidded to a halt. The driver jumped out, leaving his door open, and ran around the back of the Jeep where John met him.

"*Qué te pasa?*" The man's hoarse voice cut across the wind. He punched John's shoulder with the heel of his hand.

"*No hablo español.*"

John brushed past the man, knocking him into the Jeep's trunk as he did so. He'd almost reached the Pontiac's right taillight when the man grabbed his left arm and spun him around. The first punch landed on his chin, but the second one John blocked. He grabbed a handful of hibiscus flowers and pulled the man closer to him.

"Look, I bet you *comprende ingles muy bien*. So listen up: I need to talk to Ana and I'm either gonna do it with you standing or with you flat on your back. If you're in such a hurry to get somewhere that you won't stop unless someone runs you off the road, I'd think you'd want me to leave you able to drive when I'm done with her. Got it?"

The other man's eyes darted from side to side as John spoke, but when John finished, he nodded once sharply. John pushed him away and the man staggered into the Pontiac. He didn't move, but watched John make his way around to the passenger side where Ana waited, smoking a clove cigarette. She looked at John, the cigarette held between her lips with the first two fingers of her right hand. She dragged on the cigarette and exhaled into the wind, which snatched the fragrant blue smoke and whisked it into oblivion.

"Where is she?"

She shrugged.

In the eerie bright overcast, John glimpsed a Goddess figure on a black cord around her neck. The stone in its belly winked as she moved. He reached into the window and snatched the cigarette out of her fingers and flung it away.

"I know you know where she is."

"*La mujer del mar?*" The wind tore at the driver's words, flinging them at John's head like darts.

John looked across the front seat of the Pontiac. The man bent now and looked back at him from the other side.

"*Sí.*"

"*Jesus la sacó.*"

"What'd he say about Jesus?" John held his face near Ana's wrinkled one.

"He said that Jesus took her." Her fingers dropped to the Goddess around her neck and lifted it. Almost immediately, she dropped it back onto her shirt as if it burned her. "She wanted to be with him during the hurricane."

"No." The other man frowned. "*No es la verdad. Jesus la agarró.*" He mimed putting his arms around someone and pulling her with him.

Ana scowled and pinched her lips together.

"Where did you get that?" John pointed to the Goddess.

Ana looked down at her chest. "I found it."

"Give it to me."

She snapped her face up and looked at him. "No."

John ignored her eyes and stared instead at the glistening wire-wrapped stone in the figure's belly. Suddenly he reached into the window, grasped the Goddess, and yanked. Ana yelped. The black cord broke at the juncture with the figure, which remained in John's fist. Ana screeched and lunged, but John pulled his arm to his side and stepped away from the Pontiac. She released the door latch and began to swing the door open.

"*Amigo*, don't you have someplace to go?" John backed away from the Pontiac.

"Ay!" The man opened his car door and slid into the driver's seat. "*Carme! Tenemos que ir ahora! No tenemos tiempo para esta tontería!*"

Ana paused, her right leg outside the open car door and her hand grasping the open window. She looked at Jaime and then back at John, who now stood near the rear bumper of the Pontiac. In this dark frame, she seemed shrunken, contained. The wind howled around her, tousling her hair, and nipping at her skirt hem. At its sudden ferocity, John realized that it had stilled during their conversation. Without saying another word, she tucked her leg back inside the car's cavity and slammed the door. Its rattle underscored her silence.

John ran back to the Jeep and jumped into the driver's seat. In its close interior, he brought the Goddess up where he could study it. He'd seen several dozen of these figures lying about Valerie's kitchen and at The Mermaid's Purse. This one appeared to be identical to all those others. Absently, he rubbed the stone with his thumb. After a moment, he set the figure on the dash behind the wheel and started the Jeep. He pulled out onto 250 without looking and drove, only vaguely aware of the road in front of him. Around him, the empty sky appeared a hazy bright citrine; where he could see the harbor on his right through the dark fringe of mangrove and thorny scrub, the sickly tint contrasted with the dull aquamarine of the seawater. The road hugged the ragged coastline, wending south and north along its many coves and channels as if nature would not be hurried. As he drove, the storm held its breath.

He'd nearly passed the Wildlife Refuge Office when he saw the black car that he'd seen a few minutes earlier parked on its far side. Teresa, the wildlife manager, drove a green Chevy. John braked and turned, cutting a wide swath across the dusty verge as the Jeep skidded toward the driveway leading to the office. He pulled in front of the low concrete building and shifted into park. As he did, he realized that his breath came in gasps. For a moment, his vision dimmed as his chest constricted and the heat enveloped him in its wet wool. Then he managed to wrench open the driver's side door. Overhead, the sky had darkened and the wind picked up again.

John started to get out of the Jeep when a glint caught the corner of his eye. He stretched forward and snagged the Goddess figure from the dash and pocketed it. He slid his hand into his pocket and his fingers found the smooth gemstone. Its warmth calmed him and his breathing eased. He walked to the office door, his eyes squinting to catch any sign of movement. Plywood covered the windows and he heard nothing.

218

He rapped on the door with his left hand. When he got no response, he tried the doorknob. It was locked. He backed up and rammed the door with his left shoulder. The Goddess lying against his palm thrummed as if alive. A moment later, the door burst open.

Overhead, a fluorescent light hummed, its bright light dazzling him after the near-twilight outside. In front of him stood an old metal desk, large and sharp-cornered and dun-colored like the decade in which it was manufactured. Forms and documents fluttered around the small room as the wind swirled in behind him, searching for something or someone in the stuffy space. On the wall behind the desk hung an institutional wall clock like the kind he'd seen throughout childhood at school. Underneath it stood two old metal filing cabinets, gray and impervious. The sharp scent of burned coffee mingled with the smell of dusty carpets, stale perfume, and body odor.

John took a few steps around the end of the desk and stopped. On the floor before him lay Tamarind, a gag in her mouth and her arms awkwardly wrenched underneath her. Her t-shirt had been sliced open down the middle and her breasts lay exposed. Other than the ravaged t-shirt, she wore only a pair of pink underwear. She stared at him, unseeing. The pupils of her eyes had widened so much that the ultramarine of her irises had nearly disappeared. She looked odd. For a few wrenching heartbeats, John couldn't comprehend why. And then he understood: her head had been shorn of its signature tresses. The manic copper curls lay forlornly in severed clumps about her on the floor and scattered across her chest. Long strands sprinkled her face and blurred her features.

"Tamarind!"

He crossed the distance between them without being aware that he moved and sank down on his knees at her side. She blinked several times and made no sound. Gently, he rotated her head until he could pick at the knot in the gag, but he couldn't untie it. The bindings on her wrist had also been tied too tightly for him to manage with his fingertips. While he struggled with the knots, Tamarind lay still and silent. John sat back and grunted, running his fingers beneath his hair and raking his nails into the scalp. As he did so, the Goddess in his pocket burned his thigh through his pants and he yelped.

He dislodged the wire figure from the confines of his pocket and held it by the head away from him. Tamarind slowly turned her face towards it. Awareness precipitated in her eyes after the trajectory of her gaze intersected the gem's soft beam and her pupils shrank back to normal. Her eyes slid up to John's face and held his.

An electric shock surged through the figure and up John's hand to his spine. Something dark and steady swirled inside his chest and his eyesight sharpened. He leaned forward, rolled her onto her side and his fingers deftly untied what had seemed impossible only a moment before. Ignoring the tufts of hair clinging to the rough material, he quickly untied the gag. He picked it out of her mouth as carefully as he would have picked shards of glass from the sole of a child. When the cloth came away in his hands, he saw that it had rubbed the corners of her mouth raw. Tamarind worked her lips, but no sounds emerged. John laid a finger across her lips and she calmed. He flung the rough gag away and then set the Goddess into her palm, wrapping her fingers around it. He rested her hands across her heart.

The floor creaked behind him. Tamarind's eyes slid sideways and widened.

John swiveled his head toward the sound in time to see a blurred figure and metal winking. In the space between breaths, he flinched.

Twenty
ࠈ

JOHN FELL AWAY FROM THE RUSH OF FLESH and shadow that descended upon him. Rasping breaths filled his ears and the office walls contracted around him, burying him underneath an avalanche of clothing, carpet, and a tangle of limbs and hair. Bodies squirmed around him and John flailed his arms and legs in response. As he jerked and heaved, memories surfaced and blotted out the reality of the office. Memories of seawater drumming in his ears, of salt burning his eyes, and of choking. White spots blossomed onto his darkened vision and his chest clogged shut.

Breathe. Just breathe.

Humming echoed inside his skull and his body responded of its own accord. His lungs opened a little and his vision cleared. His world had gone topsy-turvy. Papers flew around the office like dazed birds mistakenly trapped inside a glass building. Tamarind squatted near him on the floor, her shorn head forlorn in the fluorescent light and shadows obscuring her features. She held the Goddess between her knees. Her feet were bare.

John rolled a little to the left and saw Jesus propped on one hand and two knees; he held the other hand to the right side of his face. When he heard John move, Jesus lifted his head so that John saw the blood that streamed from his damaged right eye. He

221

lurched toward John and tumbled onto him, scrabbling at John's neck until he'd found a purchase with his blood-glazed fingers. John clawed at Jesus' fingers, kicking his heels into the floor. Again, Tamarind's voice floated through his thoughts like a memory, or an epiphany.

Remember the pearl divers?

John closed his eyes. An image of a long dive filled his mind and he relaxed. He clearly saw the oyster shell waiting for him. Then Tamarind appeared next to him, her copper hair fluttering about her in the current and she smiled. She slipped her hand into his and together they swam to the bottom. Together, they reached down and lifted the oyster shell up. When John pried it open, a luminous pearl sat cushioned on the oyster's flesh. As he blinked, dazzled, Jesus' fingers released his neck.

John, surface now.

He opened his eyes and saw Jesus kneeling in front of Tamarind, who once again lay on her back. The Goddess gleamed in the dark recesses under the desk and the wind had taken on a life of its own. Now it was a banshee, howling through the office and sending papers whirling madly; now a poltergeist who ripped at the corkboard on the wall. The blinds on the windows danced and rattled. Jesus, impervious to the character of the wind, fumbled with his belt.

"*Ahora, mi cariño, ahora.* You will have a fucking like you have never had, *mi querida. Esto te prometo.*"

He lowered himself onto her.

John levered himself off the floor and launched himself onto Jesus' back. Clawing at Jesus' shirt, he managed to grasp enough cloth with both hands to wrench the other man off Tamarind. His breath grunted from deep in his chest, but his chest remained open, expanded—light. Again, the electricity that he'd felt only a few moments before while holding the wire Goddess charged through him; this time it rushed through every nerve in his system until he felt illuminated from within. He threw Jesus away from him.

Jesus fell into the desk and yelled. Clutching his side, he stood up and turned to face John, who had pulled Tamarind behind him. John darted a glance at her. She sat, listing to one side, one hand propping her upright and the other hand limp across her torn underwear. When he swung his head back, Jesus flashed his knife, which had fallen under the chair during their earlier struggle. The jagged gash along the inside corner of Jesus' right eye distorted his features and gave him a sinister, alien appearance. Dried blood and mucous—accidental war paint applied with fate's indifferent hand—bisected his cheek.

"Ssst." Air hissed through Jesus' clenched teeth. He swiped the knife at John, who barely arched his back in time to pull his stomach out of its path. "You think you're so *listo*, *gringo*. How smart are you now, eh?"

He tossed the knife to the opposite hand and swung at John again. Again, John avoided the blade. The third time, Jesus feinted to the right and John moved left; the blade traced a path across his abdomen. John understood that Jesus had sliced him, but he felt nothing. Instead, he watched as the wind caught Jesus on the far point of his pendulous arc, overbalancing him. For a moment, Jesus hung suspended in an invisible swing and then John stepped into him, shoving him into the desk. Jesus grunted as his battered side crashed into the sharp edge of the steel desk. John kicked at Jesus' bent legs and the other man collapsed, cracking his face on the desk as he fell. He lay in a crumpled heap and made no sound.

John ignored him and spun back to Tamarind, who had slid over onto her side on the rough institutional gray carpet. The t-shirt had fallen open and he saw her belly rise and fall in shallow breaths. Her skin had pallor to it that he'd never seen before. It clung to her frame, revealing fine details in bone structure and hollows under her ribcage and cheekbones. Tamarind had always been slight, but now she appeared almost emaciated, as fragile as onionskin stretched over a frame of hollow reeds.

He took a step towards her and the wound across his stomach burned and stung so sharply that he winced. She opened her eyes and looked at him. They were huge, too huge, and a dull blue like arctic seawater.

"You're hurt." Her voice no longer lilted. She sounded far away and traveling still.

"Not much. The other geeks will be in awe when I show them the scar."

He knelt at her side, consigning the pain in his gut to the recesses of his mind where it belonged.

"Tamarind, I know you're *del mar*. Did you–did you leave the sea for me?"

She took several breaths before she answered. Her eyes watched his face. "Yes." She raised a hand to his cheek; it was hot and dry. "I fell in love with you the day you came to Culebra and climbed that mangrove tree ... near the canal."

John pulled her hand into his and then touched her lips with his other hand. They were cracked and bled a little.

"You need water, don't you?"

She nodded, almost imperceptibly.

"There's water in the Jeep." He glanced over at Jesus, who hadn't moved since he'd slithered to the floor. "I'll go get some and bring it back to you."

He stood up, feeling as if his gut had come unhinged and might swing open, spilling everything inside. He braced himself for the onslaught of compressed air from the doorway, but in that moment the wind abated. He hobbled toward the open door, anticipating a fresh blast, but it didn't come. He paused in the doorway. Outside, the sky had darkened to a premature nighttime and the air smelled wet. The oppressive heat from earlier in the afternoon had disappeared as the air pressure dropped. John looked south toward the harbor and saw the palms bent horizontal and the thorny thickets shaking as if in the grip of a fever; rain blurred the edges of trees and buildings alike. He ducked his head and ran.

In the trunk of the Jeep he found a case of water that he'd meant to unload for Valerie. He hefted it, resting it on his hip as a mother rests her toddler, and shuffled awkwardly back to the refuge office. Once inside, he stopped to catch his breath and swing his gaze from Jesus' body to Tamarind, lying with her eyes closed. The slight rise and fall of her chest reassured him that she hadn't been completely desiccated yet.

He set the water on the desktop and broke the plastic seal. Grabbing a bottle, he twisted the cap off and then knelt by her side, gently lifting her until he could prop her against his bent knee. Her head lolled forward and he slipped his left hand behind to steady it. His fingers snagged on her truncated tendrils, but he ignored his first touch of her head after so many weeks of imagining it and instead focused on tipping the bottle between her parted lips. Most of what he poured dribbled out of her and down her chin and neck, but he persisted. When he saw the water on her skin disappear as if absorbed directly, he poured more recklessly. Tamarind choked and coughed, her eyelids fluttering open and then she raised a thin hand to his holding the bottle. Their gaze met and held.

Tamarind drank five one-liter bottles of water without stopping. By the last one, John had surrendered the bottle to her and had opened three more with which to douse her body. Her skin and soft tissues rehydrated enough that she no longer looked as if she was on the verge of collapsing in on herself, but John suspected that her condition remained precarious.

"You need to get back into the ocean, don't you?"

Tamarind set the empty water bottle down and shifted so that she could lean more comfortably against his bent leg.

"Yes."

"You look so human, it's hard to believe. ..." Here he touched her legs delicately, just a brush of fingertips and nothing more.

"I *am* human—almost anyway. I've been living between two worlds, *mer* and human, all summer. Even though I have legs, I can't stray too far from Mother Sea."

"Where should I take you?"

She closed her eyes as if thinking about where they should go exhausted her.

"You've got to return to town, John, before the hurricane hits. It isn't safe to be out any longer."

"I won't return until I know you'll be all right."

She opened her eyes. The pupils had returned to their normal size, but they still looked as cold and hopeless as the arctic sea.

"Take me to the nearest water and leave me."

❧❧❧

Before they left the wildlife refuge office, John shoved Jesus' limp form under the steel office desk. As he did so, he spied the Goddess figure lying on the carpet under the desk's dark bulk and he pulled it out and put it into his pocket. He'd found an old woven Mexican blanket in the Jeep's back seat and he brought it to wrap around the nearly naked Tamarind. Then he lifted her in his arms as if he were lifting a hatchling that had fallen from its nest. The knife wound in his stomach protested, but he ignored it. While he carried her to the backseat of the Jeep, the wind and rain avoided their path as if an invisible shield hung over them. John eased Tamarind down into a lying position and then returned to get the last of the bottled water and to shut the door.

When he got into the Jeep, he turned to look at Tamarind, who lay with her eyes closed. Her face had filled out again, but she was still pale; dark shadows smudged the skin under her eyes. The bright red and green of the blanket accentuated her pallor, nearly swallowing her in its cocoon. Too much space existed between them, a dark chasm of the unknown and the unknowable. He stretched out a hand and touched her on the hip. Her eyes fluttered open.

"We'll be there soon, I promise."

"I know."

He turned back around and his hand slipped away from her. The air remained eerily still around the Jeep and he found himself expecting the wind and rain to return and break upon them as waves break upon a rocky shore. It did not. So he started the Jeep and backed away from the office, heading west toward Dewey and

226

shelter. As he drove, the stillness around the Jeep moved with them so that the rain and wind always remained thirty feet beyond them.

Earlier, he'd refused to listen to the radio. Now he turned it on: he needed to know how much time he had before hurricane winds reached Culebra and anyone left outside became chaff before Marilyn's obdurate scythe. Marilyn's eye currently passed over the east end of St. Croix and the airport on the southwest of that island reported winds ranging up to 97 miles an hour. The Miami Hurricane Center had upgraded her to category two and strengthening toward a category three. As she moved through the Caribbean, she dropped torrents of rain along her outer edges.

Even at her current speed, Marilyn wouldn't pass over Culebra for four or five more hours. John squinted out the window as the Jeep reached the intersection with 251. He would make it to Posada La Diosa provided that whatever kept the wind and rain at bay continued to do so for the next half an hour. He turned off the radio and turned north.

"Is there any music?" Tamarind's voice startled him in the quiet.

John looked at her in the review mirror. Her face held a little more color and the dark smudges had lightened. In the dim light of the Jeep's interior and with the blanket obscuring her head, she looked almost normal.

"I don't know. I'll see if I can find any."

He switched the radio back on and twisted the dial, looking for something other than weather, news, or pop music from the States. At last he found a Cuban station playing Lito Peña's *Yo Vivo Enamorado*. As its smooth saxophone and cheerful rhythms incongruously filled the Jeep, John found himself humming along and remembering the warm summer evening when he'd first heard the song with Tamarind. The memory of her singing and swinging a dripping Popsicle, her wild hair dancing around her face, brought tears to his eyes.

"I wish it was turtle-watching season right now." Tamarind hummed a little with the song, but her hum didn't reach her chest and none of her joyful clicking joined in as a counterpoint.

"Me too."

On the east side of the road, wild horses stood huddled under a tree. Several eyed the Jeep as it passed and John wondered what would happen to them when Marilyn's full force bore down on Culebra. He realized that no one had mentioned any of the wildlife, outside of the departure of the nesting seabirds, during the frantic preparations of the last twenty-four hours. What would happen to Valerie's beloved hummingbirds and bananaquits? Where would they go? Or what about the rooster and hens that walked so freely around town as if parading through their demesne? Would Marilyn devastate the wild things that galloped and strolled, hovered and glided, slithered and hopped around Culebra's preserves? He came to the fork in the road where the left branch headed toward Playa Flamenco and the right toward Punta Flamenco and Playa Resaca. Between the two branches lay Laguna Flamenco, protected from the Atlantic by the pristine sands of Playa Flamenco. He knew at once where to bring Tamarind.

He took the left toward Playa Flamenco and parked in the empty sandlot. When he slid Tamarind into his arms, she sighed and leaned into his chest. He lifted her from the seat and brought her closer, trying to block the wind and rain with his back even though neither wind nor rain touched them. A thickness sealed off his throat as he clutched her to him, but his breathing remained even and steady. In his pocket, he felt the Goddess burn and a dark, steady power buoyed him. When his wound began to bleed again, he scarcely felt it.

He trudged over the sandy path to the beach and then through the thorn thickets and between palm and mangrove trees to reach the lagoon. As he walked by the trees, an odd vibrating filled his chest and the rustling of their leaves almost made sense to him, as if their whisperings called to mind something long-forgotten that was on the tip of his tongue.

228

He reached the lagoon, winded and exhausted. Tamarind had lain still and quiet in his arms and he'd lost himself to the effort of getting to his destination, forgetting for the few minutes that it took him to get there why he'd come. He stood in front of the water in the gloom of the storm-darkened evening, his arms aching and his mind blank.

"John."

He looked down at Tamarind, who looked up at him with eyes as dark as a mountain river in winter.

"John, please put me in the water. I'll be fine."

He nodded once sharply and stepped forward. The surface of the lagoon frothed under the continuous caress of the passionate wind. He expected to struggle to the water's edge, but instead he felt again the dark energy that had aided him. Now it flowed from the ground and up through his legs, passing through the Goddess with an electric burst and up to his head where it settled into a thousand bees buzzing in his thoughts.

He dropped first to one knee and then the other, holding Tamarind against the rise and fall of his chest. She looked at him again, eyes wide and unblinking, and he slowly lowered her into the lagoon. The blanket opened a little and she struggled against its clinging folds. John freed one hand from under her knees and pulled the blanket away. Her lower half slipped under water and she sighed. John felt a faint vibration in her torso and he knew that she hummed, even if the sound couldn't make it out of her chest.

"You must let me go so you can go."

"I know." Still he didn't lower her completely into the water.

"You're bleeding again." She touched his shirt with a fingertip. "You need someone to take care of you."

"I told you it's nothing."

She flinched at his tone and he felt his heart twist in his chest.

"Don't worry about me. I'll find someone at the clinic to take a look at me. I've got a few hours to kill before Marilyn gets here anyway." His words didn't come out flippantly as he intended. They sounded grim instead. "How will I find you after the hurricane?

"You won't." A voice growled at him from a few feet across the lagoon.

When he looked up, John saw a man in the water up to his chest. His long hair flowed in tangled rivers down his massive shoulders, one of which had an angry braided scar bisecting it diagonally. The blue of his eyes left no doubt who, or what, he was.

"Father!" Tamarind lifted her head and upper body away from John.

The hollow where she had lain only moments before ached with its cold emptiness.

Twenty-one
ༀ

TAMARIND PULLED HERSELF AWAY FROM JOHN at her father's voice, a sound of sand washing over broken rocks. She was a bare promontory, exposed and cold after the shelter of John's arms. Above them, the anxious wind, which had abated during their trip from the refuge office, keened through the treetops and whirled around her bare head. Fine icy raindrops prickled on her face and upper chest; she shivered even though the water in the lagoon was warm as blood.

"Release her, human." Her father spoke in a low, flat voice. His mind resembled the ocean at midday under a blazing sun; its impenetrable surface reflected Tamarind's silent entreaties, dazzling her inner eye.

John did as her father bid and she slid completely under the water, her face submerging. Her diving membranes, unused for months, slid noticeably into place. For a moment she lay there, soaking the water into her pores and extracting oxygen. Here, in the dense atmosphere so like her mother's womb, the raw world outside no longer threatened. Only distorted sounds reached her ears and for an instant even these soothed her. But the fluorescent light of the refuge office flashed across the murk in front of her, and again a dark figure bent over her.

231

She sat up. An awful sound met her ears and she flinched. Then she realized the sound emanated from her throat.

Before she could say anything, her father erupted across the lagoon, launching himself at John. He swept past her in the water, his powerful tail churning it until it foamed. His wake washed over her; when the water had streamed out of her eyes and nose, she blinked and saw her father gripping John's neck. She stared at his rigid, alien tail.

"What have you done to her, you vile squid? What happened to her hair?"

John clawed at her father's hands and arms, gurgling and choking over the implacable fingers.

Let him go, Father!

Her father ignored her. Instead, he shook John as easily as a shark brandishes a mouthful of whale flesh. John's head snapped back and fresh blood soaked his torn shirt.

No, Father, don't! Standing, she pushed her feet down into the mud of the lagoon and its ooze calmed her. The lovely dark energy she'd felt earlier at Playa Tamarindo surged through her and she stood. Water dripped off of her bare skin; she'd lost her ravaged t-shirt in the lagoon.

Father. The dark energy smoothed and deepened her voice, carrying it easily through the shrillness of the wind.

Her father looked at her, his eyes steely-blue and turbulent. John hung limp from his hands, rasping a few breaths around his grip. He'd lost his ponytail holder somewhere during the afternoon and his tangled hair hung around his face. In the storm's twilight his skin had the bleached look of old driftwood or dead coral.

What is it, daughter?

Tamarind switched to speaking aloud. "Let him go. He's not responsible for my hair."

Her father kept his hands on John's throat, but he didn't shake him again.

Does it really matter? He's responsible for you putting off your tail, isn't he?

232

"No. I am."

I'll deal with you later. You're coming home. Back to the sea where we belong. Where you belong, with your sisters and your community.

"Not if you don't let him go."

You think you love this human, don't you? Don't you realize how vile, how abominable, they are?

"I know about Mother."

Her father's eyes dilated until she couldn't see any trace of the blue and his hands tightened around John's throat. John tugged weakly at them and then slumped into her father's grip.

How could you lie to me? How could you put off your tail and walk among these foul creatures knowing what they did to her? To me? He turned so that his scar gleamed in the dim light.

"They aren't like grains of sand, one as alike as another, Father. I have spent enough time with them to see them as they are. Many of them are worth knowing. Some worth loving." She kept her gaze on his face, but her heart beat against the cave of her ribs.

Bah! This jellyfish? He's only good for feeding bottom dwellers.

"If you kill him now, when he's done nothing wrong to you, then you're no better than the men who killed Mother." Her voice remained steady, but she heard her breath, ragged and shallow.

The wind calmed after she spoke, and so did the world around them. Trees and shrubs slumped at the respite and the lagoon, which had slapped at calves and the merman's muscular tail, subsided to a flat expanse of murky water. Her father stood immobile, silent and terrible.

"Put him down, Father, and I'll come with you."

When her father said nothing, she stepped forward and touched the back of his hands with her fingers. Her fingertips felt frozen on his cool skin and she dropped them hastily, waiting. He grunted and released John, who fell into the lagoon and crumpled to his knees so that the brackish water reached his chest.

Tamarind knelt beside him and touched his face. He raised his eyes, green as the leaves of mangrove, of tamarind, of palm—of all the trees and shrubs and flowers that she'd grown to love on Culebra. "Good-bye, John. May the Creator bless you."

His mouth opened, but nothing came out. His lips moved futilely, like a fish lying on its side on the beach suffocating in the open air. Keeping his eyes on her face, he fumbled for an instant with something below the surface of the lagoon and then lifted the small wire-wrapped moonstone Goddess, dripping and gleaming, up between them. He held it out to her and when she brought her hand up to accept it, his fingers clasped hers, hard.

Come, daughter, we go now before the fury of the storm whips the sea beyond my strength.

Tamarind extricated her hand from John's grip and looked steadfastly toward the sea as her father hoisted her onto his back, although she couldn't see it through the trees and scrub north of the lagoon. She knew from her walks on Culebra that the beach at the far northeastern corner narrowed until almost nothing remained between ocean and lagoon; her father would head there for the shortest path back to Mother Sea and safety. The full force of the storm loomed on the southern horizon and when it reached the island, it would devastate it. She felt nothing, no fear nor sorrow at the thought of mangled homes, trees ripped by the roots from the soil and denuded, birds and horses and giant anoles drowned or flung against concrete and rock.

Her father swam with one arm bent back to hold her around her waist—her own indifferent hands slack around his neck, the Goddess dangling against his chest—and they'd nearly reached the corner of the lagoon when the winds died again and she heard splashing behind them. Her father quit swimming and turned awkwardly in the shallow water to peer back toward the spot where they'd left John. The sky had darkened so much that she knew John would have trouble seeing.

"Tamarind! Tamarind!" The wind enlarged and directed his voice so that it reached them easily. "Don't go. Stay with me."

A faint surge of electricity prickled around them and her father shifted. The muscles in his back bunched and tightened. When she reached her thoughts out for his, his mind had darkened and again closed to her. He looked out toward John, whose head appeared as a darker splotch against the dusky lagoon. He said nothing, but waited. After moments long enough for them to reach the open ocean and race away, John neared, slapping the water with heavy arms that hardly cleared the surface of the lagoon. He stopped to look for them every few strokes. Against her father's chest, the Goddess glowed faintly even though the clouds hid sun, moon, and stars.

Her father took the Goddess from her hand and rubbed his thumb over the moonstone gem. *It calls to him.*

She didn't respond, only shivered against his back.

This stone is warm, almost alive. You imprinted a part of yourself on it when you wrapped it within this figure.

She clutched his neck. It's only a piece of jewelry, nothing more. Throw it into the lagoon and take me away. Even the rain now falling over them felt warmer than her chilled skin. *Please, let's go, Father.*

I cannot. His imprint is on it, too. His blood and his care for you have altered its essence indelibly. You are both bound by whatever magic lies wrapped inside it.

Tamarind closed her eyes, trying again to see into her father's thoughts, but they had taken on the polished sheen of obsidian.

"Tamarind." John's voice, a few tail lengths away, sounded frail. He'd stopped swimming and only his head bobbed above the water. As the sound of her name faded, his head disappeared. It appeared again, but only long enough for him to lift his face to draw a breath and then it slid a final time below the surface.

Before Tamarind could respond, her father lashed his tail against the lagoon, propelling them to the spot where John had slipped under. Without pausing, her father dived under the surface and black water pressed on Tamarind's eardrums and eyes. She started choking before the valve in her throat closed and her skin extracted oxygen from the water around her. Her diving membranes descended and she saw John's pale face; his open eyes stared at them.

Tamarind let go of her father's neck and swam towards John. She grabbed at his hand; his fingers curled around her wrist. She kicked her awkward legs against the enveloping water and reached upward with her free arm. Suddenly her father grabbed her hand and she soared to the surface. Next to her, John's head broke free, but she knew that he'd taken in water and couldn't breathe on his own. Before she could plead with her father, he'd pulled both of them up onto the bank and turned John onto his side. Sheets of rain washed over them until her father wove a spell in the air, surrounding them with an invisible bubble into which no wind or rain penetrated.

For several moments, they said nothing. Her father bent John's prone form over one thick forearm and began massaging his back with the other hand. In a moment John vomited copious amounts of brackish water and he coughed and choked violently afterwards. Her father waved his hand over John, murmuring until he grew limp and quiet. Then he lay John down again on the ground.

In the dark, her father's eyes glistened. He studied her face for some time before speaking. "Live well, daughter, and know that I'll love you until the stars fall from the sky and the oceans dry up."

Tamarind stepped closer to her father and into his embrace. Warm saltwater dampened her cheeks and blinded her eyes. Until now, she hadn't known what she would give up when she left the ocean behind. After the briefest interval, her father pulled back, kissed her gently on the forehead, and then eased her down onto the ground next to John.

Farewell, Father. Until the stars fall. Until the oceans dry up.

And then he'd slipped out of the bubble and heaved himself onto the sandy bridge to the ocean and disappeared into the roiling night.

※※※

They remained there on the lagoon's muddy bank, trapped between the ocean and Marilyn, in the protective bubble that

Tamarind's father had woven in the air. Tamarind sat with her knees to her chest, shivering, while John lay inert at her side. Even though no wind penetrated the cocoon, its howling tore at her with vicious fingers. It sent rain at them with such a fury that Tamarind imagined waves crashing against rocky shores.

She had no way of knowing how long she sat there in the violent dark, but she'd grown so cold that her teeth began to chatter and her knees banged into each other even though she wrapped her arms around them tightly. She remembered the warm ooze at the bottom of the lagoon when she'd stood in front of her father and she wanted to lie down in that ooze, to wrap its velvety embrace around her. Occasionally the winds died down for a moment and she heard the lagoon slapping fitfully at the ground where they sat, unable to proceed higher up the bank. If John hadn't lain there next to her, she could have escaped into the lagoon and anchored herself among the mangrove roots. She shook her head and rocked on her buttocks a little. If John hadn't lain there next to her, she would have returned with her father to the sea.

She lowered her face to her knees and breathed into her cupped palms. As she did so, she saw the Goddess lying on the ground next to her. When she picked it up, it radiated a steady heat that set her to shivering even more violently. She curled herself around her hands, holding the figure against her abdomen where it warmed her enough that she finally stopped shaking.

"Hey." John pushed himself up to a sitting position, wincing. He looked towards her, but she knew that he couldn't see her. "Where are we?"

"Inside my father's glamour, on the edge of the lagoon. We won't be able to stay here when the heart of the storm moves over us. The waves from the waters to the north will surge over the beach and flood this lagoon. My father's protection won't be able to hold against them."

"You should have gone with your father. No need to save me a second time only to have a hurricane sweep me away."

"You won't be swept away." She reached out and touched his knee. She left her hand there. "We'll take the road up Mt. Resaca together and shelter in the tower until Marilyn is far out to sea."

"That sounds like a walk in the park." His tone belied his words. "Okay, let's do it then. I can't see so well in this crap so you'll have to take point."

"'Take point'?"

"Lead."

"Okay. You hold her then." She handed the Goddess to him. The moonstone glowed enough that his fingers found hers without fumbling.

"She's so warm. Makes the night seem colder still." He lifted the figure up next to his eyes and looked at Tamarind through the sphere of light she gave off. "Holy crap! You're blue!"

He scooted behind her and wrapped his arms and legs around her. The Goddess dangled in front of them, her beam swaying as John's arms pulled Tamarind closer.

She leaned back against his damp t-shirt. "My senses tell me we need to go while the winds are still gusting. In a few hours, they will shriek without let up."

He said nothing, only held her against him for a moment. When he released her, she pushed herself up and away to stand. Her toes splayed against the muddy ground and she wobbled a little until her balance asserted itself. Behind her, John stood up as well.

"Which way, sir?" She knew he meant it as a joke, but his voice trembled.

She took his hand. "This way."

Putting her hand through her father's protective glamour, she dismissed it and stepped away from the lagoon. Mt. Resaca loomed over them, a darker shadow within the night's enveloping penumbra. Together, they plunged into the cascade, their hands a lifeline between them.

જીજીજી

Tamarind clutched John's hand as hail tattooed her chest and stung her face and scalp. Not far off to her left the ocean, already

238

frenzied beyond understanding, no longer offered her any strength or comfort. The alien drops in the air around them hissed static in her thoughts and refused to yield to her numb fingertips. She could weave no protective shield around them as her father had done and whatever benign force had aided them earlier as they drove from the refuge office had disappeared in the merciless onslaught. The gusts abated for a moment and she pulled John forward a few steps before bracing for another rush; as they walked across the grain of the storm's path, every fresh gust threatened to hurl them to the sea.

During one of these brief interludes, John swung the Goddess into the hand that held hers; now they cradled the figure between their interlocked fingers. Warmth radiated up Tamarind's arm and down her trunk, flowing into her feet and then into the ground. The dark, rich energy hummed inside her and flowed back through the Goddess to John, linking them more securely than their joined hands. When the wind next whirled around them, it barely rocked them where they stood. Tamarind lowered her head and trudged forward, moving through the rain as easily as if she swam in a calm sea. They passed through the first line of trees and thorn acacia lining the eastern edge of the lagoon and the strength of the winds diminished noticeably. John came up beside her and they picked their way side-by-side through the low-lying groundcover to the road that led up the western flank of Mount Resaca. He kept one arm across his abdomen as they climbed.

Half an hour later, they'd reached the top of Mount Resaca and the observation tower there, panting and bleeding from a myriad thorn scratches. When Tamarind twisted the doorknob on its only door, it remained stubbornly closed.

"It's locked."

"Of course it is."

John stepped around her and battered the door with his shoulder. It didn't budge. After a moment, he held the glowing moonstone figure up and studied the door, whose red paint had long been weathered to a pale echo of itself. In the faint light, he was a *moulos*, a dark water sprite with tangled hair and hidden eyes. She blinked and willed the image away. He reached above her and she felt him tugging at something along the doorframe.

"Good thing this is an old door and no one thought to put locking pins on the hinges. Here." He held a short stick-like item toward her. "Hold this."

She took it; it was rough and heavy and made of metal. John's body rocked beside her as he worked the second and third pins out of the hinges. After each pin slid free, he handed it to her and then he gave her the Goddess. She pressed the small figure between her breasts.

"You might want to stand over there for a moment." He gestured away from the doorway.

She stepped back a few steps and he lifted the door away from the doorframe and propped it against the doorway so that there was a space big enough for them to enter.

"C'mon." John turned and caught her hand before leading her into the black interior of the tower.

They shuffled along the curving outside wall toward the far side away from the partially open doorway. John, who walked ahead of Tamarind, stopped abruptly and swore.

"What?" Tamarind found herself whispering.

"I just ran into the stairs. Can you hold up that Goddess so we can at least make out shapes in this pitch black?"

Tamarind grasped the Goddess by the head and dangled her at the end of her extended arm. The stairs leading up to the top of the tower came into vague outline. She swung the Goddess to the right and saw another door beneath the stairs.

"Ah, storage. Let's see if we can open this one, too." John tried the door handle and the door swung open easily. "Let me hold Her."

He took the Goddess and waved her around the space. "As far as I can tell, there's enough room for us to squat in here. It'll be warmer, I think." He took her arm and pulled her into the closet and shut the door.

They sank down onto the concrete floor. Tamarind brought her knees to her chest and wrapped her arms around them. Her shoulder touched John's arm and her flank rested against his soaking t-shirt and shorts. In the muffling darkness, their breathing rasped in unison like some monster from the fairy tales that she'd read that summer. She hummed a little and her breathing smoothed and slowed.

John's own breathing calmed somewhat. "I've missed hearing that. God, I've missed *you*."

Tamarind dropped her head to her knees. She tried to hold herself still, but her body shook beyond her control. Fluorescent light haloed her mind's eye, defining the dark figure that kept bending over her.

"I should have come for you yesterday. I'm sorry, Tamarind." His voice fractured on the last words; they lay between them as sharp as slivered glass. "But that doesn't help you, does it?"

They sat there without speaking and Tamarind bit her upper lip so hard she tasted blood. Its salty, mineral taste evoked the sea so strongly that she gasped and then the saltwater washed over her face. Mucous mingled with tears and blood and for a moment she knew nothing of her surroundings. When at last the waves stopped rolling through her, she brought her hands to her cheeks and wiped beneath her nose.

"Here." John wiggled next to her and then handed her his wet shirt. "Wipe your face with this."

As she wiped her face off, they heard the howling of the wind. It sent fingers of damp air under the door to the closet as if searching for them.

"Men killed your mother?" She could barely hear him over the wind.

"Drug runners killed her years ago."

"How did they find her? Couldn't she hide from them?"

She felt the breath sigh from her. "Yes. We *mer* have cloaking spells and glamour to protect us from people. But she didn't want to hide. Humans fascinated her. I think maybe she wanted to be human too."

"No wonder your father wanted to kill me." He shifted next to her and she felt his upper arm brush her nipple. She tingled where his skin had touched hers. "You said you were almost human. Will you always have to stay close to the ocean?"

"I only have legs until the end of the rainy season."

"That's November, isn't it?" She felt him hold his breath for her answer.

"Yes."

"And then you get your mermaid's tail back."

"Yes."

"And there's nothing I can do to stop it, is there?"

She hesitated.

"What?" His voice sounded sharp. "*Is* there something I can do?"

"I can keep my legs if I mate with a human." She almost didn't get the words out of her throat.

"Well, then, you're all set." The saltwater of his voice stung the scraped hollow of her chest so that it burned.

"What do you mean?"

"Jesus was just coming back for a little more, wasn't he? I mean, maybe he's a prick of the highest order who deserves to burn in hell, but he didn't exactly imagine that you'd be willing to have sex with him, did he? After all, you've already had sex with him on Punta Melones."

"What?" The word scarcely escaped her numb lips.

"You know I saw you. You looked right at me that night."

"What night?"

"What night? You gotta be kidding me. The night you and he went dancing at Isla Encantada."

"I didn't have sex with him. He clearly wanted me to, but I went back to Ana's." She wanted to leave this tower, plunge down Mount Resaca, and throw herself into the sea.

"It was you. I know what I saw. I went back later to Isla Encantada looking for you and while I was out, I found your Goddess. When I picked it up, I had the strongest urge to go to Punta Melones, and there you were under Jesus. You smiled at me and I dropped her—" here he held up the Goddess, "on the beach."

"I didn't make her until after you left Culebra, John. Valerie gave this moonstone to me, to give me hope that you'd come back." Saltwater slid down her cheeks again. "It wasn't me. It might have looked like me, but it wasn't me. What if I *had* given myself to Jesus? Are you telling me that you've never been with a woman? Are you telling me that you and Raimunda only ever went dancing? I heard the stories, John. I know you were with her, many times since you and I met."

John squirmed next to her. "I—"

"I think you saw what you wanted to see so you could leave Culebra and me. And now you believe what you want to believe so you won't have to act. I've waited all summer for you. I've never lain with a human even though I could have, and in a few weeks, I'll return to the sea. I won't come back, John. I won't come back." Convulsions shook her breathing and she felt lightheaded in the stifling dark.

They sat there for a long moment. The sound of John's breathing vanished and Tamarind pulled herself away from him and balled herself around her knees. She closed her eyes and hummed, rocking and weaving an ellipse in the air above her head. If she rocked long enough, her humming would clear her thoughts and the spell she wove would take hold. She would disappear inside a cloak of darkness. And then, in a silence so complete that she'd nearly closed off all awareness of John, she heard him inhale audibly.

"Tamarind." He breathed her name out steadily. "Tamarind."

She could feel him release and expand next to her. She stopped rocking and waited. He reached for her and touched her shoulder with a fingertip as light as the brush of an angelfish. She didn't pull away but held herself still. He brought his full hand down upon her shoulder tentatively; his palm was warm and his fingers firm. A surge of electricity, warm and dark, flowed down her arm and through her body, reaching the base of her spine and radiating through all of her limbs. Her breath grew shallow and the air in the closet grew close around them. Outside, the hurricane had arrived and the winds careened through the tower after flinging the loose entry door aside.

"I don't want to lose you. But I don't deserve the gift you want to give me."

She leaned toward him and he moved his hand up to her shorn head. When she cried out, he bent and kissed her head, and then he kissed the top of her ears, first the left and then the right. He kissed the back of her neck, and then he traced her face with the tips of his fingers. He held her cheeks gently and waited. She lifted her arms around his neck and he kissed her mouth at last.

He slid slow fingers over her shoulders and down her flanks and when she'd stopped trembling, he moved away from her and tugged off his shorts and sandals. And then he sat next to her. She extended her hand carefully, searching with her fingers until she felt his nearest hipbone. Moving her fingers across his abdomen, she touched the tender skin above the cut. He flinched. Murmuring, she laid her palm over it. Gradually, he relaxed and she knew the pain had faded from his awareness and the risk of renewed bleeding had gone. She raised her hand to his face; he turned, pressing his lips against her palm. By degrees he pulled her on top of him, as carefully as if she were sculpted from tissue paper, and wrapped his arms around her. He rocked her as the madness and fury descended upon the breathless world outside their tower, ripping tree and wall, shrub and roof in an ecstasy of obliteration. Together they wove a spell so exquisite that the foundations of heaven might have crumbled and still they would have known only the utter stillness of their breath.

Twenty-two
ɔȝ

MARILYN SLOWLY LOST STRENGTH, becoming first a tropical storm, and then a storm front, and finally dissipating out at sea, miles north and west of Culebra days later. The morning after she passed, John awoke to find Tamarind's head resting on his shoulder, her body curled in his lap. The storage closet in the observation tower where they huddled had lightened imperceptibly. The screaming winds and gunshot spray of rain mixed with hail had vanished, leaving a profound silence. He absorbed the feel of Tamarind against his chest, her silky scalp lying against his neck, and the slight weight of her buttocks on his thighs. He wanted to sit in this place so far from people and research and proposals, until they'd put down roots and transformed into a tree like some Greek nymph.

The reality of a full bladder, an empty stomach, an aching slash across his abdomen, and the soreness of scratches and bruises kept him from pursuing this option.

"Hey." He touched Tamarind's cheek.

She stirred and sighed. "It's quiet."

"Yeah, I guess we slept through the rest of the hurricane. I think it's still raining though."

She moved a little and he grunted. "Sorry." She brushed his wound with a fingertip.

"Oh, that's not the problem. You just pushed against a full bladder."

"Ah." She sat very still. "We can't stay here much longer. There's no food and I need something to wear."

"You sound disappointed."

"It's just that it seems so safe here. And private."

John ran his free hand along her flank, around the slight curve of her hip, and down her thigh. "Yes, private is good. Perhaps we can wait a bit longer to venture out into the world."

๛๛๛

Tamarind and John remained in the observation tower on Mount Resaca until the sun chased away the last of the rain later that morning and then they trudged down the road toward Playa Flamenco. John wore only his shorts and shoes; Tamarind had pulled on the remnants of his bloody t-shirt. She'd regained enough water since leaving the refuge office that she no longer looked emaciated and frail, but bruises purpled her arms and legs and angry scratches slashed her skin. A single long scratch marred her right cheek.

All around them lay scattered thorn acacia, ripped by the roots from the ground, and broken limbs from palm and mangrove trees. The rain and wind had gouged chunks from the land, leaving it pitted and vulnerable. Overhead, sooty terns and laughing gulls dotted the clear sky and they heard birds calling as they always did, as if the world below hadn't been devastated.

They found Valerie's Jeep sitting alone in the lot near the beach, thorny scrub caught under its chassis and in its rearview mirrors. A dead Puerto Rican ground dove lay on the Jeep's hood, its neck broken and its head lying sideways. They cleared the Jeep of the brush and carcass and drove to Ana's cinderblock house to get Tamarind's belongings. Fragments of the chicken coop and seagull house had embedded in the branches of nearby tamarind trees and littered the ground; patches of the blue tarps that had covered them

246

had been caught on limbs and wrapped in eddies around rocks and tree trunks.

The plywood covering Ana's small windows had been hurled from sight and the glass shattered, but in the corner of her house the temporary chicken roost and its occupants remained unharmed. The birds chuckled and squawked when John and Tamarind entered. Tamarind tiptoed through the debris of Ana's home and peered into the plywood box. The chickens fluttered and complained; they had large raw-looking bald patches on their rumps and piles of feather and dung cluttered the floor. She hummed and clicked a little until the birds quieted and settled into sleep, their beaks tucked under a wing.

Together, she and John maneuvered down the hidden path to Playa Tamarindo where her cache of clothes, jewelry, and books remained untouched by the rapacious waves. She stripped John's t-shirt off after exposing her things, flinging the scrap away from her and into the waves where the current caught it and sent it south before it grew waterlogged and disappeared. He watched as she waded into the saltwater of the Luís Peña Canal until it covered her head. He waited without taking his eyes from the spot where she'd gone under. When she emerged, the sun glistening on water droplets in the stubble on her scalp, he let out his breath.

Tamarind stood for a moment on the empty beach among the litter of shells and seaweed, plucking something invisible from the air around her as she murmured. Within moments, the water on her had disappeared. She seemed scarcely to notice the pile of silky underwear lying like treasure near her clothes and grabbed the first one that her hand touched. After she'd stepped into these, she remained bent over while she pulled on a clean t-shirt and shorts. She knelt down and picked through the jewelry pile until she found a pendant on a gold chain. She stripped the pendant from the chain and dumped it onto the rocks without a second glance. The chain lay curled on her palm like a tiny glittering serpent.

"Can I have my Goddess?" She held out her hand to John, who searched in his pocket for the small figure.

"I've just been keeping Her safe for you."

Tamarind accepted the gleaming figure. Grasping it around its belly, she threaded the chain through a small loop on the Goddess's head. She raised it up to her neck, but before she could fumble with the clasp, John had stepped behind her. Brushing his fingertips across the back of her neck, he took the chain from her fingers and latched the clasp for her.

She smoothed the figure between her breasts. "Thanks."

Tamarind tossed the clothes and books into a small travel bag that Valerie had given her for their trips to San Juan. The last item she packed was a small hand mirror. This she lifted to her eyes, before twisting and turning as she struggled to see more of herself in the mirror than was possible. While they lingered on Playa Tamarindo, the sun climbed to its apex and the day grew warm. As they walked back up the hidden path toward Ana's house, sweat glistened on John's shoulders and trickled down his spine. Tamarind watched it run toward the waistband of his shorts until she realized sweat also wet her shoulder blades and the hollow between her breasts. In wonder, she touched the moisture on her chest and tasted it. It tasted like the ocean.

They returned to the Jeep and drove down 251 to Dewey. For the first time since he'd driven Zoë around Culebra, John paid attention to the landscape beyond the road. As with Mount Resaca, trees and shrubs had been yanked up and raw wounds in the earth gaped. At the airport, all of the light planes were overturned and scattered, like so many pieces upended from a giant chessboard after a bitter loss. In place of the scrappy small houses clinging to the slope leading to town, there was nothing more than scattered debris, resembling an abandoned fairground for an army of careless giants. Here and there he could make out sheets of metal roofing, wooden planks, doors, piles of clothes, odds and ends of home life: pictures, a mattress, a broken chair. But mostly what he saw was unrecognizable, twisted and thrown in meaningless clumps and individual pieces as far as the eye could see.

Dewey had also been transformed. Marilyn had ripped off sheets of plywood and smashed store windows, broken light poles trailed wires like spilled entrails, and paper and glass carpeted the ground. Waves from the harbor had surged over the shore, canal, and docks, before reaching hungrily along Dewey's streets. Where they had passed, a salt residue rimed the pavement and glittered in the sun.

John drove slowly, the Jeep's tires crunching over the fragments of humanity and nature mingled on the pavement, pulverizing the smallest.

"There's Valerie." Tamarind pointed as they neared La Virgin del Mar.

Valerie stood with Sister Maria Margarita on the steps of the church, her hands covering her mouth. The nun's hands rested on her hips and her lips were pursed as she surveyed the houses and shops around them. When her gaze crossed over the Jeep, they widened and she stared at them.

She put her hand on Valerie's arm. "My friend, look, there is John and Tamarind whom you worried so much about."

Valerie looked where Sister Maria Margarita pointed and screamed a little. "John! Tamarind!"

She came to the Jeep, picking her way through the debris so quickly she was like a bananaquit fluttering. When she got to the driver's side, they saw the puffy grooves under her gray eyes and her uncombed hair. John recognized her shirt from yesterday.

"John! Tamarind! You're safe! Thank God!" She leaned as far into the Jeep as she could, wrapping her arm around John's neck. Then she pulled away and looked at Tamarind. "Oh, my God. What happened to your hair?"

Tamarind blinked and touched her head. "I–"

"We survived a bit more than a hurricane. We'll tell you about it later." John looked at Valerie, who gazed back at him for a long moment and then nodded. "Is everyone okay?"

"So far as we know. Only old Captain Joe hasn't radioed in yet, but he's a salty dog so we hope for the best. The power's out, but the Dockside has a generator so we can get some hot food once in a while until the power's restored on the island. If you two are hungry now, Sister's got a kerosene stove and has soup in the sanctuary."

"We are." John looked around for a place to park. "Just let me park your Jeep over there where the mess is only a couple feet high first. I don't suppose you could find me a t-shirt someplace, or a blanket?"

Valerie's gaze dropped to his bare chest and she saw the slash there, dark and wicked. She inhaled sharply. "Sister's got some blankets and a first aid kit, too."

"Thanks."

"I'll see you two inside then." Valerie looked at each of them in turn and then returned to the church.

After John parked and they'd scrabbled through the uneven litter to the church's steps, they heard voices and laughter. A moment later, a mewling threaded its way among the chatter. Just inside the church's doorway a group gathered, oblivious to the destruction only a few feet away. Tamarind recognized Jaime, the father-to-be from yesterday. Tucked between his left arm and his chest, he held a blanketed bundle that appeared to have a coconut wedged into one end of it. When she and John drew near, she saw that instead of a coconut, the furry brown sphere had a small mouth and cloudy blue eyes that studied the sky above its father intently. Jaime held his baby.

He turned at their footsteps. "*Madre de Dios. Qué pasó?*"

All of the people around them stopped chatting and looked at John and Tamarind, who stood just outside the church's entrance. Their eyes, so lively only moments before, lost their dark luster and their faces closed in on them as anemone tentacles close around prey. A few of them stepped back, and ducking their heads, turned away. The ones that remained shifted closer together and watched John and Tamarind, their lips pursed and their arms around each other's waists. Tamarind's hand flew to her scalp before she realized what she was doing. She let it brush the prickly soft hairs at the top of its arc and then it fell back to her side.

John wrapped an arm across her shoulders. "When *una mujer del mar* casts off her tail, she cuts her hair to show that she has left the sea forever."

"*Es la verdad?*" Jaime looked at her.

Tamarind nodded.

"So it's done then, young one?" The scent of cloves parted the watchers and Ana leaned against a pew, her legs crossed at the ankles and a hand-rolled cigarette gripped in her left hand. Blood spattered the front of her blouse and the bird's nest of white hair around her face lay matted against her forehead.

"Yes." Tamarind turned to look at Ana and her chin lifted a little. She touched the Goddess at her breast without knowing that she did so.

Ana nodded and dropped the cigarette onto the tiled floor where she ground it with her toe. She walked over to them and stopped. Without looking at John, she brought her hand to the Goddess, holding it up and away from Tamarind's chest so that the sunlight shone on the moonstone.

"She's a powerful one, this one is." She spoke so softly that only Tamarind heard her words.

Without warning, a laughing gull dropped from overhead and swooped alongside Tamarind, nipping at her chest. The delicate chain snapped and the bird continued flying through the open doorway into the sanctuary with the Goddess dangling from its beak. Tamarind cried out, lifting her hand at the same time. John lurched toward the bird as soon as his mind processed what had happened, but the bird escaped his reach. It flew on, flapping strongly as it navigated around the inside of the church; first, it sped toward the altar and then veered to the right as Sister Maria Margarita appeared in its path. It zoomed in a low curve toward the side of the sanctuary and continued on around the far side to come full circle at the altar. People crouching in the pews ducked their heads.

Tamarind kept her gaze on the gull and the Goddess in its mouth. John stood nearby, his attention also focused on the mad flight of the bird. Dark, steady energy crackled in the air between them. While they watched, the laughing gull's wings flapped a little less strongly and its height wavered. Again, it circled the sanctuary in its desperate flight. As it came around toward them, Tamarind held out her hand once more. The bird shied from her hand and wobbled toward the middle of the church where Valerie stood. It tried to veer away from her, but as it tipped, the Goddess slipped from its beak. She caught the figure before it fell to the floor.

The laughing gull swung back toward the open doorway, its wings flapping unevenly. As it passed over Tamarind and Ana, it let out a cry like an apology and then it had gone through the dark frame of the door into the brilliant sunshine where the air currents lifted it up as easily as if it were ash from a bonfire.

"I think this is yours." Valerie walked from the sanctuary to where Tamarind stood. She lifted the gold chain up and studied the break. "It looks like the clasp gave way. I can fix it easily."

Tamarind nodded her head once and Valerie closed her hand around the Goddess.

"She'll be ready in time for your wedding, and I'd like to give you two gold bands to exchange that I picked up in San Juan." Valerie looked at John, who blinked. After a moment, he grinned. He looked at Tamarind, clasping her hand in his.

"Perfect."

"Great! Sister!" Valerie turned around and called back up the center aisle to the nun, who stood in front of a table at the front of the church with a huge aluminum soup pot on it. "Go find Father! We're going to have a wedding while we wait for the clean-up crews from the mainland!"

*ૡ*ૡૡ

They got married on Playa Flamenco as the sun melted orange into the waves. Tree branches and bits of thorny acacia and cactus scrub had been cleared away and the white sand had been raked until it was smooth. Citronella stakes burned in a semi-circle around the wedding party and their flames danced in the growing dusk. John wore a pair of jeans and a t-shirt; Tamarind wore a blue batik dress purchased from the Mermaid's Purse that afternoon and the repaired chain from which the Goddess hung, mysterious and radiant. Julie, the owner of the Mermaid's Purse, presented her with a fringed black shawl decorated with huge *flamboyan* flowers that Tamarind draped over her head like a *mantilla*. They stood before the priest barefoot, their hands clasped.

During the brief ceremony in which they promised to honor each other before God and to love without end, Valerie and Sister Maria Margarita stood on either side of John and Tamarind with the gold bands that Valerie had given them. Chris, Pablo, and Teresa, John's closest friends on the island, sat on woven blankets behind them. Twenty feet away to the west, Ana squatted alone on the beach and smoked a clove cigarette. Her green peasant skirt puffed around her spindly legs and her white hair tangled in the breeze. If anyone had glanced at her, they might have seen her lips moving as the priest spoke.

Afterwards, the sun dissolved into the water, leaving behind a rich red afterglow in the deepening blue of the horizon. Stars spread north and west in the wake of the advancing night, their tiny white lights revealed against the darker background. Ana unfurled herself and came over to Tamarind, who stood apart from John and the priest while they talked. She carried a small wooden box in her hands.

"I haven't given you my gift yet, young one."

Tamarind dug her toes into the sand; the warm grains yielded to her nervous prodding and covered her feet almost to the ankles.

"Ana, you don't have to give me anything. Without you, I wouldn't have any legs."

"True, young one. But I still want you to have this. It's a box fashioned from mangrove wood and this symbol on the top is a sacred *mer* symbol for the ocean. It's inside this circle, which represents the earth. The mangrove has its roots in the ocean but isn't of the ocean. You are like the mangrove in reverse. You may try to put your roots in the earth, young one, but you will always belong to the sea. Like the mangrove, you will always live in the border between the sea and earth."

Ana's clove-rough voice abraded Tamarind's heart and she shivered even though the night was warm around her.

"I have imbued it with powerful spells for your marriage. Take it and remember me whenever you look at it."

"Thank you." Tamarind whispered as John stepped behind her and wrapped his arms around her waist.

Ana handed her the box without taking her eye from Tamarind's face; the hasty dark shadowed the normally bright eye and blurred the edges of her features. Ana glanced at John and nodded slightly before turning away from them and heading toward the dunes edging the beach. In a few minutes, she'd disappeared over the slight rise to the path that led to the sand lot and then to route 251 south.

"It's time to go. The others want us to go with them to the Dockside for dinner. Chris stopped by there and asked them to keep some tables open. Since they're the only ones with a generator, I'm sure they've got more business than they can handle right now. If we don't go, they may just give our tables away."

Tamarind still stared at the spot where Ana had disappeared. She cradled the box in her palms.

"Can I have a moment alone on the beach?" She didn't turn to look at him.

She felt him stiffen and draw in a breath. She hummed, a faint throbbing that didn't reach his hands on her waist. After a moment, he expelled the breath softly.

"Sure. I'll be in the Jeep waiting."

Tamarind waited for him to get to the other side of the beach before moving. Although the sensory pores on her sides had shrunk to almost non-existence with her final transformation, she still knew when he'd crossed over the dunes and gone out of sight. Setting the box down and dropping the scarf next to it, she tiptoed to the ragged edge where the waves lapped the soft white sand.

Hitching her dress up to her waist and clutching it in her left hand, she knelt down.

Humming again, she traced her fingertips across the damp sand and sang low a *mer* parting song, the song sung when a loved one died or faced mortal dangers, such as from sharks or encounters with rogue *mer*. Or humans. The water rolled over itself in increasing intensity, foaming and washing toward her knees, adding its voice to hers in a rising crescendo until she'd finished and then it seemed to fade away, taking the sweet sadness of her words with it.

"My God, that was haunting." It was Valerie. "Saying good-bye to your home, to the world that gave birth to you?"

"Yes." Tamarind realized that her cheeks had grown wet with more than spray. "Mother Sea has blessed me and blessed my union with John. I can leave in peace now."

Valerie came and laid her hand on Tamarind's shoulder. "Always remember, Tamarind, that you carry the Goddess's strength inside you. And that is no small gift."

Tamarind said nothing, simply stared at the phosphorescent white cresting along the edge of the waves in front of her.

After a time, Valerie spoke again and her cheerful voice rang across the susurrus of the ocean. "Come! It's time to eat your wedding feast where your friends will toast your happiness and fertility. And I must go transform John's pathetic room into a bridal suite."

❧❧❧

As they flew northwest over Culebra toward San Juan two days later, Tamarind looked down at the island, which reminded her of a spiny lobster. Below them, on Playa Tamarindo, Ana's knotty form squatted on the shore's stony mosaic, but she didn't lift her face towards their small plane. Instead, she stooped and reached, moving articles too small for Tamarind to distinguish, her arms spidery in their movements. Seaweed wove a loose web around her, forming an intricate bed for the unseen objects that she dropped. Tamarind sensed, rather than saw, a pattern to these tiny offerings,

255

the way that memories sometimes hover at the edge of conscious thought, but the brilliant sky filled her mind instead. If she ignored the frame of the plane's window at the edges of her vision and looked straight ahead, she forgot everything and flew with the sooty terns and brown boobies above the immense blue ocean.

Beneath them, Ana patiently worked. As the plane approached the far horizon, she sat back on her haunches and aimed her single eye on it.

"You'll be back, young one. Mark my words—you'll be back."

Volume II

Grounding Magic

These tales say that apples were golden only to refresh the forgotten moment when we found that they were green. They make rivers run with wine only to make us remember, for one wild moment, that they run with water.

G.K. Chesterton

Twenty-three

❈

THE DAY THAT TAMARIND WILKERSON found out that she was pregnant again was the same day that she couldn't read her husband John's mind any more. She didn't realize it at the time, but if she had, she wouldn't have been worried. They had no secrets, just happy diversions. John shielded knowledge about Christmas presents from her, and she kept her suspicions about conceiving from him. Instead, she called her friend Valerie a week after she took the home pregnancy test.

"It turned blue."

Valerie didn't ask what had. She just squealed. "*La Bella Diosa*! That's fantastic! I bet John's beside himself. He told me a long time ago how much he wanted a family."

"John doesn't know yet. I just couldn't keep it to myself."

"I'm honored you told me then. When will you tell him?"

"I was going to tell him right away, but he was at a conference. Then I decided to wait. He's been distracted with his job hunt and I don't want to add any stress. The night we go out to celebrate his first job, I'll tell him when he tries to order me some champagne. 'Oh, no, I can't,' I'll say. 'Not good for the baby.'" Tamarind laughed thinking about it. "I hope he gets a job soon. It'll be so hard to keep it from him."

"What fun! I'd love to see his face." Tamarind heard the wistfulness in Valerie's voice. "Maybe you can visit when you get settled somewhere. Sarah must be a regular chatterbox these days."

Tamarind squirmed. In four years, she'd never once returned to Culebra and the stony beach of her birth. The thought made her uneasy. Ana, midwife and mentor, squatted there, weaving her prophetic patterns. "Maybe." Another idea occurred to her. "Why don't you come visit us instead?"

Valerie sighed. "I'd love to, but I just got a huge order from my guy in New York. My hands just aren't what they used to be. I don't know when I'll be able to take time off."

Two-year-old Sarah saved Tamarind from having to respond. "Mommy, whazis?" In her hands she carried a wooden box.

"Listen, Valerie. I gotta go. My two minutes of phone time are up. Sarah's digging into my closet."

"No problem, Tamarind. Call me when you know where you're going, hear? Give my love to John."

Tamarind turned to Sarah who held an intricately carved mangrove box. A present from Ana. "Give me that, Roe. It's not a toy."

"I know dat." Sarah sounded offended. She touched the teardrop that dominated the rich red-brown lid. "Means crying."

A premonition streaked through Tamarind. She shoved it down. "No, honey. Those are special happy drawings." What she didn't say was that she couldn't remember what they meant. "My friend gave this box to me as a gift when I married Daddy."

Tamarind studied the *mer* symbol on its lid. A semi-circle surrounded the teardrop. Smaller shapes filled its inside and the area between it and the curved line. A circle enclosed all of these lines and shapes, but she was sure that it wasn't part of the symbol. She rubbed a fingertip around the engraved edges, chewing on her lower lip as she did. The grooved wood attracted and warmed her finger as it curved around the strange shapes. The more she caressed the wood, the more reluctant she became to put the box down.

"Mommy." Sarah put her hand on Tamarind's wrist. "Mommy, go see Daddy today."

Tamarind blinked and lifted her finger from the box. Its tip burned, whether pleasantly or painfully she couldn't say. She sucked on it anyway. She remembered Sarah's confident translation and uneasiness filled her.

"What?" she asked when she realized that Sarah stood watching her.

"Go see Daddy. Have lunch." The way Sarah stated it gave it the force of command. Tamarind had planned to call her friend Kerrie about lunch but seeing John supplanted that goal. Her head buzzed faintly, like a distant FM station turned down low. She shook it.

"That sounds like a fabulous idea, Roe. We'll surprise him. I'll call Uncle Stefan first, make sure Daddy's not going to some talk." She looked down at the box in her hand, perplexed at its presence. Why was she holding this? She tucked it into the cabinet in the corner where they kept the dessert plates, the good ones with fruit painted on each one. The ones from that expensive kitchen store in the mall. They opened that cabinet only on Thanksgiving.

Even after she'd put the box up, a tang in the atmosphere troubled her, something so delicate and rotten that she hummed as she always did to console herself. It was the last *mer* gift that she'd retained upon putting off her tail besides her diminished telepathy. Nothing happened. That scared her. Again she tried, forcing her diaphragm up until her chest ached. Only a rough wheeze clattered out. Too dry. Ignoring any implications that suggested, she phoned Stefan and asked him to check John's desk calendar. He told her not to worry, that John and he were supposed to walk into Oakland and grab something.

Relief dispelled the faint odor. She glanced out the living room's sliding-glass doors. For the first time in two weeks the sun shone, a rarity in gloomy Pittsburgh. She'd put Sarah in the stroller and they'd walk in from Squirrel Hill. She might even stop into Java Joe's. It was still early enough in her pregnancy that she could enjoy a latte.

It was when she went to grab her purse that her moonstone pendant, the one that she'd worn since John had returned to Culebra for her, fell to the floor. After she scooped it up, she saw that one side of its clasp curled like a scorched piece of newspaper. She would have to fix it before she could wear it again. She returned to the dining room and shuffled through the plastic boxes holding the jewelry-making supplies that she stored under the table. Even though it would have been easy to fix, she couldn't wait that long now that she'd decided on the walk. She found the box with her silver findings and tumbled the pendant among them.

Tamarind got a jolt every time that she walked into Squirrel Hill. Electricity hummed in the chatter and bustle of people swimming on the sidewalks and the traffic weaving among the neighborhood's congested streets. Sleepy undeveloped Culebra had more nesting seabirds than people and more wild horses and chickens roaming the streets than cars. Squirrel Hill's teeming shops and restaurants had more in common with the island's reefs, but she much preferred interacting with people than octopuses, no matter how complex their nervous systems were.

Once they entered Schenley Park, the thrumming life of Squirrel Hill dimmed away. Overhead shreds of old cumulus clouds dissolved into the pale sky, where a red-tailed hawk glided majestically—its raspy scream of "*kree-eee-ar*" splitting the air.

"Do, Mommy!" Sarah pointed at the hawk. "Do hawk sound."

Tamarind hesitated. One of her former gifts had been the ability to imitate the seabirds that nested on Culebra's wildlife refuge. She'd been so accurate that she'd fooled countless naturists who visited. Sometimes she'd discover drunken lovers on Playa Flamenco at night and so startle them with her birdcalls that they'd stumble off into thorny scrub where they made her feel guilty. Then she'd find them in the starless pitch and, taking them by the hand, lead them safely to the parking lot. She'd fascinated John with her skill that summer after she saved his life. It came, she said, from her childhood longing to fly, to see what only the far-sighted birds could see from their impossible altitude.

She didn't want to hear how awful she sounded now. Every time she heard herself, she knew that she sounded like someone trying to imitate a red-tailed hawk. She'd fool no one. "I don't think I can, Roe."

Sarah took her gaze from the hawk. "Yes, can."

So Tamarind tightened her palate and flexed her tongue, enunciating the three sharp syllables. To her critical ears, they sounded false. "See? I don't sound like a hawk."

"Do."

Tamarind ignored Sarah and picked up her pace into the park. After fifteen minutes, the walk had loosened her stride and opened up her chest. She didn't try to hum but sang nonsense syllables to Sarah and the sky at large. On a flat stretch of the street, she pushed the stroller at a run and then launched it, letting Sarah glide ahead of her with her fingers clutching the front of the stroller and chattering. Tamarind whooped and raced after the stroller, again singing nonsense syllables and laughing when Sarah echoed her. On the golf course to her left, golfers paused in mid-swing and looked at her. Tamarind waved.

As Schenley Drive descended toward Frew Street, Tamarind slowed down and kept a firm grip on the stroller. The brief summer term had started a few weeks ago and students' cars filled every one of the parking spots, but John rarely drove to campus on weekday mornings; instead, his bike would be locked to the rack in front of Baker Hall. Tamarind smiled at the students who looked their way. A few of them, including a young woman in a black turtleneck with black-dyed hair and black tights, smiled back.

She pushed the stroller past Baker and the cut and turned left before she reached Wean Hall. A pimply, shaggy-haired young man held the door to the main lobby open for her and Sarah. Tamarind smiled at him as she passed and he ducked his head, muttering. She laughed as the door closed behind her and then the smell of coffee assailed her nose. In another few weeks, it would make her nauseous, but today it warmed her. Combined with the effects of her sunny stroll, the rich scent satisfied her spirits. Everything was right in the world.

After passing the usual line in front of the coffee cart, Tamarind steered the stroller down the right hallway to John's office. When she reached it, the door was open and she could see Stefan's back across from her. He pounded on his keyboard and bobbed his head, earphones and motion together transforming him into some bizarre creature from one of John's science fiction movies. John wasn't at his desk or sitting in the broken-down sofa along one wall. Neon lines tumbled across his workstation monitor.

She parked Sarah next to John's desk and walked up to Stefan, laying a hand on his shoulder. He jumped and spun around to look at her, sliding the headphones down around his neck as he did. "Jesus God Almighty! You scared the hell out of me, T."

"Sorry, Stefan." She looked down and hunched her shoulders a bit, then looked up again. "I didn't mean to. Forgive me?"

Stefan grinned at her. "I can't stay upset at you, T. No one can." He looked around her shoulder toward Sarah. "Hey, Roe-baby! Come see what Uncle Stef's got for you." He pushed his swivel chair back and stood up.

Sarah's eyes turned up at the corner and she gabbled. "Stef, Stef! Get my!"

"I love it how she mixes up her pronouns, don't you? Gets right to the point, doesn't she?"

"That everything's hers?" Tamarind made a face and Stefan laughed.

He picked up a floppy red thing from his desk and brought it over to Sarah, holding it in front of him and twisting it. Tamarind couldn't tell what it was, even when he'd handed it to Sarah.

"What is it, Stefan?"

"Mushu, from *Mulan*. And here's his buddy, CriKee." He tossed her something, which she barely caught. Looking down, she saw that it was a large purple cricket.

"Thanks, Stefan." She leaned over and gave him a hug. "You're the best."

Stefan stepped back and cleared his throat before sitting down. "Yeah, well, if you ever decide to leave that louse husband of yours, I'll be right here waiting."

"So where is 'that louse'?"

No sooner had Tamarind asked than they heard voices coming down the hall, one of which belonged to John. She and Stefan turned toward the doorway and in the next moment John and his ex-girlfriend Zoë came into view carrying paper coffee cups from Buns'n Udders. Zoë, who wasn't speaking, saw Tamarind and Sarah first. She stopped walking and smiled, a cat-who's-feasted-on-stolen-fish smile. John continued talking and walking into his office, but when Zoë didn't follow him, he stopped and looked back at her with a puzzled expression.

"What's wrong?"

Silence answered him.

Sarah broke it. "Daddy!"

"I didn't actually mean 'louse.'" Stefan whispered so low in Tamarind's ear that she almost didn't hear him.

"I know," she whispered back. She knew that John ran into Zoë around campus, but she'd never liked it. Not one bit. And this looked like more than 'running into.'

John spoke to Sarah, but he looked at Tamarind. She read the apology in his eyes. And something more. Was that guilt? For the first time since they'd been married, she didn't know for sure. "Hey, Roe-girl! What're you doing here?"

"Lunch! My hung'y!"

Tamarind said nothing and then Zoë stepped into the office, put her hand on John's forearm and kissed him on the cheek. Tamarind forgot that she couldn't hum and tried to do so unobtrusively. A whispery sound filled her mouth. She truncated it.

"Good luck with everything, John. I'll look you up next time I'm in Boston." Zoë smirked at Tamarind, nodded at Stefan, and turned on her Doc Marten's and left.

Tamarind waited until her former rival had disappeared down the cinder-block hallway, her musky fragrance clouding the office, before turning to John. "What did she mean?"

John cleared his throat, looked down at the cup in his hand as if he had no idea how it got there, and then tossed it into his wastebasket. He glanced at Stefan and back. "Uh, Indian food?"

Tamarind couldn't believe he hadn't answered her. "What?" Incredulity sharpened her voice.

John blinked, surprised. "I just thought we could talk outside."

"Why not here?" Tamarind found his manner maddening.

"Well, um, we won't bore Stefan here."

"What's Stefan got to do with it?" Angry puzzlement crackled from her.

"T, I think John's trying to convey the idea that it's none of my business. I can leave." He stood up.

"No, no, that won't be necessary. Sarah's hungry. We'll just head down to the cart." John sounded shaken.

Tamarind's anger scalded her, but she agreed. "Sure." She smiled at Stefan, a wide, false, happy smile that caused him to shift and mutter. "See ya, Stefan. Thanks for the stuffed animals."

She slipped her hair behind her ear, grabbed the handle of Sarah's stroller and wheeled it around so fast that John had to step out of the way or risk having his toes run over by large, rubber wheels. She pushed so fast that he didn't catch up until she'd stopped in front of the elevator.

"Tam–" John gripped her elbow as she reached forward to punch the elevator button. "Tam, I'm sorry."

Tamarind pulled her elbow away. "Don't touch me." She didn't wait for the Indian faculty member, the middle-aged white industry visitor, or the Asian graduate student to exit the elevator; she shoved the stroller through the doors while they still slid open.

"Tam."

"What were you doing with Zoë? What did she mean about looking you up in Boston?" Her chin trembled. That's when she recognized her hurt.

"Please, let's wait." He touched her side, but she didn't react. When she looked at him, he kissed her. For the first time ever, she pulled away.

At the next floor, a group of students, undergraduates by the look of the sparse beards and full faces, boarded. John squeezed next to Tamarind, who wedged herself into the corner of the elevator. Her anger had cooled enough that the hurt took precedence. Both were strange and frightening to her.

When the elevator reached the ground floor of Wean and the doors slid open, letting in people carrying backpacks and takeout containers filled with aromatic Indian food, the intensity of these new emotions abated. The rich smell of *masala* with its complicated blend of coriander and cumin, cardamom and ginger lulled and soothed her, like incense burned during Mass or perfumed candles next to her bathtub. She relaxed and let John rest his hand on her lower back.

They reached the lobby of Building D where Star of India daily brought stacks of Styrofoam containers filled with steaming chicken curry, or *chana masala*, or beef *korma* to sell to the fortunate few who knew about the deliveries. Today, the entrees were lamb *vindaloo* and *palak paneer*. John bought two of the *palak paneer*, which came with *naan* and an order of vegetable *samosas*. Still not speaking to each other, they took the elevator back up through Wean and got out at the lobby. John guided them to the cut where dozens of people idled in the gorgeous sunlight, eating their lunches while sitting on any available flat surface: benches, the grass, and steps. John stopped in front of Hammerschlag Hall and sat down. Tamarind parked the stroller and stood waiting while John handed Sarah a *samosa*. Sarah bit into it, waving the deep-fried pillow around her head so that flecks of chunky potato and peas flew through the air.

"Thanks." Tamarind sat on the far side of the stroller. She opened the Styrofoam box that he passed to her and dipped a fork into the creamy spinach and cheese. Savoring the taste of the clove-scented *palak paneer* almost made up for not being able to hum. The clove reminded her of Ana.

John hadn't touched his food. "Zoë came to a talk I gave this morning. We got some coffee to discuss our research, that's all."

"Couldn't you have just chatted there? Why'd you go into Oakland?"

He ran the palm of his hand over his head, pulling some fine hairs from his ponytail. "Look, Tam, we're colleagues. We've spent the last four years avoiding each other at every departmental gathering and IC event. I thought it was about time I treated her with the professional respect she deserves. I didn't think you'd care after all this time."

That sounded reasonable. But then she remembered Zoë's parting comment. "What's Boston got to do with your research?"

Something flitted across his face. Again, she thought it might be guilt, but she couldn't be sure. "I got an offer this morning to work for that startup in Boston."

"I remember the interview. But she said she'd see you there." Tamarind waited until John looked at her. "Weren't you going to talk to me before you took the job first?"

He squirmed. "I should have, I admit. I just was so excited, I said yes right away. Now I can work for Dr. Mukarjee."

She knew that. She'd known that he'd wanted the job at Dr2Dr so that he could also work for Dr. Mukarjee's non-profit IndiaClinic. But he'd told Zoë first. He hadn't told *her*, his wife. "I guess I don't rate."

"What?" Now it was his turn to look bemused. "Rate? Of course you do. If you don't want to move to Boston, I'll call them back." She could see him struggling with something. Another emotion that she couldn't fathom. "I shouldn't have said yes without checking. It never occurred to me that you wouldn't want to go."

"I see that." She let hurt spike her voice. Well, if he could take away her joy by sharing his most important news with Zoë first, she'd keep her own news to herself at their celebration dinner. She calmed her tone. "No, no. You must take the job."

He reached for her hand. "Thanks for understanding, Tam. For a moment there, I didn't think you would."

"When do we go?" She found herself anxious now that the previously amorphous move had become fact.

"September. The start date's flexible since I've got a few things to wrap up for Steve here. Gives us plenty of time to find a house. I hear the market's heating up there so that's good." He frowned. "Hey, where's your Goddess pendant?"

Forgetting what had happened, Tamarind let her hand fly to her unadorned breast. She gasped and then remembered. "The clasp broke. I left it at home."

"That's a relief. I thought maybe it had fallen off somewhere. No way would anyone give such an unusual piece back to you."

"Drink," Sarah said. "My thirsty."

"Okay, okay." John leaned toward the basket beneath Sarah's seat. "What's this?"

"What?" When Tamarind looked down, she saw the mangrove box. The one that she'd put up. A chill threaded her spine. She didn't answer.

"Isn't this the box that Ana gave you after we got married?"

"Crying drawings." Sarah pointed to the symbols. This time Tamarind didn't object.

"It does look like a teardrop," John agreed. "Couldn't believe that old hag made it." Tamarind said nothing to this, just played with her plastic fork. She'd lost her appetite. "You should use it as a jewelry box."

He pulled the lid off. "I guess you already figured that out." He held her pendant by its broken chain where the mysterious moonstone gleamed around the star-fire blossoming in its milky heart. "I must have read your mind again."

Tamarind reached out a tentative finger to her beloved Goddess. How did it get in the box? Its touch restored her tranquility but answered no questions.

"Hm." She looked toward Hammerschlag and its distinctive tower, but her mind's eye superimposed the image of the curved line, the teardrop and the smaller shapes between them that dominated the lid of the box. The symbol tantalized her. She heard Ana's voice, hoarse and wise, in unexpected memory:

You are like the mangrove in reverse. You may try to put your roots in the earth, young one, but you will always belong to the sea.

Despite the glorious July afternoon, Tamarind shivered. Ana had been an oracle.

ملعمم

Ana sat in an aluminum chair on the small patio outside of Posada La Diosa, looking at the sugar feeders that Valerie kept filled for bananaquits and hummingbirds. The morning sun warmed the back of her neck and loosened her stiff fingers around the coffee cup in front of her. On the table sat a small shell-shaped dish that Valerie had given her for her clove cigarettes, which Valerie had gently asked her to smoke outside. Ana picked up the coffee and sipped it even though it still steamed. The piquant flavor of roasted tamarind seeds cleansed her palate and roused her senses. She smiled at the taste, the folds around her eyes collapsing in until it would have been impossible for someone who didn't know her to see the blindness in the left one.

"So, was I right? The roasted tamarind seeds add something to the coffee, don't they?" Valerie and her feline shadow joined Ana.

"Never doubted it." Ana picked up her clove cigarette and inhaled. "You're a wise woman. I don't ever forget it."

Valerie laughed. "You're too kind. But it's nice to hear all the same."

"We both know the uses of flattery." Ana tapped the ash from the end of her hand-rolled cigarette. "Pretty words can't fool us."

"True. Although sometimes I wish I could be deceived, especially now at my age."

"Shouldn't feed them, you know."

"Feed who?" Valerie had started to sip her coffee and paused with the cup raised partway to her lips.

"The bananaquits and the hummingbirds. They're useless. Won't know what to do if you ever leave."

270

"I don't judge the worth of my companions on their usefulness to me. Besides, they *are* useful, if you consider how beautiful they are and how well they pollinate my *flor de maga* and honeysuckle."

"You're sentimental, my friend."

Valerie shrugged and finished her coffee. "I can afford to be. Much has been given to me. It's my duty to give back." She stood up. "Can I get you more coffee? Some banana bread? No? You know where to find me if you need anything."

Ana smiled and stubbed her clove cigarette on the bottom of the dish. She watched Valerie's straight pale hair sway along her back as she walked back into the Posada La Diosa. A shadow glided across the wall behind her and she looked up to see a large laughing gull, its wings extended stiffly, riding a current of air above her. It banked sharply and descended steeply toward the feeders where the bright yellow-and-black bananaquits and emerald hummingbirds flitted and hovered. The smaller birds scattered as the laughing gull plowed through their feeding area. Its mocking, simian laughter echoed off the canal beside her.

Ana watched the bird ascend toward the morning sky again and then swallowed the final mouthful of cold coffee in her cup.

Twenty-four

ᔆ

JUST BEFORE SHE MET THE WILKERSONS, Lucy Romero dug up the pearl necklace that her husband Billy had given her after she'd discovered his first mistress twenty-five years ago. On the morning that the necklace resurfaced in her life, she'd been outside since eight a.m. clearing away the last of the dead grass in the plot on the side of the driveway, removing roots gnawed by grubs and blades made limp by August's drought, when her spade struck something. Whatever she'd hit, it was neither dirt nor rock and she dropped the spade and knelt down to free the item from the still-compacted soil. She picked up the indistinct lump and brushed at its uneven layer of dirt.

"What's this?" she asked her cat, Custard, who lay on the sun-warmed pavement near her. Custard only squeezed her eyes tighter as if the light hurt them and flicked her tail once. Almost as soon as she'd asked, Lucy realized what she gripped. "Oh, Lord."

She held a warped wood box that had once had a shell on the lid. Billy bought it for her the first summer that they took the kids to Maine, right after he got his promotion and a bigger sales territory. She saw his boyish grin again as he handed it to her while their boys played Frisbee in the surf and their eldest, Dorothy, sat reading a teen magazine.

"Open it," he'd urged when she would have continued caressing the lid.

Inside was a blue freshwater-pearl necklace that must have cost every cent of his pay raise. Lucy let him slip its cold beaded weight around her neck without a word.

Lost in this memory, she didn't hear the moving truck rumbling a few blocks away at first, its gears grinding every time the driver shifted at a corner. Not until it pulled up in front of the yellow colonial diagonally across Arbor Lane, squeaking to a halt, did Lucy look up from the dirt-encrusted box and its buried treasure.

The yellow colonial hadn't been on the market long when *Sale Pending* had appeared above the *For Sale* sign. That had been in July and whenever she'd glanced across the street Lucy had played a guessing game with herself, trying to picture what the new occupants would look like, how they would spend their time outside, whether they would be neighborly and prone to gardening or whether they would disappear within the walls of their home like hibernating bears.

She lowered her gaze again to the disintegrating box but didn't open it. After a moment, she carefully set it on the driveway next to the orange tabby, leaned back on her heels and surveyed the promise of bare earth before her. The dry, hard soil had been hard to break up with her spade and her shoulders and hands ached from the honest work. Before she could plant the mass of bulbs lying in wait along the front walk or scatter wildflower seeds in a thick blanket over their bed, she would have to work in six inches of compost.

Sighing, she shoved the spade into the dirt a few inches in front of her and leveraged herself to her feet against its handle. Pain stabbed her lower back and hips as she stood, and her knees ached from being pressed into the driveway. She walked stiffly around the nearest corner of the house toward her garden shed where she removed a red wagon, bleached pink from the sun and rusty around the inner rim. Years ago, Billy had modified the sides of the wagon with pieces of plywood so that she could scoop in more compost.

After shoveling as much compost into the wagon as her arms and back could bear, Lucy pulled it back toward the new flowerbed. She'd just rounded the corner of her house when she saw a black VW Jetta and a green Ford Taurus wagon parked in the driveway of the yellow colonial. By now, the owners had opened the front door and the movers, men who might have played college football, carried furniture and boxes through the open door. They reminded Lucy of ants at a cookout, especially when one of them hoisted a wardrobe box onto his back. There was, of course, no way to identify the owners by the nondescript boxes and tantalizing bits of beds and bookcases that she saw.

Lucy shoveled compost onto the stripped earth and returned to the composter for another load. This second load, and a third one, she added to the first until she'd brought enough to make the soil moister and spongier. She worked the compost composed of decaying leaves, grass clippings, and kitchen scraps into the new bed, turning the shovel until her hands blistered. As she worked, she stole glances at the yellow colonial.

She'd just finished working the compost into the soil when she heard voices across the street and sat back on her heels to look over her shoulder. A young couple stood next to the driveway and watched the movers lug their possessions into their new home. They didn't look her way at all but took turns directing the movers and chasing after a little girl who kept darting across the yard toward the moving truck. Both wore t-shirts and shorts, but the woman's sandals sat in a heap on the lawn.

The dark, wavy hair of the young man's neat ponytail and his muscular chest and arms put Lucy in mind of the cover of a supermarket romance novel. When the young woman stood next to him, she only reached his shoulders. Her exuberant copper hair sprang from her head and whirled about her face as she moved; her bare feet gleamed against the parched grass. As Lucy watched, she repeatedly caught the little girl up and swung her around, laughing. In those moments, her t-shirt clung to her midsection and Lucy recognized the slight swelling there. The young woman too belonged in an illustration but not for a cheap paperback. Instead, Lucy pictured her new neighbor in delicate acrylics and colored pencil inside a leather-bound edition of plays. With Mustardseed and Peaseblossom her giggling companions, she attended a languid Queen Titania in her woodland bower.

Lucy stood up and rolled her neck from side to side and then rolled her shoulders back a couple of times. She pulled off her old green sweatshirt with its large white dahlia, now faded and webbed with cracks, and folded it before laying it on the front steps. After ten years, the words *Gardening makes the heart bloom* had nearly washed away, but Lucy still remembered her youngest daughter Rachel's grin when she gave her the sweatshirt. A shy grin that curled the petals of her cheeks.

Lucy picked up her spade and turned over the center section of the bed where the tulips would go. When she'd cleared a trough the size of a large coffin, she returned to the sidewalk and grabbed the paper bags of mixed tulip bulbs that she'd mail-ordered. Stepping into the trough, Lucy scattered the bulbs with sharp twists of her wrist. After all the tulip bulbs had landed on the moist soil, she moved a few so that they wouldn't grow too close together and then shoveled dirt on top of them. She repeated this procedure for the remaining bulbs—narcissus daffodil, iris, lily, crocus, and hyacinth—until the whole plot hid the promise of beauty just beneath its surface.

Half an hour later, Lucy tossed the empty plastic bag that had contained ten thousand wildflower seeds into her red wagon. When the bulbs had expended their energy, wildflowers would riot over their resting place. Life must go on. She added the hand spreader that she'd used and the spade, cultivator, and hoe. Finally, she unwound the garden hose and turned the spigot only enough to cause a gentle rain to fall from the head before walking back to the flowerbed. Waving a hand shaking from fatigue over the dark soil, she stepped sideways, careful not to block the morning sun as it met the cascading water. She punctuated this silent ritual with a final flourish and three large stones along the driveway's edge. As she set the last stone in place, something caused her to look toward the yellow colonial.

The young mother stood still, staring at Lucy instead of chasing her little girl, and Lucy had the distinct impression that she'd been doing that for some time. Lucy's heart lurched, but she waved at the other woman. Her neighbor waved back and grinned but turned when her husband called to her to grab the little girl, determined but unsteady, who now headed toward the back yard. She sprinted after the toddler, pale soles flashing in the morning sun, while her husband read through a yellow invoice and the movers, who'd finished unloading the truck, stood on the shaggy lawn drinking from large water bottles.

Lucy, hearing the little girl's whiny cries as her mother grabbed her from behind, remembered that it was lunchtime and wondered what her neighbors were going to do for lunch. She knew without a doubt that they would turn her down if she offered to feed them and yet as soon as the idea occurred to her it wouldn't go away. *Oh well, Lucy old gal, all you can do is try, right?* She waited until the moving truck pulled away and her neighbors stood talking next to their cars, the young woman holding the struggling and fussing child on her left hip while whisking hair spirals out of her face. Then Lucy crossed the street toward them, determined to sound casual.

As she neared their yard, she caught the young man's eye. "Hey, neighbor. I thought I'd come over and introduce myself. I'm Lucy Romero and this is my alter ego, Custard." The inscrutable tabby sat down at her feet, squinting at them.

The couple walked over.

"Hey. Nice to meet you. I'm John Wilkerson." He stuck out a hand; his grip was warm and firm. "This is my wife Tamarind and our daughter Sarah. We like to call her Roe."

Lucy turned to shake Tamarind's hand and stopped short. At this distance, Tamarind's eyes were in sharp focus, arresting her with their lucid, changeable blue. It was like looking into the heart of a lagoon and watching the sun play over the surface of the water.

Lucy might have stood there speechless for longer than was polite if Sarah hadn't wriggled out of her mother's arms to dart for Custard. Tamarind bent down to her daughter, her crazy hair glinting red in the sun over her sloping shoulders.

"Gentle, Sarah. Don't pull Custard's tail—she doesn't like it, honey." Tamarind's voice was low and sweet, almost as mesmerizing as her eyes, with an odd accent.

Lucy squatted down to speak to the little girl. "She likes it if you scratch her behind her ear. Like this."

Sarah laughed and poked behind Custard's ears. She looked up at Lucy while she continued to gouge the patient feline and Lucy, somewhat better prepared than before, was less shocked when she saw the same changeable blue. Custard, tired of the prodding, stood up, yawned and stretched, further delighting the toddler.

"I don't want to keep you folks because I know it's lunchtime and Sarah sure sounds like she's hungry."

"Yes, she is." John ruffled Sarah's rose-gold halo of hair. "We were just talking about where to find something to eat. Can you recommend someplace?"

"Well, that's kind of why I came over, in fact. I know we just met, but I thought it might be a neighborly thing to offer you lunch. I was just about to make myself some."

Tamarind, who'd been kneeling next to Sarah, stood up at Lucy's words. "We'd love some lunch."

John darted a look at Tamarind. "But we don't want to impose. If you could just tell us where the closest grocery store is or someplace for takeout, we'd be grateful."

"Nonsense. At least let me get Sarah something to eat while you go get your lunch. There's Angus's Deli over on Avery Street. They've got some cold cuts and salads—macaroni and potato and such. Then there's Star Market further down Avery, near Parker. It's not a big grocery store, but it'll do for lunch. And there's always pizza and Chinese in the strip mall back towards Dennison."

"Lunch! My hung'y!" Sarah stood up and grabbed her mother's legs.

"Okay, we'll take you up on your offer for Roe. But I can fend for Tamarind and me. Tam, why don't you take Roe over to Lucy's house and I'll meet you there in a few minutes with something?"

Tamarind nodded and bent again to grab the little girl's hand. "C'mon, sweetheart. We're going over to our new friend Lucy's house for lunch. How's that sound?"

"Lunch! Lunch!" Sarah bounced up onto her toes, straining at Tamarind's grip.

"Follow me then, Sarah." Lucy led the way to her front door without looking back to see if Tamarind and Sarah were following.

At the door, however, she turned and waited while Tamarind led Sarah across the street. They paused in the driveway so that Sarah could bend down and look at the wet dirt, blanketed with the splinters of wildflower seeds. The little girl reached out toward the garden, but Tamarind murmured something and shook her head. They turned to follow Lucy, and Sarah stumbled over a lumpy clod on the driveway.

Tamarind, who gripped Sarah's small hand, reacted by pulling the little girl up before she could fall on her knees. Then she stopped and looked at the dirty item, kneeling on the hard pavement before picking it up to study. Before Lucy could say anything to her, she stood up again and led Sarah over the flagstone sidewalk and up the steps. As they climbed the steps, Lucy had a vision of Dorothy at the same age as Sarah—two, she was sure— clambering up the concrete steps of their first house in a little white dress, white ankle socks and black Mary Janes. The image punctured the layers of years insulating her memory, leaving a sharp ache in her chest.

"Is this something important?" Tamarind held the disintegrating jewelry box out toward Lucy.

"It was, once. Here, give it to me."

Lucy took Billy's peace offering as if it were a piece of crumpled trash and motioned her two guests inside. She led them down the hallway to the kitchen, where she set the box on the end of the counter. As she washed her hands, she asked Sarah if she'd like a cup of milk, glancing over to Tamarind to make sure it was okay to offer it. The pixie stood looking around as if she'd never seen a kitchen before. Lucy waited a moment, and then she rummaged around on the top shelf of the cabinet next to the sink until she found a small cup with a lid and a spout, one that she'd bought when Rachel first got pregnant. After she filled it and gave it to Sarah, Lucy asked Tamarind if grilled cheese was okay for the toddler.

"Yes, she loves it." Tamarind said, not looking at her. She fell silent, her gaze on the corkboard where Lucy had tacked dozens of photos of her grandkids, but when Lucy shut the cupboard door, she swirled and said, "I should've packed something for her. I just wasn't thinking."

Lucy looked at the young mother, a loaf of bread in one hand. "You don't have to apologize to me. It's tough enough to move with a little one and one on the way without feelin' guilty about what your neighbor thinks."

Tamarind appeared startled. Emotions played across her face like heat lightning and disappeared. Her hand twitched to her belly and then dropped. "I just thought you might be wondering."

Lucy said nothing for a few minutes while she got American cheese and butter out of the refrigerator and assembled the sandwich. When it lay on the griddle in a pool of melting butter, she turned to look at Tamarind.

"I wonder a lot of things I shouldn't, but that's neither here nor there. You sure I can't get you somethin' before John returns?" She tilted her head toward Tamarind's belly, the spatula in her hand a greasy exclamation point. "I was always hungry with mine."

This time Lucy thought that she caught a glimpse of guilt. Had she spoken out of turn? "That grilled cheese smells awesome, but I think I'd better wait for John. Maybe just some milk."

Remembering the last plate broken by a grandchild, Lucy slid the grilled cheese onto a paper plate and told the two to follow her into the dining room. They were there when John knocked fifteen minutes later on the storm door. Sarah sat in a booster seat that

Lucy kept for her grandchildren, eating her grilled cheese and calling for Custard while swinging her legs. Tamarind leaned on the doorframe between the kitchen and dining room, firing questions about the pictures and collectibles around them faster than Lucy could answer. In a momentary lull, Lucy heard a sharp rapping. When she looked down the hallway toward the storm door, she saw John gripping a plastic grocery bag in his left hand. Bagged lettuce bulged between the plastic handles. She motioned for him to open the door.

"They're in the dining room. C'mon in and join them. I was just grilling myself a tomato and cheese sandwich."

"No, thank you, that's all right. Tam and I can go back to our place and eat."

"You need bowls for that salad and I bet I can find mine quicker. Sit, sit. Relax a bit. You can't digest your food if your guts are all in a knot." Lucy waved in the direction of the dining room and ducked back into the kitchen just in time to flip her sandwich. She heard the storm door rattle shut and Sarah's happy cries a few moments later. When she joined them, grilled sandwich in one hand, she brought forks and bowls for Tamarind and John in the other.

She sat down opposite John and next to Sarah, who sat at the head of the table. "Where're you all from?"

"Pittsburgh." John swigged from a bottle of tea. "I just finished up my post-doc at Carnegie Mellon University in computer science."

"Never heard of it—the university, that is. But I recognize the Carnegie and Mellon names. What type of work do you do?"

John assembled two salads while answering. "I work on the networks—all the wires and such—between really fast workstations and the disks they store their data on. I wrote my thesis on storing large chunks of video on multiple disks and how to get that video back onto a computer quickly."

"Ah. Well, I'm afraid I missed the boat when it comes to computers and you can't teach this old dog new tricks."

"That's okay. You're not missing much."

They ate in silence for a while. Lucy kept her gaze on her plate as long as she could, but Tamarind's copper spirals drew it away. Tamarind stared at the photos on the sideboard behind Lucy while she munched slowly on a baby carrot. Orange flecks collected in the corners of her mouth, which gaped open. Lucy looked toward John, who attacked his salad as if he ate in a mess hall and had to finish before war games began.

"This a good area for the kind of work you do, isn't it? I mean, computer stuff?"

John put down his fork and finished chewing his salad before answering. "Yeah, the Boston area tends to draw us geeks. I could've gone to California—that's where my parents are—but I like the East Coast. That and I got an opportunity that I couldn't pass up."

"Are you working in Cheltham or do you have to commute into Boston?"

John grabbed his tea bottle and twirled it between his palms. "Neither. I've got a job in Waltham with a start-up company that's planning to go into telemedicine." He must have seen confusion on her face because he explained. "Telemedicine is one way doctors can collaborate over the Net. They can send each other x-rays and patient histories and symptoms, for example. My company is still in the very early stages, but we plan to build an on-line community of doctors and a database of case histories along with some software tools for the doctors to use."

Lucy wished that she'd brought a glass of ice water in with her. She pushed away from the table before speaking. "Bound to be money in it somewhere. My brother-in-law is a doctor and he isn't hard pressed for spare change."

John held her gaze. "Mrs. Romero, I won't deny that I'm hoping to make some money off this. But the big reason I took the job with Dr2Dr is altruistic. The head of the company's board is an Indian doctor from Tufts who wants to bring better medicine to India. He's gotten doctors at Tufts to agree to collaborate with Indian doctors through the Internet and Dr2Dr will supply them with the technology. I'm the link between his project, IndiaClinic, and the start-up company."

By this time Tamarind and Sarah were done with lunch; glancing around him, John tipped his bottle straight up and downed the last of the tea. He capped the tea bottle and rose from his chair.

"Thanks for letting us spend a little downtime with you, Mrs. Romero. We really should get back and set up Roe's crib so she can nap."

"Anytime." When John reached for their few lunch dishes, Lucy stopped him. "Don't worry about the dishes. I'll take care of them."

Tamarind, who'd already started for the door, squeaked a little. Lucy looked her way. A pained expression flitted across the young mother's face and then Tamarind looked at the floor surrounding Sarah's seat. She came around and bent down in front of Lucy and began picking up bits of grilled cheese and shredded carrot off the hardwood floor. At the sight of Tamarind's corkscrew curls slipping over her slight shoulders, Lucy knelt down next to her, intent on shooing her away. Tamarind looked up through a tangle of hair and smiled.

"I'm sorry Sarah made such a mess." She slipped a curl behind a shell-like ear.

"Mess? This ain't no mess. I'd give anything to have my grandkids here making a bigger mess than this."

Tamarind laid a hand on Lucy's forearm while her gaze held the older woman's. Her touch was as insubstantial and fleeting as the brush of a tall fern along the garden path, but it sent a shock up Lucy's arm and down her spine. Her vision and sense of smell sharpened. Now Tamarind's freckles popped against her tanned cheeks and she smelled as fresh as towels hung up to dry at the beach. Lucy's brow knitted and her mouth worked and then her gaze strayed to the pendant nestled on Tamarind's chest that she hadn't noticed before. A rotund figure of wire pregnant with a shimmering blue gem winked at her. In response, a bug zapper hummed inside her skull.

"If it's a mess you're looking for, I'll be sure to bring Sarah over every now and then so you don't go without. She's my little hurricane and our house always looks like a disaster area."

Before Lucy could stop her, Tamarind stood up and dusted the bits of food that she'd collected into Sarah's plate before looking over at John, who waited at the front door with Sarah in his arms. The little girl's head lay on his shoulder, asleep after her yard sprints and lunch with a stranger. Lucy saw their gaze meet in dialogue, that ages-old communication between husband and wife, and felt the air ripple with unspoken understanding. It was a look that she'd shared often with Billy, a look disrupted by her discovery of his cheating and only just emerging again when Rachel reached adolescence. A look both trusting and fragile, not yet tempered by the trials of everyday family life.

"Thanks again, Mrs. Romero, for letting us eat lunch with you. I hope we turn out to be good neighbors." Tamarind's words dropped like bright coins into still water.

"Lucy. Call me Lucy." She walked them to the front door, her head still buzzing.

"Lucy." Their voices merged, Tamarind's laughing and John's serious.

"Please let me know if I can help you unpack or anything."

"Sure." Tamarind called back as John walked ahead with the sleeping Sarah, the little girl's face lost in a nest of curls.

And then they were gone. Looking around the now empty dining room, Lucy decided to leave the plates and the crumbs just where they were for the rest of the afternoon. Maybe Tamarind had meant what she'd said on her way out, meant that they would become good neighbors and little Sarah would come and sit in her kitchen, eating cookies and chasing Custard until the tabby's hair fell out from stress. She'd give them a few days to settle in, and then she'd take them over a casserole so Tamarind wouldn't have to cook.

She stood still and closed her eyes, remembering Tamarind's haunting blue ones. They were imprinted on her memory as a camera flash burns itself onto the retina. If she stood there long enough, she'd fall into those eyes, falling away from all that she knew and trusted.

Where, she wondered, *would I find myself once I surfaced again?*

Twenty-five
ແ

SIX DAYS PASSED BEFORE THE FOUNDATIONS of Lucy's controlled life began to crack, but even then she didn't recognize the warning tremors for what they were. That Tuesday morning passed very much like every other Tuesday—like most of her mornings, in fact. She got up and dressed, consumed a breakfast of Earl Grey tea, toast, and a fried egg, read the first two sections of *The Cheltham News*, and washed her dishes carefully. Then she went out and mulched the front bed under her living-room window. When she came back in, Custard following at her heels and wearing splinters of red-dyed mulch in her orange coat, Lucy brewed her second cup of tea from the used bag. The phone rang while she leaned against the counter, sipping the weak tea and writing a shopping list. It was her granddaughter Olivia.

"Hey, Gram. Can you pick me up after school and take me to the Minuteman Medical Center? I volunteered to deliver mail to the long-term patients for my community-service project."

"Sure, lovey. No problem. I'll be waiting out front at two. I need to run over to the Farmer's Exchange for birdseed anyhow."

"Thanks, Gram. You're totally awesome."

"Anything for you, pet."

Lucy wrote herself a note on a post-it and stuck it to the cabinet door over the spot on the counter where she always left her pocketbook. Then, checking her watch, she swallowed the last of her tea, rinsed her cup, and set it in the drainer. She grabbed her pocketbook and slung its strap over her shoulder.

"All right, old gal, I've gotta go lead the old folks around the Arboretum. Enjoy the sun and I'll pour you some creamer when I get back."

Custard sat regally in the middle of the kitchen and mewed.

When Lucy returned home for lunch, she saw a white truck with the words *The Piano Man—Your Hometown Piano Mover* painted in red on its side parked in front of the Wilkersons. She wondered whether it was John or Tamarind who played. An image of John—ponytail and all—seated before a baby grand in a tuxedo sprang into her thoughts even though she would have said if asked that a man with long hair was more the rock-and-roll type than a concert pianist. Maybe if Rachel had had a piano teacher at sixteen who looked like that she would have made it into Berklee instead of getting pregnant.

Lucy dropped her purse on the counter and cracked the refrigerator door open. Half-empty condiment bottles dominated the shelves on the door. Besides half a head of drooping romaine, half a tomato, and three hard-boiled eggs, the only other items on the glass shelves were a nearly empty quart of skim milk, a plastic-wrapped chicken breast, and a chunk of butter on a plate.

She grabbed the jar of strawberry preserves from inside the door and slammed it shut. A few minutes later, she'd assembled a peanut-butter-and-jelly sandwich and mixed up a pitcher of lemonade from a canister of powdered drink mix. Taking the sandwich and lemonade into the dining room, she sat next to the front window with a gardening catalog on the table next to her right hand. She ate slowly, but she didn't taste the overly familiar flavors and lost herself instead in the pictures of patented, easy-to-grow, long-blooming perennials and shrubs. Even so, her lunch and her perusal ended after fifteen minutes and she drained the last of the lemonade and stood up to return to the kitchen.

As she turned away from the table, she glanced back over her shoulder and out the window. Her neighbors' front door was open so that she could see through the storm door into the entranceway; every now and then, Tamarind or Sarah would walk by, oblivious to her scrutiny. She turned away from the window, unaware that at that moment Tamarind had paused and looked across the street. As she stepped toward the kitchen, Lucy's head throbbed. She felt lightheaded and flushed as if she'd had too much wine.

She lurched into the kitchen, her hand at her right temple, and dropped her plate into the sink with a crash. She poured herself another glass of lemonade before crossing through the living room and out onto the porch where she sat down in a wicker rocker. Later, when she tried to remember what she'd thought about while sitting there, she didn't remember thinking anything from the time that she sat down until the persistent ringing of the phone roused her. Only a sensation of floating—or was it one of falling?— remained from nearly two hours on the porch.

The caller who rescued her from this state was none other than Olivia.

"Gram? Where are you?" Olivia's voice shrilled through the handset and pierced Lucy through the left temple, starting a headache. "I've been waiting twenty minutes outside school."

Lucy started to speak, but her words caught in her throat. She cleared it and coughed. When she spoke, her voice sounded rough. "I'm sorry. Just give me five minutes. I need to wash my face with some cool water and drink something cold."

"Okay. Just get here soon. The teachers are starting to leave and Mr. Demerest told me he was gonna call Mom if you didn't show up by two-thirty."

"Now you tell him I'm comin' and not to call her. I'll be there in five minutes, little girl."

"Okay."

Lucy hung up and dropped her face over the kitchen sink. She pushed the faucet arm up, cupping her hands together and dashing cold water on her cheeks until they tingled. After a minute, she pulled a kitchen towel around her neck to catch the trickles from her cheeks and gulped some lemonade from the Rubbermaid pitcher in the refrigerator. No longer dizzy or hot, she snatched her purse from the counter and trotted to her old Volvo. The sharp sun outside attacked her until she dug her sunglasses out of her purse.

When she picked up Olivia, who was standing outside the front doors of Kennedy Middle School, Lucy realized that she'd forgotten her knitting bag. Her heart tapped a rapid Morse code on her ribs.

First I'm late picking up Olivia because I fell asleep and now I've forgotten my knitting! What in the world is wrong with me?

Olivia slid into the passenger seat. Her pupils had grown so large that they threatened to obliterate the warm brown of her irises. "Gram! What's wrong? You're so white! Do you feel all right?"

"You don't look so great yourself." When Olivia's breath hitched at her words, Lucy relented. "Yes, Olivia, I'm fine. Just some sort of spell, but I'm okay now."

"Spell? What does that mean? Jason Archer's grandfather has Alzheimer's and sometimes he can't remember who Jason is. Was it like that?"

Lucy spoke over Olivia's questions. "Of course not! I may have a few rocks in my head, child, but I'm not losing my memory, not yet anyway. I think I've got a few more good years left in me."

"Still, maybe it's something else. Maybe a blood vessel popped or something. Isn't that what happens when someone has a stroke?"

"Nonsense! I think if I'd had a stroke I wouldn't be here driving you to the hospital. You're a smart girl, but you're not as smart as you think. Now stop bothering me about it."

Olivia, her large brown eyes staring at the side of Lucy's face, said nothing for a moment. Then she said, "Sure, Gram."

They rode in silence for a few minutes before Lucy asked her how her day had been.

"Fine. Just fine."

Lucy didn't push her granddaughter to tell her more. She drove silently, thinking about the traffic around her and noting the fall foliage along Parker Road.

After a few minutes, she said, "I spent the morning leading a bunch of folks from Acton around the Arboretum. One old coot even flirted with me a little bit until I told him he didn't know the first thing about ferns."

Olivia looked out the window as Lucy drove. "I wish I could tell a boy off like you can, Gram."

Lucy waited for Olivia to continue. Just before she turned onto Concord Avenue, only minutes from the hospital, Olivia blurted it out.

"Why do guys say the meanest things to girls? Mom says it's because they like me, but I don't think she knows what she's talking about."

"What kind of things?"

Olivia stared out the window, again brooding. "Do you really want to know?"

"Yes, Olivia, I do. Remember, you have three uncles even if you never see them."

"Patrick Callahan told me I had the biggest tits he'd ever seen and wanted to know if I stuffed my bra with Charmin. I just stood there like an idiot, Gram, with my mouth open as he and his friends laughed at me. Then, to top it off, he asked if he could feel one!"

"That sounds just like a young man whose hormones are running the show. I hope he didn't try to follow up on his request."

"I don't know if he would have tried or not because I turned and ran into the girls' room almost as soon as he asked me." Her voice sounded strangled.

Lucy parked the car and turned the engine off before looking at Olivia, who still stared out her window. "Olivia, I wish I could tell you that this is a once-in-a-lifetime occurrence. But unfortunately, little girl, women have been suffering from the brutish ways of some men from the dawn of time." She sighed, a harsh sound in the back of her throat. "One day you'll stand up to the likes of Patrick

Callahan, I know it. But for now, if he bothers you too much, I'll report him myself to the principal's office. It's not the best solution, I know, but it's the only one you've got."

"I guess." Olivia got out of the Volvo and slammed the door. She leaned down onto the open window frame. "I'll meet you in the cafeteria in forty-five minutes, Gram, okay?"

"Yeah, sure."

❧❧❧

Lucy returned from the Farmers Exchange twenty minutes later and waited for Olivia in the hospital cafeteria instead of the lounge outside the emergency room where the TV's sickly greens and yellows substituted for flesh tones. After she'd entered the hospital, she paused long enough to glimpse one of those god-awful talk shows on the lounge TV, shaking her head. Society no longer consigned the weaknesses of their guests to someplace below its notice. No, just the opposite seemed true. Celebrated by demagogues, the perverse behavior of these wild, childish people had arisen like cream to the top of media attention and now appeared rife in human relations. Such thoughts always made Lucy feel even more alone.

She'd nearly finished her second cup of chamomile tea when Olivia appeared, her round face pale behind her dark glasses; she seemed simultaneously reluctant and anxious, her legs quick in their flared jeans while her slow hands rubbed along the walls of the corridor leading to the cafeteria.

Every day she looks more and more like Billy. Not like Dorothy for all that her blond hair now comes out of a box. Not Jack, either, though his drunk's complexion makes it hard to be sure.

When Olivia caught sight of Lucy, she raced to the table.

"Gram, are you doing okay?" She sank into a chair next to Lucy.

"Yes," Lucy said, by now convinced that there had never been anything to worry about. "You can stop worrying, little girl, I'm fine."

Olivia stared at her for a moment. Then she got up and went to get a diet soda without saying a word. When she returned, she sighed.

"I can't help it I'm a worry-wart, Gram. Every time I try to tell myself there's no use in worrying, I think of Pam and then I start worrying even harder."

At that, Lucy laughed, nearly choking on her tea. "Oh, Olivia, that's rich! Well, I worry about Pam, too. She doesn't seem to have your smarts."

"She doesn't have my body, either."

Lucy put her empty Styrofoam cup on the table and stuck her wadded-up napkin inside it. "When I was your age, Olivia, I was pudgy too."

Olivia's eyes widened. "But Gram, you're as thin as a stick!"

"Exactly." Lucy paused for effect. "And I've been thin most of my adult life, except when I was pregnant and you can't count those times. Being pudgy when I was your age kept me safe: I spent my time learning to sew and studying and dreaming about the day when I would be thin. It got me through high school and gave me time to think. One day you'll be grateful you still have your baby fat at thirteen. Pam, if she knew what was good for her, wouldn't be so happy she has that womanly figure she has."

Olivia sat silent for several moments, drinking her diet soda. When she spoke again, she was as serious as Lucy had ever seen her, and Olivia was a serious young woman. Lucy wanted to cradle her granddaughter, to shelter her.

"Gram, a few weeks ago—after school started—Pam and Mom got into it over a boy Pam wants to date. Mom told her she had to wait until she was sixteen to go alone on a date with a boy. Pam just exploded. She said she was old enough to know her own mind. Mom told her that as long as she was paying the bills, Pam had to follow her rules. Well, the next night, Pam snuck out to be with Chad and Mom grounded her." She fell silent again.

"The trouble with that is your mom isn't always home to enforce her decisions, is she, Olivia?"

"No." Olivia looked down at her diet soda. "She doesn't know Pam's been having boys visit her at home for a while now and I haven't told her—Pam would take care of my fat ass for me if I did. But Mom asked me to tell her if Pam broke the rules, especially while she's grounded."

"You should watch your language, little girl."

Olivia ducked her head and nodded. "Sorry, Gram."

"As for Pam, now you've got to make sure you're never around when she brings boys home, huh?" Lucy bit her tongue to keep *herself* from swearing.

"You always understand, Gram. I hope I'm as wise as you are someday."

"It ain't nothin' a few knocks to the head can't give you, my dear. And life has a way of givin' 'em to you when you're not lookin.'"

She wished life had knocked her a little harder, a few more times, before she drove Olivia home a little while later. Maybe then she would have seen what was coming before they got there. As it was, she drove Olivia home, not anticipating the strange car in Dorothy's driveway. When she recognized it for what it was, the shock wore off quickly enough, to be replaced with sudden concern for Olivia's predicament. *How do I protect Olivia from her mother* and *her sister?*

By telling Dorothy herself, of course. But then, she had to actually see the young man in Dorothy's house and she had to do Dorothy the honor of throwing him out as well. Where would that leave her in Pam's eyes? Maybe in the same place she'd been with Dorothy for the past twenty-five years, though God knew why her daughter held her in such disdain.

Well, I can handle Pam's rejection if it comes to that.

Even with all of her experience—and the experience of her daughters—Lucy expected to find Pam necking on the sofa with a teenage boy. Instead, when Lucy entered the house alone, having ordered Olivia to remain in the Volvo so that she couldn't see anything, an empty silence greeted Lucy. Pam and her boyfriend were nowhere to be seen in the common areas of the house:

kitchen, dining room, and living room. As Lucy stood in the entranceway of the cluttered ranch, pondering where her granddaughter could be, she heard a muffled thumping from the wall on her left. Her heart sank.

She walked the few feet from the front door to the hall and then stood outside Pam's closed door, her forehead resting against it. She thought about Rachel, alone with the kid who knocked her up, and she knew what she could not do: open the door without warning. So she raised her head, cleared her throat loudly, and then rapped on the door three times. From inside the room came a cry and more muffled sounds. Then silence. Lucy waited a long time and then rapped again.

"Pam, are you in there? It's Gram—I've got something to tell you." Lucy's voice rang out.

"Yeah, just a minute, Gram." More muffled noises. The door creaked open a small fraction and Pam, pink-cheeked, looked out at her.

"What's up? Where's Olivia?"

"Never mind Olivia. I want to tell you that I know perfectly well what's going on in there, young lady."

Pam's eyes widened and the rosiness faded from her skin. Then her eyelids lowered. "I don't know what you're talking about, Gram."

"Don't play coy with me, Pam. I wasn't born witless. Or yesterday. It's pretty clear you've got a young man in there with you and that you two were engaged in intercourse. Now, I don't actually want to meet your friend—I just want him gone from here before I walk out the front door."

"How's he supposed to do that without you seeing him?"

"Don't get smart with me. You gonna play games, you better at least learn a little more discretion. Look, do I have to spell it out for you? You've got a window—open it."

Pam stared at Lucy a moment, weighing her words; then she shut her bedroom door. Next, Lucy heard voices and the shriek of a window sliding up. After a few minutes, Pam opened the door

293

again, this time wide enough for Lucy to see the rumpled bedcovers. She stood there, head back and shoulders up, begging for her grandmother to smack her. Or lash her with a serrated tongue. She was tall, like Lucy and Dorothy, and blond. Unlike Olivia, her figure wasn't distorted or hidden—just curvy like Marilyn Monroe. *If she's not careful, she'll be the pudgy one later in life.* Two short years divided Pam from her sister, but there was an eternity between her and Lucy. Lucy's heart broke, something that she didn't think could happen again. Here Pam was, a child on the cusp of womanhood, screwing a boy behind her mother's back.

"Pam. I'm not going to lecture you. It's a waste of time to talk at you and it's not my place, anyway."

"You got that right." Pam scowled at Lucy and then seemed to reconsider her tone. She asked more tentatively, "What're you going to do?"

"I should tell your mom, but I'm not going to. I was, mind you, when I thought I'd catch you out front on the sofa with a boy. I didn't though, did I?"

Pam lowered her eyes and nodded.

"Since I didn't actually see you with a young man, I'm going to keep this to myself. On one condition, Pam."

"What?" Pam asked in a low voice.

"Don't get Olivia involved in your troubles with your mom. She's got her own worries. If you're gonna mess around with boys against your mom's wishes, don't bring them home where Olivia's bound to run into them, okay?" Her voice had started out soft and hardened into nails by the end.

"Yes."

"Okay then."

Lucy left the girls, her thoughts as heavy and dark as they had ever been. She'd clearly done something wrong with her daughters. Now a granddaughter flirted with disaster.

I could be an optimist and hope the third time's a charm. Maybe Pam and Dorothy will reconcile their differences before it gets really serious. Maybe it's my lot to see my sins visited on Dorothy. At this thought, Lucy crossed herself, shoulders hunched. *Forgive me, Lord, for my lack of faith.*

How could she have faith? Dorothy ceded much of her parenting to chance moments, distracted thoughts, and impatience. Would it change the course of their personal trajectories if Lucy told her about Pam? In the end, Lucy decided that the best thing for her to do was to keep her nose out of the affair. Her daughters had long ago taken control of their own destinies for better or worse, and nothing that she could say now would change that.

❧❧❧

That night, Tamarind couldn't fall asleep after Sarah's shrieks awoke them. John sprung from the bed as if roused by a call to battle for which he'd long waited and sprinted out of their bedroom door while Tamarind sat rigid, night blind and pinned to the mattress. After several more shrieks that overrode John's soothing voice, Sarah switched to crying. Her sobs rolled down the hall and through the doorway to the master bedroom and released Tamarind from her place on the bed. She slid from under the cloying sheets and saw from their open door that John had turned Sarah's light on. He stood holding Sarah next to her crib, shushing and rocking her, but she sobbed and pointed over his shoulder.

Tamarind scurried down the hall. "What happened?" She couldn't hear her own whisper, but John turned toward her.

"A bat. A bat woke Sarah and now she's scared to death."

Tamarind scanned the room but saw nothing. "Where is it?"

"It flew out the door when I opened it. I'll find it later."

Tamarind shivered and put her hand on Sarah's back. Sarah startled and then held her arms out toward Tamarind. Tamarind reached for her, but John kept his arms around Sarah.

"I'll take care of her. You go back to bed." He turned away to walk Sarah, who'd started sobbing for Tamarind. "Go on. She'll be okay."

Tamarind hesitated. Sarah's weepy, red face and contorted mouth bruised her heart, but after a moment she turned and left. She shut the door behind her and had walked halfway down the hall when the strip of light seeping along the floor from under Sarah's door disappeared. Yet her muffled cries still reached Tamarind's ears.

She flipped on their light switch. A black shape darted around the ceiling above her and before she could scream it swooped out their bedroom door and down the darkened stairwell. Tamarind pressed a palm against her lips and swallowed the noise rising from her core, somewhere deep in her torso. She tried humming, but her chest tightened and a squeak emitted that drowned out the sound of John singing to Sarah, who no longer sobbed. She put a hand on the wall next to her and leaned into it. When her chest eased and she could make out the shape of John's dresser again in the incandescent light, she stumbled forward with her hand still supporting her on the wall.

On Tamarind's left, the carved mangrove box caught her eye where it glowed a rich red under the lamp on her nightstand. She lurched and grabbed it. As soon as her hands wrapped around its mysterious *mer* carvings, she felt better and her humming strengthened. She held the mangrove box to her chest and surveyed the bedroom. The outlines of bed, dresser, lamp and shadows returned to normal size and her room settled back into its familiar proportions of empty space and solid furniture.

She pushed through the bathroom doorway to get a drink of water. Through the sheer curtains she saw a warm yellow rectangle of window on Lucy's second floor. She went on to the sink, where she ignored the cup and tipped her mouth to the cold water streaming from the faucet. She sucked at the water until her stomach felt leaden, but very little changed in the rest of her. She still felt dry. She turned back to the window and pushed the curtains aside. Setting the mangrove box on the floor beside her, she shoved the window open as far as it would go.

Kneeling, she studied Lucy's house. She knelt this way for some moments when the dark form flapped, squeaking, into the bathroom and bounced off the screen. No scream threatened her this time. Instead, Tamarind grasped the latches on the screen with her thumbs and depressed them, sliding the screen up at the same time. The bat returned after veering off into the bedroom and raced through the opening and into the night.

Tamarind let the screen fall back into place with a screech and watched until the bat disappeared into the silhouette of a tree west of Lucy's house. She knelt by the window, watching, until John came in ten minutes later and gently led her to bed.

Twenty-six
✿

MAKING SURE THAT NO ONE SAW HER leave town, Ana set off early for Carlos Rosario, near the northwestern tip of the Flamenco Peninsula. The morning sky ahead of her glowed blue-white over the dark tops of thorn acacia and palm trees and hundreds of sooty terns peppered the sky; their high-pitched *wideawake* call badgering all within half a mile to get out of bed. Members of the colony had left Culebra over the past week and soon a thick layer of dung would be the only evidence that fifteen thousand noisy sooty terns had bred on the peninsula over the summer.

Ana meant to reach the head of the Carlos Rosario trail before anyone else had gotten up and spotted her, but her legs no longer carried her as swiftly as she needed and a Samurai Suzuki drove past her on its way into town. Pinching her lips together, she nodded briefly at the driver's honk and wave. The entire back of her body ached with the effort of standing upright, and she overcompensated so that she leaned into the walk as if the rise of the road took her up a mountainside. After she'd reached the apex of her climb, she squatted next to the side of the road and panted. Across from her a small group of wild horses stood under a stand of thorn acacia. The largest one, a chestnut stallion, stared at her for a long moment. Abruptly, he broke his gaze, whinnied to his companions, and trotted away with the others streaming behind him.

Ana's breathing slowed and energy filled her legs. She closed her eyes and sighed through parted lips. When she started walking again, she walked more quickly and easily. As she reached the parking lot for Playa Flamenco, she heard the distinct *kreeak* of a sooty tern overhead. It was followed by the mocking laugh of a gull. Shielding her good eye with her right hand, Ana squinted at the sky above her. A lone sooty tern hunted a large laughing gull.

"Ai!" Ana's cry pierced the warm air between her and the birds. "Ai! Fly, you fool, or it'll make you a fine meal!"

The laughing gull dipped its wings to acknowledge her warning. It veered down, its wings flapping rhythmically and strong. The sooty tern pursued it easily. Ana bit her lip and waited, her aching calves and neck forgotten. The laughing gull headed up and to Ana's right before darting left. The sooty tern matched the gull's maneuvers and continued to gain on the other bird. In a moment, the sooty tern overtook the laughing gull and sunk its talons into the gull's back, sending a flurry of gray feathers down toward her.

Ana watched the battle. Now morning fully brightened the parking lot as the shadows slunk away at the approach of the sunlight and the air around her grew hot. The laughing gull cried piteously, twisting and turning in mid-air in an effort to shake the sooty tern off, but still Ana did nothing. After several desperate spirals overhead, the laughing gull stopped flapping its wings, tucking them against its body and drooping its head onto its chest. As it went limp, the sooty tern lost altitude from the greater weight and lost its grip on the laughing gull's back.

The laughing gull dropped free of its attacker and suddenly its wings snapped open and it flapped in an arc away from the sooty tern. Instead of escaping, however, it banked and came back toward the sooty tern. Before the sooty tern could react, the laughing gull flew at its head, its long red bill stabbing. The sooty tern dropped toward Ana. She glanced down as it hit the parking lot near her, its eyes bleeding and its neck broken.

"Getting old, Ai." She reached into her apron and found some dried tamarind to feed the laughing gull, which now stood on her shoulder, blood and loose feathers marring its gray back. "Youth no match for age and cunning, eh, my friend?"

The laughing gull swallowed the morsel and opened its beak slightly. A soft whirring sound came from its throat and its bright eyes watched hers.

"Indeed, my friend, that's what we have in common." Ana laughed. "Still, need some youth on our side. Or youth that we control, eh?"

She raised her hand to the bird. On her palm lay a piece of dried tamarind. The gull dipped its bill to snatch the tamarind, but Ana's fingers closed on the dried fruit first.

"Ah-ah. I have a mission for you, Ai. She's been touching the box. Now my spells have found fertile ground for their mischief. Find her. Be my eyes and ears."

Ana held the bird's gaze for a moment and then she opened her hand and let it eat.

లులులు

The second secret that Tamarind kept from John, the one that he should have known about if their minds had still been in sync, flowed from the first. She wanted to tell John that she was pregnant again, but she found that she didn't quite know how to bring it up. Every time she thought about announcing it, imagining that she told John while loading the dishwasher for example, unhappiness descended upon her with its unfamiliar dark weight. It wasn't the way that she'd planned to tell him. Nor the way the news should be told. Never had she expected that carrying John's child would fill her with anything beyond simple joy. The longer she waited, the harder the telling became, the more that she needed to explain. As she struggled to choose the right moment, her unhappiness grew along with her morning sickness.

That had been a surprise, too. The morning sickness. She'd expected nausea, something triggered by an increasingly sensitive nose and strong odors. But this time it had been hideous, causing her to vomit all day long. She'd lost so much water that her ability to hum had taken on the sheen of myth, of something so wondrous as to belong to the realm of the fantastic. That's when she remembered Ana's advice to all the expectant Culebrense mothers who came to her.

"Eat seaweed. And fresh seafood, especially shrimp and spiny lobster. Babies need what's in 'em." Tamarind could still recall the fierce look on Ana's face, even wreathed in its eternal cloud of clove-scented smoke, as she spoke to them. "You do too. Got any brains, you'd make friends with the fishermen. Best friends." To Tamarind she'd once added, "They forget that all life came from the sea."

Once her morning sickness tapered off, Tamarind began to eat fish and seafood, the first since she'd left Culebra. She popped cans of sardines open during Sarah's naps and snacked on the fish like potato chips. She hid them in the diaper bag or among her lingerie. She hid them downstairs in her jewelry-making boxes. Wherever she might get the urge to nibble. She just couldn't let John, who'd adopted a vegetarian diet years ago, know. Somehow keeping this second secret challenged her more than keeping the first. It wasn't only that John hadn't started working yet, even though his presence meant that she had to sneak into the bathroom and spray deodorizer afterwards. No, carrying these two weighty secrets made her feel odd. Beyond recognizing her general unhappiness, she couldn't understand what strange riptide swirled under her surface.

They'd been in their new house a week when the undercurrent of unfamiliar emotions spiraled into a savage vortex that she couldn't calm. She'd palmed a sardine can and trod softly upstairs to the master bathroom where she sat on the toilet and ate the fish, greedy tongue licking every drop of fish-flavored oil from her fingers. She touched the tip of her tongue to the corner of her mouth to retrieve a final drop when she heard the bedroom door open.

Fear clutched her heart in its iron grip. She waited, hoping to hear the door again, but instead she heard John whistling. What if Sarah, as unconcerned about privacy boundaries as all two year olds, opened the door? She wasn't ready to face him, to tell him that she'd been eating fish because her pregnant body craved it. Tamarind looked around for someplace to hide the empty tin. She hadn't unpacked all of the master bath items, including extra towels or trash bags. What could she do?

Heart pounding, she whirled a handful of toilet paper off the roll and stood up, thought to flush, and headed for the sink. There she wrapped the toilet paper around the can. Turning the water on, she slid the bundle inside the cabinet. *Please, Creator, don't let John go under there.* She lathered her hands with soap, rinsed with hot water, and then dried them. When she'd finished, she sniffed her fingers. Her pregnancy-enhanced nose caught a whiff of fish, but she doubted John would. She *hoped* that he wouldn't. She stepped into the bedroom to find John lying on the bed, his arms behind his head.

"Where's Sarah?" Anxiety sharpened her voice.

He must have thought that the risk of their being discovered had caused her anxiety. "Watching a Disney video." He smiled his lazy, suggestive smile and patted the bed next to him. "Come here. I've got a few ideas for how we can spend our furlough."

Tamarind tasted the fish on her breath. Could she risk it? She hedged. "What if she catches us?"

John laughed. "Not likely. She's glued to that screen." His voice softened. "Come here. I don't have to be at the office to get my keys and parking pass for a while."

Tamarind wished that he'd leave, putter around with the unpacking, log onto the Internet and read email—anything that would keep him from seeing her discard the evidence.

"Don't you want to shower?"

"Sure. There's time for both. First things first." His eyelids had lowered in that sleepy, intense gaze he got when his desire began to overtake him. Soon he'd be too distracted to think clearly. That's when she decided that her best option lay in risking the fishy scent of her breath. She should encourage his loss of focus even if desire found no room in her roiling feelings.

She pulled her t-shirt over her head and pushed her pajama bottoms off her hips, stepping out of them where they landed. She hustled onto the bed next to him so that he wouldn't have time to notice the slight swelling there.

"Oh, ho! Eagerness becomes you." The green of John's eyes had deepened. He pulled her to him and kissed her. For a moment, she thought that she might get away with it. And then, he pulled back, frowning. "You taste funny."

Tamarind froze. Panic hammered her. She'd never been less than direct with John. What would she say? She tried to deflect him, to joke, as he'd do. She only sounded awkward to her ears. "I always taste funny," she said and leaned in to kiss him, her hand on his chest.

He kissed her back for a moment but then pulled away again. "I don't know, Tam. I think you ate something that didn't agree with you. It tastes fishy." He sounded apologetic. "Do you think you could brush?"

A sharp, unidentified emotion flared from the seething mix inside her. Confused and angry at being so mixed up, she pushed against John and rolled away and off the mattress. "No problem."

"Hey, wait. I didn't mean to offend you." She sensed him jumping up from the bed and sped up, but he reached the bathroom door before she did. He put his hand on her arm. "Honey, I'm sorry."

Remorse elongated his face and lightened the green of his eyes, adding a new emotional eddy to her already-overwhelming turmoil. Why did he have to look so sorry? She was the one who should apologize. "Can I brush my teeth or not?"

He sighed and stepped away. She snatched the door open and stepped in, shutting it behind her. When she looked in the mirror, she saw wild eyes and crazy hair. By the time she returned to the bedroom, John had disappeared. Dizzy with relief that her crisis had been averted, she grabbed the disguised sardine can and trotted toward the upstairs room that John intended to use as his office. He'd had the movers store some of his old gadgets and files in the closet. She'd leave the can there until she could retrieve it when John wasn't around.

The relief dissolved into uneasiness when she returned to their bedroom. What should she do? She regretted the lost intimacy, but something told her that the moment couldn't be recovered this morning, at least not without that awkward self-consciousness that had overtaken her. She hated thinking that it could be like that between them again when they'd known only open certainty before.

She couldn't decide whether to shut their bedroom door or not, temporizing by leaving it at the halfway position. Ignoring the bed, she fled to the shower. The tepid water, although lacking salt and treated with chemicals, soothed her. She stood under the spray and let it fill her eyes and roar in her ears. Faint echoes of crashing waves rose and subsided in her memory. She tilted her head back and opened her mouth to let the water pour down her throat. After twenty seconds, she began to cough and splutter. She had to stand away from the water then, acknowledging that its alien taste and substance couldn't satisfy her.

John wore a rueful smile when she came into the kitchen half an hour later. He handed her a cup of coffee. "Tam, I'm a stupid jerk. Forgive me?"

She wanted to avoid his eyes but couldn't. She smiled a little and offered up as much of the truth as she could. "It's not your fault." She picked up her cup and sipped just enough to cover her tongue. She couldn't drink the coffee. Her hand went to her belly. John would notice any time now. She had to find a way to tell him before he did.

"I could've handled that better." He kissed her. "No matter how strange you taste, it's all good to me." He changed the subject, renewing her relief. "Why don't you and Sarah come with me? I'll show you the route and the office. You'll have to drive in to go to lunch with me from now on."

"I'd love to see where you work. We can drive around Waltham, too. Just tell me when."

Two hours later, John drove them to Dr2Dr's offices, which overlooked the Charles River from a new office building. Sarah filled the silence at first, chattering about 'big bucks' that drove by, and once, a 'helo-ga-ga.' Tamarind, who usually sang a truck-and-helicopter song whenever she and Sarah drove alone for a distance greater than two miles, stared out her window without singing. After fifteen minutes, Sarah stopped talking. She'd fallen asleep by the time they reached Main Street.

John turned onto Moody Street and then parked in a lot behind the second block of businesses. He looked into the back where Sarah slumped in her car seat.

"This shouldn't take more than fifteen minutes. Why don't you let Sarah sleep? You two can visit me another time at work."

"Okay. Put the windows down, though. It's pretty warm today."

John nodded and turned the key in the ignition far enough to power the windows. He leaned over and brushed his lips across Tamarind's and then he left them.

After fifteen minutes, John still hadn't returned. Tamarind shifted in her seat. Sweat ran down her neck and between her breasts and her back melted into the car's upholstery. If John had left the keys, she could have switched on the engine and the AC or driven the car around the block, but he'd pocketed the keys and she'd left her purse at home. In the backseat, Sarah's tiny face flushed bright red and sweat blossomed on her forehead and upper lip. Tamarind opened the doors on the passenger side, but no air moved around the lot. Summer had reared up for a final huzzah.

After half an hour, Sarah began to whimper and stir and Tamarind's blouse stuck to her chest and back. By now, the illusory taste of Coke sweetened her mouth until she could think of nothing else besides the burning rush of soda down her throat. She got out of her seat, closed her door and maneuvered around the open back door to bend in and release Sarah's seatbelt. She lifted her daughter, still sleeping and very damp, from her seat and backed out before standing up so that she wouldn't bang either Sarah's head or hers on the doorframe. She positioned Sarah high on her shoulder and slammed the door shut.

Dr2Dr's offices were on the second floor over retail spaces that lined the western side of Moody. The outside door to the staircase was locked and Tamarind had to press a button to be admitted. After the door buzzed, she entered a warm, dusty stairwell carpeted with flat brown carpet. Sweat slicked her skin by the time she reached the second floor still carrying Sarah's limp form. She'd just put her hand on the door handle when the door swung open. In front of her stood a man in a white, long-sleeved shirt, dark tie, and navy slacks. White teeth glowed against his rich brown skin when he smiled.

"You must be John's wife. Come in, come in." Tamarind recognized the accented syllables from her conversations with Indian graduate students. "I'm Prasad."

She stepped inside the door, looking beyond the man in front of her for John. The room they stood in seemed to be a reception area. Across the room, a desk faced toward them. On either side, filing cabinets were tucked into corners. A small loveseat and a coffee table filled the corner on her right. On the coffee table lay a handful of magazines: *Entrepreneur, Wired, Modern Doctor.*

"Have a seat. John's still in with Mukesh, our bean counter." Prasad giggled, a sound that caught Tamarind off guard. "Can I get you something to drink? A soda perhaps?"

"That would be great. Coke, if you have it." A smile flitted across her mouth. She watched Prasad walk out, the stilts of his legs reminding her of flamingos wading through water. After he left the room, she eased Sarah off of her shoulder and onto the loveseat before sitting next to her.

The air conditioning barely cooled the room, but Tamarind no longer sweated. She plucked at the folds of her maternity smock and slipped a hand under it to the band on her bra. She eased it away from her clammy skin, releasing the sweat pent up against it. Just then, the floor creaked and she started, retrieving her hand and burying it in the crevice between her thigh and the loveseat's arm. Prasad stood over her, a can of Coke in his left hand and a cell phone pressed against his right ear.

"Yes, we're working on it." He listened again. "Yes, I understand. Yes, we'll take care of it. Wait, I'm not at my desk."

Prasad started to turn away from Tamarind without giving her the Coke. She jumped up and grabbed at the can. He paused long enough to let it slip into her hand and then he disappeared through the doorway, still nodding into the cell phone.

Tamarind drank half of the cold Coke without taking a breath. Looking toward the doorway to make sure that no one stood there, she parted her lips and let the carbonation escape. In the four years since she'd guzzled her first Coke and impressed John with her burping skills, she'd learned to release them more carefully, if less satisfyingly.

Sarah stirred next to her, rubbing a small fist into her eyes and sitting up. She blinked and frowned at the strange surroundings.

"My thirsty."

"Okay, love. Just a sip until we can get you some juice." It couldn't be long now, could it?

Sarah sipped at the Coke, wrinkling her nose at the bubbles and pushing the can away. She wiggled off the loveseat and toddled toward the coffee table. When she reached the magazines, she began paging through *Wired* with as much interest as Tamarind usually gave it. They remained in the corner of the office for another fifteen minutes without seeing anyone else. Occasionally, the phone rang somewhere down the hall and Prasad's voice burbled after a pause. Once he giggled and Tamarind's eyes widened at the ridiculous sound. While they waited, she prevented Sarah from tearing the magazines or picking up the phone on the desk whenever it rang. Eventually tiring of this reactive game,

Tamarind picked Sarah up and sat her in the corner of the loveseat and began singing silly rhymes that she'd made up.

Sarah listened as patiently as she could, but the dribble of Coke hadn't quenched her. "Mommy, my thirsty."

Tamarind stopped singing, pushed herself upright off the loveseat, and walked over to the doorway. She peered down the hallway but saw only four doors, one of which stood open. She could hear Prasad's high-pitched voice and surmised that he sat in that office. Stepping across the hallway, she stopped just in front of the doorway and watched him as he shifted papers back and forth between two piles on his otherwise-empty desk while he spoke. Sarah came along behind her and grabbed onto her jeans with one hand. Prasad looked up after a moment and saw them standing there. He waved an index finger at them and then swiveled around in his chair to face his window. Tamarind didn't move.

After several minutes, Prasad finished with his phone call and swiveled back to face Tamarind. "John's not done yet?"

"No and my little girl needs a drink. Do you have some water or juice I can give her?"

"I'll go see. I think Mukesh might have some cranberry juice." He got up and strolled past them. He passed by so closely that she recognized the smell of garlic and onion underneath his cologne. The scent of fennel on his breath pierced through the other odors when he spoke again. "Excuse me."

She nodded once and turned her face away, but not before her stomach clenched. She closed her eyes and soothed it with the memory of the smell of the ocean. When Prasad returned from the room across from his office, Tamarind and Sarah still stood in the hallway.

"Here you go." He handed Tamarind a can of cranberry juice.

"How much longer? It's already been more than an hour and we need to run some errands before lunch."

"You never can tell with bean counters." He giggled.

"I see." Tamarind turned with the cranberry juice and headed toward the reception area. When she sat down on the loveseat,

Sarah trotted across the room. Tamarind offered her the can. "Let's see if you can drink from a can without making too big a mess."

Sarah bounced on the balls of her feet and leaned in to slurp from the open can. Juice dribbled down her chin and onto her dress. Tamarind held the can steady until Sarah had drunk her fill and cranberry juice dotted the office carpet. Then she finished her own Coke, staring at the blood-red drops for a long time before going to find Prasad, who was on the phone again. When he waved his finger at her this time, she crossed her arms and frowned.

He covered the receiver with his palm. "What is it?"

"Sarah spilled cranberry juice on your carpet. I need to get water on it before it stains."

"Listen, man, I've gotta go. I've got a little emergency here. I'll call you back in five." He dropped the phone in the cradle and sprinted out of the office, nearly stepping on Sarah along the way.

Tamarind picked Sarah up and returned to the loveseat where she sat down. Her intractable stomach rumbled. She'd locked the Taurus's doors or she would have walked back down to get the diaper bag where she'd stashed a couple of cans of sardines along with Sarah's goldfish crackers. Right now, she didn't care if John caught her eating them. She looked at Sarah, who'd again stood flipping through magazines. The sagging bulge of her diaper under her dress testified to her need for a change. The drying cranberry drops on the front of her dress begged for attention, too.

Prasad hustled back into the reception area with wet paper towels and got down on his knees at the site of the stain. Tamarind slid off the loveseat and tried to take a paper towel from his hand, but he frantically blotted at the juice without loosening his grip. He'd managed to lighten the red to a pale pink when they heard a voice from the doorway.

"Prasad, what's happened here?" A short, dark man stood a couple of steps in front of John, who looked over his shoulder at Tamarind. "Why are you on your knees?"

Prasad jumped up. "Just cleaning up a little stain."

"What stain?" Mukesh looked down at the floor and then up at Tamarind. His black eyes reminded her of a shark's: cold and flat. "I see. So now our reception area looks like a daycare center?"

"No, man. I got most of it up. The office cleaners have stuff for removing stains like this. I'll leave them a note."

"Yes. Do that."

Tamarind rose from her kneeling position. "Hello."

Sarah squirmed on the loveseat next to her and grabbed her jeans again. Without looking, Tamarind knew that her daughter's middle fingers had sunk to the second knuckle in her mouth.

"Yes?" Mukesh turned his head slightly toward Tamarind.

John stepped forward and through the doorway, coming to a stop between Mukesh and Prasad, who still stood over the stain.

"Mukesh, I'd like you to meet my wife, Tamarind, and my daughter, Sarah."

Mukesh's dark eyes didn't blink as he studied Tamarind. "Tamarind?" When he spoke, the temperature dropped in the room. "In India, we have a story about tamarind trees. It's said that it's dangerous to sleep under one because it breathes out poisonous air."

John frowned and started to say something but then stopped. Prasad shifted next to her. Tamarind looked at Mukesh, longing to hum, to relieve her fear and anger. But she knew that she couldn't.

Just then, Sarah, who still clung to Tamarind's jeans, spoke. "My no like him, Mommy."

Prasad giggled.

Mukesh opened his mouth to speak, but Tamarind cut him off. "I hope the stain comes out." She turned to John. "We need to get going, John. I might poison the air here if I stay any longer."

Before John could respond, Mukesh spoke to him. "Go. We need to clean that before the investors arrive." He looked at John. It had been years since Tamarind had read more than John's mind, but Mukesh's thoughts showed plainly enough on his face.

He'd already been poisoned.

310

Twenty-seven

☙

JOHN SCOOPED SARAH UP INTO HIS ARMS and brushed past Tamarind and out the door to the stairs. He didn't look behind him to see whether she followed or not.

Clutching at Sarah, who clutched him back, he descended the stairs toward the bright square of sunlight at the bottom as if he emerged from a spelunking trip that had taken him into the suffocating bowels of the earth. With the light, came heat. And life. Behind him, Tamarind's breathing became the sound of a subterranean beast, loud and rasping. John twisted the door handle down and shoved the door open before bursting into the expanse of parking lot.

"Hey, the door nearly shut on me!" Tamarind pulled up next to him and stopped. She swiped a long, unruly strand away from her face. "I need something to eat. Let's find a coffee shop or something."

"What the hell was that all about?"

She looked at him. Her eyes narrowed and she pressed her lips together. "I could ask you the same."

John, his grip still on Sarah, ignored Tamarind and headed toward the alley on the east side of the parking lot. He heard Tamarind struggling to keep up behind him, but he didn't slow down or turn around to look at her. Mukesh's voice kept playing in his head and even the light from Tamarind's eyes hadn't dispelled the other man's presence.

"John, wait! I can't keep up."

He stopped then and waited. When Tamarind reached them, she sounded out of breath and she held her hand on her side.

"How about that coffee shop over there?" He pointed without looking at her.

"Sure."

Together, they crossed the busy street as soon as a break in traffic let them and entered the dim coffee shop. A bell clanged on the door as it shut after them, signaling the hush that replaced the sounds of car engines and pedestrians laughing on the sidewalk. A man and a woman talked behind the glass case that lined the left side of the shop; a lone customer sat reading a paper at one of the small round tables in front of the case. The shop smelled of home fries, fried eggs, bacon, and newspaper ink.

"Can I help you?" The woman stood next to the cash register, wiping her hands on her apron and focusing on them expectantly.

Tamarind brushed past John and moved closer to the case. "I'd like the cranberry-orange muffin. And a glass of milk, please. Do you have cups with lids?"

From the table nearest the register, John watched Tamarind negotiate her snack with the woman. Sarah got off his lap and walked over to the case, where she put her hands on the glass and shrieked delightedly at the pastries.

"John!" He looked at Tamarind, who faced him. "I forgot my purse at home."

He stood up to pay while she carried the milk and muffin back to the table. He sat down again and waited until she'd handed a big chunk of muffin to Sarah, who then returned to the pastry case where she squatted down and pressed her face against the glass.

"You better start remembering your purse, Tam. Waltham's too far away for me to bring you money whenever you need it."

"I know, I know." She spoke without looking at him.

He watched as she tore pieces off the muffin and stuffed them into her mouth, dropping bits on the table and floor around her in her hurry. Muffin crumbs gathered in the corners of her mouth after each bite and he almost handed her a napkin. When she finished, she drank half the milk down while making a face. A mustache rimed her upper lip afterwards.

"Why'd you order milk? You don't like it."

A shadow passed over her face, but he had no idea how to interpret it. She'd always been so obvious. "I need it." She flipped her hair away from her face, but it fell right back. "Look, John, I thought you were just dropping in today for keys and a parking pass, not to work."

"I was. I mean, getting the keys and a parking pass. But Mukesh wanted to take a few minutes to go over my salary and benefits. And then he wanted to talk about the current project and its schedule."

"A few minutes? Try more than an hour, John. That car got pretty hot after thirty minutes. You should've seen how red Sarah's face was!" He watched her milk-crowned lips as she spat the words at him.

His unhappiness flared into defensive ire. "You didn't have to stay in there. You could've put her in the stroller and gone for a walk. If you'd brought your purse, you could've gotten your own damn snack." He threw a napkin at her. "Wipe your mouth!"

She glared at him and ignored the napkin. Her earlier reason for milk drinking had just wiggled its way into his awareness when she stunned him with her next words. "I guess I really don't rate any more. You probably won't even care that I'm going to have your baby." She sounded both defiant and triumphant, attitudes he didn't recognize in her.

Her declaration hit him with the force of a nuclear bomb. "What? Are you sure?"

"Yes."

He thought about this for a moment. "So the baby will be here in late April?"

She looked down while toying with her napkin. "No. Late February. I've got to find a doctor for my first prenatal visit."

If John had been stunned before, he went blank now. All he could see in his mind's eye was Mukesh's white board and the project schedule. How had he missed the signs for the past three months? Why hadn't he had any inkling about Tamarind's state of mind? "Why didn't you tell me?" The strangled, angry voice he heard was his own.

Tamarind bristled and sat up. Her eyes shone, whether from fierceness or unshed tears, he no longer had any sense that told him. "I thought you wanted another child."

He took her hand with both of his and held her gaze. "I do." Even as he said it, a thrill of excitement sweetened his anxiety. *Another baby.* "I do," he repeated more fiercely. "I just wish you'd told me before, not today when you're mad at me." Not today when he'd just learned what he'd gotten himself into.

A tremor rolled through Tamarind. She looked away. "Me too."

Just then Sarah stood up and returned to Tamarind, putting her hands on Tamarind's thighs and bouncing until Tamarind fed her some of the muffin that she'd reserved for her. John said nothing. Mukesh's face, cream darkened with a splash of coffee, superimposed itself on Tamarind's pale freckled one and a chill lodged between his shoulder blades.

Sarah wandered away to look at the pastries again. Prints from her palms and the tip of her nose covered the glass case.

"Did you have to bait Mukesh?"

What looked like guilt fluttered across Tamarind's features and she shifted in her chair, muttering as she wiped crumbs into her palm. She looked up when she'd finished.

"I admit I wasn't very careful when she drank from the can and I did wait to get Prasad to clean it up. But I was angry by then." She raised both hands and tucked large clumps of hair behind her ears. Several strands sprang free. "I don't care if I baited Mukesh. He gave me the creeps."

"That's a bit harsh, don't you think?" Even as he asked this, John recalled sitting across from Mukesh, who was shorter and slighter than he was, but whose presence loomed over his small office. "You done?"

Tamarind gave Sarah the last bit of muffin, nodded and stood up. She bent to pick up Sarah, but John had already reached for her. Out of the corner of his eye, he saw Tamarind frown and turn on her heel, stepping briskly toward the coffee-shop door. He let her walk ahead of them to the edge of the sidewalk where the wind from passing cars toyed with her corkscrew hair. The door framed her in the bright sunlight and for a moment he saw her standing alone on an outcrop of rock on the coast of Culebra where he'd met her. Then the light changed at the corner and she crossed between two stopped cars and headed toward the alley that led to the parking lot. He hurried to follow her just as the shadow between the buildings swallowed her figure.

৵৵৵

Later, he called Dr. Mukarjee from the upstairs bedroom that he planned to turn into an office. Besides a desk and chair shoved against one wall, the room contained only a stack of boxes and a phone. Even though Sarah napped down the hall and Tamarind unloaded groceries in the kitchen, John shut the door. He'd left a voicemail for Dr. Mukarjee two weeks ago when they'd first arrived in Cheltham, but the epidemiologist hadn't returned his call yet. Today, he expected Dr. Mukarjee's assistant to offer to put him through to voicemail again, but she crisply asked him to wait while she spoke with the doctor. He began to pace.

"John! So good to hear from you!" Every time John heard Dr. Mukarjee's voice, he thought of Ben Kingsley playing Gandhi. "I'm sorry I never returned your call, but it's been a very busy month with the start of the fall term. You're not so far out of school that you've forgotten, eh?"

"No, no, I understand, Dr. Mukarjee. I don't mean to bother you...." His voice trailed off. He opened the closet door and stared without seeing at the jumble of items there.

"No bother, no bother. What is it?"

"Well, I stopped by the offices of Dr2Dr today and Mukesh told me that my salary package had been changed along with my title. When I told him that you and I had negotiated my salary and responsibilities, he said that whatever I'd discussed with you had only been conjectural pending final budget numbers for Dr2Dr and that even though you're on the company's advisory board and you recruited me for your project, you hadn't been in a position to guarantee me anything. Needless to say, I'm extremely unhappy, Dr. Mukarjee."

The closet distracted him. Something stank in there. Something *fishy*.

"Hold on a moment, John. You say Mukesh is not honoring our agreement? This distresses me to no end. I had no idea that they would refuse to pay you what you are worth."

John bent down and rummaged through the closet's contents.

"What Mukesh wants to pay me isn't even *close* to what I'm worth. Have you told him what a Ph.D. from Carnegie Mellon makes?" His hand found a wad of toilet paper inside a box of cables. He withdrew the wad and began unwrapping it. "Frankly, I'm insulted. I'd already taken a pay cut when I negotiated with you and I'm more than a little confused. I thought you had more influence with the way this startup is being managed. Was I wrong?"

The toilet paper opened to reveal a stinky sardine tin, still moist from its recent contents. He clutched it in his hand and gave his full attention to Dr. Mukarjee.

"John, I must apologize if I gave you the wrong impression about my role with Dr2Dr. I'm just an academic researcher who happens to know a couple of ambitious entrepreneurs. They don't always listen to my advice."

"Dr. Mukarjee, I can't work for what Mukesh wants to pay me. I'm not a grad student any more. I have a wife, a two-year-old daughter, and a baby on the way. We can't afford our mortgage on the salary he insists I have to accept. I don't want to abandon the

IndiaClinic project, but if you can't persuade him to honor your salary offer, I'm going to have to look for another job."

"Oh, no. No, that can't happen. IndiaClinic needs you. *I* need you, John." He paused and John heard him take a breath. "All right, John, I have to tell you the truth. I have misgivings about Mukesh and Prasad. I've known both of them a very long time, and our families in India are close, but they've always been focused on— how shall I say this—monetary issues. I fear they will choose the bottom line over helping people if left to their own counsel. I need you to be my eyes and ears at Dr2Dr to make sure the IndiaClinic project doesn't get orphaned in the mad dotcom rush."

John gripped the receiver. "I want to help you, Dr. Mukarjee. I want to do the right thing, but I can't work for those wages in good conscience. Not when I know I can make a few phone calls and have job interviews by the end of next week with companies that will pay almost twice that salary."

"Let me speak with Mukesh, John. I can't promise he'll listen to me, but I'll call him as soon as we get off the phone together. Will you give me this afternoon to do my best before you abandon my beloved IndiaClinic?"

"That sounds reasonable. Look, Dr. Mukarjee, I don't want to leave you in the lurch, you know. If you can't get Mukesh to pay me the salary I moved here for, then I promise I'll still work for you on the side if I have to get another job."

"Thank you, John, for your kind offer. Let us hope that it doesn't come to that. I don't know who else I can trust to defend my interests at Dr2Dr. It seems that everyone these days is more committed to lining their pockets than to helping people."

"Not me, Dr. Mukarjee. Not me."

John said good-bye to Dr. Mukarjee, stood up, and walked over to the bedroom window. This side of the house bordered on conservation land and a thick stand of trees met his gaze. Some of the leaves had turned orange and yellow already and in three or four weeks the leaf colors would peak in New England, blazing so gloriously that people would drive from New York and

Pennsylvania to gaze at them. He stared for several minutes and then turned to go, rushing down the stairs and out the front door before Tamarind came out of the kitchen. He didn't want her to see him. She'd know what was in his mind.

In the back of the house, he jogged across the lawn toward the trailhead between two maples. The trail meandered for a good half mile through the woods, splitting in a couple of places. One branch ended at a steep ridge where local kids had tied shoestrings together to form a thin rope with which to climb the ridge. The other continued on until it split again near a small stream. Here, the right hand trail curved off to the northeast between saplings and full-grown deciduous trees. John stopped and studied the bifurcate trail for clues about which one to take and finally decided that the northeast trail looked more worn and less wet.

John trotted between the maples and along the narrow right-hand trail, which was uneven and still soggier than he liked. Somewhere off to his right he heard voices and remembered that his neighbor's house, invisible through the trees, also backed on the conservation land. Perhaps other trails fed into this trail and he would encounter others out walking. When he met no other hikers after five minutes, he slowed his pace and looked around him. Except for the squelch of the soles of his sneakers and his ragged breath, a hush enveloped him as though the trees listened. Their arching, intertwining branches shielded him from the outside world, guiding him along a defined path where a misstep only meant muddy jeans and soaked socks.

The trail ended at a cleared area about the length and breadth of a football field. John's realtor had told him that a developer had recently purchased this parcel of land as well as more wooded acres on its northern border. When John expressed concern that the conservation land between his house and the field might be disturbed if houses were built nearby, his realtor had laughed and said that the Town of Cheltham had a conservation commissioner who could give lessons to Machiavelli. As he came out into the open, John discovered that another person already populated this leaf-rimmed sanctuary. She sat on a blanket in the center of the clearing with her back to him, her orange tabby hunched beside her. He recognized Lucy's sloping shoulders and shock of white hair before she heard his footsteps and turned to face him.

"Hey, neighbor." He hoped his voice sounded friendly and not annoyed.

"Hey." She stood up and brushed her pants with her hands. John saw nothing either on her hands or her pants. The tabby squinted at him but didn't move. "I see you found the trail."

"Yeah, the realtor let me wander around when I was here in July and I found the trail then. I decided to buy the house before I stepped inside it."

"That's pretty brave."

"Or foolish."

"You could say that. I didn't, though." She looked at him a moment, the sloping lines at the corners of her eyes reminding him of a hound's hang-dog look. "I've been comin' here for the past twenty years and I'd like to keep comin', if you don't mind."

"Mind? Why would I mind?" She started to answer when he understood. "Oh, you use our trail? Don't worry about it. You're welcome to use it whenever you like."

"Thanks." She looked over her shoulder at the clearing. "Of course, once the developer finally starts grading and tearing down trees, this won't be such a good place to sit and relax. Custard and I'll have to limit ourselves to the trail."

"Do you come here often?"

"Not as much as I used to. Before the kids all grew up and left home, I'd come here almost daily. It was the only quiet place I could find!"

John laughed. "Ah. That makes sense. I guess you don't have as much need for quiet these days, huh?"

Looking down, she shook her head. "Not quiet so much as someplace *separate*. Sometimes I just need to go somewhere where I can talk to God. My faith gets renewed out here."

John gazed off toward the top of the trees where the mid-afternoon sun had a magical quality that reminded him of childhood days spent wading streams and catching frogs with his best friend Liddy. "I haven't had much faith in faith since my nona died. I go to Mass with my parents and Sarah's been baptized, but it's all *pro forma*. You know? Nothing there."

"God's still there." Lucy stopped and reached out to her tabby, rubbing the cat's ears. "Though I've not always had faith in Him. I learned a long time ago I run hot and cold like a broken faucet. I figured out it's me. Nothin' to do with the water supply."

"Hm." John didn't know what to say to that. How would faith in God help him untangle the mess he'd found himself in? "So what do you do, leave the faucet open and hope it starts flowing again?" He laughed a little uncomfortably at the unnatural metaphor. "I'm sorry, Lucy. Right now, it's easier to believe in the unbelievable, like mermaids or magic."

She looked at him. "One thing about water, John: it finds whatever cracks will let it in." She paused, pursed her lips. "Course, it seems to me that when it comes in that way, the more fantastic it appears."

John took this in, turned it over. Tamarind, a sign of God's presence in his life? That was one way to see her, he guessed. He doubted that Tamarind would see herself that way, though. He decided to joke to change the subject. "That explains it, then. I'm so cracked, I've got the San Andreas Fault running from my crown to my big toe."

Lucy laughed. "Don't we all." She paused. "Enjoy your peace and quiet, neighbor."

John held out his hand. "You don't have to go. I'll go."

Lucy halted. Her face adopted a stern look that lost its strength in her kind eyes. "Now, young man, didn't I tell you I've been comin' here for twenty years?" At his nod, she continued. "All right then. It doesn't take me long to get in here and talk to God. After all this time, there ain't nothin' much new for me to tell Him anyway."

She bent down and grabbed the corners of the blanket, shaking it to dislodge the tabby, which mewled and unfurled itself before stalking off. John stepped in and together they folded the blanket until they'd reduced it to a square the size of a chair cushion. Lucy pushed the square under on arm and clucked at Custard. The cat's tail twitched, but otherwise it ignored Lucy's call until she'd reached the edge of the clearing and then it picked its way quickly across the grass and followed at her heels as she entered the woods.

John watched them disappear among the waving branches and sat down on the flattened grass. His gaze settled on the wavering line the treetops drew along the edge of sky and he lost track of time while he thought about his meeting with Mukesh and his phone call with Dr. Mukarjee. Somehow in this clearing, Mukesh shrank down to normal size in John's memory and Dr. Mukarjee's plight lost some of its gravity here. No matter what happened with Dr2Dr, the trees still reached for the sunlight overhead and the earth still nourished their roots. Even the future housing development couldn't touch the woods of the conservation land, no matter how closely it crowded them.

The ticking of his watch wormed its way into his reverie and he looked at its face. An hour had passed since he'd said good-bye to Dr. Mukarjee. Tamarind probably unpacked another room of boxes while Sarah played nearby, neither of them aware that he no longer worked upstairs in the office. When he began commuting on Monday, the rhythm of their lives would continue unchanged as if he'd never been there. Sarah had no way of knowing that he'd spent the first weeks of her life changing her every diaper and walking her after every feeding so that Tamarind could rest. She only knew that he'd always left her to work, whether upstairs or in an office somewhere else.

He pushed himself up from the ground and retreated to the trail without looking back at the clearing. As he walked back to his yard, the trees seemed to reach for him, stroking his arms and back and whispering as he passed. He touched their rough skin, acknowledging their efforts, before stepping out of the woods and back into his life. When he opened the front door, he saw Tamarind kneeling on the family-room floor with her arms buried inside a packing box. She looked up and her eyebrows rose.

"Where've you been? I didn't even know you'd left the house."

He shut the door behind him. "I just went for a walk in the woods. Is Roe awake?"

"No. I think our little trip wore her out. I've been taking advantage of it to get some unpacking done."

"I see that. Just let me get something to drink and I'll come in and help you."

Tamarind nodded and pulled a lamp out of the box. John stepped around her and into the kitchen. He'd managed to get a glass out of the dishwasher and pull a pitcher of iced tea out of the refrigerator when the phone rang.

"I've got it." He picked up the receiver. "Hello?"

"John." Mukesh's voice sounded reedy over the telephone.

"Yes?"

"I've just spoken with Dr. Mukarjee. He has a very high opinion of you and can be very persuasive. I told him that we're in no position to pay you market wages, but we can meet the salary you and he discussed if we don't hire any other programmers right away. That means you'll have to cover some of our programming needs until we get some more funding. We'll also double our stock offer, but you'll still have to work four years before you're fully vested." He paused a moment. "Is this acceptable to you?"

The pinball of John's thoughts bounced off the sides of his mind, lighting up too many areas for him to settle upon one.

"I need to think about it. But I appreciate you calling me."

"We need an answer by Monday, John."

"No problem." John hung up. When he turned, he found Tamarind leaning on the doorframe.

"Something wrong?" Her eyes impaled him.

"No, not at all." He grabbed the tea pitcher and poured a glass. "Let's see how far we can get in this room before Roe wakes up."

322

Tamarind let him pass her as he returned to the living room without saying anything, but he felt her gaze on him. He carried its weight with him for the rest of the weekend.

Twenty-eight

♋

TAMARIND DIDN'T NOTICE THE LAUGHING GULL until after she finished mowing the lawn and sat, sweating and tired, on the deck overlooking the back yard holding a glass of cranberry juice. She watched Sarah frolic barefooted around the grass in the mid-morning sun, the hem of her jeans dark from the dew that still clung to the short blades. In a few weeks—four or five, perhaps—the temperatures would drop below freezing at night and the grass would grow hoary. The first time she saw frost in Pittsburgh, she'd ignored John's warning to put on shoes and dashed outside to kneel in the overgrown grass of their duplex. Her soles burned wet prints where she walked; and when she pressed her knees and shins to the ground, icy damp soaked through the thin cotton of her pajamas. Ignoring her lower legs, she leaned over and pressed both palms against the grass. Her touch was magic.

"No, Roe! Stay in the yard where Mommy can see you!" She leaned back against the plastic chair, which the previous owner left with a handful of other plastic chairs and a table on the deck, and sipped the juice. That's when she heard the laughter overhead.

Looking up, she spied the distinctive grey wings and black head of a laughing gull that slowly circled over the woods behind their house. In the past two weeks, a Cooper's hawk had drifted regally several times over the conservation land, reminding her of the red-tailed hawk that she'd observed in Pittsburgh. Gulls rarely made their way so far inland, although she'd watched several fly over the parking lot of the Star Market in Waltham when she and John loaded groceries into the Taurus last week. But those had been common gulls, not laughing gulls. Tamarind frowned and tried to remember if laughing gulls even came this far north.

She followed the laughing gull as it arced away from the woods, an indistinguishable gray speck in a brilliant autumn sky, and then headed back toward her. It continued flying, turning its head to stare at her as it passed on its way to the far end of its elliptical flight path. Something in its manner as it turned away and stroked the air low over the forest reminded her of another laughing gull, one that she'd known on Culebra.

The laughing gull again passed overhead and continued on instead of swooping around and returning to the woods. Tamarind craned her neck to watch it disappear over the roofline, but then she turned back to the yard to look for Sarah, who no longer danced and sang in the grass. Tamarind's heart iced up and then wobbled against her ribcage at the sight of the empty green lawn before her. Standing up, she scanned as much of the back yard as she could while she raced down the short flight of steps to the ground.

"Sarah!"

Nothing but the sound of the wind in the treetops responded.

She ran around the side of the house and her gaze slid across the street toward Lucy's house, which stood blank and unconcerned. Dragging it back toward her house, she investigated the dense holly and rhododendron that crouched along its front foundation, prying apart the stiff branches and calling Sarah's name again and again. Still Sarah didn't respond.

Lurching up the front steps, she pulled the storm door wide and listened inside the front hall. Silence greeted her.

"Sarah, Sarah!" Tamarind's voice caught and she choked Sarah's name out a third time.

Without entering the house, she let the storm door slam shut and stumbled down the front steps. Icy saltwater ran through her veins as she ran around to the back yard and on toward the trail between the maples—where Sarah had been headed a few minutes before when Tamarind had warned her to stay in the yard. The uneven trail dipped and rose over rocky, damp ground better suited to a mountain goat than an unsteady two-year-old and the sparse undergrowth scarcely served as a barrier for an intrepid toddler who recognized no paths.

Panting, Tamarind laid a hand on her side where a sharp ache threatened her pace. For a moment, the gait of pregnant woman grew strange as her hips swung from side to side and her sneakers rebounded from the earth. She stopped at the trailhead, clutching the newly repaired Goddess pendant that thudded against her breast and bent over. Tree trunks whirled at the periphery of her vision, nauseating her. The oddness of thigh, knee, calf, and foot continued to overwhelm her. She had been born with a muscular tail, one that propelled her through saltwater. She didn't belong in this world skipping over stones and sliding along muddy ridges.

The Goddess grew warm against her palm and soothing vibrations soaked into her bones and traveled through her body until the ache in her side eased and her heartbeat steadied. The world around her lost its strangeness and the terrain no longer daunted her with its crevices and exposed roots. She focused on Sarah, listening for any sound of the little girl around her and searching her heart for deeper knowledge. Now that panic no longer dominated her, her hearing, inner as well as outer, cleared. As she walked, she looked around and called. When the path split the first time, she followed the right branch until it ended at a steep ridge. Then she backtracked and stumbled along the left branch until it split again by a small stream. Kneeling, she dipped her fingertips into the stream. Cold, alien water stung her skin, but she persisted until she knew that Sarah hadn't taken the trail along the edge of the stream so she went right. By the time that she reached the clearing, she knew that Sarah hadn't come into the woods.

As she turned back toward the trail, she caught sight of the Cooper's hawk darting into the trees on the far side of the woods. She paused to watch. Within seconds the gray-brown hunter emerged with a sparrow in its talons. Tamarind turned back to the trail and hurried along it as fast as the muddy, stony ground allowed. When she came out of the trees five minutes later, her hand on the pendant to prevent her heart from accelerating, she scanned the backyard. No Sarah.

Even with her grasp on the Goddess, Tamarind's heart thudded. Ignoring it, she headed around the house and to the only other place that she knew to go: Lucy's. No movement on the silent street distracted her as she sprinted across the asphalt. She scarcely noticed the dark blue van in the driveway, but the open front door registered long enough for her to crane her head at any number of angles to try to see past the reflection of the storm door and down the hallway. She rapped on the glass after a moment and stood waiting, her fingers curled around her pendant.

A boy, somewhere between eight and ten, came and cracked the door open. His brown eyes showed no emotion under his long bangs. He said nothing.

"Is–is Lucy here?" Her voice escaped on her breath, uneven and raspy.

He nodded. "I'll go get Gram" He let the door shut without asking her inside.

Seconds later, Lucy's tall figure hurried down the hall, her white hair like mown grass and her eyes blue as daybreak. She opened the door wide and waved Tamarind inside.

"Tamarind! I was just coming to find you. I got your number from information, but when you didn't answer, I knew you must be out looking for Sarah."

"She's here." Tamarind's knees turned into shell-less oysters, rubbery and without structure. She leaned on the doorframe.

"Mom, should I feed her? She's just tried some of Custard's food." A thin shadow appeared behind Lucy, followed by a young echo of Lucy's face. The newcomer stopped when she saw Tamarind. "Oh."

"This is Sarah's mother, Rachel." Lucy turned back to Tamarind. "Come in, come in!" She tugged on Tamarind's hand until Tamarind took a few steps toward the open door and then she let go. Tamarind followed her down the hall without speaking, Rachel trailing behind.

As they approached the kitchen, a little girl wearing a two-piece pink-and-purple outfit that didn't cover her round tummy or reach her ankles came to stand in the doorway with a lollipop in her mouth. Her tangled blond hair rested on her shoulders, but a few strands stuck to the sticky spots at each corner of her mouth.

"Hayley! Good grief! Let's wash your face, child." Lucy bent and grabbed her granddaughter's hand. "In here, Tamarind. She's following Custard around the kitchen. Custard's doing a good job of keeping her out of too much trouble."

"Except for the cat food," Rachel muttered.

Ignoring Rachel, Tamarind stepped into Lucy's white kitchen. Sarah crawled on her hands and knees in front of the kitchen sink, wriggling after Custard and shrieking. When she looked up and saw her mother, she pointed at the marmalade tabby and babbled.

"Sarah!" Tamarind rushed to the little girl and lifted her into her arms. A ligament in her groin, loosened from a rush of pregnancy hormones, pulled sharply. She winced and the pain sharpened her voice. "I told you to stay in the yard where I can see you!"

Sarah stopped squirming and looked at her mother. "My see kitty!"

"I don't care about the cat! Listen to me. You can't go where Mommy can't see you. Do you hear?"

Sarah blinked but said nothing.

"God, am I glad I don't have to follow Ben and Hayley around all day." Rachel sat down at the kitchen table and picked up a cup. "I'd blister their fannies if they disappeared."

Lucy, who'd just scrubbed pink into Hayley's cheeks where purple residue had formerly clung, stood now and grabbed the teakettle from the stove. She spoke over her shoulder while Hayley, eyeing the adults around her, sidled out of the kitchen. "Those are fine words from someone who used to routinely hide among the forsythia and stay there while I called and called. And you weren't no toddler, either. Eight or nine, I seem to recall."

She shut the tap off and turned back to Tamarind. "Tea?"

Tamarind clutched Sarah, but little tremors made the skin of her calves and triceps crawl. "I–"

"Sit down, sit down. It's no bother and you look a little sick. I'll make some ginger tea. Always good for an uneasy stomach."

Rachel tilted her cup up and then set it down hard. "When are you gonna make real coffee instead of this instant shit? It makes my tongue shrivel, it's so bitter and flat."

Lucy frowned at her but said nothing. Instead, she turned to Tamarind. "Do you want some saltines or anything? Are you still having morning sickness?"

Tamarind felt Rachel's gaze on her. "No, not really anymore. I'm fine, really. I'll just take Sarah home."

As she spoke, a blond boy with messy hair and a dirty t-shirt wandered into the kitchen. He looked close to Sarah's age. Upon seeing him, Sarah moved so strongly that Tamarind lost her grip and Sarah slid down Tamarind's front to land heavily on the linoleum. Without hesitating, Sarah headed for the boy. He shrank back, clutching onto Rachel's jeans and ducking his head behind her back.

"Here, what's the matter with you?" Rachel grabbed the boy's upper arm and pulled him around in front of her. "Go say hi, Ben. You can't stand here all morning hiding behind me."

Lucy came over and squatted down in front of Ben. "Why don't you take Sarah into the family room and show her the toy basket? I think there's a Winnie-the-Pooh tea set and an Elmo See N'Say."

Ben kept one hand grasping Rachel's jeans, but now a thumb crept into his mouth. He stared through a wavering screen of hair at Sarah.

Sarah walked over to him and stopped. "Where's toys?"

"C'mon, Sarah. I'll take you and Ben to the toys." Lucy gently pried Ben's fingers from Rachel's jeans and, taking his and Sarah's hands, led them from the kitchen. "Don't worry, Tamarind. Matthew and Hayley will keep an eye on them for us."

Rachel stood up and walked to the kitchen sink where she dumped her coffee cup out. She grabbed an apple from the fruit bowl next to the stove and returned to the kitchen table. "Might as well sit down and let Mom make you some tea. So, how far along are you?"

"Just past twelve weeks. My stomach's better, really."

Rachel nodded and bit into the apple. A sharp crunch filled the silence between them. She spoke before she'd finished chewing. "I was so sick with Ben I wanted to crawl into bed for nine months and moan. But then the rent wouldn't get paid and no one would eat."

"Why? Doesn't your husband work?"

Rachel laughed. It was a sharp, barking sound. "Who, Todd? Yeah, he works when he feels like it. I suppose your husband has a job that pays well enough you stay home?"

"Yes."

"Nice. I guess. But I wouldn't want to be stuck at home all day with the kids. They'd drive me batty." She took another bite from the apple. "What I want is a rich husband who travels on business and a nanny. Then I'd go shopping and get my nails done."

"What a fantasy." Lucy returned to the kitchen just as the kettle began to whistle. She turned off the gas and reached in the cupboard for some cups. "You don't have time to waste on such ridiculous daydreams."

Rachel's jaw dropped and Tamarind, whose chin rested on the heel of one palm, stopped worrying the edge of the placemat in front of her and raised her face to watch them.

"I can't believe you just said that."

Lucy turned in mid-pour, spilling some hot water on the counter. She set the kettle down on the stove and grabbed a kitchen cloth. "Good Lord, did I say that out loud?" Her gaze slid to Tamarind. "I've gotten in the habit of talking to myself. That's what happens when you're alone too much."

She brought a cup over to Tamarind, fumbling as she set it down. Hot water splashed on Tamarind's lap. Tamarind uttered a sound that was a cross between a yip and groan.

"Oh, no! Are you all right?" Concern sharpened Lucy's voice. Before Tamarind could say anything, Lucy swiveled and grabbed the dishtowel hanging from the oven door and blotted the hot, damp spot on her upper thigh. Tamarind put her hand on Lucy's hand, the soft, veined skin warm and loose on the fine bones.

"It's okay, Lucy. Don't worry about it." Lucy looked at her directly and Tamarind saw the down-turned lines at the corners of her eyes as if for the first time. "You know, you remind me of someone I knew on Culebra, where I'm from."

Lucy dropped the towel on the counter and wrapped a hand around a cup. "Why don't we go into the living room? It's more comfortable in there and my old bones need a soft seat at the moment."

Tamarind nodded, stood, and lifted her cup. She followed Lucy through the far doorway to the living room, stepping down onto an immaculate hardwood floor and into a room filled with so many plants that Tamarind recalled the Phipps Conservatory across Schenley Park from Carnegie Mellon. A moist, earthy smell filled the air. Custard hunched on the window seat, framed by several spider plants and table ferns. Around these crowded Wandering Jews, prayer plants, and a gorgeous monkey plant with flamboyant pink flowers. The conservatory had always soothed her.

Lucy eased herself into a rocking chair in the far corner near the window. Late morning sunlight obscured her face. "You're from Culebra? Where's that?"

Tamarind blew on her tea. "Northeast of Puerto Rico."

"Ah. That explains your accent."

Rachel dangled the gnawed apple core between a forefinger and thumb as she stepped down into the living room. "That doesn't sound like a Spanish accent to me."

Tamarind ignored Rachel. "I lived for a while with a wise woman named Ana. She always spoke her mind."

"That's not wise." Lucy sipped her tea and sighed. "Speaking your mind can be downright dangerous."

"When have you ever suffered for speaking your mind?" Rachel asked. She sat down in a plush velvet chair that swiveled and curled her feet behind her. Sun gilded her spiky brown hair and glittering brown eyes, softening the sharp angles of her face and warming her expression a little.

"I–"

Not meaning to do so, Tamarind cut Lucy off. "Ana is more like a healer. She gathered plants from the sea, like turtle grass, and animals like cone snails and she made medicine from them."

"That sounds like you, too, Mom. Always steeping tea out of some god-awful weed and telling us to drink it to regulate our cycles or get over a cold."

Tamarind giggled. "I bet she never made your dad a lotion with bird dung, did she?"

Rachel screwed up her face. "What?"

Tamarind laughed and tossed her hair. A strand fell across her face anyway and she brushed it impatiently behind her ear. "Sometimes Culebrense men who had trouble making love to their wives and girlfriends visited Ana. She made a very potent aphrodisiac for them, a lotion whose main ingredient was *guano*." She pronounced it as a Spanish speaker would.

Rachel's face remained painfully twisted. "Christ! They don't *eat* it, do they?"

Tamarind laughed so hard, the loosened ligaments in her groin stung and she instinctively put her fingers along the crease between her thighs and abdomen. "No, no. I said it was a lotion. The men, they would have to plan in advance and rub some into themselves—" here she made a circular motion vaguely above her lap—"and it would slowly take effect."

"I bet the stink sure drove their women wild." Lucy's dry voice cut across Tamarind's gurgle. "I've used enough bat guano in my time to fertilize my flowerbeds and vegetables to know."

Tamarind wiped moisture from the corners of her eyes. She felt Rachel staring at her, but the pained expression had left the other woman's face. "Yes, dried *guano* stinks. But Ana ground up certain kinds of rock and added them to neutralize the smell. She also collected a lot of other plants and substances from animals that she added to the *guano*. She used a liquid that she milked from cacti as the base for the lotion. When she was done, it smelled as clean as the sea."

"Did it work?"

Tamarind couldn't tell if Rachel sounded skeptical or not. She shrugged. "I guess so. I never personally saw it in action, but most of the men who came to her kept coming back for more."

"Did she ever give any wives a lotion to take away a man's desire?" Something in Lucy's voice suffocated the mirth in Tamarind's chest and she blinked in the older woman's direction.

"Well, yes, I think she did. When a woman named Rosalinda caught her husband making love to another woman."

"We could make a killing off something like that." Rachel's eyes glittered again, but the earlier warmth no longer softened them. "What's the key ingredient for this miracle drug?"

Unease tickled Tamarind's belly, but she spoke anyway. "Poison from a cone snail. It's very dangerous, though. Less than a drop will kill someone."

Rachel studied her for a moment, chewing her lower lip. Then she shook her head and laughed. "That's no good. Let 'im live with a tool that won't work, that's the best solution."

"Yes, well, if only we were so lucky." Lucy stood up.

Rachel looked at her mother. "I'm surprised you'd say such a thing, being such a devout Catholic and all. Where would we be if you'd poisoned Daddy?"

"Yes, where would you be?" Lucy said as she walked by Rachel on the way to the kitchen, then she turned. "Did I just say something out loud?"

Rachel looked nonplussed for the second time. Tamarind wondered if Rachel always found Lucy so surprising.

"Yes, you did. I think someone's put something in that chamomile tea of yours. Maybe you picked the wrong weed when you made it. Pretty soon you'll be speaking your mind like this friend of Tamarind's and you know where you'll be then."

Lucy ignored Rachel. "I'm going to go check in on the kids. Tamarind, help yourself to some more hot water. Rachel, there's some lemon-filled cookies in the cupboard by the stove."

"Those sound good. Whadya think?" At Tamarind's nod, Rachel stood up, picked up Tamarind's empty teacup and disappeared after Lucy into the kitchen. While she was gone, Tamarind got up and looked more closely at the photos on Lucy's mantelpiece. Five minutes later, Rachel returned with a tray that held tea and a long rectangular box of cookies.

"Is this your dad?"

Rachel set the tray down on the coffee table and looked up. "Yeah, charming bastard. You can tell by the cocky grin he's wearing in all those photos. You can also tell he had Mom wrapped around his little finger. That's the closest she's ever come to hinting he was less than perfect."

Tamarind recognized the grin that Rachel had just described as "cocky." Sometimes John grinned at her like that when he was about to win an argument and wanted to soften her anger, but most of the time earnestness ruled his demeanor. Lucy's husband appeared at ease with his power to charm those around him and Tamarind wondered how carelessly he'd done so. Lucy had sad eyes, after all.

"What's that necklace you're wearing? I've never seen anything quite like it before." Without waiting for Tamarind to answer, Rachel touched a fingertip to the moonstone. "Holy crap!"

Tamarind cried out and jumped back as Rachel brought her fingertip up to her mouth. She pressed her palm over the Goddess, which radiated heat.

"That shocked me." Rachel's voice sounded accusatory. "Don't tell me that's another one of Ana's creations."

Tamarind shook her head. "No, actually, I made this Goddess. She's a kind of talisman."

Rachel sucked on her finger, but she looked interested. "Talisman? Talisman for what?"

The unease that had prickled in Tamarind's stomach flared again, much stronger this time. She turned away from Rachel and walked back to the sofa and the tea tray as she answered as casually as she could. "It protects my marriage."

"Now that's what my mom would call a fantasy." Scorn sharpened Rachel's voice. "Only a fantasy could protect marriage in this day and age. Not too many women are as devout as good old Mom and keep the home fires burning for their men."

Tamarind didn't look up at Rachel; she already knew that the hard glints in Rachel's brown eyes would shred the dry skin of her face. Instead, she sipped at the ginger tea and concentrated on vibrating her core as low and evenly as she could. The tea eased her chest and let her hum flow through her and into her thoughts. The sound of waves echoed in her memory and she relaxed.

Rachel watched her. "I suppose you can't find a talisman like that lying around just anywhere. Magic can't be picked up for a few bucks, huh?"

Tamarind set the cup down on the tray and shrugged. Her hair cascaded around her face and she pushed it up and held it away for a moment. "Ana sells magic things, but a talisman like my Goddess can only be made by someone who believes in Her."

"Right." Rachel grabbed a couple of cookies and began eating one.

A loud wail emanated from somewhere beyond the dining room and Tamarind's heart plunged to the well of her stomach. Turning, she darted toward the kitchen door. The next few moments passed in a confused blur as she clutched a sobbing Sarah and tried to understand Lucy through the added din of Hayley, who chittered like a chipmunk, and Ben, no longer sucking on his thumb but babbling and pointing at some toys on the floor. Matthew sat in a corner watching cartoons, his chin resting in his hands. When it became clear that Sarah's distress had plenty of life left in it,

Tamarind lobbed her thanks at Lucy and retreated out the front door.

Rachel, who'd been standing in the doorway of the family room during the brouhaha, watched the writhing mass of child and petite mother cross the street.

"Mommy." Hayley stood at her side. "Mommy."

Rachel didn't look down but sighed. "What is it, Hayley?"

"Mommy, I found this. Can I keep it?"

Rachel glanced at her daughter and then looked again. Hayley held in her grimy palm the moonstone pendant that Tamarind had worn.

"Let me see that." Rachel knelt down and studied it. The delicate gold clasp was twisted and bent. "No, you can't keep it, honey. It's Tamarind's. Give it to me and I'll return it to her."

Hayley's lower lip curled stubbornly over the upper one. "But she lost it. Finders keepers."

"I said give it to me." Rachel's hand shot out and she caught Hayley's arm as her daughter turned to flee. She prised the chubby fingers, which had curled around the wire-and-stone pendant, open. "Now get out of here."

Hayley continued to pout and stomped a foot, but she left soon enough after Rachel swatted her backside hard. Rachel waited until Hayley had disappeared down the hallway to the family room and then she dangled the Goddess figure in front of her face. The deep blue stone in the figure's belly glimmered mysteriously as light played over its smooth sphere. Cool heat radiated from its depths.

"But first," she said softly, "I'll just borrow this lovely little lady for myself. Then we'll see if Tamarind's belief is strong enough."

◢◢◢

Later that evening, after Rachel and her grandchildren went home and she ate dinner alone, Lucy found the pearl necklace where she'd buried it among her panties and put it on. The pearls sank, satiny and cool, against the wattle at her lower neck. She rubbed calloused finger pads over the beads and an image of her younger self in a long black evening gown sprang to life in her thoughts. Perhaps if Billy had given her the pearls before she'd found out that he'd cheated on her she might have actually bought such a gown.

Slipping the necklace off and burying it among the dowdy lingerie that she'd resigned herself to wearing, she shut the image out and got dressed for bed. Afterwards, in the bathroom while she brushed her teeth, she had another spell. She didn't lose all sense of time during this one; rather, time seemed to open up before her. It wasn't an unpleasant feeling but an odd one: as she diligently stroked the toothbrush along her back molars, her thoughts on the Macintosh apples that she'd bought yesterday at a roadside stand in Acton, she felt her face flush and her thoughts became as slippery as darting fish.

And then he was there, in the bathroom doorway, as young and handsome as the day she met him more than forty years before.

"Billy!" She dropped her toothbrush in the sink. White foamed her mouth but she didn't care.

He said nothing but walked toward her and when she focused on her own reflection in the mirror, she saw that she was nineteen again, firm and smooth with shoulder-length blond hair. She wore the white cotton nightgown that she'd worn on their wedding night and Billy bent his head to the hollow in her throat, kissing it with a mouth of soft fire. She closed her eyes and leaned into him and he was as hard and real as her sudden desire for him. They stood that way a long time, his hand cupping her upturned breast and his breath hot on her skin, and then she opened her eyes again and she was alone once more.

Shaking her head, Lucy rinsed her mouth and then wiped her face with a warm washcloth. Even though she was sure that she'd imagined the whole interlude, she still felt Billy's presence all around her. Gingerly, she walked to her bed, almost afraid to turn out the lights. She lay and read a gardening magazine for a long time although she couldn't focus on the meaning of the words that her gaze skipped across doggedly because now Billy lay next to her, waiting patiently. Finally, she reached for the light switch, still a little dizzy and confused, and that's when she tumbled into the past.

Billy sighed and rolled over onto his side, half leaning on her. His nose nuzzled her left ear as his right hand stroked up from her waist to her breast, pausing before his thumb circled her breast in a slow spiral to the now-hard nipple. Lucy no longer cared if what was happening was some spirited hallucination; she sighed and sank down on her pillow as Billy's warm mouth captured her nipple and tugged. It had been so long, so long.

There was an audible creak as Billy's weight rolled over onto Lucy, a weight so familiar that she began to cry silently. Even as she cried, she felt herself moving beneath it, arching her back and twining her legs around his waist. She hadn't known how cold she'd been, sleeping alone these past ten years, until now when the warmth of his body heated the air above her and they began to move in a long-perfected fire-making ritual ... a ritual that ended when she felt a release deep within her.

Lucy fell asleep crying, Billy holding her close and wiping her tears with gentle fingertips.

Twenty-nine
ОЗ

TAMARIND SHIVERED SO HARD that her body rocked and her lips quivered. Her skin and scalp prickled painfully, shrunken and taut in the chill air. Beneath her body—which lay exposed like old bones from a desecrated burial—rough material scraped her shoulder blades and hipbones. Her arms wrenched behind her until her shoulders shrieked, but no sound left her. Instead, her tongue collapsed in her throat, forcing her to gag. Fluorescent light dazzled her.

"Tamarind, love, it's all right." Warm breath caressed her earlobe and gentle hands lifted her into an embrace. Her shivering increased.

"It's only a dream, love. It's not real. You're here with me now."

Tamarind tried to answer, but her tongue choked her and she whimpered and thrashed.

An arm remained secure, holding her close to warm skin while a hand fumbled below her. After several seconds, a down comforter and sheets flowed over her from the bunched material at her feet. Still she shivered, but the sensation of being exposed faded and her legs quit jerking.

"Sh, sweetheart. Sh. You're safe. I won't let anything harm you."

Fingers stroked her head and slowly she became aware that hair covered her scalp and that silky nylon and smooth cotton touched her skin—not institutional carpet. Her tongue relaxed in her throat and her shivers died away. Even as John's heat seeped into her, thawing the chill that penetrated to her marrow, white light still blinded her.

"John."

"I'm here, love."

"I can't see. The light's too bright."

"Light?" He sounded puzzled. "It's pitch black in here."

"It's bright. It blinds me!" Hysteria grabbed her by the throat.

John shifted; fingertips eased her eyelids down and then she felt his lips press each one.

"We're at home, love, in bed. It's dark. You're just dreaming."

Red and orange shapes mottled the white light, which had dimmed somewhat after John lowered her eyelids. She let herself relax a little against his chest and for the first time heard herself breathing. Shallow, ragged breaths filled ears previously clogged with fear. She listened and beneath her breathing, she heard John's own steady and quiet inhales and exhales. The color behind her lids cooled to dull orange and deep red, cooled through brown to velvety black. She sensed the space of her bedroom around her.

"Are you with me again?" he breathed into her ear, warming her.

"Yes." She reached her arms, now loose between them, around his torso and snuggled in closer. Just then, a small fluttering tickled her lower belly. She drew in her breath.

"What? What is it?" Now John sounded alarmed.

"I just felt the baby." Wonder colored her voice, then relief. "I just felt the baby, John."

He sighed and clutched her tighter. "Just remember that feeling. Let it keep you here with me, grounded."

"I will."

But even as she spoke, Tamarind felt a chill caper up her spine and down again. It had been years since she'd relived the horror of Jesus' attack.

᪥᪥᪥

"Hey, man. You look like you've been castrated."

John looked up from his monitor, fingers poised above his keyboard. "What?"

"I said you look like you've been castrated."

John flinched at Prasad's words. "That's a bit graphic, don't you think?"

Prasad giggled. "Yeah, but I got your attention, didn't I? Besides, you're pretty damn white. I don't know what else causes such pallor except blood loss, and I don't see any obvious gushing wounds on you. Hence, I suspect castration. American women psychically castrate all the time, man. Maybe your wife took it a step further."

John wished he'd put his headphones on already but doing so now would be a mistake. He thought about Tamarind, whimpering and shaking in his arms and color flooded back into his face—color that Prasad mistook.

"Ah ha! I hit the nail on the head! Man, never fear. You can always hide out here. I'll cover for you if she calls or comes by."

"Look, I'm kinda busy right now. Is there something I can do for you?" John's jaws stiffened, but he managed to sound calm.

Prasad sat on the corner of John's desk, a stilt-like leg all angles between them. His crisp white shirt deepened the color of his skin.

"I just got off the phone with my friend who works at Patriot Healthcare. He told me about something called virtual medical records. He thinks we should add them to Dr2Dr."

John frowned. "That's not as simple as it sounds, Prasad. I'm sure there are all kinds of patient confidentiality issues to take into account."

"How hard can it be? The largest insurers already have their own VEMRs, John—including Patriot Healthcare. We're not invading anyone's privacy." Prasad sounded indignant. "But they don't have Web access to these records yet. You've got to admit that our site will be much more powerful if we can offer docs more than chat and streaming video."

"That might be. But the Web is way less secure than an internal LAN. We'll have to address some serious security issues to make sure Joe Hacker doesn't come along and sneak a peek into patient records."

"No problem, John. That's why we hired you." Prasad's white teeth flashed. "Listen, man, this is the way to go. My friend says they're already talking to their internal software group about moving their patient records to the Web. We've got to show them we can do it better. And faster. Then they'll be more interested in the other stuff, the virtual consulting for their docs."

A sharp pain sliced across John's forehead. He massaged it with stiff fingers and squeezed his eyes shut for a moment. Then he looked at Prasad again.

"Okay, I get that we need to entice insurers. But Dr. Mukarjee never mentioned patient records when he talked to me back in Pittsburgh. It makes me a little nervous you're adding such a big component at this point. I thought the Patriot negotiations were in the final stages."

"They are, John. They are. But insurance companies, especially Patriot Healthcare, aren't like VCs these days. They're more cautious with their money. That's why we have to offer them something flashy, something they can't resist. Either that, or we sell out to an investor who couldn't care less about IndiaClinic."

John pinched the bridge of his nose and reached for his coffee cup. It was empty. Time to switch to Coke anyway. "All right, all right. I just don't want to do a half-assed job is all. I'm not going to be responsible for insecure patient records."

"Neither will Patriot." Prasad giggled, annoying John. "We'll sell them on the full system but write the contract such that they don't get Web access to patient records right away. Don't worry, you'll have enough time to build a secure system."

Prasad's cell phone rang—it rang constantly despite the fact that he spent most of his time in the office. Their conversation was over apparently. He waved at John, stood up and turned away. John heard him say "yes," followed by "I understand," and "we're working on it right now." Finally, he said, "Wait—I'm not at my desk. I'm on my way right now." And then he left John's cubicle, head bent and torso leaning as if he walked against a stiff wind.

John waited a few moments and then he turned to compose an email to Dr. Mukarjee outlining his concerns and warning that his increasing workload might compromise the integrity of his work and keep him from working altogether on IndiaClinic business. Messages from Patriot Healthcare programmers and their project manager already waited in his inbox, but he ignored them. The new message from Zoë commanded his attention, though.

As promised, she'd contacted him about an upcoming visit to Boston. Deep into writing her thesis, she'd landed an interview at MIT and then used that to leverage a talk at Harvard as well. She planned to stay with a friend in Cambridge, who'd told her about several great places to eat and drink around Harvard Square, including a pub called Brew Moon. She asked in typical blunt manner if he'd have dinner with her there, ostensibly to give her some job advice and look over a copy of her job talk.

That would go over well with Tamarind. He should just say no. But the chance to have dinner with someone he knew from grad school, someone very smart and capable and not employed at his small startup—which pretty much circumscribed his world right now—tempted him. Tamarind might not like it, but he'd never given her any reason to suspect his motivations or distrust his faithfulness. Perhaps she'd tolerate the invitation if he insisted upon bringing her and Sarah along.

Yes. That should satisfy everyone.

Relieved, he typed a hasty acceptance and returned to wading through Patriot Healthcare email. Anything to avoid researching and planning virtual medical records.

❧❧❧

Not constrained by the demands of working for a startup tech company or caring for a two year old, Zoë arrived before them at the restaurant and sat at the near end of the bar drinking a pint. John saw her leaning back against the bar stool with one long leg crossed over the other, wearing a mini skirt and dark tights. She chatted with the bartender, a blond woman in white shirt and black tie. Beside him, he felt Tamarind vibrate a little, but her humming never grew loud enough to leave her chest and she didn't click her tongue at all as she used to do to soothe herself. He placed his hand on her lower back and smiled at her.

The hostess walked them to the bar to collect Zoë and stood waiting during their brief hellos. Zoë towered over Tamarind, her *flamboyan*-red silk blouse and black suede skirt striking even in the dim light. She bent smoothly and pressed a cheek against Tamarind's before turning to smile at Sarah, who'd stuck her two middle fingers into her mouth. A maddening habit that perplexed John: Sarah hadn't needed her thumb or a pacifier as a baby. Then Zoë turned to him, one hand held her drink and the other lay lightly on his forearm, and leaned in to brush her lips against his cheek.

"You look tired." Her voice was low, conspiratorial. More loudly, she said, "I took the liberty of ordering you a beer, John. Improper Hopper IPA is what they call it." She turned and grabbed a glass from the bar. "Thanks, Diane. Tamarind, I know you're not drinking in your current state."

John took the pint glass from her and they all followed the hostess to a large table. While Tamarind bent her attention on getting Sarah into a high chair and distracted with a board book and a few toys, John and Zoë chatted awkwardly about Zoë's flight and where Cambridge was in location to Cheltham and Waltham. Silence descended after the waitress appeared with menus and took drink orders for Tamarind and Sarah.

Zoë broke it first. "Diane at the bar recommends the jalapeño corn chowder and the grilled portabella sandwich." She sipped her beer.

John's gaze took in her long nails, painted to match her shirt. "Not studying Tae Kwon Do anymore?"

Zoë glanced at her hands and smiled back at John. "No, as a matter of fact, I'm not. At least, not until I land a job. I thought a manicure improved my prospects a little, made me a little more polished. And intimidating. I dated a guy once who said red nails scared him."

"I want fries." Tamarind scooped some loose curls behind her ear as she studied the menu. She looked at John. "And salmon seared with sesame. I really, *really* want salmon, John."

"I couldn't follow Tamarind's example." Zoë gestured in Tamarind's direction but didn't look at her. "The John-the-Baptist look is fine for watching the kiddies all day, but no one would take it seriously in an office."

Tamarind looked across at Zoë. Her watercolor-blue eyes mirrored the glow from the candle nearest her, turning her eyes opaque. Otherworldly. John expected her to say something—ask about John the Baptist, question why red nails had anything to do with computer-security research, or comment on how differently Zoë dressed from the other women in the computer science department. But for once, Tamarind said nothing. Maybe she remembered the time that Zoë stopped by their Pittsburgh apartment shortly after they'd gotten married. Wincing, he picked up his Improper Hopper and drank half of it in one swallow.

Zoë watched him closely. She must have read his mind. "Do you recall that time I brought over a box of your stuff and Tamarind answered the door naked? I hope I didn't break anything when I dropped the box. You don't answer the door naked anymore, do you, Tamarind?" Laughing, she picked up her beer and sipped again. As she did, John realized that her lipstick matched her nail polish.

Tamarind reached for her ginger ale before answering. John had trouble hearing her over the background noise. "No."

Time to steer the conversation elsewhere. "So, what time is your job talk tomorrow?"

Zoë picked at the deep-fried onion blossom the waitress deposited on the center of the table. "Eleven. Will that give you enough time to read through my slides and give me some feedback?"

"Yeah, it should."

Twisting to reach for one of Sarah's toys that had fallen on the floor, Tamarind spoke before sitting completely upright. Her hair wafted about her head in the air from her movement, obscuring her face and muffling her words. "Will you still have time to get Sarah into bed? I wanted to work tonight."

"Sure, sure, no problem." John watched as Tamarind tried again to smooth the corkscrew curls behind her ears. *John the Baptist* was an apt description. "I promised to finish coding a module for Prasad, but I should be able to do that and look over Zoë's slides after Sarah goes to bed."

"Great!" Zoë signaled to the waitress. "Two more Improper Hoppers here."

She appeared to consider Tamarind, whose greasy fingers gave away her furtive raids on the fried onions. "What work do you do? Oh, you mean that jewelry business you ran a couple of years ago. I guess you don't have to dress up or even get dressed to string beads or twist earrings. By the way, what happened to that stunning pendant you always wore in Pittsburgh?"

Tamarind's hand flew reflexively to her chest, but John knew that she'd been unable to locate it for several weeks.

"I–I don't know what happened to it." Tamarind sounded breathless.

"Can't you just make another one?" Zoë asked.

"No. No, it was one of a kind." Tamarind darted a look at John, but he didn't meet her gaze.

"Ah, sentimental value. Maybe something John bought you in Culebra? Well, I'm sure its loss is hard, but it was just a pendant. It's not like losing it will mean the end of your marriage."

Tamarind jerked a little in her seat and frowned but said nothing. Her t-shirt billowed around her, too big on her small frame and obscuring the swelling of her waist. She didn't look pregnant, just sloppy. Some of the grease from her fingers smeared the edge of the shirt and shined the corners of her mouth. Dandruff flakes speckled her shoulders. He risked a glance at Zoë, her hair smooth and dark and the cut of her blouse flattering. She caught him looking, smiled. Said nothing.

"Boy, it's warm in here. I wonder if their thermostat is broken." John picked up his IPA and tilted it up until he'd swallowed half the new pint. "It's too bad you're looking for something academic. We could use someone like you at Dr2Dr. I've been given the task of adding patient records to the system we're going to develop for Patriot Healthcare and I'm pretty nervous about keeping them secure on the Web."

Zoë held her beer in one hand next to her face, the other arm crossed across her waist. "I never said I wasn't interested in industry. I just haven't stumbled across anything to whet my appetite. Tell me more about this startup you work for."

"Okay." John nodded and gathered his thoughts. "So the idea is to use the Web to allow doctors in a wide area to consult one another on specific patient cases. Right now, the system isn't very efficient. For example, let's say Dr. A sees a patient named John Doe and diagnoses him with a condition that he, Dr. A, can treat, but he needs some expert advice. He can try calling a colleague and describing the situation, but Dr. A might forget something or perhaps not see something that Dr. B might see if he just had the records in front of him. Of course, Dr. A could send the records to Dr. B and then call him, but that's not the same as Dr. A and Dr. B meeting in person and looking at the records together and it doesn't include the patient at all.

"What we want to do is have a network of doctors, in the Boston area for a start, who have a networked PC in their office. So when Dr. A schedules a follow-up with John Doe, he also schedules a live consult with Dr. B, who has access to John Doe's pertinent lab tests. Most likely, John Doe won't be part of the initial doctor consult, but it would be possible. When Dr. A and Dr. B are online together, they'll have a video window so they can talk face-to-face, a window for x-rays and other visuals, and a window for lab results."

"Very impressive. But why are all the doctors men?"

John laughed. "Predictable, Zoë! Maybe it's because male doctors are the ones who need the most help?" He rubbed his forehead. "Boy, it's been too long since I've had more than one beer with dinner. Either that or this IPA has a higher alcohol content than it should."

Zoë smiled and her eyes twinkled. But when she spoke, business ruled her tone. "It sounds like the system has security issues but not very complicated ones. You clearly don't want anyone to hack into a consult, but that's pretty garden-variety security. I guess I don't have a sense for how a one-time consult could hurt a patient's privacy. There's no need to have a patient name involved is there?"

"No, not if these Web consults are independent of a patient's larger profile. But we've contracted with Patriot Healthcare, the largest insurer in New England, to use our Web front-end on top of their database of patient records. Ideally, this will allow primary caregivers to situate a patient's current condition in a larger framework. So now we're going to add another window to our interface that lets Dr. A and Dr. B access these records. And patient names are clearly associated with the records."

"Can't you strip the names off before shunting them into your Web-based system?" Zoë leaned forward and her eyes gleamed in the low light. John knew that her intellect had engaged his problem.

"Yeah, but I'm concerned that our Web interface will build a portal to an otherwise secure database. I just don't have the expertise to make the two parts work together as securely as I think they should."

Zoë sat back. "Indeed you don't. But I do. I could certainly sink my teeth into the myriad issues you need to address in designing your system. Where do I apply?"

"You wouldn't like Dr2Dr." Tamarind spoke, startling John who'd forgotten that she and Sarah still sat next to him.

Zoë swiveled to look at her. "Oh, why not?" Her voice sounded airy, tolerant. She clearly didn't think Tamarind had any idea what she would like.

"Because John's bosses don't think much of women."

John squirmed and frowned at Tamarind. "Just because Mukesh got upset over the cranberry juice stains from your visit doesn't mean he doesn't think much of women."

"Are you sure they just aren't comfortable around toddlers?"

Tamarind shrugged. She looked tired. "I don't have any evidence. It's just intuition, I guess. You can believe me or not."

"If Tamarind's right, all the more reason I should consider Dr2Dr. You know me, John. It's one of my missions to combat discrimination, especially in technology." She turned to look at Tamarind. "Is there something wrong with your salmon, Tamarind? You sounded like you were going to die if you didn't get it and you've hardly touched it. I'll call the waitress over and we'll order you something else."

Later that night, John couldn't go to sleep despite the fact that he'd been so wool-headed after dinner that he'd asked Tamarind to drive him home instead of picking his car up from Dr2Dr's parking lot. He lay awake for a long time next to her, her pregnant body radiating heat in the cool October night. Outside their open window, crickets chirruped and occasionally an owl hooted in the woods behind their yard. Light from a full moon illuminated the sky beyond the window frame, sharpening his vision and increasing his alertness. A sense of expectancy loomed over him so strongly that his heart raced a little in his chest, but nothing and no one interrupted the stillness of their room.

At last he slid away from Tamarind and got up, feeling the air swirl around his overheated legs. He shivered once and headed as quietly as he could downstairs. At the dining-room table, the orange incandescent lights of the old chandelier dazzled him, but he sat there clutching a glass of iced tea until he could see the room without his eyes watering.

Around him, Sarah's artistic masterpieces consisting of blotchy paintings in primary colors settled like down on most flat surfaces, including the dining table and hardwood floor. An open box of jewelry findings, a pair of needle-nosed pliers, and some fine-gauged wire cluttered the far end of the dining table. They drew John's gaze with the strength of accusation. He flinched. He'd forgotten his promise to put Sarah to bed so that Tamarind could bead and had instead stumbled upstairs to his office and printed out Zoë's job talk. It wasn't until he'd turned to the module for Prasad that he remembered and by then Tamarind had given up waiting and lay in bed reading. He urged her to put in a few minutes on her jewelry anyway, but she only shook her head and said that she was too tired. Her puffy, lined eyes confirmed her words. So he kissed her goodnight and went back to work.

Now, surrounded by these familiar artifacts, John couldn't quite conjure the sense of excitement and suspense he'd felt when Zoë had talked about working for Dr2Dr. Instead, the more he thought about it in the cocoon of his dining room, the greater his unease. He felt a little ill, in fact. As if he'd eaten a scrumptious meal whose rich sauces and exotic herbs concealed spoiled main ingredients.

His eyes stung and he rubbed them. He couldn't explain what had come over him at dinner. Even if he had been drinking something stronger than beer, he still wouldn't have found Zoë as compelling. It was true that he found her extremely desirable physically, but the years had only clarified and settled his feelings for her. Zoë, exuding sexuality, strength, and confidence like an Amazon, lacked humor, playfulness, and gentleness. John never let his guard down around her, constantly wary that he might do or say something to earn her reproach. After a while, not even her body's strong magnetism could balance the drain on his psyche.

He sighed. Perhaps he overestimated his detachment now that he no longer benefited from constant inoculation against Zoë's charms at Carnegie Mellon. Even though he'd known that he missed the daily interaction with other grad students and research staff, he hadn't realized just how desperate he'd been for any contact from an old colleague, no matter how brief or how fraught with personal risk.

Given the look of defeat and hurt on Tamarind's face after dinner, and the prospect of Zoë rubbing shoulders with him daily at Dr2Dr, he wished he could blame his behavior on the beer.

ּשׁשׁשׁ

Zoë slouched in the black leather armchair in the living room of her friend Karen's apartment, her legs lying over an arm. She'd stripped down to a black camisole and baby-doll shorts, washed her face, and grabbed a hard cider from Karen's refrigerator to sip. Before Karen left for dinner with her boyfriend, she'd told Zoë that she wouldn't be back this evening in case Zoë cared to entertain. Karen knew full well that Zoë planned to meet John and she knew what Zoë wanted. Too bad she hadn't known that John would bring his frowsy airhead for a wife and her chatty little girl.

Not that it mattered too much. John had eyes and ears only for her. During dinner Zoë had restrained her grin, but triumph had lifted her shoulders and warmed her face. She wasn't sure what felt better: John's hungry gaze or Tamarind's deflated, dumpy posture. Even Sarah sensed something between the adults and grew quiet, watching them with her unsettling eyes.

Zoë sipped her cider and looked over at the coffee table where a small bottle sat half empty. It had been years since John had looked at her the way he'd looked at her this evening and she hated to think that the love potion the old witch on Culebra had sold her might be responsible. Hated it because she wanted him to want her without any outside stimulus. Hated it even more because she'd had the potion months before he lost his head and married an uneducated island cunt.

As it was, the potion had lain forgotten at the bottom of her nightstand until she'd started cleaning and sorting in anticipation of being done with grad school. She didn't know what had prompted her to use it tonight, and she still couldn't be sure that the amber liquid inside the palm-size bottle had anything to do with John's eagerness to have her come work with him. She hadn't managed to get him to ditch Tamarind and come back to Karen's with her. Perhaps she should have used the whole bottle? Then she'd have followed the opening its effects gave her with a full frontal assault.

She grinned, the wickedness of her thoughts satisfying.

Well, half the potion remained in the bottle. Another dose might just do the trick. Nothing wrong with taking her time, as long as the outcome remained the same.

Thirty

❧

ANA HID IN PLAIN SIGHT ON THE PLAZA under the pineapple-guava tree across from the ferry dock, her slight form wrapped in a glamour. She sat cross-legged watching the mainlanders milling outside the ferry office like fish along a reef. Among them strode a few purposeful middle-aged women, who dragged suitcases behind them as they made for the sidewalk along the taxi lane. These women wore large dark sunglasses, gold jewelry, and tailored clothes in navy, khaki, and white. Their burnished hair gleamed in the late-morning sun and their red nail polish threatened blood at their well-kept hands. They didn't scare Ana one bit. She knew that they'd come to Culebra looking for her and her remedies for the tribulations of getting old. Remedies that she no longer had for sale.

For years, Ana had brewed, fermented, distilled, and bottled any number of enhancing treatments for San Juan's wealthiest. She earned enough to keep herself in the basics: clove cigarettes, a dry house, clothes and any foodstuff that she couldn't grow or gather for herself. Anything extra, she surreptitiously funneled to needy Culebrenses through anonymous donations to Sister Maria Margarita at La Virgin del Mar or in middle-of-the-night deliveries to individuals in dire straits.

But Ana grew old and tired and her supplies from the sea had grown dangerously low ever since she'd lost her sole *mer* protégée. Now, whatever remedies she had left she guarded closely for herself. Rather than risking the loss of her wealthy customers to quack medicines, Ana chose to disappear when they came calling. At first, they sent personal assistants on the ferry, but as the weeks passed and the assistants failed to find Ana, they began to charter planes and brave the ferry themselves. They came more and more frequently, no longer waiting for convenient mid-week trips when their social calendars slowed enough to allow for personal care beyond a trip to the salon. Ana read the anger in their tight mouths and the fear in the corners of their eyes when they removed their sunglasses.

Today, she'd left a few bottles at The Mermaid's Purse, a souvenir shop along the main street of Dewey, along with word that she'd become ill and needed to travel to a remote location to restore herself. She promised to return with some of the very elixir that she sought to mend her own debilitating symptoms. This story would have to do, but she knew she had very little time to save herself and her work as midwife and healer. If she couldn't bring the one who called herself Tamarind back to Culebra in the next few months, Ana would have to retreat to the Carlos Rosario Peninsula where she would sit on the beach—that border world between land and sea—and wait to die. If she were fortunate, Mother Sea would eventually come to claim her dehydrated carcass with an act of compassion and absolution, lifting it from the sand and sending it floating out wherever the currents would take it until it sank to the forgetful depths.

A taxi van arrived and the women left their suitcases with the sweating Culebrense driver in his short-sleeved camp shirt to climb inside. After the van drove away, Ana closed her eyes and let the glamour wink out simultaneously. In the growing heat of the day, sleepiness welled up and she gave in without a struggle, letting her chin drop to her chest and her hands fall apart where they nestled in her lap. She dozed until early afternoon when something woke her—a sound perhaps, but her conscious mind lagged behind her hearing so that she couldn't be sure. She sat listening, letting her thoughts clear and sharpen. Heat shimmered from the pavement beyond the empty plaza, but nothing else moved or made a sound. A sudden urge for a clove cigarette clutched her and she fumbled for the drawstring bag at her waist where she kept papers and cloves mixed with loose tobacco. With shaking fingers she sprinkled some of the pungent mix onto a paper and rolled a thin cigarette. She flicked a thumbnail against a match and lit an end of the tapered roll, sucking eagerly on the other. Harsh air burned her throat and filled her lungs while sweet-smelling blue smoke spiraled in front of her face. She held the smoke in as long as she could and then blew it out roughly, like a winded horse. An image of the proud stallion that had ruled over the herd of wild horses not far from her former home flashed before her mind's eye, coaxing a sad smile. Ana may have lost her house to Hurricane Marilyn four years before, but the stallion had been unable to outrun the hurricane's fury. The memory of his sightless eyes and bent neck, graceful even in death, still haunted her dreams sometimes.

A flapping of wings fluttered through her reverie and Ana blinked, scowling. She looked around her, the clove cigarette burning forgotten in her right hand. At times like these, the loss of sight in her left eye infuriated and frightened her all over again, but she welcomed the feelings because they justified everything she'd ever done as midwife and healer, neither human nor mermaid.

"You look like hell," she said to the laughing gull perched on the low wall bordering the plaza. "You won't do me much good if you drop out of the sky from exhaustion. Next time, rest up with your cousins north of us." Before the laughing gull responded, Ana reached into the bag at her waist and pulled out some dried tamarind pulp. "Here." She tossed a bit to the bird, which snatched it from the air and swallowed.

"You've done well, Ai. Your eyes were my eyes and I saw that she no longer wears the pendant. That's very good, very good, for us."

The bird cocked its head and stared at her with a bright eye. It laughed.

"What? Another child? You're sure?" Ana paused for Ai's answer. "No, I didn't see the swelling of her belly. That's not good. I don't know if the spells on my mangrove box can counter the grounding magic of pregnancy by themselves. I'll have to think of something to strengthen them."

Lost in thought, she almost forgot to bring the clove cigarette to her lips for a last drag. The spicy clove fogged her thoughts for a moment, but she welcomed the distraction. When even that wore off, she sighed and tossed the butt on the pavement ten feet away where it smoldered.

"No wonder you're hiding from me," a voice called from the corner of the street. It was Valerie. "How many of those vile things have you smoked since you left the guesthouse this morning?"

"Not enough." Still Ana tightened the drawstring on her bag and tucked it out of sight under her thigh. "What brings you out during *siesta*? I thought you had an order to fill for your friend in New York."

"I do, but I just can't concentrate. My fingers fumble with every bead and wire I attempt to mold. I was about to throw everything against the wall when Tamarind called."

"Oh?" Ana wished that she could roll another cigarette to have something to do with her hands. Instead, she studied the pineapple-guava tree, which never flowered and therefore never bore fruit. It was a basic law of nature: to thrive and spawn, life needed the right environment and care. After four years locked on dry land among humans, Tamarind must by now have grown to understand, if only a little, how much out of her element she was, no matter how many children that she managed to bear.

"Yeah. She and John moved a while ago and now she's trying to find places to sell her jewelry. She called to see if she could send a few pieces along to my New York buyer, which works out well for me."

Ana pursed her lips and nodded. "That would be good for both of you. An ideal partnership." She waited for Valerie to volunteer more information.

Valerie sat down on the low wall near the tree and gazed out to sea. Wisps of long blond hair fluttered behind her as a westerly breeze picked up, bringing a strong scent of salt with it. "She doesn't sound happy."

Ana squeezed her hidden bag, feeling the various items in it. They kept her eagerness at bay. "Don't need a phone call to know that. It's a rare woman who doesn't find herself disillusioned after a while with a man."

Valerie nodded but said nothing for a while. Ana studied her pale skin. Although Valerie had lived on Culebra for more than a dozen years, she had grown paler rather than darker as time went by and Ana found herself wondering if Valerie had been outside during the day at all in weeks. Pale skin belonged on a fish's belly, not on a healthy woman. Ana frowned.

"You look like you live in a cave. Go to the beach. Take a book. Some sun would do you good."

Valerie waved her hand dismissively and continued. "Tamarind is normally so, well, quirky and upbeat that I didn't quite believe it was her at first on the phone. Her voice was so *flat*. She asked about the New York buyer as if she were arranging a funeral for a stranger."

"Ask her what was wrong?" Ana hoped that impatience hadn't too obviously roughened her already raspy voice.

"Of course. I couldn't help it. She wouldn't say anything though. Just that she was tired and all with the work of settling in to a new house and watching Sarah, who's two now and into everything. She's also pregnant again."

"Ah." Ana counted on the noncommittal sound to mask her lack of surprise. "That would make her tired."

"Yes, but there was no *joy* in her voice, not like when she was expecting Sarah."

"Needs some time on a beach too. Never forget that the sound of the surf was her first lullaby."

Valerie looked at Ana. The sun obscured her eyes, but Ana felt their gaze searching her. Not for the first time Ana wondered at the depths she sensed in Valerie but had no way to plumb. "You know, I think you're right. I'm going to go back and call her, tell her to get herself back down here. A little vacation never hurt anyone."

"No doubt. Now, my friend, get lost so I can smoke and you can pretend to have reformed me."

Valerie stood up with a tired laugh. "No problem. What should I tell the lovely ladies who plan to stop by this afternoon looking for you?"

Ana shrugged. "Tell them I've gone on vacation to get a little rest. They only have to take one look at you to know that's a good idea."

৵৵৵

"Gorgeous color, isn't it?"

At the sound of Lucy's voice from only a few feet away, Tamarind flinched and fumbled with the handle of the rake that she leaned against. She darted a look at Lucy, who stood in the street near the edge of their lawn holding a rake, and then swept her gaze guiltily over the front yard. Sarah gabbled around the base of the sugar maple, swiping her toy rake at the leaves in Tamarind's pile and spreading them around the grass again. She hadn't disappeared while Tamarind's attention wandered.

"Yes." Tamarind lifted the corners of her mouth at Lucy and turned to pull the rake through the scattered leaves.

"My daughter Dorothy called it the fairy-tale sky when she was a girl. She thought that Hansel and Gretel got lost in the autumn when the fallen leaves obscured their path." As she finished speaking, Lucy stepped next to Tamarind and began to rake, her words riding grunts as she stroked the rake toward her. Before Tamarind could protest, she continued, "She also said that Cinderella wore a ball gown that color of blue and that her hair matched the gold of new-fallen maple leaves."

"You don't have to do that." Tamarind found her voice.

Lucy looked sideways at her but didn't stop raking. "Nonsense. I couldn't sleep at night if I let you rake by yourself when I've got a perfectly fine arm and few leaves to trouble my yard."

An urge to cry welled up inside Tamarind, but she pressed her lips together and turned a little from Lucy so that she wouldn't have to face the older woman. Lucy continued to rake without appearing to notice Tamarind's response.

"You really should get one of those leaf vacuums. They mulch the leaves so they don't take up so much room. You can haul 'em in a cart around back to the woods and dump them."

Tamarind said nothing. Her arms, sore from the unaccustomed work, hung from her shoulders and only reluctantly pulled the rake around her. The color of the sky reminded her of Culebra and she longed to smell saltwater and hear the sounds of hundreds of terns, brown-footed boobies, gulls, and ducks. When Lucy interrupted her moments ago, she'd been trying to recall the particular calls of masked and ruddy ducks—both of whom had bills the color of today's late October sky—but even though she'd spent countless hours listening to and emulating them when she lived in the waters near Culebra, she couldn't recall what they sounded like now.

"Livy! Livy!" Sarah's high-pitched warble announced the arrival of Lucy's granddaughter Olivia, who often walked to Lucy's house after school.

Tamarind looked up, dragging the rake halfheartedly toward her feet. Olivia stood at the edge of the yard listing under the weight of a backpack high on her left shoulder. Shaggy dark hair and dark-framed eyeglasses obscured her face so that Tamarind could never read her expression.

"Hungry?" Lucy rested both gloved hands on the tip of her rake handle as she spoke. "I baked some apple pies today. I have iced tea, too."

Olivia shifted on her feet and clutched the backpack straps. "Um, okay."

Lucy turned to look at Tamarind and Sarah, who'd dropped her rake and capered through the leaf pile. "Tell you what, I'll go over and slice up some pie, pour a few glasses of tea. When it's ready, I'll call for you, Olivia, and we'll bring over a blanket and enjoy the afternoon properly."

Olivia bit her lower lip and nodded. Lucy smiled at Tamarind, who tried to smile back, and then she strode across the street without looking back. They watched her go silently, her erect posture and spiky white hair somehow both reassuring and vulnerable. Tamarind wanted to go inside and sit down on the couch, but even that seemed like too much effort, requiring some explanation to Lucy that she couldn't give. Meanwhile, Sarah danced around Olivia and sang "and Bingo was his name-o" over and over again. After a few moments Olivia let the backpack slide off her shoulder to plop onto the street near her feet and Tamarind went and sat down on her front steps without dropping the rake. Olivia still stood at the edge of the yard, her baggy clothes melting from her like wax.

"You don't have to hang out here," Tamarind called. "You should go to your grandmother's and eat pie there."

Olivia shook her head and waved her left foot in an arc around her. "I don't think Gram would be too happy if I did that. She'd tell me I was being anti-social."

Tamarind watched Olivia, who'd spoken without looking at her. "Maybe you could just tell her I'm the one being anti-social."

Olivia stopped smoothing the street with her toe and looked at Tamarind. The frame of glasses magnified her dark eyes. "Are you really from an island in the Caribbean?"

"Yeah."

"It must be hard living here, then."

Tamarind studied Olivia, but she could see nothing to explain the fourteen-year-old girl's insight. She sighed. "Sometimes." Her gaze lifted to the sky unconsciously, to the intense blue. "Especially on days like today." She looked back at Olivia to see the teenager looking at the sky too.

360

"Fairy-tale sky," Olivia said. "Sometimes I wish I lived in a fairy tale and a prince came to rescue me. Then we could live happily ever after."

"That would be nice." Tamarind leaned over her belly, its hard mass pushing uncomfortably against her upper chest, and laid the rake down on the sidewalk. Sarah came over and sat down on the steps near her.

"My wan' bubbles."

"Okay." Tamarind grabbed the railing next to her and pulled herself from her seat to stand. Inside the house, a plastic bottle of bubbles sat on the hall table among picture frames and stacks of bills. She grabbed the sticky bottle and carried it back out to Sarah, who sat crushing ants with the tip of her sneaker.

Olivia now sat on her backpack staring at the sky. "My favorite fairy tale is *Beauty and the Beast*. Actually, it's a version called *Beauty* by a writer named Sharon McKinley."

"You read a lot?" Tamarind watched Sarah dip the bubble wand into the bottle and pull it out. She touched the wand to pursed lips and blew wetly, spraying soapy water across the front sidewalk.

Olivia kept her gaze on the sky. "Yeah. I dream of being a writer someday, but that seems as real as a fairy tale."

Lucy's storm door opened and she stuck her head and shoulders outside. "Olivia, can you come get this tray for me?"

Olivia jumped up. "Yeah, sure."

Tamarind watched her walk up Lucy's driveway and into the cape. Even though her round face testified to some pudginess, her loose shirt and drooping pants fit her so poorly that Tamarind suspected that Olivia hid inside them. In fact, she thought Olivia's clothes seemed even baggier than they had a month ago when they'd first met.

Ten minutes later, the four of them sat on a Mexican wool blanket under the maple tree in the front yard, surrounded by drifts and heaps of golden leaves and eating apple pie on paper plates. Custard sat, regal and implacable on a throne of green and gold, watching them and blinking at Sarah, who offered her tidbits of crust on a wet forefinger. Tamarind, a Buddha with crossed legs and loose belly, ate two pieces of pie slowly. She felt sugar graining the corners of her mouth and licked them with the tip of her tongue.

"You around for Thanksgiving?" Lucy asked after they'd all eaten several bites.

"No." Tamarind cleared her throat and sipped iced tea before continuing. "I mean, John's staying here. He's too busy at work. They have some kind of test they're running a few days before Thanksgiving and he'll have to be here."

"Where'll you and Sarah be then? Will you travel home?"

"We're flying to Culebra for the week." Not home. She could never go home again.

"Will you see your folks there?"

"No. My mother died a long time ago. My father and I are —" Tamarind struggled for the right word, "estranged."

"That's too bad." Lucy's voice held a note that Tamarind didn't recognize at first, but she saw Lucy's gaze shift toward Olivia and wondered if Olivia had her own experience with estrangement.

"John and I have a friend named Valerie there. She's the one who taught me how to wire-wrap beads and gems into pendants and earrings."

"Ah." Lucy took a bite and chewed thoughtfully. "So John'll be here alone for Thanksgiving? He can stop over for dinner with us. I'm hosting again this year."

Olivia shifted a bit on the blanket and set her plate on her thighs. "I thought Mom and Aunt Rachel said they wanted to start hosting Thanksgiving so you wouldn't have to, Gram."

Lucy sighed. "So they said. But Thanksgiving's in three weeks and when I pinned them down to something this week, they both begged me to do it again because they're too swamped to be in charge."

"I don't think you need John to add to your stress."

"Now John wouldn't do that. If anything, he'd defuse my stress by keeping Rachel and Dorothy on their best behavior, not that *that's* saying much given how sharp tongued those two are." Lucy shook her head. "I'm sorry, Tamarind. I always say more than I mean to when I'm around you. My mother always used to say 'loose lips sink ships.'"

"What does that mean?" Tamarind's curiosity flared for the first time in weeks. "Do ships have lips and if they're loose the ship will take in water?"

Lucy chuckled. "That's fabulous! Whoo-whee! What an image! Do you see it too, Olivia?"

Olivia nodded and smiled a little, her gaze not quite meeting Tamarind's. "I bet Pam could create a wicked Photoshop image of that."

"Yeah, I bet. You'll have to tell her." Lucy rubbed away her tears with the edge of her index finger.

Tamarind winced and looked toward the trees that lined the cul-de-sac opposite them. Curiosity always led her into a display of mock-worthy ignorance.

"Oh, Tamarind, I'm not laughing at you, hon." Lucy laid a warm, rough palm onto Tamarind's forearm. "Please don't look so devastated. Your innocence is refreshing."

"I wondered what that saying meant, too," Olivia said. "I was afraid to ask."

"Well, GIs used it in World War Two to mean 'Don't tell anyone what you know.' Something they said could cause the Nazis or their allies to sink a ship."

"Cool. I can use it in the presentation I'm working on for history. Thanks, Gram." Tamarind felt Olivia's gaze on her, but she continued staring at the trees. "Thanks, Tamarind, for asking."

"So why did you say it just now?" Tamarind heard the confusion in her voice. And a trace of hurt that she hadn't managed to suppress.

Lucy cut a sliver of pie from what remained in the dish between them. "Well, I guess relationships are a kind of 'ship' after all and saying too much out of turn can 'sink' them."

"I won't say anything."

Lucy took a long time cutting a bite with the edge of her fork. "I was talkin' about *my* loose lips, not yours," she said. "Maybe it'd be better for all concerned if I did speak my mind to my daughters. Sometimes 'ships' are so old and leaky, they have to be scuttled anyway. It wouldn't take much to send these two 'ships' to the bottom."

"It's not like Mom'll care," Olivia said.

"Because she doesn't care what I think of her?" Lucy's soft voice barely reached Tamarind. Her pie now resembled clumpy sand, but still she twisted the fork in it. "You're right of course, little girl. She stopped listening to me a long time ago."

Silence fell between them, opposed only by the sound of Sarah's giggles as she swung a thin branch with dead leaves still clinging to it over Custard, who batted languorously at the branch. At last Lucy folded the paper plate in half and then folded it in half again and wedged it under the pie plate on the tray.

"You look a little out of sorts, Tamarind. Is everything okay?"

Tamarind licked her fork clean. Butter coated cinnamon and sugar along her tongue and filled her nostrils with their warm scent, reminding her of Ana's clove cigarettes. She'd even be happy to see Ana on her visit.

She shrugged. "I've just got a lot to do. I'm supposed to bring some jewelry pieces to Valerie when I visit. She's going to sell them for me or send them to a buyer she has in New York."

"Maybe Olivia can come over a few afternoons a week and play with Sarah so you can get some made. How 'bout it, lovey? Can you help Tamarind out?" Lucy's face had grown serious. "Of course, you wouldn't be home when Pam's around."

"It's okay. I'm sure Olivia has homework ..." Tamarind's voice trailed away when she saw the grin on Olivia's face.

"You don't have to ask me twice." Olivia stood up. "Can I start today?"

Thirty-one

ॐ

ON THE FLIGHT FROM SAN JUAN TO CULEBRA, homesickness slammed into Tamarind's chest and slid down the well of her stomach. She realized that it had stalked her for weeks, maybe months. While she caressed the lifeless replacement pendant nestled between her breasts, her other hand clutched Sarah's shirt to keep her from climbing over the seats in front and back of them. Unlike the American Airlines flight from Boston the day before where attendants cosseted Sarah and salvaged the four-hour flight for Tamarind, nobody brought them anything to eat or drink and no movies played. Only the view of the ocean below—the sixteen-passenger plane had no center aisle bisecting its eight rows of seats for Sarah to cruise—offered them any entertainment.

After a few minutes Sarah stopped trying to stand up again and asked for her Winnie-the-Pooh audio book that Tamarind carried in her tote bag. Tamarind dug past the sippy cup and the bags of goldfish crackers and raisins to find the small silver Walkman and handed it to Sarah. When she'd helped Sarah to slide the headphones over her ears and push play, Tamarind turned to study the ocean tableau beneath them.

Yesterday, she'd either spent all her time taking Sarah to the bathroom or reading picture books aloud while she blocked the exit to the aisle and she'd only glimpsed a sliver of the ocean over the shoulder of the college student slouched in the window seat. Now the brilliant blue surrounded her on all sides, so close below the Trislander commuter plane that she fought the urge to open the door on her side and drop into its saline embrace. She went so far as to put her hand on the door handle when a sudden tumbling staccato inside her swollen abdomen brought her back to who and where she was. One set of fingertips abandoned the handle and the other quit worrying the moonstone and together pressed into the hard flesh beneath her belly button. The baby quieted and her gaze, no longer misted with emotion, settled on the undulating surface of the ocean. *Mother Sea.* That's what the *mer* people called the ancient, amniotic fluid that had nurtured and defined them over the eons of their existence. Eventually, everything subject to saltwater erodes or dissolves and the *mer* people had only their collective memory, and its imprint on the very molecules of saltwater around them, to record their history.

She shifted in her uncomfortable seat. It had been four years since she'd tried sending her thoughts out to her brethren, four disconnected years without another *mer* kind's thoughts swimming inside her head. In that moment, the silence and emptiness loomed large over her thoughts and she acknowledged how alone, how on her own she'd been, since she'd put off her tail for John. She shook her head. *That's not true.* When she and John survived Hurricane Marilyn together, they'd been as connected as any *mer* couple. When had swirling mists obscured John's thoughts from her?

A ripple of energy droplets sprayed the sky around the Trislander in a fine cloud, jolting Tamarind from her musing and drawing her gaze to the window. Dark blue-gray smudged the southern horizon where Vieques lay. The energy droplets streamed north and west from the nearly invisible island, but Tamarind didn't need to see its shoreline to know what artifacts lay there. A *mer* festival had been held recently, probably on the far eastern tip where the U.S. Navy tested live weapons and where the ragged shoreline provided a perfect canvas for *mer* artisans to create a kind of performance art. Using found objects such as wrappers and plastic soda bottles, old tires and rusty gas cans, *mer* artisans built walls and towers that both mocked and revered the humans responsible for them. Only the concerted effort of young *mer* swimming along the shore and sending out mental support kept these strangely beautiful structures together until the lead artisan coaxed a wave to stunning height and then slammed it down onto the art. The resulting destruction and cathartic energy release showered the ether for miles around.

Echoes of older festivals filled her mind. Their lingering traces had a bright quality that meant these festivals had been held within the last year—which was why she could hear the echoes at all. Three or four echoes magnified and took on a red-orange tinge in her thoughts; the others fell away as she recognized the signature of the *mer* artisan responsible. He had no name that humans would even be able to hear, let alone understand. The sounds, low on the register, captured the sound of the ocean floor shifting along fault lines. It was an ominous, dark, core-reverberating sound. Perhaps the best way to translate his name, if she had to tell a human about him, was Silent Heart. He'd loved her, had built fanciful creations on remote outcrops in her honor, but she had never felt the same for him. He had always been satirical toward humanity, but his art had been miniature, private, for her alone. These larger echoes had a tang of bitter wildness to them; she sensed that Silent Heart lashed out at the *mer*, too. Although his art still depended upon the adoring participation of other young *mer*, she feared that Silent Heart's recent frenzy would escalate until he'd transformed into a *moulos*, strange and lost. If that happened, he'd spend the rest of his life creating larger and more outlandish art closer and closer to humans until he'd become a kind of energy bomb. She shivered. At the movement, Sarah watched her for the rest of the flight.

Tamarind brooded within the cloud of dispersed energy until the Trislander, emerging into the clear sunlight, banked and headed for the runway on Culebra. The sight of the island, its arms open to greet them, cheered her more than she'd anticipated, especially given that she'd seen it from the sky only once in her life. Sarah leaned her forehead on the plane's window the entire time the plane descended. When they disembarked into the brilliant afternoon, Tamarind stood, dazzled, on the bleached asphalt with Sarah clinging to her leg.

"Tamarind!" Valerie appeared before them, her hair a halo. She'd kissed Tamarind's cheek before Tamarind could respond and knelt down to face Sarah. She smelled of polishing cream, orange, and, oddly, cheese. "You must be Sarah. I'd recognize those crystal-blue peepers anywhere."

Sarah smiled at Valerie. "My hungry." She slipped her hand into Valerie's. "Lunch with you?"

Valerie laughed. "Certainly, darlin'." She turned to Tamarind. "Let's get your bags. I've got a few things I can throw together for lunch."

"Okay." Tamarind watched Valerie push herself to her feet and frowned. Valerie's pale hair had more gray in it than blond, but it was the waver in her posture and the tremble in her hands that alarmed Tamarind. "No, don't worry. I can carry the bag. It's not really heavy with only shorts and t-shirts."

They walked to Valerie's Jeep, Valerie holding Sarah's hand and chatting as though Tamarind had never left the island. Tamarind answered questions absentmindedly; the dry heat from the open window and the familiar view of dusty guinea grass and stunted trees distracted her, but Valerie didn't seem to notice. Even though she'd packed away her long pants and fleece outerwear, she grew warm and sleepy in the bright, still afternoon. If only Sarah hadn't given up napping most days, she'd have reverted to the luxury of a *siesta* while on Culebra. She must have dozed because Posada La Diosa appeared suddenly before them, its cheerful pastels and hanging baskets of flowers an oasis in the arid street. Four or five chickens chuckled and clucked on the sidewalk outside the front door. The scent of cloves wafted to them from the hidden patio on the side of the inn.

"Ana's here?" Tamarind heard the wary surprise in her voice.

Valerie paused with her hand on the door handle. "Yeah. She's been staying with me."

A hidden current snagged Tamarind's attention. "A long time?"

Valerie didn't look at her. "Since Marilyn."

"What about her house?" Tamarind let her shock raise her voice. "Her chickens? Her seagulls?"

Now Valerie did look at her. "Tamarind, Ana's too old to live out in the brush with chickens and seagulls. When I saw how much losing nearly everything cost her, how much losing you cost her, I asked her to stay."

Tamarind bit her lower lip. "I'm sorry, Valerie. I was just surprised. You hadn't said anything before."

"You never asked about Ana either."

An awkward silence created a fissure inside the easy camaraderie that had renewed itself between them. Sarah filled it. "Lunch, Valrie? My hungry. My want grilled cheese." She paused. "Please?"

"Sure, love bug. Let's get you outta that seat first."

Tamarind glanced across the sidewalk to the fence around the patio. Uneasiness and guilt jostled queasily inside her. Ana loomed in memory as hard as dead coral, as opaque and shifting as sand. She had never been anything but helpful, in her own way. Tamarind should have been concerned about Ana's fate, but she hadn't been. Probably only Valerie had cared for what had happened to the ancient woman, had cared and noticed that Tamarind hadn't. Would Ana be happy to see her after all this time? She reached for the pendant at her neck, but it didn't feel right. The moonstone didn't fit in the heart of her palm the way her other moonstone had. It never burned but lay cold on her breast.

Tamarind took their bags to their room while Valerie escorted Sarah, who chattered nonstop, to Posada La Diosa's kitchen. Tamarind found Sarah kneeling on a bar stool petting the cat that Valerie had finally domesticated with a collar. The kitchen looked much the same since Tamarind had last been a guest at its counter, save for more jewelry findings and bags of herbs and other dried organic material, some of which must surely be from Ana. Even so, there was something about the kitchen, some greater disorder that disturbed her. She sat next to Sarah and let her knees splay open to accommodate her belly while Valerie filled trays with olives and sliced tomatoes, almonds, feta, and toasted pita. She managed a grilled cheese sandwich using pita, provolone, and a heart-shaped cookie cutter. They sat at the counter to eat, mostly silent as they watched Sarah on her precarious perch. Tamarind wondered when Ana would decide to join them.

"What happened to your Goddess?"

Tamarind fingered the wire-wrapped figure. "Nothing. Why?"

"'Cause that's not the moonstone I gave you. Much more inferior."

"She's around. I just misplaced her in the new house. This one is a stand-in."

"Must be important if you have to wear a fake." Ana's gruff voice grated along Tamarind's shoulder blades. "Does it work as well for you?"

Tamarind put her food down and slid around on the stool to face Ana. She'd never spoken to Ana about the power that she'd imbued in the Goddess when she'd polished its moonstone. "What do you mean?" She gripped the pendant, shielding it from Ana's keen eye. She tried to depreciate its worth. "I just like the weight on my chest."

Ana said nothing to this, just pursed her lips and walked to the last bar stool. Tamarind studied her. Ana had grown yet spindlier, if that were possible, and almost frail looking. Her wild hair resembled finely spun glass and it had thinned enough that Tamarind saw freckled scalp. She couldn't help but stare at Ana's bare feet, whose worn soles and shriveled, flaky skin looked too frangible to carry her weight. Ana had no trouble walking and mounting the bar stool, however, so Tamarind looked away from her old mentor and pretended to eat but not before she caught Ana's gaze.

370

Ana asked Valerie for a glass of lemonade and the sound of the ceiling fan, ice chinking against glass, and Sarah's gabble filled the silence between the three women for the next two or three minutes. Tamarind couldn't stand the weight where words should be.

"Valerie says you've been living here. Do you like living in town?"

Ana tilted her head and looked at Tamarind, whether in hostility or unconcern, Tamarind couldn't tell. "It's not home. No sound of waves to put me to sleep. No chickens clucking out back." She shrugged and spread her hands wide on the counter. "What is, is."

Sarah, who'd stopped eating, leaned against Tamarind and watched Ana. Ana looked down at her and smiled. Her teeth, small and white, contrasted with her shrunken cheeks and pale lips. They were young teeth.

"Who's this?" She extended a bony finger to Sarah, who shrank and hid her face against Tamarind's shoulder. "*Mer* daughter for sure."

Tamarind started. "She's human."

"Course she is. But those eyes aren't."

Tamarind wrapped an arm around Sarah. She shouldn't be shocked, but she was. "As you said, she's my daughter."

Valerie set a plate of peanut butter cookies on the counter and picked one up. "Some say seeing through a child's eyes makes the world new. Sarah probably sees the world more completely than any of us."

"Sarah?" Ana asked and took a cookie. She broke some off and offered it to Sarah. "Some of my cookie?"

But Sarah refused to accept the offering until Tamarind, ashamed at the little girl's stubbornness, took it from Ana and gave it to her instead.

❧❧❧

Valerie led them on a walk around Dewey later, when the afternoon had cooled but before the seabirds that clustered in the skies over Culebra had settled like down in the mangroves along the shore and on the protected grounds of the wildlife reserve. They hadn't walked more than four or five blocks when the scent of saltwater with its undertones of seaweed, fish, and plankton hit her jaded nostrils and catalyzed homesickness in the very pit of her until she thought that she'd get sick from it. She craved the feel of saltwater on her feet so violently that she started to tremble.

"Valerie, I need to get to the dock."

Valerie looked at her. "La Diosa Marvelosa! You're so pale! C'mon, Sarah-bug, let's go this way."

Valerie led them to the town docks where Tamarind had met John four years before with her real legs so recently and so painfully gained. The hungry mist that consumed her didn't entirely obliterate her memory of John on the deck of the Triton or the way her heart had leapt when she saw his grin. Ignoring Sarah in her extremity, she kicked off her clogs and sat down to dangle her feet over the water. It was no good. The skin of her feet and calves felt like dried whale skin and there was no way it would absorb any of the good energy of Mother Sea without being fully immersed.

"It's not working, is it?" Valerie held Sarah's hand.

"No." Tamarind heard the despondency in her voice. "No, I need to swim. I suddenly feel as though I'll die if I don't get in the water."

"Let's go then. Playa Melones isn't so far. Unless you want to jump in here."

"No." Tamarind shook her head. No need to attract any more attention to herself. She put her hand on the dock to push herself up, but her belly had grown enough to throw off her center of gravity and she tottered. Valerie squeaked and put out a hand to steady her, letting go of Sarah's hand at the same time. Tamarind saw Valerie's hand coming toward her, saw the gilded-red of Sarah's curls as she stepped away from Valerie, and understood too late that Sarah toddled to the edge of the dock fearlessly. She lurched forward to grab her daughter, but Sarah stepped out of reach and in the next instant had toppled into the harbor.

Without thinking, Tamarind turned and dropped over the side after her. The water hit her closed pores with the strength of bone and for a heartbeat she choked. She couldn't breathe water anymore. The thought seized her and she reacted. She kicked and popped to the surface. Gasping, she stroked blindly toward Sarah. Her muscles, with the memory of countless years, worked on their own accord. She'd snatched Sarah's head from the water before she recognized what her hands had grasped.

Sarah didn't kick or thrash. She didn't choke or suck in air. She remained calm even as water streamed over her face and from her mouth. She'd only been under for fifteen seconds, not long enough to get truly scared or swallow more than a mouthful of water. Tamarind's heart hammered in her ears. Never, not even when Jesus wielded his knife, had she been so scared. She lifted Sarah out of the water and Valerie grabbed her up into her arms and held her dripping against her chest. Tamarind, drained by her swift response, tried three times to lift herself out of the harbor before her trembling arms let her rise out of the water enough to hook a leg onto the dock. After she finally struggled out, she lay on her side breathing hard.

"I'm so sorry." Valerie whispered as she knelt above Tamarind. "It's all my fault. It's all my fault."

Tamarind closed her eyes behind their curtain of waterlogged hair. "No." She shook her head. Her sopping clothes and tired muscles made her feel as heavy and helpless as a beached whale. "No. I brought us here. I was thinking only of myself."

"Mommy! Mommy! I heard music." Sarah leaned, calm and dripping, over Tamarind. "Go again. Go again in water."

Tamarind pushed herself to a sitting position. "No, Sarah. Not here, not now. We'll go to the beach later. Oh, Valerie. I feel so weak, like I just used up my last energy. I don't think I can make it back to Posada La Diosa."

"Let's go to the Dockside."

Valerie waited while Tamarind rolled over onto her hands and knees and, groaning, dragged herself to a standing position. She moderated her steps to keep pace with Tamarind's slower waddle and distracted Sarah when she begged to be carried by Tamarind. They arrived at the Dockside too early for dinner, but everyone on Culebra knew Valerie and so Carol, the bartender, good-humoredly let them in and took them to a table not far from the bar.

"Forget your swimsuits?" she asked Tamarind, who was mostly dry but looked like she'd gone swimming in her clothes. "I'd probably wear shorts and a t-shirt if I were pregnant too."

Tamarind smiled, but the curve of her lips didn't lift her eyes. "Can I get some fish? I haven't had any good fish in ages."

Carol looked surprised but not put out. "Sure, we've got mahi-mahi on special tonight. I can fire up the grill early."

"Can I have it raw? You know tartar? With some lime juice." Tamarind pushed her drying hair from her face without looking at Carol to see her reaction.

"Su-ure. Do you want anything else? Drinks? Salad?"

"Shrimp. Do you have shrimp? I'd love some shrimp."

Valerie, who'd placed Sarah next to her at the table, interrupted. "Why don't you bring a round of ice water and the fried plantains for now. We'll figure out what we want when Joe gets here so you don't have to cook anything else."

"Okay. I'll be right back with the drinks then."

Tamarind refused to watch Carol on the off chance that she'd catch a disapproving posture. "I could eat a whole mahi-mahi, Valerie. I can't tell you how I crave fresh fish."

"Don't you eat it then?" Valerie sounded surprised, but she didn't look at Tamarind. Instead, she helped Sarah with some crayons and paper.

"Sometimes I sneak sardines when John isn't looking, but I'm supposed to watch how much and what kind of fish I eat." She patted her belly. The baby kicked back.

"John's still doing the vegetarian thing?" Now Valerie did look at her and Tamarind saw the hollows below her eyes, the newer wrinkles at the corners of her mouth.

374

"Yes. We eat turkey at the holidays with his family, but we don't bring any meat or fish home with us."

"But you grew up eating seafood. Maybe your body needs it, especially in pregnancy."

"I guess so."

"Has he told you not to eat seafood?"

Tamarind squirmed and sipped her ice water, which soothed her dry throat, before answering. "No, not specifically. I just don't think he'd be happy to have it in the house."

Valerie toyed with her own glass but didn't drink. "I almost hate to ask this." There was apology in her voice. "But didn't John become a vegetarian for his old girlfriend Zoë?"

Tamarind couldn't help it. Anguish and something like rage sprung up whole, apparently grown within the shade of her subconscious these past weeks. "Yes, he did."

"Perhaps it's just a habit, a reflex—something he hasn't really thought about since he adopted it. You should discuss it with him." This was said so gently that Tamarind didn't at first feel the admonition it carried.

The rebuke, no matter how mildly delivered, stung Tamarind. "Just like he discusses dinner dates with Zoë with me?"

"What?" Amazement sharpened Valerie's question.

Sarah startled and then began crying. Tamarind let Valerie soothe her daughter, glad that she could vent her own unhappiness without needing to console Sarah. She watched as Carol placed a basket of fried plantains and a chipotle-lime dipping sauce in front of them. Valerie coaxed Sarah into trying one and after she'd learned to dip it into the sauce, Valerie turned back and looked at Tamarind. Her brows were pinched, but her voice was calm.

"John snuck out for a dinner date with Zoë? Doesn't she live in Pittsburgh?"

"No, we all met her in Cambridge. She was interviewing for some jobs and got in touch with John."

"So he brought you and Sarah along?"

"Yes." Tamarind could see where Valerie was going with her questions and she didn't like the implications. "You don't understand, Valerie. I shouldn't have been there. Zoë compared me to 'John the Baptist' and said it didn't matter what I looked like since I made jewelry at home. I didn't understand until I looked up John the Baptist and read about his wild appearance."

"Ah. And John didn't defend you."

"No. He may have brought us along, but it was like we didn't exist. He was too busy staring at Zoë like a starving man." She paused while Carol placed a plate of raw mahi-mahi in front of her. "He told me he'd put Sarah to bed so I could make some jewelry, but he just went to the upstairs office like he was bewitched and read her job talk."

"That does sound bad, Tamarind. When did this happen?"

"About a month ago."

"Did you speak to him about it?"

"No." She felt belligerent and hurt all at once. "Why should I? *I* didn't make the dinner date, *I* didn't break an agreement."

"John isn't a mind reader, is he?" A pointed question. Tamarind recalled her earlier thoughts about losing her own telepathy. How did humans manage? Or maybe they didn't.

"He told her she should work for his company."

"Did she seem interested?"

"Yeah, she did." She didn't bother telling Valerie that John had also shared his fears with his ex-girlfriend instead of her. What did it matter if John didn't talk to her about his work? Zoë not only understood what he did, she could act as a partner to him.

"Then I guess you'd better clear the air with him or you're going to let your hurt fester until it turns into a nasty wound."

Tamarind glumly bit into the mahi-mahi. Where once she might have complained about its freshness, she could only sigh as it melted on her tongue. Valerie let her eat in silence. Sarah, however, begged for a bite and when Tamarind would have denied her, Valerie urged her to let Sarah have some. Together, they cleaned the plate so well that Valerie waved Carol over and ordered more along with the special for herself. She waited until Carol had walked away before bringing up another topic.

"About the Goddess pendant."

Tamarind frowned and her hand flew to the inferior stone on her breast. "I can't believe I lost it. I've scoured the house and our cars, but I don't know where it could be."

"It's just a pendant."

"No, it's not!" Tamarind's voice squeaked. Angry with herself, she shoved the ever-dangling curls behind her ear and reminded herself to wipe her mouth. "How can *you* say that?"

"Easy. All I have to do is take a look at *that*." Here she pointed at Tamarind's belly. "You're the living incarnation of the Goddess, Tamarind."

"A lot of good it does me."

"It should, if you let it. You have more power in your little finger than all the moonstones in my collection. It's your job to take care of yourself, to nurture the life within you and the other one you've given birth to already." Here she laid a hand on Sarah's head. "Birth is the most powerful force in our lives that nothing else on land or under wave exceeds. Nursing a child comes close, though. It cements a bond between mother and infant that lasts a lifetime."

Tamarind watched Sarah as Valerie spoke. Perhaps that helped explain her ability to read Sarah so well, to understand Sarah's moods and meanings with her two-year-old, truncated speech. Now that she thought of this, she realized that John acted enviously whenever she anticipated Sarah's needs or interpreted her verbal stumbling. Once, he'd even alluded to Sarah's *mer* blood as the reason that she seemed so connected to Sarah. Then a thought came to her.

"If that's so, why do I feel so lost without my Goddess? Why have John and I started bickering more? Why doesn't he understand me?"

"I said you have more power in you than ever before. I didn't say it was mature or directed. The Goddess came to you through your pendant because you sealed your love in the moonstone. Your love is eternal but fragile. It's up to you—and John too—to nurture it, to tend it until it grows sturdy and healthy enough to withstand even major storms.

"Not everyone gets this gift, Tamarind." She said this mildly, but Tamarind caught a trace of regret and remembered that Valerie had never had children. "And even those who do don't always master that energy. They let it diffuse until it's nothing but a pale shadow of what might have been. Don't let that happen to you and John."

"I wish I could bring you back with me. I could use your advice more often."

Valerie sighed.

"That's not going to happen, Tamarind. You'll have to make do without me. Besides, I'm not the best mentor when it comes to nurturing love. Steve finally ended it last spring." Her voice caught on 'ended,' but before Tamarind could respond, she continued, "Don't worry, though. You met me when you needed your moonstone. Someone will come into your life just when you need her most."

Thirty-two
 CB

ANA WAITED TEN MINUTES after Valerie left with Tamarind and her whelp before going through Tamarind's bag. There was nothing she could pilfer that would give her some hold over her former protégée, no item even remotely as valuable as that vile Goddess pendant had been. She sat back on her haunches, frustrated. What would she do now? Idly, she ran her fingers around the piping on the Little Mermaid backpack that obviously belonged to Sarah, she of the *mer* eyes. Ana felt disdain sour her throat. Those eyes were a waste on a human. She hadn't counted on Tamarind propagating so successfully. The opposite, in fact. She'd counted on Tamarind being barren. She was a mule, after all.

Ana opened the backpack and rummaged around. Board books, things that rattled and squeaked, a couple of stuffed animals, crayons and a coloring book. None of this stuff could help her. Or could it? Ana pursed her lips and hummed, a pale sound compared to the reverberating hum that she'd produced as a young mermaid. She set an item or two aside and then returned to Tamarind's bag. She pulled out the book that Tamarind had packed. A *Widow for One Year* by someone named John Irving.

"Not a very compelling cover," she said aloud and opened it to the front flap. "A mother leaves her child and womanizing husband ... hmm. That's the right track."

She slipped the book back and zipped the bag closed. The items she'd put aside she studied, trying to choose. A worn book. A chewed plastic thing. A queer-looking purple cricket. She closed her eyes and whispered a charm that was more mantra because in the end she'd have to choose with nothing to go on but instinct. She reached for one; something stuffed. When she opened her eyes she saw that she'd picked the cricket.

"Have to do."

She returned the other items and carefully zipped the backpack shut. Grabbing the edge of the dresser near her, she leveraged her old bones upright, feeling every angle of rotation in her knees and hips. She scanned the floor to ensure that she'd left everything in the same position and then clutched the unlucky cricket to her chest.

"No time like now."

If she worked diligently and quickly, she'd have set recovery plans in motion before her quarry returned from dinner.

જ્જ્જ્

Two days later, Tamarind lay on her side on the powdered sugar of Playa Flamenco watching Sarah dart in and out of the tickling waves. Sarah giggled each time the water playfully curled around her toes. For the first time, Tamarind considered what her life as a *mer* mother might have been, how Sarah would have had dolphins as playmates. If she'd never met John, would she now be an apprentice *dragos*, a *mer* leader in training? Ana had said that Tamarind's father had wanted that for her and there was no reason to think that Ana had been wrong. A pang knifed between Tamarind's ribs when she thought about her father and sisters. She'd been so focused on herself these past four years, so caught up in the drama of her life with John and Sarah that she'd forgotten her other family, her rejected destiny. They were lost to her now.

She and Sarah couldn't stay long. Even with the heavy-duty sunscreen that she'd slathered onto every inch of Sarah's pixie body, Tamarind knew that Sarah would burn quickly under the Caribbean sun. After so many months away even she would do well

380

to watch her exposure. Or so she told herself. But it was hard to believe given how desperately her skin soaked in its life-giving energy.

That wasn't all she soaked in so close to the ocean. Her pores had opened in the ever-present salt air and her skin had grown pliable and soft again. She hadn't realized how tired she'd been, how heavy her burgeoning stomach had become. The baby felt her relaxed state so much that he—her dreams told her that she carried a son—kicked during the day and slept at night with her. And what sleep she had. Washed by a benevolent moon that guarded her through an open window, Tamarind drifted deeper to the hidden well of self and woke feeling replete.

Being around Ana again had been surprisingly low-key and calm. As always, the old woman rose with the birds and took her coffee on the patio. Sarah still avoided her, but Ana spoke patiently to her and even brought little gifts—a rose conch pearl the size of the tip of Sarah's little finger, two or three pieces of sea glass, and a whole, fragile scotch bonnet. Tamarind watched the exchanges from the side, the careful offering and the reluctant acceptance.

If Ana resented her forgetfulness, she didn't show it. She asked Tamarind when her baby was due and who delivered babies where they lived now. Tamarind told her that they'd found a birth center so that she could have a midwife and Ana seemed surprised that midwives existed elsewhere. When Tamarind asked if she'd delivered any babies in the past four years, the old woman shook her head and showed Tamarind her hands, now veined and unsteady.

"These hands? Mothers go to the clinic now. Some go to stay with relatives on the big island." She tapped Tamarind's hand with a talon-like finger. "Your hands are still strong. Better take off that wedding band though. Wouldn't want to have to cut it off from the swelling."

Ana asked polite questions about John's job and family, their house, Tamarind's jewelry business. Tamarind hadn't experienced this side of Ana before, the casual friendship without an expectation of more. It was both pleasant and unsettling.

When they returned to Posada La Diosa later that afternoon for a *siesta*, Tamarind found Ana in Valerie's kitchen surrounded by bowls and bottles of liquids and powders, both sweet smelling and foul, colorless and tinted the hues of the earth and sea. She paused to watch a moment, remembering her life with the old woman. Afterwards, she lay down with Sarah for a nap, but instead of sleeping next to her daughter as she'd first intended, she got back up. Sarah had settled into sleep, her cheeks rosy and her breathing soft. Tamarind kissed her forehead and tiptoed from the room.

Ana didn't look up when she returned and helped herself to lemonade.

"Your hair has darkened," she said. "Not much time in the sun?"

Tamarind sighed, surprising herself. "No. Pittsburgh is rather gloomy and I doubt Cheltham's much better. This time of year, it's even worse with the short days."

"Hm." Ana grunted. She rolled out a sheet of dried seaweed and began sprinkling a tan powder along its surface. "I lived further south, in New Orleans. Not as sunny as here, made a big difference in how I felt."

"You lived in New Orleans?" Tamarind didn't try to hide her amazement. "When?"

"When I was married."

Tamarind remembered something about this. "So you didn't marry a Culebrense?"

"No, a sailor. U.S. Navy. The guys who bombed Carlos Rosario for years."

"It didn't work out?"

"Never had a chance." Ana stopped, lit a cigarette, which she held in a cupped palm. "Lasted ten years, most of them dreary. He shipped out a lot, left me alone."

"What'd you do?" Eagerness threaded Tamarind's voice: she found herself more alone as John's work hours stretched into the evening. Perhaps Ana had advice, some insight to share.

Ana, who'd taken a puff on the cigarette, snorted smoke from her nostrils. "Not a helluva lot, young one. Learned to read, like you. Took a lot of walks, learned to cook. Always waiting for the baby that never came."

"You wanted children?" This was fascinating, fascinating beyond belief. She'd never looked at Ana as anything but an old woman. "Why didn't you have any children?"

Ana laid her cigarette on the edge of the counter with the ash hanging over the side. "Don't tell Valerie I'm smoking in here."

She fell silent and continued working for so long that Tamarind thought that she'd overstepped some hidden boundary, one of those emotional reefs that she hadn't known existed in her youth, something that needed a psychic lateral line to detect. *Mer* minds also had boundaries, boundaries with unique mental signatures as variable as fingerprints or the patterns on shells. There were pockets and rooms, sometimes vast recesses, sealed off from other *mer* minds. For instance, she'd never guessed at her father's anger and pain, which he'd kept from her. The problem was that she hadn't learned to read the subtleties of her own race before she'd transformed into another. She had little hope of reading Ana, who was neither *mer* nor entirely human.

"Children weren't important to me." Ana interrupted Tamarind's musing, surprising her again. "Not really important to *him*, either. His mother, now that was a different story. She wanted grandkids, constantly bitched about not having them."

"Why'd you finally leave?"

"Read this novel. I was in this reading group at the library and one of the women suggested a book set in New Orleans. *The Awakening*. The main character just walked into the ocean one day. The end."

Tamarind frowned. "You don't mean she went swimming, do you?"

Ana barked a laugh. "Not hardly. It was winter, cold even for the Gulf of Mexico. No, young one, she drowned herself."

"How'd that help you?"

Ana picked up the cigarette, now almost a stub, took a final drag, and then pinched the burning tip between her thumb and forefinger. She put it into her skirt pocket.

"Didn't have to gloss over the ending like the other wretched housewives. They tittered over their lunchtime cocktails, talked about stripping off their clothes and following suit. I just left."

Tamarind stepped around the counter and began laying out seaweed sheets next to Ana. The rhythm of their joint movements reminded her of the rhythm of the waves.

"You walked into the sea naked?" she asked after they'd finished sprinkling powder. "You swam home?"

"How'd I do that?" Ana gave her a sideways glance that told Tamarind how stupid the questions had been. "No. Flew back to Puerto Rico, took the ferry here. Had some absurd notion I'd go back to being a mermaid like nothing'd ever happened."

For once Tamarind didn't lead with the obvious, didn't question the outcome. She saw that there was no point in asking what really happened. She wondered whether Ana's blind eye and the vestigial webbing between finger and toe had resulted from the first transformation or the attempt to transform back. Ana had warned her that putting off her tail was dangerous, but only now did she begin to comprehend how dangerous it had been.

Ana put all of the seaweed in a stack to the side. She lined up a series of bowls, several containing powders, one with dried seaweed flakes, and a final one with a milky liquid. Tamarind guessed that it was cactus juice, Ana's favorite base for lotion. She wondered whether she had ever helped Ana compound this particular lotion.

"Can I help?"

"If you want." Ana pulled two wooden bowls from a stack and handed one to Tamarind. "Just watch. No need to get the midwives' book."

She set a deep-bowled wooden spoon near each ingredient and began ladling amounts of powders into her wooden bowl. Tamarind moved to the opposite side of the counter where she could watch and imitate Ana's measurements. Ana sifted the whole amount and then she finished with a level spoon of seaweed flakes.

"Know what we're making?

Tamarind dipped a delicate fingertip into a grayish powder and sniffed. *Guano.* "It could be a few things."

Ana smiled her old smile. "True. But you know what we're making. Thought you'd like to take some home with you."

Tamarind washed her finger off. "It won't work if the intended isn't around to use it."

"John doesn't sleep at home?"

"No, he does. Just not for long. He falls into bed most nights after I've gone to sleep already and he gets up before I do. I don't think your lotion will help much."

"Perhaps a love potion? Something to turn his eyes towards home more."

"What I need is a truth powder." Tamarind said this lightly, but she knew that she meant it as soon as it came out of her mouth.

Ana finished up her lotion and began filling round tins with it. Tamarind remembered that she offered a discount to any repeat customers who reused their tins.

"Truth and marriage are often incompatible." Ana copied Tamarind's light tone, but Tamarind sensed something in her stance. "Always best to ask straight out if you want to know something." She sounded like Valerie. Tamarind got annoyed.

"You can make a truth powder. I've seen the recipe in that book of yours."

"I can also make a doppelganger mix. Much more effective with the truth powder."

"'Doppelganger'? What's that?"

"Someone who looks like someone else. One of my favorites."

Tamarind remembered reading the recipe for such a transformation when she was Ana's assistant. Something tickled at the back of her mind. She ignored it and finished mixing her own libido lotion. "How does that help me?"

"Only works if there's another woman."

The tickle returned, but Tamarind didn't let it distract her. "What makes you think there's another woman?"

"Didn't say that." Ana looked around and then pulled out another clove cigarette, lit it. "Do you?" she asked after smoke obscured her face.

"Yes." Tamarind felt disloyal telling Ana about Zoë, but that only made her angrier. "That's why I want the truth powder."

"Ah." Ana took a drag on the cigarette. "Combine that with the doppelganger mix and get to the heart of the matter. Go to John in the guise of this other woman and give him the truth powder. Then ask straight out what you want to know."

"How will I know it works?" Tamarind heard suspicion and anxiety in her voice. "What if the powder is defective?"

"Simple. Ask him something you know the answer to first, something about another woman would be best."

Tamarind frowned, thinking. "The only other woman I know about is that Culebrense woman."

Ana had gone still. "You know of no others? A man who cheats once has no reason not to cheat again."

"No, I don't. What does it matter? Isn't Raimunda good enough? He slept with her."

Ana shrugged, pinched her second cigarette out and pocketed it, too. "Doesn't matter. She'll work fine. Get something from the other woman, a hair or fingernail clipping. Or treasured item, like a locket." She gestured toward Tamarind's swollen belly. "Can't use it while you carry his child. Needs to ripen anyway."

Tamarind tapped the final lid into place and set the tin onto her stack. "I want both. How much?"

Ana shook her head. "For an old friend? Nothing. It's enough to know I'm helping."

୬୬୬

It was the dry half of the year. Not the best time to imbue her mixes with strength and vitality. There was so little moisture in the air that Ana needed to work on the shore with living water. Fortunately for her, there was a three-quarter moon—the old

386

woman's moon, Mother Sea's ancient face. It was her time and she would make the most of it.

As she walked to Playa Tamarindo that night, she congratulated herself on her patient pursuit of Tamarind, who had not only given Ana the means to recover her but had also willingly become a player in the process. Ana chuckled and shifted the rucksack on her shoulder. Tamarind wouldn't knowingly give John a libido mix along with the truth powder, but that's what Ana intended her to do. It would take a lot of energy to craft the mixes, so much that she expected to see little of Tamarind and her child before they left, but even that would benefit her plans. Sympathy would feed Tamarind's feelings of indebtedness and gratitude until they blinded her. Which was a good thing since there were no names besides Raimunda's with which to test the efficacy of the powder. Ana quashed the misgivings that filled her at this detail; the risk, slight as it was, was worth the reward.

❧❧❧

In the middle of chewing a mouthful of creamed onions—the kind of Thanksgiving dish that he'd eat only from politeness—John wanted Tamarind so badly he went deaf. He literally couldn't hear any of the chatter and clatter around Lucy's dining table. He'd missed Tamarind all week of course, but he'd been busy at work and her absence had nagged at him indirectly, like when he tried and tried to remember something, but it never came to him. Or when he walked down familiar stairs and missed the last step. His balance was off; his timing was poor. He missed her most of all at night when he allowed himself to go to sleep. That's when his nightmare began. The hurricane nightmare, dark and gusting.

He knew full well why he'd started dreaming about the hurricane. It was as plain as day. He had no one to support him as he designed and programmed the prototype for Dr2Dr and its success or failure rested on him alone. This wasn't what he'd wanted when he took the job, but he reminded himself that it was a startup and it was what he'd agreed to, like it or not. Even if he wanted out, wanted a stable job with an established tech company, 'he had no time to cut his fingernails let alone send out feelers to all the local CMU graduates he knew.

He and Tamarind hadn't had time to chat in weeks, since before that disastrous dinner with Zoë, and he suspected that they needed to clear the air, but it would have to wait until after the release next week. They hadn't made love in two weeks, either, and when the hurricane stopped wailing in his nightmares he was overtaken by a lust so strong he could taste it. It was sweet and sour and left him with a stomachache.

"More stuffing? Turkey?" Rachel, Lucy's daughter, cracked the silence with her pointed question. "You look like you've been eating too much pizza and Chinese lately."

"I have," he said. She scooped stuffing onto his plate and waited with a quizzical look, her spoon hand held high. "Thanks." She set the bowl down and forked several slices of turkey onto his plate without asking. John said nothing. The turkey tasted good and he was glad she'd taken it upon herself to give him more. He wouldn't have served himself.

"You look lost in thought," she said as she sat back down next to him. The serving dishes were back in the kitchen where there was room for them. "Missing your wife and daughter?"

"Yes, I am." He didn't elaborate, just shoveled stuffing into his mouth to kill the taste of creamed onion.

Rachel clicked her tongue and shook her head. "Guess absence does make the heart grow fonder."

Before John could answer, Rachel's husband Todd sat down next to her. He'd been outside a long time on his cell phone. If Tamarind and Sarah had been there, John would never have noticed the affection between Rachel and Todd. Now he was keenly aware of Todd's hand on Rachel's upper back, his lingering kiss. They acted like newlyweds for all that they had three young kids.

"Listen, Rache. I gotta go into work a little early. There's a backlog and it ain't gonna get better tomorrow."

Rachel didn't seem to mind. Tamarind would have minded but so would John. It *was* Thanksgiving. Maybe that came from being married longer.

"Okay, babe. Take a slice of Mom's pumpkin pie with you."

Lucy, who'd been sitting at the other end of the table, came around collecting plates and flatware. "Just like Billy," she said, not very loudly but John heard her. "Always had work to do on the holidays, always takin' off and leavin' us."

"You talking to us, Mom?" John saw surprise, and something else—resentment? anger?— on Rachel's face. "Speak up if you've got something to say."

Lucy looked up. Her basset-hound eyes had a faraway look in them. "Billy's gone again. I told him. I told him I wasn't always going to be so forgiving."

"What the hell are you talking about, Mom? Dad's been dead ten years."

John decided that he was finished. Pushing back from the table, he said, "Lucy, that was the best Thanksgiving dinner I've had in some time. Tamarind tells me your pie is beyond good. Where can I get a piece?"

Lucy blinked several times as though clearing something from her eyes. The faraway look dissolved. "Pie? Did you ask for pie?"

Rachel started to say something, but John pretended not to hear her and answered. "Yes. Can I help clear dishes first?"

He avoided looking at Rachel and no one else had heard the bizarre interchange. Without waiting for an answer, he headed for the smaller children's table in the family room where Rachel's children had eaten. They'd left a mess of shredded paper napkins, bits of ham and stuffing clung to the plastic tablecloth, and a puddle of apple juice dripped like a leaky faucet from the youngest one's chair. He stacked all their paper plates and grabbed all of the flatware and napkin bits that one hand could hold and returned to the kitchen.

Rachel was there with Dorothy, Lucy's other daughter. They were talking in the far corner, near the doorway to the living room. They didn't see him right away.

"She's losing her goddamn marbles, Thee. You shoulda heard her, shoulda seen the look on her face. It's not the first time, either."

"Livy's said Mom doesn't seem herself lately. She forgot to pick Livy up from school once. Told Livy she had a spell." Dorothy was as tall as Lucy, but Rachel looked more like their mother—except for her hard brown eyes.

John made noise as he set the flatware on the counter. He busied himself throwing away the paper plates and napkins. When he looked up, Rachel had moved to the coffee maker and Dorothy was pulling cups down to stack on the counter. A couple of feet along the white laminate sat two pies: pumpkin and apple. A warm, spicy scent came from the oven where more pies awaited.

Lucy came in from the dining room. "You like mincemeat? Or cherry? I also got a pecan in the oven that tastes divine with vanilla ice cream."

John accepted a slice from the pecan and cherry and promised to take a whole pumpkin pie home with him. Lucy told him to bring his coffee and follow her into the living room while Dorothy and Rachel loaded the dishwasher and wiped every surface down. They sat eating for a few moments before John asked about the piano.

"It's Rachel's, but she doesn't play much anymore. I hope Matthew takes it up. He's always plunking on the keys."

"But there's a picture of you over there sitting at the keyboard."

Lucy said nothing at first, just sipped her coffee. "I took lessons for a while, before Rachel came. Guess I just lost interest."

John set his cup down and stood up. "Why don't you come play with me?"

Lucy blushed and fidgeted. For an instant, John glimpsed the beautiful young woman she'd been in the tilt of her face and the grace of her long fingers. "Don't think I could. You play though."

John held his hand out to her. "Please, Mrs. Romero?"

Sighing, she set her cup down and wiped her hands on her napkin. "All right, young man."

She sat next to him on the bench. She smelled of cloves and cinnamon and, faintly, of musk and jasmine. Something old fashioned and reassuring. John flipped through the books stacked on the back of the piano until he found one. *Fur Elise* by Beethoven. An easy arrangement. He laid his right hand on the keyboard. She looked at him and then put her left hand on the correct keys.

He hadn't played much since they came to Cheltham and he missed it. There was something reassuring about sitting next to Lucy, the way she strained to read the music, her tentative fingering. He abandoned himself to the soothing melody, hearing it whole in his head even as they fumbled the notes. He sensed Lucy relaxing next to him and her playing became more confident, more fluent. The piece took on life and they swayed together during the final measures.

Clapping resounded from the doorway after they finished. Dorothy stood there, her pale blond hair marred with a brown part. Pam and Olivia crowded the doorway behind her.

"That was fabulous. Play something else," Dorothy said.

Lucy demurred. "You go on," she said to John. "You don't need me throwing a wrench in the works."

"You play beautifully."

But Lucy slid away and sat in the wingback chair next to the piano. Pam and Olivia sat down on the sofa behind him and Dorothy sat in the corner with Custard in her lap, but Rachel's kids watched a Disney movie in the family room. John remembered family holidays at Nona's house when he'd play his recital piece for everyone while they sat without speaking and listened intently. Then he'd bring out the Christmas songs or something from a Broadway musical and the room would fill with singing and laughter. He imagined he was at Nona's house and the smells of baccala, lobster ravioli, and stuffed calamari hung heavy around him. Nona had infused every dish with love and those occasions had a warm glow in his memory. It was a little different here. No one broke into singing when he began playing *Winter Wonderland*, but he persisted and the songs lifted his spirits anyway. When he got up, Lucy and Olivia clapped. He bowed and grinned.

Rachel had come to lean in the doorway while he played and now she walked toward the piano.

"May I?"

John nodded and went to sit in the easy chair in the far corner. No one spoke while Rachel sorted through the stack of music and then, running her hands through her hair once, she pushed the books aside and placed her fingers on the keyboard. John expected a Christmas hymn, but Rachel had something else in mind. Without any prelude, she began playing with such skill that John was ashamed of his own proud performance. Everyone sat entranced. It was a dark, ferocious piece that rolled over the room before subsiding into a calm that built again in intensity only to end in a dazzling lighthearted tap dance. Mussorgsky's *Hut on Chicken's Legs*.

"That was totally awesome." John let admiration color his voice.

Rachel turned to look at him. Her eyes gleamed in the light from the piano stand and her expression was hard to read. "My audition piece for Berklee."

"You must have wowed them."

She said nothing, just slid the cover down on the keyboard and stood up. He watched her walk from the room wondering whether he'd said anything he shouldn't have, but he caught Lucy's eye and she shook her head slightly. It wasn't until later, as Lucy stacked containers of leftover turkey and stuffing into a plastic bag for him, that John learned the reason behind Rachel's abrupt exit.

"She never played it for them. She took a pregnancy test two days before the audition and decided to get married instead." She said this matter-of-factly, but John heard the note of regret anyway.

"She can always come back to it. It's not like she lost her talent."

Lucy shrugged, wrapped the pumpkin pie with aluminum. "It's never about talent. Only about choices. Then again, that's true for most things, isn't it?"

Thirty-three
ೞ

IF TAMARIND HAD LONGED FOR CULEBRA before her trip, she thirsted for it in the weeks leading up to Christmas. Her thoughts drifted there at the most inappropriate times. As she read *Dr. Seuss's One Fish, Two Fish, Red Fish, Blue Fish* to Sarah for the fiftieth time, she remembered sitting on a darkened Playa Resaca waiting for sea turtles to waddle ashore while John read to her. Sometimes when John was telling her about the ins and outs of the scaled-down system he was programming for Patriot Healthcare, she heard sooty terns crying *wideawake wideawake*. Once, during lovemaking, she drifted in and out of the memory of gentle waves. Today, when she should be in the dining room beading bracelets for holiday shopping, she stared unseeing at the darkening December afternoon and imagined that she glided through silent seawater.

"Mrs. Wilkerson? Sarah wants an apple." Olivia materialized beside her. "Can I get her one?"

"Hm?" Tamarind shook her head and blinked, frowning. "Get her what?"

"An apple." Olivia looked at her, her eyes dark and serious inside their frames. "Is everything okay? I thought you wanted to make some jewelry."

Tamarind sighed and shoved her lank hair behind both ears where it lay meekly. "I'm fine, Livy. Just tired. Sure, get Roe an apple." As Olivia headed toward the kitchen, she added, "You know to slice it, right?"

She turned away from the chilly glass and went into the brightly lit dining room. On other days, its mess of toddler artwork and crusty dishes cheered her, but this afternoon they increased her fatigue. Her feet hurt in her slippers and a sharp twinge grew between her eyebrows. She sat down to work on a silver charm bracelet, but clumsiness dominated her and she couldn't string any beads. She dropped the piece onto the table and massaged her fingers, now swollen into fat pink sausages. Her wedding band squeezed the flesh of her third finger to a glossy white. She should have listened to Ana and taken it off weeks ago.

Sarah walked through the far end of the dining room, a sippy cup filled with juice tucked under one arm. She gnawed on an apple slice.

"Sit down!" Olivia commanded and tugged Sarah into a seat. "Don't walk while you're eating. You can choke."

Sarah, her blue eyes popping against rosy skin, grinned. "Livy's not mad. She's pretending."

Olivia frowned and sat down next to her. "Of course I'm mad. I'm so mad, I'm gonna turn into an ogre and eat you!" At this, she bared her teeth in mock fury and raised curled finger to emulate claws. "Little girls are very tasty," she growled. Sarah giggled.

Tamarind watched, but she felt detached from the scene before her. Detached and a little dizzy. She fingered the pile of silver beads. They clicked and clacked against their glass bowl.

Olivia looked at her. "Sure you're okay? Your eyes are puffy. Mine get puffy when I cry."

"Well, I haven't been crying." Tamarind stopped fingering the beads and touched the substitute Goddess at her breast. It didn't help. She pulled her fingertips away. "How's your grandma? We found that bunch of pine with the ribbon on our storm door. I suspect her."

"She gets the swags from her church, St. Ann." Olivia looked down and began playing with a piece of paper in front of her. She continued to play long enough that the sense that she was struggling with something began to seep through Tamarind's fog. "Gram's okay, I guess. She's just been different lately."

"Different? How?" Tamarind squeezed her eyes shut and massaged her temples. It was no good. Her headache now spread across her forehead and the light had begun to hurt her eyes.

"She's absentminded. She never used to forget anything, but she's forgotten me at school four or five times this semester."

"You should see me these days. You wouldn't be so worried about your grandma." Tamarind tried to sound lighthearted, but the pain in her head added an edge to her words.

Olivia had shredded the paper by now. Tamarind hoped that it wasn't one of Sarah's favorite masterpieces. "That's not all. She keeps saying things to Mom and Aunt Rachel she never would've said before. When they respond, she seems totally surprised she said anything out loud, like she meant to only think it. Mom thinks she's going senile, but Aunt Rachel's getting angry."

Tamarind ignored the headache and focused on Olivia. "Like that day she talked about loose lips?" She wondered what Olivia would think of her own inability to filter the thoughts that passed through her lips. Maybe she was rubbing off on Lucy....

"Yeah." Olivia's fingers quieted and she looked at Tamarind. "The worst part," she said, her voice lowered, "is that sometimes she doesn't know who she's talking to. Sometimes she talks to Great Aunt Louise, sometimes to Mom or Aunt Rachel as if they were little again. Once, I caught her sitting in her living room talking to Grandpa."

"I used to talk to my mom all the time, but she died when I was too young to really remember her. I missed her anyway."

"But Grandpa's been dead ten years! Mom says Gram should be over it by now."

"I'm still not over my mom's death." Tamarind's voice caught as she said this. She hadn't thought about it before, but it was true.

"Olivia, I'm not the best person to talk to about how other people act. I'm generally clueless. But I can tell you that your grandma is a strong, gentle soul who loves you. That's all that matters."

Olivia nodded but said nothing.

Tamarind stood up. The room wobbled. "I need some juice. Can I get you something?"

Olivia shook her head. "I've gotta go to the bathroom." She darted a glance at Sarah, who sucked on the spout of her cup. "Is that okay?"

Tamarind waved her away. "Of course you can go to the bathroom. Go, go!" She watched as Olivia left the dining room.

Sarah put the cup down. "Livy's tummy hurts, Mommy. She has accidents like me."

Tamarind frowned and compressed her lips together. She'd noticed that Olivia went to the bathroom a lot, like a pregnant woman. Or a child who was potty training. More like a child who was potty training. She'd discovered the truth when she once went to borrow a highlighter and pulled out a grocery bag from the front pocket of Olivia's backpack. She'd caught a whiff of excrement from the tightly wrapped lump. Perhaps she should mention Olivia's accidents to Lucy if they continued.

"Livy wants everyone happy." Sarah's blue eyes held Tamarind's. "Live like Prince Eric and Ariel."

Tamarind remembered Olivia's remark about fairy tales. She'd obviously not read any of the original stories or she'd know that not everyone lives happily ever after. And most of the time there was violence and bloodshed along the way. "Me, too, honey. Me, too."

She helped Sarah down, but when she stood upright again, dizziness snatched her up in its hurricane and she had to clutch the table to keep from falling. Her stomach lurched. The floor rocked beneath her. Somewhere in the back of her mind she wondered if this was how seasickness felt for some people, wondered why *she* felt seasick—seasick on land.

"Mommy." Sarah still stood next to her. "Mommy, sit down." Her tone was a perfect imitation of Olivia's earlier command. Tamarind eased herself into Olivia's seat without opening her eyes.

"Mrs. Wilkerson?" Olivia had returned. She sounded alarmed. "Should I call Gram?"

"No," Tamarind said. Her voice sounded weak. "No." The room still rocked and a fierce ache threatened to split her head, but the nausea had eased. Her body felt bloated inside its skin casing, thick and unwieldy. "I just need some Tylenol and a glass of juice, Livy."

"I'll get them. Stay there."

Tamarind had no intention of standing up again. In fact, if she could stay in this chair until she gave birth, she wouldn't complain. Her feet had swollen towards the end of her pregnancy with Sarah, but she'd had no idea that the rest of her body could hold so much water. She endured the time it took for Olivia to search the cabinets for the Tylenol, too sick to call out where she kept it. At last Olivia returned with the juice, which she drank in two long swallows, pausing only long enough to take a breath and to pop the Tylenol capsules into her mouth.

"Maybe I should lie down?" It was supposed to be a statement, but her voice rose at the end. She didn't feel capable of deciding on her own.

"Yes, yes. I'll help you." Olivia took up a position next to Tamarind, who braced herself against the young woman's bony shoulder.

Together, like some lumping three-legged beast, they stumbled to the loveseat in the family room. The dizziness whirled around Tamarind and she sat panting. Heat flushed through her and there was a roaring in her ears.

"I'm going to be si—" she began and vomited.

Olivia ran to the kitchen. Tamarind heard water running and then Olivia hurried back and wiped her face clean.

Sarah watched Olivia's ministrations. "Call Daddy," she commanded when Olivia turned to cleaning Tamarind's blouse and the floor.

"Okay, bossy pants." Olivia tossed the dirty cloth into the kitchen where it skidded on the linoleum floor. "First, let's get your mom a clean shirt."

Sarah nodded once and turned to run to the stairs, her short legs going faster than she did. Olivia called over her shoulder as she followed, "Be right back."

Tamarind tilted her head to acknowledge the news. The baby kicked once, twice, and was still. Whatever this was, it was worse than morning sickness, which got better once she threw up. The headache had abated a little and she no longer felt nauseous, but dizziness still wobbled her thinking and fatigue weighed her heavy body down. Her chest felt so heavy that she knew humming would be impossible, but still she tried to regulate her breathing. The effort died, stillborn. Instead, she waited in a near stupor while Olivia and Sarah were gone.

The sound of clattering on the wood stairs announced their return.

"Is this okay?" Olivia said. "It was the only clean one in your closet."

"It's okay." Tamarind didn't even open her eyes before answering. Her mouth tasted terrible.

Olivia said nothing for a long moment. Tamarind heard her feet shift. "Um, do you want me to help you change? Or do you want to go to the bathroom?"

"Help," Tamarind said.

Olivia nodded and, laying the clean blouse onto the loveseat, she removed the vomit-slick Goddess pendant and dropped it onto the coffee table. Tamarind scarcely felt it go. Olivia turned back and tugged on the soiled blouse. After five minutes of working the material over Tamarind's head and lifting her arms to pull the sleeves off, she managed to remove it. She slid the fresh blouse into place, jarring Tamarind's aching head in the process. Tamarind moaned a little.

"Did I hurt you?"

"No." Tamarind sighed. How would her headache go away now that she'd thrown up the Tylenol? "My head hurts, that's all."

"I'm going to call Mr. Wilkerson now. What's his number?"

Tamarind listened while Olivia dialed, but she could tell by the tone of Olivia's voice that she'd gotten John's voicemail.

She interrupted before Olivia could make her condition sound worse than it was. Before the dinner with Zoë she might have been happy to play up how ill she felt, but now she didn't want to give John any more reasons to disdain his "John-the-Baptist" stay-at-home wife.

"Don't ask him to come home early. Just tell him to pick up a pizza on the way home." Her voice sounded thin and unconvincing even to her.

Olivia left the message anyway and came back. "How about I stay until Mr. Wilkerson gets here? He can give me a ride home."

"It might not be until eight or nine. Don't you have homework?" Tamarind didn't want Olivia to know how much she wanted her to stay. "Won't your mom want you home sooner?"

Olivia looked away. "No, tonight's her date night. She leaves cash in the drawer with the takeout menus and we're supposed to order dinner. Pam usually grabs some of it and goes to the mall with her friend Michelle."

"Okay, then. Put a video on for Roe and you can do your homework. We'll get pizza delivered if John's not home by six."

Tamarind, knowing that Olivia was on duty, let the stupor take control. When she came around again, the sky outside the family room window had darkened and cold stars glittered. The house was quiet except for the scratching of Olivia's pen in her spiral notebook. She studied the teenager across from her in an easy chair, absorbed in her writing. Sarah must still be in the living room watching a video.

"What time is it?" Her voice scratched her throat. A dull ache crucified the base of her skull.

Olivia looked up and for an instant Tamarind glimpsed uncertainty and something else. Happiness. And then recognition slid over Olivia's face and the happiness got tucked away. "It's four thirty. I think."

"Get any homework done?"

Olivia clutched the notebook to her chest; she appeared unaware that she'd done so. "Most of it. I was just working on a story."

"Olivia."

"What, Mrs. Wilkerson?"

"Thanks for staying. I don't know what I'd do without you."

"No problem." Olivia continued to squeeze the notebook. "Can I ask you something?"

"Only if I don't have to stand up to answer."

"Do you think I'm normal?"

Tamarind frowned. "I don't understand. You have two arms, two legs, two eyes ... are you hiding something under your sweatshirt and jeans?"

Olivia shrugged. "I don't think so." She paused. Something flitted across her features that her glasses couldn't disguise. "It's not on the outside. It's my inside."

"Don't you have organs and blood like everyone else?"

Olivia flipped her head. When she spoke, she sounded peevish. "I'm sorry I asked." She stood up and laid her notebook on the coffee table.

Tamarind had said something wrong, but she didn't know what. And the persistent pounding in her head got in the way of thinking. "Why're you mad? I don't understand."

"You're mocking me, that's why." Olivia looked down at Tamarind, who recognized hurt now.

"No, I'm not. If you're not asking about organs and blood, then I don't know what you mean." She heard pleading in her voice.

Olivia sighed and then plopped back into the easy chair. "I mean, how I think. How I feel. You don't know what I mean because you're so normal."

That struck Tamarind as exceedingly funny. She started laughing. It jarred her eyeballs.

"What?" Olivia bristled again, like a puffer fish facing a shark. "How's that funny?"

The dizziness and headache clamored for attention, but Tamarind ignored them. "I'm as far from normal inside as you can get and still be human, trust me."

Olivia leaned over and picked up her pencil. She tapped it on her fingers, the sole of her sneaker, her forehead. Finally, she said, "I don't get this new body I have or all the new feelings that come with it. I find myself crazy happy around this girl I know, Britney, almost like I've got a crush on her."

"New body? Crush?"

Olivia looked hard at Tamarind. Tamarind saw irritation. And suspicion. After a moment, Olivia's gaze went to the darkened windows. "You're like Amelia Bedelia, aren't you? You take everything literally." Tamarind didn't know who Amelia Bedelia was, but it didn't sound like a compliment. "I'm talking about puberty. I can still remember not having these." She pounded her breasts, none too gently. "Along with them came all of these … these wants. I'm all mixed up. And now I think I'm in love with a girl."

Tamarind, whose body felt as inflated and strange as the puffer fish she'd just compared Olivia to, didn't understand the teenager's anxiety. "What's wrong with being in love?"

Olivia beat a rapid tattoo on her sole as she answered. "It's hard to be happy if everyone else thinks you shouldn't be. Or would if they knew anyway."

"Who? Your mom? Your grandma?"

"And all the kids at school, including Britney."

Tamarind recognized loneliness in Olivia's voice. She'd felt it more than once since she'd put off her tail. Maybe that's what Ana had meant long ago when she'd said that it took more than legs to be human. It took fortitude to stand on your own. She didn't know what to say.

So she said the only thing that came to mind. She repeated her earlier assertion. "Your grandma loves you." The terrible taste surged in her throat.

"I know." Olivia sounded sure. Sure and sad. "As long as I don't disappoint her. Please don't tell her what I told you."

The dizziness whirled around Tamarind, carrying off Olivia's words while she vomited again. She moaned, heard Olivia's voice as though underwater, and the headache erupted into a shrieking pain that blinded her and she lost consciousness.

જ⁓જ⁓જ

When Olivia called, voice trembling so much that Lucy almost didn't understand her, Lucy had a gardening catalog open, but she hadn't turned a page in a quarter of an hour. For the first time that she could remember, she couldn't find anything worth getting her hands dirty for. It was all stuff and nonsense. She almost didn't answer the phone, thought perhaps it was Carol from the gardening club about the trip to tour "magnificent homes and gardens of the Old South" or possibly Janice from the daily Mass group at St. Ann's. The answering machine had picked up, though, and Olivia's frightened warble propelled her from her easy chair quick enough.

"—passed out and she looks awful. Please, Gram, if you're there—"

"Olivia, slow down, love. What's the matter?"

"Something's wrong with Tamarind! She keeps vomiting and she's passed out. Her face and hands are all puffy. I'm so scared, Gram."

"I'll be right there." Lucy hung up without waiting to hear Olivia's response.

When she got to her front door, she could see light blazing from her neighbor's house. She hurried across her driveway, her chest heavy from fright and unaccustomed exertion. By the time she reached Tamarind's yard, Olivia stood holding the storm door open. Sarah huddled in the cramped front hall, her blue eyes shocked and shocking.

"Where is she?" Lucy panted.

Tamarind lay sideways on the loveseat, an avalanche waiting for a loud noise to crumble to the floor. Watery mucous slimed her chest and pregnant belly. Lucy hurried to her, knelt and took one of

402

her hands, swollen so much that it hurt Lucy just to touch it, and kissed her forehead. She wasn't feverish. And she didn't stir.

"Call 911, child," she said.

"Okay." After Olivia told the 911 operator where to send the ambulance, she turned to Lucy. "They're on their way." The relief in her voice didn't dissolve the worry in Lucy's heart.

"Call Mr. Wilkerson, too."

"What if he's not there?"

Exasperation colored Lucy's voice. "Just leave a message, Olivia. The man needs to get to the hospital. Tell him either way that I'll stay with her. You stay here with Sarah."

"Yes, Gram."

Lucy's chest ached when the dark-blue jacketed EMTs appeared in the doorway with their collapsed gurney. What was wrong with Tamarind? Were she and the baby in danger? She hovered in the kitchen doorway, shooing Olivia and Sarah into the living room when it looked like they would get in the way.

"How many weeks is she?" The EMT nearest her asked over his shoulder.

"I think she said her due date was mid-February," Lucy said. She watched as they listened to Tamarind's heart and lungs, tried to rouse her.

"How long has she been this way?" The EMT turned to face her now.

"My granddaughter called me when she passed out, but I think she started vomiting an hour ago. What's wrong with her?" Lucy's voice wavered. She clenched the edge of her cardigan to strengthen it.

"Severely dehydrated. Happens to pregnant women sometimes, usually early on. We're starting her on an IV, but she'll have to get checked out at the hospital. She's having some contractions and we don't want those to get any stronger."

"Can I ride with her?"

"Sure."

They lifted Tamarind, who for all her girth appeared diminutive and vulnerable between them. Lucy snatched Tamarind's purse from the counter and her coat from the hall closet before following the EMTs to the ambulance, its pulsing red light a beacon in the dark December evening. When she got in next to Tamarind, her heart seized. Tamarind's once crazy, brilliant hair lay limp and dull around her wan face, so puffy that her delicate bone structure had been submerged. She leaned closer, slid a few hairs behind Tamarind's ears, wondered how long it would be before John got the message and came to the hospital, his face drawn. She remembered going into labor early with Bill Jr.—six weeks—back when six weeks meant you might lose the baby. Billy had stayed in the waiting room overnight and when she saw him next, his haggard, stubble-blackened face had never looked dearer to her. He'd rushed to her bedside and, kneeling, buried his face against her chest. They'd both cried from all the stress and the relief and the uncertainty.

Lucy whispered a Hail Mary and then offered up her own wordless prayer to the Mother who understood better than anyone the trials of motherhood. When they got to the ER, she kissed Tamarind's forehead and squeezed her hand, telling her that God and the Virgin Mary watched over her and her baby. She waited until the EMTs had wheeled Tamarind through the swinging doors to the mysterious reaches of the emergency department and then made her way to a pay phone in the waiting room. She called Dorothy, got her answering machine, and stood there for ten seconds before hanging up. Rachel turned out to be at home, but Lucy found that she had nothing to say to her either, and when Rachel grew irritated with both her silence and the kids clamoring in the background, Lucy said goodbye. On the third try, she got Olivia. This time, she spoke.

"Sweetheart, I love you." Her voice didn't waver.

జ్ఞ్యైజ్ఞ్

Nearly 1700 miles away, Ana nursed a feverish Valerie, whose embattled immune system had already begun to fail her. She dipped a soft cloth in tamarind water and wiped it along Valerie's shining forehead. In the darkened room, Valerie's harsh breathing broke along the walls like implacable surf.

Perhaps it was the white noise surrounding Valerie's illness or perhaps it was the force of her attention on her friend, but it was more than an hour before Ana heard the echoes of Tamarind's plight. By then, the IV had reconstituted Tamarind's body and halted her early contractions. Ana's suspicions had been correct, then. The baby Tamarind carried had no *mer* elements within him. She felt certain that it was a male child, a child whose grounding magic was so strong it would suck the water from its mother remorselessly—quite possibly to its death.

She'd gambled on this possibility and sent Tamarind home with a charm to strengthen the baby's grounding magic. She smiled. What a lucky purple cricket that had been.

Thirty-four

✆

AFTER TAMARIND'S TRIP TO THE EMERGENCY ROOM, John's hurricane nightmare returned, howling in his thoughts during waking hours when he should have been wrestling with the design specifications for Patriot's Web portal. Even Prasad's cheerful news that he could advertise for a system administrator and an entry-level programmer added to his anxiety instead of detracting from it. Too many variables beyond his control had the potential to upset the precarious balance that he'd achieved between work and home. Tamarind's weekly visits for an IV trumped every other subject vying for his attention, but he could ill afford to hire incompetent—or worse, unpleasant and difficult—tech support. He'd emailed all the CMU connections that he had in the Boston area looking for good, reliable people, but it was the week before Christmas and responses had trickled back.

The real test of his composure walked into his cubicle this morning unannounced.

Zoë had blown in from an interview with a Waltham-based network-security firm. John had been forced to introduce her to Prasad, who'd let her into Dr2Dr's main office. Prasad, jerking his long limbs with the grace of a marionette, had hopped around Zoë's Amazon form, his white teeth splitting his face and lighting his eyes.

Before John knew what was happening, Prasad had taken Zoë to meet Mukesh and Mukesh had stood there, jaw slack, as she dominated the conversation. The upshot was that Zoë had maneuvered Mukesh into a second, formal meeting the next day so that she could present some security research relevant to Dr2Dr's mission.

Tomorrow, Dr. Mukarjee was scheduled to visit, and John hadn't made as much progress on the IndiaClinic Web site as he'd promised. He didn't need Zoë's unsettling presence looming over their meeting. If he had any luck at all, she'd arrive after the good doctor had gone to lunch. He might even take the good doctor to lunch and leave Mukesh to her mercy. It would serve the uptight bastard right.

John spent the rest of the afternoon trying to focus on work, but Zoë's perfume lingered in his cubicle and gave him a headache like the one he'd had after their dinner back in October. He remembered thinking that he'd been inoculated against her sexual magnetism at CMU, but now he wondered if he'd developed an allergy to her presence—all he needed was a whiff and he felt ill. If she managed to worm herself into consulting for Dr2Dr, would he build up a tolerance to her again or wreck his immune system?

Mukesh came in while he toyed with the video module for the prototype. Mukesh's starched shirt and gray slacks made John wish he'd worn ripped jeans and a scruffy beard just to further distinguish them. He didn't worry that Mukesh would write him up for improper office attire; even though Mukesh had handed out a policy and procedures handbook in November, John had since realized how much power he, John, had in the scheme of things. He might not have time to look for a better job or want to disappoint Dr. Mukarjee, but Mukesh had no time to replace him in a tight market. For now, they were stuck with each other.

"John, I need to talk to you." As usual, Mukesh didn't wait for John to finish what he was doing or ask to schedule a meeting when he was free. "I just got off the phone with Dr. Pendyala. He's bringing in an ad agency next week to see the prototype."

"Ad agency?" John's head buzzed. Maybe he shouldn't have had that last cup of coffee so late in the day. "Why?"

Mukesh compressed his lips. He obviously didn't want to answer John's question. "Patriot plans to subscribe consumers to a Web-based consulting service via the Dr2Dr portal. The prototype will feed the ad agency's brainstorming for its campaign."

The news blindsided John, who knew that subscribing consumers to Dr2Dr was akin to opening Pandora's box—at least for him. Not only did this new service promise to complicate the Web site design, but he also feared that he hadn't heard everything.

"Good thing you told me this now," John said, keeping his irritation in check. "I need to know as much as possible about intended uses so that I can address them in the site design. Serving up confidential information on the open Internet poses unique problems. Anything else you leave out?" He locked his gaze on Mukesh's face, but Mukesh didn't blink.

"Hey, man!" Prasad walked in, his nearly perpetual good cheer jolting the office. "Did you tell John the good news?"

John heard the almost inaudible intake of breath from Mukesh, whose lips had tightened further. He almost expected the straight-laced Mukesh to roll his eyes.

"What good news?" John asked, hoping to get it out of Prasad before Mukesh could step in.

"We're going to start selling advertising." Prasad sounded eager, smug. "Now that we've signed with Patriot, we can target individual doctors and consumers. With enough 'eyeballs' we can get ad revenue from pharmaceutical and medical supply companies."

He had to hand it to Mukesh and Prasad: they had grand plans for Dr2Dr and they hadn't even launched a working site. Correction: *He* hadn't even designed a site. Well, that gave him more power in the employment equation. He looked at Mukesh, who appeared as taut as a pulled bowstring, and recognized Mukesh's awareness of his conclusion. It felt good to move up from interchangeable cog to essential control valve.

He nodded, his face magnanimous and thoughtful. "I see. Guess I'd better get those job descriptions posted on The Monster Board. It might take some time to find the right people."

John remained calm for the rest of the afternoon; in fact, he found his focus after the impromptu strategy session and solved a sticky problem related to how the Web site pulled data from Patriot's servers. His calm only delayed the storm of conflicting emotions that whirled around him on the drive home, however. His distrust of Mukesh rose daily. He doubted that Prasad lost any sleep over how Dr2Dr's Web site might be abused, but he'd started to fear that Mukesh would knowingly deceive doctors and patients if it meant lining his own pockets. Neither man cared about how they could use the wonder of the burgeoning Web to help people. He for one didn't want to start advertising drugs and medical supplies to Joe User. It was one thing to advertise to doctors, who were educated professionals—or should be. John feared that the next step would be selling, and he had no confidence in the ethical or legal strength of *that* possibility. Poor Dr. Mukarjee had allied with some shady characters.

When he arrived home, John's anxiety about Tamarind and the baby surfaced through his roiling thoughts. Nothing else mattered. He opened the front door to find Tamarind propped against the arm of the loveseat, her legs stretched before her. Her curls, once spunky and wild, lay unfurled on her shoulders in a dull mass; her eyes, no longer brilliant, had sunken into a smoky smudge in her swollen, wan face. She looked toward the front hall where he stood, and worry and love stabbed his chest.

Lucy appeared with a cup of tea, set it on the coffee table, and, seeing Tamarind's gaze, turned to face John.

"John!" Lucy's face crinkled with pleasure. "You're home! I was just relieving Tamarind so she could put her feet up a bit."

As she was speaking, Sarah trotted to Lucy's side. John set his laptop bag down, dropped his coat, and strode into the family room before Sarah could say anything. He lifted her into the air where the simple act of defying gravity made her shriek happily.

"Roe! How's my girl?"

"Daddy!" Her giggles cut through his anxiety, dispelling the bulk of it as sunshine banishes morning fog. He lowered her for a kiss, which she accepted before pulling back to look at him. Her grave eyes brooked no disobedience. "Kiss Mommy, too."

"Yes ma'am," he said and slipped her to the floor.

He bent over Tamarind, who lifted her face. Her lips, warm and dry, lay under his. It was like kissing his grandmother's cheek.

"Hey. How're you?"

She shrugged. "About the same. Lucy wouldn't let me make dinner."

"No sense in her peeling potatoes at the dining-room table when I've got two good legs and can stand at the sink," Lucy said behind him. John tilted his face and when their gazes met, he let her see his gratitude.

John stood and wiggled his fingers at Lucy. "These could use something else besides keyboarding. What can I do?"

Lucy smiled. "Good thing you got here when you did. Tamarind was going to tell me how to make something called a vegetable *korma.* Afraid I was going to have to sprinkle some curry powder on a pot of soup and hope you wouldn't notice."

John laughed for the first time in weeks. "I've eaten your cooking, Lucy. I bet it would've tasted great."

They went into the kitchen and John insisted that Lucy delegate the rest of the vegetable chopping to him while she searched for spices in the pantry. As he worked, he heard Sarah talking steadily in the family room. He glanced into the room to see her sitting on a plastic stool at Tamarind's shoulder, her copper curls obscuring her face, reading a picture book. Tamarind's eyes had closed and she'd relaxed back against the armrest. He longed to caress her shoulder, put his hand on the nape of her neck and kiss her. They hadn't made love for several weeks, since before she'd gone to the ER, and he had no idea when they would make love again.

Lucy stood at the sink near him, busy washing out a pot. She spoke over the running water but not loud enough for her voice to carry into the family room.

"I'd like to take Sarah in the mornings so Tamarind can stay in bed." She didn't look at John.

"That would be great," he said. He was sure Tamarind hadn't heard Lucy, but he couldn't help looking towards the family room anyway. "But I don't know how Tamarind would feel about that."

"I take it she told you they want her on bed rest then?" The rhythm of her scrubbing lessened, but she didn't look at him. The question took him by surprise.

"What?" John's knife missed the carrot he'd been chunking and skidded on the plastic cutting board. He stopped chopping and turned to face her. "She never said anything."

Something about the slope of her shoulders suggested that Lucy wasn't surprised—and she'd held something back.

"Is there more she hasn't told me?"

"Maybe she doesn't want you to know." Her voice barely rose above the sound of the water.

John's fear, waiting to be tapped, welled up in the column of his throat. "Is she all right?" His question came out as a harsh whisper.

Lucy darted a glance at his face, looked back over her shoulder toward the family room where Sarah's voice persisted, and then back to John.

"As far as I know, John, Tamarind just needs to stay off her feet as much as she can. That's not what I was speaking about." She paused, shifted her shoulders back a fraction, and then went on. "They had to cut her wedding band off last Friday. She got really upset, tried to keep them from doing it. They had to sedate her first."

John didn't know whether to be relieved or worried. His fear abated somewhat at the look of sympathy on Lucy's face. "She puts a lot of weight on symbols. Like this necklace she made when she was waiting for me to realize I was in love with her."

411

Lucy turned the water off. Neither of them looked toward the family room, but they moved closer and lowered their voices even more.

"The one with the figure of a pregnant woman twisted in wire?" she asked.

"Yeah." He nodded. "She lost it a couple of months ago. She misses it."

"I thought I saw her wearing it the day she got sick."

"No." John shook his head. "That wasn't the real one, the one that matters to her. It was a substitute."

"Ah." Lucy looked thoughtful. "I'll let you talk to Tamarind about bringing Sarah over in the mornings then."

She left the pot on the stove and filled the rice cooker with water and rice. John poured some clarified butter into the pot and was just dropping handfuls of sliced onions into it when Lucy came over with diced garlic. When she spoke, her voice had returned to normal.

"Tamarind told me you all haven't been to Mass since you moved from Pittsburgh. I wondered if you'd like to come to Mass with me on Christmas Eve."

Lucy's invitation had solved a dilemma for John. His parents, who arrived on the twenty-third, would expect to go to Mass. "Sure," he began when Tamarind's sharp voice cut him off.

Grabbing a towel for his messy hands, John hurried into the family room, Lucy not far behind. Tamarind was on her knees in front of the fireplace while Sarah stood on the hearth blocking her way.

"Let me get in there," Tamarind said.

"No, Mommy, no!" John had never heard Sarah sound so negative before, although everyone had warned them that two year olds often wielded the word 'no' with great relish. She looked like a fierce cherub.

"Here, here," John said and knelt next to Tamarind, who collapsed onto his shoulder. "What's the matter?"

412

"She's put that stuffed animal Stefan gave her into the fireplace," Tamarind said. "I want to rescue it, but she's acting as if she's a *moulos*."

"'*Moulos*'?" Lucy asked.

John spared her a glance. "Like a demon." He turned to Sarah. "Roe, sweetheart, let me get CriKee out of the fireplace. He doesn't like sleeping in such a dirty bed."

"No!" Sarah's firm voice rose. She didn't shriek. "No, CriKee's bad. Very bad. Has to burn."

"No," John said, his voice soothing, and reached around Sarah for the handle to the fireplace door.

Sarah put her small hand on his wrist and looked at him. For the first time he realized how much like Tamarind's they were, how much they reminded him of the blue-green ocean around Culebra. Something tickled his thoughts, dislodged his intentions.

"No, Daddy."

"Let's get Tamarind back on the loveseat," said Lucy before John could respond.

He shifted and Tamarind came into his arms. He pressed her to his side for a moment, and then he let Lucy brace her until he could get to his feet. Together, they helped Tamarind stand and return to the loveseat where she sat down and sighed.

"I don't care. Let it stay in the fireplace or throw it away." Tamarind sounded weary.

Lucy sat down and picked up Tamarind's teacup. "Here, drink this. It has raspberry leaf, dandelion, and lemon balm. Raspberry leaf eases labor and increases milk. You should start drinking it now, before the baby comes."

Tamarind sipped the tea.

John picked Sarah up and asked, "What about the dandelion and lemon balm?" He hoped the ridiculous stuffed cricket had been forgotten.

Lucy looked at him. "Dandelion is said to help with edema. Lemon balm calms." Her sad eyes held his.

413

"Ah." John pressed his lips together and nodded. "Calm is good." He looked at Sarah, whose gaze belonged on an older face. "How about a video while Daddy finishes dinner?"

"'kay," she said. No sign of a *moulos*.

John tried to rescue CriKee when Sarah went to bed, but the fireplace was empty. As he started to shut the mesh curtain, something caught his eye. He peered at the metal covering over the ash chute until he understood what had made him pause. Two black threads tipped with tiny purple balls of cloth extended just beyond the edge of the covering. The unfortunate CriKee waited to fall to oblivion.

❧❧❧

Later, after Tamarind had fallen asleep, John pressed himself against her rounded back and listened to her breathing in the dark. Her hair, free of its band, slid off her shoulder and into his face; it smelled of cloves, garlic and onion, with a faint underlying scent of shampoo. Even pregnant, she was so slight that he wanted to lay himself across her like a down comforter. Nuzzling her neck, he slipped his left arm under her own left arm and touched her hardened belly with his fingertips. Beneath his palm, the baby jumped and darted. Wonder and disbelief welled up in him and he held his breath for a moment until the baby seemed to settle under his hand; he imagined that his child was snuggling close to him.

He kissed Tamarind's bare shoulder and moved his hand up to her full breast. He might not get to make love to her, but he could at least appease himself a little by touching her. He lay there for several long minutes, savoring the sweet agony of his erection until it passed. In the morning, in the shower alone, he would take a few minutes and relieve himself, but it would only dampen the need down for a few days. Perhaps feeling the heat of his groin, Tamarind stirred, murmuring, and rolled over into his arms but didn't waken. Holding her against his side, John closed his eyes and drifted to sleep—perchance to dream of happier days.

❧❧❧

414

Lucy stood at her dining-room window, watching John and Sarah romping in the deep snow that had fallen the night before. It was obvious that they adored each other. She smiled. It had been a long time since she'd seen a father and daughter playing together. Without warning, a vivid memory of Billy and a two-year-old Dorothy commandeered her thoughts. It was summer, and Dorothy's chunky little calves were covered with white knee socks and her wispy blond hair was clipped back with a plastic barrette. Billy grabbed her and dropped her over his shoulder, like a sack of potatoes. He started down the street toward the drugstore that they'd lived near back then, Dorothy giggling. Lucy watched them return, Billy holding a Coke and Dorothy a vanilla ice cream cone, her faced bearded with melted cream.

As quickly as the image came, it fled, leaving Lucy dizzy and weak. She half turned and put out a hand to steady herself on a dining chair, but her knees gave way before she could. She slid to the floor, striking her forehead on the chair on the way down. Her fall was quick and silent.

"Mom!" Dorothy, who'd been walking through the doorway from the kitchen, set the bowl she was carrying onto the sideboard and rushed to Lucy's side. "Are you all right? Mom, I said, Are you all right?"

Lucy's thoughts whirled in a brisk wind of nostalgia and regret; she struggled to gather them back to the present. Even when the wind quieted, she sensed it drawing into the recesses in her mind, not dampened, just waiting. She raised a shaky hand to her forehead and felt along the welt rising there.

"I think so," she said, her voice mirroring her uncertainty.

"Rache, bring Mom a cup of tea and a cold washcloth," Dorothy called into the kitchen.

Rachel appeared in the doorway, took in the scene, and disappeared.

"Mom, what happened?" It was the first note of concern that Lucy had heard out of Dorothy in years. She helped Lucy into a chair and her hands were firm, gentle.

"Guess my blood sugar's low." Lucy's laugh was shaky. "Dinner about ready?"

Dorothy frowned. She sat in the chair next to Lucy and leaned closer. "Your eyes are dilated, Mom. Like you've been to the eye doctor."

Rachel came in with a wet washcloth and handed it to Dorothy. "Tea's brewing. What happened?"

"Beats me," Dorothy said. She looked up at her sister. Lucy saw the look that passed between them. "I saw her collapse as I was bringing in the salad. She says her blood sugar's low."

Rachel bent over, pressed warm lips to Lucy's forehead. "She feels cool if anything. We need to watch her this afternoon, see if she acts funny." It was almost as if Lucy weren't sitting there. Or she was a child who didn't understand them.

"I don't have a concussion," Lucy said. It came out sharper than she intended and Rachel bristled. "I'm sorry." Lucy laid her hand on Rachel's forearm. "Thank you for your concern."

Rachel muttered and stood up. "I'll get your tea. Sit there while we finish setting out dinner."

"Sure thing." Lucy tried to smile at Rachel.

It was good to sit, although she didn't want to dwell on the possible reasons for her fall. She prided herself on being pragmatic, willing to accept that she was getting old, but she'd be foolish not to be a little scared. These vivid flashbacks and dizzy spells weren't normal. She sipped her tea—lemon balm, the same that she'd given Tamarind—and now she did smile. Her fear slipped away. Rachel, for all her gruff remarks about Lucy's herbal medicines, had brought the right remedy, even if she thought it was only a placebo.

Lucy listened to the sounds of her family waiting for Christmas dinner. Rachel's kids played in the family room, their childish voices raised in argument that morphed into shrill excitement. Todd yelled for them to shut up so that he could talk on his cell phone; when that failed to quiet them, Lucy heard him walk out the front door. She looked out the window and saw him, breath frosting the air, shoulders hunched as he talked.

Rachel and Dorothy came back carrying steaming mashed potatoes and candied yams. The smell of butter made Lucy's stomach grumble. They were absorbed in their conversation and seemed to have forgotten her.

"He's always on that goddamn phone." Lucy winced at Rachel's profanity and sent a silent prayer to God that he'd forgive her daughter. "Even late at night. He tells me it's work or his buddy Joe, but I've heard his tone of voice. That ain't no guy he's talking to."

Dorothy, arranging all the dishes on the sideboard, didn't look at Rachel. "Thought things had gotten dramatically better between you two. You were certainly all over each other at Thanksgiving. I was goin' to tell you to get a room." She laughed.

"That's the thing, Thee. It's still like that. But something's changed." Rachel sounded frustrated, confused. "I don't know if this makes sense at all, but it's almost like Todd makes love to me against his will."

They left the dining room again and Lucy heard cabinet doors banging and the electric carving knife. Pam passed through the kitchen, heading toward the bathroom. After several minutes, Lucy caught low voices in the living room; they were hard to understand through the noise in the kitchen. It was Pam and Olivia. She moved her chair nearer to the living-room doorway. She wasn't a snoop, but experience with teenagers urged her to listen.

"How about a mint?" It was Olivia.

"No." Pam's voice sounded strained. "I don't think my stomach can handle them."

"Just try." There was a pause and Lucy imagined Olivia holding out a mint to her sister. "I used to get sick before class presentations. I took one of these just to make my breath smell better. It made the nausea go away, too."

There was silence and Lucy thought the girls had finished when Olivia spoke again. "Just keep one on the roof of your mouth."

"I didn't know you threw up before class presentations."

"I used to."

"You don't throw up anymore." It was a statement. "But you still get stressed out."

Olivia didn't answer.

"That's what the stains are in your panties. You've just. ..." Pam's voice trailed away.

"... switched to the other end," Olivia said. Lucy heard anguish in her voice. "Please don't tell anyone, Pam."

Dorothy walked in behind Lucy, holding a turkey high before her and talking over her shoulder to Rachel, who followed with the ham. While they settled their platters in the places of honor on the sideboard, Lucy moved her chair back. When Rachel turned to her, she was sipping the last of the lemon balm tea.

Lucy watched Olivia and Pam throughout dinner. How could she not have seen Olivia's weight loss, the baggy clothes? The chunky teenager who'd met her at the hospital cafeteria and lamented about her "fat ass" a few months ago no longer had a moon-shaped face or pudgy hands. She still hid behind dark glasses and dark hair, but it was plain to see. Lucy's heart ached. She studied Pam next. Surly as usual, Pam only played with the food on her plate even though she looked as though she'd gained some of the weight Olivia had lost. Her curves had gotten curvier, too. They'd never been as close as she and Olivia were, but ever since the day that Lucy had caught her with a boy, Pam had avoided looking at her. Today she looked at no one, not even Olivia, who also watched her.

Lucy let the conversation flow around her, cut little Ben's turkey and ham, and chatted with Hayley, who wore gravy and cranberry sauce on her holiday sweater. She said nothing more important than "Would you like more stuffing, dear?" and passed the rolls. She sat when Dorothy and Rachel insisted that they would clear the table. The whole time she listened to what wasn't said between Rachel and Todd.

It was a Christmas dinner rife with secrets and only she was paying attention to all of them.

They'd finished their pie and the little kids had grabbed handfuls of Christmas cookies to take to the family room when the doorbell rang. It was John and Tamarind, whose rosy face and sparkling eyes startled Lucy. The puffiness that had erased every angle of her cheek and jaw had disappeared and she looked healthier, the Lord be thanked.

"Merry Christmas!" Tamarind held out a wrapped present. "We hope you like it."

"Goodness! You didn't need to do that." Lucy took the gift. "Come in, come in. I have something for you folks, too."

"We can only stay a moment," John said as they stepped inside. "Mom and Dad insisted on cleaning up after dinner."

"I understand. I won't keep you." Lucy went into the living room where two packages lay under the tree. As she bent to retrieve them, an angry voice erupted from the kitchen, shattering the cheerful hubbub. Lucy arrived in the doorway to the dining room in time to see the jam of people in her foyer as Todd pushed past John and Tamarind while Rachel stomped behind him, grabbing for his hood.

"You son-of-a-bitch. Don't tell me they're backed up at work again and you've got to go in. It's Christmas."

The foyer seethed. The next few minutes were a turmoil of coats and shocked faces and sharp words. Lucy found Tamarind's hand and tugged her into the dining room; John, who'd put an arm around Tamarind, came along. Thanksgiving had been a peaceful anomaly, a blip. It had been too much to ask that they could make it to the end of Christmas without a scene.

"I'm sorry," Lucy said. Her voice trembled. "Afraid my daughters can't go long without some high drama."

In the next minute Todd was through the front door and Rachel followed, screaming. Her fury resonated in the silence. Dorothy came into the dining room, a coffee mug gripped in her hand, and sat down next to Lucy. She took a sip, looked around, and set the mug down.

"Well, I'd say they're headed for Splitsville." She didn't sound too sorry.

Lucy picked at some crumbs on the tablecloth. "That'd make you happy. Then you two could go out manhuntin' together."

Dorothy's eyebrows rose. "Well, now," she said, sounding surprised. "Don't hold back, Mom. Tell me what you really think."

Lucy looked up, unexpected pain stabbing her forehead. Dorothy glared at her. She slid her gaze away, across Tamarind and John's anguished faces and toward the doorway which framed Pam on her way to the front door. In that instant, Pam glanced into the dining room and they stared at one another. And then Pam had disappeared through the front door. When Lucy looked out the window, she saw the red glow of taillights in the street.

She tried to keep silent, but the words came out anyway. "Wait a few more years and you two can take Pam with you," she said. Her hand flew to her mouth.

Thirty-five
☙

"YOU SURE YOU DON'T WANT any help?" Valerie called from the patio.

Ana, in the act of reaching for a tin hidden on the back of the top shelf of Valerie's kitchen, paused.

"No, old friend," she called through the open sliding door. "No need for you to get up."

She found the tin and pulled it down. Rust dotted the surface and she had to find a towel to get a good grip on the lid. She twisted and twisted, but she had to expend precious energy on a tiny spell to break the rusty seal before she could open it. Inside, a dusty green powder rimed the bottom. Not enough. Not nearly enough. She would have to hitch a ride to Playa Flamenco, secrecy be damned. She tilted the tin and tapped its bottom until all of the powder had slipped to the side. She scooped the powder into the waiting cup.

She poured coffee into the cup and another for herself, stirred milk and sugar into Valerie's and carried them both out onto the patio. Valerie sat looking out over the canal, her frail neck wobbly under the weight of her head. The fever had left her thinner than ever.

"Here." Ana handed Valerie a cup. "That'll give you a boost." She sat down next to Valerie. The clove cigarettes in her skirt pocket lay against her thigh, but she wouldn't bring them out. Valerie's lungs didn't need the smoke.

"Thank you." Valerie smiled at Ana, a tired smile that didn't curl the numerous creases that marred the skin around her eyes. She raised the cup and took a tiny sip. It looked like it was more effort than she could manage. She set the cup down. "I called my lawyer, Ana."

Ana couldn't look at Valerie. She traced a fingertip around the rim of her cup. Whatever Valerie had to say to her, she didn't want to hear it. Across from them the bananaquits sang high and sweet as they fluttered around their feeders. Valerie couldn't reach the feeders anymore. Ana kept them filled.

"Didn't you say pretty words can't fool us?" Valerie asked.

Ana grunted, took a sip of her coffee. It burned her tongue.

"Posada La Diosa's paid for. It's pretty much all I've got left of my life's savings. I'm leaving it to you."

Ana's head snapped up at that. Valerie, her eyes steady, didn't flinch at Ana's look. "Don't talk that way. I can help you."

Valerie sighed and shook her head. "No, you can't." Her voice was gentle but firm. "I want you to stay and care for my birds."

Ana said nothing. What could she say?

"I'm leaving all my jewelry findings and the pieces I've already made to Tamarind." Valerie lifted her coffee, sipped, and set the cup down too hard. Coffee splashed over the side onto the aluminum table. Ana stifled a groan. Every drop counted. "I talked to Tamarind yesterday. She called while you were at the *mercado*. She gave birth to a boy two weeks ago."

Now Ana did groan. How had she missed sensing this? How had her spell failed? Did Tamarind know? She covered the groan. "Oh?"

"She sounded overwhelmed."

"Like last October?" Ana leaned closer. Perhaps all wasn't lost.

"Worse. John didn't get any time off when she had the baby. He's been working at home as much as he can, but she doesn't have a lot of help this time around, only a neighbor who stops in."

"That's too bad." Ana looked down at her coffee cup to hide the smile quivering on her lips. "Too bad, indeed."

≈≈≈

Tamarind dreamt that she was floating again on the waters near Culebra. She turned onto her back to stare into the endless blue sky and marveled at the buoyancy of the water, something that she'd always taken for granted before. As she drifted on the slight current, she raised her cupped hand high and let the water, warm and delicious, run down her arm. She felt so at peace, so light, that it was several minutes before reality intruded and woke her from her dream: Sarah's over-full diaper had seeped through her nightgown and the sheets under them. She lay, wedged between the stink of cooling urine on her arm and Sarah's soft respirations in the otherwise still morning. How had she gotten here? And then Tamarind remembered.

She'd brought Sarah to bed with her this morning after John left at dawn. Sarah must have heard John on the stairs and woke unhappy, crying about the bat that scared her so many months ago. Tamarind, just finished nursing Adam, scooped Sarah up and hustled back to the master bedroom before Sarah could wake fully. In the quiet warmth of the pale morning, they'd both fallen deeply asleep.

Her bed felt nothing like the buoyant sea. Nothing.

She turned her face toward the window, timid light held at bay behind the blinds. Still, the room's murkiness stemmed more from her mood than the actual lack of light. She'd never felt so *dark* inside before. Even when she swam too far below the water's surface for sunlight to reach, she'd never had her internal light dimmed. Ana's call had done it. Or more precisely, Ana's news had done it. The old woman had called yesterday afternoon, the first time she'd ever called Tamarind.

"Valerie told me about the baby." Ana's rough voice sounded odd, contained and powerless over the phone. Tamarind wondered why it had ever left her uneasy. "Said it wasn't easy, this pregnancy."

"No, it wasn't." The words slipped out. It was a relief to talk to someone. Someone who knew who she'd been before John. "I got so dehydrated I had to go to the hospital every week for an IV. I began to think Adam was sucking the water out of me."

Ana made clucking noises. Tamarind had heard the ancient woman soothing new mothers on Culebra and was surprised how much the sympathy meant to her. She didn't deny Tamarind's conjecture. "It never got dangerous, did it?"

"They had to cut my wedding ring off."

"Ah. Warned you." Ana's voice held no trace of smugness, which surprised Tamarind.

"I got a reprieve during the last six weeks. The doctors had no clue why."

"Odd." Ana, who had great experience delivering babies, volunteered no theories. "Labor? Easier this time?"

"No." Tamarind felt petulance seep into her voice. "Everyone said it would be shorter and easier than the first, but it was longer and more painful. It was like putting off my tail all over again. They threatened a C-section. And John had to go right back to work the next day."

"You should be here. I would nurse you."

Affection wiped away the petulance. "That would be wonderful." She paused, wondered if her next words would offend Ana. "My neighbor helps out. She's not you though."

"I'm sure she'll do just fine." Something in Ana's voice suggested doubt. "Ever need something only I can give, just call Valerie."

"I will."

There was a telling silence, as if Ana, never one to grapple with tact, had difficulty retreating back into brusqueness. At last she said, "Valerie's dying."

Her words knocked the breath from Tamarind. Somewhere in the back of her thoughts she wondered if this was how John had felt when he'd suffered his panic attacks, but for an interminable moment she couldn't get air in.

"You're sure?" Her voice croaked. "You're sure?"

"I'm sure."

ৰ্ঝ্ঝ

Nothing in Tamarind's past had prepared her for the brevity or the intensity of human bonds. *Mer* kind lived far beyond the span of even the oldest human. So long, in fact, that the thoughts and emotions of the eldest *mer* individuals became a mental artifact, a meme, transmitted as a memorial through younger generations until the wisdom of the ancients resided in the very tissue of the living *mer* mind. Only violent, untimely death—the end of a *moulos* or a victim like her mother—ever ripped away the essence of a *mer* from the rest of the community. Even so, when her mother died, Tamarind's father had cushioned his children from the worst pain and sustained them with his strong memory of her. But Tamarind was human now. When Valerie died, there would be nothing left for Tamarind to carry within her, except perhaps grief. Even that would fade.

Why hadn't Valerie told her when she'd called? Bitter orange shot through Tamarind's dark thoughts like a flare across a night sky. Valerie hadn't deemed her close enough to share the grave nature of her illness, instead mentioning only that she'd been sick and that Ana had been taking care of her.

At last the stink of urine got to Tamarind. She extricated herself from the sheets and Sarah's clinging form, pulling the breastmilk-stained nightgown over her head and dropping it onto the wood floor. Adam stirred in his bassinet and began making the kissing sound that signaled his hunger. Tamarind, shivering in the cool room, grabbed her robe and bent to pluck him up. He smelled sweet, a mixture of baby wipes, spit-up, and diaper cream overlaying his own natural scent. Her dark mood lightened and the tightness in her chest eased. She sat down, snuggling Adam to her breast, and guided him to suckle. His warm weight along her forearm ignited a fierce protectiveness that she hadn't felt before, not even for Sarah. A protectiveness fed by her realization of how fragile human life was. How fragile *her* life was.

Grief and love. Fear and hope. A complex brew churned and fermented in the hollow core of her body, leaving her stomach aching too much to eat. By early afternoon, faintness challenged her and Tamarind knew that she needed food, but nothing in her pantry promised to survive the toxic effects of her emotions.

When Lucy came calling that afternoon, Tamarind, sipping mint tea to stave off dehydration, had just finished nursing Adam to sleep and Sarah stood at the kitchen sink washing toy dishes. Ever since Tamarind's emergency trip to the hospital, Lucy had found one reason or another to stop by and she'd watched Sarah for a few hours every day the week after Adam was born so that Tamarind could nap. Tamarind's gaze latched onto Lucy, who stood on her front steps holding a cardboard box, and smiled. Lucy's stiff white hair stood up in the cold air like dandelion fluff and the folds around her wise eyes sagged.

"Thought you might like some apple pie." Lucy lifted the box. "I brought lasagna, too."

Tamarind's stomach gurgled, surprising her. They both laughed.

"Come in." Tamarind held the door wide. As happy as she was to see Lucy, she didn't miss the deep lines under the older woman's eyes, the sloping of her shoulders, the slower gait. She led the way into the kitchen, talking over her shoulder. "Want some pie now?"

"Not much of a gift if I eat some," Lucy said, setting the box on the kitchen floor.

"Of course it is! I'm just trading some for your company. I insist," she said when she saw that Lucy was going to speak again. "How about some iced tea?"

Before Lucy could respond, Tamarind had opened the cabinet and pulled down two glasses, then two plates. The smell of cinnamon and cloves made her stomach gurgle again.

"Iced tea sounds great." Lucy leaned against the counter, her arms folded across her chest while Tamarind cut and served the pie.

Tamarind, torn between her fear of being nosy and her concern for Lucy, finally said without looking at the other woman, "You look tired today. Do you feel all right?"

Lucy, about to turn toward the dining room, stopped. "Didn't sleep so well last night—had the strangest dream." She didn't elaborate. After a moment she went on. "I woke up pretty early. Couldn't get back to sleep so I started baking pies. Never made much sense to me to waste my time awake when there's always something I can do or needs doing."

Tamarind, plate and glass in hand, fixed her gaze on Lucy. "I hope it wasn't a bad dream." What she didn't say was *I hope I didn't have anything to do with it.* She'd once had the power to come to John in dreams, but that was before she'd put off her tail. Still, something in Lucy's voice bothered her.

Lucy turned and walked into the dining room. "No, I wouldn't say a bad dream, just a disturbing one. I dreamt about Billy. Seems I do a lot of that lately."

Tamarind followed Lucy to the old maple table that John had found at a used-furniture store in Pittsburgh. Its edges were pitted and rough in places, but John had laughed once and said that people paid good money these days for such 'antiquing' effects. Then when Sarah had joined them at the table and added her own distressing by banging her fork along the edge, he'd told Tamarind that they'd have to put the next child at the other end to even out the marks. If Lucy noticed the dilapidated condition of the table, she gave no sign.

"You'd never know it to eat my pie today, but I couldn't bake worth a damn when I got married," Lucy said, digging into her slice.

Tamarind chewed slowly. Even after four years of human food, she'd never gotten tired of sugary desserts. "That's hard to believe," she said after swallowing. "This tastes so good."

427

"You get good with enough practice. The first pie I ever made was cherry. I'd just met Billy and fallen head-over-heels and wanted to impress him. I think I must've worked most of the morning on it and I wouldn't let my mother anywhere near me to help. When he came calling, I offered him a piece and he managed to choke all of it down, me hoverin' over him like a nervous hen, and then asked for more to boot! After he ate half the pie, we took a stroll and that's when he started singing."

Lucy's eyes had a faraway look as she sang.

"'Can she bake a cherry pie, Billy boy, Billy boy? Can she bake a cherry pie, charming Billy? She can bake a cherry pie quick as a cat can wink its eye, but she's a young thing and cannot leave her mother.'" I thought my heart was goin' to burst, it was so big. Then he asked me if I was ready to leave my mother and I knew all my dreams were coming true. I said yes, and we got married three months later. That was 1958. Even after thirty years of marriage, he swore that was the best cherry pie he'd ever tasted."

Lucy looked at her plate and spent a long time cutting a piece of pie with the edge of her fork. Tamarind, who sensed that Lucy had never told this story before, felt something dissolve in her, some worry that she would say or do something that would drive Lucy away. Lucy had trusted Tamarind enough to share something so important.

"The funny thing is, I later tasted that first cherry pie I'd worked so hard on and it was awful! I'd used too much salt. That's when I knew I'd made the right decision when I said yes."

Tamarind sighed. "John doesn't love me that much after four years of marriage, let alone *thirty*."

"Why would you say such a thing?" Lucy asked, her voice sharpening.

How could she tell Lucy about Zoë? Lucy, whose husband had loved her so much that he'd lied to protect her feelings? She shrugged, made a joke. "My specialty's food poisoning."

Lucy caught her gaze and held it.

"Let me tell you something, Tamarind. You'll get much better as a cook whether you try or not and much worse as a housekeeper. If John has any problems with that, he can always help out. Do some laundry."

"Why will I get better as a cook but worse as a housekeeper?" asked Tamarind, her mouth half full and her eyes darting to take in the mess of Sarah's artwork on the end of the table.

"Your family will make sure you cook better or they won't eat, and as I said, practice makes perfect. As for housework, your kids will see to it that you get worse. With kids, you can't ever catch up. You just fall behind at different rates, depending on whether you're tired and sick or just sick and tired of cleaning. Or whether one of the kids is sick or in a school play."

Tamarind swallowed her bite, pushing her plate away from her. "Great," she said. "Something to look forward to." The darkness from the morning began to seep back into her.

"Life's about cleaning—one damn dirty dish at a time. All you can hope for is a little help and fewer dishes as time goes on." Lucy drained her glass of tea.

Seeing this, Tamarind stood up. "I'll get us more tea. Maybe you can teach me how to make a pie sometime."

"I'd be happy to."

When Tamarind returned, she set Lucy's glass down and asked, "Do you miss him?" She kept her gaze on the tea, sloshing around the glass's rim, as if its upheaval mattered more than her question.

Lucy picked up her fork and twisted its tines against her empty plate. Tamarind studied the exposed knuckles, the skin sunken and veined between their bony knobs. These were hands that had wiped butts and noses for five children, tilled soil and planted vegetables, cooked countless meals, and caressed a stubble-coarsened cheek in passion and concern. They reminded her of Ana's hands, yet they had more grace, more compassion in their still-nimble movements.

"Yes." Lucy's voice, when her answer came, was low and rough with emotion.

Tamarind sat down then. "Valerie's dying." Her voice trembled.

Lucy's warm hands covered hers. "I'm sorry Tamarind."

"She didn't even tell me herself," Tamarind said. She heard her outrage, her anger. "She didn't even tell me herself," she repeated. "I thought we were close."

"Maybe it's too hard to talk about with you," Lucy said. Her gentle tone with its shades of rebuke reminded Tamarind of Valerie. "Perhaps this way she can stay strong, for you. For herself."

In that moment, Tamarind understood that she had thought of only herself and that she continued to think only about herself. She squirmed and scowled, pushed her hair from her eyes. Sarah, soapy and dripping, came in from the kitchen, and finding her mother's lap free, climbed up. Tamarind brushed Sarah's misty rose-gold curls into a semblance of neatness with her fingers.

"You're right," she said and looked at Lucy's down-turned eyes. "Tell me how you learn to let someone you love go."

"I don't know," Lucy said, never blinking. "If I knew that, Billy's ghost wouldn't haunt me all these years later."

ર્જા ર્જા ર્જા

After Lucy returned home, she wandered around the house for a few minutes. It had been a long day: she woke at 5 a.m. after tossing and turning most of the night. The night before, she'd fallen asleep after crying, a heavy sleep that only served to make her feel more tired than before. She woke first at eleven-thirty, then again at two-thirty; it wasn't until the sun had lightened the horizon that she had at last felt alone again and then she knew that she couldn't go back to sleep. Hence the morning spent baking pies.

Now she was completely drained. Lord knew what in the world was wrong with her.

She'd long since stopped thinking about Billy except at the periphery of her thoughts, her mind focusing on other people and places. Why did he now return to haunt her? Was she doing this to herself? If she hadn't been so exhausted, she might have felt a shock of fear pierce her gut; as it was, she reminded herself that people nearing the ends of their lives often began to recall the past with a

430

clarity that they had lost even in the present. Perhaps her dreams, that spell last fall, and the persistent buzzing that had nagged at her for weeks were all simply omens that she was dying. Funny, she'd always thought that death would either sneak up and hit her a mortal blow over the head or she'd grow obviously frailer and frailer until she winked out into nothingness. She wouldn't have said that she would feel as healthy as a horse, shying away from the shadows of her own mortality.

Lucy drifted into her bedroom and toward her dresser. She meant to open the nightgown drawer but instead pulled open the top one where she kept her panties. Her sure hand reached under the prudent cotton to grasp the pearl necklace, hard and silky. And waiting. She trembled, adrenaline flowing from heel to crown, and then two fingers plucked the necklace from the drawer to dangle gleaming in the warm incandescent light before her.

She lifted the strand with both hands around her neck, the metallic blue beads lying against the ridge of her collarbone, and screwed the clasp together. The weight of the pearls burned against the folds of skin. When she looked at herself in the mirror, she saw herself at thirty-five again, the year that Billy brought her the necklace, begging her to accept it. Accept his apology. She'd never worn it. She'd stuffed it back into the wooden jewelry box that he'd bought in Maine and buried it. Even when she found out that she'd conceived Rachel, she left the necklace underground.

The ubiquitous buzzing swelled louder, insistent. Turning her head, she caught a ghostly outline in the bedroom door. She walked back to the darkened hall, heart thudding. Nothing but a sense of expectation greeted her. Her hand on the pearl necklace, she lurched toward the living room where a light she'd turned off only ten minutes before glowed and staggered into her chair.

Her gaze riveted on the picture of her and Billy, his hand on her shoulder and that devilish grin on his face. She clutched at the pearls. That grin had snagged her heart when she first met him in 1957. She was a soda jerk at Cat's drugstore in St. Joe, Mo. He was an Army vet going to the junior college on his GI bill. That grin and the cocky way he carried himself, so worldly wise and sure, that's what got her. She was just out of high school and hoping to land a job as a secretary—she'd won the typing medal and had good grades, especially in English. Maybe she could one day take some classes at the junior college, too. Maybe she'd study nursing or become a high-school English teacher.

None of those plans were firm, and they didn't have to be. She was young and the rest of her life was ahead of her. It was enough to know that she was at last in charge of herself and that she could decide when she was ready. But first, she wanted a little excitement. Excitement that could only be found when a good-looking fellow paid you some attention. Billy Romero was just the right prescription for that, excitement with a capital E. The other girls at Cat's needled her about her handsome war hero and sniped in good-humored jealousy about the luck the south-end girl was having with the dreamiest dish to walk through the drugstore's door in months. It was enough to turn any girl's head, but especially Lucy's, which had spent too much of its time dreaming about escape.

Who wouldn't want to escape from Karl and Mabel Schneider's house? Even if Mabel, a seamstress, hadn't been crazy—and she had been—it wasn't a place any hope-filled, eager young woman would want to remain, not if she wanted to keep from disintegrating inside until she became nothing but the hollow shell left behind when an insect molts. Her parents spent most of their time trying to deny her mother's sickness, a sickness that came and went unpredictably, usually entrapping her father, a taciturn butcher who owned his own shop, like quicksand. It kept them from having any friends and cut them off from her father's family, who lived in Kansas City. Her mother had been an only child whose parents died when Lucy was still a baby.

Lucy and her younger sister, Louise, were oblivious to Mabel's illness when they were children, but somewhere around the age of twelve Lucy began to comprehend that her mother's behavior went beyond the pale. She'd leave for school with her mother lying on her bed and smoking cigarette after cigarette, staring at the wall in front of her. When she returned home, her mother would be in the same position; this time, however, there would be a coffee cup on the bedside table near her head.

Sometimes Mabel would leave little notes around the house and in Karl's car, often with obscene and graphic drawings of men and women. Once, Lucy found a picture of her father glued onto a poster-size drawing of Superman. Her mother had drawn a grossly swollen penis between the Man of Steel's legs and colored it red. Whenever she found any notes, no matter what they said—and she always read them in an effort to decipher her mother's scrambled logic—Lucy threw them away.

On the days that Mabel's madness reigned, she and Louise would duck and run when they heard their father's hand on the front doorknob: Mabel was prone to throwing things, including hot coffee, and cursing before Karl, smelling of blood, had cracked the door. Lucy would snatch a loaf of bread, some butter, and jam from the kitchen, and the two girls would lock themselves in their room during dinner. Sometimes they would hear shouts from downstairs, their father's deeper voice contrasting with Mabel's shrill one.

Mabel never directed her anger at Lucy or Louise; it wasn't until she was much older, and married, that Lucy began to suspect that Mabel wasn't crazy at all, or at least not crazy for being crazy. What else did a seamstress in a small Midwestern town with two young daughters do to vent her frustration and outrage at her lot in life—a calculated venting necessary to pretend that all was well the rest of the time?

Almost as quickly as it came, Mabel's insanity would disappear, a storm cloud passing across the sun. She always acted unaware of the ludicrous and bizarre things that she'd said and done during her episodes as if she'd lent her body to a mischievous spirit and wasn't responsible. Karl, who sometimes threatened to end the whole thing by shooting her and then himself or hit her when she was particularly incessant in her vocal attacks, would sheepishly and without apology buy Mabel some flowers or a pretty little trinket that she'd set her eyes upon.

When Lucy met Billy, she wanted to escape the monotony of the predictably unpredictable outbursts at home. She wanted to see the world outside of St. Joe—and Billy had done that, of course, having been stationed in California before fighting in Korea. She wanted to secure for herself a life chaotic with children and pets, overflowing with noise and laughter, where love and anger were two sides of the same coin, acknowledged but never pandered to. In short, she wanted a life that was evenly and richly hued, not a dull gray that was illuminated with jagged bursts of tawdry neon.

If she thought her own family life had been far from that depicted by Norman Rockwell, Lucy felt lucky to have had even what she did: Billy was an orphan raised by a farmer cousin in Severance, Kansas. His father was killed in Germany during World War II and his mother struggled for four years to support them on her own until she herself died after becoming ill; Billy had no idea what her illness was, only that they couldn't afford any medical care.

He was thirteen when his mother's cousin, Bob, took him in. Bob wasn't cruel or crazy, just completely uncaring. He treated Billy like a hired hand, made him sleep in the back of the barn, which had been converted into quarters for a hired man, and kept him out of school most of the time for chores. Billy hadn't been so young when his parents were both alive that he couldn't remember Christmas and Thanksgiving and his mother's cooking; he'd sit in the loft, he told Lucy, and watch the cows with their calves and miss his mother so much that his stomach hurt like some wild beast tried to eat its way out of him.

Lucy sighed in her chair and scooted further down, closing her eyes on the picture and easing her grip on the pearls. Even today, her pity for Billy was undiluted. She'd believed him more than forty years ago when he'd told her that he too wanted a large, rambunctious family. If she'd stayed with him after learning about his adultery because she had nowhere else to go, Lucy admitted now that she'd also stayed with him because of this shared dream and because he, too, had been affected by its fulfillment.

While she had often felt like a mute boulder around whom the tumultuous rushing waters of five children flowed, Billy must have often felt locked out by that very floodwater which he'd helped release. Their fledgling intimacy, nurtured for a scant two years before Dorothy's birth, was stifled even without considering his long absences while traveling for work.

At least he got to travel. I had to stay home while he got to satisfy himself with Marge and Silvia and who knows who else. And here I was, waiting for him, waiting for him to come to my bed and beget another child on me. A divorcée and an old widow, only one child between the two of them. When no sitter could be found for this child, he just arranged to be with the other woman. He didn't really have to compete with children for time with either of them. Damn him!

Envy welled up in her, envy she'd never recognized before now. *Is this why I couldn't forgive him all these years? Because he was free to love women while I couldn't even love him? If we'd never had any children, what would our life together have been like?*

She opened her eyes. It was stupidity and a waste of time to think about what might have been, especially if she really were receiving portents of her imminent end.

Maybe it would be better if I forgive Billy and remember him only with love.

Dying with bitter hurt in her heart was likely to leave her own spirit in limbo, wandering the nether reaches of her loved ones' dreams until she had worked out her penance. She crossed herself at this thought. Better to get it over with now so that she and Billy could reconcile in the afterlife without tormenting anyone still living.

She caressed the pearls, which warmed under her fingertips, radiating eagerness. Peace. Acceptance.

The buzzing exploded in dazzling light inside her skull, blinding and deafening her in a tsunami too ferocious to filter into its constituent waves. When she could see again pearls winked at her from their landing places on couch, carpet, and keyboard.

Movement outside her front window drew her dazed gaze. John Wilkerson's black Jetta pulled into his driveway. She watched as he got out of his car, turning to pull a leather satchel from the passenger seat out after him. He walked to the front door, which was open to reveal Sarah waiting behind the glass of the storm door, the slow cadence of his step speaking of fatigue. Or despair.

Lucy knew that she had no idea what motivated John or gave meaning to his days. It didn't matter in the least. Instead, she hoped that he didn't let his family get away from him or, more importantly, that he didn't let his family get in the way between him and Tamarind.

"Please God," she said.

Thirty-six
ଔ

TAMARIND REMAINED HAUNTED by Lucy's expression for days after her visit. The lightning view into the older woman's tormented soul terrified her. She'd been wrong, terribly wrong to think that humans carried nothing of their dead with them, that their grief was transitory. Lucy carried her grief like a grain of painful sand in an oyster's shell. Time had yet to transform it into something hard and beautiful, as rare as an iridescent-blue Tahitian pearl.

She waited up for John, thinking about Lucy and Valerie and nursing Adam. The house was quiet. Sarah, still disappointed that she hadn't conjured John up by staring out the storm door, had trudged up to her bath with her fingers in her mouth and refused to play at all with her tub toys. She listened while Tamarind read her a story before bed, a story that John had written late one night after Tamarind had told him about Sarah's vigils at the front door. He'd titled it *Little Sarah Waits*, and once Sarah had heard it, she insisted that Tamarind read it to her every night.

Tamarind heard the front door open and the sound of keys followed by a bag dropped on the floor. A moment later John appeared in the doorway, surprise fighting the fatigue that drooped his face. She'd stopped waiting up for him weeks ago, stopped leaving pots filled with dinner on the stove and a place setting on the table. He'd never eaten off the plate anyway. He told her that there was no point in sitting down alone and that he usually stood at the counter reading mail or the newspaper while eating from the pot. Now she filled a microwaveable plate and left it in the refrigerator for him to reheat in case he hadn't ordered takeout at work.

"Hey," he said and came to her. He bent down and kissed her, a real kiss and not one of those brush-of-the-lips he pulled off on his way out the door. He smelled like coffee and stale sweat. And something darker. "What are you doing up?"

"Waiting for you," she said. She hadn't told him about Valerie yet. Maybe Sunday morning, if he'd had a chance to sleep in a little, she'd tell him on the way to Mass. He'd once told her that he'd found irreplaceable comfort in the prayers of the faithful when his Sicilian grandmother, a devout Catholic, had died. Perhaps he would again.

Adam had fallen asleep, letting her nipple slip from his mouth. His warm breath and tiny fist lay on her skin like peace. An energy that she'd never felt before, a weight and substance like the lifeblood of mountains flowed between her and Adam, grounding them to the rocker, the floor, even the house around them. She looked at his profile and then held him up to John, whose naked adoration lit his face. She watched John snuggle the tiny bundle against his chest, remembering the first time that he'd pulled her into his arms. Until then, she'd had only faith that he loved her. She wished that her faith were still as pure, that she hadn't considered using the truth powder after Adam's birth.

"There's focaccia and white-bean chili," she offered. She thought about the sardines that she and Sarah had eaten as well and guilt jabbed her. She'd never followed Valerie's advice to talk to John about relaxing their diet. It never seemed to be the right time.

"Thanks. I ate a sub earlier." Apology colored his voice. "I wanted to talk with Ted and Jim about the specs for the APIs for Patriot's databases so I bought them dinner."

"Um," she said. What else could she say? "It going well?"

He sighed and sat down on the loveseat. "As well as can be expected. I'm not too impressed with Patriot's programming staff or the system they use internally. When I tell Prasad, he just laughs about our 'dog-and-pony show' and continues to tell anyone—including funders—about the wonderful new Web interface we're building. Mukesh, he just squints and tells me to make sure it all works together."

Tamarind listened to John's complaints, surprised at the bitterness. He'd always spoken in vague terms about his two bosses, and while she'd sensed that he didn't like them, she'd had no proof. For a moment in the darkened family room, he seemed adrift, separated from her by more than a coffee table. Startled by this insight, Tamarind realized how far into herself that she'd fallen, how little she knew about what troubled John these days. She saw how she'd accepted the opacity of his thoughts and for the first time it occurred to her to consider if she could do anything about it. Her instinct told her to close the distance, anchor him to her. So she got up and came over to the loveseat. John opened his free arm and she sank against him. He sighed.

"I suppose Adam needs a change," he said. He didn't sound as though he wanted to get up.

"Do it later. I changed him an hour ago."

"I should go up and kiss Sarah." He made no move and she said nothing. "I'm not working this weekend. At. All. I'm taking Sarah swimming at the Y and I'm taking you both to dinner."

"Mmm." She snuggled closer. "That sounds good." It had been too long since they'd sat together like this, just talking. She slipped her hand under his pullover and ran tentative fingertips over the skin of his stomach. Gooseflesh answered her touch.

"I ran into Lucy this morning," he said, his voice shading into husky. He settled further down the cushions, giving her better access to his midsection. "It's not the first time. Seems she's taken to walking the neighborhood before the sun's up."

"She bakes too." She buried her nose into his neck, his skin warm against its cold tip. He wriggled and laughed. "Sorry," she said, waited. "Bad dreams keep her up all night."

"Bad dreams." This was a statement and something made her think that he wasn't speaking about Lucy. Her own nightmare, the nightmare of Jesus above her in a harsh fluorescent eternity lay quiescent but not purged. Whatever had triggered its return last fall, she knew it was only a matter of time before it caught her in its steel grip. Would John be there to rescue her? Shivering, she pushed herself against him, her arms wrapped around his torso under the pullover.

His arm tightened around her and he looked down. The green of his eyes, so steady and alive, warmed her. "You haven't dreamt about him again, have you?"

"No."

"Good." She thought he was about to say something else and then he changed his mind. His hand moved to her upper arm. "Tamarind, when are you going to tell me about your wedding ring?"

The question caught her off guard. She sat up and looked away. "Lucy told you."

"Yes."

"When?" Anger and hurt covered her guilt, hid her fear. The circle, the sign of eternal love, had been severed. First the Goddess pendant. Now her wedding ring. A cold thrill of premonition ran up her spine.

"Before Adam was born. No, don't get up. Don't blame Lucy. She was concerned about you."

Tamarind let John tug her back into the hollow next to him. Still she didn't look at him. "I didn't want you to find out. I asked Valerie how to get it fixed. She gave me the name of a goldsmith in New York I can send it to." She held her hand up. "But I think my finger needs to be sized. I think it's grown."

John's free hand took her left hand and he rubbed his thumb over the third finger. "Really? Maybe we should remake it."

440

"Remake it?" Tamarind's mind went blank. "What do you mean?"

"If you need a bigger band, we can have a goldsmith melt your old one down and add it to a new one."

She shivered again. Was that a good idea? She looked at John, who watched her. Her fear melted into restlessness at his calm. "I don't know."

"Where is it? There's a goldsmith on Moody Street. I can take it over at lunch one day."

"My jewelry box. The one from Ana." She didn't want to tell him. The words unraveled from the fabric of her fear. "Don't take it. Just leave it."

John tipped her chin up so he could look her in the eyes. "What's wrong?"

"I don't know." She moved away from him. "Can you just wait?"

"Sure, love." His arm slipped around her shoulder, pulled her back to him. Adam, snug against his inner arm, slept on.

Tamarind reached over and touched the tiny nose. He looked so much like John, down to his feet, which were beautiful. An image of John's feet, one foot wedged into an unnatural black flipper and the other with its long arch and sturdy toes, filled her thoughts. She'd pulled John from the ocean before she'd known what he'd looked like, responding only to a soul's call for rescue, but when she'd brought him ashore she couldn't take her gaze from his feet. An urge to see them now moved her.

She slipped away from him and onto her knees. Ignoring his low exclamation of surprise, she tugged at the laces of his boots, which he'd forgotten to take off. His feet, warm from their time inside socks and boots, goose-pimpled in the cooler air. Tamarind took one between her hands, her thumbs pressing and stroking along the arch. A sigh escaped John, but she continued rubbing and running her fingers along the edges and around the heel. She pored over his soles and toes as if she read them with her hands, a blind woman who finds meaning in every callus and seam. Only after she'd massaged both feet did she look up, her hands gripping his

441

lower calves under his jeans. In focusing on John's tired feet, she'd banished the fear over her broken ring.

"Come up to bed," she said.

John's face held hunger and uncertainty. "It's too soon."

"I think," she said, "that we may have other options." And was rewarded with a smile not at all dimmed with fatigue.

ዺዺዺ

John woke to the soft stirrings of Adam in his bassinet at the side of the bed. Tamarind lay half sprawled on top of him, her leg covering his lower legs and her arm across his chest. Her hair, darker now than when they'd met, cloaked her face and shoulders. Her heavy breasts pressed against him, leaking. He ran his hand up the silky line of her waist and along the ridge of her backbone until he found her shoulder under the mass of hair and tugged her closer. Her weight fit against him.

His fingers strayed to her hair, toying with a strand. He smoothed it back from her face, feeling the curves of her cheeks and her warm breath on his palm. When she'd gotten better before Adam's birth, he'd told her that Zoë had interviewed with Dr2Dr, downplaying it as much as he could. Tamarind, who'd been sitting on the toilet next to the tub where Sarah splashed among soap bubbles and plastic dolphins that whistled when their heads were tapped, stiffened at his announcement. He could still remember the subtle change in air pressure between them, some shift in molecules or temperature that signaled her distress. Still, she'd said nothing.

Once upon a time, back when she'd been a fairy-tale creature incarnated and before she'd suffered at the hands of a sociopath, Tamarind's thoughts had flowed unchecked from her mouth. She'd kept only the truth of what she was from him but not the truth of *who* she was, innocent and trusting. And totally wild about him. He'd known it, too, and strung her along until he'd been forced to decide or lose her forever. Somewhere along the line he'd lost her faith in him. Maybe it was just the way things had to be between husband and wife. Scales had to fall off of eyes, especially if the faith had been misplaced. Maybe now that reality had set in, he couldn't disappoint her. Even so, he was surprised at how much it hurt to lose her adoration. He wanted to be held to a high standard, to work to justify how she saw him. There was something intensely deflating knowing that she expected less of him.

That's why he couldn't tell her that Zoë's first day had been today. Not yet. Not after she'd surprised him by waiting up. Not after she'd reacted with anger when he'd asked about her wedding band. Not after *she'd* initiated intimacy. He called up her hands on his feet, the sensuous pressure of her fingertips on their arches, the desire that had crackled like static electricity between them. But when he closed his eyes, Zoë's perfume filled his nostrils. His stomach clenched.

She'd stopped by his cubicle that morning.

"Hey," she'd said and sat on the corner of his desk. She wore a tight black skirt with a slit on one side. It fell open to reveal a sculpted thigh. "Prasad gave me an API spec but it's dated January fifteenth. Got anything newer? I meet with the Patriot team on Wednesday."

She could have sent him an email for that request. John counted to five before he answered. "Sure. I'll email it to you now. I'm sure you'll find plenty to work with."

Zoë had lingered. "I was just in talking to Susan Henry. She needs to grow a spine, that one."

John had wanted Zoë to leave; he didn't want to return to the casual collegiality that they'd maintained back at CMU. But he really didn't have a choice. They had to work together.

"She seems like a sweet girl. Not everyone has to be as assertive as you."

"God, John! How offensive! She's 'a sweet girl,' is she? You're as bad as Mukesh and Prasad are."

John hadn't expected that. It annoyed him. "What? I'm not denigrating her. She's smart and funny, too."

"Yeah, but she's letting them walk all over her. Mukesh told her she has to answer the phones."

John, who had a nail of pain piercing the bone over his left eye, had frowned. "Everyone answers the phones here, Zoë. We're a low-budget operation, but you'll figure that out when you get your first paycheck."

"John, Mukesh told her he wanted only *her* to answer the phones from now on. Because she's a woman and people expect a woman's voice to answer. When I asked her if she'd been told she'd be the secretary as well as a tech writer when she interviewed, she just hunched her shoulders and mumbled no."

John massaged his temple. "You're right. But Tamarind warned you, didn't she?"

It had been Zoë's turn to frown. "That's all you've got to say?"

John sighed. "No. I'll go tell Mukesh he can't make Susan answer the phone just because she's a woman. I'll tell him I'm happy to answer the main line too. Satisfied?"

"I'm going to send him a link to an EEOC Web site."

"Subtle, Zoë, real subtle." John had nearly followed these words up with a request for her to leave. Zoë was as subtle as an intensely red, showy hibiscus with its alluring, slightly ominous smell.

"Well, you know me." She'd leaned closer. "I believe in standing up for my rights."

A tiny tic started in John's armpit and kept time with his breathing.

"Always looking for the good fight?" he'd asked, trying to sound casual but feeling as though his words fought their way through cotton batting in his chest.

"Susan reminds me of someone." Zoë sat up and folded an arm across her midsection, tapping her nails along her front teeth. John was sure it was for show. He also had a sinking feeling that he knew where she was going. "Hm. You called her sweet. Tamarind's a sweet girl, too, wouldn't you say? I don't know her well enough to know if they share the same sense of humor." Zoë didn't bring up the other attribute that John had assigned to Susan: smart. That wasn't an oversight either.

Remembering this conversation while lying next to Tamarind, John groaned. Tamarind stirred and rolled over, her arm curling around his neck.

"Whazit?" she said, still asleep.

"Shhh." John wrapped both arms around her. She sighed and burrowed her nose into his chest.

He played the scene with Zoë over again. He'd known when she came for the interview what she wanted. He'd known why she sat on the corner of his desk reeking of musk and heat. He'd just kept it down in his lizard brain, that part of his brain that handled basic functions like breathing and driving to work. It was his lizard brain that had sent up distress signals, jabbing his higher-order thinking into acknowledging that he had to bring reasoning and logic to handle Zoë.

Like a groggy beast, his ego swung round to issue a clumsy defense.

"Good thing they both have you looking out for their interests." Zoë's eyes narrowed as he warmed to the topic. "You women got to stick together, right? Otherwise us guys might think it's really a matter of the strong taking advantage of the weak."

He could see her mulling this over, trying out the puzzle of his argument like a safecracker manipulating a lock. Was she a champion of women's rights or a bully? When she found the right combination, he could almost hear the wheels line up. She smiled.

"I always fight the good fight, John. I'm always for women's rights." She'd leaned down so far this time that he could see the compact mounds of her breasts as her blouse drooped open. "Of course, sometimes that means helping another woman learn to stand up for herself by knocking her down. She's better off in the long run. It's all about intentions. I mean well, I do."

He hadn't thought about how to parry this challenge before Prasad walked by. He swiveled when he heard Prasad's footsteps, catching Prasad's open-mouthed gape. Prasad blinked and snapped his jaws shut. A grin spread across his face like water on a grease fire.

"Collaborating already?" John hated the glints dancing in Prasad's dark eyes, the mixed mirth and jealousy he heard in Prasad's high-pitched voice. "I'm sure Zoë's got some good ideas."

Zoë snorted and slid off of John's desk. John saw the irritated curl of her lip. How long would she tolerate Prasad before she smacked him down? When she walked out of the office, she didn't look at her new boss. Instead, she smiled over her shoulder at John.

"I'll look for that spec. Thanks." The ionized field of her presence burned through the air around them even after she'd gone. It was only a matter of time before the inevitable lightning strike. Prasad waved his hand, grinned, and left.

Here, in the dark with Tamarind floating on the life raft of his body, John knew what he should have said to Zoë about her planned assault on Tamarind. He knew that she'd framed the argument wrong, but his rational mind hadn't worked it out yet, fogged as it had been in her cloying scent. What he should have told her was that her fight wasn't with Tamarind at all. It was with him. And he had no intention of lying down.

Thirty-seven
ೞ

WHEN OLIVIA SHOWED UP LATE a week after Tamarind found out that Valerie was dying, Tamarind didn't notice right away. She'd spent the previous twenty minutes chasing Sarah, who'd slid a chair over to the open pantry and snuck a box of graham crackers into the living room where she ate less than she left spread out in crumbs all over the floor. She'd tried putting Sarah into a chair for timeout after she spied a moist crumble clinging to the corners of Sarah's mouth, but Sarah hadn't agreed to sitting still no matter how sharp Tamarind's tone grew.

Olivia slouched into the doorway to the dining room, paused to watch them scurrying around the table, and then stepped in and snatched Sarah, whose happy shriek came to an abrupt halt when Olivia swatted her buttocks once. Into the chair she went. Tamarind saw Sarah's lips quiver and splotchy red break out along her forehead, but the tears stayed in her eyes. Tamarind was a lot less bothered by the swat than she thought she'd be.

It wasn't until Olivia almost misjudged her own seat that Tamarind noticed anything amiss. She didn't ask right away, though. She was learning that sometimes it's better to gather more information, to wait until the right moment to draw someone out, especially Olivia who was as skittish as a young amberjack.

"Want some pie? Your grandma's been baking again."

"That's not all she's been doing," Olivia pushed her words through her teeth. She seemed to have lost control of her tongue.

"What else has she been doing?" Tamarind asked, as curious about Olivia's state as Lucy's alleged behavior. She'd been to enough grad student parties and other social events to recognize the signs of drinking, but she needed to hear more to be sure.

"She's not herself. She's writing letters to the editor."

Tamarind remembered the last conversation that they'd had, the one in which her limited insight had been further challenged by her water retention. Perhaps it would be better to just apologize now.

"I'm sorry, Livy. Don't get mad. I just don't understand what's wrong with writing letters to the editor."

Olivia didn't get mad. She blinked and tears rolled down her cheeks instead.

"I think she's had a stroke, Mrs. Wilkerson." Olivia struggled to get the words out. She slurred her consonants so much that Tamarind had to translate her speech into something that she understood. "She used to keep her opinion to herself, unless you asked. She used to be so matter-of-fact, so even."

An ache dented Tamarind's brow. "She does keep saying she's sorry for saying things."

"Yes!" Olivia shouted. Sarah, sitting so quietly in her chair that Tamarind had all but forgotten her, gasped. Tamarind told her to get down, but Sarah's gaze was riveted to her beloved Olivia's face. "She's so odd lately, Mrs. Wilkerson. She's off in LaLa Land, mooning around like she's one of my classmates who's crushing."

"Crushing?"

A look of extreme patience washed over Olivia's features. "In love."

"Ah."

"Sometimes she's sad. Sometimes she's wistful. Now she's angry. Or she sounds angry in her letters."

"What are they about?" Tamarind sat down. She could smell the booze on Olivia's breath now, intensely sour. There was also a pungent smell—garlic?—mixed with it.

"Everything. She wrote one about Bill Clinton and Monica Lewinsky, but she never cared about politics before. She blasted him for using his position to take advantage of a twenty-two-year old idiot with stars in her eyes. That's what she called her."

Tamarind hadn't seen the news in weeks and they didn't take the paper. She remembered John telling her about the President getting caught with his trousers down last summer. John had been pretty disgusted. He'd said that his sister Cassie almost got an internship at the White House.

"What else?" She didn't say that this letter didn't sound so crazy to her.

"There are four more, each sounding angrier than the last. First she wrote about how sloppy and rude teenagers are these days. Then she wrote how parents aren't around enough to be good role models. At Christmas, she wrote a letter about how no one pays attention to the true meaning of Christmas. I figured she was writing all the stuff she couldn't say to Mom or Aunt Rachel."

Again, understandable. But Tamarind just nodded. "I can see how that would bother you."

"That's only three though. It's the last one that weirded me out the most. I don't know why she wrote it."

A premonitory chill streaked down Tamarind's spine. "What was it about?"

"Gram rambled on and on about busybodies who didn't want any woman to have an abortion. I thought a demon had taken control of her."

"Why?" The chill seeped into Tamarind's torso.

"'Cause she's so devout, Mrs. Wilkerson. It just doesn't sound like her." She paused for a moment and looked down at her fingers, which picked at each other. Her speech had improved, but she still had tearstains on her cheeks. "I almost think she knows Pam's pregnant."

The chill in Tamarind exploded and she shivered.

"That's not good, is it?" She found that she wasn't surprised. When she'd met Pam last fall, she'd identified her as a jellyfish: capable of stinging, but at the mercy of the waves and the predatory hunger of sea turtles.

"It's the worst." Olivia sounded sober.

"Is that why you've been drinking?"

Olivia's hand flew to her mouth. Her dark eyes widened behind her glasses. She hiccupped. "I thought the garlic toast would hide it," she said.

"I've got a good nose."

Olivia's tears rushed out and she gasped like an angelfish stranded onshore. Tamarind put her hand over Olivia's fingers and they stilled their nervous movement.

"That's not why," she whispered. She looked over her shoulder at Sarah whose blue eyes shone as bright as Tamarind's moonstone.

Tamarind understood. "Roe, Livy has to tell me something secret."

"I know Mommy," Sarah said. "A stranger hurt her."

Olivia startled and her tears stopped. She looked at Tamarind.

Tamarind stood up. "Let's go put on a video, lovey. You can keep Adam company."

Sarah, who'd been so difficult before, looked solemn. She slid down from her chair and came over to Olivia. Putting her tiny hand on Olivia's cheek, she said, "Forget it, Livy. It's not real."

A tremor rolled down Olivia's body and she sighed. Sarah's hand dropped to her side and she followed Tamarind to the living room.

When Tamarind returned to the dining room, she brought two glasses of iced tea. "Here, drink this." She set one glass in front of Olivia. "It'll help wake you up. Take this ibuprofen, too."

Olivia did what she was told. When she spoke again, her voice was calm and her words clear. Her pupils were dilated, giving her a dazed look. "Are you going to tell Gram?" She sounded so vulnerable, so in need of protecting that the same fierce tenderness that Tamarind felt when she held Adam flooded her.

"No."

"Thanks."

Tamarind watched Olivia toy with the rim of the glass. "Where'd you get the alcohol?"

"It was my mom's. She left a bottle of wine in the refrigerator. From her date last night."

"Why'd you drink it?"

"I went to check my email. My friend Sean invited me to come over and do homework with him this weekend. Mrs. Thompson wrote me about the school newsletter. And somebody called 'NetSlug' sent me one. It had a video attached."

Tamarind waited. Her heart told her that Olivia had to do this on her own or not at all.

"The mail said 'I've been watching you.' When I opened the video, a clip played with a-a naked man. His-his penis was erect."

Tamarind was shocked. Who would send such a thing to a fourteen year old?

"That's not all." Olivia whispered. "A picture of me came on the screen and slid over on top of the man's penis. Then it disappeared. A woman's face appeared. She-she sucked on the man's penis. He grabbed her head and wouldn't let her go. He called her horrible things and she looked like she was choking. He just laughed." Her voice was so low that Tamarind almost didn't hear her. She covered her face with her hands and her voice got a little louder. "I couldn't help it. I watched it over and over. Then I vomited."

Olivia shivered and sat silent. At last she let her hands drop. "I could still see it, Mrs. Wilkerson, with my eyes open. That's why I drank my mom's wine. But it didn't help. I could still see that poor woman until Sarah touched my cheek just now." She shivered again. "He's watching. He said so."

If she'd been shocked before, Tamarind was stunned now. She'd had no idea such things existed. All at once, the image of Jesus standing over her, the bright fluorescent light haloing his head and

451

darkening his face, filled her thoughts. For a moment all she knew was fear and then, like sunlight burning away a smothering fog, her anger blazed blue-white across the memory of Jesus and lashed out at the stranger who'd terrorized and sickened Olivia.

"Don't worry," she said. "I'm sure John knows just how to track this shithead down." She'd never sworn before. She didn't even know where the word came from, but she rolled the sound of it around her palate. It came from someplace powerful and dark inside her. Like the earth beneath her feet.

It wasn't until later, after Lucy had come to pick Olivia up to take her to a movie that Tamarind recalled Sarah's consoling words in wonder and consternation.

ﻉﻉﻉ

Lucy woke up from where she lay on her couch with a confused start. Across from her, the luminous gray window of her living room told her that it was still early on an overcast afternoon and that she couldn't have slept long. She shook her head, trying to jar her thoughts into coherency in the hope that some explanation for her nap would occur to her. She hadn't felt at all sleepy when she came into the room after lunch looking for a magazine and her knitting, but she couldn't even remember sitting down with either.

A pain in her left shoulder and hip brought her fully awake and aware of her awkward position on the cushions. Looking down as she pushed herself upright, she had the odd feeling that she'd landed, rather than eased, onto her back and that she hadn't exactly gotten comfortable as she dozed off. The way her head throbbed now, she would swear that she'd been struck unconscious instead.

As she sat up, the back of her neck tingled and the hairs on her forearms wiggled along her skin. The atmosphere in the room around her was charged with an energy that only comes from the presence of another person, yet her reason—her hope!—told her that she must be alone. She forced herself to listen for what seemed like an unnecessarily long time, but in reality must have been only a minute or two. The house was silent.

452

She released her breath, which she'd been holding, and reached over for the phone on the end table nearest her. She picked up the handset. Hearing the dial tone, she sighed, reassured. No stranger had cut the phone lines while she slept. Yet even as she sighed and replaced the handset, the presence in the room increased until she was more convinced than ever that she wasn't alone. Closing her eyes for a moment, she let it envelope her and then she remembered what she'd been thinking as she walked into the family room: the presence, she knew somehow, wanted her to remember.

She'd been replaying the shock of seeing Ruth Corcoran at the Feast of the Holy Family a few weeks ago. When Mass first started, she'd been busy helping Tamarind get Sarah settled with a picture book and a sippy cup of milk and didn't see the woman sitting alone in the front center pew. If she had, she might have recognized the upright bearing, the petite square shoulders, the short auburn hair cut close up the back of the head. By the time that the three of them were settled in, the pews around them had filled up enough that Ruth's form had become obscured and Lucy had no idea that her old friend was present. Even if she had, it probably wouldn't have prevented the shock she felt later in Mass when Father Shaughnessy introduced Ruth as the guest speaker.

In the five years since Ruth had severed their friendship, little had changed in her demeanor or appearance—and apparently nothing had changed in her opinions. Father Shaughnessy invited her to describe her work at a nearby pregnancy-crisis center, Crisis Pregnancy, and with the political group, Mass Mothers for Life. Lucy, after she recovered from her shock at hearing Ruth's bell-like voice again, recalled their five-year-old parting as if it had been yesterday.

"I've come over to return some of your things, Lucy," Ruth had said at Lucy's front door, holding up a small box.

"Okay," she'd said. "C'mon in and have a cup of tea, won't you?"

"No, Lucy, that won't be a good idea. This isn't a social visit and if there's one thing that you and I do have in common, it's our dislike of pretense. I'm returning your things because it's become clear to me that you and I can't remain friends."

"Why?" Lucy asked, her hand frozen on the doorknob to her front door.

Ruth sighed. "I see you're going to make me spell it out for you, when it's as obvious as the nose on your face: there's no place in my heart or in my home for anyone who would condone baby killing, Lucy Romero."

"Baby killing? I don't condone baby killing." Even as Lucy said it, her head buzzed and ached. What was Ruth talking about? She must have some idea, but she just couldn't think right now.

"What a piece of work you are! You stand there doe-eyed and acting as if you haven't a clue in the world what I'm talking about. You know damn well, Lucy, I'm speaking about Claire Reynolds killing her unborn baby."

The buzzing exploded into a thousand chattering fragments inside Lucy's skull. She put her fingertips to her forehead hoping to coax them into a dull roar.

"Claire Reynolds had to have an abortion. She wanted that baby, Ruth, she *wanted* it."

"She had to *bear* that child. Abortion is murder, no ifs, ands or buts. There can be no equivocating and you know it."

"She would have died. The cancer would have spread until it killed her. Her baby would have cost her her life."

"So she says. Doctors can't say for sure when cancer's going to be fatal. The point is, it was in God's hands, not Claire's. And instead of condemning what she did, you took her in with open arms and let her think what she did could be forgiven."

"Maybe God put it into Claire's hands," Lucy said, bile rising into her mouth.

"God was testing her, like he tested Abraham with Isaac. He was calling her to have faith."

"God asked Abraham to sacrifice his son," Lucy said, the buzzing silent now. "Abraham showed his faith by willingly tying up Isaac and holding a knife to his throat. He would have murdered his son with his own hands and God wanted him to be ready to murder his son. Not only that, but God *rewarded* him for being so willing to murder."

She paused a moment, meeting Ruth's wide eyes and clinched mouth. This was the final blow, she knew. "We don't live in Old Testament times, Ruth. Christ calls us to love, to heal wounded hearts. And Claire's heart is wounded, whether you want to believe it or not. I won't judge her and I don't believe God gave you the right to judge her, either."

Then, while Ruth stood there spluttering, Lucy had reached over and taken the box from her. She didn't bother to shut the door behind her as she turned to go inside.

Today, sitting here with the firm cushion of her couch behind her and the warm presence of another around her, Lucy thought about the Feast of the Holy Family and Ruth's admonition to the parishioners at Sacred Heart to do God's will and protect the unborn. She finished her appeal by sharing a personal story about her years trying to conceive, which were interspersed with several miscarriages. Lucy, who never knew that Ruth had suffered this cruel heartbreak, remembered envying Ruth's status as a mother of one—she'd thought back then that Ruth had been lucky. When Ruth finished, she asked her audience to imagine their lives devoid of children.

"Just think for a moment how empty your lives would be, how much less rich, how much less hopeful. Then go and do, as God wants each and every one of us to do with every fiber of our beings: protect the unborn. Thank you."

Lucy snorted, remembering. Was her life any less empty than Ruth Corcoran's life? Her sons, real and not wish-children, lived in New York, Maryland, and Pennsylvania, but they might as well live on the moon for all she got to see them. And their children were as real to her, and she to them, as figments of the imagination. And why indeed should children get all the credit for richness and hope? She herself had felt mostly relief when the bulk of her noisy, energetic brood had left home. Then, she felt, she finally had time to spend with Billy and Rachel, and her garden. That's all she'd wanted. Apparently Ruth's desire for the children she'd never had, and her quest to make sure no other woman refused to bring a baby into this world, gave more meaning to her life than the friendship she and Lucy had shared for more than twenty years.

"Ah, what am I sittin' here thinkin' about that woman for?" she asked herself, waving her hand and standing up.

At that moment, her doorbell rang. Startled, she stumbled on stiff legs across the living room and down the hall, all the time muttering about surprise visits from salesmen and schoolchildren. But when she opened the front door, it was neither. Instead, she saw Rachel, her face pale and drawn, with little Ben in her arms. Around her huddled Matthew, his dark eyes wide, and Hayley, her dress too short for her pudgy frame, tears and snot streaming down her face.

"Good heavens! What's happened?" Lucy asked.

"Mom, I'm leaving Todd," Rachel said, her voice quiet and certain.

"Why? What happened?"

"He's been fooling around for the last year and I just found out about it." Rachel's voice cracked a little. "We need someplace to stay for a few days. Will you let us stay here?"

Lucy didn't hesitate for a moment. "Of course I will."

Thirty-eight
❧

JOHN FOUND A WHOLE NEW WAY to appreciate the pithy saying about March, lions, and lambs. With Zoë acting as a predatory lioness, that unpredictable month roared onto his calendar. John doubted that she'd leave as a lamb once she understood that her prey had claws and fangs of his own. He didn't want to butt heads with her. He'd rather convince her that he wasn't the same man that she'd dominated in grad school, but he knew Zoë well enough to understand that, even after four years, a wife and two children, he wouldn't be able to do it. Something told him that it was as much about her pride as any desire for him.

Zoë would be chagrined to know that she didn't dominate his thoughts either. At Dr2Dr, he'd finally hired two software engineers to code the system that he'd designed for Patriot Healthcare, freeing him up for more project management and longer-term design issues related to enrolling multiple insurers, doctors and consumers. Now he focused on these complex problems and managing Ted and Jim, who often didn't roll into the office until the decent hour of ten. With more time at his day job, he'd been able to add some functionality to the IndiaClinic site to let Tufts doctors access chat logs, something that he'd been meaning to do for six weeks. And Tamarind had asked him to track down some punk who'd sent Olivia seriously demented email. Even though he hadn't pinpointed the loser's exact account or IP address, he'd confirmed that it had come from a Cheltham PC. It was only a matter of time. He'd glimpsed the hint of steel in Tamarind when he told her. Nothing would satisfy him more than to help her sharpen it. Zoë had gotten one thing right: Tamarind needed to stand up for herself. Standing up for Olivia was a perfect way to practice.

Even though he wished that Zoë would lose interest in him, he was relieved that such an outstanding security architect worked for Dr2Dr. Mukesh had hired Zoë to make sure that their algorithms and tools were impregnable. What Mukesh might not realize, John suspected, was that Zoë would let no one leave doctors and patients vulnerable. If the two interests ever conflicted, it would be a cold day in hell before Zoë would let Dr2Dr's interests win out. She'd already told John about a software key that she'd developed that would let her lock the system up if Mukesh or Prasad tried to override her.

But none of his challenges, not Zoë, his workload, or his sleepless nights with a newborn and an inscrutable wife, exempted him from more trouble. March showed its malign influence on the season one early morning in mid-month when he took a disturbing phone call.

Alone in Dr2Dr's dark offices, he was sipping scalding coffee and typing an agenda for a project meeting when the main phone rang.

"Hello, Dr.2Dr. John Wilkerson here." Even as he answered, his mind began processing a script for talking to Bill, the new system administrator, about remote logins and configuring drives.

"Hi, this is Tom Anderson from Tufts. I'd like to speak with Dr. Prasad Vishnavi."

"Sorry, Dr. Vishnavi is in India. Can I help you?" He halted the background mental process and focused on the caller.

"Not sure. I'm a colleague of Dr. Anil Mukarjee. Do you know anything about the Rajasthan study?"

"I suggest you call Dr. Mukarjee. He's the PI." John's scalp prickled. Why would someone from Tufts call Prasad about Dr. Mukarjee's study?

"Well," Dr. Anderson said and there was an edge in his voice, "I'm on Tufts' institutional review board. I've been reviewing the procedure for recruiting test subjects for Dr. Mukarjee's study. That's why I'm calling Dr. Vishnavi. He's listed as an investigator. Can you help me or not?"

John, who'd been busy with Dr2Dr's prototype when Dr. Mukarjee won the grant to run a study for Phoenix Pharmaceuticals through IndiaClinic, had barely read the award documents. Yes, Tom Anderson had been listed as one of Tufts' IRB members, but John had spoken to someone else when the study began, a doctor named Rujit something or other.

"Maybe. I work for Dr. Mukarjee on IndiaClinic, but I thought another doctor from the IRB was assigned to the study. Someone named Rujit."

"Rujit Pendyala, Yes, well, I've just been following up on some areas that Dr. Pendyala normally handles, including the Rajasthan study. It's a bit unusual for us, you know, overseeing a study where the data is gathered overseas and monitored via the Internet. We're anxious to make sure that the research protocols are strictly followed."

"I understand. But I also understand that the Board approved Dr. Mukarjee's study, including the informed-consent form and his advertisements through the IndiaClinic Web site."

"It did. But we're required to review the recruiting process at least once a year, and in the case of an overseas study, we feel it's necessary to review it more often, especially given the numbers being gathered."

"I wrote the program for analyzing the numbers." John heard the stiffness in his voice. "Are you suggesting they aren't being accurately presented?"

459

"No, not necessarily. I've just found some results that seem highly remarkable and I want to verify that everything has been reported correctly. Really, it's standard procedure."

"Okay." Now he sounded dubious. "I can take a look at the numbers for you and re-run them. Is there anything I should be looking for?"

"Not yet. I just want to make sure the right numbers are being analyzed and that the program does what it's supposed to do. Can you email me the equations you used to analyze the data and let me know if any of the raw data is incorrect?"

John, trying not to bristle at the implication that he didn't know how to analyze statistics, swallowed before responding.

"I really should talk with Dr. Mukarjee before I send you anything."

The other man sighed loudly, taking John by surprise.

"Listen, I'd rather you didn't, Mr. Wilkerson. The truth is that Dr. Pendyala, who sits on the IRB, is under investigation here at Tufts and I've been asked to look at every study he's taken a lead on for the Board. When I started looking into the Rajasthan study, I discovered that Dr. Pendyala also sits on the Dr2Dr.com advisory board. There's an obvious conflict of interest there, and I don't want Dr. Mukarjee alerting Dr. Pendyala that he's being investigated. It might compromise the investigation."

"Wait a minute," John said, confused. He tried hard to think. "Even if Dr. Pendyala is on Dr2Dr.com's advisory board, what's that have to do with the numbers being collected in the study? Why would Dr. Mukarjee tell Dr. Pendyala that he's being investigated if I tell him that you want to verify some data?"

"You'll just have to trust me on this. I can't tell you much more than I already have, unfortunately. Let's just say that Dr. Pendyala has a reason for championing an overseas study run by a colleague of his and that any extra scrutiny of the study may cause the parties involved to alter records."

"And what if I don't cooperate?" John wished that he'd never taken the call. Damn Zoë for making him feel that he needed to answer the phone. "Won't you have to deal directly with Dr. Mukarjee then?"

"Yes. And that will make our investigation that much more difficult and time consuming because I'll be forced to make a site visit to the IndiaClinic to make sure that the test subjects are being informed according to the protocol. It would be a lot easier and speedier for all concerned—including Dr. Mukarjee and Phoenix Pharmaceuticals—if I can rule out a site visit by looking over the raw data first."

"I've got to think about it first." John's mind raced. "You've got to understand. I owe a lot to Dr. Mukarjee and it goes against the grain not to check with him first."

"I understand. I respect you for being so concerned. I just want to assure you that I'm not asking this lightly or trying to cause difficulties for a Tufts investigator." Dr. Anderson paused. "But it's my job as an IRB member to make sure that people are safe and fully informed about the risks of the clinical trials they're participating in. Without their trust, we wouldn't get very far."

John sighed. "All right, Dr. Anderson. I'll let you know if I can help you out by the end of the week. Is that soon enough?"

"Yes. That's soon enough."

After he hung up, John squeezed his eyes shut and massaged his forehead.

"Problems?" Zoë's sure voice startled him. She leaned against the frame of his cubicle, her face shadowed against the darkened hallway behind her. Even without distinct features, her curves and her scent filled the cubicle. His stomach tightened.

"Maybe." He didn't look at her; he didn't want to invite her in. Maybe she'd take the hint and move along.

She didn't leave. "You want to talk about it?"

"I don't think so, Zoë."

"Does it have something to do with that new kid Mukesh hired?" That startled John. Who had Mukesh hired? "I see you haven't met Kevin yet."

461

Now John did look at her. She'd stepped just inside the cubicle but remained a safe distance away with her arms folded across her midsection. She wore a gray sweater and black slacks, all business today.

"No, I haven't. Should I?" He played it casual. After all, there wasn't any reason to believe that he should know who was going to be hired and when, provided it wasn't for any position that he should manage. He had no desire to interface with marketing research types, for instance.

"I don't know. You tell me. I overheard Prasad giving Kevin instructions about some study before he left to buy a bride. He mentioned test pages and security. Sound familiar?"

John scowled. It did sound like he'd been left out of an important loop. "Yes. What else do you know about Kevin?"

"Other than he's got a lisp and a rat tail? I saw his resume or something like it before I started. Mukesh emailed me a poorly written letter and a transcript from an MIT student. He said you were too busy looking for real programmers to bother with an intern. I looked at some sample code, talked to some friends at MIT about the classes listed on the resume, and told Mukesh he'd pass for a grunt job."

John's hands went to his head and tugged at his ponytail. Part of him was unsurprised that Mukesh had done an end-run around him. It wasn't in Mukesh's make-up to treat John as anything but an inferior underling. But would Mukesh really hire a programmer, even an intern, for the Rajasthan study without talking to Dr. Mukarjee first? Was it just coincidence or was there a relationship between today's call and Zoë's news?

"This isn't a big office, Zoë. Where's Kevin been hiding? Mukesh's office?" It was a joke, but as soon as he said it, John knew that it was true. His foreboding intensified.

"What's this study that Kevin's working on? I thought we were all about the money here."

John sighed, tugged at his ponytail again. "Oh, we are that. But we're so much more than that too." He couldn't help it. The sarcasm

462

crept in. "Remember that silver-haired gentleman who visited the day you interviewed? The one who smells like rubbing alcohol and curry? Dr. Mukarjee is the reason I came to work for Mukesh and Prasad. He couldn't afford to pay me much to work on his pet project, the IndiaClinic, so he got me an interview with them. In return for helping them find a Ph.D. from CMU at bargain-basement rates, they let him use Dr2Dr machines to connect Tufts doctors with their Indian colleagues for consults. Now IndiaClinic is in the first stage of a drug study set in Rajasthan. That's the other reason Prasad's in India, by the way. He's supposed to handle some of the details in person."

"I heard enough just now to know that someone is looking for some answers about Dr. Mukarjee."

"Yes, I guess you can say that." He hadn't thought about the query in those terms, but Zoë was right: Dr. Mukarjee was the nexus among all the questionable players, from Dr. Pendyala at Tufts to Mukesh and Prasad. How could such a warm-hearted, kind man rub shoulders with such lizards? The skin on John's face tightened as if he'd been dehydrated under a heat lamp. "But I really can't talk about it right now, Zoë." He paused, thought. Whatever their personal struggles, Zoë would be a good man to have on his side in a fight. "I've got to poke around a bit, check on some work I did for Dr. Mukarjee. I don't want to go all Oliver Stone and invent some sort of conspiracy if I can clear up my questions. I am curious about Kevin, though. I suspect Mukesh, control-freak that he is, just wanted to make sure I stayed busy on the paid work."

Zoë squinted, nodded, started to turn away. "Okay, that's reasonable. But let me know if there *is* something funny going on. I like to stay on top of things, make sure I can plan for contingencies if I need to."

John looked at her. "We work at a startup, Zoë. You should definitely have a contingency plan." And as he said it, he knew that he needed one, too.

ﻼﻼﻼ

"Are crocuses blooming yet?" Valerie, who still hadn't told Tamarind the nature of her illness, sounded as strong as a tern chick over the phone.

Tamarind looked out the window. Nothing but a handful of snow patches relieved the damp brown grass of her front lawn. Lucy's yard across the cul-de-sac lay in shadow, its layer of snow crusty and thick.

"I can't see any from where I'm standing."

"Haven't you been outside lately?" Tamarind heard the faint reproof in Valerie's voice. Resentment flared, but then she reminded herself that she had no time for that.

"Not really."

"Why not? Is it still really snowy and cold?"

Tamarind sighed. "It hasn't snowed in a few weeks. I've just been hibernating, I guess."

She looked behind her into the dining room where paper, play dough, glitter, scissors, stickers, and a dozen other art supplies covered the surface of the table. A microcosm for the whole house, for her mental state. No telling when she'd find time to clear a corner for her jewelry making.

"Go. Get outside. It's been six weeks, you're fit enough to take walks. To smell the muddy ground, hear the peepers, feel the sun on your cheeks. You need to connect with the world around you. It'll revitalize you. You sound wan."

"I could say the same of you." Tamarind's heart beat faster.

"I know you know," Valerie said after a pause. She sounded sad. "I didn't want to darken your joy from Adam's birth. I wish Ana hadn't told you."

"I know." Tamarind's grief scalded her, but she spoke without tears melting her voice—at least until her next words. "What am I going to do without you?"

She could hear Valerie crying and for the next ten minutes they cried together until at last Valerie spoke again.

"You'll live," she said. "You'll raise two beautiful children and love one wonderful man. Whatever else you do, whatever other friendships you make or amazing jewelry you create, you'll live more fully than I ever did."

Tamarind didn't want to hear about the future or other friendships. Or jewelry. She wanted to hold onto Valerie, nothing else. "None of it matters without you."

"Ridiculous." Now Valerie's voice grew firm. "Don't make a mockery of our friendship by turning me into some sort of idol, Tamarind. Dying is part of the Wheel of Life, which turns for all of us. You chose to cross over to mortality and you must take its sorrows along with its beauties. Even Ana accepts this."

For the first time, Tamarind thought to wonder about Ana's fate. "What will happen to her?"

"She'll stay at Posada La Diosa, making and selling her herbal concoctions. She has little power left to her, but she always uses what she has to the utmost. Don't worry about her."

Tamarind thought about Valerie's words while she readied Sarah for an outing into the thin-blue March afternoon. Sarah, who'd been confined to the house and rare visits to the library or the pool at the Y since Adam's birth, gabbled as Tamarind helped her slip on a jacket and sturdy boots. While Sarah wandered in a small arc around the front yard, stooping to study thick green blades slicing through the mud or darting among the shriveled rhododendrons in the bed against the house, she bundled Adam larvae-like into a carrier, his face hidden against her chest.

They headed for the backyard and the trail, which Tamarind hadn't followed since the day that she'd hurtled down it in a desperate search for Sarah. As they walked, a speck resolved above them into a lone bird, reminding Tamarind that it had been a long time since she'd practiced birdcalls in the warm Pittsburgh sunshine. She watched the bird, but it caught an updraft and soared away to the north, somewhere over the woods.

Maples guarded the trailhead in august silence, their bare limbs dark against the aloof sky. Tamarind and Sarah passed them, Sarah trotting ahead, chattering, while Tamarind walked by and laid reverent palms on the crenellated gray-brown bark. When she did, a rich, dark energy tingled along the surface of her skin and danced along the nerves of her forearms, traveling a rapid circuit across her chest and the living conduit of Adam's body. A loamy scent, mixed with pine and the cold dust of rocks, filled her nostrils. She snatched her hands away, shoved them into her pockets, and trudged after Sarah, who waited at the edge of the stream, dancing and stretching out a big toe to a nearby stepping stone. Adam continued to vibrate on an invisible plane as if the contact had struck a pure dark tone in his being.

Tamarind led Sarah toward the clearing at the northeast side of the woods. When they reached it, she stood in the middle, studying the bowl of heaven above while Sarah ran in a circle around her, arms held up and laughing. Another bird soared, dark wings stretched against the pale blue, and Tamarind wondered if it was the same one that she'd noticed before. The bird stayed too high for her to identify so she brought her gaze back to the woods.

The wall of leafless trees made her feel sheltered, safe, and yet part of the world around her. Her hands still tingled. After several minutes, she grew aware that the prickling in her hands echoed a vaster energy flowing under her feet. It had always been here. She'd just been too focused on finding Sarah and relying on her Goddess pendant to recognize it for what it was before. Pulling her hands from her pockets she held them out, flexing the fingertips. For the first time in more than four years, she relived the terrifying day that Marilyn descended on Culebra, the howling wind and lashing rain a white, inchoate fury sent by the Creator to scourge land and sea alike. She shivered. Adam stirred in the carrier and yawned but didn't awaken. Though faint, the pure tone still resonated from him.

"Mommy?"

Tamarind looked down at Sarah, who'd stopped dancing and stared at her with haunting blue eyes filled with awareness. Ana had been right. *Mer* eyes.

"Yes, Roe?" She didn't recognize her own voice. It sounded awestruck.

"Don't be afraid, Mommy. We're home now."

Tamarind blinked and then Sarah had started dancing again, a little girl who would be three in the summer, whose fine rose-gold hair haloed her tender cheeks.

Her first contact with the dark, steady lifeblood of the earth had been from an impulse, an instinct about the dual nature of the moonstone in the Goddess pendant. Even then, she'd only had time to taste the energy before Jesus grabbed her. But later, when she faced her father's rage, it had flowed through her again as she stood planted in the mud of the lagoon. It had flowed between her and John, channeled through the Goddess pendant, as they struggled through the wild night to the observation tower on Mount Resaca. Without her hand-polished moonstone, she'd never thought to feel it again.

"Thinking about your wedding ring?" Lucy's voice startled Tamarind. She whirled around, her hands clutched into fists. "Sorry, didn't mean to startle you, young one."

Tamarind blinked and looked at Lucy. There was something about Lucy beyond the endearment—perhaps the wildness of her hair or her lined, world-weary features—that reminded Tamarind of Ana.

"It's okay. I just didn't expect to see anyone in this lonely field."

They both turned at Sarah's shriek of happiness. The little girl had seen Custard and now bent over to wrap her arms around the patient cat's neck. Tamarind wondered if she should tell Lucy about Olivia's email, but Lucy's sloping shoulders made her want to protect her neighbor. She suspected that Lucy had heard a lot of distressing news over the years.

"That's why I come here," Lucy said and stepped up beside Tamarind. She was tall, straight and true as a maple. "I told John I've been coming here for twenty years. I started when my kids were young and I needed to get away from the noise. Now that Rachel's staying with me, I have to sneak over here more often."

"Then I should leave." Tamarind couldn't help the regret that colored her voice. She kept her gaze from Lucy's face.

"No, don't go." Lucy laid a hand along Tamarind's upper arm. The dark energy flared and spiked down Tamarind's leg and then quieted. "I'd like to share this retreat with you today, Tamarind."

A strange, sore lump blocked Tamarind's throat. After a moment, she managed to speak. "Okay."

Lucy nodded and then shuffled her feet. She frowned a little and cleared her throat. "Tamarind, I really don't want to pry. But you didn't answer my question. Are you thinking about your wedding ring?"

Now it was Tamarind's turn to shuffle her feet. "No. I was thinking about my pendant. The one with the blue stone in the belly."

"Ah." There was a note of understanding in Lucy's voice. "John told me that it meant a lot to you, that it was a symbol of your faith in his love." She paused and in the brief silence Tamarind's heart pinged so hard in her chest that she was sure that Lucy could hear it. When Lucy continued, it appeared as if she'd only just come to believe the import of her words herself. "Symbols are important, Tamarind. If you believe this pendant holds your faith, then it does. That's why I'm giving it back to you."

As Tamarind stood, stunned, Lucy reached into her jacket pocket and fumbled for a moment.

"I'm sorry, Tamarind. I'm afraid Rachel took it. She was desperate to save her marriage. What she didn't get is that you can't borrow someone else's magic. There's no magic that can fix what's wrong in a bad marriage. Even a good one needs faith and elbow grease."

Tamarind accepted the Goddess pendant. She lay on Tamarind's palm, insubstantial as an old dream. The moonstone, which had captivated Tamarind ever since Valerie had shown her how to polish its dusty surface to a fine sheen, winked in the watery March sunlight. She clutched the Goddess, but nothing happened. No heat warmed her palm, no electricity surged along her nerves, no glow emanated from between her curled fingers. The moonstone, though lovely and rare, had lost its magic.

She managed to say a lukewarm "thanks" before a peculiar *cuk-cuk-cuk-cuk-cuk* from the nearby trees stole their attention. Tamarind looked around to see a gray-brown hawk swoop from the woods across from them. It sped across the clearing and descended into the leafless stand, using its long legs like a spear. When it headed back, they saw a plump bird struggling against its claws.

Lucy issued a low whistle. "Cooper's hawk! I haven't seen one of those in years. They're endangered. Won't the Conservation Commission love to hear about this."

Tamarind, who remembered seeing one last fall, frowned as she tried to identify what kind of bird that it had brought down. "Is that a sea gull it's got?"

Lucy peered as the Cooper's hawk passed overhead. "Yup. Odd. We're quite some ways from the coast."

The sea gull jerked and squeaked, but the merciless Cooper's hawk circled the field twice, shaking and clutching until the smaller bird's head flopped. Something fell from the conjoined birds and landed not ten feet from Tamarind and Lucy. Sarah, who'd stopped stroking Custard's ears, skipped over to the spot before Tamarind could call out to her. When she brought the conch shell wrapped with a bit of twine, Tamarind accepted it.

"That's odd," Lucy said. "It almost looks as though someone tied that to the gull."

Tamarind, who hadn't spoken to Ana since her old mentor had told her the terrible news about Valerie, rubbed the striped shell with her fingertip. "Someone did. The question is, why?"

Thirty-nine
෪

NEARLY A MONTH AFTER RACHEL and her three children moved in, Lucy, who'd agreed to let them stay for a few days, found herself wondering if her solitary life had come to an end for the indefinite future. Rachel did all that she could between working two jobs, talking with a divorce lawyer, and shuttling children half an hour each way to school and daycare, to find an apartment that she could afford. When Lucy asked her why she didn't just stay in her current apartment, Rachel rolled her eyes and explained in the voice she often used with her children that it had taken all of Tom's unemployment and occasional paychecks to supplement her income so that they could pay the rent.

"Mom, you just have no idea how outrageous rent is these days. So many people clamoring for apartments means landlords can charge whatever they like for the nastiest dive around. I can't get a two-bedroom apartment for less than twelve hundred."

"Good heavens! Twelve hundred dollars? That's more than the mortgage your father used to pay. Don't tell me how much houses cost."

"Okay, I won't. Even if I could afford the mortgage, I don't have enough money to put down on a house—yet. You're lucky, Mom.

You own your house. I bet it's worth a lot more these days than you think."

"Really?" Lucy asked. She'd often flipped through the real estate section, of course, but it hadn't actually occurred to her that her house might be worth much more than what it had been appraised for before Billy died ten years ago.

Remembering this conversation a few days later, Lucy found herself thinking about Rachel's future. Rachel insisted that she and the kids would be out of Lucy's hair as soon as she could manage it, but she admitted that it probably meant moving further west, to Marlboro or Worcester even, where she could afford the rents. If that was the case, Lucy knew that Rachel would want to keep Matthew and Hayley in school in Holliston until the end of the year, something that she supported; however, that meant that she must also give them a place to stay until June, another four months away. Did she really want to do that?

She sat at her breakfast table, alone at last after a morning of Rachel screeching at her children to hurry or they'd all be late amid whines, cries, and spilled cereal, and drank her second cup of Earl Grey tea. As she drank, she ignored the scattered breakfast dishes still surrounding her and refused to look under the table for the large chunks of scrambled eggs and toast that Ben had dropped onto her carpet. Yet she still felt the air vibrating around her and heard the echoes of their squabbling. What in the world was the matter with her? Only a month ago she sat on her sofa deriding Ruth Corcoran for not understanding the pain of a forgotten mother and today she wondered whether she could withstand four more months of noise, mess, and tension from her daughter's family.

I'm not really much different from Ruth after all, she thought: *when it comes down to it, the thought of children is much more pleasant than the reality of children.*

She put her empty cup down and began to massage her temples. Now her head was vibrating in concert with the disturbed air around her. Heart racing, she felt woozy and a little nauseous as though she'd drunk too much tea on an empty stomach. It was difficult to think when she felt this way, her thoughts leaping around like a monkey in a tree. Maybe she should go lie down until her heart stopped tapping at her ribcage in a bid to spring free from the confines of her chest.

She stood very carefully, feeling the walls around her tilt off vertical, and stepped away from the table. She was forced to stop after only two steps as a rush of vertigo overcame her and brought bile to her mouth; only after several long moments in which she thought she might add to the bits of Ben's breakfast littering the carpet did she calm her stomach. Once the wave of nausea passed, she walked slowly down the hallway toward her room. As she paused at her doorway, she looked across the hall at the door to Bill Jr.'s old bedroom, which was standing ajar; inside she could see the unmade bed, piles of dirty laundry on the floor, empty soda cans, and a few toys. Rachel had never been the neatest of her children, but now she was a downright slob.

Lucy went into her room and shut the door behind her, feeling safer and less wobbly. Her room was the sunniest in the whole house and even this early in spring it was cheerful and bright. Sighing, she tossed her decorative pillows onto the floor, lay down on the quilt she'd sewn herself and closed her eyes. It was almost as though she'd lain back against Billy's chest and she let herself imagine his arms around her.

"Why, oh why, did we ever have children?" she murmured to the listening silence; a warm breath tickled her ear, but there was no response.

"You wouldn't have needed to cheat on me, would you?" She snuggled deeper into the bed. "I would have kept things so hot here at home that you wouldn't have glanced twice at another woman. And you would have worked harder to get a job closer to home, one that didn't make you travel so much. I could have done something with myself, learned to sell houses or become a florist."

She paused, considering what she was saying to him. "Yes, I could have found my own way in the world and you might have thought twice about hurting me. I wouldn't have sat home and kept

472

my mouth shut, you know. I would have left, and there wouldn't have been any children caught in the middle, not like Matthew, Hayley and Ben are."

The air vibrated again as it had done in the dining-room, this time filling her whole chest with its humming; Lucy felt the bed beneath her moving in time with the vibration. The vibration swelled until her very core ached with it, a hurt both familiar and long forgotten: it was the euphoria she'd felt as she held Dorothy in her arms for the first time upon waking in the hospital. It was the bittersweet pain that impaled her as she held Rachel, after bearing this child of reconciliation fully awake and completely aware. Among these stronger chords of intense joy and pain were other threads begun at the birth of her sons, no less important because they hummed more steadily and evenly. Together, all these chords bound her to Billy, bound her and made her both more and less than whom she might have been. She hadn't heard the full music, except in snatches, while their children grew up; it had been years since she'd heard any of it.

Keeping her eyes closed, she allowed the music to swell to its fullest voice as it conjured up images of her children that she'd thought were long gone: a nine-year-old Bill Jr., his hair freshly shaved in neat imitation of his father, wearing a white, short-sleeved dress shirt and dark blue jeans; James and Thomas, five and four, covered in mud and holding the garden hose under the hot sun; Rachel, almost ten, her dark hair curled, looking solemnly over her left shoulder as she held her fingers above the keyboard; Dorothy, just after her sixteenth birthday, her long blond hair resting on her shoulders, smiling a dazzling smile in her pale-blue prom dress.

And then the images came so fast that she hadn't the time to sort and study them as though they were photographs in an album left out on the coffee table for casual perusal. It was as though someone was throwing them at her, saying, *Here, here, here, here— look at your children! Do you really wish that they'd never been born? Do you really want to get back at Billy that way?*

473

"No, no!" She wanted the images to slow down so that she could linger over them, and their attendant grief, but they stopped coming and the music halted. Loud ringing replaced it. She opened her eyes and reached for the phone at her bedside.

"Hello?"

"Mom? Is that you?" It was Rachel.

"Yes. Who did you expect?"

"You just didn't sound like yourself there for an instant."

"I was just lying down." Lucy paused, took a breath. "What's the matter, Rachel? Shouldn't you be at work by now?"

"I *am* at work. Mom, I need your help. Ben's daycare center just called. He's got a fever and they want him to go home. I really can't miss work right now with tax deadlines coming up. Can you go get him for me?"

Lucy pushed herself upright against the headboard and cleared her throat before answering.

"Yes, dear. Aren't you lucky I was home this morning?"

✍✍✍

By Thursday morning, John knew that there was a problem with the Rajasthan study. He'd already checked his program and none of the equations that he'd used to analyze the raw data being collected had any flaws. Before he sent the tool to Dr. Anderson, however, he wanted to re-run the data through it and check the results against the file that Dr. Mukarjee had submitted to the IRB. He'd processed about twenty percent of the raw data that he'd stored on his PC when he saw that his results didn't match up with the numbers that Dr. Anderson had sent him. Dr. Anderson's numbers showed that the experimental abortion drug Tamarifex had a modest effect in inducing miscarriage in the first trimester. John's analysis, however, showed a statistically significant rate of abortion in first- and even second-trimester pregnancies.

Dr. Mukarjee had told him last summer that most studies of promising drugs failed to deliver on their promise when they'd moved from animal to human trials. Often, the money spent developing the drug ended up being a gamble, a roll of the dice that

474

ended up in snake eyes. Even when a drug did work as hoped, it had unacceptable side effects. No matter what the final outcome, the first weeks of a drug trial almost always presented mixed results. The increased abortion rate should have been good news, for Phoenix Pharmaceutical anyway. John, an American Catholic who'd sworn to uphold his conscience in matters of faith, had mixed feelings about abortion now that he had two children.

But he didn't have the current study data that had been used to generate the IRB report. Without running all of the latest numbers, he couldn't be sure that the statistical significance hadn't just been an artifact of his data set. Yet when he tried to access the IndiaClinic files on the Dr2Dr server, he found that he'd been locked out.

Frustrated and uneasy, John tried all morning to get into the IndiaClinic files. He needed access. Without asking Dr. Mukarjee or Kevin.

He could just give Dr. Anderson the copy of the data he had, wash his hands of the whole thing. Or he could stall, send the analysis tool and the equations to the good doctor. Write an email that sounded appropriately cooperative, perhaps a tad incompetent. Admit he hadn't been able to track down the current data because an intern had been hired to process it. How long would he have to get into the files before Dr. Anderson gave up on him?

He fretted over the email's wording off and on for most of the morning. He'd never had such trouble hitting the send button before, but every time he reread his sentences, their tone and implications grew distorted, grew sullen and wooden or defiant and cold. Sometimes the voice in his head read the words onscreen as if a non-native English speaker had written them. Then he suspected that English wasn't *his* native tongue. He wasn't cut out for this subterfuge. Why did he have to sneak around behind Dr. Mukarjee's back?

He returned to the unsent email until it occurred to him that a simple, stupid answer waited to be discovered. He hadn't been asked to oversee any reporting so there was a chance that Kevin had run the fake data file that he'd created to test the tool. Dr. Mukarjee had then submitted the wrong results. An accident. Easy to rectify.

But why did they lock you out of the IndiaClinic data? a skeptical voice asked inside him.

He'd kept a copy of the test file on his hard drive. He could run the file through the tool and then compare the results to Dr. Anderson's numbers. He'd have enough analyzed by lunch to know whether his simple answer was the correct answer.

He tugged off his ponytail holder and ran his fingers through his hair. *Maybe I should cut this short*, he thought. An idle thought interrupted by Zoë.

"I always loved your hair down. Makes you look like Fabio." He twitched and blinked. "Here. Coffee." She held out a cup.

John accepted it. His hand brushed Zoë's but he ignored the touch. "Mm." He sipped, grunted and swallowed. "Hot. And it tastes weird. You didn't put any fake stuff in here?"

Zoë laughed and sat in the gray office chair he kept for visitors. A musky vanilla-and-clove scent wafted in the draft of her movement. Once John smelled it, his nostrils filled with its spicy warmth and he felt lightheaded. He sipped the coffee again.

"No. Nothing but the real thing in there," she said. "You look troubled. Difficulty finding the bug in the storage algorithm?"

John's eyesight blurred and a slight, sharp pain notched the spot between his brows. Zoë's image wavered until he blinked. Sighing, he rubbed a fingertip on the spot and sipped the coffee. "No. Ted found it."

"Something else." She shifted and her legs parted. John noticed that she wore a skirt, the same black-suede skirt that she'd worn the night that they'd eaten at Brew Moon. Her long legs, muscular from years of Tae Kwon Do, tempted him. An urge to stroke her calf jolted him.

"Just checking some results for the IndiaClinic. All my equations are solid for the analysis tool I wrote, but when I run the raw data that resides on this PC, I get very different results from the ones we sent to the review board. It didn't occur to me until just now that Kevin could've run the test file I used to develop the tool." He turned back to his monitor to see the results scrolling by. He studied them against the IRB results in a parallel window. "Well, I've got my answer. He didn't."

"The review board? Is that who called the other day?" Zoë's dark eyes pulled his gaze to her face like a magnet. Her glossy hair enticed him.

"Yeah. Now I need to get some patient data. I just can't get into the files on the server."

"Maybe I can help." Zoë stood up and leaned over him. Her vibrant scent, the heat of her upper arm pressed into his, crept under his awareness making it hard to focus on the task at hand. How could he have forgotten how incredibly sexy she was? She logged into her PC via the network. John saw that she'd mirrored the server's contents on a back-up hard drive. "I did this after our talk the other day. Remember my private key? It lets me in as well as locks others out."

"Ah." He couldn't help sounding admiring. He'd been right. Having Zoë around had come in handy. He searched for the file with the latest study data. When he found it, he began analyzing it. The numbers scrolled by in a new window. Together they peered at the results, comparing them to Dr. Anderson's data set.

"They don't look the same to me."

"Me either." Disappointed bitterness roughened his speech. "I'll send them through the comparison checker, but that's just putting off the inevitable. Now I need to track down the author of the false data set. I doubt Kevin is clever enough to create one on his own." He closed his eyes and rubbed his forehead. He pulled the ponytail holder back around his hair and sighed.

"I'll help." Was she purring? A lurid image of her, sweaty and flushed, flickered like lightning across the dark screen of his thoughts. "You'll have to tell me more over lunch."

"Lunch?" he asked, dazed.

"Yes." She stood up and laughed. "That was my stomach you heard just now." She glanced over her shoulder. "Besides, I think we should take this topic off-site, don't you?"

"Sure. I'd love to get out of here." What was happening to him? Zoë had always been overwhelmingly sexy, luring men with her dark fragrance and animal aura. But he knew, better than anyone, the shallowness of that attraction. The dissatisfaction of one-dimensional passion.

By the time they got to the Cheltham Applebee's, John's headache had burrowed itself into his eyeball. The vanilla musk had degraded in his nostrils like a heady wine turned to vinegar. A tic tattooed his left eyelid. He was grateful for the dim booth where the hostess seated them.

"Listen," he began. His voice creaked. "I feel a little strange."

"What's wrong?" She slid next to him in the booth. The contact points of upper thigh and hip burned him. His stomach churned.

"I feel like someone thrust an ice pick in my eye. It's making me a little sick to my stomach."

She looked at him. Was that guilt that he read in her gaze? "You are? Maybe a soda would help." She put her hand on his knee and he jumped. She let it fall off and bit her lip.

He said nothing about her touch and his reaction. "Maybe."

They sat in awkward silence while the waitress delivered their drinks. As soon as they were alone, however, Zoë cleared her throat.

"Did you feel all right before I came to see you?" There was a tentative quality to her question that he'd never heard from her before. The oily mash in his belly gurgled and sloshed around. He felt seasick and he'd always had sea legs.

"Yeah." He put his palms to his forehead and leaned onto his elbows. "Fine. I didn't even eat breakfast this morning. I was in such a hurry to get in before Mukesh got there. It must be nerves over this IndiaClinic nonsense. Either that, or Tamarind made some bad cocoa chili last night and it's just now hitting me."

"Are you that worried about the drug study?" She no longer looked at him. Instead, she played with the paper wrapper from her set of flatware.

He closed his eyes. If only this damn headache would just go away! He could handle the clinching belly and the twisting intestines. "Yes. I've been so busy I haven't had the chance to follow up on some contacts I made back in December. If I need to walk away from Dr2Dr, I won't have any place else to go. What if I can't get another job for months?"

"That won't happen, John." She put her hand on his forearm. Her fingers branded him and he groaned. She pulled her hand away as if she was the one who'd been burned. "You're not one of those fruity AI guys trying to build believable agents. You make networks work better to store important data. EMC or even DEC would snap you up in a heartbeat."

"What if something illegal's going on, Zo? I told Dr. Anderson at the review board I'd help him track the raw data down. If I give it to him now, Dr. Mukarjee might get in trouble. I can try to find out who ran false numbers for the report beforehand, but that could lead to any number of bad outcomes. I might not find the culprit in time. I might get fingered as some sort of accomplice. I might not like what I find out." He couldn't bring himself to say that he might find out that Dr. Mukarjee, the man that he'd idealized for his good works, had turned out to be a fraud.

"John." He twisted his face to look at her. Her pupils were huge. "I think I know who generated that file. Me."

His thoughts reeled. "You? Why? How could you?"

She bristled. "Because I didn't know what I was doing when I did it. They gave me your equations and told me to create a test file, to really stress the tool. They gave me a target range for my results. I laughed because I knew you'd think it was funny I was tackling your work, just like I tackled you back in grad school. Even back then, I think I knew I couldn't beat you." She sounded wistful. And resigned.

"Who told you to create the file? Mukesh? Prasad? Dr. Mukarjee?" He could hear the strain in his voice. His gut gurgled again.

"Dr. Pendyala. Said he was a colleague of Dr. Mukarjee's. I've seen him in the office so I didn't question." She squinted at him. "What's the real issue, John? So the wrong file got analyzed. Just send Dr. Anderson the real data. Let him sort out if it was deliberate or not."

"I don't know, Zo. The drug study, the one Dr. Pendyala tampered with? It's to test an abortion drug for poor women in developing countries like India. Does it sit well with you knowing some guy maybe manipulated data about that drug?"

"When you put it that way—" Her eyes glowed with a new fire. "I get fired up, yes."

"What if Dr. Anderson comes back wanting more snooping? I could still get burned. My family—my wife and children—Tamarind—" He writhed. His intestines roiled in sudden warning. "Excuse me." He jumped up, knocking over his Sprite as he raced to the restroom.

When he returned, Zoë sat tearing a napkin into bits. Her pale face heightened the red, bitten look of her lips. She looked up at him with bright eyes.

"I'm sorry." Her whisper almost didn't reach him.

John's visit had turned him inside out and wrung him dry. He sank into his seat and grabbed his refilled Sprite glass. He sipped it, sighed. "What'd you give me? Some new date drug?"

"No." She shook her head. "I gave you the rest of a love potion some old witch gave me on Culebra years ago. I put some of it in your beer at Brew Moon. When I saw how well it worked, I resolved to give you the rest."

John's thoughts reeled. She'd put something in his beer that night? That's why he'd gone all raging lust and hot eagerness. Then his mind caught up with the phrase "old witch" and Ana's face flashed into his memory. "Damn her."

"Who?"

"Ana, a–a—" he stumbled. How to describe that freak of nature? "A friend of Tamarind's. She wanted to run me off."

Tears ran down Zoë's face. "God, John! It's like I've been bewitched! For five fucking years I've had something eating at my insides, gnawing at me. That's why I've never kept a boyfriend for more than a few months. When I found that bottle while I was packing, something even stronger came over me. It's been riding me like a demon until we left for lunch. It fought me, but when you cried out Tamarind's name just now, it withered away. All that's left is the taste of ashes and something sour, like that juice you served me on Culebra."

When John touched the back of her hand, nothing happened. "It's over, whatever it was. Forget about it. I'm going to."

She nodded but said nothing.

John pursed his lips and hunched his shoulders. A weight had lifted that he hadn't even realized he'd carried. Without Zoë's feral lust misting the atmosphere, he felt clean and renewed. Almost hopeful.

"I'll send the real data to Dr. Anderson, explain that your test file was used. It's over and done with, too, at least for us."

Even as he said it, he remembered that Zoë had a key to the locked files. Could he let it go without finding out why the mysterious Dr. Pendyala would suppress a significant success rate for an abortion drug?

Forty
☙

TAMARIND SAW JOHN AND ZOË returning to Dr.2Dr after lunch, but they never saw her. Later she wondered what she'd have done if either of them had looked over and caught her eye. As it was, they got out of an unfamiliar car, their gazes never straying from one another as they talked, and she never found out. Through her shock at seeing Zoë, whose confident walk and ID badge confirmed that she was no stranger to John's office, Tamarind recognized an ease between them that had never been there before, an acceptance or closeness that replaced the tension that she'd always taken for sexual attraction. She squinted and tried to hum, but it had been months since any relief had come from her old ability, something that had failed her that day she'd passed out from lack of fluids. She stared at them, trying to interpret this change in their demeanor towards each other. Without her *mer* telepathy, she hadn't a clue how to read them.

Heart pounding, she waited for them to enter the office building. Whether she felt relief at the close call or anger at discovering a crucial truth that John had kept from her, she didn't know. Her very confusion signaled something deep had changed in her; when it had happened she didn't know. The transformation hadn't been instantaneous. It had accreted over time, starting out tiny with annoyance about eating only vegetarian meals and growing into outraged silence following John's slavering attention to Zoë at Brew Moon. Here she was, witness to her husband's deceit, perhaps infidelity, and instead of confronting him and her rival, she'd cringed behind a parked car.

Her heart continued to pound, so hard in fact that Tamarind wondered if something had broken in her chest, perhaps some mooring for the stressed organ. She climbed back into her wagon almost unaware of Sarah behind the driver's seat. Adam slept next to her, emanating a faint dark tone that made Tamarind's ears ring.

She sat so long without starting the car that Sarah said, "We're not going to see Daddy." It wasn't a question.

"No." The pounding had moved from her chest to her head, dull and slow.

She started the car and headed out of the parking lot and up Moody, so glazed and lost that she almost didn't see the red lights in her rearview mirror. Pulling over, she felt a stabbing pain in her chest. She'd never been pulled over, not in the four years since she'd gotten her driver's license. She lowered the window.

"License and registration please." All she could see was the light tan and black uniform, the holster on the hip, the clipboard. She felt blank, unable to process visual information. She'd grown deaf to all but the officer's next words.

"Ma'am, where're you going?" He'd bent over and looked at her.

"Home." The word crystallized between her numb lips.

"You just ran through two red lights. I was going to let you go through the first, but then you went through the second." He paused and looked into the backseat. "Ma'am, I'm just going to give you a warning today, but you've got two young children back there. They're depending on you. Pay attention."

"I will." She didn't look at him. His eyes were too sharp, his gaze too direct. He handed her back her license and registration.

When she pulled out, she signaled, something that she'd never done, even when John had told her that she needed to learn the rules before breaking them. But the cruiser tailed her for several blocks so she struggled to focus on half-learned arcane driving etiquette even though her thoughts had scattered beyond the boundaries of her skull. She surprised herself when a modicum of sense returned along with her effort to stay out of trouble. The pounding was gone, but the headache had stayed and brought along a dry mouth and eyes.

Sarah spoke, but she'd used up all her attention on driving and couldn't do more than note the sounds of her daughter's speech. They passed out of the urban landscape of Waltham into the tree-lined, two-lane state highway that took them to Cheltham. Green grass rimed the wakening ground and deep purple and occasional yellow dotted the front beds of colonials. She couldn't see the tiny leaves and flowers budding on maples and magnolias, apples and dogwood, but her inner sense quivered with the thousands of pinpricks of life verging on exploding around her. It made her nauseous.

Olivia. She'd gone to see John about Olivia's stalker. Olivia had gotten so distressed about another email that she'd refused to go home after school every day this past week. Her bouts of diarrhea had grown so intense that there was no longer any pretense between them. Tamarind recalled Olivia's shrunken figure, the large haunted eyes behind her thick glasses, and her anger flared, shattering the numbness that had dominated her since leaving Dr2Dr's parking lot. She'd wanted to tell Lucy, but Olivia had pleaded with her not to tell her grandmother, who'd grown so strange that Olivia worried that she'd break the older woman's fragile mind. So Tamarind had held her tongue and held out hope that John would track down the pervert tormenting Olivia. After what she'd seen today, she knew that she couldn't count on John. She couldn't wait for him to deliver the culprit before doing something to help Olivia. She'd start by telling Lucy, whose plainspoken manner and sad eyes she suspected cloaked the indomitable heart of a mountain.

Lucy answered the door when Tamarind knocked twenty minutes later. Behind her, Hayley stood sucking on a Popsicle, her mouth stained red and her hair a mess. Ben, his cheeks pink and wearing only a t-shirt and diaper, hid his face against Lucy's chinos. Toys, shoes, and picture books littered the floor of Lucy's once-immaculate front hall. Splotches of dirt blossomed on the marble tile. In the distant family room, the TV muttered.

"Tamarind! What's wrong? You look like thunder." Lucy stood holding the storm door open. "Do you want some tea? Tell me what's wrong?"

Sarah, who waited in the station wagon, shouted. "Yes! Tea! Yes!"

Adam began to wail, the peculiar trilling wail of the hungry newborn. Tamarind, who'd navigated her way home by the fiery sun of her anger, felt her milk let down and her breasts tingle. Two warm wet spots sprouted on her chest. She ignored him.

"Lucy, I've got to tell you something. It's about Olivia." She paused and bit her lip. Olivia's anxious face filled her thoughts.

"What is it?" Lucy's voice sliced the air between them. Her gaze searched Tamarind's face. "She hasn't had a fight with Dorothy, has she? Pam?"

"No." How did she tell Lucy about the violent video of the man laughing as he choked a woman with his penis? How could she not tell Olivia's family what was going on?

Lucy saved her. "It's about the diarrhea, isn't it?" At Tamarind's wide-eyed response, she went on, "I overheard her and Pam at Christmas. She's losing weight fast. Something's stressing her so much it's all going right out her. Do you know what?"

Tamarind nodded. Details didn't matter. The substance did. "She got two emails that frighten her. She thinks someone's watching her and she won't go home after school. She didn't want to worry you so I asked John to see if he could trace who's sending the email so we could stop it. John found out that it's coming from a computer in Cheltham but not who's sending it. Olivia looked so bad yesterday that I asked John what I should do. He told me to go to the police, but when I saw them they wanted to see John's evidence. But he's, ah, a little too busy today and I couldn't talk to him. I don't know what else to do."

Lucy stood there, blinking and confused. She looked ancient and brittle. Tamarind's heart lurched and she wished that she'd never brought this to Lucy's doorstep. And then the indomitable heart rose up to level Lucy's shoulders. "I do. Olivia stays with me tonight. We'll get John's evidence later and get it to the police. It'll get taken care of. Thank you for telling me."

She paused and Tamarind realized that Adam's wails had turned into desperate screams. Her leaking breasts had soaked her blouse. Lucy put a bony hand on Tamarind's wrist. A spark of dark energy crackled from her touch, but she seemed unaware of it. "That's not what's eatin' you, is it? Come in and talk. Sarah can play with Ben and Hayley. You can nurse Adam."

"Mommy! I want tea!" Sarah called over Adam's wails.

Tamarind stood rooted to Lucy's stoop. Her wrist tingled and ached from Lucy's touch. Should she go in and tell Lucy about what she'd seen? She scanned Lucy's lined face, so familiar and concerned, and saw something there, something that stirred her heart. It had flitted across her father's features the last time that she'd seen him. And then she slipped her hand into her pocket and felt the conch shell that she'd recovered from the field in the woods. While she turned it over as she considered what to do, she recognized the deep lines of sadness drooping Lucy's eyes and she remembered Olivia. She couldn't stay and burden Lucy.

"I wish I could, Lucy. Maybe another time."

Lucy nodded and dropped her hand from Tamarind's wrist. Tamarind felt the other woman's gaze on her back as she returned to the station wagon where a cacophony of misery greeted her. Sarah looked at her and stopped crying for tea. Her gaze bore into Tamarind. Whatever message those eyes contained, Tamarind didn't want to know what it was.

Time took on an odd quality for the rest of the afternoon. As always, it dragged. She nursed and changed Adam, played pretend and read to Sarah, ran through shopping lists and dinner menus in her head, and categorized all the waiting chores. She picked up a novel to read while nursing Adam again and then abandoned it to entertain Sarah, whose naps had dwindled to one so late in the afternoon that Tamarind had to wake her up after fifteen or twenty minutes or she'd stay up until eleven. Of course, for an hour afterwards, Sarah fussed and whined while Tamarind made dinner. Lucy called it the witching hour. Yet even as her afternoon crawled, Tamarind's emotions seethed and churned. Her heart raced. She envisioned confronting John, watching him as she told him that she knew about Zoë. Watching him squirm. But then her visions failed. What next? Maybe he wouldn't squirm. Maybe he'd be relieved that his secret was out. She couldn't begin to imagine what might happen after that.

The worst part of the afternoon came when Olivia showed up and Tamarind had to send her across the street knowing that she wasn't coming back. She knew that Olivia would be upset that she'd told Lucy about the creepy email, but that didn't bother her. She'd gotten attached to the afternoons that Olivia came over, true, but Olivia didn't come every day—except for last week, when Olivia's visits had little to do with helping Tamarind out. No, she missed Olivia because they would have talked and that would have distracted her, kept her from worrying the conch shell, which reminded her about the doppelganger and truth potions that Ana had given her.

By the time that John came home Tamarind was exhausted. She felt as if she'd run one of the long foot races that had fascinated her ever since seeing one in Pittsburgh. For weeks afterwards, she'd pretended to run in one whenever she went into the Carnegie Mellon campus. She'd start down Schenley Drive just inside the entrance to Schenley Park. The feeling of her feet on the pavement and the wind in her hair had been glorious and surreal. Those runs had been the only times that she'd even come close to reliving her speedy ocean swimming around Culebra and its cays. She'd catch the shadow of a red-tailed hawk gliding over the park and for a few minutes they would both soar together, she on the ground and the hawk in the air.

After dinner, John read to Sarah while holding Adam. Tamarind cleaned up and then went into the dining room where her neglected jewelry-making supplies waited in a set of white- plastic stacking drawers. She pulled out her needle-nosed pliers and her wire cutters, a tray of glass beads and design board and sat down. Nothing inspired her, but she played with the beads on the board until she heard John and Sarah head upstairs. Even though Sarah had catnapped at four, she begged to stay downstairs and play dress up. It took John an hour to get her through her bath and a picture book. Tamarind didn't know how he handled Adam because she didn't go upstairs and get the baby as she usually did. Instead, she pushed the beads and the wire aside and went to the bottom drawer of the stacking drawers where she'd hidden her potions from Ana. She studied the tins, opened their lids and sniffed. Was her future bound up in their repulsive scents?

John came down after he'd gotten Sarah tucked in, Adam nestled into the pocket made by his bent arm. She looked at his face, not aware of the small frown that knitted her brow.

He halted in the doorway. "Something wrong?"

She shook her head, her lips pressed together. She no longer had a diving membrane, that blue inner eyelid that slid down to shield a mermaid's eyes underwater, but her vision had altered after seeing him with Zoë. What puzzled her, what she couldn't be sure about, was whether she saw John as he really was or whether her eyesight was distorted.

"I don't know. You tell me. I came to Dr2Dr today to get some evidence from you about whoever's sending Olivia email. I called first, but I didn't wait for you to call back. You were out when I got there so I came back home." Despite all her fantasies, she didn't say any more. She wanted to give him a chance to tell her, to avoid the truth potion.

Something wild and dark winged across his features. He sighed and sat down. Adam mewled in his sleep and turned his nose into John's armpit.

"I'm sorry. I missed your voicemail. I was distracted by a problem I didn't want to tell you about."

Tamarind's heart thudded. *Here goes*, she thought. *The truth comes out and it's a problem named Zoë.* But his answer surprised her.

"On Monday I got a call from a doctor at Tufts—you know, the university where Dr. Mukarjee teaches. This doctor works for the review board that oversees all the medical research at Tufts. He had some questions about the Rajasthan study. That night I stayed late this week? I-I well I found out that someone submitted false data to the review board."

Tamarind knew that John was lying. She didn't know how that she knew, but it was true.

"But you were out. Were you meeting with the doctor from Tufts?" She watched his reaction.

The shadow didn't reappear. "No. I had to get out, think about what to do about the false data. I don't want to get Dr. Mukarjee in trouble for nothing."

Tamarind's disappointment blinded her. She looked down and blinked to clear it from her eyes. She heard Valerie's voice telling her to ask John about Zoë. She blinked harder and clamped her lips together. She didn't need to ask John. *He* needed to come clean. He'd cheated on her before with Raimunda. They might not have been dating or lovers, but he'd slept with Raimunda as a way of avoiding his feelings for her. Ana had as much equated his actions with infidelity, hadn't she?

She forced a sigh and looked at him. "No problem. Olivia's staying with Lucy who plans to take whatever you have to the police. I told her when I couldn't find you."

John ran his hand through his loose hair. Fine short hairs fuzzed around his face making him look unkempt. For the first time, Tamarind found his appearance less than appealing.

"I'm sorry you had to tell Lucy. Probably for the best though." Adam stirred and began uttering little *ah-ah-ahs*. He turned his head into John's armpit and rooted. "I don't think I've got what he's looking for." John stood up and handed Adam to her before going into the kitchen to wash the dinner dishes.

Tamarind aided Adam's search for her nipple and sank back into the chair. She lifted her tired feet to the seat of the chair across from her. A surge of oxytocin filled her as she nursed Adam, a deep, rich tone of protective love that swelled her chest and dampened her unhappiness at John's lying. Adam, peacefully solid even for a newborn, curled his hand around her breast. She traced the edge of his hairline and encircled his perfect ear. Tomorrow, she would give him his first tub bath. Unlike mothers who'd forgotten their own watery births, she planned to cradle him in her lap as she sponged him clean. There was no feeling quite like the feeling of warm, slippery skin-upon-skin between infant and mother.

As Adam nursed, she hummed, a deep sound reminiscent more of whale song than her old *mer* clicks and vibrations. Adam pulsed and hummed in response. That's when she saw it. A long, coarse hair, too dark and straight to be John's, lay on the long sleeve of Adam's sleeper. It was Zoë's hair. She hooked her nail under the hair and wrapped it around the finger for later, after Adam's two a.m. feeding. She'd slip downstairs and add it to the doppelganger potion. Ana had said that she needed a hair or a fingernail. It had been delivered to her just in time. Ana said it needed to ripen. She'd find out the truth one way or another. It didn't occur to her to wonder what she'd do with it once she knew it.

※ ※ ※

Ana leaned against the side of Posada La Diosa where Valerie could neither see nor smell her smoking. It had been weeks since Valerie had been outside on the patio, weeks since Ana had left out sugar water for the hummingbirds and bananaquits, who still continued to flutter around the empty feeders ever hopeful that their easy nectar would return. As long as Valerie's *flor de maga* bloomed, they would likely fly by the feeders to check. She had yet to decide if she'd maintain the flowers as Valerie wanted, but she didn't relish the drudgery of cleaning the feeders every couple of days to prevent the syrup from spoiling. Caring for Valerie was more than enough work for her, more than she'd ever wanted to take on. What Valerie didn't know wouldn't hurt her.

She scanned the sky above. Rainy season approached, bringing life-giving moisture to the air. Her tired skin tingled in anticipation. She stretched and reached above her head, feeling renewed—as much as any dried-up piece of driftwood could be renewed by a fine mist—and wondering why Ai hadn't yet returned from reconnoitering Tamarind's house. She'd given him instructions to return to Culebra while Tamarind's potent brew matured. He needed to rest and eat a restorative diet, filled with fresh fish, dried tamarind pulp, and her own nutritious mix of seeds and seaweed. Ai had a crucial role to play in guiding her wayward protégée home. He would act as a directional amplifier for her magic.

Of course, if he hadn't delivered the conch shell, there'd be no receiver. But Ai had never let her down.

She finished the clove cigarette, inhaling the spicy smoke. It burned down her throat, but she held it, tamed it, let it out only when she'd extracted every last stimulating particle. She smiled and dropped the smoldering stub on the pavement where it joined a host of mates.

Inside she went to the kitchen and washed her hands and face. She picked at the front of her blouse and sniffed. She couldn't smell any clove smoke, but she didn't want Valerie wasting any breath on admonishing her. She harbored no malice toward her host; she wanted a clear conscience after the good—misguided and weak, but good—woman died. So she changed her blouse. She put on the white one that she'd often worn as Raimunda, the one that displayed her illusory breasts to the gullible John Wilkerson. She chuckled when she thought about him. Horny men had always been easy to manipulate. She'd share this joke with Tamarind after she arrived.

491

Valerie still napped so she made a pitcher of lemonade. The lemons were expensive, but it was the only thing that Valerie could keep down any more and Ana fortified it with tamarind syrup and a drop or two of cone-snail poison for the pain. She shrugged. It wasn't her money anyway. If she spent her own money, it wouldn't be on fresh lemons imported from the main island. She'd buy a few cases of good beer and get shit-faced, maybe smoke a few joints.

She poured a glass, grabbed the New York Times that Valerie had delivered late at great expense and went into Valerie's bedroom. It was dark and cool. An overhead fan whirred, its blades stirring the hot air but not cooling it. Next to Valerie, who lay on her right side, the long-tamed stray cat curled. Its cool green eyes blinked. Ana didn't fool it one bit. Ana narrowed her eyes. Perhaps she should shoo it away. The cat blinked again and yawned, its fangs a warning. Of course she couldn't get rid of it, not until Valerie was dead anyway. The no-name feline had attached itself to Valerie as a daemon and would stay at her side as long as she breathed.

"I'm awake." The form on the bed spoke. The slight voice betrayed no bitterness or pain, but Ana suspected that it took everything Valerie had to speak so evenly.

"I brought you some lemonade."

"Here, put it on the nightstand. Help me sit up or I'll pour it all down me."

Ana set the sweat-beaded glass down and turned to clutch Valerie's hand and pull her upright. For all her growing weakness, lifting Valerie's slight figure took little effort. She grabbed two pillows and plumped them to support Valerie, who sighed when she slipped back onto them.

Ana slid the slippery glass into Valerie's feeble grasp, wrapping her own gnarly fingers around Valerie's wrist and guiding the glass to Valerie's lips. It took forever, but at last Valerie swallowed more than half of the lemonade and Ana set the glass back down on the nightstand.

"Thanks."

Ana sat in the wicker chair near the head of the bed. "More of *Pride and Prejudice*? Although can't see why you find Elizabeth Bennet charming. She's a dolt."

"She does make some bad choices, doesn't she? Maybe too trusting." Valerie panted a little. Ana waited for her to continue. "But the real dolt is the little sister, Lydia. Elizabeth just needs to learn a few lessons. So does Darcy. The key, Ana, is that they do learn. Don't you find it at all hopeful?"

Ana snorted. She wished that she could smoke right now. An icy Medalla would be welcome as well. Maybe a foolish man to manipulate too. Darcy hadn't met someone like Raimunda, who'd make that simpering idealist Elizabeth look like the wan doll that she was.

"Hope is for storybooks, my friend. You know that. No pretty words, remember?"

Valerie sighed again. She struggled to speak. "Ah, Ana. Not for us. Not for us. We've lived our lives, made our choices. We have to hope for those who come after us. For Tamarind and John."

Ana started. What had prompted that comment? She calmed herself. No need to argue with a dying woman. Let her believe what she wanted to believe. Ana knew that *her* hope depended on Tamarind coming home.

She pressed her lips together and hummed. She hoped that she sounded thoughtful. She was searching for the right words. She didn't do that often so she struggled and failed. "Why? True love's just a fairy tale. My barren marriage and your no-show at the altar prove it. How much more evidence do you need?"

Valerie closed her eyes. "Tons. It only takes one real-life happy ending to justify having faith." She coughed. "Not everyone gets to play the same part in the fairy tale. Someone has to be the godmother." She panted some more.

Ana stood up and reached for the lemonade. She urged Valerie to sip between pants and then she helped the other woman to lie down again. No reading a romance novel today.

"Rest. I'll read to you later."

Valerie nodded and murmured so that Ana had to lean closer. "Besides, there's no point in living without faith. That's why I gave Tamarind my own Goddess. She can use all the faith I imbued in it."

Ana jerked her head up, stunned. What had Valerie done? Perhaps she wasn't as weak and misguided as Ana had assumed. Ana had to get to the shore right away, pull out her last stores of seaweed, poison from a young octopus, the heart of a dolphin, and the remnants of Tamarind's tail that she'd been living off for the past five years. She had to craft a final potent brew that would give her the power to overcome a lifetime of faith of a good woman.

As she got to the door, Valerie's weak voice drifted to her, clear even against the humming of the ceiling fan.

"I'm sorry I don't have much faith left for you, Ana. You're going to have to find your own. Maybe when you realize your neglect won't kill the hummingbirds and bananaquits, you'll experience the joy they bring."

Forty-one
∞

LUCY KEPT THINKING ABOUT Tamarind's stricken face—those preternatural eyes that saw into your soul even though she hadn't learned to look into her own—while she cooked spaghetti and meat sauce for dinner that night. She made a salad, toasted some garlic bread, set the table and poured the milk—all the usual things that you do when there are children to feed, no matter what's in your head or your heart. She'd had a trying afternoon after Olivia arrived. She'd watched Olivia shrink in the past few months, biting her tongue and praying to the Virgin Mary that her beloved granddaughter would seek her out. How could Dorothy not see what was happening? Did she think that Olivia, studious and responsible, could take care of herself, leaving her plenty of time for celebrity-gossip magazines, manicures, hair appointments and cocktail hour after work? Dorothy lived to chase after the next man. To chase after the ephemeral, just-the-next-date chance meeting with Prince Charming.

To tell the truth, Olivia had needed to lose twenty pounds. Her clothes, which Lucy suspected that she'd traded with Pam, fit pretty well. A trip to the hair salon and some contacts and she'd be transformed from nerdy bookworm to someone to notice—not that Olivia wanted that kind of attention. Or did she? Had Olivia sought out the solace of reading and academics because she had no other choices? Lucy shook her head. No. Olivia had her head on straight. No matter what her body or her heart longed for, she had plenty of examples around her to show the danger of selling out one dream for another. Give her ten years, ten years to grow into herself, and she'd be ready to knock the socks off of some lucky young man.

But Lucy had had to deal with today's Olivia. Her granddaughter, looking bewildered at Tamarind's distracted and easily irritated manner, traipsed over to Lucy's five minutes later. She didn't say anything, just went into the kitchen and poured herself some iced tea. Lucy left her alone, at least until she heard Olivia snapping at the little cousins while she set water for the pasta on the stove. Sighing, she grabbed her teacup and went to the family room.

"Olivia, bring your tea. I want to talk to you." She forced herself to speak firmly, to turn and head to the dining room without waiting for Olivia's verbal compliance. She'd gathered long ago that children respond to confident authority.

After Olivia slipped into the room as though arriving late for algebra, her head down and shoulders hunched, Lucy waited for her to sit down. Olivia didn't look up.

"Do you know why Mrs. Wilkerson sent you here instead of having you help her today?"

Olivia hesitated and then nodded.

"I'm not going to press you for details. You tell me when you're ready. Deal?" She waited for Olivia's one-shoulder shrug. "Don't hold it against Mrs. Wilkerson. She didn't want to tell me, but she's got her plate full. She wanted to help you. Understand?"

Olivia tilted her chin down. A bare acknowledgement.

"Olivia Chapman, look at me." Lucy's tone would have prodded a sleeping grizzly. Olivia raised her eyes, unhappiness and resentment roiling their darkness. "Good. Now, call and leave your mom a message. You're staying here tonight. You'll have to stay in your mom's old room upstairs, but there's a TV. And a lock on the door. You can even eat dinner up there if you don't want to listen to your cousins."

Olivia shot up from her seat as soon as she understood that Lucy had finished. Lucy heard her on the phone talking to Pam and then her steps sounded on the stairs. She got up and returned to the kitchen where she found the pot with the boiling water half empty. She refilled it to the right level and browned the hamburger, her thoughts returning to Tamarind. Who did her young neighbor have to turn to for advice? That's when she remembered Tamarind's anguish a month ago. She'd said that her friend Valerie was dying. In the short time that Lucy had known her, Tamarind had mentioned only one other friend, a woman named Ana, a folk healer. Lucy closed her eyes and stood with a wooden spoon poised above the saucepot while she intoned a silent Our Father. *Let Tamarind's friend find peace. Let Tamarind find peace. Let me be the friend that Tamarind needs.* She crossed herself.

Rachel came in late looking wrung out, dropped her briefcase full of printouts in the front hallway next to her black pumps, and walked into the kitchen in her stocking feet. When they heard the front door close, Hayley and Ben came running into the kitchen from the family room and began talking at Rachel, who now leaned against the refrigerator door while watching Lucy strain the spaghetti.

"That smells great, Mom," Rachel said while ignoring Hayley, who was at that moment tugging on the sleeve of her blouse. "I don't know what I'd do without you right now."

"Put something in the microwave," Lucy said. She dumped the spaghetti back into its pot then poured the sauce over it. "Why don't you have your kids help set the table?"

Lucy put the spaghetti in a large serving bowl and brought it to the table. It had been years since she'd made such a large meal, years since she'd had spaghetti at home, in fact. Spaghetti was a family meal, not a meal for one. Now she had a family in the house again. If she didn't focus on the voices in the dining room but listened instead to the general din, she could almost imagine that the noise emanated from Dorothy and the boys. Billy was out of town, of course.

Rachel divided up the tasks between Matthew and Hayley, who complained that she didn't want to set out forks and spoons for everyone. Rachel told her to do as she was told, but Hayley continued to balk. Lucy, who still stood lost in reverie, heard a smack and her eyes snapped open. Rachel leaned over the table setting out the contentious forks and spoons while Hayley stood off to one side sobbing and holding her right palm over her deep-red cheek.

"Did you have to smack her?"

Rachel stopped laying down utensils and straightened.

"Yes, I did. I don't have time for this goddamn nonsense right now. She can either help out or not eat, for all I care."

Lucy felt a now-familiar tingle and buzz inside her head. "Watch your tongue, Rachel." Somewhere inside her a voice began warning her to stop, but the buzzing drowned it out. "I don't want to hear that kind of language in my house and I don't want to ever see you smack that child's face again."

Rachel's lips were a thin, white line now. "I'm not a child any more, Mom. I'll discipline my children the way I see fit."

"Discipline is one thing, but abuse is another. Stick her in the corner until she cooperates, take away one of her videos, make her earn a new toy, but don't hit her in anger."

"I don't want to talk about parenting theories right now. I'm hungry and so are the kids."

Around the two of them, the children stood watching. Ben gripped the tablecloth nearest him instead of Rachel's skirt, his thumb in his mouth, while Hayley hadn't moved her hand or her gaze since Lucy started speaking. Matthew stood in a far corner, his narrowed eyes imitating Rachel's, his hands holding cups of milk.

"Well, I'm not," Lucy said and left the dining room.

She went down the hall to her room and shut the door. The buzzing was gone now, but it had left behind a hollow, empty place inside her head and she thought that she might faint. She lay down

498

on her bed and closed her eyes in the dark room, which was insulated against any sounds from the next-door dining room. As she lay there, breathing deeply and slowly, she caught the scent of Billy's cologne, like a reward. *It's a start*, she thought.

The next afternoon, she went to Cheltham High with Ben and waited outside for Pam to leave the building and walk by her wagon, which was parked on the street across from the school. She'd thought about driving over to Dorothy's house and waiting there for Pam, but she was afraid that Pam might not come straight home after school and she wasn't going to chance missing her, not today. As the wise man said, there is a time to keep silence, and a time to speak.

Teenagers streamed out through the front door for a good ten minutes before she caught sight of Pam, who was walking next to another girl. Lucy's heart lurched, missed a beat, and then went on beating faster. Pam's jacket hung open to reveal a large gray sweatshirt and faded jeans that were frayed at the cuffs. Her long blond hair hung to the open collar of her jacket, large strands of it falling into her eyes as she walked so that she needed to swipe them away with one hand. Little had changed in her appearance since Lucy had last seen her at Christmas, but Lucy's knowing gaze already saw a difference.

She got out of the Volvo and headed toward the sidewalk to intercept the two girls. "Pam," she called as they neared her.

Both girls' heads swung her way and they stopped talking. When Pam saw who'd called out to her, her eyes widened. She stopped walking and waited where she was, her backpack slipping off her shoulder and down to the sidewalk next to her.

"Gram." She sounded resigned.

"Pam, I'd like to talk with you." Lucy looked at Pam's friend, who appeared concerned. "You two going somewhere? Maybe I can give you both a ride there in exchange for a few minutes of Pam's time."

"We're going to T.G.I.Friday's. Michelle's got her driver's license so we don't need a ride, thanks."

"You can meet her there. That'll give me a chance to talk to you alone."

Pam exchanged looks with Michelle and then shrugged. "Sure, Gram. I have a feeling you won't give up until I hear what you've got to say."

"That's right." Lucy motioned toward her car.

Pam followed Lucy to the car. As she opened her door, she saw Ben in the backseat. "I thought you said you wanted to talk to me alone."

"I do. Don't worry about Ben, Pam—he's too young to understand what we're saying." Lucy got into the driver's seat.

They said nothing while Pam dropped her backpack next to Ben's car seat before sliding into the front. Although it was still March, the inside of the wagon was warm enough that Pam asked if she could roll down her window. Lucy said yes, but nothing more as she navigated the traffic departing the high school. When at last they'd headed south on 87 toward T.G.I.Friday's, it was Pam who spoke first.

"So. You know."

"Yes." Lucy looked at her granddaughter and then out the front window. "I overheard you and Olivia at Christmas dinner. I've already talked to her about her stress diarrhea."

"You know about the creep who's been emailing her too?" There was anger in Pam's voice, but Lucy sensed that it was directed at Olivia's stalker.

Lucy sighed. "Yes. My neighbor Tamarind told me. Her husband is helping us track him down." She squinted at Pam again. She hadn't suspected that Pam cared so much about Olivia's welfare, but frankly she was more than pleased that Pam did. "We'll catch him, that I promise. Then I'm going to roast his *cajones* on a grill, little girl."

"Gram!" Pam sounded shocked. And delighted.

Lucy fell silent.

"Aren't you going to lecture me?"

"No. To lecture you means I know what you should've done and what you should do now. But it's a little late to tell you to stop sleeping around and to use birth control, isn't it?"

"But you could still tell me what to do now, couldn't you?" It almost sounded like a plea.

"Yes, I guess." Lucy sighed. "But I don't know what you should do."

"What would you do?"

"If it were me?" At Pam's assent, Lucy went on. "If it were me … if it were me, Pam, I'd have an abortion."

The silence between them reverberated with shock.

"You would?" Pam asked at last. "I'd never have guessed, Gram. Never. Did you … did you … I mean, you never had an abortion, right?"

"No," Lucy said, shaking her head. "But you asked me what I would do if I were just sixteen, still in high school, and pregnant by a no-good-for-nothing jackass. And I told you."

"I'm sure that's what Mom will say too. What if I don't want to have an abortion, Gram? What then?"

Lucy, whose gaze still focused on the road before her, heard tears in Pam's voice. Ahead of her was the parking lot for Pitney Bowes and she turned into it. Pulling into the nearest free spot and turning off the engine, she turned to look at her granddaughter. Pam sat looking out the passenger window, chewing her lower lip; her hands lay still and palm up in her lap. Lucy picked up her left hand and held it in her own until Pam looked at her.

"Listen, Pam: no matter what you decide to do, I love you. I've made enough of my own mistakes to know the best thing I can do for you is love you no matter what."

Pam's eyes glistened in the late afternoon sun. "Thanks, Gram," she whispered.

సంసంస

A week later, Lucy sat next to Dorothy, who was sobbing. It had been so long since Dorothy had even shown her more than dismissal that she had no idea what Dorothy wanted from her except a listening ear. What *she* wanted however, more than anything else, was to wrap her arms around Dorothy's shoulders and squeeze until that wretched sound softened and stilled. Dorothy had called her twenty minutes before rambling about a meeting with a teacher and needing to talk with her right away. Lucy had agreed that Dorothy could come over and then was surprised when Dorothy begged her to stay on the line until she pulled up in front of Lucy's cape.

Clearly, Dorothy's anguish had something to do with one of her daughters. Lucy's instinct told her that it wasn't Pam's pregnancy or her obstinate refusal to have an abortion that had rent Dorothy's soul. Indeed, Dorothy was more likely to come here in a high dither to accuse her of filling Pam's head with pro-life "nonsense" than to sob about the possibility of becoming a young grandmother.

Making soothing noises reminiscent of ones that she'd made when Dorothy was a girl and had lost or broken something dear, Lucy slipped her arms around Dorothy's shoulders, half expecting her eldest daughter to slip out from under them. Instead, Dorothy, a tear dangling from the tip of her nose, turned with a sigh toward her mother and rested her face against Lucy's chest. Lucy pulled her daughter close and rocked and hushed, smoothing Dorothy's hair away from her damp face. It didn't matter that she was an old woman or that Dorothy was an adult who must shoulder her own burdens; Lucy wished with all her might that she could erase Dorothy's pain as easily as she'd done when Dorothy was a child, simply by holding her and making her believe that parents had infinite power.

"Mom," Dorothy said at last, her voice cracking. "Mom, I'm sorry."

"Sorry? Sorry for what, dear?"

"For being a lousy daughter."

Lucy sighed to clear a sudden catch in her throat. "Ah, Dorothy. That's not why you're here. Do you want to tell me about it?"

"Not yet." Dorothy fell silent. She didn't begin crying again, however, and Lucy knew the worst was past.

After a few more moments in which Lucy felt certain that Dorothy was quite aware that she'd succumbed to her mother's embrace and still hadn't pulled away, Dorothy spoke again.

"I'm sorry for being mad at you all these years."

Lucy caught her breath and went still.

"I've been angry ever since I discovered that Dad was cheating on you with those two women from Worcester."

"How do you know about that?"

Now Dorothy turned and looked up at her. "I was the one who hid your vacuum bags and brush before your meeting so you'd have to get into his work case," she said in a rush. "I'd gotten into Dad's case to search for candy, and I found the notes and pictures. And condoms."

Lucy's brow furrowed. "You were how old then? Thirteen."

"I waited for you to yell at Dad, to get angry, to *throw him out.* Instead, all you did was get pregnant again." Dorothy's voice quavered.

"With Rachel." Lucy paused. "I had no idea you knew. I wanted to keep it all as quiet as possible while I sorted everything out, Dorothy. You don't just leave your husband and the father of your children without at least trying to fix things. Especially when you don't have any skills, any way to support yourself."

"So you reconciled with him even though he'd fathered a child with someone else." Accusation sharpened Dorothy's voice.

Stillness fell between them then, stillness so deep and complete that Lucy didn't know how to bridge it. When she spoke at last, it felt like falling.

"Yes. Yes, I swallowed my hurt and anger and followed my priest's advice to reconcile with a philandering bastard who'd planted his seed half an hour away and what I got was another child to raise."

Dorothy looked away at the raw hurt that she must have seen in Lucy's eyes. "I–I couldn't forgive you for forgiving him. I decided that I wasn't ever going to let any man do what Dad did to you. I wasn't ever going to trust a man."

"I didn't forgive him, not even after he died. I wanted to but couldn't. All this time, I've been angry with Billy Romero for betraying and hurting me. And he's been dead ten years." She paused then went on. "Well, since we're clearing the air, maybe we can speak about your abortion at last."

Dorothy squirmed and moved away from her mother's embrace. "What's to tell, Mom? I had one, end of story."

"Is it because you didn't want to end up like me? Rachel wasn't that old, maybe five then. Did you hate her?"

"No! No. Actually, I adored Rachel. I couldn't believe how incredibly sweet and funny a baby could be. But I'd gotten pregnant by some football player who diddled me after practice and home games and I knew that he wouldn't marry me, even if I could accept such a marriage. I didn't want to feel trapped by love of a child, if that makes any sense."

"Yes. Would it surprise you to know that I forgave you a long time ago for not telling me you were pregnant and then going to the clinic for an abortion?"

"No," Dorothy said, dragging it out into a two-syllable word. "No, I believe you." She sighed. "I thought I could control things better than you, Mom. I married someone I didn't love so he couldn't hold that over me. I decided when to have children and how many. I left my husband when things didn't work out. I see now they couldn't have worked out. I've been living my life like it's my own, like I'm free to continue dating the wrong man and free to run from hurt. But all I've done is run from my responsibilities. My children've paid the price."

Her voice started to crack and Lucy feared that she'd begin sobbing again.

"Mom, Mom," Dorothy went on. "Mom, I had a meeting with Pam's art teacher. Pam confided to her that she was raped by a man I dated. I brought him home, I brought him right to her and didn't even notice when it happened, I was so wrapped up in pity for myself."

Lucy reared back. *Holy Mother of God!* She'd had no idea. The latent buzzing under her thoughts exploded into a white fury. Where moments before she'd wanted to wrap her arms around Dorothy and erase her pain, her fingers now itched to slap her, to shake her from her ingrown selfishness.

"And that's what you're doing now." Lucy enunciated each word with frosty precision, clearly catching Dorothy off guard. "Wrapping yourself in pity so that you don't have to face what you've done. I know you feel bad, but damn it, Dorothy, now is not the time to cry for your mistakes. Now is the time to take care of Pam, for Lord's sake, before it's too late. Don't wait twenty-five years to clear the air with her, like you did with me. Life is too short for any of us to be playing the silence game."

Dorothy appeared to let the words sink in.

"You're right, Mom," she said at last. "And I'm not going to make the same mistake again." Bending over, she kissed Lucy on the cheek then stood up to go. But she paused at the dining-room door and turned around, her eyes large and shiny.

"By the way, Mom. I think you'd better consider your own advice. Hasn't it been far too long for you to hold Dad's affairs against him? Why don't you let it go? I can tell you from experience that it's a lot easier to forgive than to carry your hurt around with you all of the time."

And with that she was gone.

৵৵৵

Saturday afternoon Mass feels very different from a Sunday morning one, possibly because the average age of attendees differs greatly at each. Lucy preferred the Sunday morning liturgy because it was filled with families and all their attendant noise and family-related activities. But lately, with Rachel's kids filling her house with noise and activity, she found herself drawn to the quieter and shorter Saturday Mass.

Today she found herself thinking that perhaps she should have waited and gone to the Sunday Mass when she'd be less likely to let her mind wander during the familiar repetitions to her

505

conversation with Dorothy. Dorothy was right about forgiving Billy, but knowing that she should forgive him and accomplishing it were two separate things. After all, she'd invested more than twenty-six years in hurt, resentment, and loss.

The best I can do, she thought, *is to keep petitioning God for a change of heart and hope that it comes before I die.*

She'd hoped to have one of her strange dreams the night before, certain that if anything could call forth Billy's ghost it would be discussing his infidelity with their eldest child, but in this too she'd been disappointed. Instead, she dreamt of climbing a ladder to an infinite height, so far above the world that the clouds misted around her shoulders and blocked her vision. She woke up several times, her nightgown wet with sweat and the covers pushed to the side; it reminded her of the long months she spent going through menopause as her hormone levels roller-coasted ever downward. But that had been over for several years now and there was no reason to think that her previous night's travails would visit her again.

The priest reached the part of the liturgy where he should deliver a homily, but this afternoon he introduced an elderly couple to the congregation instead. Lucy listened, her mind no longer wandering, as the priest spoke about the couple's lifelong service to the Church and to each other, having recently celebrated their fiftieth wedding anniversary. As a way to mark their continued devotion to each other and their faith, they had asked for a renewal ceremony during the scheduled Mass rather than a smaller, private one with their friends and family.

Lucy clutched the missal in her lap as she watched, intent on learning the parts of this ceremony of renewing. Was it at all like a wedding? She hadn't been to a wedding in nine years, not since Rachel married Todd, and that hadn't been a particularly joyous occasion. As she listened, she realized that it *was* like a wedding with its talk of love and devotion, its vows of faithfulness. But it was something more: an ode to their strength and steadfastness in the face of a lifetime together and a promise of sweetness in the years remaining to them. Lucy imagined them clinging to each other through the storms of childrearing, working, and caring for others—weathered certainly but unbelievably strong together.

As they faced one another, a glow on their cheeks—not of hope but of knowing—Lucy felt a pressure on her chest and then her heart opened like a lotus blossom. She remained in her seat where she sensed, but did not hear, the remainder of the Mass as people moved around her. Rachel found her still sitting in her pew half an hour after the Mass had ended, tears coursing down her face.

"Hey, Mom," she said in a low voice. "I thought I'd find you here today. You all right?"

Lucy turned to her, oblivious to her wet cheeks. "I've never been better. Why?"

Rachel shrugged and looked around her at the few remaining people talking in small groups along the sides and back of the church. "Don't see anyone else sitting and crying in a pew, do you?"

"There should be hundreds of people sitting and crying, but that's beside the point. Why are you here, Rachel?" Lucy asked, drying her face.

Rachel looked at her. "Thee called a little while ago. It seems that she told Pam about her meeting with the high-school art teacher and Pam got upset, saying it was just like a teacher to tell a parent something told in confidence. She left the house before Thee could think of anything to say to her and Thee hoped she'd come to your house."

Lucy nodded. "She might. Then again, she might not. Children have a way of doing unpredictable things."

They were silent for a moment before Lucy turned to Rachel and took her hands. "Listen, Rachel, I've got something to say to you and I want you to let me say it all without interrupting me."

"Does it have something to do with your conversation yesterday with Thee? She told me that you two finally made peace."

Lucy nodded, her eyes bright and sharp like an eagle's. "Rachel, Dorothy and I talked about your father and some affairs he had before you were born. I won't go into all the details right now, but suffice it to say that I was very, very hurt and never forgave him even after he died. Talking with Dorothy yesterday made me admit that. But it made me realize something else, too: I've resented you all these years."

Rachel started to speak, but Lucy shook her head and continued.

"No, hear me out, Rachel. I was done having children when I found out about your father's cheating. I tried to forget what had happened I went through the motions of reconciling with him. You came out of that effort and, if I'd truly forgiven him, I would've recognized your worth. Instead, I resented you and at the same time refused to admit that I resented you."

She sighed. "Do you remember the story of Abraham and Isaac?" At Rachel's nod, she continued. "Some people think it's about faith—God testing Abraham's. But I just realized it's about the gifts God gives us. God asked Abraham to give Him a life, a life most dear to Abraham, and God gave it back. Isaac, you see, is a *gift*. He belonged to God, but God gave him to Abraham. I'm sorry, Rachel, that I didn't treat you as the gift you are all these years. My gift from God."

Rachel heard the tremor in Lucy's voice, the fear that her apology wouldn't be accepted. She studied the lined face, the soft, puffy pouches under the eyes, the trembling chin. She reached out and took her mother's soft hand, spotted with age and crossed with prominent veins.

"Well, then, if I'm truly a gift, Mom, I'd better find a way to give back a little. Come home and I'll make you a cup of tea and we'll wait for Pam together."

Lucy smiled, wide and shaky. "Earl Grey and shortbread *does* sound good about now."

Forty-two
ଓଃ

NOT LONG AFTER SHE AND JOHN had settled into their duplex in Pittsburgh, Tamarind overheard the assistant dean of the School of Computer Science telling one of the professors that a watched pot never boils. She hadn't understood why Sheryl had said this because no one had been speaking about cooking, but she couldn't wait to test Sheryl's revelation the next time she made pasta. The water boiled. It took ten minutes, but it boiled. Puzzled, she'd repeated the test three more times with different burners and different pots, but they all boiled after more or less the same time. She spent an hour and forgot to cook the pasta. When John got home, he'd laughed and explained what Sheryl had meant and then they'd gone for Chinese. Idioms continued to trip her up, but she never forgot them once they'd been explained to her. How could she? She learned her lesson through repeated embarrassment. That idiom mocked her as she tiptoed every morning to the shelf in the garage where she'd left Ana's doppelganger potion. The truth potion she'd mix just before she needed it—its potency peaked within twenty minutes.

John seemed much more relaxed since the day that she'd seen him with Zoë. He whistled while he made coffee in the morning and came home at five-thirty most nights. He tickled Sarah, who giggled and made him wear the long gowns that Tamarind had found for her at the Salvation Army. He squeezed Tamarind as she stood stirring the curry, brought her juice while she nursed, and took Adam upstairs while he supervised Sarah's nightly bath. When she asked him why he'd started coming home on time, he said that Ted and Jim had hit their stride and needed minimal management. Once he wrote some code after Sarah went to bed, but mostly he washed the dishes and watched TV. She found it hard to string jewelry knowing that he sat in the family room.

The night that he came home from a haircut she couldn't speak. For as long as she'd known him, John had had shoulder-length hair pulled into a ponytail. With his hair cropped close, he'd been transformed. Into what, she didn't know. He waited for her in the doorway to the kitchen, his expression tentative and boyish. His eyes seemed greener, his jaw leaner. She noticed the strength of his neck and the breadth of his shoulders. They made love that night and she couldn't get enough of him, this stranger in her bed. Did she love him? She didn't know, but he made her breath stutter in her chest.

Tamarind had never felt so confused.

She wanted to be alone with him. She wanted to hide from him. She wanted the truth.

She had no time to consider what to do. Not really. Even though she kept returning to the foul-smelling liquid that fermented in the garage and tried to figure out what John's new behavior meant, she found her mind wandering off to the grocery list or to nothing at all as she pretended to make soup with Sarah. She'd blink and it would be the witching hour and she'd be too hungry to do more than remember that she had no answers.

John catalyzed her confusion with a new wedding band. He'd decided, he said, to risk her unhappiness by taking the severed band to a goldsmith in Waltham and having it remade. The simple gold band lacked any decoration other than the words *faith, hope, and love* that were engraved on the inside. It fit perfectly. He kissed her, brushing her unwashed hair from her face with tender fingers—as if she didn't smell of breastmilk and grilled cheese, spit-up and body odor. As if she were as beautiful as the day that he'd married her.

Tamarind wore the heavy band, playing with it as she'd done with the original after they'd gotten married. It felt heavier, stranger. She was sitting nursing Adam and rubbing her thumb along it when Ana called. Sarah picked up the phone, listened with a frown, and then handed the receiver to Tamarind.

"Tamarind?"

"Yes." Tamarind's spine ached in foreboding.

Ana cleared her throat, coughed, and cleared her throat again. "It's Valerie, young one. She's dead."

A dull pain threatened to wedge Tamarind's forehead open, and she closed her eyes. It wasn't unexpected. Did it hurt more for the anticipation or less? "When?"

"Last night. Asked me to scatter her ashes over the ocean. She made all the arrangements some time ago, but if you want to be here, I can wait."

Tamarind caught her breath. Go back to Culebra? "I–I don't know, Ana. Can I have some time? I–I'm waiting for the doppelganger potion to develop."

"Ah." There was a world of meaning in that one syllable that Ana released. "I see. When do you, ah, plan to use it?"

"Soon. Zoë's hair reacted strongly with your powder. I didn't think it would develop so fast."

"Good. That's a good sign. Means she's got a strong life force, easy to copy." A note of triumph lightened the old woman's smoke-roughened voice. "Have your truth in no time. No time."

Tamarind didn't tell Ana that that was what she was afraid of. She didn't want Ana to suspect that she didn't have the nerve.

She hadn't seen Olivia or Lucy all week. She went to the dining-room window and looked into the hopeful April sunlight. Rachel's silver minivan blocked the view of Lucy's front door. Next to the driveway, bright green shoots glowed against the rich brown earth in the rectangular plot that Lucy had planted in the fall. Tamarind

511

stared at the garden, blinking to clear her vision, but it wouldn't clear. If anything, the aura that emanated from the new growth became more distinct, sharp and crisp as a taste of green apple or the scent of turned loam. Tamarind shivered. There was power, deep and silent.

She turned away from the window and went to the kitchen, green and brown tinting her vision like the afterglow from fireworks. She missed Olivia, but she missed Lucy more. Lucy might not have magic like Ana, but her friendship almost made up for it. It had been weeks since she'd brought over an apple or a chocolate-pecan pie, protest that she couldn't possibly eat any of it, and then stay to chat over tea. Her family needed her. That's just the way it was.

The internal timer that most mothers of two year olds develop warned her that Sarah had been quiet far too long.

"Roe!" Nothing. "Roe! Where are you?"

Stillness answered her so she went to the living room via the family room. No Sarah. That's when she saw that the gate on the stairs swung wide. She must have forgotten to shut it after going upstairs for a change of clothes for Adam. She climbed the stairs, foreboding coloring her vision. Sarah often disappeared when she was up to no good.

Dear God, don't let it be anything dangerous or destructive.

Sarah's bedroom door was wide open and her room empty. A quick sweep of Adam's room and the office showed that she wasn't playing in them either. Tamarind hurried to look in the hall bath, afraid that Sarah had figured out how to defeat the child locks on the cabinets or climbed on the counter to get into the medicine cabinet. Tamarind shoved the door to the master bedroom open. Sarah turned to look at her. In one hand she held the carved mangrove box that Ana had given Tamarind, in the other, an open brown marker. God had only heard half of her request.

"I made it pretty. See?" Sarah held the box out. Tamarind saw controlled dashes and swirls over the symbols. In that instant, she realized what the symbols meant: they were the *mer* symbols for fertility and life.

"No!" She rushed forward and snatched the box from Sarah. "What've you done? They're ruined!"

She sat on the edge of the bed. Rubbing her fingertip around the teardrop, she felt hot tears rise. Ana had said she'd used spells for her marriage. Ana had helped her even after the disaster of her own marriage to a human. What would happen now that Sarah had defaced the symbols?

Tamarind looked up to see Sarah studying her, her changeable blue eyes unreadable. *Mer* eyes. She opened the box. Inside rested both moonstone Goddesses, one beautiful and mysterious even though it lacked the fire of her faith, the other lovely if imperfect. The conch shell lay next to them. She took the pendants out. Maybe she should return to Culebra with Valerie's and offer it to Mother Sea when Ana scattered Valerie's ashes? It would be fitting.

Tucking the pendants back into the box, she stood up. She'd wear Valerie's one last time, when she transformed into Zoë. That's when she heard the doorbell. Sarah shrieked, jumped up, and ran for the stairs. She slid the conch shell into her pocket and followed Sarah downstairs. Lucy stood just inside the doorway, her hands filled with a pie. On top sat a brown-paper bag, its top rolled down.

Tamarind laughed. "How'd you read my mind?"

Lucy, who'd been chatting with Sarah, looked up. Tamarind stopped on the last step, astonished. Lucy's eyes, always so sad, no longer sank into the soft smudged flesh beneath them. Instead, they sparkled like sunlight on waves and the skin appeared smoother, less dark. Her shoulders levitated without any visible effort, her crown reached for the ceiling as a tree reaches for the sky. She looked ten years younger.

"Lucy, you look fabulous! No more dreams disturbing your sleep?"

Lucy smiled. A hidden dimple popped at the corner of her mouth. "No, no more dreams. I haven't slept this well in almost thirty years."

513

"Come in. I'll make some tea." Tamarind set the mangrove box on the hall table and held out her hands for the pie. "Let me carry that."

Lucy snatched the brown bag but let Tamarind take the pie. "Sarah, love, I brought apple. That's your favorite, right?"

Sarah nodded and smiled. Tamarind saw something flash between her and Lucy, some recognition that she hadn't known that Sarah was capable of. "I love apple."

"Good." Lucy bent down. "Can you take this to the dining table for me? I want to show it to you and your mom."

Sarah nodded again and skipped away. Adam, who'd been asleep in a bassinet in the family room, began mewling.

"Go on, get him. I can make the tea." Lucy took the pie back before Tamarind could stop her. A scent of loam and green apple clung to her, filling Tamarind's nose. Did faint green tinge her white hair?

Tamarind scurried off to get Adam, who hadn't yet reached a full-throated cry. She snuggled him against her chest where he rooted, determined to satisfy his hunger. Her milk let down, prickling her breasts as though they'd been asleep and had awoken hard. When she got to the kitchen, Lucy hummed as she filled the teakettle and motioned Tamarind into the dining room with a warm smile. Tamarind shrugged, sighed, and turned toward the sunny room where Sarah kneeled in her chair, delicate fingers setting beads into Tamarind's necklace design board.

"What are those?" Tamarind sat down near her daughter and helped Adam latch on.

"Pretty. Like the night sky," Sarah said.

Tamarind looked up to study the beads. Steely-blue pearls. "Are these Tahitian pearls? They don't look regular enough."

Lucy came in with two steaming cups, set them down, and laughed. "What? Tahitian? Oh, no. Billy couldn't afford those! No, no. Those are freshwater pearls."

Tamarind picked one up and rolled it between forefinger and thumb. "Amazing. I had no idea there were any mollusks in freshwater that could produce such beautiful pearls."

"I read up on them years ago, right after Billy gave me that necklace. Freshwater pearls are made differently." She walked into the kitchen but continued talking. "Instead of a grain of sand, pearl farmers stick pieces of other mollusks into cuts in their mantles. They can take dozens of cuts and produce multiple pearls at a time."

Tamarind thought about that. "It's not something foreign? They use bits of other mollusks?"

Lucy came back with three slices of apple pie and set one in front of Sarah. "I'll get you milk, Sarah love." Again she continued talking over her shoulder on her way to the kitchen. "That's what I read. Made me think of motherhood at the time. How we take all these cuts and hurts from our loved ones and make something precious. Pearls of wisdom."

"Wisdom?" Tamarind latched her bra shut and pulled her blouse down. Adam dozed, sweet and serene against her, thrumming with a dark energy not unlike that which she sensed in Lucy's garden. She picked up the largest pearl and cupped it in her palm. "There's an endless lore associated with pearls. Some people identify pearls with marriage and fertility. Jews, Christians, and Muslims link them to purity and perfection. Some believe that pearls ward off evil."

Lucy set milk in front of Sarah and sat down. She lifted her cup and blew a little before sipping. "That's fascinating. Tell me more."

Tamarind frowned and looked up at Lucy. "Some ancient people associate pearls with tears."

"Tears?" Now Lucy frowned. "That doesn't sound good."

"It could be good or bad, depending on whose tears." Tamarind shifted Adam's weight and reached to set the pearl onto the necklace guide. "Some think that pearls are tears from angels, nymphs, mermaids." She stopped and sipped her tea again to keep from disparaging *that* idea aloud. "Some say that giving pearls to your love is bad luck because they represent the tears of separation. Pearls show up in stories of pain and suffering."

Lucy sighed and, picking up her fork, toyed with her pie. "That rings true to me."

Tamarind looked at her friend, saw the shoulders slump a little. "I believe that pearls are sacred symbols of love, like the ancient Greeks and Hindus did." She leaned forward and touched a fingertip to a line of pearls. "Blue pearls mean you'll find love. If your husband gave them to you that fits."

Lucy set her fork down, sighed again. She looked up at Tamarind, who saw the old sadness flash across her face and then it disappeared. "Both myths are right, Tamarind. You can't have love without some tears. I want to believe—no, I *do* believe—Billy gave me those pearls out of love. But they caused me too much pain."

Tamarind pushed her pie away. From the corner of her eye, she saw Sarah studying Lucy. Her daughter's eyes had deepened to a stormy blue. Tamarind turned to look at Sarah while she asked, "Is that why these are loose? There are enough here for a necklace."

Lucy looked down and nodded. "I ripped it from me in rage." Her voice didn't rise above a whisper. "He gave it to me after he told me he'd had an affair."

Tamarind put her hand over Lucy's fragile one. The older woman's skin, spotted and veined, felt soft and warm. Questions came, but she refrained from asking any. Lucy would tell her whatever she wanted to share. "Do you want me to restring them?"

Lucy darted a glance and then looked back at the table, but not before Tamarind saw the water spilling over her lower lids. They sat there for two or three minutes before Lucy spoke. "Yes." She sounded confident. "Yes. Will you?" This time when she looked up, her eyes shone.

Tamarind studied the pearls laid around the necklace guide. Under the table, she felt for the remade wedding band. Warm, it reflected dark energy from Adam's leg. "It won't be the same. Why don't I design another one using these? Something with Swarovski crystal. Maybe some gold or silver spacer beads."

516

Lucy sat up. Her shoulders rose and stayed level. "Thank you, Tamarind. Whatever you choose. It means a lot, you helping me."

Tamarind smiled. "That's what friends are for."

"Speaking of friends. How's your friend Valerie?"

The question caught Tamarind like an unexpected blow to the forehead. The grief, lying at the base of her skull, flared. She couldn't see or hear for an indeterminate time, but when sound and vision penetrated her awareness, Lucy stood over her, shaking hands resting on Adam.

"Holy Mary, Mother of God," Lucy said. "Here, let me take him." She lifted the sleeping baby to her shoulder. "Drink your tea before you fall out of your chair."

Tamarind sipped the cool tea but didn't taste it. She started to set the cup down before she dropped it.

"All of it."

She did as she was told. "Dead. She's dead." The cup clattered on the tabletop, but Sarah steadied it. "Our friend Ana called and told me after lunch." Tamarind frowned as she gazed at her daughter. What did she see in Sarah's eyes?

Lucy flinched, crossed herself over Adam. "I'm sorry."

Tamarind rubbed her forehead. The pain lost its edge. "I can't believe she's gone." She gestured around the room toward the jewelry findings and tools. "She taught me how to make jewelry. She taught me all about different gemstones, minerals, beads. She gave me that perfect moonstone in the Goddess pendant Rachel took, taught me how to polish it. She made me believe that I put love and faith into the moonstone, made it magic somehow."

Lucy sat down. She looked at the steel-blue pearls from her husband's broken peace offering. "She sounds like a wise woman. Symbols have only as much power as we give them. Or refuse to give them."

Tamarind wanted to snap, wanted to ask, then why doesn't my Goddess work? She didn't. She changed the subject instead. "How's Olivia? Did you talk to the police?"

517

Lucy squinted at her. For half a minute Tamarind feared that her neighbor would ignore the question. "Olivia's Internet stalker has been caught, thanks to John's evidence. Turned out to be a disturbed young man in her life science class. He's been suspended. Probably going to transfer to a special program for troubled teens this fall."

Tamarind sighed. She hadn't realized how worried she'd been until the relief flooded her. "That's great, Lucy."

"All thanks to you. Who knows if she'd ever have confided in us."

"You think so?" Tamarind experienced a sense of fulfillment that she'd never felt as a human before. "I really did good?"

"Yes, you really did." Lucy pulled her half-eaten pie toward her but didn't take a bite. "Tamarind, I can watch Sarah and Adam. Why don't you get out of the house for a while? Go see John, tell him. He can leave work for this."

Tamarind stiffened. "I don't know. John wasn't there last week when I went to see him."

"Does he have lots of meetings out of the office?"

She hedged. "Sometimes he goes to see a doctor at Tufts. Sometimes he meets with some guys at Patriot Healthcare or Phoenix Pharmaceutical."

"Call him. Tell him you need to see him."

"His ex-girlfriend works there." Tamarind blurted it out. She hadn't meant to tell Lucy about Zoë. Once she'd said it though, the bitter words tumbled in a rush to escape her. "He went to lunch with her last week. That's where he was when I tried to find him."

"How do you know?" Adam stirred at Lucy's sharp tone and she patted him. "Did he tell you?"

"No." Tamarind swallowed, trying to get rid of the vile taste that word left in her mouth. "His employee Ted told me he'd gone to lunch with a co-worker. I waited for him in the parking lot and saw them returning. He never told me she got a job there."

Lucy shook her head. "Then you must call him, Tamarind. Go. Don't wait for him to come home. You need to clear the air with him. You need to get the truth from him."

Tamarind had started to shake her head when Lucy's words sunk in. They echoed advice from Valerie *and* Ana. It was a sign. She would do as Lucy said. She would call, but not John. She'd call the technical writer, Susan Henry, whom she'd talked to at the holiday party back in December. If the synchronicity held and John was in while Zoë was out, she'd take the doppelganger potion before she drove to Dr.2Dr. The shake turned to a nod.

Heart pounding at the enormity of her task, she almost didn't get words out. "Yes. I'll get the truth from him. I will."

வ்வ்வ்

For the first time in almost five years, John wished that Zoë were at his side, her sharp tongue and muscular energy shoring up his confidence. He could use a quick-thinking, unflappable partner who'd jump into any breach and drag him to safety. He had to face Tom Anderson alone, however. Even if Zoë hadn't gone to Patriot Healthcare for the day to work with their team, he couldn't bring her to this meeting until he had a chance to explain her role if it came up. He knew that she'd never fake data for a research study.

He sat at the bar where he could see the entrance. It was a silly, James-Bondish thing to do, but he wanted to size up the good doctor before he sat down to lunch with him. He'd emailed the real data off two weeks ago wanting to believe that it was all over and done with, a simple mistake corrected, nothing more to worry about. When he received nothing more than a thank-you email, he had believed that his little drama had ended, even felt foolish for getting so anxious. Not so foolish that he hadn't sent out some feelers to local storage companies, big and small. He'd also hunted down the date for the next Carnegie Mellon "clan" meeting in Boston. Time to network but no hurry.

And then this morning around ten Dr. Anderson called and asked if he had lunch plans. He'd been curt, not unfriendly but all business. John's palms started sweating and hadn't stopped yet. He

519

arrived twenty minutes early, his stomach aching. Medical research studies and falsifying patient data—serious situations that must have been covered in the handbook on adulthood that he forgot to pick up at graduation.

Through the front windows he saw a man in a crisp white dress shirt and gray slacks get out of a dark sedan, a Lexus or some other tasteful luxury car. He carried what looked like a leather portfolio. When he came into the darkened restaurant, he smoothed his short hair back and then stood blinking until the blond college hostess hurried up to him. John couldn't hear her, but the doctor's voice carried to the bar. He said he was meeting someone, would hit the restroom before she seated him. John kept his gaze on Dr. Anderson until he'd disappeared down the short hall to the restrooms. The other man's assured gait and polished appearance made his heart beat faster.

He grabbed his iced tea and sought out the hostess, a vacuous, tanned and heavily eye-lined young woman who frowned at him when he said that he was the guy that her last patron intended to meet.

"Just seat me in that booth. When the guy in the gray slacks and carrying the portfolio gets out of the restroom, bring him over."

A light flipped on in her brain and she smiled. "Oh, yeah. Him." She said it as if Brad Pitt had walked into Applebee's.

John sighed. His heart stuttered but he ignored it and ordered another iced tea when the waitress showed up. Behind her stood Dr. Anderson.

"John Wilkerson?" More a statement than a question, the doctor held his expectant hand out. John took it, glad that he'd just had his hand on a sweaty glass to explain his damp palm. Dr. Anderson shook his hand hard once and slid into the booth across from him. "Water, with lemon." The waitress murmured something and disappeared.

Dr. Anderson set his portfolio on the tabletop between them and lay his long tapered fingers along its edges. John took in their manicured cleanliness, wondered idly if Dr. Anderson performed surgery.

"John, I had to thank you in person for sending over that data file. It was a real eye-opener."

John slid one hand under his thigh where it couldn't pick at anything on the table and pulled his empty glass closer with the other. "How so?"

"Until you sent it to us, we had no idea that anything illegal was going on in the Rajasthan drug study."

John stared at the other man. The doctor's hard gray eyes and close haircut encased him in an impenetrable field devoid of anything as soft as sympathy. "Illegal?" John asked. The tip of his tongue flicked across his dry lips. Where were their drinks?

"Yes. Those results are astounding, better even than Phoenix Pharmaceutical needs to move along in the drug trials. Except they were never given permission to test the Tamarifex on women in the third trimester. It was deemed too risky. And there are more subjects in that file than we approved for this round of study."

The waitress set their glasses down and asked if they wanted to order. John ordered pasta, a menu item that needed no thought, and Dr. Anderson ordered a salad with the Balsamic dressing on the side. When she'd left, John sat mute, waiting for the rest of the explosive news.

"Any idea how the subjects are being recruited off line?" The gray eyes hooked into John's face and kept his gaze level.

"Not really. Look, I've already told you all I know, Dr. Anderson. I didn't find anything else, and I've got work to do." He covered his fear with a fine layer of annoyance.

Dr. Anderson studied him for a moment. Then he moved the portfolio around on the table between them, delicate but firm fingertips on its edges. John felt as though they pinned *him* down.

"I understand and appreciate all the time you spent, John." Dr. Anderson paused. "But I need your help again. We found evidence that Dr. Pendyala has been taking kickbacks from Phoenix Pharmaceutical to get the Rajasthan study through the IRB without too much scrutiny. When we confronted him, he implicated Dr. Mukarjee. We'd like you to look at the informed consent documents for any abnormalities, any evidence that the patients who are participating aren't aware they're being given a drug that stimulates abortion instead of preventing it."

John's head reeled. Before, he hadn't wanted Dr. Mukarjee knowing that he'd been disloyal enough to go electronic snooping. Now he didn't want to find out that Dr. Mukarjee was the biggest slime bag of them all. Not the Gandhi-like saint who had set out to bring the best of modern medicine to his fellow Indians. Yet if he wanted to clear Dr. Mukarjee, he had to risk discovering that the truth might not match his beliefs.

"Also," said Dr. Anderson, apparently unfazed by John's silence, "we think some of the Indian patients being studied are being charged for using the Tamarifex. You may be able to piece together an electronic-payment trail showing that Dr. Mukarjee is already selling this drug in India before it's even been approved as an abortifacient."

This was worse than he'd feared when Dr. Anderson had first called him about the connection between Dr. Pendyala and Dr. Mukarjee. Back then, he'd convinced himself that Prasad and Mukesh were eager for the Rajasthan study to go well so that Dr2Dr and telemedicine looked good, thereby enhancing the value of their dotcom and possibly Dr. Pendyala's wallet. But he'd never imagined all this. Not in his wildest dreams.

"I don't know if I can help you," he said at last. "When do you need me to find this evidence?"

"As soon as possible. The IRB meets this Friday to tell Dr. Mukarjee that Dr. Pendyala has been relieved of his position as lead investigator and to inform him that Dr. Pendyala has implicated him in unethical and illegal activities in a clinical trial. Until then, he'll have no reason to alter his records."

John felt a cold stone drop in his stomach. That left him two days to investigate and either confirm Dr. Pendyala's claims or clear Dr. Mukarjee's good name.

"I'll see what I can dig up."

"Okay, John. Oh, I'd like you to track down whoever created that false data file. He's a potential accomplice."

❧❧❧

When the time came, Ana couldn't get rid of the stray cat. She'd found the creature that last morning pressed against Valerie's back as she lay curled in a fetal position. It stared at Ana, green eyes glittering in the dim dawn, burning a hole in her cheek as she came around the end of the bed. The sun hadn't risen yet, no seabirds stirred on the northwest coast, no brown boobies and terns woke the island with their incessant chattering. Ana knew even before she bent over to check Valerie's breathing that her friend's spirit had left her body's ravaged shell behind.

She'd looked over Valerie's scrawny shoulder at the stray only to shiver at the awareness that she recognized in its eyes. Later, when she'd brought the EMTs into the room to collect the body, the cat had disappeared. She found it sitting on the patio, blinking in the morning sun as it watched the bananaquits and hummingbirds.

Ana hurried past the cat, certain that its gaze had shifted to that powerful spot between her shoulder blades, and out onto the sidewalk. The sun warmed her skin as she walked through Dewey toward Playa Melones where she kept her dwindling supplies. She rubbed her hands along her upper arms. Her thin flanks didn't retain heat well anymore; her old bones had hollowed and her hair had grown as tufted as a chick's down. She could have saved the rest of Tamarind's tail, desiccated and ground into a fine powder, to extend her life for a handful of years or more to come. She could have shuffled between guesthouse and patio until she'd become desiccated herself, finally blowing away across the harbor in a stiff wind. Instead, she'd drawn on Mother Sea one last time, using up the last of her sea-harvested ingredients and the remainder of Tamarind's tail to prepare a final potent drink.

When she got to the rocky beach, she stopped in the thorn scrub along the shore and searched the sky overhead. Dozens of seabirds fluttered like dark pennants against the vibrant blue, but none of the laughing gulls she heard answered her heartfelt call. None tucked its wings and dropped down toward her; none glided, regal and nonchalant, around her head. She knew Ai hadn't returned, wouldn't return until Tamarind headed for the coast. Still, Ana missed him.

After ten heart-aching minutes spent studying a friendless expanse, she left the shrub and crossed the narrow beach to the water. It had been months since she'd cast an oracle. There'd been no need: Valerie's fate had been written all over her. She could ask Mother Sea about Tamarind. She *should* ask Mother Sea before she swallowed the last of her magic. She shrugged. She'd decided long ago what path to take. No point in laying questions out if she had no use for the answers.

Forty-three
og

JOHN LINGERED FOR A GOOD HALF an hour after Dr. Anderson
handed him a manila folder before leaving. The artificial dusk
inside the chain restaurant closed in on him, a simultaneous
darkness descending over his thoughts. The folder's contents
documented Dr. Pendyala's allegations against Dr. Mukarjee. More
than that, it contained the blueprint for his own disillusion. Even
should he tiptoe through the labyrinthine corridors of Dr.2Dr's
directories, he might not find any evidence beyond the
circumstantial. As it was, he'd have to persuade Zoë to work her
magic on the system's security. That shouldn't be too difficult. Not
only could he count on Zoë, Wonder Woman's heir, to take on the
modern "Nazis" who manipulated study data for a drug being
tested on poor Indian women, but she'd also relish the chance to
clear herself. No man would manipulate and outsmart *her*.

Why couldn't he open the folder then?

It took half an hour, but John did let the answer surface. He
didn't want to open the folder because he'd have to act. He'd have to
do something to discover the truth and then do something about it.
He couldn't do that for the Tufts IRB and those poor Indian women,
however, if he hadn't even told Tamarind the truth. He'd wanted to
believe that he didn't need to tell her about what happened with

Zoë, that he'd find some way to mention Zoë's presence at Dr.2Dr. He'd convinced himself that Tamarind didn't need to know the details.

But Tamarind deserved the truth. Why not tell her? He'd remained faithful to her. Even Zoë had overcome whatever madness that Ana had tortured her with. At this point, what did he have to fear? Tears and loss of trust? Did he want to wait for her to stumble upon Zoë first? Would she see them together and recognize the truth: that Zoë no longer pursued him? Would she even ask him?

It was that last possibility that troubled him the most. After discovering the sardine tin last fall, he'd realized that Tamarind no longer let her thoughts run through her mouth like water through an open spigot. She hadn't told him that she needed bed rest after her ER trip. She hadn't told him about the wedding band cut from her finger. She hadn't told him that she'd found her Goddess pendant, the one that had lit their way through a hurricane, drawing upon some power of sea, earth and love that his rational mind couldn't begin to comprehend. He only knew that she had it again because he'd discovered it in that carved mangrove box that Ana had given her. What else had she kept to herself?

John twisted his wedding band. His own finger had gotten fleshy, either from the ten pounds that he'd gained over the winter—his first not spent commuting on a bike—or from a temporary swelling. Either way, the band resisted his efforts. It wouldn't be easy to remove. How would he feel if it had to be cut off his finger? Wouldn't he feel unsure, naked? Maybe even a little superstitious about what it meant to sever such a symbol of eternal love?

Whatever Tamarind felt, she hadn't told him. He'd had to pry the truth about her wedding band out of her and even then she wouldn't look at him, wanted him to wait to get it fixed. He had waited, but after the showdown with Zoë he'd determined that a new wedding band would make Tamarind happy, if she had it. Now he saw that he'd had *faith, hope, and love* inscribed in lieu of coming clean. As if it was all an exercise for himself and didn't need

Tamarind's overt understanding and agreement. He shifted in the booth, reached for his watery iced tea, and swallowed what was left. Icy remnants slid down his throat. He'd seen her face after she asked him where he'd been that day, the day that Zoë poisoned him with Ana's "love potion." Tamarind knew that he'd lied to her.

Well, he'd come clean, about Zoë and about the trouble at IndiaClinic. He'd put it all out there tonight, and he'd understand if she got upset about him keeping everything from her. He just hoped that she would understand that he had to spend the next two nights working in proximity to his former she-wolf girlfriend. He grinned, nervous and resolved. Zoë might be a she-wolf, but only Tamarind had the power to shred him.

John looked at his watch. He'd delayed long enough. Pulling the manila folder closer, he opened it.

ﺀﺀﺀ

Tamarind's entire scheme teetered long before she confronted John. She'd dug her breast pump out two weeks ago when she'd decided to make the doppelganger potion, but although she'd managed to collect almost a hundred ounces of milk since, she had no idea whether Adam would take a bottle or whether the potion would affect her later supply. She'd have to throw away several feedings anyway. She couldn't feed Ana's potion to him, filtered though it might be in her milk. That would be tantamount to poisoning her newborn son.

She called Susan Henry first, before showering and changing. No point in getting ready and drinking Zoë's essence only to find that John had traveled off site today and that Zoë prowled the cubicles. Susan sounded thrilled to take her call, chatting so much that Tamarind had to interrupt her. She told her first lie ever, leavened with the truth. Taking a leap, she confided in Susan that John hadn't told her about Zoë, his ex-girlfriend, and that she wanted to come in to Dr.2Dr to meet her old rival for a little heart-to-heart. Fear and excitement flattened Susan's voice. She liked John and Zoë, she said, and hoped that there wasn't going to be any trouble.

527

Tamarind sought to reassure Susan. When she spoke, she recognized shades of Ana in her smooth tones. "Me either, Susan. I just want everyone to know where they stand is all."

Susan whinnied nervously. "Maybe you should just talk to John, Tamarind. Zoë's gone today anyway. Out at Patriot Healthcare all week, in fact. John's got a lunch meeting off site, but he's supposed to be here all afternoon."

Tamarind scowled at Susan's suggestion, but when she answered, she focused on being nice. "You're right. I should talk to John first. That's what I'll do." That at least wasn't a lie.

"Good." Susan paused but went on before Tamarind could say good-bye. "You know, Tamarind, I don't think you've got anything to worry about. John and Zoë don't seem at all interested in anything outside of work. All John ever talks about is you and your kids."

This observation dented Tamarind's confidence, but she deflected it. Susan, sweet as she was, had no boyfriend, let alone a husband. What did she know about the emotional eddies that swirled between a husband and wife with an ex-girlfriend like Zoë around? She didn't understand Zoë if she didn't recognize her threat. And that, Tamarind decided, put Susan in a special category. Even she, as a naïve mermaid, had identified Zoë at first sight. Black Urchin, that's what she'd nicknamed her. Long, needle-like spines filled with venom.

"I'm not worried. Just need to talk." Tamarind tried to sound nonchalant but failed. "Guess I'll have to find Zoë another time. Thanks anyway."

She showered and dressed in one of her few silk blouses and a pencil skirt, an outfit that John's sister Cassie had helped her buy for his graduation three years ago. She smoothed the luscious red material over her full breasts. It reminded her of the *flamboyan*-red blouse Zoë wore to such devastating effect at Brew Moon. She admitted to herself that she was jealous of Zoë, who exuded sexual magnetism as naturally as breathing. She would enjoy transforming into her rival. Ana told her that the potent glamour lasted two hours or more. Maybe she'd stop to get gas, swagger about on her heels. Just before she headed downstairs to feed Adam one last time, she dug the conch shell out of her jeans pocket and slipped it into the front pocket of her skirt. It reminded her of Ana, and she needed to channel her old mentor if she wanted to succeed.

As she flitted about, trying to make sure that Lucy had whatever she might need, she avoided looking at Sarah, who played at her toy kitchen. Lucy caught her after fifteen minutes and made her sit with her feet up to nurse Adam, a steaming cup of herbal tea, the kind nursing mothers drank to build their milk supply, on the table at her side. She tried to get Tamarind to eat a sandwich, but Tamarind pleaded that anxiety had killed her appetite. It wouldn't do to get sick from the taste of Zoë. An empty stomach would speed the transformation anyway.

"You look gorgeous, Tamarind. I'm sure that's what you're going for." Lucy stood in the kitchen doorway, hands on hips. "Nice to see you dressed up."

"Thanks." Tamarind smiled. A twinge of guilt flitted through her thoughts, but she let it fly away.

Lucy didn't leave even though Tamarind no longer felt like chatting. "Just make sure you listen to what John has to say."

That surprised Tamarind. "What do you mean? Of course, I'll listen to him."

Lucy sighed and came in to sit on the loveseat next to Tamarind's easy chair. "Just what I said. Listen. I agree that where there's smoke, there's often fire. No one knows better than me. But so far you have nothing but your insecurity to go on. Give him a chance to explain. Maybe he has no idea how much this bothers you. Men can't read our minds, you know. Though I admit it'd be nice if they did." She sounded like she spoke from hard-earned wisdom.

Tamarind bristled. "He should know. She's never been anything but nasty to me. She's always made it clear that she wants him."

"Then maybe John's trying to protect you. How much control does he have over Zoë working at his company?" Lucy looked at her, a concerned frown marring her kind face.

Tamarind's frustration and unhappiness flared, despite the protective rush of oxytocin from nursing. "So it's up to me then? Why does this have to be so hard?"

"Because a successful marriage is hard, Tamarind. But a failed marriage is harder. Just ask Rachel."

Tamarind didn't know what to say to that so she said nothing.

"That's a new wedding ring, isn't it?" Lucy had just noticed Tamarind's left hand.

Tamarind looked down at the heavy gold band. It hummed faintly against Adam.

"Yes. John had it remade." She twisted it. "I'm not sure I like the way it feels."

"Almost like getting married all over." Lucy's soft voice matched her faraway look. Her gaze returned to Tamarind's face. "Promise me you'll leave it on. Don't take it off, even if he hurts you. Please. Promise me."

Tamarind screwed up her face and looked away. She hadn't planned to wear the band while transformed! John might notice it. "I-" she began.

"Please," Lucy interrupted. "Its weight will remind you, keep you grounded. You've got to fight for John. If this Zoë thinks he's worth fighting for, you've got even more reason."

"Are you saying I should let him cheat on me?" Incredulity lent a tang to Tamarind's question.

"No." Lucy shook her head. "I'm saying don't give up on him until you know for sure. There's too much at stake."

Perhaps she should humor Lucy. John wasn't very observant. He hadn't noticed last fall that she'd made a substitute Goddess pendant until she'd told him that Valerie had traded it for a better one. She had no idea when Lucy told him about them cutting off her first wedding band, but he'd clearly not noticed *that* right away. Distract him with Zoë's overwhelming charms and he'd never see the new wedding band. She'd risk it. "I don't see why it matters, but I promise to keep it on, Lucy." She smiled at the relief on Lucy's face. "Time to change Adam."

"Hand him here. I don't mind." Lucy reached for Adam, who squeaked as only newborns and sleeping mice can do. When Tamarind handed him off, a chill rushed in to replace his sweet warmth against her chest. She shivered but pushed her unease to the back of her thoughts.

The unease returned when she caught sight of Sarah watching her as she pulled out of the driveway. The storm door, silvered in the sunlight, revealed only Sarah's disembodied head. Against the surrounding opaque glass, her rose-gold curls haloed and magnified her disconcerting blue eyes. Those eyes penetrated to Tamarind's soul as if her little girl knew full well that she'd just gulped a foul-tasting transformative drink from that plastic tumbler now in the sink. As if she'd seen the tin that Tamarind had palmed into her handbag.

Tamarind forgot Sarah, forgot everything, when the transformation began. She'd meant to pull into a deserted parking lot or an empty side street before it worked, but she'd just turned onto route 87 going through Cheltham when weakness washed down her like heavy rain down a windowpane. She managed to turn into the strip mall with the Stop-N-Shop and the Friendly's and crept into a spot along the roadside embankment.

As she sat there, icy heat nauseated her. Her vision blurred and heartburn enflamed her chest. She'd dropped her head to her steering wheel when she heard a rapid tapping on her window. She looked up, saw a construction worker in dirty denim and orange vest, concern on his face.

"Yes?" she asked as soon as her window slid down. Her voice sounded strange, causing her gaze to slide across to the rearview mirror. Zoë's wide black eyes met it.

"Are you all right?" When she looked back, Tamarind saw that he looked at her chest.

"Why wouldn't I be?" Annoyance and fear colored her voice. She'd never felt the strength of a leer before. *What would Zoë do?* she thought. And laughed inside her head at the unintended echo of the popular bracelets that asked *What would Jesus do?* Even as she found the comparison funny, she felt Zoë's personality channeling through her, mocking it. She turned this force onto her errant knight. "Hello? I'm up here."

The guy raised his face and made a tiny movement, something more than a blink and less than a flinch. "I saw you weavin' all the way down Parker. Just thought I'd make sure you hadn't had a heart attack or nothin'."

Tamarind's anger rose. Or was it hers? Whatever it was, it felt good. Powerful. "I'm fine. Thanks for asking. You can move along now."

The construction worker turned away, mumbling and shuffling to his pickup. Tamarind waited until he'd gone and then got out of the car. John drank more coffee these days than Coke, so she planned to buy him one of those expensive drinks at Starbuck's coffee shop and spike it before she got to Dr2Dr. If the construction worker's leer had scared her, the sweet goofiness of the handsome young barista behind the counter at Starbucks filled her with giddiness. She smiled and brought her chin up and her shoulders back. This young man, too sensitive to turn her into a pair of breasts, spent the whole time chatting while ignoring the line that formed behind her. Zoë's aspect whispered a disdainful laugh that he'd be jealous of Adam—he'd not know whether he wanted to be suckled for sustenance or pleasure or both. Tamarind heard this whisper as one hears a humming bee and ignored it.

She turned the radio on as she drove through Cheltham, pushing the search button until she hit on classic rock. The words *More Than A Feeling* swelled through the car. She found herself humming along, unknown lyrics stuck in her mind as flotsam sticks in mangrove roots along the shore. For a terrifying instant she didn't know who she was and then the glint of gold drew her gaze to her wedding band and she remembered. By the time she pulled into the parking lot behind Dr2Dr, Tamarind had absorbed Zoë's personality to such an extent that even the sensation of a mental dichotomy had subsided. She was Tamarind. She was Zoë.

Zoë anticipated the need to park on the far side of the lot, under some oak trees and next to a white electrician's van. Better to leave it where John would have little chance of recognizing Tamarind's car. His spot was empty; he hadn't returned from lunch. She turned the engine off to wait, leaving the radio on and mixing the truth powder into the short coffee cup. Energy rippled through her arms and thighs. She had the urge to get out of the car, kick off her pumps, hike up her skirt, and launch a few kicks. She giggled. Shook her head to clear it.

She'd just decided to look at herself in the review mirror, twisting her head and manipulating her cheek muscles as if she'd transformed into a bear or a monkey and not the sexiest woman she'd met, when she glimpsed John's car turning in to the lot. Her heart thudded like a terrified rabbit in a cage. Then Zoë looked out at her from those hard black eyes.

"Let's put this body through its paces."

Together they left the car, smoothing skirt and blouse as they walked. Anticipation and apprehension mingled in a heady mix. Ahead of them on the sidewalk John's muscular back and shorn head snagged at their gaze. Zoë missed the long hair. Tamarind wanted to run her hands along his shoulders. They'd drawn within fifteen feet when John glanced over his shoulder, did a double take, and then stopped.

"Zoë, am I glad to see you!" His relief showed on his face. Zoë exulted. Tamarind felt a pang.

"Trouble holding the fort down without me?" Her eyelids lowered before Tamarind knew what she'd done. Looking at John through slanted eyelashes, she sensed Zoë gathering herself to toy with him. As with Zoë's earlier anger, this teasing power to seduce felt good. She handed him the spiked coffee. "I stopped off at Starbucks. Thought you might like something."

"Not trying to poison me again, are you?" he joked, but they recognized the truth in what he said. Zoë felt guilt. Tamarind wondered.

Still Zoë came to the rescue. "Why would I do that?" It came out as affronted purr.

John laughed and sipped the coffee. They both noticed his worried tic. That the hand holding the coffee cup shook a fraction. He brushed his other palm across his head. "You'll never guess who called and wanted to meet me for lunch."

Tamarind's jealousy flared, but Zoë kept it under control. "Another woman?"

John's gaze darted beyond her and back over his shoulder. He grabbed her by the elbow. "Let's go to that bagel place across the street."

"This is gotta be something," Zoë said. "Lead on, good man."

They crossed over Moody to the same café that Tamarind and John had gone to last fall after he'd left her waiting for so long. It was empty except for the tired-looking twenty-something behind the counter who eyed John's cup pointedly but said nothing when he ordered Zoë a black coffee.

"So, you were about to tell me about the other woman," Zoë said as they took their seats. She nodded toward his coffee. "Might as well drink that since you offended Miss Thing over there."

John gulped from the cup and then shook his head. His green eyes wilted where they showed around the enlarged irises. "Cut the jokes, Zo. Tom Anderson called, that's who. Pendyala claims Mukarjee is in on this big scam. Anderson gave me until Friday morning to track down any evidence of lying to the pregnant women in the study or illegal payments."

This wasn't what they'd come for! Still, they had to stay calm. "Illegal payments?"

"For the Tamarifex. Anderson said that Phoenix might be selling it already in India. To women who don't know it induces abortion."

Zoë's anger erupted again, but Tamarind struggled to understand. "Why would they do that?" Even as she asked, she tried to think about how to test the truth potion before unleashing Zoë on him. So far, he'd done nothing to confirm or deny interest let alone unfaithfulness.

John shook his head and finished his coffee. "That part doesn't make any sense. None of it does." He frowned and smacked his lips. "That was the shittiest Starbucks I've ever had. Reminds me of that nasty stuff you snuck into my coffee last week. Hope I'm not going to upchuck again." He laughed. It was a mirthless sound. "What am I going to do, Zo? You know I'm no good at confrontations."

Ah ha. This may lead us into the subject. Tread softly. "You'll do fine. You broke up with me, remember?" Angry hurt thrummed in Zoë's voice, negating any attempt at softness. Tamarind marveled at Zoë's pain but shoved any empathy to the back of her thoughts.

John studied her. The green of his eyes deepened, called to mind the color of August leaves in cool woods. "I'm sorry," he said. Zoë heard and quivered. Tamarind ached and angered together. "I know I said it before, but I'll say it again. I was a total shit and I deserved to get stomped, but you restrained yourself."

"Was she worth it?" Zoë and Tamarind were of one mind as they asked. "Raimunda, that is. You cheated with her, not Tamarind. Right?"

John's gaze didn't waiver. He looked like he welcomed this talk. That would be the potion taking effect. "No, she wasn't worth it. If I'd been stronger, I wouldn't have been susceptible to Ana's tricks. I know it. I didn't want to let you go, but I didn't want to get involved with Tamarind either. I wanted you both. So Ana, smelling weakness like a shark smells blood, came for me."

He'd told the truth. Zoë and Tamarind followed the opening and ignored his mention of Ana. "Now you have us both, eh?" Nothing like going right after the heart of the matter.

"Both of you?" John screwed up his face, belched a little. His fingertips came to his temples and rubbed. He closed his eyes and sat silent for two or three minutes until Tamarind and Zoë worried that he'd succeed in fighting off the potion. He opened them again; they'd turned a sickly yellow-green. "If I didn't know better, I'd think you tried to poison me again." He looked at her hard. "You told me you'd used all that crap she gave you, that you'd been under some spell but I'd broken it. Not going back on me, are you?"

Zoë grew wary, but Tamarind became confused. What was John saying? They tried to laugh and play down his suspicion. "Doesn't hurt for a girl to try, does it?" They started to slide off the seat. Something in John's face warned them that he'd switched roles and now interrogated Zoë.

John's hand came down and snatched her wrist. "No, Ana. It doesn't. It *is* you, isn't it, Ana? You've changed into Zoë somehow, just like you turned yourself into Raimunda. Your love potion failed, the one you gave Zoë. So here you are trying to trap me yourself."

Tamarind and Zoë flinched from the ferocity of his gaze, his painful grip. Tamarind's wedding band throbbed beneath the touch of John's palm. The solution had failed in some horrible, unpredictable way. They needed to get away from the blazing green fire in his eyes. A whimper escaped her.

The woman behind the counter called out. "Hey, what's going on?"

John ignored her. "Why? Isn't it enough you seduced me back on Culebra?" He shook her wrist but not hard. A light of understanding tempered the anger. "You're after Tamarind, aren't you? You want her back."

The woman interrupted. "Let her go." She stood next to John, a mop held like a baseball bat. "I'll call the cops, so help me."

Still John ignored her. A heartbeat later, too many things happened at once for Tamarind and Zoë to take in. John yelped and dropped Zoë's wrist, his eyes darting down to her hand where it lay on the table. The wedding band gleamed against her smooth flesh. "Wha–?" he asked just as another voice spoke from the doorway to the street.

"Don't!" It was the real Zoë.

Tamarind and Zoë felt the wind of the mop handle's swing as it cracked the table between them and John. And then the real Zoë sprang between the café employee and their table and wrested the mop from the determined, if obviously frightened, woman—who grew more frightened when she saw who'd taken the mop from her.

She took a step away from the table and asked in a breathless voice, "Twins?"

Zoë cradled the mop in an elbow. "Yup. Afraid you've already met my crazy sister. She sometimes forgets to take her meds." She glanced down at the table. "Right, Sis? Her husband here gets a little forceful trying to keep her from hurting herself." A look passed between her and John.

In that instant, Tamarind who was Zoë and was not Zoë, jumped to her feet and ran.

Forty-four
ଔ

ZOË, STILL REELING FROM SEEING John with what looked like her identical twin, whirled toward the other woman, swinging the mop around and catching her behind the knees. Her double sprawled on the floor, a tangle of legs and skirt. Her own heart tattooed against her rib cage, but she felt exhilarated and triumphant, not scared. From the moment she recognized herself outside Dr2Dr, her martial arts training, always latent, had gone on alert status. She felt poised to spring like a crouching panther watching a deer.

"Oh, Christ!" Zoë gasped. If she played this right, the heroic café employee would never suspect that she'd subdued her own 'sister.' "Here, let me help you up." She bent over and grabbed for the evil twin's hand.

The other woman's hand clasped her wrist and yanked. Zoë, although expecting trouble, lost a fraction of her balance anyway and took two steps forward. As she did, the other woman got her knees under herself and pushed off from the floor with her free hand. Zoë caught herself but not before the other woman had regained her feet. They faced each other across the open space in front of the café door.

"Guess you've got some of my reflexes, eh, Sis?" Zoë asked in a low voice. She'd started to sweat in her gabardine slacks and button-down shirt. At least she wasn't wearing a tight skirt like her opponent, who could only be that vile old woman from Culebra. She didn't know how the old woman had adopted her aspect, but it didn't matter. Looking like her and displaying her martial arts prowess were two very different things. "Don't have a mop though." She held the mop out and shook it playfully.

The fake Zoë, a mad gleam in her black eyes, laughed a little wildly. "Don't need one to mop the floor with you." Her hands tugged the skirt almost as high as her crotch and then she acted. Zoë just had time to brace for the side kick the other woman launched toward the mop hand. She blocked, but barely. For the next frenzied five minutes they whirled and kicked, testing each other and knocking tables and chairs over. The whole time Zoë and her double avoided John, who'd dragged the café employee behind the counter.

Fighting herself disconcerted Zoë more than she would have predicted.

They broke off and circled one another, panting softly and watching each other's eyes as only panthers can. No longer certain that she had the advantage, Zoë's earlier exhilaration evaporated. When the café door, now behind and to the left of her, opened, she kept her gaze on her opponent. Even panthers sometimes eat their own kind.

"Holy crap!" A young man's voice squeaked in the breathless silence. "It's like Street Fighter two in here."

"Shut the fuck up," Zoë commanded. She had to think, second-guess herself, and then do something unexpected.

"Trying to second-guess me?" taunted her double. "Won't work."

"Zoë," John called in a strangled voice. They both looked at him. His darkened eyes blazed from a shockingly pale face as they swung from the double to Zoë and back again. "Zoë, stop."

"John?" The double sounded tentative. She took a step toward him. "Are you all right?"

"I feel like shit. Worse than last time." He gripped the counter, hung his head. Started to convulse. Zoë recognized the minute pivot when it began and instantly understood.

"John!" she screamed and bolted for him as he fell. So did her twin.

Zoë, closer than the old woman, pressed her palms into the glass and vaulted the counter. She landed on panther's feet next to John. The young woman that he'd rescued, petrified only moments before, had knelt and caught his head before it hit the floor. Zoë dropped to her own knees and turned John's face as he began to vomit. Her own stomach clenched.

"Oh, God!" Zoë's evil twin moaned. Zoë looked up to see the other woman leaning over the counter, her eyes dilated. "Oh, God!"

"See what you've done, you old hag!" Fury and fear shot like a geyser through Zoë, burning her esophagus and superheating the air between them. How dare she act so terrified? "What'd you give him? Another 'love' potion? Don't you get it? He doesn't love me! He loves Tamarind!"

The dilated eyes never left John, who continued to vomit a black tarry liquid. From the smell of it, it had been coffee. Zoë turned away from her double to reach for a dingy rag on the back counter next to the coffee machine to mop up the mess.

"Truth potion." Zoë almost didn't hear the whisper. "I only wanted to know the truth."

But Zoë *did* hear. In the space between two heartbeats she'd erupted from the floor to grab her opponent by the front of her silk blouse. She gripped so much of the slippery material that the blouse cut into the other woman's neck. Her twin didn't flinch or struggle. "I'll give you the truth." Zoë shook the other woman so hard her teeth rattled and then she slapped her.

Someone clutched Zoë's ankle. She looked down to see a green-tinged John struggling to raise himself off the floor. "Let her go." His hoarse voice serrated her soul. Could he be in danger? Maybe they should call an ambulance. She let her double go. The other woman sagged against the counter.

Zoë dropped again to John, who heaved but nothing more came from his bloodless lips. She clamped her gaze on the monster above them. "Get out of here," she hissed, "before I ignore him and beat the crap out of you, old woman or no."

Her double darted a glance at John, met Zoë's gaze one last time, and then whirled around. Zoë regretted the impulse to get rid of the woman as soon as she'd left her field of vision, but when she put her hand down onto the floor to push herself to her feet, John fought to speak again.

"Not Ana." He took in a great sobbing breath. "It wasn't Ana. It was Tamarind."

చచచ

Hardly pausing to look left for oncoming traffic, Tamarind dashed across Moody Street toward the alley leading to the parking lot behind Dr2Dr's offices. Her eyesight caught only fractured images of glass, steel, and concrete while her heartbeat pulsed in her ears. No other sensory stimuli pierced her. There were no smells, no tastes, no hot or cold, no pounding or sweating or swinging arms. Only disjointed sight and garbled sound. Somewhere off in the periphery of her awareness she heard tires squealing and a car horn followed by rapid words, but she understood nothing. She flew over the pavement. When she'd arrived at her car, she couldn't remember how she'd gotten there.

Zoë again rescued her as she stood, blinking and blank. Tamarind watched from a distance, as though she'd projected her subtle body through space—something that she hadn't done since John lived in San Juan. Zoë pulled out her keys, unlocked the car and hustled into the driver's seat. Tamarind moved to the ceiling of her station wagon, floating like a numb ethereal balloon tethered to the dark-haired woman below her. She watched as Zoë swung her head in a slow arc, all caution in the absence of hot pursuit.

From her height, Tamarind glimpsed slices of street and building as Zoë navigated her way out of the parking lot and through Waltham onto the 128/95 loop around Boston. The slices slid by in meaningless concrete gray broken by odd splashes of living green and patches of robin's egg blue. Zoë drove south, although Tamarind had no idea how she knew this to be true. She began to lose altitude as a balloon loses helium around the time that Zoë took the exit for 93 so that she sat on Zoë's shoulder. Zoë sped on, nearly sideswiping a minivan trying to merge into the right lane. Tamarind, free from driving duty, looked back to see the other driver gesturing and heard the van's horn. Zoë seemed not to notice.

They drove among the early afternoon traffic, weaving in and out of lanes in unthinking escape. Tamarind grew aware of a nagging ache that crept up on her, a dull pain that throbbed through her numb distance. She believed that it had been there for some time. The pain anchored her to Zoë's corporeal body—no, *her* corporeal body transformed into her rival. She puzzled over this, the source of pain. From the corner of her subtle body's eye she caught a glimpse of gold. Her wedding band.

As soon as she recognized it, Tamarind swooped back into the body below to rejoin Zoë, who was still in charge. Their vision blinked in and out while their foot plunged the gas pedal down. At the same time, the sphincter at the entrance to their esophagus hiccoughed sporadically. Tamarind, no longer numb, wanted to pull over, squeeze her eyes shut, and sob. Zoë had something else in mind. She gripped the wheel and concentrated on bringing their foot up while veering left to avoid rear-ending the sedan in front of them. As she did, another car swerved behind them into the far left lane, its horn blaring.

Zoë took the exit to 495 before Tamarind realized what she'd done. They'd traveled forty miles south of Waltham where John lay poisoned and more than fifty miles from home. Tamarind groaned. Zoë ignored her. Tamarind, grateful that the transformation still had life in it, let Zoë's borrowed aspect stay in control. She played with the gold band instead, forcing Zoë to drive one handed while she rubbed it with her thumb. It continued to burn and throb.

Zoë concentrated on driving, her disdain for Tamarind clear as the peal of a glass bell. Tamarind didn't blame her. She'd totally

542

messed the situation up, although she didn't know how. Ana hadn't warned her not to use coffee. And she'd followed Ana's instructions for ripening the solution. If anything, she'd used it before it had reached its full strength. She shouldn't have worn the wedding band, but that hadn't caused John to get sick or the real Zoë to show up and challenge her. She frowned. Zoë frowned. Had John gotten sick before or after the real Zoë showed up? It hurt to think. She reached her left hand up to rub her temple. There was something else. John and Zoë had both said something else. Something about Ana.

Tamarind conjured up a vague image of Ana sitting outside her shack in the heat of a Culebra afternoon, dozing with a clove cigarette dangling from her right hand. What she'd long taken as folds of dry old skin, Tamarind remembered now as remnants of *mer* webbing. She'd been so scared of Ana! Scared of that single eye boring into her. Scared of the coarse voice and wild hair and the unknowable thoughts of someone who controlled magic in a way no *mer* ever could. Ana had been human. And married. Ana had failed at both. Hadn't she known all along that if Ana couldn't make it that she had no right to expect success? Hadn't Ana told Tamarind as much when she asked about putting off her tail?

Once she'd started thinking about Ana, Tamarind couldn't stop thinking about her. She remembered the first time that she met the old woman, long before John visited Culebra and stole her imagination along with her heart. She'd still been a child, barely allowed by her father and sisters to wander out of mind's eye when she swam closer to Culebra's western flank. Culebra had been a towering, hard-edged mystery: unlike the smaller cays surrounding it, her father and sisters wouldn't let her go near Culebra or tell her anything about it.

That day she played a game with herself to help her work up the courage to disobey her father. She swam towards the rocky beach that she came to call La Playa Tamarindo and then turned around and headed out swiftly, all the time expecting her father or sisters to catch her and drag her away. At last, after about the fifteenth run, she went far enough ashore to touch her belly to the bottom. Pleased and excited about her daring, Tamarind didn't notice the human who'd been watching her game from the beach.

Not safe to come ashore without a glamour, a strange thought warned her as she lay sunning herself. Humans come here. *Trouble if they see you.*

Tamarind swiveled her head around. Seeing a strange face amongst the scrub lining the beach, she forgot to breathe air, something that she hadn't mastered yet. She watched the eyes, her heart pounding. There was something wrong with the left eye. It was opaque and shiny like mother of pearl. Blind. It gave the face, surrounded by tangled white hair, a furious, vengeful aspect. In the silence that bound them, Tamarind's sudden intake of breath sounded harsh and shuddering. Fearful.

Feeling lightheaded, she managed to send a question to her unexpected guardian. *Humans? What are humans?*

"I'm human." The creature stood up. "Know who you are, *mer* child. Won't harm you."

Tamarind stared, not sure what she was seeing or hearing. The other had a recognizable head and torso, although its scrawny arms and sunken chest hadn't the muscle necessary to propel itself through Mother Sea. Its voice had all the mellifluous sound of shell scraping stone above water. Yet it took her astounded eyes dozens of waves to realize what was wrong with the creature. The old one—the *human*—didn't have a tail. This had so startled her that she'd shoved off into the water and swam away.

That had been their first meeting.

But she'd been more curious than fearful as a child so once she'd recovered from her initial shock she thirsted to know more about humans. She knew, without asking, that this was the reason that her father and sisters kept her from Culebra. She must not tell them what she'd found there. After many more furtive trips, she saw the human again. The old woman appeared between some thorny bushes, her limited gaze swimming over the seawater near the shore. When her gaze met Tamarind's, the swimming ceased.

This time Tamarind played no games, heading straight for the beach. She lay there, mesmerized by the other's blank eye, which sparkled like Mother Sea under a bright sky.

Thought you might come back. The old woman's thoughts bore into Tamarind's tender mental ear, discordant and jangling. She lowered her torso, wrapping her arms around the bony protrusions that appeared where a tail should be. She studied Tamarind, squinting out of her good eye. After several heartbeats loud enough to threaten Tamarind's inner ear, the old woman pulled something from a pouch at her waist, waved one hand around her face, and then stuck what looked like a piece of dead coral in her mouth. *Too curious for your own good.*

That was the beginning of their secret friendship.

Tamarind continued to meet the withered human, whose name she learned was Ana, off and on for a long time, perhaps two years. In that time, Ana taught her simple drawing-upon magic and told her stories about the humans living on Culebra. In exchange, Tamarind brought sea plants and creatures, sometimes some coral. When she asked Ana why she wanted them, the old woman told her that she used them in healing concoctions for humans.

The secret friendship ended when Tamarind's father caught her talking to Ana. She'd never seen him so angry and lay mute as he assaulted the very air around her with furious energy. Ana remained calm and said nothing, not even when Tamarind's father compelled Tamarind to return to the water and forbade her to go near Ana. She simply fixed Tamarind with a stare that would not let her go. When Tamarind reached the age of maturity, she returned to Culebra against her father's command. She'd never told him what she did. He never spoke of Ana. But she'd seen his eyes, read the echo of his angry hurt. He'd known.

She hadn't thought about Ana's unspoken invitation in years now, but having recalled it, she felt again the power of its pull. Ana's eye blazed in her memory and then the salt tang of home filled her nostrils. She blinked and shook her head. Her eyes focused on the road outside the car's front window. She found that she'd pulled the conch shell from her pocket and worried it between her fingers.

She'd returned to herself just in time. Zoë's aspect, a shade of its former self, clung to the steering wheel even though her power faded away. Tamarind wrested control of her body as she shrank back into her petite height. She glanced in the rearview mirror, saw that it was angled too high and adjusted it. As she did so, the conch shell fell to the floorboards but she didn't care. Zoë's hair lengthened and curled as she watched, lightening from glossy black to reddish-brown. She brought her gaze back to the road. She didn't need to see her hair grow as light as a dull copper penny to know that she'd transformed back into herself.

About two hundred yards ahead Tamarind saw a highway sign and recognized the next exit. John had taken her to visit Woods Hole and the state beach at Buzzard's Bay while he was a post-doc. Zoë had brought her back. A rush of certainty washed over her. This was her destination. She exited the highway and headed for the state beach. At this time of year, the parking lot was deserted and she parked close to the sand.

As soon as Tamarind opened the car door, she smelled home. Nothing else mattered.

Overhead, the shrill laughter of seagulls welcomed her and Tamarind cried out to them. Slipping off her heels, she ran forward onto the sand without shutting her car door or grabbing her purse. The sound of the car's reminder chime receded into the *shush-shush* of the ocean's waves.

Tamarind's toes dug into the forgiving sand, warm in the April sunshine. She stopped and hugged herself, laughed, then threw out her arms and raised her face to the sky. After a moment, she darted off down the beach in a diagonal until her feet touched wet sand. Then she stopped and squatted down and squeezed clumpy handfuls, letting sand spurt out until her hands were covered with a fine, beaded layer. For long moments she stayed like this, so lost in the sound and smell and feel of this place that she forgot who she was and how she came here. Eventually, though, the faint chiming

546

pierced her reverie and she looked up and out over the undulating horizon. Even through the welcoming noises of water and bird cry, there was stillness as though the world waited for her to decide something.

"Oh, Mother! I miss you!"

There was no answer, just the ever-continuous suspiration of the waves.

"Please!" she said, not knowing what she was asking for exactly. After another moment, she sat down and sobbed. An image of John, tarry liquid spewing from his mouth and his green eyes dark as moss, tormented her. She couldn't do it, couldn't be human. She didn't have enough faith, in herself or John. She couldn't live in a world without magic. A world where the man she loved couldn't read her thoughts or she his. A world that required her to struggle, solitary and unsure, with mistakes and false steps. She'd already made the worst mistake she ever could. She'd poisoned John. How could she fix that? She couldn't think beyond the image of him lying on the floor.

Even Sarah, she with the *mer* eyes, had declared Tamarind's fate. Sarah had obliterated the protective spells that Ana had woven into the box. She'd turned the *mer* symbols for life and fertility into nothing more than carvings. Without Ana's spells, what hope did she and John have?

A wind began to blow, forcing the tears into her hairline even as her hair fluttered out behind her like a dark pennant. She wrapped her arms around her knees and dropped onto the wet sand where she rocked in unison with the waves. She sat only three or four feet away, and soon they began to lick at her toes. She heaved a sigh that left her feeling simultaneously heavy and empty, a feeling unrelieved by the hiccoughing that followed her bout of weeping. Her wedding band had grown heavy and cold, making her finger ache, but when she tried to remove it, she found that it wouldn't budge.

"Not surprised to find you crying," a voice said, startling Tamarind so much that she ceased hiccoughing.

She sprang up and flung her arms forward, as if warding off an attack. There in front of her, as ephemeral as fog billowing over a warm ocean, stood Ana. Her white hair, wild and unkempt as it had always been, remained untouched by the wind that blew in toward Tamarind. Tamarind had forgotten how much like a piece of driftwood Ana resembled, so twisted and brown. A wreath of clove smoke hung so heavily about her features that Tamarind could almost smell it.

"Ana." Her voice trembled, whether from relief or surprise, she didn't know.

"That's me." Ana smiled her familiar crooked smile. Even across the ether, her voice had lost none of its crackle. "Suspected you'd need me after using the truth potion. I was right."

Tamarind looked away at her words. "I did something wrong, Ana. John got sick, so sick, from the potion." She felt sick herself.

"Fighting it, sounds like. Can't keep the truth in once he's drunk the potion."

"That explains it." Tamarind latched onto Ana's excuse. She welcomed the bitterness that edged her voice. "He started to get sick after I got him to admit he'd cheated with Raimunda. He must've wanted to take the words back, cover for letting them out."

"Ah. Same spineless jellyfish he was. Been better off if Jesus had taken you. Save you a lot of pain."

Tamarind looked back at Ana, her eyes dry. Something about Ana's statement niggled, but she couldn't remember what. "Maybe." Her icy wedding band stung her hand. She hid it in her lap.

"Know so." Ana squinted at her. "Come home, young one. I'll take care of you."

Tamarind hunched her shoulders and looked down. Her breasts felt heavy. She thought of Adam, and Sarah, who'd watched as she left to confront John. Guilt flared in her, but she batted it away. "I don't know."

"You can say good-bye to Valerie."

At Valerie's name, Tamarind's sorrow flooded her again. Valerie had believed in her. Valerie had believed in love. She'd failed

Valerie, who'd said that Tamarind would live more fully than she had. Well, Tamarind didn't deserve to live more fully than Valerie.

"We'll draw on Mother Sea together." When Tamarind looked up at her old mentor, she felt the familiar power in her gaze. "Come home. Say good-bye to Valerie."

Still Tamarind hesitated. Beneath her buttocks, the damp sand seeped into her pants. She realized then that she sat between two worlds, the wild magnificence of the untamed sea and the rich, sustaining mystery of the earth. Where did she belong?

"Don't have much time." Ana's rough voice grew urgent. "Don't have the strength I used to. It'll take everything we have to get you home. Give over your thoughts. I'll channel Mother Sea."

Tamarind felt the pull of the land, the dark energy that her Goddess had channeled through her during Hurricane Marilyn. Some part of her had rooted deeply into the earth. To tear herself away now would not be easy.

Ana grew petulant. "Suppose you'd rather stay with him, let him cheat on you. Better to live with lies than to live free." She paused, anger wavering through her form and clearing the smoke from her face. "After all I've done to help you."

That was enough for Tamarind and she hesitated no more. She relaxed her shoulders first, breathing deeply.

"Good, good." Ana's murmurs rolled with the waves. "Let go of everything. I'll bring you home, Tamarind."

Tamarind's angry hurt struggled against Ana's descending thoughts, only to fall back to confused guilt and sorrow before Ana's mental assault. She might want to let go, but these had a hold on her.

"No, no," Ana said, her voice caressing the raw places in Tamarind's heart until they began to close over, releasing the potent brew of her emotions into the ground beneath her. As they drained away, she surrendered to Ana's mind.

"That's it." Ana led her towards the water. "Bringing you home, young one. Bringing you home."

Ana's words became a song that wove itself through Tamarind's consciousness until she was aware of nothing else, not the warmth from the sun, or the icy embrace of the ocean, as she walked, unblinking, into the surf.

Forty-five
ﻌ

JOHN SLOUCHED AGAINST THE PASSENGER door of Zoë's car, no longer wracked by violent waves of nausea but far from free of its effects. He could well believe that he'd been poisoned. The last time that he'd felt so weak he'd just had day surgery for a hernia and needed a wheelchair to get out to his ride home. Without Zoë, he never would have made it from the bagel shop back to the parking lot behind Dr2Dr. He'd had to lie for some time on the floor before she could prop him in a chair. He sat there for almost an hour as she mopped up his vomit and straightened up the mess that her fight with Tamarind had made. Fortunately, nothing had been broken or damaged so a little sweet talking and a large donation to the tip jar had forestalled a call to the cops. After that, she'd wedged her shoulder under his arm, which she'd draped over her own shoulders, and half-dragged, half-carried him the whole way. She'd wanted to drive him straight to the Waltham Hospital, but he'd refused. He might feel like a newborn puppy, eyes glued shut and legs wobbly, but he didn't need the ER. He needed to get home, make sure that Tamarind was all right.

Zoë broke the silence, except for a few terse words, that had overtaken them he'd stopped her from following her double. "Sure it was her?"

"Yeah." He looked at her. Her sleek black hair obscured her profile. "She had on that new wedding band I had made for her."

"Ah." Zoë looked at him, her head tilted away from the late afternoon sun and her face in shadow. She turned back to the road ahead. "That seems pretty certain then. That old witch helped her though."

John couldn't be sure. Tamarind had been Ana's protégée once upon a time. Maybe she'd learned all she needed to know about potions and herbal tinctures and deception then. "Probably."

"If I hadn't seen it with my own eyes, I never would've believed it." Zoë seemed to be talking to herself. "Even after what that stuff I gave you did. She looked and acted *just like me.*"

John said nothing. What could he say? *You ain't seen nothing. You should've seen her when she had a tail.*

"Why'd she do it?" Again, that tilted shadow face. "I take it she suspects we're up to something. Did she know I'd gotten the job at Dr2Dr?"

John sighed and looked out the open side window. "No. There never seemed to be a good time to mention it. I'd just decided today that I needed to tell her before she found out."

"Guess you're too late for that."

"Guess so."

John continued to stare out the window as Zoë turned onto 87 toward Cheltham. While he'd been distracted, spring had quit acting coy and turned on her full charm. Forsythia rioted yellow over clumps of shy daffodils and confident red tulips; tender green leaves unfurled tentative banners to the strengthening sun. He wondered if the maples behind their house had leafed out yet and whether plush grass and grape hyacinth softened the hidden meadow where he and Lucy had met last fall. Lacy white and pink apple blossoms canopied the lawns of colonials and more contemporary houses set far back from the road. In the distance he heard the peculiar drone of a lawn mower. The smell of growing vegetation lifted his spirits.

"Not too late to clear the air, though." He heard the determination in his voice. "We need to clear the air about a lot of things." He thought about how they'd never had to speak to know the other's thoughts. That had been magic, but he now saw that kind of magic never survived suburbia, two kids, a mortgage, and a start-up—not to mention a determined ex-girlfriend and criminals for bosses.

Tamarind had had real magic, too.

She'd hidden in the water around Culebra, flirting with him before showing herself. She'd worn a magical aspect, a glamour, so that she could walk on land with him. She'd come to him at night, more substantial than a dream, once in San Juan and again in Pittsburgh. Her magic had crafted the Goddess pendant, the one that bound them together during Hurricane Marilyn. It had brought him to her rescue, it had kept her father from taking her back home, and it had lit their way during the blinding rain and dark.

Even as he remembered these surreal incidents, other, more powerful ones replayed themselves in his memory: Tamarind sweating and moaning in a hospital room as she walked in labor with Sarah, Tamarind above him as they made love, Tamarind nursing Adam early in the morning as he got ready for work. These too were magic but far more real and substantial. Would he, if he could, trade all these experiences, and everything else in their lives, for one night in a bioluminescent Caribbean bay with a mythical woman? No, and he couldn't wait to tell Tamarind so.

He continued, almost as if to himself. "*That's* why I was such a shit," he said, realization dawning as the words came out. "You wanted something more, but I couldn't bring myself to tell you I didn't want more with you. Falling in love with Tamarind was a kind of fairy tale. I put her off, too. I ran back to Pittsburgh the first excuse I got. I wanted the promise of happy-ever-after without the work."

"You never were good at dealing with problems." Zoë said this lightly, but John wondered if she still regretted his inept handling of their relationship and its dissolution.

He laughed, not without a touch of bitterness. "That's what I said to her, too." He reached out and touched Zoë's upper arm. "Thought it was you so I apologized again. I'll say it a third time. I'm sorry, Zo. I really am. You deserve better than me."

"Damn right." She said it gruffly, but he thought he heard a trace of laughter, too. "So what were you meeting me for anyway?"

John groaned. "Crap! I forgot. Tom Anderson called me this morning, insisted I meet him. Dr. Pendyala claims he and Dr. Mukarjee have set up a scam that involves lying to the pregnant women in the study and taking illegal payments."

"No shit?" It came out as an angry growl. Zoë shifted in the driver's seat. "Rotten to the core, this bunch. Good thing I had another interview this morning. They made me an offer, John. I can get the hell out of this hole."

"Not me. Anderson gave me until Friday morning to track down evidence. I have a feeling it could drag on even longer than that."

"What about Tamarind? Don't you think you should focus on her right now?"

John remembered the wide black eyes staring down at him from the shop counter. He'd read the terror and the guilt in them. They'd been easy enough to see once he recognized the wedding band. He thought about Anderson's implication that whoever had created the false data set for Dr. Mukarjee was involved in the larger fraud. He couldn't let Anderson implicate Zoë. He didn't want to worry her, either. She was on her way out. He had to cover her back.

"I can't let Mukarjee get away with it, Zo. If I don't snoop around before the board meeting, the good doctor might be able to cover his tracks. I'll just have to work things out with Tamarind in stages."

Zoë glanced at him, her expression inscrutable. "You sound better. That stuff must be wearing off."

"I didn't keep much of it in me, that's for sure."

They'd arrived in Cheltham so John gave Zoë directions to the house. Zoë was right. He *did* feel better, especially after admitting his own shortcomings just now. He felt stronger, but more than that. He felt satisfied, as though he'd solved a particularly intractable problem—one that had had so many sticky variables and unknowns that it had overwhelmed him to the point of avoidance. One that his subconscious had tackled until he could pull it out in the light of day and fit all of the parts of the answer together in an elegant solution.

Now he understood what Tamarind had fed him. What she'd been after.

"'The truth will set you free,'" he murmured.

"What?"

"Oh, I just figured out what Tamarind 'poisoned' me with, though that should have been obvious. A truth serum."

"Why didn't she just ask?" Zoë, ever direct, sounded perplexed and a shade disdainful.

"Probably for the same reasons I didn't tell."

"To avoid confrontation? Maybe she thought it was *your* job, not hers."

John saw the reason in that. He sighed. "More to do penance for, I guess. I made my inquisitive wife close herself off."

"Oh, she still should have asked. Marrying you taught her to be cautious, but that doesn't mean she can sit and wait for you to do the right thing. Trust me, that was a bad move."

John laughed. His weakness had fled. The warm spring afternoon had recharged him. He could almost taste the hope of new life on the air, feel it quivering on a spiritual plane that hovered just out of sight. The looming storm clouds that had darkened his soul for the past few months broke, letting sunshine stream through. There might be more rain, but the worst had passed. Besides, there couldn't be any new growth without a little rain.

He considered this insight as they turned down Arbor Lane. Now that he'd faced his first test with Tamarind, he couldn't quite remember what he'd feared. He grinned to himself. It wasn't as if he'd been able to anticipate the worst part. Nasty truth serum and Tamarind disguised as Zoë had never crossed his mind. Next to those possibilities, a terrifying shouting match and some broken dishes seemed rather tame. He thought about Lucy's poor granddaughter, Olivia, the one who'd had a pervert sending her depraved videos. Now *that* was some real heavy stuff for loved ones to deal with, a crisis that they hadn't brought upon themselves.

John had the sickening image of the assault in his mind as Zoë pulled into his driveway. Just as she turned the engine off, his front door swung open and Sarah burst through the storm door. She shot a glance at Zoë but trotted around the front of the car toward John's door. When her gaze met his through the windshield, a premonition flashed through John. He popped open his door before she reached it, careful not to swing it into her path.

"Roe, what's up?"

She came around the open door and slid into his arms. "Daddy, where's Mommy?" Her gaze again fell on Zoë. This time she kept it there.

John's heart lurched. "She's not back?"

The storm door opened and Lucy, feeding Adam a bottle, descended the front steps. Behind her, he caught sight of Olivia's dark hair and black glasses through the glass door. John's heart plummeted to the well of his stomach.

"Guess Tamarind's visit didn't go so well," Lucy said as she came to a halt at the driveway's edge. She nodded at Zoë. "I suppose she caught you two together again?"

Her question stunned John until he realized that Tamarind must have confided in Lucy about her reasons for visiting him without the kids. "So she talked to you." He heard the bitterness and shook it off. "Lucy, this is my good friend Zoë. I wasn't feeling well after–after talking with Tamarind so she drove me home."

Lucy nodded at Zoë. It wasn't an unfriendly nod, but John felt her holding herself aloof. Good old loyal Lucy. Tamarind was lucky to have a friend like her. *He* could use more friends like her, one who could take the truth head on and shoulder it. Inspired, he went on. "Look, Zoë and I are friends and colleagues, nothing more. I'm sorry that Tamarind found out before I told her."

"This isn't just about Zoë." Lucy's aged velvet voice hid an edge of steel. "She needs you, John. She just found out that her friend Valerie died."

John, who'd pushed Valerie's illness to the back of all the other troubles fermenting in his mind, staggered against the side of Zoë's car. "When?" The weakness had crept back into his voice.

"Today, I think. I came over this morning and she told me. I urged her to call you, that this was important enough to leave work for. That's when she told me about Zoë. She didn't want to go, but I told her it was time to clear the air between you."

John pinched the bridge of his nose and then rubbed his hand over his head. "We never got around to talking about Valerie. She–" here he looked at Zoë, "she ran out on us. We came here to find her."

"She hasn't come back yet. I was just going to leave the kids with Olivia so I could pick my grandson Ben up from daycare."

Just then Olivia propped the storm door open with one hand. She held a phone up with the other. "Mr. Wilkerson? It's for you," she called out as she stepped onto the stoop. "It's a state trooper named Sean Halloran. He's says it's about Mrs. Wilkerson."

A lightning bolt struck John and zipped down his spine. Storm clouds, blue-purple and threatening, thickened on his interior landscape. All the heat drained out of his body; he felt it leave through every pore in his skin, escape his mouth and nose, evaporate from the surface of his eyes, and flush his scalp on its way through his hair. After it left, he was as icy as if he stood naked in a hailstorm. So icy he burned from it.

≈≈≈

Tamarind had only been in the water for a few minutes when Ana's focus wavered and her head slipped under, saltwater burning her eyes and tongue. Groggy, she didn't feel any alarm at this. A gull cried overhead at that moment, reminding her of something, but she didn't know what. Ana's mind refocused and Tamarind glided through the water again, invisible to human eyesight, and gathering speed for her journey. In that brief dip, Tamarind had recovered an awareness of her surroundings and how she traveled, but it didn't matter. She'd let Ana detach her subtle body from her physical one. Her tongue tasted salt and her eyes blinked from the sunlight that fractured and sparkled on moving water, but these stimuli meant nothing to her.

She might have traveled to Culebra like this, with no regret and no fear, if something hadn't tickled the back of her thoughts. It sounded like a gull's cry, but that wasn't it, she was sure of it. *What is it then?* She tried but couldn't replay the sound of the gull and her memory seemed locked away from her. Then she became aware of heavy weight on her breastbone and pain in her chest, an aching fullness that even the cold sea hadn't deadened yet.

A gull cried again and she felt a prickling in her breasts and a release—a momentary heat trickling along her wet chest. She pressed a hand against Valerie's forgotten—and useless—Goddess pendant. Dear Lucy, standing tall as a maple in the doorway, her kind eyes never wavering, sprang to life in Tamarind's mind as plainly as if she'd had the power to project her subtle body through space. Lucy's left arm cradled Adam and her right hand rested on Sarah's head. Tamarind understood what Lucy wanted her to know. Sarah and Adam needed her. Here she was hovering over dark fathoms, speeding away from them. As soon as she thought of her baby, more milk let down—its heat washed away by the salty cold.

"No." Her protest sounded weak to her ears, but Tamarind gathered her strength and tried again. "No!"

Ana struggled to respond. Tamarind felt how difficult it was for the old woman to keep her head above water and still focus on her words. *What? What are you saying?*

"My children! My baby! I have to go to Adam!"

Ana's mind probed Tamarind's. The other woman's fury howled through her thoughts. *Forget it. Hear me, Tamarind? It's nothing to you, nothing! You're mine now. You're coming home with me.*

"No!" Tamarind lashed out at Ana's control. It slipped and Tamarind's head dipped again under water. She lifted it, gasping and spluttering.

You will *forget it!* This time when she sank under, it was because Ana forced her there.

Fear and regret suffused Tamarind. And understanding. John had been true. He loved her. And then the thing that had bothered her at Buzzard's Bay returned. Jesus. Ana had mentioned Jesus.

Before she could solve the mystery of Ana's remark, the old woman pulled her head up above the water. Tamarind gasped for air. The memory of John struggling in Luís Peña Canal filled her thoughts. There was no one, no *mer* kind, here to rescue her if Ana chose to hold her under. She'd lost the ability to breathe seawater. She would die.

But not without a fight. In linking herself to Tamarind, Ana had given Tamarind a way in to her mind. Tamarind, long unused to navigating the thoughts of others, searched for a crack in Ana's mental barricade.

Ana laughed. It was an eerie soundless echo in Tamarind's head. *No hope of controlling me, young one. Might as well give in. Always get what I want in the end.*

That's when Tamarind saw the truth: Ana had set her up for Jesus. How else could Ana know about his assault? Ana had always been for Ana, only tangentially for anyone else when it benefited her. Ana didn't care if she knew.

Panic and ocean threatened to drown Tamarind. She renewed her desperate struggle, now a matter of life and death, against Ana's weakening control. Her mind, half-caught and flickering from oxygen-deprivation, searched for something to hold onto. As seawater rushed into her lungs, power surged through her body.

With the force of revelation, Tamarind propelled Ana away. *Better to live free than with lies.*

Ana's mind darted back weaker still but looking for a way into Tamarind's thoughts. *Ungrateful! I'll bring you home or die trying.*

Tamarind's mind dodged Ana's. She tried to hold onto consciousness long enough to free herself. Again, she pulled on Mother Sea and this time the energy that came through her swallowed Ana's presence, obliterating her.

559

Exhausted from the effort, Tamarind felt seawater extinguish her own breath. She sank into Mother Sea's waiting arms.

Forty-six
ငၟ

JOHN, PETRIFIED FOR THE SPACE of a heartbeat, swiveled his head around to meet first Lucy's gaze, then Zoë's, and at last Sarah's. Their uncanny blue shocked him. So like Tamarind's. He felt something stir inside him, a tiny flame that thawed his frozen spirit. Gathering his courage, he held out his hand for the phone. Olivia told the caller to hold on. She appeared at the end of the sidewalk as if she'd teleported and slipped the receiver into his clammy palm.

"This is John Wilkerson." He trembled, but his voice held steady.

"Sir, this is Sergeant Sean Halloran with the Massachusetts Highway Patrol. Are you Tamarind Wilkerson's next of kin?"

"I'm her husband." What an effort to say those three impartial words when he wanted to shout *what's wrong? Is she hurt? Is she dead?*

"Mrs. Wilkerson, sir, has been transported to Jordan's Hospital in Plymouth. You'd better get here as soon as you can. Where will you be coming from?"

"Plymouth?" John couldn't comprehend where that was.

"Yes, sir. Sir, where are you?"

John's pleading gaze sought out Lucy's. He slipped his hand over the receiver. "Where are we?"

Lucy didn't blink or look alarmed, thank God. "Cheltham, John."

"Cheltham. I'm coming from Cheltham. I mean, I've got to stop in Waltham to get my car first." Anxiety and fear burst through his polite answers. "What's happened? Is she okay? What's wrong?"

"Sir, Mrs. Wilkerson is unconscious and in serious condition, but the doctors say she's not in danger. I'd rather wait until you get here to discuss what happened."

Relief that Tamarind wasn't in any danger overwhelmed John's immediate fears. He'd deal with what happened later. He looked at his watch. It was three. "I'll be there by five, unless traffic is heavy around Boston."

"See you then, sir."

John punched the button to close the line. He looked at the expectant faces around him. Adam, snug against Lucy's chest, squirmed and mewled as though he'd been unable to bear the tension that bound them there.

"Tamarind's had some sort of accident. He won't say what happened on the phone, wants me to drive to Jordan Hospital in Plymouth."

"Go now," said Lucy as Zoë added, "I'll drive you."

John looked at Zoë. "I appreciate the offer, Zo, but I've got to go on my own. Whatever's caused Tamarind to need an ambulance–" here his voice broke, but when Sarah slipped her hand into his, he steadied it. "Whatever's happened to her is because she was upset when she left this afternoon. I heard the car horns and tires screeching, Zo. I know she almost got herself killed on Moody."

Zoë studied him, her dark eyes intent. "Okay. Do you need to do anything here first?" She glanced at Sarah.

John nodded and squatted down to look Sarah in the face. Peer to peer. "Roe, honey. I've got to go see Mommy. She might be hurt."

Sarah lifted gentle hands to his face, cupping it. "She needs you, Daddy. Everything be all right when you go there."

John blinked tears back. He hugged his prescient daughter tight and then looked at her one more time. "Help Lucy and Olivia with baby Adam, okay?"

"Okay." She nodded and then extricated herself. She went to stand next to Olivia, wrapping an arm around Olivia's left leg.

John stood up and looked at Lucy.

"Just go," she said before he could say anything. "We'll be fine."

"What're you feeding Adam?" It just dawned on him that Lucy had been giving Adam a bottle when they'd arrived.

"Breastmilk. Tamarind had a bunch stored away. It should last for a few more hours, but we'll get some formula for him if we have to. Take Tamarind's pump. Maybe they'll let her pump if she feels like it."

That seems pretty unlikely, John thought but wouldn't have said aloud for anything. Maybe Tamarind didn't want to pump. Maybe she'd been running away. He blinked back tears again. What an ever-loving idiot he'd been!

"Thanks, Lucy." John leaned down and kissed Adam, who smelled as sweet as innocence. As sweet as love, pure and uncompromised. On impulse, he reached up and kissed Lucy's soft, wrinkled cheek. She smelled like cinnamon, sugar, and cloves. That too smelled like love, but the hands-on love of kneading, chopping, and mixing. Of devotion and patience and communion.

Lucy squeezed his shoulder. "Go with God, John."

He and Zoë got back into Zoë's car and they retraced their route to Waltham. Zoë waited until they were on 87 before breaking the silence that enveloped them in regret.

"What about Mukarjee, John? You don't have much time to get the evidence that Anderson wants."

"Fuck Mukarjee. My wife is more important than doing my part to prove his guilt."

"No chance you're going to take any heat for this?"

John thought again about Dr. Anderson's accusation. "No," he said. "I'm not worried. Let them do their own dirty work."

"Hm." Zoë said nothing for several minutes. She spoke again without looking at him. "What if I snoop around, John? Maybe I can find something."

"Leave it, Zoë. Just get out and don't look back. Don't let yourself get tangled up in the scam."

"I can always lock up the data before I go." There was mischief in her tone.

Weariness overcame John. "Whatever, Zo. I can't think about any of that now. None of it matters. None."

Zoë looked at him and back at the road. "Thank God." She exaggerated her relief. "You've finally figured out how to deal with your problems. I wrote you off when you said you'd deal with Tamarind in stages. You've finally realized she's your number one priority. That's a damn good start. Everything else will fall into line."

꒰꒱꒰

John drove to Jordan's Hospital, sick to his stomach but numb. The sun had sunk low on the western horizon when he pulled into the visitor's parking lot. After all his anxiety and the constant struggle not to speed and risk getting pulled over, John parked as far from the ER entrance as he could and then dawdled along the sidewalk. He halted and stood looking at the automatic glass doors that would lead him to his wife's side. The last time he'd been at the ER, he'd rushed there from work to find Lucy pacing in the waiting room, her fingers telling off the beads of her rosary. Tamarind's severe dehydration had been scary, but he'd focused on what needed to be done to get her through the crisis and to protect Adam. He'd ignored any unlikely statistical scenario of maternal distress or fetal danger and his faith had been justified. What needed to be done this time couldn't be fixed with a few hours in a hospital bed with IV fluids. She might be lying broken from a car crash. She might have swallowed something. The Lord knew that Ana was capable of poisoning Tamarind if she couldn't have her for herself.

He longed to cross himself, but his hands ached from clutching the steering wheel for so long. Instead, he massaged them there on the sidewalk until he realized that he appeared as guilty as the hand-wringing Lady Macbeth. It dawned on him that he could pray. Lucy's kind face floated before his mind's eye. He had a feeling that she'd be praying for them, too. He'd follow her example. He'd get on his knees before facing what must be faced. He forced himself to enter and look for the hospital chapel while his heart pounded. He found the small brown room with a nondescript stained-glass window filtering the last of the day's sunlight onto the rows of cushioned benches that faced an undistinguished wooden podium. Nothing about the room uplifted him nor did he think it could uplift. Yet it exuded a quiet presence unlike the sterile indifference of the fluorescent hallway outside its slow-closing door.

John padded across the institutional carpet. Ignoring the benches, he fell on his knees before the stain-glassed light, crossed himself, and then waited. What should he say to God?

Oh, Lord. Let her be all right. I'm sorry.

That seemed to be adequate. Acceptance of whatever was to come washed over him like peace. His heart slowed to normal. He crossed himself again, pushed himself to his feet, and straightened his spine. He went to the nearest nursing station, but the nurses refused to release any information until he'd spoken with Sgt. Halloran, whom he found in the ICU waiting room five minutes later.

John approached the state trooper, who was tall and martial, and held out his hand. His moist palm didn't keep John from gripping the other man's.

"Sir, please sit," Halloran said as soon as John identified himself.

"I'll stand, thanks," John said, his voice shaking slightly. He'd take whatever he needed to hear on his feet. "You found my wife?"

"Sir, I suggest you sit." Sgt. Halloran waited a moment but then went on when John remained standing. "Yes, I found your wife at Horseneck Beach in Buzzard's Bay."

John gulped and squeezed his hands into fists. "What happened? The hospital staff won't tell me anything."

"She nearly drowned, but by some miracle she survived."

"Nearly drowned? I don't understand. She's a really good swimmer...."

"Sir, that may be, but maybe she didn't want to swim."

"What do you mean?"

"Listen, sir, I have to be honest with you. I don't know what happened at Buzzard's Bay today. Another trooper had radioed your wife's license plate number and said she was driving recklessly, someone should watch out for her. I picked her up on 88 South, not far from the beach, but she wasn't speeding. In fact, sir, she didn't match the description of the driver that was reported. Witnesses described a woman with short dark hair. I decided to follow your wife, see if she'd had some trouble. Give her a warning if need be. When I pulled in to the parking lot at Horseneck Beach, I saw her running up and down the beach throwing sand."

Sgt. Halloran paused. He was clearly choosing his words with care.

"I thought maybe I should wait and see what was going on. I got within fifteen feet of her at one point. She took no notice of me. She stopped running and squatted down for a while. Next thing I know, she cries out, starts weeping and rocking back and forth. I decide to get out of my car, go over. See what's wrong. Obviously she's upset and may need help. But before I reach her, she jumps up and throws her arms out, like she's fending off an attack. Then a moment later, she starts talking to herself and next thing I know, she's walking into the water."

The trooper paused again, fingered his holster then started pacing.

"I yelled for her to come back, but she kept going, didn't even turn around to look at me. The damnedest thing happened then. One moment she was there, the next she wasn't. I must've blinked or something and she slipped under because she was gone, not even a ripple. I dashed in to where I'd last seen her, you know I thought maybe I could find her, pull her out before it was too late. But she was gone."

He stopped pacing and fell silent while John tried to wrap his mind around what he'd said, but it made no sense. No sense, he realized, unless it had to do with some ability Tamarind retained from her previous life as a mermaid. She'd not wanted to talk about that life after he'd come back for her, simply saying that Ana had helped her become human and wanted to make her an apprentice. Could Ana have anything to do with it? Or was he just looking for a scapegoat?

Sgt. Halloran finally went on. "So I went to her car, got her driver's license and radioed the event in. While I was waiting for the search team to arrive, I got out of my car and walked back to the beach. I have to be honest, Mr. Wilkerson. I was wondering why such a beautiful woman was so upset she walked into the ocean and drowned herself. And then, while I was standing there, she reappeared. I nearly flipped. There she was, floating face down but coming back in to shore even though the tide was going out. It was almost like the ocean didn't want to keep her.

"When I went to her, I thought for sure she was gone. I pulled her out and lay her down on the sand, not even careful to lay her on her side so she wouldn't choke. Mr. Wilkerson, you've got to understand." Unnatural pleading threaded his tough voice. "She'd been under for fifteen minutes. Then all of the sudden she starts coughing and spitting up water. I was giving her mouth-to-mouth when the search team showed up. The doctors here say she shows no signs of oxygen deprivation. She's here only as a precaution. They don't understand how that can be. "

He finished and stood there, looking at John, a slight crease between his brows. Clearly, he was hoping that John could provide some explanation for the unexplainable. But John had no answers for him. He had no answers for himself.

"Thanks." That's all he could say.

After that he was finally shown into Tamarind's room. She lay in the middle of a bed, her hair spread around her on the pillow, a bit of flotsam washed up by the tide. He stood there looking down at her, aware of how fragile she looked, how human. He reached out and stroked her temple. As he did so, she opened her eyes, the lids heavy and low.

"John." Her weak voice almost didn't reach his ears. "John, I want to go home."

He felt tears on his cheeks and knew he was crying, but not whether from happiness or sadness.

"Soon," he said, "we're going home soon."

Epilogue
ଓଃ

TAMARIND WAITED UNTIL THE EARLY SPRING sun had melted all but the most shade-covered patches of snow before fetching the mangrove box from the back of the shelf in her closet. Its *mer* symbols for life and fertility, though no longer powerful to her, would serve as fitting tribute to Valerie. She lifted Adam in his backpack from the dining-room table to her shoulders, and, handing Sarah the box, followed the little girl to the stream behind their house. The narrow trail through the woods still had an icy crust, but Tamarind didn't worry about slipping or stumbling, even with Adam's weight challenging her balance. As he kicked and chattered just outside her range of vision, Tamarind watched Sarah negotiate the muddy ruts in her toddler construction boots, carrying the box before her as parishioners carried the gifts up the aisle before Communion.

Life, long slumbering in the frigid winter, hummed around them, in earth and tree. Tamarind inhaled deeply, letting the rich loamy scent churned up by their passage ignite hunger in her for growing things. Green ryegrass. Crinkle-edged oak leaves. Deep-purple crocus and white snowdrop and grape hyacinth. Sweet pink apple blossoms. As they passed a maple, sticky sap sugared the tree's heart. Her tongue tingled at the taste. She reached out fingertips to caress the coarse bark along the trail, playing the trunks as one played a xylophone. Deep, smooth tones emanated around them, floating and swirling on the chill air so clearly that she could see them. They were the color of fertile black soil.

Out of the corners of her eyes, Tamarind could see a faint green aura outlining the twigs and branches of the deciduous trees guarding the trail. Through the limbs arching above them, the robin's egg blue of the sky lent clarity to the morning that dazzled her. Birdsong trilled somewhere further to the right, lending a counterpoint to the crackle of the ice underfoot and the thumping of their feet on muddy ground. Tamarind, who'd long missed her ability to hum along the whole of her torso while clicking out a melody, cheered as she recognized this different music. She jounced Adam on her back, who giggled his delightful belly laugh, and then glanced down at Sarah, who looked back at her.

"*Kree-eee-ar. Kree-eee-ar.*" Even though she hadn't tried the red-tailed hawk's cry since they'd moved from Pittsburgh, Tamarind hadn't forgotten it. She still sounded like a human imitating a wild bird. She laughed at the startled look on Sarah's face and began to hum. Like a human, too.

They reached the place where the trail split next to the stream. Tamarind stopped on the trail where the ground was more even. "Where should we dig?" she asked.

Sarah considered the ground around the stream, muddy and hidden by clumps of soggy half-decayed leaves. "Over there." She pointed to a bare spot edging the stream, whose movement sparkled in the sun. "Near the water."

Tamarind pursed her lips and pretended to weigh the decision. It didn't need to be weighed, however. Sarah had honed in on the perfect resting place. Perhaps she'd read Tamarind's thoughts. It wouldn't be the first time.

"Okay, then, Roe. Let's dig a hole."

Sarah squatted and set the mangrove box on a flat rock near the stream's edge. Tamarind handed her the hand spade that she'd stuck into her belt and she scooped out the muddy top layer until she'd managed to dig a hole that was eight inches in diameter.

"Got the box?" It was an unnecessary question. Sarah had dropped the spade to clutch it to her chest before she leaned in to study the brown ooze at the bottom of the depression. She started to set the box into it, but Tamarind stopped her. "Wait! Open it first."

"Okay, Mommy." Sarah pulled the lid off. Inside gleamed a wire-wrapped moonstone. She reached in and pulled the figure out. It hung in the still spring air between them.

"Think she'll like it here, near the water?"

Sarah nodded. "She's home now."

Tamarind let her gaze polish the moonstone a final time. Her inner eye caught the faint gleam from its heart. "Good-bye, Valerie. Thank you."

Sarah placed the Goddess pendant on the velvet cushion that Tamarind had made for it and dropped the lid back on the box. She traced over the marker scribbles she'd made, the ones that had broken Ana's spells. Then she settled the box into the hole before scooping the dirt over it. Sarah had just finished and Tamarind had begun to tamp the soil down when a shadow passed overhead. They looked up to see the silhouette of a hawk, a Cooper's hawk, sail across the brilliant river of sky. Tamarind wondered if it was the Cooper's hawk that she'd seen nesting last season or the hawk's daughter. She was glad that the developer had lost its ferocious battle with the conservation commissioner. Nothing threatened the Cooper's hawk's reign in these woods now.

Tamarind waited until the majestic shadow disappeared over the bare treetops to the northeast, likely headed for the field hidden there. She grabbed Adam's fist, which clutched a handful of her hair, and gently pried his fingers loose. She adjusted him on her back. "Ready to go to Lucy's?"

"Yes." Such a grave answer, spoiled by Sarah's next words. "I want pie! I want to see Custard. Will Ben be there? Ben won't share his LEGOs with me."

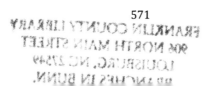

Tamarind laughed. "Let's worry about that when we get there."

Lucy came to the door smiling. Her pale eyes reflected the steel blue of freshwater pearls clearly visible at the base of her throat. When she pushed her storm door open, the sun flashed from the crystal and gold beads that Tamarind had strung between them. From the living room the sound of a piano concerto swelled to a passionate crescendo.

And from the kitchen drifted the warm, sweet scent of cinnamon and clove, apple and butter.

ACKNOWLEDGEMENTS

Thanks first and foremost go to my family, especially my wonderful husband, Scott, who refused to read anything I'd written until I finished a draft. And then he read each version. Without his faith in me, I never would have believed in myself. I also owe him more than I can say for protecting my writing time and treating it as work so that our children know that their mother has work to do. Every novelist who's ever toiled at home without pay knows how important this is.

I'd also like to thank Alan Sloan, who sent me cards from famous authors to encourage me and always asked about my writing. Outside of Scott, he's been my longest and staunchest supporter. I hope someday to repay him in kind.

Chris Hughes, oldest friend and toughest critic, renewed our friendship just when I needed a critique partner. I owe you. Literally. Money isn't likely to be forthcoming, however. Just my everlasting gratitude.

Emmett Hamilton, an incomparable artist, took my verbal description of the crucial Goddess pendant and turned it into a virtual reality. Emmett, thank you doesn't seem to be enough.

There is a veritable litany of other saints, friends and readers, who gave of their time and their insight. I wish that I could list you all here by name, but I'm sure that I'd forget someone and that would be unforgiveable. Please, if you ever listened to me discussing my novel, its characters, or the agony of writing and publishing, know that I'm grateful. If you gave of your time to read one of the iterations, I'm not only grateful but aware that I wouldn't have been able to succeed without your generosity and insight.

A NOTE ON THE AUTHOR

LeAnn Neal Reilly graduated with a master's degree in professional writing from Carnegie Mellon University. She lives outside Boston with her husband and three children. This is her first novel. Her Web site is www.nealreilly.com.

Zephon Books presents

Reading Group Guide

୭୭୭୭୭୭

The

Mermaid's Pendant

LeAnn Neal Reilly

Inspiration for *The Mermaid's Pendant*

As with most books I read as a child, I discovered fairy tales on my own, devouring them at an early age. My earliest reading memories center on the mystery, excitement, sense of adventure, and thrill of possibility *and* danger that fairy tales elicited in me. I moved on to childhood fantasy like *Ozma of Oz* and *The Littles* and then later to fantasy novels such as Stephen Donaldson's *The Chronicles of Thomas Covenant the Unbeliever* and Julian May's *Saga of Pliocene Exile*. Yet fairy tales, situated as they were in that part of my childhood where magical thinking dominated, retained an undimmed patina.

When I read excerpts of Bruno Bettelheim's *Uses of Enchantment: The Meaning and Importance of Fairy Tales* in college, fairy tales took on a new importance for me. Although his theories about the allegorical nature of fairy tales have become controversial, Bettelheim's belief that fairy tales taught—and continue to teach— important developmental lessons to children still has merit. One of those lessons is that the world can be a dark, frightening, and dangerous place. Another is that not everything is as it seems to be, and that sometimes what is hidden can be fatal. The children in the stories have to be alert, clever, resourceful, and careful not to trust strangers without reservations. The stories don't all have happy endings. For example, in the original *Snow White*, the evil stepmother is forced to dance herself to death wearing fiery shoes at Snow White's wedding.

Unfortunately, modern treatment of fairy tales sanitizes them, either deliberately changing the endings or softening them until the very concept of "fairy tale" has shifted to some unrealistic ideal limited mainly to romantic love. This weakened concept has permeated modern culture at all levels. Adults talk about "fairy-tale

2

romance," "fairy-tale weddings," "living a fairy-tale life," and "looking for Prince Charming." Novels and movies either treat this ideal as a wonderful escape or something to disdain. We've stripped fairy tales of their power to inspire and guide us.

After having children, I found myself watching Disney's *Little Mermaid*. Even though I loved the movie and its music, it got under my skin. I'd married a prince of man and had no complaints, but the happily-ever-after still required work. I resented the implication that the young couple had already overcome all their problems and could sail off into the sunset. On the contrary, I knew that the real tests of true love were about to begin. Knowing that Disney had altered the original, I then read Hans Christian Anderson's *The Little Mermaid* and discovered that the Little Mermaid sacrificed herself for love, earning a soul and a place in heaven with other angels. She didn't have the chance to see if she'd still love the prince after marriage and children. Nor did I read whether his marriage to the princess, made after he mistook her for his rescuer, worked out. Not entirely satisfying for someone hoping for a vision of life after magic brings two lovers together.

As I wrestled with my conflicted feelings about fairy tales and my conviction that they were meant to help their audience experience the darker side of life along with the light, the alchemy of my own young marriage and parenthood motivated me to rehabilitate *The Little Mermaid* for a modern adult audience. I began by imagining conversations between a young mother who'd thought she'd made a fairy-tale marriage and an older, wiser, sympathetic neighbor. This wise-woman neighbor became Lucy in *The Mermaid's Pendant*. After that I imagined the young mother that Lucy advises, a former mermaid who leaves the sea for a scientist. From there, the "fairy tale" took lots of twists and turns in the writing and revising, but always I knew it included a sea witch with her own agenda and a happily-ever-after that incorporated darker elements.

Questions and Topics for Discussion

1. In *Volume One: An Ordinary Drowning*, John travels to "La Isla Encantada" where he meets two women, Raimunda and Tamarind, after nearly drowning. What choice does each woman offer John to escape his growing dissatisfaction with the path his life has drifted along?

2. John's ex-girlfriend Zoë interrupts him on his first date with Tamarind, accusing him of "playing Pygmalion" with an uneducated island girl. What does John's response say about his relationship with Zoë? With Tamarind? What does it say about him?

3. Tamarind's mentor Ana tempts the vulnerable mermaid with power and knowledge upon learning about John's response to Zoë. Ana also portrays all humans as unworthy of Tamarind's trust and love by choosing to tell her the story of her mother's murder. How does Tamarind reject Ana's offer for a half-life between the *mer* and the human world? Why?

4. In rescuing Tamarind, John imprints his love with hers onto the Goddess pendant, thereby preventing her return to the sea with her father. Tamarind, however, warns John that if she returns to the sea once Hurricane Marilyn passes, she "won't come back." What does this mean for the magic that binds them together? When John makes love to Tamarind, what does her physical transformation mean for both of them? When does John fully understand and accept what he's done?

4

Throughout *Volume Two: Grounding Magic*, several pieces of jewelry symbolize different aspects of love, faith, trust, and forgiveness for the characters. They also play key roles in how they learn about themselves and interact with each other.

5. How does Tamarind and John's relationship change after the Goddess pendant breaks? After Tamarind loses it? After Lucy returns it?

6. Why does Rachel keep Tamarind's Goddess pendant? Does it work for her? Why or why not?

7. What does Lucy's digging up her husband's pearl necklace mean? Why does she break it? Why does she ask Tamarind to repair it?

8. Tamarind's wedding band has to be cut off during pregnancy. How does she feel about this? Does she want John to repair it? What does John do with the band? How does it affect Tamarind's later escape efforts?

Throughout the novel, Ana, Valerie, and Lucy advise the young lovers and act as role models for them.

9. How does Ana use her magic to manipulate John and Tamarind? How does Ana's experience as a wife influence her motivations and actions?

10. Valerie shows Tamarind how to make a pendant that draws on Mother Earth in Volume One, but in Volume Two she urges Tamarind not to rely on its powerful magic. Why? How does her use of magic contrast with Ana's? How does her romantic past compare to Ana's? How does it influence her motivations and actions?

11. Does Lucy have any magic? Why or why not? How does Lucy's marriage compare to Ana's? What does her friendship mean to Tamarind? John?

The second volume also explores the theme of silence and secrets and the pain and misunderstanding that festers in their presence.

12. Both Valerie and Lucy advise Tamarind to discuss her needs and fears with John. Why does Tamarind choose to listen to Ana instead?

13. Why does John not say anything to Tamarind about his immediate misgivings about Dr2Dr and later about Zoë's presence there? Why does he keep the investigation at work from her? How do his feelings for Dr. Mukarjee influence his actions?

14. Lucy realizes at Christmas that her family members are hiding many secrets from each other. What secret has she kept from them? From herself? How has it affected their lives? What does meeting Tamarind and John do to her efforts to keep silent?

CPSIA information can be obtained at www.ICGtesting.com
Printed in the USA
LVOW041448310512

284114LV00002B/5/P